**"My name is Templar**

*SIMON TEMPLAR: a/k/a The Saint, the Happy Highwayman, the Brighter Buccaneer, the Robin Hood of Modern Crime.*

*DESCRIPTION: Age 31. Height 6 ft., 2 in. Weight 175 lbs. Eyes blue. Hair black, brushed straight back. Complexion tanned. Bullet scar through upper left shoulder; 8 in. scar on right forearm.*

*SPECIAL CHARACTERISTICS: Always immaculately dressed. Luxurious tastes. Lives in most expensive hotels and is connoisseur of food and wine. Carries firearms and is expert knife thrower. Licensed air pilot. Speaks several languages fluently. Known as "The Saint" from habit of leaving drawing of skeleton figure with halo at scenes of crimes.*

# By Leslie Charteris

DARE DEVIL
THE BANDIT

THE WHITE RIDER
X ESQUIRE

## The Saint Series (in order of sequence)

MEET THE TIGER!
ENTER THE SAINT
THE LAST HERO
KNIGHT TEMPLAR (THE
   AVENGING SAINT)
FEATURING THE SAINT
ALIAS THE SAINT
ANGELS OF DOOM (SHE WAS A
   LADY, THE SAINT MEETS HIS
   MATCH)
THE SAINT V. SCOTLAND YARD
GETAWAY
THE SAINT AND MR. TEAL
THE BRIGHTER BUCCANEER
THE MISFORTUNES OF MR. TEAL
THE SAINT INTERVENES
THE SAINT GOES ON
THE SAINT IN NEW YORK
THE SAINT OVERBOARD
ACE OF KNAVES
THIEVES' PICNIC
THE SAINT PLAYS WITH FIRE
FOLLOW THE SAINT
THE HAPPY HIGHWAYMAN
THE SAINT IN MIAMI
THE SAINT GOES WEST
THE SAINT STEPS IN
THE SAINT ON GUARD
THE SAINT SEES IT THROUGH
CALL FOR THE SAINT

SAINT ERRANT
THE SAINT IN EUROPE
THE SAINT ON THE SPANISH
   MAIN
THANKS TO THE SAINT
THE SAINT AROUND THE WORLD
SENOR SAINT
THE SAINT TO THE RESCUE
TRUST THE SAINT
THE SAINT IN THE SUN
VENDETTA FOR THE SAINT
THE SAINT ON T.V.
THE SAINT RETURNS
THE SAINT AND THE FICTION
   MAKERS
THE SAINT ABROAD
THE SAINT'S CHOICE
THE SAINT IN PURSUIT
THE SAINT AND THE PEOPLE
   IMPORTERS
CATCH THE SAINT
THE SAINT AND THE
   HAPSBURG NECKLACE
SEND FOR THE SAINT
THE SAINT IN TROUBLE
THE SAINT AND THE TEMPLAR
   TREASURE
COUNT ON THE SAINT
SALVAGE FOR THE SAINT
THE FANTASTIC SAINT

(Parentheses indicate alternate titles)

# LESLIE CHARTERIS

*Dec. 1990*

## THE FIRST **SAINT** OMNIBUS
### AN ANTHOLOGY OF SAINTLY ADVENTURES

**INTERNATIONAL POLYGONICS, LTD.**
**NEW YORK CITY**

**THE FIRST SAINT OMNIBUS**

Library of Congress Card Catalog No. 90-80771
ISBN 1-55882-060-4

Printed and manufactured in the United States of America.
First IPL printing June 1990.
10 9 8 7 6 5 4 3 2 1

*The villains in this book are entirely imaginary, and have no relation to any living person.*

"I HAVE BEEN TRYING *to make a picture of a man. Changing, yes. Developing, 1 hope. Fantastic, improbable—perhaps. Quite worthless, quite irritating, if you feel that way. Or a slightly cockeyed ideal, if you feel differently. It doesn't matter so much, so long as you feel that you would recognise him if you met him tomorrow.*"

# CONTENTS

# CONTENTS

# FOREWORD

I SUPPOSE *it has long been obvious to every addict of these Immortal Works that sooner or later there would have to be an omnibus, anthology, or hash of selected adventures of the Saint. Some twenty volumes covering the exploits of a single character would be a fair crowd even in the spacious library (you remember—the place where the body is found in Chapter One) of one of the Stately Homes of England; and so few of us are keeping up our Stately Homes any more, what with the present rate of income tax and the falling birth-rate among butlers and one thing and another. Furthermore, the entire residue of the reading public which has never yet read a Saint story, and which is anxious to catch up on his background before joining up with the series, have both pointed out to us that twenty volumes is a lot of volumes to have to wade through before they can look their contemporaries in the eye.*

*So, for the benefit of all those who want to do it the easy way, here it is at last, in a mere nutshell of a quarter of a million words—*
*THE FIRST SAINT OMNIBUS*

*Note that we have called it a "Saint" Omnibus. Not a Charteris Omnibus.*

*I am inclined to think that one of the most salutary experiences that can befall a writer is to realise that he has created something much bigger and more life-like than himself. It isn't much good telling yourself that this is only a tribute to your own superlative genius and scintillating technique. The plain truth is that your unregenerate personal vanity stands up and takes it on the chin.*

*What happens to me, with exhilarating frequency, is that some*

# viii      FOREWORD

*charming person to whom I have been introduced will say: "Oh, so you're the Saint!"*

*(That is, when they don't say: "Tell me . . . what name do you write under?")*

*But not so long ago, when a certain periodical held a poll on "My Favourite Author", the name at the head of the final results was not (as you were thinking) Leslie Charteris. No. No. A thousand times No. By a comfortable majority, their favourite author was The Saint.*

*A situation like that has one curious consolation. It is not often that an author can honestly stand back and review one of his own creations objectively, as he would review the living subject of a factual biography. But it has become almost weirdly easy for me to do so with the Saint. So much so that at certain delirious moments I have almost started to believe that perhaps after all the Saint is the real person and Leslie Charteris is the literary myth. And from such mild hallucinations to the stage where one is firmly convinced that one is a scrambled egg is, I am credibly informed, hardly more than a step.*

*It may be a matter of some satisfaction to a few thousand members of what (when in the company of rival authors) I complacently refer to as My Public, to know that the daily consignments of mail which I receive from them brings me steadily closer to the crossing of this psychic Rubicon, this point of destiny at which I shall spread myself on a piece of toast and wait with pathetic confidence for somebody to surround me with slices of crisp bacon. Files of correspondence which my indomitable secretary struggles to keep in order—in spite of my most determined efforts to frustrate her—overflow with letters in which readers bombard me with questions about the Saint, demanding to know this and that about him which I have not yet stated in any of the stories, as if these were actual facts which I were withholding from them. Where was he born? What was his childhood like? How did he get his name? What started him off on his career? What did the bishop say to the actress? Is he married to Patricia? Or when is he going to marry her? Why does he have romantic interludes with other women? Has he ever been to Kalamazoo, does he play golf, does he like mashed potatoes, who is his favourite film star, what school did he go to? And trying*

*to answer—or, I must admit, quite often trying to dodge—such seri-
ous questions, in the same serious vein, has done its full share towards
catching me in the net of my own fable.*

*The only other character I can think of whom I know to have
been subjected to the same remorseless investigation is Sherlock
Holmes. Several societies have been formed in his name, some of
them with a most distinguished list of members, who know every
word of his exploits as well as a preacher knows his Bible, and who
meet at intervals to discuss the finer nuances of the Master's career.
Monographs of the most profound and ingenious scholarship have
been written, soberly purporting to piece together the missing fragments of the Master's life from various piquant allusions in the
stories. But most of this has taken place since the death of his creator,
since speculation and deduction have become the only methods at
the disposal of these insatiable students. Leslie Charteris, on the other
hand, is unfortunately still alive, and therefore no such intellectual
efforts are required of those devotees of the Saint who want to
know more than I have told them. All they have to do is to write
and ask me.*

*One object of this Foreword, then, is to try and forestall some of
the more common questions which I get shot at me, in the faint hope
that this may save me a certain amount of future letter-writing, and
thereby give me more time to write more stories to make more
money to finance the Commissioners of Taxes, who are feeling the
draught pretty badly these days on account of not being able to take
more than three-quarters of my income away from me.*

*The plain fact of the situation is this: that just about everything I
have found out about the Saint, so far, has been passed on in the
Saint stories. If, for instance, the few references which are made to
his early life are vague, it is because he himself is reticent on the
subject. If his origin, and the circumstances of his youth, seem to be
shrouded in mystery, it is not because I am wilfully trying to hide
anything, but simply because I don't know. When, if ever, he
chooses to reveal it, you can be sure that I shall put it into print. But
until then, it is no good at all to ask me.*

*My personal first-hand knowledge of the Saint's biography goes
back exactly as far as the first published Saint story, which appeared
about ten years ago under the title of* Meet the Tiger. *This was the*

*only Saint story which did not bear the imprint of Hodder &
Stoughton, the publishers of the present volume and also of all the
other Saint books. Although this book has been listed in the bibliog-
raphy printed at the beginning of every new Saint book for several
years, the fact that it is on another publisher's list seems to have
caused a good many readers to overlook it. This book tells the
story of his first meeting with Patricia Holm, and is therefore a
complete and detailed answer to one of the questions which I am
most frequently asked.*

*However, it does not tell anyone whether he married her, or if
he is going to marry her, or when he is going to do so, which seems
to be the next most common source of popular anxiety.*

*Now this again is something which it is no use asking me. As to
whether he has married her, the internal evidence of subsequent
stories should make the question superfluous. At no time is there any
quoted reference by either Simon or Patricia to any wedding ceremony in which both of them took part. On the contrary, certain
passages in the story entitled* The Melancholy Journey of Mr Teal
*(not included in the present volume) may be illuminatively studied
in this connection. As to whether they intend to marry, and, if so,
when—that is putting too great a strain either on my capacity for im-
pertinence or on my gifts of prophecy. I am not going to hold them
up at the point of a gun and ask them; and I am not going to risk my
reputation by trying to predict it. As soon as I know the answer, it
will be told. And until then, once again, it is no use asking me.*

*The same thing applies to the associated question of his relation-
ships with other women, of whom there have been quite a few. No
one would want to deny that he has his human weaknesses in that
direction, and at the same time that he has less than the ordinary
human burden of repressions. But it should also be unnecessary to
point out that very few stories ever go by before Patricia is with him
again; and I defy anyone to discover any rift between them, or to
catch her making any really bitter thrusts about his other adventures.
On the contrary, I think that a recent Saint novel,* Prelude for War,
*throws a good deal of useful light on that situation. And since
Patricia is the party chiefly concerned, I feel that no one else needs
to worry unduly over a state of affairs about which she is so imperturbably serene.*

*And so it goes. There are a large number of Saint books, an even larger number of Saint stories. For more than ten years now I have been industriously putting into print everything that I knew or could find out about the Saint. It isn't much use asking me to amplify, in a letter, anything that I haven't already been able to say in a couple of million words.*

*I have done all this, frankly, because I love him. Over all this time, he has grown into me, and I have grown into him, so much that there may after all be some excuse for a confusion of our identities. And these stories were brought together especially for those people who have flattered me by coming to share my affection for him.*

*He, after all, is still the main character in this book—not myself. And I have held you back from him for too long already. It seems to me that he should be able to answer these questions better for himself. It is as true of him as it would be of anyone else, that anything you can be told about him is only a shadow of the man, reflected in some other person's mind. You still have to meet him. You have to hear him talk, and watch him move, and see what he does.*

*The purpose of this book is to show him in a few representative episodes, selected from different stages in his career. The first of them is so old as to be almost an antique, but for that very reason it may be of interest to the archæologists whose white beards I can see waving in the audience. It is called:*

# THE MAN WHO WAS CLEVER

## From ENTER THE SAINT

---

THIS WAS THE FIRST SAINT STORY *I ever wrote at this length—the first of many, as the present volume shows. In those days we called them "novelettes", and blushed faintly when we said it. Recently I have gathered from some reading of book reviews that an attempt is being made by a few publishers and authors more highbrow than myself to popularise this length as "a new literary form". Only now they call them* novellas, *and instead of the blush there are traces of a lofty preening. Which just goes to prove something or other; I forget exactly what.*

*Whether you call it a novelette or a* novella *or a piece of cheese, I don't think I shall ever lose my affection for it as a literary form. The short story is inevitably an artistic anecdote. The "full-length novel", on the other hand, must always be open to suspicion of having been artificially inflated in order to bring it up to a purely conventional size. But the novelette leaves room for all the meaty development that could be asked for, while at the same time calling for a fairly ruthless conciseness. It is a nice length to read, since it can be consumed completely, at one sitting, in any idle hour, such as while lying in bed before going to sleep, or while waiting for the wife to put on her hat. It is a particularly nice length to write, since it can be finished before the author gets tired of it.*

*This story, like the two following it, has no particularly brilliant originality of plot, and there are perceptible crudities in the telling. However, I have left it in its original form, except for revising a few minor allusions which dated it too unmistakably. It belongs to a period when the Saint was younger, more boisterous, and less subtle than he has since become.*

# THE MAN WHO WAS CLEVER

MR "SNAKE" GANNING was neither a great criminal nor a pleasant character, but he is interesting because he was the first victim of the organization led by the man known as the Saint, which was destined in the course of a few months to spread terror through the underworld of London—that ruthless association of reckless young men, brilliantly led, who worked on the side of the Law and who were yet outside the Law. There was to come a time when the mere mention of the Saint was sufficient to fill the most unimaginative malefactor with uneasy fears, when a man returning home late one night to find the sign of the Saint—a childish sketch of a little man with a straight-line body and limbs, and an absurd halo over his round blank head—chalked upon his door, would be sent instinctively spinning round with his back to the nearest wall and his hand flying to his hip pocket, and an icy tingle of dread prickling up his spine; but at the date of the Ganning episode the Saint had only just commenced operations, and his name had not yet come to be surrounded with the aura of almost supernatural infallibility which it was to earn for itself later.

Mr Ganning was a tall, incredibly thin man, with sallow features and black hair that was invariably oiled and brushed to a shiny sleekness. His head was small and round, and he carried it thrust forward to the full stretch of his long neck. Taking into the combination of physical characteristics the sinuous carriage of his body, the glittering beadiness of his expressionless black eyes, and the silent litheness with which he moved, it was easy to appreciate the aptness of his nickname. He was the leader of a particularly tough race-course gang generally known as "The Snake's Boys," which subsisted in unmerited luxury on the proceeds of blackmailing bookmakers under threat of doing them grievous bodily harm; there

3

were also a number of other unsavoury things about him which may be revealed in due course.

The actual motive for the interference of the Saint in the affairs of the Snake and his Boys was their treatment of Tommy Mitre on the occasion of his first venture into Turf finance. Tommy had always wanted to be a jockey, for horses were in his blood; but quite early in his apprenticeship he had been thrown and injured so severely that he had never been able to ride again, and he had had to content himself with the humble position of stable boy in a big training establishment. Then an uncle of Tommy's, who had been a publican, died, leaving his nephew the tremendous fortune of two hundred pounds, and Tommy decided to try his luck in the Silver Ring. He took out a licence, had a board painted ("Tommy Mitre— The Old Firm—Established 1822") and enlisted a clerk. One day he went down to Brighton with this paraphernalia and the remains of his two hundred pounds, and it was not long before the Snake's Boys spotted the stranger and made the usual demands. Tommy refused to pay. He ought to have known better, for the methods of the Snake had never been a secret in racing circles; but Tommy was like that—stubborn. He told the Snake exactly where he could go, and as a result Tommy Mitre was soundly beaten up by the Snake's Boys when he was leaving the course, and his capital and his day's profits were taken. And it so happened that Simon Templar had elected to enjoy a day's racing at Brighton, and had observed the beating-up from a distance.

Snake Ganning and a select committee of the Boys spent the evening in Brighton celebrating, and left for London by a late train. So also did Simon Templar.

Thus it came to pass that the said Simon Templar wandered up the platform a couple of minutes before the train left, espied the Snake and three of the Boys comfortably ensconced in a first-class carriage, and promptly joined them.

The Saint, it should be understood, was a vision that gave plenty of excuse for the glances of pleased anticipation which were exchanged by the Snake and his favourite Boys as soon as they had summed him up. In what he called his "fighting kit"—which consisted of disreputable grey flannel bags and a tweed shooting-jacket of almost legendary age—the Saint had the unique gift of appearing so immaculate that the least absent-minded commissionaire might have been pardoned for mistaking him for a millionaire duke. It may be imagined what a radiant spectacle he was in what he called his "gentleman disguise."

His grey flannel suit fitted him with a staggering perfection, the whiteness of his shirt was dazzling, his tie shamed the rainbow. His soft felt hat appeared to be having its first outing since it left Bond Street. His chamois gloves were clearly being shown to the world for the first time. On his left wrist was a gold watch, and he carried a gold-mounted ebony walking-stick.

Everything, you understand, quietly but unmistakably of the very best, and worn with that unique air of careless elegance which others might attempt to emulate, but which only the Saint could achieve in all its glory. . . .

As for the man—well, the Snake's Boys had never had any occasion to doubt that their reputation for toughness was founded on more substantial demonstrations than displays of their skill at hunt-the-slipper at the YMCA on Saturday afternoons. The man was tall—about six feet two inches of him—but they didn't take much count of that. Their combined heights totted up to twentyfour feet three inches. And although he wasn't at all hefty, he was broad enough, and there was a certain solidity about his shoulders that would have made a cautious man think carefully before starting any unpleasantness—but that didn't bother the Snake and his Boys. Their combined widths summed up to a shade over six feet. And the Saint had a clear tanned skin and a very clear blue eye—but even that failed to worry them. They weren't running a beauty competition, anyway.

The important point was that the Saint had a gold cigarette-case and a large wad of bank-notes. In his innocent way, he counted over his pile before their very eyes, announced the total at two hundred and fifty pounds odd, and invited them to congratulate him on his luck. They congratulated him, politely. They remarked on the slowness of the train, and the Saint agreed that it was a boring journey. He said he wished there was some sort of entertainment provided by the railway company for the diversion of passengers on boring journeys. Somebody produced a pack of cards. . . .

It can be said for them that they gave him the credit for having been warned by his grandmother about the danger of trying to find the Lady. The game selected was poker. The Saint apologetically warned them that he had only played poker once before in his life, but they said kindly that that didn't matter a bit.

The fight started just five minutes before the train reached Victoria, and the porters who helped the Snake and his Boys out of the compartment were not thanked. They gave the Boys a bucket of water with which to revive the Snake himself, but they couldn't do anything about his two black eyes or his missing front teeth.

Inspector Teal, who was waiting on the platform in the hope of seeing a much-wanted con-man, saw the injured warriors and was not sympathetic.

"You've been fighting, Snake," he said brightly.

Ganning's reply was unprintable, but Mr Teal was not easily shocked.

"But I can describe him to you," said the Snake, becoming less profane. "Robbery with violence, that's what it was. He set on us——"

" 'Sat' is the past tense of 'sit,' " said Teal shifting his gum to the other side of his mouth.

"He's got away with over three hundred quid that we made to-day——"

Teal was interested.

"Where d'you make it?" he enquired. "Have you got a real printing-press, or do you make it by hand? I didn't know you were in the slush game, Snake."

"Look here, Teal," said Ganning, becoming more coherent. "You can say what you like about me, but I've got my rights, the same as anybody else. You've got to get after that man. Maybe you know things about him already. He's either on a lay, or he's just starting on one, you mark my words. See this!"

Mr Teal examined the envelope sleepily.

"What is it?" he asked. "A letter of introduction to me?"

"He gave it to Ted when he got out. 'That's my receipt,' he said. Didn't he, Ted? You look inside, Teal!"

The envelope was not sealed. Teal turned it over, and remarked on the flap the crest of the hotel which had provided it. Then, in his lethargic way, he drew out the contents—a single sheet of paper.

"Portrait by Epstein," he drawled. "Quite a nice drawing, but it don't mean anything to me outside of that. You boys have been reading too many detective stories lately, that's the trouble with you."

## II

The Saint, being a man of decidedly luxurious tastes, was the tenant of a flat in Brook Street, Mayfair, which was so far beyond his means that he had long since given up worrying about the imminence of bankruptcy. One might as well be hung for a sheep, the Saint reflected, in his cheerfully reckless way, as for a foot-and-mouth-diseased lamb. He considered that the world owed him a good time, in return for services rendered and general presentability and good-fellowship, and, since the world hitherto had been close-fistedly reluctant to recognise the obligation and meet it, the Saint had decided that the time had come for him to assert himself. His invasion of Brook Street had been one of the first moves in the campaign.

But the locality had one distinct advantage that had nothing to do with the prestige of its address; and this advantage was the fact that it possessed a mews, a very small and exclusive mews, situated at a distance of less than the throw of a small stone from the Saint's front door. In this mews were a number of very expensive garages, large, small, and of Austin Seven size. And the Saint owned two of these large garages. In one he kept his own car; the other had been empty for a week, until he had begun smuggling an assortment of curious objects into it at dead of night—objects which only by the most frantic stretch of imagination could have been associated with cars.

If the Saint had been observed on any of these surreptitious trips, it is highly probable that his sanity would have been doubted. Not that he would have cared; for he had his own reasons for his apparent eccentricity. But as it was, no one noticed his goings-out or his comings-in, and there was no comment.

And even if he had been noticed, it is very doubtful if he would have been recognized. It was the immaculate Saint who left Brook Street and drove to Chelsea and garaged his car near Fulham Road. Then, by a very subtle change of carriage, it was a not-nearly-so immaculate Saint who walked through a maze of dingy back streets to a house in which one Bertie Marks, a bird of passage, had a stuffy and microscopical apartment. And it was a shabby, sloppy, down-at-heel Bertie Marks who left the apartment and returned to the West End on the plebeian bus, laden with the packages that he had purchased on his way; and who shambled inconspicuously into the mews off Brook Street and into the garage which he held in his own name. The Saint did not believe in being unnecessarily careless about details.

And all these elaborate preparations—the taking of the second garage and the Chelsea apartment, and the creation of the character of Bertie Marks—had been made for one single purpose, which was put into execution on a certain day.

A few hours after dawn on that day (an unearthly hour for the Saint to be abroad) a small van bearing the name of Carter Paterson turned into the mews and stopped there. Bertie Marks climbed down from the driver's seat, wiping grimy hands on his corduroys, and fished out a key, with which he opened the door of his garage. Then he went back to his van, drove it into the garage, and closed the doors behind him.

He knew that this action must have excited the curiosity of the car-washing parade of chauffeurs congregated in the mews, but he wasn't bothering about that. With the consummation of his plan, the necessity for the continued existence of Bertie Marks was rapidly nearing its end.

"Let 'em wonder!" thought the Saint carelessly, as he peeled off his grubby jacket.

He switched on the light, and went and peeped out into the mews. The car-washing parade had resumed its labours, being for the moment too preoccupied to bother about the strange phenomenon of a Carter Paterson van being driven into a garage that had once housed a Rolls.

The Saint gently slid a bar across the door to shut out any inquisitive explorers, and got to work.

The van, on being opened, disclosed a number of large, wooden packing-cases, which the Saint proceeded to unload on to the floor of the garage. This done, he fetched from a corner a mallet and chisel, and began to prise open the cases and extract their contents. In each case, packed in with wood shavings, were two dozen china jars.

As each case was emptied, the Saint carried the jars over to the light and inspected them minutely. He was not at all surprised to find that, whereas the majority of the jars were perfectly plain, all the jars in one case were marked with a tiny cross in the glazing. These jars the Saint set aside, for they were the only ones in which he was interested. They were exactly what he had expected to find, and they provided his entire motive for the temporary and occasional sinking of his own personality in the *alias* of Mr Marks. The other jars he replaced in their respective cases, and carefully closed and roped them to look as they had been before he tampered with them.

Then he opened the marked jars and poured out their contents into a bucket. In another corner of the garage was a pile of little tins, and in each jar the Saint placed one of these tins, padding the space that was left with cotton wool to prevent rattling. The jars so treated were replaced one by one and the case in its turn was also nailed up again and roped as before—after the Saint, with a little smile plucking at the corners of his mouth, had carefully laid a souvenir of his intervention on the top of the last layer of wood shavings.

He had worked quickly. Only an hour and a half had elapsed from the time when he drove into the garage to the time when he lifted the last case back into the van; and when that had been done he unbarred the garage doors and opened them wide.

The remains of the car-washing parade looked up puzzledly as the van came backing out of the garage; it registered an even greater perplexity when the van proceeded to drive out of the mews and vanish in the direction of Bond Street. It yelled to the driver that he had forgotten to close his garage after him, but Mr Marks either did not hear or did not care. And when the parade perceived that Mr Marks had gone for good, it went and peered into the garage, and scratched its head over the litter of wood shavings on the floor, the mallet and chisel and nails and hammer, and the two or three tins which the Saint had found no space for, and which he had accordingly left behind. But the bucket of white powder was gone, riding beside Mr Marks in the front of the van; and very few people ever saw Mr Marks again.

The van drove to an address in the West End, and there Mr Marks delivered the cases, secured a signature to a receipt, and departed, heading further west. On his way, he stopped at St George's Hospital, where he left his bucket. The man who took charge of it was puzzled, but Mr Marks was in a hurry and had neither the time nor the inclination to enlighten him.

"Take great care of it, because it's worth more money than you'll ever have," he directed. "See that it gets to one of the doctors, and give him this note with it."

And the Saint went back to the wheel of his van and drove away, feeling that he was nearing the end of an excellent day's work.

He drove to the Great West Road, and out of London towards Maidenhead. Somewhere along the road he turned off into a side lane, and there he stopped for a few minutes out of sight of the main traffic. Inside the van was a large pot of paint, and the Saint used it energetically. He had never considered himself an artist, but he man-handled that van with the broad sweeping touch of a master. Under his vigorous wielding of the brush, the sign of Carter Paterson, which he had been at some pains to execute artistically the night before, vanished entirely; and the van became plain. Satisfied with the obliteration of the handiwork which only a few hours before he had admired so much, Simon resumed the wheel and drove back to London. The paint he had used was guaranteed quick-drying, and it lived up to the word of its guarantee. It collected a good deal of dust on the return voyage, and duly dried with a somewhat soiled aspect which was a very fair imitation of the condition in which Mr Marks had received it.

He delivered it to its home garage at Shepherd's Bush and paid twentyfour hours' hire. Some time later, Mr Marks returned to Chelsea. A little later still, the not-so-immaculate Simon Templar turned into another garage and collected his trim blue Lagonda speedster, in which he drove to his club in Dover Street. And the Simon Templar who sauntered through to the bar and called for a pint of beer must have been one of the most impeccably immaculate young men that that haunt of impeccably immaculate young men had ever sheltered.

"We don't often see you as early as this, sir," remarked the barman.

"May it be as many years before you see me as early as this again, son," answered the Saint piously. "But this morning I felt I just had to get up and go for a drive. It was such a beautiful morning."

### III

Mr Edgar Hayn was a man of many interests. He was the proud proprietor of "Danny's", a night club in a squalid street of Shaftesbury Avenue, and he also controlled the destinies of the firm of Laserre, which was a small but expensive shop in Regent Street that retailed perfumes, powders, rouges, creams, and all the other preparations essential to modern feminine face-repair. These two establishments were Mr Hayn's especial pets, and from them he derived the greater part of his substantial income. Yet it might be mentioned that the profits of "Danny's" were not entirely earned by the sale of champagne, and the adornment of fashionable beauty was not the principal source of the prosperity of the house of Laserre. Mr Hayn was a clever organiser, and what he did not know about the art of covering his tracks wouldn't have been missed from one of the microscopical two-guinea alabaster jars in which he sold the celebrated Crême Laserre.

He was a big, heavy-featured man, clean-shaven, pink complexioned, and faintly bald. His name had not always been Hayn, but a process of naturalisation followed by a Deed Poll had given him an indisputable legal right to forget the cognomen of his father—and, incidentally, had eliminated for ever the unpleasant possibility of a deportation order, an exercise of forethought for which Mr Hayn was more than once moved to give his sagacity a pat on the back. The police knew certain things about him which made them inclined to regard him with disfavour; and they suspected a lot more, but there had never been any evidence.

He was writing letters at the big knee-hole desk in his private office at "Danny's" when Ganning arrived. The knock on the door did not make him look up. He said "Come in!"—but the sound of the opening and closing of the door was, to him, sufficient indication that the order had been obeyed; and he went on to finish the letter he had been drafting.

Only when that was done did he condescend to notice the presence of his visitor.

"You're late, Snake," he said, blotting the sheet carefully.

"Sorry, boss."

Mr Hayn screwed the cap on his fountain pen, replaced it in his pocket, and raised his eyes from the desk for the first time. What he saw made him sag back with astonishment.

"Who on earth have you been picking a quarrel with?" he demanded.

The Snake certainly looked the worse for wear. A bandage round his head covered one eye, and the eye that was visible was nearly closed up. His lips were bruised and swollen, and a distinct lack of teeth made him speak with a painful lisp.

"Was it Harrigan's crowd?" suggested Hayn.

Ganning shook his head.

"A bloke we met on the train coming back from Brighton last night."

"Were you alone?"

"Nope; Ted and Bill were with me. And Mario."

"And what was this man trooping round? A regiment?"

"He was alone."

Hayn blinked.

"How did it happen?"

"We thought he was a sucker," explained the Snake disgustedly. "Smart clothes, gold cigarette-case, gold-mounted stick, gold watch —and a wad. He showed us his wad. Two-fifty, he said it was. We couldn't let that go, so we got him into a game of cards. Poker. He said he didn't know anything about the game, so it looked safe enough—he struck us as being that sort of mug. We were geeing him along nicely right up to ten minutes or so before Victoria, and we'd let him take fifty off us. He was thinking himself the greatest poker player in the world by then, you'd have said. Then we asked him to be a sport and give us a chance of getting our money back on a couple of big jack-pots with a five-pound ante. He agreed, and we let him win the first one. We all threw in after the first rise. 'What about making it a tenner ante for the last deal?' I said, tipping the wink to the boys. He wasn't too keen on that, but we jollied him along, and at last he fell for it. It was his deal, but I shuffled the boards for him."

"And your hand slipped?"

Ganning snorted.

"Slipped nothin'! My hand doesn't slip. I'd got that deck stacked better than any conjuror could have done it. And I picked up a straight flush, just as I'd fixed it. Mario chucked in right away, and Ted and Bill dropped out after the first round. That left the Mug and me, and we went on raising each other till every cent the boys and I could find between us was in the kitty. We even turned in our links and Mario's diamond pin to account for as much of the Mug's wad as possible. When we hadn't another bean to stake, he saw me. I showed down my straight flush, and I was just getting set to scoop in the pool when he stopped me. 'I thought you told me this was next to unbeatable,' he says, and then he shows down five kings."

"Five?" repeated Mr Hayn frowning.

"We were playing deuces wild, and a joker. He'd got the joker."

"Well, didn't you know what he was holding?"

"It wasn't the hand I fixed for him to deal himself!"

Mr Hayn controlled his features.

"And then you cut up rough, and got the worst of it?"

"I accused him of cheating. He didn't deny it. He had the nerve to say: 'Well, you were supposed to be teaching me the game, and I saw you were cheating all the time, so I thought it was allowed by the rules!' And he started putting away our pile. Of course we cut up rough!"

"And he cut up rougher?" suggested Mr Hayn.

"He didn't fight fair," said Ganning aggrievedly. "First thing I knew he'd jabbed the point of his stick into Ted's neck before Ted had a chance to pull his cosh, so Ted was out of it. Bill was all ready for a fair stand-up fight with the knuckle-dusters, but this man kicked him in the stomach, so *he* took the count. Mario and me had to tackle him alone."

The Snake seemed disinclined to proceed further with the description of the battle, and Hayn tactfully refrained from pressing him. He allowed the Snake to brood blackly over the memory for a few moments.

"He wasn't an amateur," said Ganning. "But none of us could place him. I'd give the hell of a lot to find out who he was. One of these fly mobsmen you read about, I shouldn't wonder. He'd got all the dope. Look at this," said the Snake, producing the envelope. "He shoved that at Ted when he got out. Said it was his receipt. I tried to get Teal to take it up—he was at the station—but he wouldn't take it seriously."

Hayn slipped the sheet of paper out of the envelope and spread it out on his desk. Probably he had not fully grasped the purport of Ganning's description, for the effect the sight had on him was amazing.

If Ganning had been disappointed with Inspector Teal's unemotional reception of the Saint's receipt, he was fully compensated by the reaction of Mr Edgar Hayn. Hayn's pink face suddenly turned white, and he jerked away from the paper that lay on the blotter in front of him as if it had spat poison at him.

"What's it mean to you, boss?" asked the bewildered Ganning.

"This morning we got a consignment over from Germany," Hayn said, speaking almost in a whisper. "When Braddon opened the case, there was the same picture on top of the packing. We couldn't figure out how it came there."

"Have you looked the stuff over yet?" demanded the Snake, instantly alert.

Hayn shook his head. He was still staring, as though hypnotised, at the scrap of paper.

"We didn't think anything of it. There's never been a hitch yet. Braddon thought the men who packed the case must have been playing some game. We just put the marked jars away in the usual place."

"You haven't had to touch them yet?"

Hayn made a negative gesture. He reached out a shaky hand for the telephone, while Ganning sat silently chewing over the startling possibilities that were revealed by this information.

"Hello. . . . Regent nine double-o four seven . . . please." Hayn fidgeted nervously as he waited for the call to be put through. It came after what seemed an eternity. "Hullo. . . . That you, Braddon? . . . I want you to get out the marked jars that came over in the case with the paper in—you remember? . . . Never mind why!"

A minute ticked away, while Hayn kept the receiver glued to his ear and tapped out an impatient tattoo on the desk.

"Yes? . . . What's that? . . . How d'you know? . . . I see. Well, I'll be right round!"

Hayn clicked the receiver back and slewed his swivel chair around so that he faced Snake Ganning.

"What's he say?" asked the Snake.

"There's just a tin of Keating's powder in each," Hayn replied. "I asked him how he knew what it was, and he said the whole tin was there, label and all, packed in with cotton wool to make it fit. There was ten thousand pounds' worth of snow in that shipping, and this guy has lifted the lot!"

## IV

"You may decant some beer, son," said Simon Templar, stretched out in an armchair. "And then you may start right in and tell me the story of your life. I can spare you about two minutes."

Jerry Stannard travelled obediently over to a side table where bottles and glasses were already set out, accomplished his task with a practised hand, and travelled back again with the results.

"Your health," said the Saint, and two foaming glasses were half-emptied in an appreciative silence.

Stannard was then encouraged to proceed. He put down his glass with a sigh and settled back at his ease, while the Saint made a long arm for the cigarette-box.

"I can't make out yet why you should have interested yourself in me," said Stannard.

"That's my affair," said the Saint bluntly. "And if it comes to that, son, I'm not a philanthropic institution. I happen to want an assistant, and I propose to make use of you. Not that you won't get anything out of it. I'm sufficiently interested in you to want to help you, but you're going to pay your way."

Stannard nodded.

"It's decent of you to think I'm worth it," he said.

He had not forgotten—it would have been impossible to forget such an incident in two days—the occasion of his first meeting with the Saint. Stannard had been entrusted with a small packet which he had been told to take to an address in Piccadilly; and even if he had not been told what the packet contained, he could not have helped having a very shrewd idea. And therefore, when a heavy hand had fallen suddenly on his shoulder only a few minutes after he had left Mr Hayn, he had had no hope.

And then the miracle had happened, although he did not realize at the time that it was a miracle. A man had brushed against him as the detective turned to hail a taxi, and the man had turned to apologize. In that crisis, all Stannard's faculties had been keyed up to the vivid supersensitiveness which comes just before breaking point; and that abnormal acuteness had combined with the peculiarly keen stare which had accompanied the stranger's apology, so that the stranger's face was indelibly engraved on Stannard's memory. . . .

The Saint took a little package from his pocket, and weighed it reflectively in his hand.

"Fortyeight hours ago," he murmured, "you assumed, quite rightly, that you were booked for five years' penal servitude. Instead of that, you're a free man. The triumphant sleuths of Vine Street found nothing on you, and had to release you with apologies. Doubtless they're swearing to make up for that bloomer, and make no mistakes about landing you with the goods next time; but that can't hurt you for the moment. And I expect you're still wondering what's going to be my price for having picked your pocket in the nick of time."

"I've been wondering ever since."

"I'm just going to tell you," said the Saint. "But first we'll get rid of this."

He left the room with the packet, and through the open door came the sound of running water. In a few moments he was back, dusting his hands.

"That disposes of the evidence," he said. "Now I want you to tell me something. How did you get into this dope game?"

Stannard shrugged.

"You may as well know. There's no heroic or clever reason. It's just because I'm a waster. I was in the wrong set at Cambridge, and I knew most of the toughs in Town. Then my father died and left me without a bean. I tried to get a job, but I couldn't do anything useful. And all the time, naturally, I was mixing with the same bad bunch. Eventually they roped me in. I suppose I ought to have fought against it, but I just hadn't the guts. It was easy money, and I took it. That's all."

There was a short silence, during which the Saint blew monotonously regular smoke-rings towards the ceiling.

"Now I'll tell you something," he said. "I've made all the enquiries I need to make about you. I know your family history for two generations back, your early life, your school record—everything. I know enough to judge that you don't belong where you are now. For one thing I know you're engaged to a rather nice girl, and she's worried about you. She doesn't know anything, but she suspects. And you're worried. You're not as quiet and comfortable in this crime racket as you'd like to make out. You weren't cut out for a bad man. Isn't that true?"

"True enough," Stannard said flatly. "I'd give anything to be out of it."

"And you're straight about this girl—Gwen Chandler?"

"Straight as a die. Honest, Templar! But what can I do? If I drop Hayn's crowd, I shan't have a cent. Besides, I don't know that they'd let me drop out. I owe money. When I was at Cambridge, I lost a small fortune—for me—in Hayn's gambling rooms, and he's got I O U's of mine for close on a thousand. I've been extravagant—I've run up bills everywhere. You can't imagine how badly in the cart I am!"

"On the contrary, brother," said the Saint calmly, "I've a very good guess about that. That's why you're here now. I wanted an agent inside Hayn's gang, and I ran through the whole deck before I chose you."

He rose from his chair and took a turn up and down the room. Stannard waited; and presently the Saint stopped abruptly.

"You're all right," he said.

Stannard frowned.

"Meaning?"

"Meaning I'm going to trust you. I'm going to take you in with me for this campaign. I'll get you enough out of it to square off your debts, and at the end of it I'll find you a job. You'll keep in with Hayn, but you'll be working for me. And you'll give me your word of honour that you'll go straight for the rest of your life. That's my offer. What about it?"

The Saint leant against the mantelpiece languidly enough, but there had been nothing languid about his crisp incisive sentences. Thinking it over afterwards, it seemed to Stannard that the whole thing had been done in a few minutes, and he was left to marvel at the extraordinary force of personality which in such a short time could override the prejudice of years and rekindle a spark of decency that had been as good as dead. But at the instant, Stannard could not analyse his feeling.

"I'm giving you a chance to get out and make good," the Saint went on. "I'm not doing it in the dark. I believe you when you say you'd be glad of a chance to make a fresh start. I believe there's the makings of a decent man in you. Anyway, I'll take a chance on it. I won't even threaten you, though I could, by telling you what I shall do to you if you double-cross me. I'll just ask you a fair question, and I want your answer now."

Stannard got to his feet.

"There's only one answer," he said, and held out his hand.

The Saint took it in a firm grip.

"Now I'll tell you exactly where you stand," he said.

He did so, speaking in curt sentences as before. His earlier grimness had relaxed somewhat, for when the Saint did anything he never did it by halves, and now he spoke to Stannard as a friend and an ally. He had his reward in the eager attention with which the youngster followed his discourse. He told him everything that there was any need for him to know.

"You've got to think of everything, and then more, if you're going to come out of this with a whole skin," Simon concluded, with some of his former sternness. "The game I'm on isn't the kind they play in nurseries. I'm on it because I just can't live happily ever after. I've had enough adventures to fill a dozen books, but instead of satisfying me they've only left me with a bigger appetite. If I had to live the ordinary kind of safe civilized life, I'd die of boredom. Risks are food and drink to me. You may be different. If you are, I'm sorry about it, but I can't help it. I need some help in this, and you're going to give it to me; but it wouldn't be fair to let you whale in without showing you what you're up against. Your bunch of bad hats aren't childish enemies. Before you're through, London's likely to be just about as healthy for you as the Cannibal Islands are for a nice plump missionary. Get me?"

Stannard intimated that he had got him.

"Then I'll give you your orders for the immediate future," said the Saint.

He did so, in detail, and had everything repeated over to him twice before he was convinced that there would be no mistake and that nothing would be forgotten.

"From now on, I want you to keep away from me till I give you the all-clear," he ended up. "If the Snake's anywhere around I shan't last long in Danny's, and it's essential to keep you out of suspicion for as long as possible. So this'll be our last open meeting for some time. But you can communicate by telephone—so long as you make sure nobody can hear you."

"Right you are, Saint," said Stannard.

Simon Templar flicked a cigarette into his mouth and reached for the matches.

The other had a queer transient feeling of unreality. It seemed fantastic that he should be associated with such a project as that into which the Saint had initiated him. It seemed equally fantastic that the Saint should have conceived it and brought it into being. That cool casual young man, with his faultless clothes, his clipped and slangy speech, and his quick clear smile—he ought to have been lounging his amiable easy-going way through a round of tennis and cricket and cocktail-parties and dances, instead of . . .

And yet it remained credible—it was even, with every passing second, becoming almost an article of the reawakened Stannard's new faith. The Saint's spell was unique. There was a certain quiet assurance about his bearing, a certain steely quality that came sometimes into his blue eyes, a certain indefinable air of strength and recklessness and quixotic bravado, that made the whole fantastic notion acceptable. And Stannard had not even the advantage of knowing anything about the last eight years of the Saint's hell-for-leather career—eight years of gay buccaneering which, even allowing for exaggeration, made him out to be a man of no ordinary or drawing-room toughness. . . .

The Saint lighted his cigarette and held out his hand to terminate the interview; and the corners of his mouth were twitching to his irresistible smile.

"So long, comrade," he said. "And good hunting!"

"Same to you," said Stannard warmly.

The Saint clapped him on the shoulder.

"I know you won't let me down," he said. "There's lots of good in you, and I guess I've found some of it. You'll pull out all right. I'm going to see that you do. Watch me!"

But before he left, Stannard got a query off his chest.

"Didn't you say there were five of you?"

His hands in his pockets, teetering gently on his heels, the Saint favoured Stannard with his most Saintly smile.

"I did," he drawled. "Four little Saints and Papa. I am the Holy Smoke. As for the other four, they are like the Great White Woolly Wugga-Wugga on the plans of Astrakhan."

Stannard gaped at him.

"What does that mean?" he demanded.

"I ask you, sweet child," answered the Saint, with that exasperatingly seraphic smile still on his lips, "has anyone ever seen a Great White Woolly Wugga-Wugga on the plains of Astrakhan? Sleep on it, my cherub—it will keep your mind from impure thoughts."

## V

To all official intents and purposes, the proprietor and leading light of Mr Edgar Hayn's night club in Soho was the man after whom it was named—Danny Trask.

Danny was short and dumply, a lazy little tub of a man, with a round red face, a sparse head of fair hair, and a thin sandy moustache. His pale eyes were deeply embedded in the creases of their fleshy lids; and when he smiled—which was often, and usually for no apparent reason—they vanished altogether in a corrugating mesh of wrinkles.

His intelligence was not very great. Nevertheless, he had discovered quite early in life that there was a comfortable living to be made in the profession of "dummy"—a job which calls for no startling intellectual gifts—and Danny had accordingly made that his vocation ever since. As a figurehead, he was all that could have been desired, for he was unobtrusive and easily satisfied. He had a type of mind common to his class of lawbreaker. As long as his salary—which was not small—was paid regularly, he never complained, showed no ambition to join his employer on a more equal basis of division of profits, and, if anything went wrong, kept his mouth shut and deputised for his principal in one of His Majesty's prisons without a murmur. Danny's fees for a term of imprisonment were a flat rate of ten pounds a week, with an extra charge of two pounds a week for "hard." The astuteness of the CID and the carelessness of one or two of his previous employers, had made this quite a profitable proposition for Danny.

He had visions of retiring one day and ending his life in comparative luxury, when his savings had reached a sufficiently large figure; but this hope had received several set-backs of late. He had been in Mr Hayn's service for four years, and Mr Hayn's uncanny skill in avoiding the attentions of the police was becoming a thorn in the side of Danny Trask. When Danny was not in stir, the most he could command was a paltry seven pounds a week, and living expenses had to be paid out of this instead of out of the pocket of the Government. Danny felt that he had a personal grievance against Mr Hayn on this account.

The club theoretically opened at 6 pm, but the food was not good, and most of its members preferred to dine elsewhere. The first arrivals usually began to drift in about 10 pm, but things never began to get exciting before 11 o'clock. Danny spent the hours between 6 o'clock and the commencement of the fun sitting in his shirtsleeves in his little cubicle by the entrance, sucking a foul old briar and tentatively selecting the next day's losers from an evening paper. He was incapable of feeling bored—his mind had never reached the stage of development where it could appreciate the ideas of activity and inactivity. It had never been active, so it didn't see any difference.

He was engaged in this pleasant pursuit towards 8 o'clock on a certain evening when Jerry Stannard arrived.

"Has Mr Hayn come in yet, Danny?"

Danny made a pencil note of the number of pounds which he had laboriously calculated that Wilco would have in hand over Man of Kent in the Lingfield Plate, folded his paper, and looked up.

"He don't usually come in till late, Mr Stannard," he said. "No, he ain't here now."

Danny's utterances always contrived to put the cart before the horse. If he had wanted to give you a vivid description of a death-bed scene, he would have inevitably started with the funeral.

"Oh, it's all right—he's expecting me," said Stannard. "When he arrives you can tell him I'm at the bar."

He was plainly agitated. While he was talking, he never stopped fiddling with his signet ring; and Danny, whose shrewd glances missed very little, noticed that his tie was limp and crooked, as if it had been subjected to the clumsy wrestling of shaky fingers.

"Right you are, sir."

It was none of Danny's business, anyway.

"Oh—and before I forget. . . ."

"Sir?"

"A Mr Templar will be here later. He's OK. Send down for me when he arrives, and I'll sign him in."

"Very good, sir."

Danny returned to his study of equine form, and Stannard passed on.

He went through the lounge which occupied the ground floor, and turned down the stairs at the end. Facing these stairs, behind a convenient curtain, was a secret door in the panelling, electrically operated, which was controlled by a button on the desk in Hayn's private office. This door, when opened, disclosed a flight of stairs running upwards. These stairs communicated with the upstairs rooms which were one of the most profitable features of the club, for in those rooms *chemin-de-fer*, poker, and roulette were played every night with the sky for a limit.

Hayn's office was at the foot of the downward flight. He had personally supervised the installation of an ingenious system of mirrors, by means of which, with the aid of a large soundproof window let into the wall at one end of the office, without leaving his seat, he was able to inspect everyone who passed through the lounge above. Moreover, when the secret door swung open in response to the pressure of his finger on the control button, a further system of mirrors panelled up the upper flight of stairs gave him a view right up the stairway itself and round the landing into the gaming rooms. Mr Hayn was a man with a cunning turn of mind, and he was pre-eminently cautious.

Outside the office, in the basement, was the dance floor, surrounded with tables; but only two couples were dining there. At the far end was the dais on which the orchestra played, and at the other end, under the stairs, was the tiny bar.

Stannard turned in there, and roused the white-coated barman from his perusal of *La Vie Parisienne*.

"I don't know what would meet the case," he said, "but I want something strong in corpse-revivers."

The man looked him over for a moment with an expert eye, then busied himself with the filling of a prescription. The result certainly had a kick in it. Stannard was downing it when Hayn came in.

The big man was looking pale and tired, and there were shadows under his eyes. He nodded curtly to Jerry.

"I'll be with you in a minute," he said. "Just going to get a wash."

It was not like Mr Hayn, who ordinarily specialised in the boisterous hail-fellow-well-met method of address, and Stannard watched him go thoughtfully.

Braddon, who had remained outside, followed Hayn into the office.

"Who's the boy friend?" he asked, taking a chair.

"Stannard?" Hayn was skimming through the letters that waited on his desk. "An ordinary young fool. He lost eight hundred upstairs in his first couple of months. Heaven knows how much he owes outside—he'd lost a packet before I started lending him money."

Braddon searched through his pockets for a cigar, and found one. He bit off the end, and spat.

"Got expectations? Rich papa who'll come across?"

"No. But he's got the clothes, and he'd pass anywhere. I was using him."

"*Was?*"

Hayn was frowningly examining the postmark on one of his letters.

"I suppose I shall still," he said. "Don't bother me—this artistic hijacker's got me all ends up. But he's got a fiancée—I've only recently seen her. I like her."

"Any good?"

"I shall arrange something about her."

Hayn had slit open the letter with his thumb-nail, but he only took one glance at what it contained. He tossed it over to Braddon, and it was the manager of Laserre who drew out the now familiar sketch.

"One of those came to my house by the first post this morning," Hayn said. "It's as old as the hills, that game. So he thinks he's going to rattle me!"

"Isn't he?" asked Braddon, in his heavily cynical way.

"He damned well isn't!" Hayn came back savagely. "I've got the Snake and the men who were with him prowling round the West End just keeping their eyes peeled for the man who beat them up in the Brighton train. If he's in London, he can't stay hid for ever. And when Ganning's found him, we'll soon put paid to his joke!"

Then he pulled himself together.

"I'm giving Stannard dinner," he said. "What are you doing now?"

"I'll loaf out and get some food, and be back later," said Braddon. "I thought I'd take a look in upstairs."

Hayn nodded. He ushered Braddon out of the office, and locked the door behind him, for even Braddon was not allowed to remain in that sanctum alone. Braddon departed, and Hayn rejoined Stannard at the bar.

"Sorry to have kept you waiting, old man," he apologised, with an attempt to resume his pose of bluff geniality.

"I've been amusing myself," said Stannard, and indicated a row of empty glasses. "Have a spot?"

Hayn accepted, and Stannard looked at his watch.

"By the way," he said, "there's a man due here in about an hour. I met him the other day, and he seemed all right. He said he was a South African, and he's sailing back the day after tomorrow. He was complaining that he couldn't get any real fun in England, so I dropped a hint about a private gambling club I might be able to get him into and he jumped at it. I thought he might be some use—leaving England so soon, he could hardly make a kick—so I told him to join us over coffee. Is that all right?"

"Quite all right, old man." A thought struck Mr Hayn. "You're quite sure he wasn't one of these clever dicks?"

"Not on your life," scoffed Stannard. "I think I know a busy when I see one by now. I've seen enough of 'em dancing here. And this man seems to have money to burn."

Hayn nodded.

"I meant to come to some arrangement with you over dinner," he said. "This bird can go down as your first job, on commission. If you're ready, we'll start."

Stannard assented, and they walked over to the table which had been prepared.

Hayn was preoccupied. If his mind had not been simmering with other problems, he might have noticed Stannard's ill-concealed nervousness, and wondered what might have been the cause of it. But he observed nothing unusual about the younger man's manner.

While they were waiting for the grapefruit, he asked a question quite perfunctorily.

"What's this South African's name?"

"Templar—Simon Templar," answered Jerry.

The name meant nothing at all to Mr Hayn.

## VI

Over the dinner, Hayn made his offer—a twenty percent commission on business introduced. Stannard hardly hesitated before accepting.

"You don't want to be squeamish about it," Hayn argued. "I know it's against the law, but that's splitting hairs. Horse-racing is just as much a gamble. There'll always be fools who want to get rich without working, and there's no reason why we shouldn't take their money. You won't have to do anything that would make you liable to be sent to prison, though some of my staff would be jailed if the police caught them. You're quite safe. And the games are perfectly straight. We only win because the law of probabilities favours the bank."

This was not strictly true, for there were other factors to influence the runs of bad luck which attended the players upstairs; but this sordid fact Mr Hayn did not feel called upon to emphasize.

"Yes—I'll join you," Stannard said. "I've known it was coming. I didn't think you went on giving and lending me money for looking decorative and doing an odd job or two for you now and again."

"My dear fellow——"

"Dear-fellowing doesn't alter it. I know you want more of me than my services in decoying boobs upstairs. Are you going to tell me you didn't know I was caught the other day?"

Hayn stroked his chin.

"I was going to compliment you. How you got rid of that parcel of snow——"

"The point that matters is that I did get rid of it," cut in Stannard briefly. "And if I hadn't been able to, I should have been on remand in Brixton Prison now. I'm not complaining. I suppose I had to earn my keep. But it wasn't square of you to keep me in the dark."

"You knew——"

"I guessed. It's all right—I've stopped kicking. But I want you to let me right in from now on, if you're letting me in at all. I'm joining you, all in, and you needn't bother to humbug me any longer. How's that?"

"That's all right," said Mr Hayn, "if you must put things so crudely. But you don't even have to be squeamish about the dope side of it. If people choose to make fools of themselves like that, it's their own lookout. Our share is simply to refuse to quibble about whether it's legal or not. After all, alcohol is sold legally in this country, and nobody blames the publican if his customers get drunk every night and eventually die of DT's."

Stannard shrugged.

"I can't afford to argue, anyhow," he said. "How much do I draw?"

"Twenty percent—as I told you."

"What's that likely to make?"

"A lot," said Hayn. "We play higher here than anywhere else in London, and there isn't a great deal of competition in the snow market. You might easily draw upwards of seventy pounds a week."

"Then will you do something for me, Mr Hayn? I owe a lot of money outside. I'll take three thousand flat for the first year, to pay off everybody and fit myself up with a packet in hand."

"Three thousand pounds is a lot of money," said Hayn judicially. "You owe me nearly a thousand as it is."

"If you don't think I'm going to be worth it——"

Mr Hayn meditated, but not for long. The making of quick decisions was the whole reason for his success, and he didn't mind how much a thing cost if he knew it was worth it. He had no fear that Stannard would attempt to doublecross him. Among the other purposes which it served, Danny's formed a working headquarters for the Snake's Boys; Stannard could not help knowing the reputation of the gang, and he must also know that they had worked Hayn's vengeance on traitors before. No—there was no chance that Stannard would dare to try a doublecross. . . .

"I'll give you a cheque tonight," said Hayn.

Stannard was effusively grateful.

"You won't lose by it," he promised. "Templar's a speculation, granted, but I've met him only once. But there are other people with mints of money, people I've known for years, that I can vouch for absolutely. . . ."

He went on talking, but Hayn only listened with half an ear, for he was anxious to turn the conversation on to another topic, and he did so at the first opportunity.

Under pretence of taking a fatherly interest in his new agent's affairs, he plied him with questions about his private life and interests. Most of the information which he elicited was stale news to him, for he had long since taken the precaution of finding out everything of importance that there was to know about his man; but in these new enquiries Mr Hayn contrived to make Stannard's fiancée the centre of interrogation. It was very cleverly and surreptitiously done, but the fact remains that at the end of half an hour, by this process of indirect questioning, Hayn had discovered all that he wanted to know about the life and habits of Gwen Chandler.

"Do you think you could get her along here to supper on Thursday?" he suggested. "The only time I've met her, if you remember, I think you rather prejudiced her against me. It's up to you to put that right."

"I'll see what I can do," said Stannard.

After that, his point won, Hayn had no further interest in directing the conversation, and they were chatting desultorily when Simon Templar arrived.

The Saint, after weighing the relative merits of full evening dress or an ordinary lounge suit for the auspicious occasion, had decided upon a compromise and was sporting a dinner jacket; but he wore it, as might have been expected, as if he had been an Ambassador paying a state visit in full regalia.

"Hullo, Jerry, dear angel!" he hailed Stannard cheerfully.

Then he noticed Mr Hayn, and turned with outstretched hand.

"And you must be Uncle Ambrose," he greeted that gentleman cordially. "Pleased to meet you. . . . That's right, isn't it, Jerry? This is the uncle who died and left all his money to the Cats' Home? . . . Sorry to see you looking so well, Uncle Ambrose, old mongoose!"

Mr Hayn seemed somewhat taken aback. This man did not wear his clothes in the manner traditionally associated with raw Colonials with money to burn; and if his speech was typical of that of strong silent men from the great open spaces of that vintage, Mr Hayn decided that the culture of Piccadilly must have spread farther abroad into the British Empire than Cecil Rhodes had ever hoped for in his wildest dreams. Mr Hayn had never heard of Rhodes—to him Rhodes was an island where they bred red hens—but if he had heard of Rhodes he might reasonably have expressed his surprise like that.

He looked round to Jerry Stannard with raised eyebrows, and Stannard tapped his forehead and lifted his glass significantly.

"So we're going to see a real live gambling hell," said the Saint, drawing up a chair. "Isn't this fun? Let's all have a lot of drinks on the strength of it."

He called for liqueurs, and paid for them from a huge wad of banknotes which he tugged from his pocket. Mr Hayn's eyes lit up at the sight, and he decided that there were excuses for Templar's eccentricity. He leant forward and set himself out to be charming.

The Saint, however, had other views on the subject of the way in which the conversation should go, and at the first convenient pause he came out with a remark which showed that he had been paying little attention to what had gone before.

"I've bought a book about card tricks," he said. "I thought it might help me to spot sharpers. But the best part of it was the chapter on fortune-telling by cards. Take a card, and I'll tell you all your sins."

He produced a new pack from his pocket and pushed it across the table towards Hayn.

"You first, Uncle," he invited. "And see that your thoughts are pure when you draw, otherwise you'll give the cards a wrong impression. Hum a verse of your favourite hymn, for instance."

Mr Hayn knew nothing about hymns, but he complied tolerantly. If this freak had all that money, and perhaps some more, by all means let him be humoured.

"Now, isn't that sweet!" exclaimed the Saint, taking up the card Hayn had chosen. "Jerry, my pet, your Uncle Ambrose has drawn the ace of hearts. That stands for princely generosity. We'll have another brandy with you, Uncle, just to show how we appreciate it. Waiter! . . . Three more brandies, please. Faceache—I mean Uncle Ambrose—is paying. . . . Uncle, you must try your luck again."

Simon Templar pored over Hayn's second card until the drinks arrived. It was noticeable that his shoulders shook silently at one time. Mr Hayn attributed this to repressed hiccups, and was gravely in error. Presently the Saint looked up.

"Has an aunt on your mother's side," he asked solemnly, "ever suffered from a bilious attack following a meal of sausages made by a German pork butcher with a hammer toe and three epileptic children?"

Mr Hayn shook his head, staring.

"I haven't any aunts," he said.

"I'm so sorry," said the Saint, as if he were deeply distressed to hear of Mr Hayn's plight of pathetic auntlessness. "But it means the beastly book's all wrong. Never mind. Don't let's bother about it."

He pushed the pack away. Undoubtedly he was quite mad.

"Aren't you going to tell us any more?" asked Stannard, with a wink to Hayn.

"Uncle Ambrose would blush if I went on," said Templar. "Look at the brick I've dropped already. But if you insist, I'll try one more card."

Hayn obliged again, smiling politely. He was starting to get acclimatized. Clearly the secret of being on good terms with Mr Templar was to let him have his own irrepressible way.

"I only hope it isn't the five of diamonds," said the Saint earnestly. "Whenever I do this fortune-telling stuff, I'm terrified of somebody drawing the five of diamonds. You see, I'm bound to tell the truth, and the truth in that case is frightfully hard to tell to a comparative stranger. Because according to my book, a man who draws the five of diamonds is liable at any moment to send an anonymous donation of ten thousand pounds to the London Hospital. Also, cards are unlucky for him, he is an abominable blackguard, and he had a repulsively ugly face."

Hayn kept his smile nailed in position, and faced his card.

"The five of diamonds, Mr Templar," he remarked gently.

"No—is it really?" said Simon, in most Saintly astonishment. "Well, well, *well!* . . . There you are, Jerry—I warned you your uncle would be embarrassed if I went on. Now I've dropped another brick. Let's talk of something else, quickly, before he notices. Uncle Ambrose, tell me, have you ever seen a hot dog fighting a cat-'o-nine-tails? . . . No? . . . Well, shuffle the pack and I'll show you a conjuring trick."

Mr Hayn shuffled and cut, and the Saint rapidly dealt off five cards, which he passed face downwards across the table.

It was about the first chance Mr Hayn had had to sidle a word in, and he felt compelled to protest about one thing.

"You seem to be suffering from a delusion, Mr Templar," he said. "I'm not Jerry's uncle—I'm just a friend of his. My name's Hayn—Edgar Hayn."

"Why?" asked the Saint innocently.

"It happens to be the name I was christened with, Mr Templar," Hayn replied with some asperity.

"Is that so?" drawled the Saint mildly. "Sorry again."

Hayn frowned. There was something peculiarly infuriating about the Saint in that particular vein—something that, while it rasped the already raw fringe of his temper, was also beginning to send a queer indefinable uneasiness creeping up his back.

"And I'm sorry if it annoys you," he snapped.

Simon Templar regarded him steadily.

"It annoys me," he said, "because, as I told you, it's my business never to make mistakes, and I just hate being wrong. The records of Somerset House told me that your name was once something quite different—that you weren't christened Edgar Hayn at all. And I believed it."

Hayn said nothing. He sat quite still, with that tingling thrill of apprehension crawling round the base of his scalp. And the Saint's clear blue gaze never left Hayn's face.

"If I was wrong about that," the Saint went on softly, "I may quite easily have been wrong about other things. And that would annoy me more than ever, because I don't like wasting my time. I've spent several days figuring out a way of meeting you for just this little chat—I thought it was about time our relationship became a bit more personal—and it'd break my heart to think it had all been for nothing. Don't tell me that, Edgar, beloved—don't tell me it wasn't any use my finding out that dear little Jerry was a friend of yours—don't tell me that I might have saved myself the trouble I took to scrape an acquaintance with the said Jerry just to bring about this informal meeting. Don't tell me that, dear heart!"

Hayn moistened his lips. He was fighting down an insane unreasoning feeling of panic; and it was the Saint's quiet level voice and mocking eyes, as much as anything, that held Edgar Hayn rooted in his chair.

"Don't tell me, in fact, that you won't appreciate the little conjuring trick I came here especially to show you," said the Saint, more mildly than ever.

He reached out suddenly and took the cards he had dealt from Hayn's nerveless fingers. Hayn had guessed what they would prove to be, long before Simon, with a flourish, had spread the cards out face upwards on the table.

"Don't tell me you aren't pleased to see my visiting cards, personally presented," said Simon, in his very Saintliest voice.

His white teeth flashed in a smile, and there was a light of adventurous recklessness dancing in his eyes as he looked at Edgar Hayn across five neat specimens of the sign of the Saint.

## VII

"And if it's pure prune juice and boloney," went on the Saint, in that curiously velvety tone which still contrived somehow to prickle all over with little warning spikes—"if all that is sheer banana oil and soft roe, I shan't even raise a smile with the story I was going to tell you. It's my very latest one, and it's about a loose-living land-shark called Hayn, who was born in a barn in the rain. What he'd struggled to hide was found out when he died—there was mildew all over his brain. Now that one's been getting a big hand everywhere I've told it since I made it up, and it'll be one of the bitterest disappointments of my life if it doesn't fetch you, sweetheart!"

Hayn's chair went over with a crash as he kicked to his feet. Strangely enough, now that the murder was out and the first shock absorbed, the weight on his mind seemed lightened and he felt better able to cope with the menace.

"So you're the young cub we've been looking for!" he rasped.

Simon raised his hand.

"I'm called the Saint," he murmured. "But don't let us get melodramatic about it, laddie. The last man who got melodramatic with me was hanged at Exeter six months back. It doesn't seem to be healthy."

Hayn looked around. The diners had left, and as yet no one had arrived to take their places; but the clatter of his chair upsetting had aroused three startled waiters, who were staring uncertainly in his direction. But a review of these odds did not seem to disturb the Saint, who was lounging languidly back in his seat with his hands in his pockets and a benign expression on his face.

"I suppose you know that the police are after you," grated Hayn.

"I didn't," said the Saint. "That's interesting. Why?"

"You met some men in the Brighton train and played poker with them. You swindled them right and left, and when they accused you you attacked them and pinched the money. I think that's good enough to put you away for some time."

"And who's going to identify me?"

"The four men."

"You surprise me," drawled Simon. "I seem to remember that on that very day, just outside Brighton racecourse, those same four bums were concerned in beating up a poor little coot of a lame bookie named Tommy Mitre and pinching *his* money. There didn't happen to be any policemen about—they arranged it quite cleverly— and the crowd who saw it would most likely all be too scared of the Snake to give evidence. But yours truly and a couple of souls also saw the fun. We were a long way off, and the Snake and his Boys were over the horizon by the time we got to the scene, but we could identify them all, and a few more who were not there—and we shouldn't be afraid to step into the witness-box and say our piece. No, sonnikins—I don't think the police will be brought into that.

That must go down to history as a little private wrangle between Ganning and me. Send one of your beauty chorus out for a Robert and give me in charge if you like, but don't blame me if Ganning and the Boys come back at you for it. Knowing their reputations, I should say they'd get the cat as well as their six months' hard, and that won't make them love you a lot. Have it your own way, though."

The argument was watertight, and Hayn realized it. He was beginning to cool down. He hadn't a kick—for the moment, the Saint had got him right down in the mud with a foot on his face. But he didn't see what good that was doing the Saint. It was a big bluff, Hayn was starting to think, and he had sense enough to realize that it wasn't helping him one bit to get all hot under the collar about it. In fact—such was the exhilarating effect of having at last found an enemy whom he could see and hit back at—Hayn was rapidly reckoning that the Saint might lose a lot by that display of bravado.

Clearly the Saint didn't want the police horning in at all. It didn't even matter that the Saint knew things about Hayn and his activities that would have interested the police. The Saint was on some racket of his own, and the police weren't being invited to interfere. Very well. So be it. The cue for Hayn was to bide his time and refuse to be rattled. But he wished the Saint hadn't got that mocking self-possessed air of having a lot more high cards up his sleeve, just waiting to be produced. It spoilt Hayn's happiness altogether. The Saint was behaving like a fool; and yet, in some disconcertingly subtle way, he managed to do it with the condescending air of putting off a naturally tremendous gravity in order to amuse the children.

Hayn righted his chair and sat down again slowly. The alert waiters relaxed—they were a tough crowd and selected more for their qualities of toughness than for their clean fingernails and skill at juggling with plates and dishes. But as Hayn sat down his right hand went behind his chair—his back was towards the group of waiters—and with his fingers he made certain signs. One of the waiters faded away inconspicuously.

"So what do you propose to do?" Hayn said.

"Leave you," answered the Saint benevolently. "I know your ugly face isn't your fault, but I've seen about as much of it as I can stand for one evening. I've done what I came to do, and now I think you can safely be left to wonder what I'm going to do next. See you later, I expect, my Beautiful Ones. . . ."

The Saint rose and walked unhurriedly to the stairs. By that time, there were five men ranged in a row at the foot of the stairs, and they showed no signs of making way for anyone.

"We should hate to lose you so soon, Mr Templar," said Hayn.

The Saint's lounging steps slowed up, and stopped. His hands slid into his pockets, and he stood for a moment surveying the quintet of waiters with a beatific smile. Then he turned.

"What are these?" he enquired pleasantly. "The guard of honour, or the cabaret beauty chorus?"

"I think you might sit down again, Mr Templar," suggested Hayn.

"And I think not," said the Saint.

He walked swiftly back to the table—so swiftly that Hayn instinctively half rose from his seat, and the five men started forward. But the Saint did not attack at that moment. He stopped in front of Hayn, his hands in his pockets; and although that maddening little smile still lurked on his lips, there was something rather stern about his poise.

"I said I was going to leave you, and I am," he murmured, with a gentleness that was in amazing contrast to the intent tautness of his bearing. "That's what I came here for, ducky—to leave you. This is just meant for a demonstration of all-round superiority; you think you can stop me—but just watch. I'm going to prove that nothing on earth can stop me when I get going. Understand, loveliness?"

"We shall see," said Hayn.

The Saint's smile became, if possible, even more Saintly. Somehow that smile, and the air of hair-trigger alertness which accompanied it, was bothering Edgar Hayn badly. He knew it was all bravado—he knew that for once the Saint had bitten off more than he could chew—he knew that the odds were all against a repetition of the discomfiture of the Ganning combine. And yet he couldn't feel happy about it. There was a kind of quivering strength about the Saint's lazy bearing—something that reminded Edgar Hayn of wire and whipcord and indiarubber and compressed steel springs and high explosives.

"In the space of a few minutes," said the Saint, "you're going to see a sample of rough-housing that'll make your bunch of third-rate hoodlums look like two cents' worth of oxtail. But before I proceed to beat them up, I want to tell you this—which you can pass on to your friends. Ready?"

Hayn spread out his hands.

"Then I'll shoot," said the Saint. "It's just this. We Saints are normally souls of peace and goodwill towards men. But we don't like crooks, blood-suckers, traders in dope and damnation, and other verminous escrescences of that type—such as yourself. We're going to beat you up and do you down, skin you and smash you, and scare you off the face of Europe. We are not bothered about the letter of the Law, we act exactly as we please, we inflict what punishment we think suitable, and no one is going to escape us. Ganning got hurt, but still you don't believe me. You're the next on the list, and by the time I've finished with you, you'll be an example to convince others. And it will go on. That's all I've got to say now, and when I've left you, you can go forth and spread the glad news. I'm leaving now!"

He stooped suddenly, and grasped the leg of Hayn's chair and tipped it backwards with one jerking heave. As Hayn tried to scramble to his feet, the Saint put an ungentle foot in his face and upset the table on top of him.

The five tough waiters were pelting across the floor in a pack. Simon reached out for the nearest chair, and sent it skating over the room at the height of six inches from the ground, with a vimful swing of his arms that gave it the impetus of a charging buffalo. It smashed across the leader's knees and shins with bone-shattering force, and the man went down with a yell.

That left four.

The Saint had another chair in his hand by the time the next man was upon him. The waiter flung up his arms to guard his head and tried to push into a grapple; but the Saint stepped back and reversed the swing of his chair abruptly. It swerved under the man's guard and crashed murderously into his short ribs.

Three. . . .

The next man ran slap into a sledge-hammer left that hurled him a dozen feet away. The other two hesitated, but the Saint was giving no breathing space. He leapt in at the nearest man with a pile-driving, left-right-left tattoo to the solar plexus.

As though crumpled up with a choking groan under that battering-ram assault, some sixth sense flashed the Saint a warning.

He leapt to one side, and the chair Hayn had swung to his head swished harmlessly past him, the vigour of the blow toppling Hayn off his balance. The Saint assisted his downfall with an outflung foot which sent the man hurtling headlong.

The last man was still coming on, but warily. He ducked the Saint's lead, and replied with a right swing to the side of the head

which staggered the Saint on his feet. Simon Templar decided that
his reputation was involved, and executed a beautiful feint with his
left which gave him an opening to lash in a volcanic right squarely
upon the gangster's nose.

As the man dropped, the Saint whipped round and caught Stannard.

"Fight, you fool," the Saint hissed in his ear. "This is for local
colour."

Stannard clinched, and then the Saint broke away and firmly but
regretfully clipped him on the ear.

It was not one of the Saint's heftiest punches, but it was hard
enough to knock the youngster down convincingly; and then the
Saint looked around hopefully for something else to wallop, and
found nothing. Hayn was rising again, shakily, and so were those
of the five toughs who were in a fit state to do so; but there was no
notable enthusiasm to renew the battle.

"Any time any of you bad cheeses want any more lessons in
rough-housing," drawled the Saint, a little breathlessly, "you've
only got to drop me a postcard and I'll be right along."

This time, there was no attempt to bar his way.

He collected hat, gloves, and stick from the cloakroom, and went
through the upstairs lounge. As he reached the door, he met Braddon returning.

"Hullo, Sweetness," said the Saint genially. "Pass right down the
car and hear the new joke the Boys of the Burg downstairs are
laughing at."

Braddon was still trying to guess the cause for and meaning of
this extraordinary salutation by a perfect stranger when the Saint,
without any haste or heat, but so swiftly and deftly that the thing
was done before Braddon realized what was happening, had reached
out and seized the brim of Braddon's hat and forced it well down
over his eyes. Then, with a playful tweak of Braddon's nose and a
cheery wave of his hand to the dumbfounded Danny, he departed.

Danny was not a quick mover, and the street outside was Saint-
less by the time Braddon had struggled out of his hat and reached
the door.

When his vocabulary was exhausted, Braddon went downstairs
in search of Hayn, and stopped open-mouthed at the wreckage he
saw.

Mr Hayn, turning from watching the Saint's triumphant vanish-
ment, had swung sharply on Stannard. The Saint's unscathed exit

had left Hayn in the foulest of tempers. All around him, it seemed, an army of tough waiters in various stages of disrepair were gathering themselves to their feet with a muttered obbligato of lurid oaths. Well, if there wasn't an army of them, there were five—five bone-hard heavyweights—and that ought to have been enough to settle any ordinary man, even on the most liberal computation of odds. But the Saint had simply waded right through them, hazed and manhandled and roasted them, and walked out without a scratch. Hayn would have taken a bet that the Saint's tie wasn't even a millimetre out of centre at the end of it. The Saint had made fools of them without turning a hair.

Hayn vented his exasperation on Jerry, and even the fact that he had seen the boy help to tackle the Saint and get the worst of it in their company did not mitigate his wrath.

"You damned fool!" he blazed. "Couldn't you see he was up to something? Are you taken in by everyone who tells you the tale?"

"I told you I couldn't guarantee him," Stannard protested. "But when I met him he wasn't a bit like he was tonight. Honestly, Mr Hayn—how could I have known? I don't even know what he was after yet. Those cards . . ."

"South African grandmothers!" snarled Hayn.

Braddon intervened.

"Who was this gentleman, anyway?" he demanded.

"Gentleman" was not the word he used.

"Use your eyes, you lunatic!" Hayn flared, pointing to the table, and Braddon's jaw dropped as he saw the cards.

"You've had that guy in here?"

"What the hell d'you think? You probably passed him coming in. And from what the Snake said, and what I've seen myself, he's probably the very man we're looking for—the Saint himself."

"So was the gentleman!" said Braddon, only once again he described Simon Templar with a more decorative word.

Hayn snorted.

"And that fool Stannard brought him here," he said.

"I've told you, I didn't know much about him, Mr Hayn," Stannard expostulated. "I warned you I couldn't answer for him."

"The kid's right," said Braddon. "If he put it over on the Snake, he might put it over on anybody."

There was logic in the argument, but it was some time before Hayn could be made to see it. But presently he quieted down.

"We'll talk about this, Braddon," he said. "I've got an idea for stopping his funny stuff. He didn't get clean away—I put Keld on to follow him. By tonight we'll know where he lives, and then I don't think he'll last long."

He turned to Jerry. The boy was fidgeting nervously, and Hayn became diplomatic. It wasn't any use rubbing a valuable man the wrong way.

"I'm sorry I lost my temper, old man," he said. "I can see it wasn't your fault. You just want to be more careful. I ought to have warned you about the Saint—he's dangerous! Have a cigar."

It was Mr Hayn's peace-offering. Stannard accepted it.

"No offence," he said. "I'm sorry I let you down."

"We won't say anything more about it, old man," said Hayn heartily. "You won't mind if I leave you? Mr Braddon and I have some business to talk over. I expect you'll amuse yourself upstairs. But you mustn't play any more, you know."

"I shan't want to," said Stannard. "But, Mr Hayn——"

Hayn stopped.

"Yes, old man?"

"Would you mind if I asked you for that cheque? I'll give you an I O U now. . . ."

"I'll see that you get it before you leave."

"It's awfully good of you, Mr Hayn," said Stannard apologetically. "Three thousand pounds it was."

"I hadn't forgotten," said Hayn shortly.

He moved off, cursing the damaged waiters out of his path; and Stannard watched him go, thoughtfully. So far it had all been too easy, but how long was it going to last?

He was watching the early dancers assembling when a waiter, whose face was obscured by a large piece of sticking-plaster, came through with a sealed envelope. Stannard ripped it open, inspected the cheque it contained, and scribbled his signature to the promissory note that came with it. He sent this back to Hayn by the same waiter.

Although he had disposed of several cocktails before dinner, and during the meal had partaken freely of wine, and afterwards had done his full share in the consumption of liqueurs, his subsequent abstemiousness was remarkable. He sat with an untasted brandy and soda in front of him while the coloured orchestra broke into its first frenzies of syncopation, and watched the gyrating couples with a jaundiced eye for an hour. Then he drained his glass, rose, and made his way to the stairs.

Through the window of the office he saw Hayn and Braddon still engaged in earnest conversation. He tapped on the pane, and Hayn looked up and nodded. The hidden door swung open as Stannard reached it, and closed after him as he passed through.

He strolled through the gaming rooms, greeted a few acquaintances, and watched the play for a while without enthusiasm. He left the club early, as soon as he conveniently could.

The next morning, he hired a car and drove rapidly out of London. He met the Saint on the Newmarket road at a prearranged milestone.

"There was a man following me," said the Saint happily. "When I got out my bus, he took a taxi. I wonder if he gave it up, or if he's still toiling optimistically along, bursting the meter somewhere in the wilds of Edmonton."

He gave Stannard a cigarette, and received a cheque in return.

"A thousand pounds," said Stannard. "As I promised."

The Saint put it carefully away in his wallet.

"And why I should give it to you, I don't know," said Stannard.

"It is the beginning of wisdom," said the Saint. "The two thousand that's left will pay off your debts and give you a fresh start, and I'll get your I O U's back for you in a day or two. A thousand pounds isn't much to pay for that."

"Except that I might have kept the money and gone on working for Hayn."

"But you have reformed," said the Saint gently. "And I'm sure the demonstration you saw last night will help to keep you on the straight and narrow path. If you kept in with Hayn, you'd have me to deal with."

He climbed back into his car and pressed the self-starter, but Stannard was still curious.

"What are you going to do with the money?" he asked. "I thought you were against crooks."

"I am," said the Saint virtuously. "It goes to charity. Less my ten percent commission charged for collecting. You'll hear from me again when I want you. *Au revoir*—or, in the Spanish, *hasta la vista* —or, if you prefer it in the German, *auf Wiedersehen*."

## VIII

About a week after the Saint's mercurial irruption into Danny's, Gwen Chandler met Mr Edgar Hayn in Regent Street one morning

by accident. At exactly the same time, Mr Edgar Hayn met Gwen
Chandler on purpose, for he had been at some pains to bring about
that accidental meeting.

"We see far too little of you these days, my dear," he said, taking
her hand.

She was looking cool and demure in a summer frock of printed
chiffon, and her fair hair peeped out under the brim of her picture
hat to set off the cornflower blue of her eyes.

"Why, it seems no time since Jerry and I were having supper
with you," she said.

"No time is far too long for me," said Mr Hayn cleverly. "One
could hardly have too much of anyone as charming as yourself, my
dear lady."

At the supper-party which she had unwillingly been induced to
join, he had set himself out to be an irreproachable host, and his
suave geniality had gone a long way towards undoing the first instinctive dislike which she had felt for him, but she did not know
how to take him in this reversion to his earlier pose of exaggerated
heartiness. It reminded her of the playful romping advances of an
elephant, but she did not find it funny.

Mr Hayn, however, was for the moment as pachydermatous as
the animal on whose pleasantries he appeared to have modelled his
own, and her slightly chilling embarrassment was lost on him. He
waved his umbrella towards the window of the shop outside which
they were standing.

"Do you know that name, Miss Chandler?" he asked.

She looked in the direction indicated.

"Laserre? Yes, of course I've heard of it."

"I am Laserre," said Hayn largely. "This is the opportunity I've
been waiting for to introduce you to our humble premises—and how
convenient that we should meet on the very doorstep!"

She was not eager to agree, but before she could frame a suitable
reply he had propelled her into the glittering red-carpeted room
where the preparations of the firm were purveyed in a hushed and
reverent atmosphere reminiscent of a cathedral.

A girl assistant came forward, but in a moment she was displaced
by Braddon himself—frock-coated, smooth, oleaginous, hands at
washing position.

"This is my manager," said Hayn, and the frock-coated man
bowed. "Mr Braddon, be so good as to show Miss Chandler some
samples of the best of our products—the very best."

Thereupon, to the girl's bewilderment, were displayed velvet-lined mahogany trays, serried ranks of them, brought from the shelves that surrounded the room and set out with loving care on a counter, one after another, until she felt completely dazed. There were rows upon rows of flashing crystal bottles of scent, golden cohorts of lipsticks, platoons of little alabaster pots of rouge, orderly regiments of enamelled boxes of powder. Her brain reeled before the contemplation of such a massed quantity of luxurious panderings to vanity.

"I want you to choose anything you like," said Hayn. "Absolutely anything that takes your fancy, my dear Miss Chandler."

"But—I—I couldn't possibly," she stammered.

Hayn waved her objections aside.

"I insist," he said. "What is the use of being master of a place like this if you cannot let your friends enjoy it? Surely I can make you such a small present without any fear of being misunderstood? Accept the trifling gift graciously, my dear lady. I shall feel most hurt if you refuse."

In spite of the grotesqueness of his approach, the circumstances made it impossible to snub him. But she was unable to fathom his purpose in making her the object of such generosity. It was a hot day, and he was perspiring freely, as a man of his build is unhappily liable to do, and she wondered hysterically if perhaps the heat had temporarily unhinged his brain. There was something subtly disquieting about his exuberance.

She modestly chose a small vanity case and a little flask of perfume, and he seemed disappointed by her reluctance. He pressed other things upon her, and she found herself forced to accept two large boxes of powder.

"Make a nice parcel of these things for Miss Chandler, Mr Braddon," said Hayn, and the manager carried the goods away to the back of the shop.

"It's really absurdly kind of you, Mr Hayn," said the girl confusedly. "I don't know what I've done to deserve it."

"Your face is your fortune, my dear young lady," answered Hayn, who was obviously in a brilliant mood.

She had a terrified suspicion that in a moment he would utter an invitation to lunch, and she hastily begged to be excused on the grounds of an entirely fictitious engagement.

"Please don't think me rude, hurrying away like this," she pleaded. "As a matter of fact, I'm already shockingly late."

He was plainly crestfallen.

"No one can help forgiving you anything," he said sententiously. "But the loss to myself is irreparable."

She never knew afterwards how she managed to keep her end up in the exchange of platitudes that followed, until the return of Braddon with a neat package enabled her to make her escape.

Hayn accompanied her out into the street, hat in hand.

"At least," he said, "promise me that the invitation will not be unwelcome, if I ring you up soon and ask you to suggest a day. I could not bear to think that my company was distasteful to you."

"Of course not—I should love to—and thank you ever so much for the powder and things," she said desperately. "But I must fly now."

She fled as best she might.

Hayn watched her out of sight, standing stock still in the middle of the pavement where she had left him, with a queer gleam in his pale eyes. Then he put his hat on, and marched off without re-entering the shop.

He made his way to the club in Soho, where he was informed that Snake Ganning and some of the Boys were waiting to see him. Hayn let them wait while he wrote a letter, which was addressed to M Henri Chastel, Poste Restante, Athens; and he was about to ring for the Snake to be admitted when there was a tap on the door and Danny entered.

"There are five of them," said Danny helpfully.

"Five of whom?" said Hayn patiently.

"Five," said Danny, "including the man who pulled Mr Braddon's hat down over his eyes. They said they must see you at once."

Mr Hayn felt in the pit of his stomach the dull sinking qualm which had come to be inseparable from the memory of the Saint's electric personality. Every morning without fail since the first warning he had received, there had been the now familiar envelope beside his plate at breakfast, containing the inevitable card; and every afternoon, when he reached Danny's, he found a similar reminder among the letters on his desk.

He had not had a chance to forget Simon Templar, even if he had wished to do so—as a matter of fact, the Snake and his Boys were at that moment waiting to receive their instructions in connection with a plot which Hayn had formed for disposing of the menace.

But the Saint's policy was rapidly wearing out Hayn's nerves. Knowing what he did, the Saint could only be refraining from passing his knowledge along to Scotland Yard because he hoped to gain more by silence, yet there had been no attempt to blackmail—only those daily melodramatic reminders of his continued interest.

Hayn was starting to feel like a mouse that has been tormented to the verge of madness by an exceptionally sportive cat. He had not a doubt that the Saint was scheming and working against him still, but his most frenzied efforts of concentration had failed to deduce the most emaciated shred of an idea of the direction from which the next assault would be launched, and seven days and nights of baffled inaction had brought Edgar Hayn to the verge of a breakdown.

Now the Saint—and the rest of his gang also, from all appearances—was paying a second visit. The next round was about to begin, and Hayn was fighting in a profounder obscurity than ever.

"Show them in," he said in a voice that he hardly recognized as his own.

He bent over some writing, struggling to control his nerves for the bluff that was all he had to rely on, and with an effort of will he succeeded in not looking up when he heard the door opening and the soft footsteps of men filing into the room.

"Walk right in, souls," said the Saint's unmistakable cheery accents. "That's right . . . Park yourselves along that wall in a row and stand easy."

Then Hayn raised his eyes, and saw the Saint standing over the desk regarding him affectionately.

"Good morning, Edgar," said the Saint affably. "And how is Swan?"

"Good morning, Mr Templar," said Hayn.

He shifted his gaze to the four men ranged beside the door. They were a nondescript quartet, in his opinion—not at all the sort of men he had pictured in his hazy attempts to visualize Templar's partners. Only one of them could have been under thirty, and the clothes of all of them had seen better days.

"These are the rest of the gang," said the Saint. "I noticed that I was followed home from here last time I called, so I thought it'd save you a lot of sleuthing if I brought the other lads right along and introduced them."

He turned.

"Squad—shun! Souls, this is dear Edgar, whom you've heard so much about. As I call your names, reading from left to right, you will each take one pace smartly to your front, bow snappily from the hips, keeping the eyebrows level and the thumb in line with the seam of the trousers, and fall in again. . . . First, Edgar, meet Saint Hodgkins of Booth. Raise your hat, Hodgkins. . . . On his left, Saint George of Pruge. Eyebrows level, George. . . . Next, Saint Herbert Hawkins of Mile End Road, and no relation to the celebrated admiral. Wave your handkerchief to the pretty gentleman, Herb! Last, but not least, Saint Harry Johnston. Keep smiling, Harry—I won't let Edgar bite you. . . . That's the lot, Edgar, except for myself. Meet me!"

Hayn nodded.

"That's very considerate of you, Mr Templar," he said, and his voice was a little shaky, for an idea was being born inside him. "Is that all you came to do?"

"Not quite, Precious," said the Saint, settling down on the edge of the desk. "I came to talk business."

"Then you won't want to be hurried," said Hayn. "There are some other people waiting to see me. Will you excuse me while I go and tell them to call again later?"

The Saint smiled.

"By all manner of means, sonny," he said. "But I warn you it won't be any use telling the Snake and his Boys to be ready to beat us up when we leave here, because a friend of ours is waiting a block away with a letter to our friend Inspector Teal—and that letter will be delivered if we don't report safe and sound in ten minutes from now."

"You needn't worry," said Hayn. "I haven't underrated your intelligence."

He went out. It was a mistake he was to regret later—never before had he left even his allies alone in that office, much less a confessed enemy. But the urgency of his inspiration had, for the moment, driven every other thought out of his head. The cleverest criminal must make a slip sooner or later, and it usually proves to be such a childish one that the onlooker is amazed that it should have been made at all. Hayn made his slip then, but it must be remembered that he was a very rattled man.

He found Snake Ganning sitting at the bar with three picked Boys, and beckoned them out of earshot of the bartender.

"The Saint and the rest of his band are in the office," he said, and Ganning let out a venomous exclamation. "No—there won't be any rough business now. I want to have a chance to find out what his game is. But when the other four go, I want you to tail them and find out all you can about them. Report here at midnight, and I'll give you your instructions about Templar himself."

"When I get hold of that swine," Ganning ground out vitriolitically, "he's going to——"

Hayn cut him short with an impatient sweep of his hand.

"You'll wait till I've finished with him," he said. "You don't want to charge in like a bull at a gate, before you know what's on the other side of the gate. I'll tell you when to start—you can bet your life on that."

And in that short space of time the Saint, having shamelessly seized the opportunity provided by Hayn's absence, had comprehensively ransacked the desk. There were four or five I O U's with Stannard's signature in an unlocked drawer, and these he pocketed. Hayn had been incredibly careless. And then the Saint's eye was caught by an envelope on which the ink was still damp. The name "Chastel" stood out as if it had been spelt in letters of fire, so that Simon stiffened like a pointer. . . .

His immobility lasted only an instant. Then, in a flash, he scribbled something on a blank sheet of notepaper and folded it into a blank envelope. With the original before him for a guide, he copied the address in a staggeringly lifelike imitation of Hayn's handwriting. . . .

"I shall now be able to give you an hour, if you want it," said Hayn, returning, and the Saint turned with a bland smile.

"I shan't take nearly as long as that, my cabbage," he replied. "But I don't think the proceedings will interest the others, and they've got work to do. Now you've met them, do you mind if I dismiss the parade?"

"Not at all, Mr Templar."

There was a glitter of satisfaction in Hayn's eyes; but if the Saint noticed it, he gave no sign.

"Move to the right in column o' route—etcetera," he ordered briskly. "In English, hop it!"

The parade, after a second's hesitation, shuffled out with expressionless faces. They had not spoken a word from the time of their entrance to the time of their exit.

It may conveniently be recorded at this juncture that Snake Ganning and the Boys spent eleven laboriously profitless hours following a kerbstone vendor of bootlaces, a pavement artist, and a barrel-organ team of two ex-Service men, whom the Saint had hired for ten shillings apiece for the occasion; and it may also be men-

tioned that the quartet, assembling at a near-by dairy to celebrate
the windfall, were no less mystified than were the four painstaking
bloodhounds who dogged their footsteps for the rest of the day.

It was the Saint's idea of a joke—but then, the Saint's sense of
humour was sometimes quite infantile.

## IX

"And now let's get down to business—as the bishop said to the
actress," murmured Simon, fishing out his cigarette-case and tapping
a gasper on his thumbnail. "I want to ask you a very important
question."

Hayn sat down.

"Well, Mr Templar?"

"What would you say," asked the Saint tentatively, "if I told
you I wanted ten thousand pounds?"

Hayn smiled.

"I should sympathize with you," he answered. "You're not the
only man who'd like to make ten thousand pounds as easily as that."

"But just suppose," said Simon persuasively—"just suppose I told
you that if I didn't get ten thousand pounds at once, a little dossier
about you would travel right along to Inspector Teal to tell him
the story of the upstairs rooms here and the inner secrets of the
Maison Laserre? I could tell him enough to send you to penal
servitude for five years."

Hayn's eye fell on the calendar hung on the wall, with a sliding
red ring round the date. His brain was working very rapidly then.
Suddenly he felt unwontedly confident. He looked from the calendar to his watch, and smiled.

"I should write you a cheque at once," he said.

"And your current account would stand it?"

"All my money is in a current account," said Hayn. "As you
will understand, it is essential for a man in my position to be able to
realise his assets without notice."

"Then please write," murmured the Saint.

Without a word, Hayn opened a drawer, took out his cheque-
book, and wrote. He passed the cheque to Templar, and the Saint's
eyes danced as he read it.

"You're a good little boy, son," said the Saint. "I'm so glad we
haven't had any sordid argument and haggling about this. It makes
the whole thing so crude, I always think."

Hayn shrugged.

"You have your methods," he said. "I have mine. I ask you to observe the time." He showed his watch, tapping the dial with a stubby forefinger. "Half-past twelve on Saturday afternoon. You cannot cash that cheque until nine o'clock on Monday morning. Who knows what may have happened by then? I say you will never pay that cheque into your bank. I'm not afraid to tell you that. I know you won't set the police on to me until Monday morning, because you think you're going to win—because you think that at nine o'clock on Monday morning you'll be sitting on the Bank's doorstep waiting for it to open. I know you won't. Do you honestly believe I would let you blackmail me for a sum like that—nearly as much money as I have saved in five years?"

The crisis that he had been expecting for so long had come. The cards were on the table, and the only thing left for Edgar Hayn to wonder was why the Saint had waited so many days before making his demand. Now the storm which had seemed to be hanging fire interminably had broken, and it found Edgar Hayn curiously unmoved.

Simon looked at Hayn sidelong, and the Saint also knew that the gloves were off.

"You're an optimist," he said. "Your trouble is that you're too serious. You'll lose this fight because you've no sense of humour—like all second-rate crooks. You can't laugh."

"I may enjoy the last laugh, Templar," said Hayn.

The Saint turned away with a smile, and picked up his hat.

"You kid yourself," he said gently. "You won't, dear one." He took up his stick and swung it delicately in his fingers. The light of battle glinted in his blue eyes. "I presume I may send your kind donation to the London Hospital anonymously, comrade?"

"We will decide that on Monday," said Hayn.

The Saint nodded.

"I wonder if you know what my game is?" he said soberly. "Perhaps you think I'm a kind of hijacker—a crook picking crooks' pockets? You're wrong. I'm losing money over this. But I'm just a born-an'-bred fighting machine, and a quiet life of the moss-gathering would just be hell for me. I'm not a dick, because I can't be bothered with red tape, but I'm on the same side. I'm out to see that unpleasant insects like you are stamped on, which I grant you the police could do; but to justify my existence I'm going to see that the insects contribute a large share of their illgotten gains to charity, which you've got to grant me the police can't do. It's always seemed a bit tough to me that microbes of your species should be able to make a fortune, and then be free to enjoy it after they've done a year or two in stir—and I'm here to put that right. Out of the money I lifted off the Snake I paid Tommy Mitre back his rightful property, plus a bonus for damages; but the Snake's a small bug, anyway. You're big, and I'm going to see that your contribution is in proportion."

"We shall see," said Hayn.

The Saint looked at him steadily.

"On Monday night you will sleep at Marlborough Street Police Station," he said dispassionately.

The next moment he was gone. Simon Templar had a knack of making his abrupt exits so smoothly that it was generally some minutes before the other party fully realized that he was no longer with them.

Hayn sat looking at the closed door without moving. Then he glanced down, and saw the envelope that lay on the blotter before him, addressed in his own hand to M Henri Chastel. And Hayn sat fascinated, staring, for although the imitation of his hand might have deceived a dozen people who knew it, he had looked at it for just long enough to see that it was not the envelope he had addressed.

It was some time before he came out of his trance, and forced himself to slit open the envelope with fingers that trembled. He spread out the sheet of paper on the desk in front of him, and his brain went numb. As a man might have grasped a concrete fact through a murky haze of dope, Hayn realized that his back was to the last wall. Underneath the superficial veneer of flippancy, the Saint had shown for a few seconds the seriousness of his real quality and the intentness of his purpose, and Hayn had been allowed to appreciate the true mettle of the man who was fighting him.

He could remember the Saint's last words. "On Monday night you will sleep at Marlborough Street Police Station." He could hear the Saint saying it. The voice had been the voice of a judge pronouncing sentence, and the memory of it made Edgar Hayn's face go grey with fear.

## X

The Saint read Edgar Hayn's letter in the cocktail bar of the Piccadilly, over a timely Martini, but his glass stood for a long time untasted before him, for he had not to read far before he learned that Edgar Hayn was bigger game than he had ever dreamed.

Then he smoked two cigarettes, very thoughtfully, and made certain plans with a meticulous attention to detail. In half an hour he had formulated his strategy, but he spent another quarter of an hour and another cigarette going over it again and again in search of anything that he might have overlooked.

He did not touch his drink until he had decided that his plans were as foolproof as he could make them on such short notice.

The first move took him to Piccadilly Post Office, where he wrote out and despatched a lengthy telegram in code to one Norman Kent, who was at that time in Athens on the Saint's business; and the Saint thanked his little gods of chance for the happy coincidence that had given him an agent on the spot. It augured well for the future.

Next he shifted across from the counter to a telephone booth, and called a number. For ten minutes he spoke earnestly to a certain Roger Conway, and gave minute directions. He had these orders repeated over to him to make sure that they were perfectly memorised and understood, and presently he was satisfied.

"Hayn will have found out by now that I know about his connection with Chastel," he concluded, "that is, unless he's posted that letter without looking at it. We've got to act on the assumption that he *has* found out, and therefore the rule about having nothing to do with me except through the safest of safe channels is doubly in force. I estimate that within the next forty-four hours a number of very strenuous efforts will be made to bump me off, and it won't be any good shutting your eyes to it. It won't be dear Edgar's fault if I haven't qualified for a funeral by Monday morning."

Conway protested, but the Saint dealt shortly with that.

"You're a lot more useful to me working unknown," he said. "I can't help it if your natural vanity makes you kick at having to hide your light under a bushel. There's only need for one of us to prance about in the line of fire; and since they know me all round and upside down as it is, I've taken the job. You don't have to worry. I've never played the corpse yet, and I don't feel like starting now."

He was in the highest of spirits. The imminent prospect of the violent and decisive action always got him that way. It made his blood tingle thrillingly through his veins, and set his eyes dancing recklessly, and made him bless the perfect training in which he had always kept his nerves and sinews. The fact that his life would be charged a five hundred percent premium by any cautious insurance company failed to disturb his cheerfulness one iota. The Saint was made that way.

Anxiety was a sensation that had never troubled his young life. For the next few hours there was nothing that he could do for the cause which he had made his own, and he therefore proposed to enjoy those hours on his own to the best of his ability. He was completely unperturbed by the thought of the hectic and perilous hours which were to follow that interlude of enjoyment—rather, the interlude gathered an added zest from the approach of zero hour.

He could not, of course, be sure that Hayn had discovered the abstraction of the letter; but that remained a distinct probability in spite of the Saint's excellent experiment in forgery. And even without that discovery, the cheque he had obtained, and Hayn's confidence in giving it, argued that there were going to be some very tense moments before the Monday morning. Simon Templar's guiding principle, which had brought him miraculously unscathed through innumerable desperate adventures in the past, was to assume the worst and take no chances; and in this instance subsequent events were to prove that pessimistic principle the greatest and most triumphant motto that had ever been invented.

The Saint lunched at his leisure, and then relaxed amusingly in a convenient cinema until half-past six. Then he returned home to dress, and was somewhat disappointed to find no reply to his cable waiting for him at his flat.

He dined and spent the night dancing at the Carlton with the lovely and utterly delightful Patricia Holm, for the Saint was as human as the next man, if not more so, and Patricia Holm was his favourite weakness.

It was a warm evening, and they walked up Haymarket together, enjoying the fresh air. They were in Hanover Square, just by the corner of Brook Street, when the Saint saw the first thunder-cloud, and unceremoniously caught Patricia Holm by the shoulders and jerked her back around the corner and out of sight. An opportune taxi came prowling by at that moment, and the Saint had hailed it and bundled the girl in before she could say a word.

"I'm telling him to take you to the Savoy," he said. "You'll book a room there, and you'll stay there without putting even the tip of your pretty nose outside the door until I come and fetch you. You can assume that any message or messenger you receive is a fake. I don't think they saw you, but I'm not risking anything. Refuse to pay any attention to anything or anybody but myself in person. I'll be around on Monday at lunch-time, and if I'm not you can get hold of Inspector Teal and the lads and start raising hell—but not before."

The girl frowned suspiciously.

"Saint," she said, in the dangerous tone that he knew and loved, "you're trying to elbow me out again."

"Old darling," said the Saint quietly, "I've stopped trying to elbow you out and make you live a safe and respectable life. I know it can't be done. You can come in on any game I take up, and I don't care if we have to fight the massed gangs of bad hats in New York, Chicago, Berlin and London. But there's just one kind of dirty work I'm not going to have you mixed up in, and this is it. Get me, old Pat? . . . Then s'long!"

He closed the door of the taxi, directed the driver, and watched it drive away. The Saint felt particularly anxious to keep on living at that moment. . . . And then the taxi's tail-light vanished round the corner, and Patricia Holm went with it; and the Saint turned with a sigh and an involuntary squaring of the shoulders, and swung into Brook Street.

He had observed the speedy-looking closed car that stood by the kerb directly outside the entrance to his flat, and he had seen the four men who stood in a little group on the pavement beside it conversing with all apparent innocence, and he had guessed the worst. The sum total of those deceptively innocuous fixtures and fittings seemed to him to bear the unmistakable hallmarks of the Hayn confederacy; for the Saint had what he called a nasty suspicious mind.

He strolled on at a leisurely pace. His left hand, in his trouser pocket, was sorting out the key of his front door; in his right hand he twirled the stick that in those days he never travelled without. His black felt hat was tilted over to the back of his head. In everything outward and visible he wore the mildest and most Saintly air of fashionable and elegant harmlessness, for the Saint was never so cool as when everything about him was flaming with red danger signals. And as he drew near the little group he noticed that they fell suddenly silent, all turning in his direction.

The Saint was humming a little tune. It all looked too easy— nothing but a welcome and entertaining limbering-up for the big stuff that was to follow. He had slipped the front door key off the ring and transferred it to a side pocket of his jacket, where it would be more easily found in a hurry.

"Excuse me," said the tallest of the four, taking a step forward to meet him.

"I'm afraid I can't excuse you, Snake," said the Saint regretfully, and swayed back from his toes as Ganning struck at him with a loaded cane.

The Saint felt the wind of the blow caress his face, and then a lightning left uppercut came rocketing up from his knees to impact on the point of the Snake's jaw, and Ganning was catapulted back into the arms of his attendant Boys.

Before any of them could recover from their surprise, Simon had leapt lightly up the steps to the portico, and had slipped the key into the lock. But as he turned and withdrew it the other three came after him, leaving their chief to roll away into the gutter, and the Saint wheeled round to face them with the door swinging open behind him.

He held his stick in both hands, gave it a half-turn, and pulled. Part of the stick stripped away, and in the Saint's right hand a long slim blade of steel glinted in the dim light. His first thrust took the leading Boy through the shoulder, and the other two checked.

The Saint's white teeth flashed in an unpleasant smile.

"You're three very naughty children," said the Saint, "and I'm afraid I shall have to report you to your Sunday School teacher. Go a long way away, and don't come near me again for years and years!"

The rapier in his hand gleamed and whistled, and the two Boys recoiled with gasps of agony as the supple blade lashed across their faces. And then, as they sprang blindly to attack, the Saint streaked through the door and slammed it on them.

He turned the sword back into a stick, and went unhurriedly up the stairs to his flat, which was the first floor.

Looking down from the window, he saw the four men gathered together engaged in furious deliberation. One of them was mopping about inside his coat with an insanitary handkerchief, and the Snake was sagging weakly back against the side of the car holding his jaw. There were frequent gesticulations in the direction of the Saint's windows. After a time, the four men climbed into the car and drove away.

The brief affray had left the Saint completely unruffled. If you had taken his pulse then, you would have found it ticking over at not one beat above or below its normal 75. He sauntered across the room, switched on the lights, and put away his hat and stick, still humming gently to himself.

Propped up on the table, in a prominent position, was a cable envelope. Without any hurry, the Saint poured himself out a modest Vat 69, lighted a cigarette, and then fetched a small black notebook from its hiding-place behind a picture. Provided with these essentials, the Saint settled down on the edge of the table, ripped up the envelope, and extracted the flimsy.

"Elephant revoke," the message began. A little further on was the name Chandler. And near the end of the closely-written sheet were the words: "Caterpillar diamonds ten spades four chicane hearts knave overcall."

"Elephant" was the code word for Hayn; Chastel was "Caterpillar." "Revoke" meant "has changed his mind." And the Saint could almost decode the sentence which included the words "chicane" and "overcall" at sight.

In his little black book, against the names of every card in the pack, and every bridge and poker term, were short sentences broadly applicable to almost any purpose about which his fellowship of freebooters might wish to communicate; and with the aid of this book and a pencil, the Saint translated the message and wrote the interpretation between the lines. The information thus gleaned was in confirmation of what he had already deduced since purloining and reading Hayn's letter to Chastel, and the Saint was satisfied.

He opened his portable typewriter, and wrote a letter. It was the Saint's first official communique.

*To Chief Inspector Teal*
*Criminal Investigation Department*
*New Scotland Yard*
*S W 1*

*Dear Claud:*
*I recommend to your notice Edgar Hayn, formerly Heine, of 27 Portugal Mansions, Hampstead. He is the man behind Danny's Club in Soho, and a well-timed raid on that establishment, with particular attention to a secret door in the panelling of the ground floor lounge (which is opened by an electric control in Hayn's office in the basement) will give you an interesting insight into the methods of card-sharping de luxe.*

*More important than this, Hayn is also the man behind Laserre, the Regent Street perfumers, the difference being that George Edward Braddon, the manager, is not a figurehead, but an active partner. A careful watch kept on future consignments received from the Continent by Laserre will provide adequate proof that the main reason for the existence of Laserre is cocaine. The drug is smuggled into England in cases of beauty preparations shipped by*

*Hayn's foreign agents and quite openly declared—as dutiable products, that is.
In every case, there will be found a number of boxes purporting to contain
face powder, but actually containing cocaine.*

*Hayn's European agent is a French national of Levantine extraction named
Henri Chastel. The enclosed letter, in Hayn's own handwriting, will be suffi-
cient to prove that Hayn and Chastel were up to their necks in the whole
European dope traffic.*

*Chastel, who is at present in Athens, will be dealt with by my agent there.
I regret that I cannot hand him over to the regular processes of justice; but
the complications of nationality and extradition treaties would, I fear, defeat
this purpose.*

*By the time you receive this, I shall have obtained from Hayn the donation
to charity which it is my intention to exact before passing him on to you for
punishment, and you may at once take steps to secure his arrest. He has a
private Moth aeroplane at Stag Lane Aerodrome, Edgware, which has for some
time been kept in readiness against the necessity for either himself or one of
his valued agents to make a hasty getaway. A watch kept on the aerodrome,
therefore, should ensure the frustration of this scheme.*

*In the future, you may expect to hear from me at frequent intervals.*

*Assuring you of my best services at all times,*

*I remain, etc,*

THE SAINT.

With this epistle, besides Hayn's letter, Templar enclosed his
artistic trademark. So that there should be no possibility of tracing
him, he had had the paper on which it was drawn specially obtained
by Stannard from the gaming rooms at Danny's for the purpose.

He addressed the letter, and, after a preliminary survey of the
street to make sure that the Snake had not returned or sent deputies,
he walked to a nearby pillarbox and posted it. It would not be delivered until Monday morning, and the Saint reckoned that that
would give him all the time he needed.

Back in his flat, the Saint called up the third of his lieutenants,
who was one Dicky Tremayne, and gave him instructions concerning the protection of Gwen Chandler. Finally he telephoned another
number and called Jerry Stannard out of bed to receive orders.

At last he was satisfied that everything had been done that he had
to do.

He went to the window, drew the curtains aside a cautious half-
inch, and looked down again. A little further up Brook Street, on
the other side of the road, a blue Lagonda sports saloon had drawn
up by the kerb. The Saint smiled approvingly.

He turned out the lights in the sitting room, went through to his
bedroom, and began to undress. When he rolled up his left sleeve
there was visible a little leather sheath strapped to his forearm, and

in this sheath he carried a beautifully balanced knife—a mere six inches of razor-keen leaf-shaped blade and three inches of carved ivory hilt. This was Anna, the Saint's favourite throwing-knife. The Saint could impale a flying champagne cork with Anna at twenty paces. He considered her present place of concealment a shade too risky, and transferred the sheath to the calf of his right leg. Finally, he made sure that his cigarette-case contained a supply of a peculiar kind of cigarette.

Outside in the street, an ordinary bulb motorhorn hooted with a peculiar rhythm. It was a prearranged signal, and the Saint did not have to look out again to know that Ganning had returned. And then, almost immediately, a bell rang, and the indicator in the kitchen showed him that it was the bell of the front door.

"They must think I'm getting old," murmured the Saint.

But he was wrong—he had forgotten the fire-escape across the landing outside the door of his flat.

A moment later he heard, down the tiny hall, a dull crash and a sound of splintering wood. It connected up in his mind with the ringing of the front door bell, and he realized that he had no monopoly of prearranged signals. That ringing had been to tell the men who had entered at the back that their companions were ready at the front of the building. The Saint acknowledged that he had been trapped into underrating the organising ability of Edgar Hayn.

Unthinkingly, he had left his automatic in his bedroom. He went quickly out of the kitchen into the hall, and at the sound of his coming the men who had entered with the aid of a jemmy swung round. Hayn was one of them, and his pistol carried a silencer.

"Well, well, *well!*" drawled the Saint, whose mildness in times of crisis was phenomenal, and prudently raised his hands high above his head.

"You are going on a journey with me, Templar," said Hayn. "We are leaving at once, and I can give no date for your return. Kindly turn round and put your hands behind you."

Templar obeyed. His wrists were bound, and the knots tightened by ungentle hands.

"Are you still so optimistic, Saint?" Hayn taunted him, testing the bonds.

"More than ever," answered the Saint cheerfully. "This is my idea of a night out—as the bishop said to the actress."

Then they turned him around again.

"Take him downstairs," said Hayn.

They went down in a silent procession, the Saint walking without resistance between two men. The front door was opened and a husky voice outside muttered: "All clear. The flattie passed ten minutes ago, and his beat takes him half an hour."

The Saint was passed on to the men outside and hustled across the pavement into the waiting car. Hayn and two other men followed him in; a third climbed up beside the driver. They moved off at once, heading west.

At the same time, a man rose from his cramped position on the floor of the Furillac that waited twenty yards away. He had been crouched down there for three-quarters of an hour, without a word of complaint for his discomfort, to make it appear that the car was empty and the owner inside the house opposite which the car stood.

The self starter whirred under his foot as he sidled round behind the wheel, and the powerful engine woke to a throaty whisper.

The car in which the Saint rode with Hayn flashed up the street, gathering speed rapidly; and as it went by, the blue sports Lagonda pulled out from the kerb and purred westwards at a discreet distance in its wake.

Roger Conway drove. The fit of his coat was spoiled by the solid bulge of the automatic in one pocket, and there was a stern set to his face which would have amazed those who only knew that amiable young man in his more flippant moods.

From his place in the leading car Simon Templar caught in the driving mirror a glimpse of the following Lagonda, and smiled deep within himself.

## XI

Gwen Chandler lived in a microscopic flat in Bayswater, the rent of which was paid by the money left her by her father. She did the housekeeping herself, and with this saving on a servant there was enough left over from her income to feed her and give her a reasonably good time. None of the few relations she had ever paid much attention to her.

She should have been happy with her friends, and she had been, but all that had stopped abruptly when she had met and fallen in love, head over heels, with Jerry Stannard.

He was about twentythree. She knew that for the past two years he had been leading a reckless life, spending most of his time and money in night clubs and usually going to bed at dawn. She also knew that his extravagant tastes had plunged him into debt, and that since the death of his father he had been accumulating bigger and bigger creditors; and she attributed these excesses to his friends, for the few people of his acquaintance she had met were of a type she detested. But her advice and inquiries had been answered with such surliness that at last she had given up the contest and nursed her anxiety alone.

But a few days ago her fiancé's grumpiness had strangely vanished. Though he still seemed to keep the same Bohemian hours, he had been smiling and cheerful whenever she met him; and once in a burst of good spirits he had told her that his debts were paid off and he was making a fresh start. She could get no more out of him than this, however—her eager questions had made him abruptly taciturn, though his refusal to be cross-examined had been kindly enough. He would be able to tell her all about it one day, he said, and that day would not be long coming.

She knew that it was his habit to lie in bed late on Sunday mornings—but then, it was his practice to lie in bed late on all the other six days of the week. On this particular Sunday morning therefore, when a ring on the front door bell had disturbed her from the task of preparing breakfast, she was surprised to find that he was her visitor.

He was trying to hide his agitation, but she discerned that the agitation was not of the harassed kind.

"Got any breakfast for me?" he asked. "I had to come along at this unearthly hour, because I don't know that I'll have another chance to see you all day. Make it snappy, because I've got an important appointment."

"It'll be ready in a minute," she told him.

He loafed about the kitchen, whistling, while she fried eggs and bacon, and he sniffed the fragrant aroma appreciatively.

"It smells good," he said, "and I've got the appetite of a lifetime."

She would have expected him to breakfast in a somewhat headachy silence, but he talked cheerfully.

"It must be years since you had a decent holiday," he said. "I think you deserve one, Gwen. What do you say we get married by special licence and run over to Deauville next week?"

He laughed at her bewildered protests.

"I can afford it," he assured her. "I've paid off everyone I owe money to, and in a fortnight I'm getting a terribly sober job, starting at five pounds a week."

"How did you get it?"

"A man called Simon Templar found it for me. Have you ever met him, by any chance?"

She shook her head, trying to find her voice.

"I'd do anything in the world for that man," said Jerry.

"Tell me about it," she stammered.

He told her—of his miraculous rescue by the Saint and the interview that followed it, of the Saint's persuasiveness, of the compact they had made. He also told her about Hayn; but although the recital was fairly inclusive it did not include the machinations of the Maison Laserre. The Saint never believed in telling anybody everything, and even Hayn had secrets of his own.

The girl was amazed and shocked by the revelation of what Stannard's life had been and might still have been. But all other emotions were rapidly submerged in the great wave of relief which swept over her when she learned that Stannard had given his word to break away, and was even then working on the side of the man who had brought him back to a sense of honour—even if that honour worked in an illegal way.

"I suppose it's crooked, in one sense," Stannard admitted. "They're out to get Hayn and his crowd into prison, but first they're swindling them on behalf of charity. I don't know how they propose to do it. On the other hand though, the money they've got back for me from Hayn is no more than I lost in cash at his beastly club."

"But why did Hayn let you keep on when he knew you'd got no money left?"

Stannard made a wry grimace.

"He wanted to be able to force me into his gang. I came in, too —but that was because Templar told me to agree to anything that would make Hayn pay me that three thousand pound cheque."

She digested the information in a daze. The revelation of the enterprise in which Jerry Stannard was accompliced to the Saint did not shock her. Womanlike, she could see only the guilt of Hayn and the undoubted justice of his punishment. Only one thing made her afraid.

"If you were caught——"

"There'll be no fuss," said Jerry. "Templar's promised me that, and he's the kind of man you'd trust with anything. I haven't had to do anything criminal. And it'll all be over in a day or two. Templar rang me up last night."

"What was it about?"

"That's what he wouldn't tell me. He told me to go to the Splendide at eleven and wait there for a man called Tremayne, who may arrive any time up to one o'clock, and he'll tell me the rest. Tremayne is one of Templar's gang."

Then she remembered Hayn's peculiar behaviour of the previous morning. The parcel she had brought away from Laserre still lay unopened on her dressing-table.

Jerry was interested in the story. Hayn's association with Laserre, as has been mentioned, was news to him. But he could make nothing of the incident.

"I expect he's got some foolish crush on you," he suggested. "It's only the way you'd expect a man like that to behave. I'll speak to Templar about it when I see him."

He left the dining room as soon as he had finished breakfast, and was back in a moment with his hat.

"I must be going now," he said, and took her in his arms. "Gwen, dear, with any luck it'll all be over very soon, and we'll be able to forget it. I'll be back as soon as ever I can."

She kissed him.

"God bless you. And be careful, my darling!"

He kissed her again, and went out singing blithely. The world was very bright for Jerry Stannard that morning.

But the girl listened to the cheerful slamming of the door with a little frown, for she was troubled with misgivings. It had all seemed so easy at the time, in the optimistic way in which he had told her the story, but reviewed in cold blood it presented dangers and difficulties in legion.

She wished for both their sakes that he had been able to stay with her that day, and her fears were soon to be justified.

Half an hour after he had gone, when the breakfast things had been cleared away and she was tidying herself to go out for a walk, there was a ring on the front door bell.

She answered it; and when she saw that it was Edgar Hayn, after what Jerry had been able to tell her, she would have closed the door in his face. But he had pushed through before she could collect her wits.

He led the way into the sitting room, and she followed in mingled fear and anger. Then she saw that there were dark rings round his eyes, and his face was haggard.

"What is it?" she asked coldly.

"The police," he said. "They're after me—and they're after you, too. I came to warn you."

"But why should they be after me?" she demanded blankly.

He was in a miserable state of nerves. His hands fidgeted with his umbrella all the time he was talking, and he did not meet her eyes.

"Drugs!" he said gruffly. "Illicit drugs. Cocaine. You know what I mean. There's no harm in your knowing now—we're both in the same boat. They've been watching me, and they saw me with you yesterday and followed you."

"But how do you know?"

"I've got friends at Scotland Yard," he snapped. "It's necessary. Policemen aren't incorruptible. But my man let me down—he never gave me the tip till the last moment. They're going to raid this flat and search it this morning."

Her brain was like a maelstrom, but there was one solid fact to hold on to.

"There's nothing for them to find."

"That's where you're wrong! Those things I gave you—one of our other boxes got mixed up in them. I've just found that out. That's why I'm here. There's six ounces of cocaine in this flat!"

She recoiled, wide-eyed. Her heart was thumping madly. It all seemed too impossible, too fantastic. . . . And yet it only bore out and amplified what Jerry had been able to tell her. She wondered frantically if the excuse of innocence would convince a jury. Hayn saw the thought cross her mind, and shattered it.

"You know how Jerry's lived," he said. "No one would believe that you weren't both in it."

He looked out of the window. She was impelled to follow his example, and she was in time to see two broad-shouldered men in bowler hats entering the house.

"They're here," said Hayn breathlessly. "But there may be a chance. I recognized one of the men—he's a friend of mine. I may be able to square him."

Outside, a bell rang.

Hayn was scribbling something on a card.

"Take this," he muttered. "My car's outside. If I can get them away from you for a moment, slip out and show the card to the chauffeur. I've got a house at Hurley. He'll take you there, and I'll come down later and discuss how we're going to get you and Jerry out of the country."

The bell rang again, more urgently. Hayn thrust the pasteboard into the girl's hand.

"What're you hesitating for?" he snarled. "Do you want to stand in the dock at the Old Bailey beside your fiancé?"

Hardly knowing what she did, she put the card in her bag.

"Go and open the door," Hayn commanded. "They'll break in if you don't."

As he spoke, there came a yet more insistent ringing, and the flat echoed with the thunder of a knocker impatiently plied.

The girl obeyed, and at the same time she was thinking furiously. Jerry—or his chief, this man Templar—would know how to deal with the crisis; but for the moment there was no doubt that Hayn's plan was the only practicable one. Her one idea was to stay out of the hands of the police long enough to make sure that Jerry was safe, and to give them time to think out an escape from the trap in which Hayn had involved them.

The two broad-shouldered men entered without ceremony as she opened the door.

"I am Inspector Baker, of Scotland Yard," said one of them formally, "and I have a warrant to search your flat. You are suspected of being in illegal possession of a quantity of cocaine."

The other man took her arm and led her into the sitting room. Hayn came forward, frowning.

"I must protest about this," he said. "Miss Chandler is a friend of mine."

"That's unlucky for you," was the curt reply.

"I'll speak to Baker about this," threatened Hayn hotly, and at that moment Baker came in.

He was carrying a small cardboard box with the label of Laserre. "Poudre Laserre," the label said; but the powder was white and crystalline.

"I think this is all we need," said Baker, and stepped up to Gwen. "I shall take you into custody on a charge——"

Hayn came between them.

"I should like a word with you first," he said quietly.

Baker shrugged.

"If you must waste your time——"

"I'll take the risk," said Hayn. "In private, please."

Baker jerked his thumb.

"Take Chandler into another room, Jones."

"Jones had better stay," interrupted Hayn. "What I have to say concerns him also. If you will let Miss Chandler leave us for a minute, I will guarantee that she will not attempt to escape."

There was some argument, but eventually Baker agreed. Hayn opened the door for the girl, and as she went out gave her an almost imperceptible nod. She went into her bedroom and picked up the telephone. It seemed an eternity before the paging system of the Splendide found Jerry. When he answered, she told him what had happened.

"I'm going to Hayn's house at Hurley," she said. "It's the only way to get out at the moment. But tell Tremayne when he comes, and get hold of Templar, and do something quickly!"

He was beginning to object, to ask questions, but there was no time for that, and she hung up the receiver. She had no means of knowing what Hayn's methods of "squaring" were, or how long the negotiations might be expected to keep the detectives occupied.

She tiptoed down the hall and opened the door.

From the window, Hayn, Baker, and Jones watched her cross the pavement and enter the car.

"She's a peach, boss," said Baker enviously.

"You've said all I wanted you to say," Hayn returned shortly. "But it's worked perfectly. If I'd simply tried to kidnap her, she'd have been twice as much nuisance. As it is she'll be only too glad to do everything I tell her."

Dicky Tremayne arrived two minutes after Hayn's car had driven off. He should have been there over an hour ago, but the cussedness of Fate had intervened to baulk one of the Saint's best-laid plans. A bus had skidded into Tremayne's car in Park Lane, the consequent policeman had delayed him interminably, the arrangements for the removal of his wrecked car had delayed him longer, and when at last he had got away in a taxi a series of traffic blocks had held him up at every crossing.

Now he had to act on his own initiative.

After a second's indecision, Tremayne realized that there was only one thing to do. If Hayn and his men were already in the flat, he must just burst in and hope for the best; if they had not yet arrived, no harm would be done.

He went straight into the building, and on the way up the stairs he met Hayn and two other men coming down. There was no time for deliberation or planning a move in advance.

"You're the birds I'm looking for," Tremayne rapped, barring the way. "I'm Inspector Hancock of Scotland Yard, and I shall arrest you——"

So far he got before Hayn lashed out at him. Tremayne ducked, and the next instant there was an automatic in his hand.

"Back up those stairs to the flat you've just left," he ordered, and the three men retreated before the menace of his gun.

They stopped at the door of the flat, and he told Hayn to ring. They waited.

"There seems to be no reply," said Hayn sardonically.

"Ring again," Tremayne directed grimly.

Another minute passed.

"There can't really be anyone at home," Hayn remarked.

Tremayne's eyes narrowed. It was something about the tone of Hayn's sneering voice. . . .

"You swine," said Tremayne through his teeth. "What have you done with her?"

"With whom?" inquired Hayn blandly.

"With Gwen Chandler!"

Tremayne could have bitten his tongue off as soon as the words were out of his mouth. That fatal thoughtless impetuosity which was always letting him down! He saw Hayn suddenly go tense, and knew that it was useless to try to bluff further.

"So you're a Saint," said Hayn softly.

"Yes, I am!" Tremayne let out recklessly. "And if you scabs don't want me to plug you full of holes——"

He had been concentrating on Hayn, the leader, and so he had not noticed the other men edging nearer. A hand snatched at his gun, and wrenched. . . . As Dicky Tremayne swung his fist to the man's jaw, Hayn dodged behind him and struck at the back of his head with a little rubber truncheon. . . .


## XII

Jerry Stannard never understood how he managed to restrain himself until one o'clock. Much less did he understand how he waited the further half-hour which he gave Dicky Tremayne for grace. Perhaps no other man in the world but Simon Templar could have inspired such a blind loyalty. The Saint was working out some secret stratagem of his own, Stannard argued, and he had to meet Tremayne for reasons appertaining to the Saint's tactics. In any case, if Gwen had left when she telephoned, he could not have reached the flat before she had gone—and then he might only have blundered into the police trap that she had tried to save him from.

But it all connected up now—Gwen's Laserre story, and what Stannard himself knew of Hayn, and more that he suspected—and the visions that it took only a little imagination to conjure up were dreadful.

When half-past one came and there was still no sign of Tremayne, the suspense became intolerable. Stannard went to the telephone and fruitlessly searched London over the wires for Simon Templar. He could learn nothing from any of the clubs or hotels or restaurants which he might have frequented, nor was he any more successful with his flat. As for Dicky Tremayne, Stannard did not even know him by sight—he had simply been told to leave his card with a pageboy, and Tremayne would ask for him.

It was after two o'clock by that time, and Tremayne had not arrived. He tried to ring up Gwen Chandler's flat, but after an interminable period of ringing, the exchange reported "No reply".

Jerry Stannard took a grip on himself. Perhaps that emergency was the making of him, the final consolidation of the process that had been started by the Saint, for Stannard had never been a fighting man. He had spoken the truth when he told Templar that his weakness was lack of guts. But now he'd got to act. He didn't know nearly everything about Hayn, but he knew enough not to want to leave Gwen Chandler with that versatile gentleman for a moment longer than was absolutely necessary. But if anything was going to be done, Stannard had got to do it himself.

With a savage resolution, he telephoned to a garage where he was known. While he waited, he scribbled a note for Tremayne in which he described the whole series of events and stated his intentions. It was time wasted, but he was not to know that.

When the car arrived he dismissed the mechanic who had brought it round, and drove to Hurley.

He knew how to handle cars—it was one of his few really useful accomplishments. And he sent the Buick blazing west with his foot flat down on the accelerator for practically every yard of the way.

Even so it was nearly five o'clock when he arrived there, and then he realized a difficulty. There were a lot of houses at Hurley, and he had no idea where Hayn's house might be. Nor had the post office, nor the nearest police.

Stannard, in the circumstances, dared not press his enquiries too closely. The only hope left to him was that he might be able to glean some information from a villager, for he was forced to conclude that Hayn tenanted his country seat under another name. With tnis forlorn hope in view, he made his way to the Bell, and it was there that he met a surprising piece of good fortune.

As he pulled up outside, a man came out, and the man hailed him.

"Thank the Lord you're here," said Roger Conway without preface. "Come inside and have a drink."

"Who are you?" asked a mystified Jerry Stannard.

"You don't know me, but I know you," answered the man. "I'm one of the Saint's haloes."

He listened with a grave face to Stannard's story.

"There's been a hitch somewhere," he said, when Jerry had finished. "The Saint kept you in the dark because he was afraid your natural indignation might run away with you. Hayn had designs on your girl friend—you might have guessed that. The Saint pinched a letter of Hayn's to Chastel—Hayn's man abroad—in which, among other things, Edgar described his plot for getting hold of Gwen. I suppose he wanted to be congratulated on his ingenuity. The rough idea was to plant some cocaine on Gwen in a present of powder and things from Laserre, fake a police raid, and pretend to square the police for her. Then if she believed the police were after you and her—Hayn was banking on making her afraid that you were also involved—he thought it would be easy to get her away with him."

"And the Saint wasn't doing anything to stop that?" demanded Jerry, white-lipped.

"Half a minute! The Saint couldn't attend to it himself, having other things to deal with, but he put Tremayne, the man you were supposed to have met at the Splendide, on the job. Tremayne was to get hold of Gwen before Hayn arrived, and tell her the story— we were assuming that you hadn't told her anything—and then bring her along to the Splendide and join up with you. The two of you were then to take Gwen down by car to the Saint's bungalow at Maidenhead and stay down there till the trouble had blown over."

The boy was gnawing his fingernails. He had had more time to think over the situation on the drive down, and Conway's story had only confirmed his own deductions. The vista of consequences that it opened up was appalling.

"What's the Saint been doing all this time?"

"That's another longish story," Conway answered. "He'd got Hayn's cheque for five figures, and that made the risk bigger. There was only one way to settle it."

Roger Conway briefly described the Saint's employing of the

four phony Cherubs. "After that was found out, Simon reckoned Hayn would think the gang business was all bluff, and he'd calculate there was only the Saint against himself. Therefore he wouldn't be afraid to try his scheme about Gwen, even though he knew the Saint knew it, because the Saint was going to be out of the way. Anyhow, Hayn's choice was between getting rid of the Saint and going to prison, and we could guess which he'd try first. The Saint had figured out that Hayn wouldn't simply try a quick assassination, because it wouldn't help him to be wanted for murder. There had got to be a murder, of course, but it would have to be well planned. So the Saint guessed he'd be kidnapped first and taken away to some quiet spot to be done in, and he decided to play stalking-horse. He did that because if Hayn was arrested, his cheques would be stopped automatically, so Hayn had got to be kept busy till to-morrow morning. I was watching outside the Saint's flat in a fast car last night, as I'd been detailed to do, in case of accidents. The Saint was going to make a fight of it. But they got him somehow— I saw him taken out to a car they had waiting—and I followed down here. Tremayne was to be waiting at the Splendide for a phone call from me at two o'clock. I've been trying to get him ever since, and you as well, touring London over the toll line, and it's cost a small fortune. And I didn't dare to go back to London, because of leaving the Saint here. That's why I'm damned glad you've turned up."

"But why haven't you told the police?"

"Simon'd never forgive me. He's out to make the Saint the terror of the Underworld, and he won't do that by simply giving information to Scotland Yard. The idea of the gang is to punish people suitably before handing them over to the law, and our success over Hayn depends on sending five figures of his money to charity. I know it's a biggish risk. The Saint may have been killed already. But he knew what he was doing. We were ordered not to interfere and the Saint's the head man in this show."

Stannard sprang up.

"But Hayn's got Gwen!" he half sobbed. "Roger, we can't hang about, not for anything, while Gwen's——"

"We aren't hanging about any longer," said Roger quietly.

His hand fell with a firm grip on Jerry Stannard's arm, and the youngster steadied up. Conway led him to the window of the smoke-room and pointed.

"You can just see the roof of the house, over there," he said.

"Since last night, Hayn's gone back to London, and his car came by again about two hours ago. I couldn't see who was in it, but it must have been Gwen. Now——"

He broke off suddenly. In the silence, the drone of a powerful car could be heard approaching. Then the car itself whirled by at speed, but it did not pass too quickly for Roger Conway to glimpse the men who rode in it.

"Hayn and Braddon in the back with Dicky Tremayne between them!" he said tensely.

He was in time to catch Stannard by the arm as the boy broke wildly away.

"What the hell are you stampeding for?" he snapped. "Do you want to go charging madly in and let Hayn grab you as well?"

"We can't wait!" Stannard panted, struggling.

Conway thrust him roughly into a chair and stood over him. The boy was as helpless as a child in Conway's hands.

"You keep your head and listen to me," Roger commanded sharply. "We'll have another drink and tackle this sensibly. And I'm going to see that you wolf a couple of sandwiches before you do anything. You've been in a panic for hours, with no lunch, and you look about all in. I want you to be useful."

"If we phone the police——"

"Nothing doing!"

Roger Conway's contradiction ripped out almost automatically, for he was not the Saint's right-hand man for nothing. He had learnt the secret of the perfect lieutenant, which is the secret of divining at once, in any emergency, what your superior officer would want you to do. It was no use simply skinning out any old how—the emergency had got to be dealt with in a way that would dovetail in with the Saint's general plan of campaign.

"The police are our last resort," he said. "We'll see if the two of us can't fix this alone. Leave this to me."

He ordered a brace of stiff whiskies and a pile of sandwiches, and while these were being brought he wrote a letter which he sealed. Then he went in search of the proprietor, whom he knew of old, and gave him the letter.

"If I'm not here to claim that in two hours," he said, "I want you to open it and telephone what's inside to Scotland Yard. Will you do that for me, as a great favour, and ask no questions?"

The landlord agreed somewhat perplexedly.

"Is it a joke?" he asked good-humouredly.

"It may grow into one," Roger Conway replied. "But I give you my word of honour that if I'm not back at eight o'clock, and that message isn't opened and phoned punctually, the consequences may include some of the most un-funny things that ever happened!"

## XIII

The Saint had slept. As soon as they had arrived at the house at Hurley (he knew it was Hurley, for he had travelled that road many times over the course of several summers) he had been pushed into a bare-furnished bedroom and left to his own devices. These were not numerous, for the ropes had not been taken off his wrists.

A short tour of inspection of the room had shown that, in the circumstances, it formed an effective prison. The window, besides being shuttered, was closely barred; the door was of three-inch oak, and the key had been taken away after it had been locked. For weapons with which to attack either window or door there was the choice of a light table, a wooden chair, or a bedpost. The Saint might have employed any of these, after cutting himself free—for they had quite overlooked, in the search to which he had been subjected, the little knife strapped to his calf under his sock—but he judged that the time was not yet ripe for any such drastic action. Besides, he was tired; he saw strenuous times ahead of him; and he believed in husbanding his energies. Therefore he had settled down on the bed for a good night's rest, making himself as comfortable as a man can when his hands are tied behind his back, and it had not been long before he had fallen into an untroubled sleep. It had struck him, drowsily, as being the most natural thing to do.

Glints of sunlight were stabbing through the interstices of the shutters when he was awakened by the sound of his door opening. He rolled over, opening one eye, and saw two men enter. One carried a tray of food, and the other carried a gun. This concession to the respect in which the gang held him, even when bound and help-less, afforded the Saint infinite amusement.

"This is sweet of you," he said; and indeed he thought it was, for he had not expected such a consideration, and he was feeling hungry. "But, my angels of mercy," he said, "I can't eat like this."

They sat him down in a chair and tied his ankles to the legs of it, and then the cords were taken off his wrists and he was able to stretch his cramped arms. They watched him eat, standing by the door, and the cheerful comments with which he sought to enliven the meal went unanswered. But a request for the time evoked the surly information that it was past one o'clock.

When he had finished, one of the men fastened his hands again, while the other stood by with his automatic at the ready. Then they untied his ankles and left him, taking the tray with them.

The searchers had also left him his cigarette-case and matches, and with some agility and a system of extraordinary contortions the Saint managed to get a cigarette into his mouth and light it. This feat of double-jointed juggling kept him entertained for about twenty minutes; but as the afternoon wore on he developed with practice a positively brilliant dexterity. He had nothing else to do.

His chief feeling was one of boredom, and he soon ceased to find any enjoyment in wondering how Dicky Tremayne had fared in Bayswater. By five o'clock he was yawning almost continuously, having thought out seventeen original and foolproof methods of swindling swindlers without coming within reach of the law, and this and similar exercises of ingenuity were giving him no more kick at all.

He would have been a lot more comfortable if his hands had not been bound, but he decided not to release himself until there was good cause for it. The Saint knew the tactical advantage of keeping a card up his sleeve.

The room, without any noticeable means of ventilation, was growing hotter and stuffier, and the cigarettes he was smoking were not improving matters. Regretfully, Simon resigned himself to giving up that pleasure, and composed himself on the bed again. Some time before, he had heard a car humming up the short drive, and he was hazily looking forward to Hayn's return and the renewed interest that it would bring. But the heaviness of the atmosphere did not conduce to mental alertness. The Saint found himself dozing. . . .

For the second time, it was the sound of his door opening that roused him, and he blinked his eyes open with a sigh.

It was Edgar Hayn who came in. Physically he was a much worse case than the Saint, for he had had no sleep at all since the Friday night, and his mind had been much less carefree. His tiredness showed in the pallor of his face and the bruise-like puffiness of his eyes, but he had the air of one who feels himself the master of a situation.

"Good evening," murmured Simon politely.

Hayn came over to the bedside, his lips drawn back in an unlovely smile.

"Still feeling bumptious, Templar?" he asked.

"On the contrary," answered the Saint winningly, "my shyness is half my charm."

The man who had held the gun at lunch stood in the doorway. Hayn stood aside and beckoned him in.

"There are some friends of yours downstairs," said Hayn. "I should like to have you all together."

"I should be charmed to oblige you—as the actress said to the bishop," replied the Saint.

And he wondered whom Hayn could be referring to, but he showed nothing of the chill of uneasiness that had leaped at him for an instant like an Arctic wind.

He was not left long in doubt.

The gunman jerked him to his feet and marched him down the corridor and down the stairs, Hayn bringing up the rear. The door of a room opening off the hall stood ajar, and from within came a murmur of voices which faded into stillness as their footsteps were heard approaching. Then the door was kicked wide, and the Saint was thrust into the room.

Gwen Chandler was there—he saw her at once. There were also three men whom he knew, and one of them was a dishevelled Dicky Tremayne.

Hayn closed the door and came into the centre of the room.

"Now what about it, Templar?" he said.

"What, indeed?" echoed the Saint.

His lazy eyes shifted over the assembled company.

"Greetings, Herr Braddon," he murmured. "Hullo, Snake. . . . Great heavens, Snake!—what's the matter with your face?"

"What's the matter with my face?" Ganning snarled.

"Everything, honeybunch," drawled the Saint. "I was forgetting. You were born like that."

Ganning came close, his eyes puckered with fury.

"I owe you something," he grunted, and let fly with both fists.

The Saint slipped the blows, and landed a shattering kick to the Snake's shins. Then Braddon interposed a foot between the Saint's legs, and as Simon went down Ganning loosed off with both feet. . . .

"That'll do for the present," Hayn cut in at last.

He took Templar by the collar and yanked him into a sitting position on a chair.

"You filthy skunks!" Tremayne was raving, with the veins stand-

ing out purply on his forehead. "You warts—you dirty verminous. . . ."

It was Braddon who silenced him, with a couple of vicious back-
hand blows across the mouth. And Dick Tremayne, bound hand
and foot, wrestled impotently with ropes that he could not shift.

"We'll hear Edgar's speech first," Simon interrupted. "Shut up,
Dicky! I don't mind your language myself, but you'll be having
Gwen blushing!"

He looked across at the girl, fighting sobbingly in Hayn's hold.

"It's all right, Gwen, old dear," he said. "Keep smiling, for God's
sake. We don't mind Edgar getting melodramatic, but you don't
have to make it a competition!"

Hayn passed the girl over to Braddon and Ganning, and went
over to the Saint's chair.

"I'm going to ask you one or two questions, Templar," he said.
"If you don't want to let the Snake have another go at you, you'll
answer them truthfully."

"Of course," said the Saint briefly. "George Washington was the
idol of my childhood."

Everything he had planned had suffered a sudden reversal. Gwen
Chandler had been caught, and so had Dicky. Their only hope was
in Roger Conway—and how long would it be before he discovered
the disaster and got busy? . . . The Saint made up his mind.

"How many of you are there?"

"Seventysix," said the Saint. "Two from five—just like when you
were at Borstal."

There was no one behind him. He had got his legs well back
under the chair. His arms were also reaching back, and he was edging his little knife out of its sheath.

"You can save the rest of your questions," he said. "I'll tell you
something. You'll never get away with this. You think you're going
to find out all about my organization, the plans I've made, whether
I've arranged for a squeal to the police. Then you'll take steps
accordingly. Hold the line while I laugh!"

"I don't think so," said Hayn.

"Then you don't think as much as a weevil with sleeping sickness," said the Saint equably. "You must think I was born yesterday! Listen, sweetheart. Last night I posted a little story to Inspector Teal which he'll get Monday morning. That letter's in the post
now—and nothing will stop it—and the letter to Henri Chastel I enclosed with it will make sure the dicks pay a lot of attention to the

rest of the things I had to say. You haven't an earthly, Edgarvitch."

Hayn stepped back as if he had received a blow, and his face was horribly ashen. The Saint had never imagined that he would cause such a sensation.

"I told you he'd squeak!" Braddon was raging. "You fool—I told you!"

"I told him, too," said the Saint. "Oh, Edgar—why didn't you believe your Uncle Simon?"

Hayn came erect, his eyes blazing. He swung round on Braddon.

"Be quiet, you fool!" he commanded harshly. "We knew it might come to this—that's why we've got those aeroplanes. We leave to-night, and Teal can look for us tomorrow as long as he likes."

He turned on the Saint.

"You'll come with us—you and your friend. You will not be strapped in. Somewhere in mid-Channel we shall loop the loop. You understand . . . Templar, you've undone years of work, and I'm going to make you pay for it! I shall escape, and after a time, I shall be able to come back and start again. But you——"

"I shall be flitting through Paradise, with a halo round my hat," murmured the Saint. "What a pleasant thought!"

And as he spoke he felt his little knife biting into the cords on his wrists.

"We lose everything we've got," Braddon babbled.

"Including your liberty," said the Saint softly, and the knife was going through his ropes like a wire through cheese.

They all looked at him. Something in the way he had spoken those three words, something in the taut purposefulness of his body, some strange power of personality, held them spellbound. Bound and at their mercy, for all they knew, an unarmed man, he was yet able to dominate them. There was hatred and murder flaring in their eyes, and yet for a space he was able to hold them on a curb and compel them to listen.

"I will tell you why you have lost, Hayn," said the Saint, speaking in the same gentle leisured tones that nevertheless quelled them as definitely as if he had backed them up with a gun. "You made the mistake of kidding yourself that when I told you I was going to put you in prison, I was bluffing. You were sure that I'd never throw away such an opening for unlimited blackmail. Your miserable warped temperament couldn't conceive the idea of a man doing and risking all that I did and risked for nothing but an ideal. You judged me by your own crooked standards. That's where you went

wrong, because I'm not a crook. But I'm going to make crooks go
in fear of me. You and your kind aren't scared enough of the police.
You've got used to them. You call them by their first names and
swap cigarettes with them when they arrest you. It's become a
game to you, with prison as a forfeit for a mistake, and bull-baiting's
just the same as tiddlywinks in your lives. But I'm going to give
you something new to fear—the Unknown. You'll rave about us
in the dock, and all the world will hear. And when we have finished
with you, you will go to prison, and you will be an example to make
others afraid. But you will tell the police that you cannot describe
us, because there are still three left whom you do not know; and
if we two came to any harm through you, the other three would
deal with you, and they would not deal gently. You understand?
You will never dare to speak. . . ."

"And do you think you will ever be able to speak, Templar?"
asked Hayn in a quivering voice, and his right hand was leaping to
his hip pocket.

And the Saint chuckled, a low triumphant murmur of a laugh.

"I'm sure of it!" he said, and stood up with the cords falling from
his wrists.

The little throwing-knife flashed across the room like a chip of
flying quicksilver; and Hayn, with his automatic half out of his
pocket, felt a pain like the searing of a hot iron across his knuckles,
and all the strength went out of his fingers.

Braddon was drawing at that moment, but the Saint was swift. He
had Edgar Hayn in a grip of steel, and Hayn's body was between
the Saint and Braddon.

"Get behind him, Snake!" Braddon shrilled; but as Ganning
moved to obey, the Saint reached a corner.

"Aim at the girl, you fool!" Hayn gasped, with the Saint's hand
tightening on his throat.

The Saint held Hayn with one hand only, but the strength of
that hold was incredible. With the other hand, he was fumbling
with his cigarette-case.

Braddon had turned his gun into Gwen Chandler's face, while
Ganning pinioned her arms. And the Saint had a cigarette in his
mouth and was striking a match with one hand.

"Now do you surrender?" Braddon menaced.

"Like hell I do," said the Saint.

His match touched the end of his cigarette, and in the same
movement he threw the cigarette far from him. It made an explosive

hiss like a launched rocket, and in a second everything was blotted out in a swirl of impenetrable fog.

Templar pushed Hayn away into the opacity. He knew to a fraction of a square inch where his knife had fallen after it had severed the tendons of Hayn's hand, and he dived for it. He bumped against Tremayne's chair, and cut him free in four quick slashes.

From the direction of the window came the sound of smashing glass. A shadow showed momentarily through the mist.

"Gwen!"

It was Jerry Stannard's frantic voice. The girl answered him. They sought each other in the obscurity.

A sudden draught parted the wreathing clouds of the Saint's quick-action smoke-screen. Stannard, with the girl in his arms, saw that the door was open. The Saint's unmistakable silhouette loomed in the oblong of light.

"Very very efficient, my Roger," said the Saint.

"You can always leave these little things to me," said Mr Conway modestly, leaning against the front door with Edgar Hayn, Braddon, and Snake Ganning herded into a corner of the hall at the unfriendly end of his automatic.


## XIV

They took the three men into a room where there was no smoke.

"It was my fiancée," pleaded Jerry Stannard.

"That's so," said the Saint tolerantly. "Dicky, you'll have to be content with Braddon. After all, he sloshed you when your hands were tied. But nobody's going to come between the Snake and me."

It lasted half an hour all told, and then they gathered up the three components of the mess and trussed them very securely into chairs.

"There were two other men," said the Saint hopefully, wrapping his handkerchief round a skinned set of knuckles.

"I stuck them up, and Jerry beaned them with a spanner," said Conway. "We locked them in a room upstairs."

The Saint sighed.

"I suppose we'll have to leave them," he said. "Personally, I feel I've been swindled. These guys are such lousy fighters when it comes to a showdown."

Then Conway remembered the message he had left in the landlord's hands at the Bell, and they piled hurriedly into the car in which Conway and Stannard had driven up. They retrieved the message, tidied themselves, and dined.

"I think we can call it a day," said the Saint comfortably, when the coffee was on the table. "The cheque will be cashed on Monday morning, and the proceeds will be registered to the London Hospital as arranged—less our ten percent commission, which I don't mind saying I think we've earned. I think I shall enclose one of my celebrated self-portraits—a case like this ought to finish in a worthily dramatic manner, and the opportunity's too good to miss."

He stretched himself luxuriously, and lighted a fresh cigarette which did not explode.

"Before I go to bed tonight," he said, "I'll drop a line to Teal and tell him where to look for our friends. I'm afraid they'll have a hungry and uncomfortable night, but I can't help that. And now, my infants, I suggest that we adjourn to London."

They exchanged drinks and felicitations with the lord and master of the Bell, and it should stand to the eternal credit of that amiable gentleman that not by the twitch of an eyebrow did he signify any surprise at the somewhat battered appearance of two of the party. Then they went out to their cars.

"Who's coming back with me?" asked Tremayne.

"I'm going back without you, laddie," said Jerry Stannard. "Gwen's coming with me!"

They cheered the Buick out of sight; and then Simon climbed into the back of the Lagonda and settled himself at his ease.

"Mr Conway will drive," he said. "Deprived of my charming conversation, you will ponder over the fact that Jerry is undoubtedly hooked. You may also rehearse the song which I've just composed for us to sing at his funeral—I mean wedding. It's about a wicked young lover named Jerry, who had methods decidedly merry. When the party got rough, was he smart with his stuff? Oh, very! Oh, very! . . . Oh, very! . . . Take me to the Savoy, Roger. I have a date. . . . Night-night, dear old bacteria!"

# THE WONDERFUL WAR

## From WANTED FOR MURDER

---

AT VARIOUS POINTS *in the chronicle of the Saint's exploits there are vague references to his adventures in the far corners of the earth. This particular story, however, is the only one of its kind which is completely on record; and his followers have mentioned it often enough to convince me that it is one of their favourite recollections of his early days. The Saint himself derives so much obvious fun from it that I am bound to believe that it must still be one of his most enjoyable memories. I suppose that one of the so-called "comic opera" South American republics has at one time or another been almost every man's imaginative playground; and it is only to be expected that Simon Templar would have used such a setting for one of his most riotous escapades.*

# THE WONDERFUL WAR

---

THE REPUBLIC OF PASALA lies near the northward base of the Yucatan peninsula in Central America. It has an area of about 10,000 square miles, or roughly the size of England from the Tweed to a line drawn from Liverpool to Hull. Population about 18,000. Imports, erratic. Exports, equally erratic, and consisting (when the population can be stirred to the necessary labour) of maize, rice, sugarcane, mahogany, and—oil.

"You can hurry up and warble all you know about this oil, Archie," said Simon Templar briskly, half an hour after he landed at Santa Miranda. "And you can leave out your adventures among the *señoritas*. I want to get this settled—I've got a date back in England for the end of May, and that doesn't give me a lot of time here."

Mr Archibald Sheridan stirred slothfully in his long chair and took a pull at a whisky and soda in which ice clinked seductively.

"You've had it all in my letters and cables," he said. "But I'll just run through it again to connect it up. It goes like this. Three years ago almost to the day, a Scots mining engineer named McAndrew went prospecting around the hills about fifty miles inland. Every one said he was crazy—till he came back six months later with samples from his feeler borings. He said he'd struck one of the richest deposits that ever gushed—and it was only a hundred feet below the surface. He got a concession—chiefly because the authorities still couldn't believe his story—staked his claim, cabled for his daughter to come over and join him, and settled down to feel rich and wait for the plant he'd ordered to be shipped over from New Orleans."

"Did the girl come?" asked Templar.

"She's right here," answered Sheridan. "But you told me to leave

77

the women out of it. She doesn't really come into the story anyway. The man who does come in is a half-caste bum from God
knows where, name of Shannet. Apparently Shannet had been
sponging and beachcombing here for months before McAndrew
arrived. Every one was down on him, and so McAndrew, being one
of these quixotic idiots, joined up with him. He even took him into
partnership, just to defy public opinion; and, anyhow, he was wanting help, and Shannet had some sort of qualifications. The two of
them went up into the interior to take a look at the claim. Shannet
came back, but McAndrew didn't. Shannet said a snake got him."

Simon Templar reached for another cigarette.

"Personally, I say the snake's name was Shannet," remarked
Archie Sheridan quietly. "Lilla—McAndrew's daughter—said the
same thing. Particularly when Shannet produced a written agreement signed by McAndrew and himself, in which it was arranged
that if either partner should die, all rights in the claim should pass to
the other partner. Lilla swore that McAndrew, who'd always
thought first of her, would never have signed such a document,
and she got a look at it and said the signature was forged. Shannet
replied that McAndrew was getting over a bout of malaria when he
signed it, and his hand was rather shaky. The girl carried it right
to the top court of what passes for justice here, fighting like a hero,
but Shannet had too big a pull with the judges, and she lost her case.
I arrived just after her appeal was turned down."

"What about McAndrew's body?"

"Shannet said he buried it by the trail; but the jungle trails here
are worse than any maze that was ever invented, and you can almost see the stuff grow. The grave could quite reasonably be lost
in a week. Shannet said he couldn't find it again. I took a trip that
way myself, but it wasn't any use. All I got out of it was a bullet
through a perfectly good hat from some sniper in the background—
Shannet for a fiver."

"After which," suggested Simon Templar thoughtfully, "Shannet
found he couldn't run the show alone, and sold out to our dear
friend in London, Master Hugo Campard, shark, swindler, general
blackguard, and promoter of unlimited dud companies——"

"Who perpetrated the first sound company of his career, Pasala
Oil Products, on the strength of it," Sheridan completed. "Shares
not for public issue, and sixty percent of them held by himself."

Simon Templar took his cigarette from his mouth and blew a long
thin streamer of smoke into the sunlight.

"So that's what I've come over to deal with, Archibald?" he murmured. "Well, well, *well*. . . . Taken by and large, it looks like a diverting holiday. Carol a brief psalm about things political, laddie."

"Just about twice as crooked as anything south of the United States border," said Sheridan. "The man who matters isn't the President. He's under the thumb of what they call the Minister for the Interior, who finds it much more convenient and much safer to stay in the background—they never assassinate Ministers for the Interior, apparently, but Presidents are fair game. And this man— Manuel Concepción de Villega is his poetic label—is right under the wing of Shannet, and is likely to stay there as long as Shannet's money lasts."

The Saint rose and lounged over to the verandah rail. At that hour (which was just after midday) the thermometer stood at a hundred and two in the shade, and the Saint had provided himself suitably with white ducks. The dazzling whiteness of them would have put snow to shame; and he wore them, as might have been expected of him, with the most cool and careless elegance in the world. He looked as if he would have found an inferno chilly. His dark hair was brushed smoothly back; his lean face was tanned to a healthy brown; altogether he must have been the most dashing and immaculate sight that Santa Miranda had set eyes on for many years.

Sheridan was in despair before that vision of unruffled perfection. His hair was tousled, his white ducks looked somewhat limp with the heat, and his pleasantly ugly face was moist.

"What about the rest of the white, or near-white, inhabitants?" inquired the Saint.

"A two-fisted, rip-roaring giant of a red-headed Irishman named Kelly," was the reply. "His wife—that's two. Lilla McAndrew, who's staying with them—I wouldn't let her put up at the filthy hotel in the town any longer—three. Four and five, a couple of traders, more or less permanently drunk and not worth considering. Six— Shannet. That's the lot."

The Saint turned away and gazed down the hillside. From where he stood, on the verandah of Sheridan's bungalow, he could look down to the roofs of Santa Miranda—the cluster of white buildings in the Moorish style which formed the centre, and the fringe of adobe huts on the outskirts. Left and right of him, on the hill above the town, were other bungalows. Beyond the town was the sea.

The Saint studied the view for a time in silence; then he turned round again.

"We seem to be on to the goods," he remarked. "Shannet the small fish, but an undoubted murderer—and, through him, our real man, Campard. I had a hunch I shouldn't be wasting your time when I sent you out here as soon as I heard Campard was backing Pasala Oil Products. But I never guessed P.O.P. would be real until I got your first cable. Now we're on a truly classy piece of velvet. It all looks too easy."

"Easy?" queried Sheridan sceptically. "I'm glad you think it's easy. With Shannet's claim established, and the concession in writing at Campard's London office, and Lilla McAndrew's petition dismissed, and Shannet twiddling the Government, the Army, the police, and the rest of the bunch, down to the last office-boy, round and round his little finger with the money he gets from Campard— and the man calls it easy. Oh, take him away!"

The Saint's hands drove even deeper into his pockets. Tall and trim and athletic, he stood with his feet astride, swaying gently from his toes, with the Saintly smile flickering faintly round his mouth and a little dancing devil of mischief rousing in his blue eyes.

"I said easy," he drawled.

Sheridan buried his face in his hands.

"Go and put your head in the ice-bucket," he pleaded. "Of course, it's the sun. You're not used to it—I forgot that."

"How big is the Army?"

"There's a standing army of about five hundred, commanded by seventeen generals, twentyfive colonels, and about fifty minor officers. And if your head hurts, just lie down, close your eyes, and relax. It'll be quite all right in an hour or two."

"Artillery?"

"Three pieces, carried by mules. If you'd like some aspirin——"

"Navy?"

"One converted tug, with 5.9 quick-firer and crew of seven, commanded by two admirals. I don't think you ought to talk now. I'll put up the hammock for you, if you like, and you can sleep for an hour before lunch."

"Police force?"

"There are eleven constables in Santa Miranda, under three superintendents. And in future I shouldn't have any whisky before sundown."

The Saint smiled.

"I'm probably more used to the sun than you are," he said. "This is merely common sense. What's the key to the situation? The Government. Right. We don't propose to waste any of our good money bribing them—and if we did, they'd doublecross us. Therefore they must be removed by force. And at once, because I can't stay long. Long live the Revolution!"

"Quite," agreed Sheridan helplessly. "And the Revolutionary Army? This State is the only one in South America that's never had a revolution—because nobody's ever had enough energy to start one."

Simon fished for his cigarette-case.

"We are the Revolutionary Army," he said. "I ask you to remember that we march on our stomachs. So we'll just have another drink, and then some lunch, and then we'll wander along and try to enlist the mad Irishman. If we three can't make rings round six hundred and fifteen comic dagoes, I'm going to retire from the fighting game and take up knitting and fancy needlework!"

## II

"My dear soul," the Saint was still arguing persuasively at the close of the meal, "it's so simple. The man who manages the Government of this two-by-four backyard is the man who holds the fate of Pasala Oil Products in his hands. At present Shannet is the bright boy who manages the Government, and the master of P.O.P. is accordingly walking around under the Shannet hat. We'll go one better. We won't merely manage the Government. We'll *be* the Government. And Pop is ours to play hell with as we like. Could anything be more straightforward? as the actress said when the bishop showed her his passbook."

"Go on," encouraged Sheridan weakly. "Don't bother about my feelings."

"As the actress said to the bishop shortly afterwards," murmured the Saint. "Blessed old Archie, it's obvious that three months in this enervating climate and the society of Lilla McAndrew have brought your energy down to the level of that of the natives you spoke of so contemptuously just now. I grant you it's sudden, but it's the only way. Before I knew the whole story I thought it would be good enough if we held up the post office and sent Campard a phony cable purporting to come from Shannet, telling him the Government had been kicked out, the concession revoked, and the only thing to do

was to sell out his Pop holdings as quickly as possible. What time
our old friend Roger, back in London, snaps up the shares discreetly, as fast as they come on the market."

"Why won't that work now?"

"You're forgetting the girl," said Templar. "This oil is really her
property, so it isn't good enough just to make Campard unload at a
loss and sell back to him at a premium when the rumour of revolution is exploded. The concession has really got to be revoked. Therefore I propose to eliminate the present Government, and make
Kelly, your mad Irishman, the new Minister of the Interior. That is,
unless you'd take the job."

"No, thanks," said Sheridan generously. "It's not quite in my
line. Pass me up."

The Saint lighted a cigarette.

"In that case Kelly is elected unanimously," he remarked with
charming simplicity. "So the only thing left to decide is how we
start the trouble. I've been in South American revolutions before,
but they've always been well under way by the time I arrived. The
technique of starting the blamed things was rather missed out of my
education. What does one do? Does one simply wade into the Presidential Palace, chant 'Time, gentlemen, please!' in the ear of his
Illustrious Excellency, and invite him to close the door as he goes
out? Or what?"

"What, probably," said Sheridan. "That would be as safe as
anything. I might get you reprieved on the grounds of insanity."

The Saint sighed.

"You aren't helpful, Beautiful Archibald."

"If you settle down to talk seriously——"

"I am serious."

Sheridan stared. Then:

"Is that straight, Saint?" he demanded.

"From the horse's mouth," the Saint assured him solemnly. "Even
as the crow flieth before the pubs open. Sweet cherub, did you
really think I was wasting precious time with pure pickled onions?"

Sheridan looked at him. There was another flippant rejoinder on
the tip of Archie Sheridan's tongue, but somehow it was never
uttered.

The Saint was smiling. It was a mocking smile, but that was for
Sheridan's incredulity. It was not the sort of smile that accompanies
a test of the elasticity of a leg. And in the Saint's eyes was a light
that wasn't entirely humorous.

Archie Sheridan, with a cigarette in his mouth, fumbling for matches, realised that he had mistaken the shadow for the substance. The Saint wasn't making fun of revolutions. It was just that his sense of humour was too big to let him plan even a revolution without seeing the funny side of the performance.

Sheridan got a match to his cigarette.

"Well?" prompted the Saint.

"I think you're pots, bats, and bees," he said. "But if you're set on that kind of suicide—lead on. Archibald will be at your elbow with the bombs. You didn't forget the bombs?"

The Saint grinned.

"I had to leave them behind," he replied lightly. "They wouldn't fit into my sponge-bag. Seriously, now, where and how do you think we should start the trouble?"

They were sitting opposite one another at Sheridan's bare mahogany dining table, and at the Saint's back was the open door leading out on to the verandah and commanding an uninterrupted view of the approach to the bungalow.

"Start the thing here and now and anyhow you like," said Sheridan, and he was looking past the Saint's shoulder towards the verandah steps.

Simon Templar settled back a little more lazily into his chair, and a very saintly meekness was spreading over his face.

"Name?" he inquired laconically.

"Shannet himself."

The Saint's eyes were half-closed.

"I will compose a little song about him immediately," he said.

Then a shadow fell across the table, but the Saint did not move at once. He appeared to be lost in a daydream.

"*Buenos días*, Shannet," said Archie Sheridan. "Also, as soon as possible, *adiós*. Hurry up and say what you've got to say before I kick you out."

"I'll do any kicking out that's necessary, thanks," said Shannet harshly. "Sheridan, I've come to warn you off for the last time. The *Andalusia* berthed this morning, and she sails again on the evening tide. You've been nosing around here too long as it is. Is that plain enough?"

"Plainer than your ugly face," drawled Sheridan. "And by what right do you kick me out? Been elected President, have you?"

"You know me," said Shannet. "You know that what I say here goes. You'll sail on the *Andalusia*—either voluntarily or because you're put on board in irons. That's all. . . . What's this?"

The Saint, perceiving himself to be the person thus referred to, awoke sufficiently to open his eyes and screw his head round so that he could view the visitor.

He saw a tall broad-shouldered man of indeterminate age, clad in a soiled white suit of which the coat was unbuttoned to expose a grubby singlet. Shannet had certainly not shaved for two days; and he did not appear to have brushed his hair for a like period, for a damp sandy lock drooped in a tangle over his right eye. In one corner of his mouth a limp and dilapidated cigarette dangled tiredly from his lower lip.

The Saint blinked.

"Gawd!" he said offensively. "Can it be human?"

Shannet's fists swept back his coat and rested on his hips.

"What's your name, Cissy?" he demanded.

The Saint flicked some ash from his cigarette, and rose to his feet delicately.

"Benito Mussolini," he answered mildly. "And you must be one of the corporation scavengers. How's the trade in garbage?" His gentle eyes swept Shannet from crown to toe. "Archie, there must have been some mistake. The real scavenger has gone sick, and one of his riper pieces of refuse is deputising for him. I'm sorry."

"If you——"

"I said I was sorry," the Saint continued, in the same smooth voice, "because I'm usually very particular about the people I fight, and I hate soiling my hands on things like you."

Shannet glowered.

"I don't know who you are," he said, "and I don't care. But if you're looking for a fight you can have it."

"I am looking for a fight, dear one," drawled the Saint. "In fact, I'm looking for a lot of fights, and you're the first one that's offered. 'Cissy' is a name I particularly object to being called, O misbegotten of a pig!"

The last words were spoken in colloquial Spanish, and the Saint made more of them than it is possible to report in printable English. Shannet went white, then red.

"You——"

His answering stream of profanity merged into a left swing to the Saint's jaw, which, if it had landed, would have ended the fight there and then. But it did not land.

Simon Templar swayed back, and the swing missed by a couple

of inches. As Shannet stumbled, momentarily off his balance, the Saint reached round and took the jug of ice water off the table behind him. Without any appearance of effort or haste, he side-stepped and poured most of the contents of the jug down the back of Shannet's neck.

Shannet swung again. The Saint ducked, and sent the man flying with a smashing jab to the nose.

"Look out, Saint!" Sheridan warned suddenly.

"Naughty!" murmured the Saint, without heat.

Shannet was getting to his feet, and his right hand was drawing something from his hip pocket.

The Saint took two steps and a flying leap over Shannet's head, turning in the air as he did so. Shannet had only got to his knees when the Saint landed behind him and caught his opponent's throat and right wrist in hands that had the strength of steel cables in their fingers. Shannet's wrist was twisted behind his back with an irresistible wrench. . . .

The gun clattered simultaneously with Shannet's yelp of agony, and the Saint picked up the gun and stepped away.

"A trophy, Archie," he said, and tossed the weapon over to Sheridan. "Guns I have not quite been shot with—there must be a drawer full of them at home. . . . Let's start, sweet Shannet!"

Shannet replied with a chair, but the Saint was ten feet away by the time it crashed into the opposite wall.

Then Shannet came in again with his fists. Any one of those whirling blows carried a kick that would have put a mule to sleep, but the Saint had forgotten more about ringcraft than many professionals ever learn. Shannet never came near touching him. Every rush Shannet made, somehow, expended itself on thin air, while he always seemed to be running his face slap into the Saint's stabbing left.

And at last the Saint, scorning even counter-attack, dropped his hands into his pockets, and simply eluded Shannet's homicidal onslaught by sheer brilliant footwork—ducking, swaying, swooping, as calm and unruffled as if he were merely demonstrating a few ballroom steps, and as light and graceful on his toes as a ballet dancer—until Shannet reeled limply back against the wall with the sweat streaming into his eyes, utterly done in.

The Saint's mocking smile had never left his lips, and not one hair of his head had shifted.

"Want a rest?" he asked kindly.

"If you'd come in and fight like a man," gasped Shannet, his tortured chest heaving, "I'd kill you!"

"Oh, don't be silly," said the Saint in a bored voice, as though he had no further interest in the affair. "Hurry up and get out—I'm going to be busy."

He turned away, but Shannet lurched after him.

"Get out yourself!" snarled the man thickly. "D'you hear? I'm going right down to fetch the police——"

The Saint sat down.

"Listen to me, Shannet," he said quietly. "The less you talk about police when I'm around, the better for you. I'm telling you now that I believe you murdered a man named McAndrew not so long ago, and jumped his claim on a forged partnership agreement. I'm only waiting till I've got the proof. And then—well, it's too much to hope that the authorities of this benighted republic will execute the man who pays half their salaries, and so in the name of Justice I shall take you myself and hang you from a high tree."

For a moment of silence the air seemed to tingle with the same electric tension as heralds the breaking of a thunderstorm, while the Saint's ice-blue eyes quelled Shannet's reawakening fury: and then, with a short laugh, the Saint relaxed.

"You're a pawn in the game," he said, with a contrasting care-lessness which only emphasised the bleak implacability of his last speech. "We won't waste good melodrama on you. We reserve that for clients with really important discredit accounts. Instead, you shall hear the epitaph I've just composed for you. It commemorates a pestilent tumour named Shannet, who disfigured the face of this planet. He started some fun, but before it was done he was wishing he'd never began it. That otherwise immortal verse is greatly marred by a grammatical error, but I'm not expecting you to know any better. . . . Archibald—the door."

Archie Sheridan had no reason to love Shannet, and the kick with which he launched the man into the garden was not gentle, but he seemed to derive no pleasure from it.

He came back with a grave face, and resumed his chair facing the Saint.

"Well," he said, "you've done what you wanted. Now shall we sit down and make our wills, or shall we spend our last hours of life in drinking and song?"

"Of course, we may be shot," admitted the Saint calmly. "That's up to us. How soon can we expect the Army?"

"Not before five. They'll all be asleep now, and an earthquake wouldn't make the Pasala policeman break off his siesta. Much less the Army, who are inclined to give themselves airs. We might catch the *Andalusia*," he added hopefully.

The Saint surveyed him seraphically.

"Sweetheart," he said, "that joke may now be considered over. We've started, and we've got to keep moving. As I don't see the fun of sitting here waiting for the other side to surround us, I guess we'll bounce right along and interview Kelly. And when you two have coached me thoroughly in the habits and topography of Santa Miranda, we'll just toddle along and capture the town."

"Just toddle along and which?" repeated Sheridan dazedly.

The Saint spun a cigarette high into the air, and trapped it neatly between his lips as it fell.

"That is to say, *I* will capture the town," he corrected himself, "while you and Kelly create a disturbance somewhere to distract their attention. Wake up, brother. Get your hat, and let's go!"

## III

The Saint's breezy way of saying that he would "just toddle along and capture the town" was a slight exaggeration. As a matter of fact, he spent nearly four days on the job.

There was some spade work to be done, and certain preparations to be made, and the Saint devoted a considerable amount of care and sober thought to these details. Though his methods, to the uninformed observer, might always have seemed to savour of the reckless, tip-and-run, or hit-first-and-ask-questions-afterwards school, the truth was that he rarely stepped out of the frying pan without first taking the temperature of the fire beyond.

Even in such a foolhardy adventure as that in which he was then engaged, he knew exactly what he was doing, and legislated against failure as well as he might; for even in the most outlandish parts of the world the penalty of unsuccessful revolution is death, and the Saint had no overwhelming desire to turn his interesting biography into an obituary notice.

He explained his plan to Kelly, and found the Irishman an immediate convert to the Cause.

"Shure, I've been thinkin' for years that it was time somebody threw out their crooked Government," said that worthy, ruffling hand like a ham through his tousled mop of flaming hair. "I'm just wonderin' now why I niver did ut meself."

"It's a desperate chance," Simon Templar admitted. "But I don't mind taking it if you're game."

"Six years I've been here," mused Kelly ecstatically, screwing up a huge fist, "and I haven't seen a real fight. Exceptin' one or two disagreements with the natives, who run away afther the first round."

The Saint smiled. He could not have hoped to find a more suitable ally.

"We might easily win out," he said. "It wouldn't work in England, but in a place like this——"

"The geography was made for us," said Kelly.

On a scrap of paper he sketched a rough map to illustrate his point.

Pasala is more or less in the shape of a wedge, with the base facing north-east on the seacoast. Near the centre of the base of the wedge is Santa Miranda. In the body of the wedge are the only other three towns worth mentioning—Las Flores, Rugio, and, near the apex, Esperanza. They are connected up by a car-track of a road which includes them in a kind of circular route which starts and finishes at Santa Miranda, for the State of Pasala does not yet boast a railway. This is hardly necessary, for the distance between Santa Miranda and Esperanza, the two towns farthest apart, is only one hundred and forty miles.

It should also be mentioned that the wedge-shaped territory of Pasala cuts roughly into the Republic of Maduro, a much larger and more civilised country.

"Of course, we're simply banking on the psychology of revolutions and the apathy of the natives," said the Saint, when they had finished discussing their plan of campaign. "The population aren't interested—if they're shown a man in a nice new uniform, and told that he's the man in power, they believe it, and go home and pray that they won't be any worse off than they were before. If we take off a couple of taxes, or something like that, as soon as we get in, the mob will be with us to a man. I'm sure the Exchequer can stand it—I don't imagine Manuel Concepción de Villega has been running this show without making a substantial profit on turnover."

"That'll fetch 'em," Kelly averred. "They're bled dry with taxes at present."

"Secondly, there's the Army. They're like any other army. They obey their officers because it's never occurred to them to do anything else. If they were faced with a revolution they'd fight it. So instead of that we'll present the revolution as an accomplished fact. If they're like any other South American army, they'll simply carry on under the new Government—with a bonus of a few *pesos* per man to clinch the bargain."

They talked for a while longer; and then they went out and joined Archie Sheridan, who had not been present at the council, being otherwise occupied with Lilla McAndrew on the verandah.

The Saint had a little leisure to admire the girl. She was rather tall, fair-haired and blue-eyed, superbly graceful. Her sojourn in that sunny climate had coloured her skin a pale golden-brown that was infinitely more becoming than mere pink-and-white; but the peach-like bloom of her complexion had not had time to suffer.

It was plain that Archie Sheridan was fatally smitten with the inevitable affliction, and the Saint was mischievously delighted.

"You want to be careful of him, Miss McAndrew," he advised gravely. "I've known him since he was so high, and you wouldn't believe what a past he's collected in his brief career of sin. Let's see. . . . There was Gladys, the golden-haired beauty from the front row of the Gaiety chorus, Susan, Beryl—no, two Beryls—Ethel, the artist's model, Angela, Sadie from California, Joan—two Joans—no, three Joans——"

"Don't believe him, Lilla," pleaded Archie. "He's been raving all day. Why, just before lunch he said he was Benito Mussolini!"

The girl laughed.

"It's all right," she told Simon. "I don't take him seriously."

"There's gratitude for you," said Sheridan wildly. "After all I've done for her! I even taught her to speak English. When she arrived here she had a Scots accent that would have made a bawbee run for its life. She reeked of haggis——"

"Archie!"

"Haggis," persisted Sheridan. "She carried one around in her pibroch till it starved to death."

"What are pibroch?" asked the Saint curiously. "Are they something you wear under a kilt?"

When the girl had recovered her composure:

"Is he really so impossible?" she asked.

"I don't know you well enough to tell you the whole truth,"

said the Saint solemnly. "The only hope I can give you is that you're the first Lilla in his life. Wait a minute—sorry—wasn't Lilla the name of the barmaid——"

"Go away," said Sheridan morosely. "With sudden death staring you in the face, you ought to be spending your time in prayer and repentance. You'll be shot at dawn tomorrow, and I shall look over the prison walls and cheer on the firing squad."

He watched Kelly and the Saint retire to the other end of the verandah, and then turned to the girl with his pleasant face unusually serious.

"Lilla," he said, "I don't want to scare you, but it isn't all quite as funny as we make out. The Saint would still be laughing in the face of the firing squad I mentioned; but that doesn't make the possibility of the firing squad any less real."

She looked at him with sober eyes.

"Then it's easily settled," she said. "I won't let you do it."

Sheridan laughed.

"It isn't me you've got to deal with," he replied. "It's the Saint. Nothing you could say would stop *him*. He'd simply tell me to beat it with you on the *Andalusia* this evening if I was scared. And I'd rather face the said firing squad than have the Saint say that to me."

She would have protested further, but something in the man's tone silenced her. She knew that he was making no idle statement. She had no experience whatever of such things, and yet she realised intuitively what she was up against, recognised the heroic thing when she met it—the blind unswerving loyalty of a man to his friend, the unshakable obedience of a man to a loved leader. And she knew that any attempt she made to seduce her man from that reality would only lower herself in his eyes.

Perhaps there are few women who could have shown such an understanding, but Lilla McAndrew was—Lilla McAndrew.

She smiled suddenly.

"I've always wanted to see a revolution," she said simply.

Moments passed before Sheridan could grasp the completeness of her sympathy and acquiescence. And then his arms went round her, and her hands tousled his hair.

"Dear Archie!" she said, and found herself unaccountably breathless.

"I admit every girl the Saint mentioned," said Sheridan defiantly. "And a few more. But that doesn't alter the fact that I love you, and as soon as this comic revolution's over I'm going to marry you."

"I'll believe that when you do it," she teased him; but her heart was on her lips when he kissed her. . . .

Some almost offensively discreet coughing from the Saint interrupted them ten minutes later.

"I tried to save you," said the Saint, declining to avert his shamelessly quizzical gaze from the girl's efforts to straighten her hair inconspicuously. "And I'm sorry to have to butt in on your downfall, but your boy friend and I have work to do. If you look down towards the town you'll see a file of men advancing up the main street in our direction, led by two men on horseback in the uniform of commissionaires. The entire police force of Santa Miranda, as far as I can make out from this distance, is on its way up here to arrest me for assaulting and battering one of their most prominent citizens, and to arrest Archie as an accessory before, after, and during the fact. They have just woken up from their afternoon snooze, and have been put on the job by the aforesaid citizen with commendable rapidity. Will you excuse us if we escape?"

They went to the edge of the verandah and looked down. Below them, about a mile away, Santa Miranda, as yet hardly astir from its siesta, lay bathed in the afternoon sunshine.

The town, indeterminately vignetted at the edges, had a definite core of nearly modern white buildings ranged down its principal streets. These numbered two, and were in the form of a T. The top of the T ran parallel with the waterfront; the upright, half-way down which was the Presidential Palace, ran inland for nearly a mile, tailing off in the mass of adobe huts which clustered round the core of the town.

From where they stood they could look down the length of the street which formed the upright of the T; and the situation was even as the Saint had diagnosed it. . . .

"One minute for the fond farewell, Archie," said the Saint briskly, and Sheridan nodded.

Simon Templar drew Kelly inside the bungalow.

"By the way," he said, "do you happen to have such a thing as a good-looking pot of paint?"

"I've got some enamel," replied the mystified Kelly.

He produced a couple of tins, and the Saint selected one with every appearance of satisfaction.

"The very idea," he said. "It's just an idea of mine for dealing with this arrest business."

Kelly was suspicious.

"I don't seem to have much to do," he complained aggrievedly. "It's hoggin' the best of the fightin' yez are. Now, if I had my way, I'd be sthartin' the trouble with these policemen right away, I would."

"And wreck the whole show," said the Saint. "No, it's too soon for that. And if you call being fifty percent of an invading army having nothing to do I can't agree. You're one of the most important members of the cast. Besides, if your bus doesn't break down, you'll be back here just when the rough stuff is warming up. You get it both ways."

He adjusted his hat to an appropriately rakish and revolutionary angle on his head, and went out to collect Archie Sheridan.

They shook hands with the still grumbling Kelly; but the Saint had the last word with Lilla McAndrew.

"I'm sorry I've got to take Archie," he said. "You see, he's the one man I can trust here who can tap out Morse fluently, and I sent him out from England for that very reason, though I didn't know it was going to pan out as it's panning out now. But I'll promise to get him back to you safe and sound. You needn't worry. Only the good die young. I wonder how you've managed to live so long, Lilla?"

He smiled; and when the Saint smiled in that particularly gay and enchanting manner, it was impossible to believe that any adventure he undertook could fail.

"Archie is marked 'Fragile—With Care' for this journey," said the Saint, and went swinging down the verandah steps.

He walked back arm-in-arm with Sheridan to the latter's bungalow at a leisurely pace enough, for it was his last chance to give Sheridan his final instructions for the opening of the campaign.

Archie was inclined to voice much the same grievance as Kelly had vented, but Templar dealt shortly with that insubordination.

"I'm starting off by having the most boresome time of any of you," he said. "If I could do your job, I promise you I'd be making you do mine. That being so, I reckon I deserve a corresponding majority ration of excitement at the end. Anyway, with any luck we'll all be together again by Thursday, and we'll see the new era in in a bunch. And if you're going to say you've thought of another scheme that'd be just as effective, my answer is that you ought to have spoken up before. It's too late to change our plans now."

At the bungalow the Saint made certain preparation for the arrival of the police posse which to some extent depleted Archie

Sheridan's travelling athletic outfit. That done, he sent Sheridan to his post, and himself settled down with a cigarette in an easy chair on the verandah to await the coming of the Law.

## IV

The *guindillas* came toiling up the last two hundred yards of slope in a disorderly straggle. The hill at that point became fairly steep, they were in poor condition, and, although the sun was getting low, the broiling heat of the afternoon had not yet abated; and these factors united to upset what might otherwise have been an impressive approach. The only members of the squad who did not seem the worse for wear were the two *comisarios*, who rode in the van on a pair of magnificent high-stepping horses, obvious descendants of the chargers of Cortés' invading Spaniards, the like of which may often be seen in that part of the Continent. The Saint had had an eye on those horses ever since he spied them a mile and a half away, which was why he was so placidly waiting for the deputation.

He watched them with a detached interest, smoking his cigarette. They were an unkempt and ferocious-looking lot (in Pasala, as in many Latin countries, Saturday night is Gillette night for the general public), and every man of them was armed to somewhere near the teeth with a musket, a revolver, and a sabre. The Saint himself was comparatively weaponless, his entire armoury consisting of the beautifully-fashioned little knife strapped to his left forearm under his sleeve, which he could throw with a deadly swiftness and an unerring aim. He did not approve of firearms, which he considered messy and noisy and barbarous inventions of the devil. Yet the opposition's display of force did not concern him.

His first impression, that the entire police force of Santa Miranda had been sent out to arrest him, proved to be a slight overestimate. There were, as a matter of fact, only ten *guardias* behind the two mounted men in resplendent uniforms.

The band came to a bedraggled and slovenly halt a few yards from the verandah, and the *comisarios* dismounted and ascended the short flight of steps with an imposing clanking of scabbards and spurs. They were moustached and important.

The Saint rose.

"*Buenas tardes, señores*," he murmured courteously.

"*Señor*," said the senior *comisario* sternly, unfolding a paper overloaded with official seals, "I regret that I have to trouble a visitor illustrious, but I am ordered to request your honour to allow your honour to be taken to the *prevención*, in order that in the morning your honour may be brought before the *tribunal* to answer a charge of grievously assaulting the Señor Shannet."

He replaced the document in his pocket, and bowed extravagantly.

The Saint, with a smile, surpassed the extravagance of the bow.

"*Señor polizonte*," he said, "I regret that I cannot come."

Now the word *polizonte*, while it is understood to mean "policeman", is not the term with which it is advisable to address even an irascible *guardia*—much less a full-blown *comisario*. It brought to an abrupt conclusion the elaborate ceremony in which the *comisario* had been indulging.

He turned and barked an order; and the escort mounted the steps and ranged themselves along the verandah.

"Arrest him!"

"I cannot stay," said the Saint sadly. "And I refuse to be arrested. *Adiós, amigos!*"

He faded away—through the open door of the dining-room. The Saint had the knack of making these startling abrupt exits without any show of haste, so that he was gone before his audience had realised that he was on his way.

Then the *guardias*, led by the two outraged *comisario*, followed in a body.

The bungalow was small, with a large verandah in front and a smaller verandah at the back. The three habitable rooms of which it boasted ran through the width of the house, with doors opening on to each verandah. The dining-room was the middle room, and it had no windows.

As the *guardias* surged in in pursuit, rifles at the ready, with the *comisarios* waving their revolvers, the Saint reappeared in the doorway that opened on to the back of the verandah. At the same moment the doors to the front verandah were slammed and barred behind them by Archie Sheridan, who had been lying in wait in an adjoining room for that purpose.

The Saint's hands were held high above his head, and in each hand was a gleaming round black object.

"*Señores*," he said persuasively, "I am a peaceful revolutionary, and I cannot be pestered like this. In my hands you see two bombs. If you shoot me, they will fall and explode. If you do not immediately surrender I shall throw them—and, again, they will explode. Is it to be death or glory, boys?"

He spoke the last sentence in English; but he had already said enough in the vernacular to make the situation perfectly plain. The *guardias* paused, irresolute.

Their officers, retiring to a strategic position in the background from which they could direct operations, urged their men to advance and defy death in the performance of their duty; but the Saint shifted his right hand threateningly, and the *guardias* found the counter-argument more convincing. They threw down their arms; and the *comisarios*, finding themselves alone, followed suit as gracefully as they might.

The Saint ordered the arsenal to be thrown out of the door, and he stepped inside the room and stood aside to allow this to be done. Outside, the guns were collected by Archie Sheridan, and their bolts removed and hurled far away into the bushes of the garden. The cartridges he poured into a large bag, together with the contents of the bandoliers which the Saint ordered his prisoners to discard, for these were required for a certain purpose. Then the Saint returned to the doorway.

"*Hasta la vista!*" he murmured mockingly. "Until we meet again!"

And he hurled the two gleaming round black objects he carried, and a wail of terror went up from the doomed men.

The Saint sprang back, slamming and barring the doors in the face of the panic-stricken stampede; and the two tennis-balls, which he had coated with Kelly's providential enamel for the purpose, rebounded off the heads of the cowering *comisarios*, leaving great splashes of paint on the gorgeous uniforms and the gorgeous moustachios of Santa Miranda's Big Two, and went bouncing insolently round the room.

The Saint vaulted over the verandah rail and ran round to the front of the bungalow. Sheridan, his bag of cartridges slung over his shoulder, was already mounted on one of the police horses, and holding the other by the bridle. From inside the dining-room could be heard the muffled shouting and cursing of the imprisoned men, and on the panels of the barred doors thundered the battering of their efforts to escape.

The Saint sprang into the saddle.

"*Vamos!*" he cried, and smacked his hand down on the horse's quarters.

The pounding of departing hoofs came to the ears of the men

in the locked room, and redoubled the fury of their onslaught on the doors. But the mahogany of which the doors were made was thick and well seasoned, and it was ten minutes before they broke out. And then, on foot and unarmed, there was nothing for them to do but to return to Santa Miranda and confess defeat.

The which they did, collaborating on the way down to invent a thrilling tale of a desperate and perilous battle, in which they had braved a hundred deaths, their heroism availing them naught in the face of Simon Templar's evil cunning. But first, to restore their shattered nerves, they partook freely of three bottles of Sheridan's whisky which they found. And it may be recorded that on this account the next day found them very ill; for, before he left, Archie Sheridan had liberally adulterated the whisky with Epsom Salts, in anticipation of this very vandalism. But since *guardia* and *comisario* alike were unfamiliar with the flavour of whisky, they noticed nothing amiss, and went unsuspecting to their hideous fate.

But when they returned to Santa Miranda they said nothing whatever about bombs, wisely deeming that the inclusion of that episode in their story could not but cover them with derision.

Meantime, Simon Templar and Archie Sheridan had galloped neck and neck to Kelly's bungalow, and there Kelly was waiting for them. He had a kitbag already packed with certain articles that the Saint had required, and Simon took the bag and lashed it quickly to the pommel of his saddle.

Sheridan dismounted. The Saint shook hands with him, and took the bridle of the spare horse.

"All will be well," said the Saint blithely. "I feel it in my bones. So long, souls. See you all again soon. Do your stuff—and good luck!"

He clapped his heels to his horse, and was gone with a cheery wave of his hand.

They watched him till the trees hid him from view, and then they went back to the bungalow.

"A piece of wood, pliers, screws, screwdriver, and wire, Kelly, my bhoy!" ordered Sheridan briskly. "I've got some work to do before I go to bed tonight. And while I'm doing it you can gather round and hear the biggest laugh yet in this revolution, or how the Battle of Santa Miranda was nearly won on the courts of Wimbledon."

"I thought you weren't coming back," said the girl accusingly.

"I didn't know whether I was or not," answered the shameless

Archie. "It all depended on whether the Saint's plan of escape functioned or not. Anyway, a goodbye like you gave me was far too good to miss just because I might be coming back. And don't look so disappointed because I got away. I'll go down to the town and surrender, if that's what you want."

Towards sundown a squadron of cavalry galloped up to the bungalow, and the officer in command declared his intention of making a search. Kelly protested.

"You have no right," he said, restraining an almost irresistible desire to throw the man down the steps and thus precipitate the fighting that his fists were itching for.

"I have a warrant from the Minister of the Interior, El Supremo é Ilustrisimo Señor Manuel Concepción de Villega," said the officer, producing the document with a flourish.

"El Disgustando y Horriblisimo, Señor!" muttered Kelly.

The officer shrugged, and indicated the men who waited below.

"I do not wish to use force, Señor Kelly," he said significantly, and Kelly submitted to the inevitable.

"But," he said, "I do not know why you should suspect me to be hiding him."

"You are known to be a friend of the Señor Sheridan," was the brief reply, "and the Señor Sheridan is a friend of this man. We are looking for both of them."

Kelly followed the officer into the house.

"What did you say was the name of this man you are looking for?" he inquired.

"To the Señor Shannet, whom he attacked," said the officer, "he gave his name as Benito Mussolini."

He was at a loss to understand Kelly's sudden earthquaking roar of laughter. At last he gave up the effort, and put it down to another manifestation of the well-known madness of all *ingleses*. But the fact remains that the joke largely compensated Kelly for the indignity of the search to which his house was subjected.

The officer and half a dozen of his men went through the bungalow with a small-toothed comb, and not a cubic inch of it, from floor to rafters, escaped their attention. But they did not find Archie Sheridan, who was sitting out on the roof, on the opposite side to that from which the soldiers had approached.

At last the search party allowed themselves to be shepherded out, for barely an hour's daylight was left to them, and they had already fruitlessly wasted much valuable time.

"But remember, Señor Kelly," said the officer, as his horse was led up, "that both Sheridan and Mussolini have been declared outlaws for resisting arrest and assaulting and threatening the lives of the *guardias civiles* sent to apprehend them. In the morning they will be proclaimed; and the Señor Shannet, who has heard of the insolence offered to the Law, has himself offered to double the reward for their capture, dead or alive."

The troopers rode off on their quest, but in those latitudes the twilight is short. They scoured the countryside for an hour, until the fall of night put an end to the search, and five miles away they found the horses of the two *comisarios* grazing in a field, but of the man Mussolini there was no trace. The Saint had had a good start; and what he did not know about the art of taking cover in the open country wasn't worth knowing.

He was stretched out on a branch of a tall tree a mile away from where the horses were found when the troop of cavalry reined in only twelve feet beneath him.

"We can do no more now," said the officer. "In the morning we shall find him. Without horses he cannot travel far. Let us go home."

The Saint laughed noiselessly in the darkness.

## V

That night there came into Santa Miranda a *peón*.

He was dirty and disreputable to look upon. His clothes were dusty, patched in many places, and threadbare where they were not patched; and his hair was long, and matted into a permanent thatch, as is the slovenly custom of the labourers of that country.

Had he wished to do so, he might have passed unnoticed among many other similarly down-at-heel and poverty-stricken people; but this he did not seem to want. In fact, he went out of his way to draw attention to himself; and this he found easy enough, for his poverty-stricken appearance was belied by the depth of his pocket.

He made a fairly comprehensive round of the inferior cafés in the town, and in each he bought wine and *aguardiente* for all who cared to join him. Naturally, it was not long before he acquired a large following; and, since he seemed to account for two drinks to everybody else's one, there was no surprise when he became more and more drunk as the evening wore on.

It was not to be expected that such display of affluence on the part of one whose outward aspect argued against the probability that he

would have more than a few *centavos* to his name could escape
comment, and it was not long before the tongues that devoured the
liquor which he bought were busy with rumour. It was whispered,
as with authority, that he was a bandit from the Sierra Maduro,
over the border beyond Esperanza, who had crossed into Pasala to
spend his money and rest until the *rurales* of Maduro tired of seeking him and he could return to his old hunting-grounds with safety.
Then it was remarked that on his little finger was a signet ring bearing a heraldic device, and with equal authority it was said that he
was the heir to a noble Mexican family indulging his hobby of
moving among the *peones* as one of themselves and distributing
charity where he found it merited. Against this, another school of
thought affirmed that he was a *peón* who had murdered his master
and stolen his ring and his money.

The *peón* heard these whisperings, and laughingly ignored them.
His manner lent more support, however, to either of the two former
theories than to the third. He was tall for a *peón*, and a man of great
strength, as was seen when he bought a whole keg of wine and
lifted it in his hands to fill his goblet as if it weighed nothing at all.
His eyes were blue, which argued that he was of noble descent, for
the true *peón* stock is so mixed with the native that eyes of that sea-
blue colour are rare. And again, the bandit theory was made more
plausible by the man's boisterous and reckless manner, as though
he held life cheap and the intense enjoyment of the day the only
thing of moment, and would as soon be fighting as drinking. He
had, too, a repertoire of strange and barbarous songs which no one
could understand.

"Drink up, *amigos!*" he roared from time to time, "for this is the
beginning of great days for Pasala!"

But when they asked him what they might mean, he turned away
their questions with a jest and called for more wine.

Few of his following had seen such a night for many years.

From house to house he went, singing his strange songs, and bearing his keg of wine on his shoulder. One or two *guardias* would have
barred his way, or, hearing the rumours which were gossiped about
him, would have stopped and questioned him; but the *peón* poured
them wine or flung them money, and they stood aside.

Towards midnight, still singing, the man led his procession up the
Calle del Palacio. The crowd followed, not sure where they were
going, and not caring, for they had drunk much.

Now, the Calle del Palacio forms the upright of the T which has been described, and half-way down it, as has been stated, is the Palace from which it takes its name.

In the street opposite the palace gates the *peón* halted, set down his keg, and mounted unsteadily upon it. He stood there, swaying slightly, and his following gathered round him.

"*Viva! Viva!*" they shouted thickly.

The *peón* raised his hands for silence.

"Citizens!" he cried, "I have told you that this is the beginning of great days for Pasala, and now I will tell you why. It is because at last we are going to suffer no more under this Manuel Concepción de Villega. May worms devour him alive, for he is a thief and a tyrant and the son of a dog! His taxes bear you down, and you receive nothing in return. The President is his servant, that strutting nincompoop, and they are both in the pay of the traitor Shannet, who is planning to betray you to Maduro. Now I say that we will end this tonight."

"*Viva!*" responded a few doubtful voices.

"Let us finish this slavery," cried the *peón* again. "Let us storm this palace, which was built with money wrung from the poor, where your puppet of a President and this pig of a de Villega sleep in luxury for which you have been tortured! Let us tear them from their beds and slay them, and cast them back into the gutter from which they came."

This time there were no "*Vivas!*" The awfulness of the stranger's blasphemy had sobered the mob as nothing else could have done. It was unprecedented—incredible. No one had ever dared to speak in such terms of the President and his Minister—or, if they had, it was reported by spies to the *comisarios*, and *guardias* came swiftly and took the blasphemers away to a place where their treason should not offend the ears of the faithful. Of course, the *peón* had spoken nothing but the truth. But to tear down the palace and kill the President! It was unheard of. It could not be done without much discussion.

The stranger, after his first speech, had seen the sentries at the palace gates creep stealthily away; and now, over the heads of the awestruck crowd, he saw a little knot of *guardias* coming down the street at the double. Whistles shrilled and the mob huddled together in sudden terror.

"*Amigos,*" said the stranger urgently, in a lower voice, "the hour of liberation will not be long coming. Tonight you have heard me sing many strange songs, which are the songs of freedom. Now, when you hear those songs again, and you have thought upon the words I have said tonight, follow the man who sings such songs as I sang, for he will be sent to lead you to victory. But now go quickly, or you will be taken and punished."

The mob needed no encouragement for that. Even while the *peón* spoke many of them had sneaked away into the dark side streets. As he spoke his last sentence, it was as if a cord had been snapped which held them, and they fled incontinently.

The *peón* straightened up and shook his fists at their backs.

"Fools!" he screamed. "Cowards! Curs! Is it thus that ye fight? Is it thus that ye overthrow tyrants?"

But his audience was gone, and from either side the *guardias* were closing in on him with drawn sabres.

"*Cabrón!*" challenged one of them. "What is this raving?"

"I speak for liberty!" bawled the *peón*, reeling drunkenly on his pedestal. "I speak against the President, who does not know the name of his father, and against the Minister for the Interior, Manuel Concepción de Villega, who I call Señor Jugo Procedente del Estercolero, the spawn of a dunghill—*guarros, cabrones, hijos de putas. . . .*"

He let loose a stream of the vilest profanity and abuse in the language, so that even the hardened *guardias* were horrified.

They dragged him down and hustled him ungently to the police station, where they locked him up in a verminous cell for the night; but even then he cursed and raved against the President and the Minister for the Interior mingling his maledictions with snatches of unintelligible songs, until the jailer threatened to beat him unless he held his tongue. Then he was silent, and presently went to sleep.

In the morning they brought him before the magistrate. He was sober, but still rebellious. They asked him his name.

"Don Fulano de Tal," he replied, which is the Spanish equivalent of saying "Mr So-and-So, Such-and-Such."

"If you are impertinent," said the magistrate, "I shall order you to receive a hundred lashes."

"My name is Sancho Quijote," said the *peón* sullenly.

He was charged, and the sentries from the palace testified to the treason of his speeches. So also did the *guardias* who had broken up his meeting. They admitted, in extenuation of his offence, that he had been very drunk.

He was asked if he had anything to say.

"I have nothing to say," he answered, "except that, drunk or not,

I shall spit upon the name of the President and the Minister for the Interior till the end of my days. As for you, *señor juez*, you are no better than the *guindillas* who arrested me—you are all the miserable hirelings of the oppressors, paid to persecute those who dare speak for justice. But it will not be long before your pride is turned to humiliation."

"He is mad," whispered one *guardia* to another.

The *peón* was sentenced to seven years' imprisonment with hard labour, for there are limits to the powers of summary jurisdiction in Pasala. He heard the verdict without emotion.

"It does not matter," he said. "I shall not stay in prison seven days. It will not be long before you know why."

When he reached the prison he asked to be allowed to send a message by telegraph to Ondia, the capital of Maduro.

"I am of Maduro," he confessed. "I should have returned to Ondia tomorrow, and I must tell my wife that I am detained."

He had money to pay for the telegram, but it was evening before permission was received for the message to be sent, for nothing is done hurriedly in Spanish America.

Twentyfour hours later there came from Ondia a telegram addressed to Manuel Concepción de Villega, and it was signed with the name and titles of the President of Maduro. A free translation would have read:

*I am informed that a citizen of Maduro, giving the name of Sancho Quijote, has been imprisoned in Santa Miranda. If he is not delivered to the frontier by Wednesday noon my armies will advance into Pasala.*

Shannet was closeted with de Villega when the message arrived, and for the moment he was no better able to account for it than was the Minister.

"Who is this man Quijote?" he asked. "It's a ridiculous name. There is a book called 'Don Quijote,' Quixote in English, and there is a man in it called Sancho Panza."

"I know that," said Don Manuel, and sent for the judge.

He heard the story of the *peón's* crime and sentence and was not enlightened. But he had enough presence of mind to accuse the magistrate of inefficiency for not having suspected that the name Sancho Quijote was a false one.

"It is impossible," said de Villega helplessly, when the magistrate had been dismissed. "By Wednesday noon—that hardly gives us enough time to get him to the frontier even if we release him imme-

diately. And who is this man? A labourer, a stranger, of whom nobody knows anything, who suddenly appears in Santa Miranda with
more money than he could have ever come by honestly, and
preaches a revolution to a mob that he has first made drunk. He
deserves his punishment, and yet the President of Maduro, without
any inquiry, demands his release. It means war. . . ."

"He knew this would happen," said Shannet. "The judge told
us—he boasted that he would not stay in prison seven days. . . ."

They both saw light at the same instant.

"An *agent provocateur*——"

"A trap!" snarled de Villega. "And we have fallen into it. It is
only an excuse that Maduro was seeking. They sent him here, with
money, for no other purpose than to get himself arrested. And then
this preposterous ultimatum, which they give us no time even to
consider. . . ."

"But why such an intrigue?" demanded Shannet. "This is a poor
country. They are rich. They have nothing to gain."

Don Manuel tugged nervously at his moustachios.

"And we cannot even buy them off," he said. "Unless we appeal
to the *Estados Unidos*——"

Shannet sneered.

"And before their help can arrive the war is over," he said. "New
Orleans is five days away. But they will charge a high price for
burying the hatchet for us."

Don Manuel suddenly sat still. His shifty little dark eyes came
to rest on Shannet.

"I see it!" he exclaimed savagely. "It is the oil! You and your
accursed oil! I see it all! It is because of the oil that this country is
always embroiled in a dozen wars and fears of wars. So far Pasala
has escaped, but now we are like the rest. My Ministry will be over-
thrown. Who knows what Great Power has paid Maduro to attack
us? Then the great Power steps in and takes our oil from us. I shall
be exiled. Just now it is England, through you, who has control
of the oil. Perhaps it is now America who tries to capture it, or
another English company. I am ruined!"

"For God's sake stop whining!" snapped Shannet. "If you're
ruined, so am I. We've got to see what can be done about it."

De Villega shook his head.

"There is nothing to do. They are ten to one. We shall be beaten.
But I have some money, there is a steamer in two days. If we can
hold off their armies so long I can escape."

It was some time before the more brutally vigorous Shannet could bring the Minister to reason. Shannet had the courage of the wild beast that he was. At bay, faced with the wrecking of his tainted fortunes, he had no other idea but to fight back with the desperate ferocity of a cornered animal.

But even when Don Manuel's moaning had been temporarily quietened they were little better off. It was useless to appeal to the President, for he was no more than a tool in de Villega's hands. Likewise, the rest of the Council were nothing but figureheads, the mere instruments of de Villega's policy, and appointed by himself for no other reason than their willingness, for a consideration, to oppose nothing that he put forward.

"There is but one chance," said de Villega. "A *radiógrafo* must be sent to New Orleans. America will send a warship to keep the peace. Then we will try to make out to Maduro that the warship is here to fight for us, and their armies will retire. To the *Estados Unidos* then, we will say that we had made peace before their warship arrived; we are sorry to have troubled them, but there is nothing to do."

It seemed a flimsy suggestion to Shannet, but it was typical of de Villega's crafty and tortuous statesmanship. Shannet doubted if America, having once been asked to intervene, would be so easily put off, but he had no more practicable scheme to suggest himself, and he let it go.

He could not support it with enthusiasm, for an American occupation would mean the coming of American justice, and Shannet had no wish for that while there were still tongues wagging with charges against himself. But he could see no way out. He was in a cleft stick.

"Why not let this *peón* go?" he asked.

"And will that help us?" demanded Don Manuel scornfully. "If we sent him away now he would hardly have time to reach the border by noon tomorrow, and they would certainly say that they had not received him. Is it not plain that they are determined to fight? When they have taken such pains to trump up an excuse, will they be so quickly appeased?"

A purely selfish train of thought led to Shannet's next question.

"This man Sheridan and his friend—has nothing been heard of them yet? They have been at large two days."

"At a time like this, can I be bothered with such trifles?" replied de Villega shortly. "The squadron of Captain Tomare has been looking for them, but they are not found."

This was not surprising, for the searchers had worked outwards from Santa Miranda. Had they been inspired to work inwards they might have found Simon Templar, unwashed and unshaven, breaking stones in their own prison yard, chained by his ankles in a line of other unwashed and unshaven desperadoes, his identity lost in his official designation of Convicto Sancho Quijote, No. 475.

It was the Saint's first experience of imprisonment with hard labour, and he would have been enjoying the novel adventure if it had not been for the various forms of microscopic animal life with which the prison abounded.

## VI

There came one morning to the London offices of Pasala Oil Products Ltd (Managing Director, Hugo Campard) a cable in code. He decoded it himself, for it was not a code in general use; and his pink face went paler as transliteration proceeded.

By the time the complete translation had been written in between the lines, Hugo Campard was a very frightened man. He read the message again and again, incredulous of the catastrophe it foreboded.

> *Maduro declared war on Pasala on impossible ultimatum. Believe deliberately instigated by America or rival combine. Pasala army hopelessly outnumbered. No chance. Villega appealed America. Help on way but will mean overthrow of Government. Concession probably endangered. Sell out before news reaches London and breaks market.* Shannet.

Campard's fat hands trembled as he clipped the end of a cigar.

He was a big florid man with a bald head and a sandy moustache. Once upon a time he had been a pinched and out-at-elbows clerk in a stockbroker's office, until his ingenuity had found incidental ways of augmenting his income. For a few years he had scraped and saved; then, with five hundred pounds capital, and an intimate knowledge of the share market, he had gone after bigger game.

He had succeeded. He was clever, he knew the pitfalls to avoid, he was without pity or scruple, and luck had been with him. In fifteen years he had become a very rich man. Innumerable were the companies with which he had been associated, which had taken in much money and paid out none. He had been "exposed" half a dozen times, and every reputable broker knew his stock for what it was; but the scrip of the Campard companies was always most artistically engraved and their prospectuses couched in the most attractive terms, so that there was never a lack of small investors ready to pour their money into his bank account.

It is said that there is a mug born every minute, and Campard had found this a sound working principle. Many others like him, steering narrowly clear of the law, have found no lack of victims, and Campard had perhaps found more suckers than most.

But even the most triumphant career meets a check sometimes, and Campard had made a slip which had brought him into the full publicity of a High Court action. He had wriggled out by the skin of his teeth and some expensive perjury, but the resultant outcry had told him that it would be wise to lie low for a while. And lying low did not suit Campard's book. He lived extravagantly, and for all the wealth that he possessed on paper there were many liabilities. And then, when his back was actually to the wall, had come the miracle—in the shape of the chance to buy the Pasala concession, offered to him by a man named Shannet, whom he had employed many years ago.

Pasala oil was good. In the few months that it had been worked, the quality and quantity of the output had been startling. Campard enlisted the help of a handful of his boon companions, and poured in all his resources. More plant was needed and more labour, more expert management. That was now to be supplied. The directors of Pasala Oil Products sat down to watch themselves become millionaires.

And then in a clear sky came the cloud.

Hugo Campard, skimming through his newspaper on his way to the financial pages, had read of the early manifestations of the Saint, and had been mildly amused. In the days that followed he had read of other exploits of the Saint, and his amusement had changed gradually to grave anxiety. . . . And one day there had come to Hugo Campard, through the post, a card. . . .

Each morning thereafter the familiar envelope had been beside his plate at breakfast; each morning, when he reached the offices of Pasala Oil Products, he had found another reminder of the Saint on his desk. There had been no message. Just the picture. But the newspapers were full of stories, and Hugo Campard was afraid. . . .

Then, two days ago, the Saint had spoken.

Campard could not have told why he opened the envelopes in which the Saint sent his mementoes. Perhaps it was because each time Campard hoped he would be given some indication of what the Saint meant to do. After days of suspense, that had painted the black hollows of sleeplessness under his eyes and brought him to a state of nerves that was sheer physical agony, he was told.

On that day, underneath the crude outline, was pencilled in small writing:

*In a week's time you will be ruined.*

He had already had police protection—after the Lemuel incident* there had been no difficulty in obtaining that, as soon as he showed the police the first cards. All night there had been a constable outside his house in St John's Wood. All day a constable stood in the corridor outside his office. A plainclothes detective rode in his car with him everywhere he went. Short of some unforeseeable masterpiece of strategy, or a recourse to the machine-gun fighting of the Chicago gangsters, it was impossible that the Saint could reach him as he had reached Lemuel.

Now, at one stroke, the Saint brought all these preparations to naught, and broke invisibly through the cordon. Against such an attack the police could not help him.

*In a week's time you will be ruined.*

An easy boast to make. A tremendous task to carry out.

And yet, even while he had been racking his brains to find out how the Saint might carry out his threat, he had his answer.

For a long time he stared blindly at the cablegram, until every letter of the message was burned into his brain as with a hot iron. When he roused himself it was to clutch at a straw.

He telephoned to the telegraph company, and verified that the message had actually been received from Santa Miranda via Barbados and Pernambuco. Even that left a loophole. He cabled to an agent in New York, directing him to obtain authentic information from Washington at any cost; and by the evening he received a reply confirming Shannet's statement. The USS *Michigan* was on its way to Santa Miranda in response to an appeal from the President.

There was no catch in it. Shannet's code message was not a bluff, not even from an agent of the Saint in Santa Miranda. It was a grimly sober utterance of fact.

But the gigantic thoroughness of it! The colossal impudence of

*See *Wanted for Murder*.

the scheme! Campard felt as if all the strength and fight had ebbed out of him. He was aghast at the revelation of the resources of the Saint. Against a man who apparently thought nothing of engineering a war to gain his ends, he felt as puny and helpless as a babe.

His hand went out again to the telephone, but he checked the impulse. It was no use telling the police *that*. They could do nothing—and, far too soon as it was, the news would be published in the Press. And then, with the name of Campard behind them, POP shares would tumble down the market to barely the value of their weight in waste paper.

Before he left the office that night he sent a return cable in code to Santa Miranda:

*Believe war organised by criminal known as the Saint, who has threatened me. Obtain particulars of any strange Englishman in Pasala or Maduro. Give descriptions. Report developments.*

What the Saint had started, Campard argued, the Saint could stop. Campard might have a chance yet, if he could bargain . . .

But the declaration of war was announced in the evening paper which he bought on his way home, and Hugo Campard knew that it was too late.

He had no sleep that night, and by nine o'clock next morning he was at the office, and speaking on the telephone to his broker.

"I want you to sell twenty thousand POP's for me," he said. "Take the best price you can get."

"I wish I could hope to get a price at all," came the sardonic answer. "The market's full of rumours and everyone's scared to touch the things. You're too late with your selling—the bears were in before you."

"What do you mean?" asked Campard in a strained voice.

"There was a good deal of quiet selling yesterday and the day before," said the broker. "Somebody must have had information. They're covering today, and they must have made thousands."

During the morning other backers of the company came through on the telephone and were accusing or whining according to temperament, and Campard dealt with them all in the same formula.

"I can't help it," he said. "I'm hit twice as badly as any of you. It isn't my fault. The company was perfectly straight; you know that."

The broker rang up after lunch to say that he had managed to get rid of six thousand shares at an average price of two shillings.

"Two shillings for two-pound shares?" Campard almost sobbed. "You're mad!"

"See if you can do any better yourself, Mr Campard," replied the broker coldly. "The market won't take any more at present, but I might be able to get rid of another couple of thousand before we close at about a bob each—to people who want to keep them as curios. A firm of wallpaper manufacturers might make an offer for the rest——"

Campard slammed down the receiver and buried his face in his hands.

He was in the same position three hours later when his secretary knocked on the door and entered with a buff envelope.

"Another cable, Mr Campard."

He extracted the flimsy and reached out a nerveless hand for the code book.

He decoded:

*Maduro armies advancing into Pasala. Only chance now sell any price. Answer inquiry. Man arrived nearly four months ago——*

With a sudden impatience, Campard tore the cablegram into a hundred pieces and dropped them into the wastepaper basket. There was no time now to get into touch with the Saint. The damage was done.

A few minutes later came the anticipated message from the firm that he had induced to back him over Pasala Oil Products. Rich as he had become, he would never have been able to acquire his large holding in the company without assistance. How, with his reputation he had got any firm to back him was a mystery. But he had been able to do it on the system known as "margins"—which, in this instance, meant roughly that he could be called upon immediately to produce fifty percent of the amount by which the shares had depreciated, in order to "keep up his margin."

The demand, courteously but peremptorily worded, was delivered by special messenger; and his only surprise was that it had not come sooner. He scribbled a cheque, which there was no money in the bank to meet, and sent it back by the same boy.

He sent for his car, and left the office shortly afterwards. The paper which he bought outside told of the panic of POP's, and he read the article with a kind of morbid interest.

There was a letter, delivered by the afternoon post, waiting at his house when he got back.

*I sold POP's and covered today. The profits are nearly twelve thousand pounds.*

*The expenses of this campaign have been unusually heavy; but even then, after deducting these and my ten percent collecting fee, I hope to be able to forward nine thousand pounds to charity on your behalf.*

*Received the above-named sum—with thanks.*

THE SAINT

Enclosed was a familiar card, and one Pasala Oil Product share certificate.

Hugo Campard dined well that night, and, alone, accounted for a bottle of champagne. After that he smoked a cigar with relish, and drank a liqueur brandy with enjoyment.

He had dressed. He felt the occasion deserved it. His mind was clear and untroubled, for in a flash he had seen the way out of the trap.

When his cigar was finished, he exchanged his coat for a dressing-gown, and passed into his study. He locked the door behind him, and for some time paced up and down the room in silence, but no one will ever know what he thought. At ten o'clock precisely the pacing stopped. The constable on guard outside heard the shot; but Hugo Campard did not hear it.

## VII

The men serving sentences of hard labour in the prison of Santa Miranda are allowed an afternoon siesta of three hours. This is not due to the humanity and loving kindness of the authorities, but to the fact that nothing will induce the warders to forego the afternoon nap which is the custom of the country, and no one has yet discovered a way of making the prisoners work without a wide-awake warder to watch them and pounce on the shirkers.

The fetters are struck off the prisoners' ankles, and they are herded into their cells, a dozen in each, and there locked up to rest as well as they can in the stifling heat of a room ventilated only by one small barred window and thickly populated with flies. The warders retire to their quarters above the prison, and one jailer is left on guard, nodding in the passage outside the cells, with a rifle across his knees.

It was so on the third day of the Saint's incarceration, and this was the second hour of the siesta, but the Saint had not slept.

His cell-mates were sprawled on the bunks or on the floor, snoring heavily. They were hardened to the flies. Outside, the jailer dozed, his sombrero on the back of his head and his coat unbuttoned. Through the window of the cell a shaft of burning sunlight cut across the moist gloom and splashed a square of light on the opposite wall.

The Saint sat by the gates of the cell, watching that creeping square of light. Each afternoon he had watched it, learning its habits, so that now he could tell the time by it. When the edge of the square touched a certain scar in the stone it was four o'clock. . . . That was the time he had decided upon. . . .

He scrambled softly to his feet.

The jailer's head nodded lower and lower. Every afternoon, the Saint had noted, he set his chair at a certain point in the passage where a cool draught from a cross-corridor would fan him. Therefore on that afternoon the Saint had taken pains to get into the nearest cell to that point.

He tore a button off his clothes, and threw it. It hit the jailer on the cheek, and the man stirred and grunted. The Saint threw another button. The man shook his head, snorted, and roused, stretching his arms with a prodigious yawn.

"*Señor!*" hissed the Saint.

The man turned his head.

"Loathsome disease," he growled, "why dost thou disturb my meditations? Lie down and be silent, lest I come and beat thee."

"I only wished to ask your honour if I might give your honour a present of fifty *pesos*," said the Saint humbly.

He squatted down again by the bars of the gate and played with a piece of straw. Minutes passed. . . .

He heard the jailer get to his feet, but did not look up. The man's footsteps grated on the floor and stopped by the cell door. In the cell the other convicts snored peacefully.

"Eater of filth and decomposing fish," said the jailer's voice gruffly, "did I hear thy coarse lips speak to me of fifty *pesos?* How hast thou come by that money?"

"Gifts break rocks," replied the *peón*, quoting the Spanish proverb. "I had rather my gifts broke them than I were compelled to break any more of them. I have fifty *pesos*, and I want to escape."

"It is impossible. I searched thee——"

"It was hidden. I will give it to your honour as a pledge. I know where to find much more money, if your honour would deign to release me and let me lead you to where it is hidden. Have you not heard how, when I was arrested, it was testified that in the town I spent, in one evening, enough to keep you for a year? That was nothing to me. I am rich."

The jailer stroked his stubbly chin.

"Verminous mongrel," he said, more amiably, "show me this fifty *pesos* and I will believe thee."

The Saint ran his fingers through his tangled hair, and there fell out a note. The jailer recognised it, and his avaricious eyes gleamed.

He reached a clawlike hand through the bars, but the Saint jerked the note out of his reach. The jailer's face darkened.

"Abominable insect," he said, "thou hast no right to that. Thou art a convict, and thy goods are forfeit to the State. As the servant of the State, I will confiscate that paper, that thy low-born hands may defile it no longer."

He reached for his keys, but the Saint held up a warning hand.

"If you try to do that, *amigo*," he said, "I shall cry out so loudly that the other warders will come down to see what has happened. Then I shall tell them, and they will make you divide the fifty *pesos* with them. And I shall refuse to tell you where I have hidden the rest of my money. Why not release me, and have it all for yourself?"

"But how shall I know that thou dost not lie?"

The Saint's hands went again to his hair, and a rain of fifty *peso* notes fell to the floor. He picked them up and counted them before the jailer. There were thirty of them altogether.

"See, I have them here!" he said. "Fifteen hundred *pesos* is a lot of money. Now open this door and I will give them to you."

The jailer's eyes narrowed cunningly. Did this fool of a *peón* really believe that he would be given his liberty in exchange for such a paltry sum? Apparently.

Not that the sum was so paltry, being equal to about two hundred pounds in English money; but if any prisoner escaped, the jailer would be blamed for it, and probably imprisoned himself. Yet this simpleton seemed to imagine that he had only to hand over his bribe and the jailer would risk punishment to earn it.

Very well, let him have his childish belief. It would be easily settled. The door opened, the money paid over, a shot. . . . And then there would be no one to bear witness against him. The prisoner was known to be violent. He attempted to escape and was shot. It would be easy to invent a story to account for the opening of the cell door. . . .

"*Señor*," said the jailer, "I see now that your honour should not be herded in with these cattle. I will set your honour free, and your honour will give me the money, and I shall remember your honour in my prayers."

He tiptoed back to his chair and picked up his rifle. Then with elaborate precautions against noise he unlocked the cell door, and the *peón* came out into the passage.

The other prisoners still snored, and there was no sound but the droning of the flies to arouse them. The whole colloquy had been conducted in whispers, for it was imperative for the jailer as for the *peón* that there should be no premature alarm.

"Now give me the money," said the jailer huskily.

The Saint held out the handful of notes, and one broke loose and fluttered to the floor. As the jailer bent to pick it up, the Saint reached over him and slid the man's knife gently out of his belt. As the man straightened up the Saint's arm whipped round his neck, strangling his cry of fear before it could pass his throat. And the man felt the point of the knife prick his chest.

"Put thy rifle down against the wall," breathed the Saint in his ear. "If it makes a sound thou wilt not speak again."

No rifle could ever have been grounded more silently.

The Saint withdrew the knife and picked the man off his feet. In an instant, and without a sound, he had him on the floor, holding him with his legs in a jiu-jitsu lock so that he could not move.

"Be very quiet," urged the Saint, and let him feel the knife again

The man lay like one dead. The Saint, his hands now free, twisted the man's arms behind his back and tied them with the sling of his rifle. Then he rolled the man over.

"When you searched me," he said, "I had a knife. Where is it?"

"I am wearing it."

The Saint rolled up the man's sleeve and unstrapped the sheath from his forearm. With loving care he transferred it to his own arm, for he had had Anna for years, and she was the darling of his heart. That little throwing-knife, which he could wield so expertly, had accompanied him through countless adventures, and had saved his life many times. He loved it like a child, and the loss of it would have left him inconsolable.

With Anna back in her place, the Saint felt more like himself—though it is doubtful if anyone could have been found to agree with him, for he could never in his life have looked so dirty and disreputable as he was then. He, Simon Templar, the Saint, the man who was known for his invariable elegance and his almost supernatural power of remaining immaculate and faultlessly groomed even in the most hectic rough-house and the most uncivilised parts of the world, had neither washed nor shaved for nearly four days. There was no provision for such luxuries in the prison of Santa Miranda. And his clothes had been dreadful enough when Kelly had borrowed them from his under-gardener for the purpose; now, after having been lived in day and night on the stone pile and in the filthy cell which they had just left, their condition may be imagined. . . .

His greatest wish at that moment was to get near some soap and water; and already the time of grace for such a diversion was getting short. The square of light on the cell wall told him that he had barely half an hour at his disposal before Santa Miranda would be rousing itself for the second instalment of its day's work; and the other warders would soon be lurching down, yawning and cursing, to drive the prisoners back to their toil. It was time for the Saint to be moving.

He unfastened the jailer's belt and used it to secure the man's legs; then he rolled him over and stuffed his handkerchief into his mouth for a gag. He straightened up, hands on hips; and the helpless man glared up at him with bulging eyes.

"But I had forgotten!" cried the Saint, under his breath, and stooped again to take his money from the jailer's pocket.

The man squirmed, and the Saint swept him a mocking bow.

"Remain with God, my little ape," he murmured. "There will now be nothing to disturb thy meditations."

Then he was gone.

He ran lightly down the corridor, and out at the end into the blazing sunlight of the prison courtyard. This he crossed swiftly, slowing up and moving a little more cautiously as he neared the gates. Within the courtyard beside the gates was a little sentry-box where the gatekeeper might take shelter from the sun.

The Saint stole up the last few yards on tiptoe, and sidled one eye round the doorway of the box.

The gatekeeper sat inside on a packing case with his back propped against the wall. His rifle was leaning against the wall in one corner. He was awake, but his eyes were intent on a pattern which he was tracing in the dust with the toe of his boot.

The bare prison walls were too high to scale, and the only way out was by way of the gates.

The Saint's shadow suddenly blocked the light from the sentry-box and the gatekeeper half rose to his feet with a shout rising to his lips. It was rather like shooting a sitting rabbit, but the issues involved were too great to allow of making a more sporting fight of it. As the warder's head came up, the Saint hit him on the point of the jaw scientifically and with vim, and the shout died stillborn.

The Saint huddled the man back against the wall, and tipped his sombrero over his eyes as if he was asleep—which in fact he was. Then he scrambled over the gates, and dropped cat-footed into the dust of the cart-track of a road outside.

The prison of Santa Miranda lies to the east of the town, near the sea, among the slums which closely beset the bright main streets; and the Saint set himself to pass quickly through the town by way of these dirty, narrow streets where his disreputable condition would be most unnoticed, avoiding the Calle del Palacio and the chance of encountering a *guardia* who might remember him.

Santa Miranda had not yet awoken. In the grass-grown lanes between the rude huts of the labourers a child in rags played here and there, but paid no attention to his passing. In the doorway of one hut an old and wizened Indian slept in the sun, like a lizard. The Saint saw no one else.

He threaded the maze quietly but with speed, steering a course parallel to the Calle del Palacio. And then, over the low roofs of the adobe hovels around him, he saw, quite close, a tall white tower caught by the slanting rays of the sun, and he changed his plans.

That is to say, he resolved on the spur of the moment to dispense with making plans. His original vague idea had been to make for Kelly's bungalow, get a shave, a bath, some clean clothes, and a cigarette, and sit down to deliberate the best way of capturing the town. So far, in spite of his boast, the solution of that problem had eluded him, though he had no doubts that he would be given inspiration at the appointed time.

Now, looking at that tower, which he knew to be an ornament of the Presidential Palace, only a stone's throw away, the required inspiration came; and he acted upon it at once, branching off to his left in the direction of the tower.

It was one of those gay and reckless, dare-devil and foolhardy, utterly preposterous and wholly delightful impulses which the Saint could never resist. The breath-taking impudence of it was, to his way of thinking, the chief reason for taking it seriously; the suicidal odds against success were a conclusive argument for having a fling at bringing off the lone hundred-to-one chance; the monumental nerve that was plainly needed for turning the entertaining idea into a solemn fact was a challenge to his adventurousness that it was simply unthinkable to ignore.

The Saint took up the gauntlet without the faintest hesitation.

For this was the full effrontery of his decision:

"Eventually," whispered the Saint, to his secret soul—"why not now?"

And the Saintly smile in all its glory twitched his lips back from his white teeth. . . .

His luck had been stupendous, and it augured well for the future. Decidedly it was his day. A clean getaway from the prison, with no alarm. And he reached the high wall surrounding the palace grounds unobserved. And only a dozen feet away from the walls grew a tall tree.

The Saint went up the tree like a monkey, to a big straight branch that stuck out horizontally fifteen feet from the ground. Measuring the distance, he jumped.

The leap took him on to the top of the wall. He steadied himself for a moment, and then jumped again, twelve feet down into the palace gardens.

He landed on his toes, as lightly as a panther, and went zigzagging over the lawn between the flower-beds like a Red Indian. The gardens were empty. There was no sound but the murmuring of bees in the sun and the soft rustle of the Saint's feet over the grass.

He ran across the deserted gardens and up some steps to a flagged terrace in the very shadow of the palace walls. Eight feet above the terrace hung a low balcony. The Saint took two steps and a jump, hung by his fingertips for a second, and pulled himself quickly up and over the balustrade.

An open door faced him, and the room beyond was empty. The Saint walked in, and passed through to the corridor on the other side.

Here he was at a loss, for the geography of the palace was strange to him. He crept along, rather hesitantly, without a sound. In the space of a dozen yards there was another open door. Through it, as he passed, the Saint caught a glimpse of the room beyond, and what he saw brought him to a sudden standstill.

He tiptoed back to the doorway, and stood there at gaze.

It was a bathroom.

Only a year ago that bathroom had been fitted up at enormous cost for the delectation of the Saturday nights of His Excellency the President and the Minister of the Interior. A gang of workmen specially sent down by a New York firm of contractors had affixed those beautiful sky-blue tiles to the walls, and laid those lovely sea-green tiles on the floor, and installed that superlative pale green porcelain bath with its gleaming silver taps and showers and other gadgets. Paris had supplied the great crystal jar of bath salts which stood on the window-sill, and the new cakes of expensive soap in the dishes.

The Saint's glistening eyes swept the room.

It was not Saturday, but it seemed as if some one was making a departure from the usual habits of the palace household. On a rack above the washbasin were laid out razor, shaving-soap, and brush. On a chair beside the bath were snowy towels. On another chair, in a corner, were clothes—a spotless silk shirt, a sash, wide-bottomed Mexican trousers braided with gold, shoes. . . .

For a full minute the Saint stared, struck dumb with wonder at his astounding good fortune. Then, in fear and trembling, he stole into the room and turned on a tap.

The water ran hot.

He hesitated no longer. War, revolution, battle, murder, and sudden death meant nothing to him then. He closed the door and turned the key.

Blessings, like misfortunes, never come singly. There was even a packet of Havana cigarettes and a box of matches tucked away behind the bath salts. . . .

Ten minutes later, already shaved, the Saint was stretched full length in a steaming bath into which he had emptied the best part of the Presidential jar of bath salts, innocently playing submarines with the sponge and a cake of soap.

A cigarette was canted jauntily up between his lips, and he was without a care in the world.

## VIII

Archie Sheridan mopped his moist forehead and smacked viciously at a mosquito which was gorging itself on his bare forearm.

"Thank the Lord you're back," he said. "This blistered place gives me the creeps. Have you fixed anything?"

Kelly settled ponderously on the spread ground-sheet.

"I have arranged the invadin' army," he said. "Anything come through while I've been away?"

"Nothing that matters. One or two private messages, which I duly acknowledged. I wonder what they're thinking at the Ondia end of the line."

"There'll be a breakdown gang along sometime," pronounced Kelly. "It's now the second day of the wire bein' cut. Within the week, maybe, they'll wake up and send to repair it. What's the time?"

Sheridan consulted his watch.

"A quarter past eleven," he said.

They sat under a great tree, in a small clearing in the jungle near the borders of Maduro, some ten miles east of Esperanza. A mile away was the rough track which led from Esperanza across the frontier to Maduro, and which formed the only road-link between the two countries; and there Kelly's Ford, in which they had made most of the journey, waited hidden between the trees at a little distance from the road.

But for all the evidence there was to the contrary they might have been a thousand miles from civilisation. At the edge of the tiny clearing colossal trees laced together with vines and creepers hemmed them in as with a gigantic palisade; high over their heads the entangled branches of the trees shut out the sky, and allowed no light to pass but a ghostly grey twilight, in which the glaring crimsons and oranges and purples of the tropical blooms which flowered here and there in the marshy soil stood out with shrieking violence.

Now and again, in the stillness of the great forest, there would be a rustle of the passing of some unseen wild thing. Under some prowling beast's paw, perhaps, a rotten twig would snap with a report like a rifle-shot. Sometimes the delirious chattering of a troop of monkeys would babble out with a startling shrillness that would have sent a shudder up the spine of an impressionable man. And the intervals of silence were not true silence, but rather a dim and indefinable and monotonous murmur punctuated with the sogging sound of dripping water. The air was hot and steamy and heavy with sickly perfumes.

"You get used to it," said Kelly with a comprehensive wave of the stem of his pipe.

"Thanks," said Sheridan. "I'm not keen to. I've been here two days too long already. I have nightmares in which I'm sitting in an enormous bath, but as soon as I've finished washing a shower of mud falls on me and I have to start all over again."

Now this was on the morning of the day in the afternoon of which the Saint escaped from prison.

On Sheridan's head were a pair of radio headphones. On the ground sheet beside him was a little instrument, a Morse transmitter, which he had ingeniously fashioned before they left Santa Miranda. Insulated wires trailed away from him into the woods.

The telegraph line, for most of its length, followed the roads, but at that point for some inexplicable reason it took a short cut across country. They had decided to attack it at that point on grounds of prudence; for although the road between Esperanza and the Maduro frontier was not much used, there was always the risk of some one passing and commenting on their presence when he reached his destination.

The afternoon before, they had cut the line and sent through to Esperanza, to be relayed to Santa Miranda, the ultimatum purporting to come from the President of Maduro. Since then, night and day, one of them had sat with the receivers upon his ears, waiting for a reply. The arrangement was complicated, for Kelly could not read Morse, while Sheridan's Spanish was very haphazard; but they managed somehow. Several times when Archie had been resting Kelly had roused him to take down a message; but the translation had had no bearing on the threat of war, except occasionally from a purely private and commercial aspect. There had been no official answer.

Sheridan looked at his watch again.

"Their time's up in half an hour," he said. "What do you say to sending a final demand?—the 'D' being loud and explosive, as in 'Income Tax'."

"Shure—if there's no chance of 'em surrenderin'," agreed Kelly. "But we can't let anything stop the war."

The message they sent was worded with this in view:

*Understand you refuse to release Quijote. Our armies will accordingly advance into Pasala at noon.*

While they waited for zero hour, Kelly completed the task of breaking camp, strapping their tent and equipment into a workmanlike bundle. He finished this job just before twelve, and returned to his prostrate position on the ground sheet.

"I wonder what that blayguard Shannet is doin'?" he said. "I only hope he hasn't missed the news by takin' a thrip to the concession. It'd be unlucky for us if he had."

"I think he'll be there," said Sheridan. "He was in Santa Miranda when we left, and he's likely to stay there and supervise the hunt for the Saint."

"He's a good man, that," said Kelly. "It's a pity he's not an Irishman."

Sheridan fanned himself with a handkerchief.

"He's one of the finest men that ever stepped," he said. "If the Saint said he was going to make war on Hell, I'd pack a fire extinguisher and go with him."

Kelly sucked his pipe, and spat thoughtfully at an ant.

"That's not what I call your duty," he remarked. "In fact, I'm not sure that yez should have been in this at all, with a girl like Lilla watchin' for yez to come back, and worryin' her pretty head. And with a crawlin' sarpint like Shannet about. . . ."

"He's tried to bother her once or twice. But if I thought——"

"I've been thinkin' a lot out here," said Kelly. "I'm not sayin' what I've thought. But it means that as soon as we've done what we're here to do we're goin' to hurry back to Santa Miranda as fast as Tin Lizzie'll take us. There's my missus an' Lilla without a man to look afther them; an' the Saint——"

Sheridan suddenly held up a hand for silence. He wrote rapidly on his little pad, and Kelly leaned over to read.

"What's it mean?"

"The war's on!" yelled Kelly ecstatically. "Don Manuel ain't the quitter I thought he was—or maybe he didn't see how he could get out of it. But the war's on! Hooroosh! There's goin' to be fightin'! Archie, me bhoy, the war's on!"

He seized Sheridan in a bear-hug of an embrace, swung him to the ground, dropped him, and went prancing round the clearing uttering wild Celtic cries. It was some minutes before he could be sobered sufficiently to give a translation of the message.

It was short and to the point:

*The armies of Pasala will resist aggression to the death.*

Manuel Concepción de Villega, being a civilian official, had thought this a particularly valiant and noble sentiment. In fact, he was so pleased with it that he used it to conclude his address to the Army when, with the President, he reviewed it before it rode out of Santa Miranda to meet the invaders. Of course the speech should have been made by the President, but His Excellency had no views on the subject.

At lunch-time the news came through from Esperanza that the enemy were attacking the town.

Although there had been ample warning, few of the inhabitants had left. The bulk of the population preferred to stay, secure in the belief that wars were the exclusive concern of the professional soldiers and had nothing to do with the general public, except for the inconvenience they might cause.

There was a small garrison stationed in the town, and they had barricaded the streets and settled down to await the attack. It came at about one o'clock.

The "invading armies" which Kelly had prepared had been designed by Archie Sheridan, who was something of a mechanical genius.

In the woods on the east, three hundred yards from the front line of improvised fortifications, had been established a line of ten braziers of glowing charcoal, about twenty yards apart. Above each brazier was suspended a string of cartridges knotted at intervals of a few inches into a length of cord. The cord passed over the branch of a tree into which nails had been driven as guides. All these cords were gathered together in two batches of five each at a point some distance away, in such a way that one man using both hands, could slowly lower the string of cartridges simultaneously into all ten braziers, and so give the impression that there was firing over a front of two hundred yards. If they had had fireworks they could have saved themselves much trouble; but they had no fireworks, and Archie Sheridan was justly proud of his ingenious substitute.

Sheridan worked the "invading armies" while Kelly lay down behind a tree some distance away, sheltered from any stray bullets, and loaded his rifle. To complete the illusion it was necessary that the firing should seem to have some direction.

Sheridan, with a low whistle, signalled that he was ready, and the battle began.

The cartridges, lowered one by one into the braziers and there exploded by the heat, provided a realistic rattle up and down the line; while Kelly, firing and reloading like one possessed, sent bullets smacking into the walls of houses and kicking up spurts of dust around the barricades. He took care not to aim anywhere where anyone might be hit.

The defence replied vigorously, though no one will ever know what they thought they were shooting at, and there were some spirited exchanges. When another whistle from Sheridan announced that the strings of cartridges were exhausted, Kelly rejoined him, and they crawled down to the road and the waiting Ford, and drove boldly towards the town, Kelly waving a nearly white flag.

The car was stopped, but Kelly was well known.

"They let me through their lines," he explained to the officer of the garrison. "That is why the firing has ceased. I was in Ondia when war was declared, and I came back at once."

He told them that he was on his way to Santa Miranda.

"Then travel quickly, and urge them not to delay sending help," said the officer, "for it is clear that we are attacked by a tremendous number. I have sent telegrams but you can do more by telling them what you have seen."

"I will do that," promised Kelly, and they let him drive on.

As soon as the car was clear of the town he stopped and assisted Sheridan to unearth himself from under the pile of luggage; for, being now an outlaw, Sheridan had had to hide when they passed through the towns on the journey up, and it was advisable for him to do the same for most of the return.

A little further down the road they stopped again, and Sheridan climbed a tree and cut the telegraph wires, so that the news of the fizzling out of the attack should not reach Santa Miranda in time for the troop that had been sent out to be recalled. Instead of organizing the "invasion" they might have tapped the wire there and sent on messages from the commander of the garrison describing the progress of the battle, and so saved themselves much labour and thought; but the short road between Esperanza and Las Floras (the next town) was too well frequented for that to be practicable in broad daylight.

The Minister of the Interior was informed that it was no longer possible to communicate with Esperanza, and he could see only one explanation.

"Esperanza is surrounded," he said. "The garrison is less than a hundred. The town will fall in twentyfour hours, and the advancing armies of Maduro will meet our reinforcements at Las Floras. It will be a miracle if we can hold the invaders from Santa Miranda for five days."

"You should have kept some troops here," said Shannet. "You have sent every soldier in Santa Miranda. Once that army is defeated there will be nothing for the invaders to overcome."

"Tomorrow I will recruit the *peones*," said Don Manuel. "There must be conscription. Pasala requires the services of every able-bodied citizen. I will draft a proclamation tonight for the President to sign."

It was then nearly five o'clock, but none of them had had a siesta that afternoon. They were holding another of many unprofitable conferences in a room in the palace, and it was significant that Shannet's right to be present was undisputed. The President himself was also there, biting his nails and stabbing the carpet nervously with the rowels of his spurs, but the other two took no notice of him. The President and de Villega were both still wearing the magnificent uniforms which they had donned for the review of the troops that morning.

Shannet paced the room, the inevitable limp unlighted cigarette drooping from his loose lower lip. His once-white ducks were as soiled and sloppy as ever. (Since they never became filthy, it is apparent that he must have treated himself to a clean suit occasionally, but nobody was ever allowed to notice this fact.) His unbrushed hair, as always, flopped over his right eye.

Since the day before, Shannet had had much to think about. Campard's amazing cable, attributing the war to a criminal gang, had arrived, and Shannet had replied with the required information. He had passed on the suggestion of his employer to the Minister for the Interior, pointing to the undoubtedly lawless behaviour of Sheridan and the unknown; but that two common outlaws could organise a war was a theory which de Villega refused to swallow.

"It is absurd," he said. "They are ordinary criminals. Two men cannot be a gang. In due time they will be caught, the man Sheridan will be imprisoned, and the man Mussolini will be hanged."

Shannet, asked for the name of the man who had assaulted him, had replied indignantly: "He told me his name was Benito Mussolini!" Since then, he had been impelled to make several protests against the conviction of the officials that this statement was to be believed; but the idea had taken too firm a root, and Shannet had had to give up the attempt.

But now he had an inspiration.

"There can be no harm in finding out," he urged. "Send for the *peón* that all the trouble is about, and let us question him."

"I have a better idea than that," exclaimed de Villega, jumping up. "I will send the *peón* to the garotte tomorrow, for an encouragement to the people. They will enjoy the spectacle, and it will make them more ready to accept the proclamation of conscription. I will make a holiday——"

But Shannet's brain had suddenly taken to itself an amazing brilliance. In a flash it had soared above the crude and elementary idea of sending for the *peón* and forcing him to speak. He had no interest in de Villega's sadistic elaboration of the same idea. He had seen a much better solution than that.

## IX

Rapidly Shannet explained his inspiration to the others. It was as simple as all great inspirations.

He was now firmly convinced in his mind that Sheridan and the Unknown were at the bottom of all the trouble, and this belief was strengthened by the fact that no trace of them had been found since their escape, although both police and military had searched for them. Some of the things that the Unknown had said—before and after the interlude in which words were dispensed with—came back to Shannet with a dazzling clarity. It all fitted in.

And ready to his hand lay the key to the trap in which he was in. He saw that what the Unknown had started the Unknown could stop.

It was Campard's own idea, but Shannet was more conveniently placed to apply it than his master had been. Also, he had the necessary lever within a few minutes' reach.

Lilla McAndrew.

She was the master card. Sheridan, he knew, was infatuated. And Sheridan was an important accomplice of the Unknown. With Lilla McAndrew for a hostage Shannet could dictate his own terms.

"I know I have reason!" Shannet said vehemently, while he inwardly cursed the limitations of his Spanish, which prevented him driving his ideas home into the thick skulls of his audience more forcibly. "I know well the Señor Campard, for whom I have worked for years. Perhaps it sounds fantastic to you, but I know that he is not an easy man to frighten. If I had suggested this to him myself, that these two men could have plotted a war, he would have laughed me to scorn. But he has said it of his own accord. Therefore I know that he must have some information."

"I think everyone has gone mad," said de Villega helplessly. "But you may proceed with your plan. At least it can do no harm. But I warn you that it is on your own responsibility. The Señorita Mc-Andrew is a British subject, and questions may be asked. Then I shall say that I know nothing of it; and if the authorities demand it, you will have to be handed over to them."

It was significant of the way in which Shannet's prestige had declined since the commencement of the war for which de Villega was inclined to blame him; but Shannet did not care.

"I will take the risk," he said, and was gone.

In the Palace courtyard his horse was still being held by a patient soldier—one of the half-dozen left behind to guard the palace. Shannet clambered into the saddle and galloped out as the gates were opened for him by a sentry.

His first course took him to an unsavoury café at the end of the town, where he knew he would find the men he needed. He enrolled two. They were pleased to call themselves guides, but actually they were half-caste cut-throats available for anything from murder upwards. Shannet knew them, for he had used their services before.

He explained what he wanted and produced money. There was no haggling. In ten minutes the three were riding out of the town.

Kelly, too late, had thought of that very possibility, as he had hinted to Sheridan in the jungle clearing that morning. But Kelly and Sheridan were still twenty miles away.

And the Saint, in the President's palatial bathroom, was leisurely completing the process of dressing himself in the clean clothes which he had found. They fitted him excellently.

Meanwhile, the men whom Shannet had left in conference were receiving an unpleasant surprise.

"God!" thundered de Villega. "How did this *peón* escape?"

"Excellency," said the abashed governor of the prison, "it was during the siesta. The man fell down moaning and writhing as if he would die. The warder went to attend him, and the man grasped him by the throat so that he could not cry out, throttled him into unconsciousness, and bound and gagged him. He also surprised the gatekeeper, and hit him in the English fashion——"

De Villega let out an exclamation.

"What meanest thou, pig—'in the English fashion'?"

The governor demonstrated the blow which the gatekeeper had described. It was, in fact, the simple left uppercut of the boxer, and no Latin American who has not been infected with our methods ever hits naturally like that.

"What manner of man was this *peón?*" demanded Don Manuel, with understanding dawning sickeningly into his brain.

"Excellency, he was tall for a *peón*, and a man of the strength of a lion. If he had washed he would have been handsome, with an aristocratic nose that such a man could hardly have come by legitimately. And he had very white teeth and blue eyes——"

"Blue eyes!" muttered de Villega dazedly, for, of course, to the Latin, all Englishmen have blue eyes.

He turned to the governor with sudden ferocity.

"*Carajo!*" he screamed. "Imbecile, dost thou not know whom thou hast let slip through thy beastly fingers? Dost thou not even know whom thou hast had in thy charge these three days?"

He thumped upon the table with his fist, and the governor trembled.

"Couldst thou not recognise him, cross-eyed carrion?" he screeched. "Couldst thou not see that he was no true *peón?* Maggot, hast thou not heard of the outlaw Benito Mussolini, for whom the *rurales* have searched in vain while he sheltered safely in the prison under thy gangrenous eyes?"

"I am a worm, and blind, Excellency," said the cringing man tactfully, for he knew that any excuse he attempted to make would only infuriate the Minister further.

De Villega strode raging up and down the room. Now he believed Shannet, wild and far-fetched as the latter's theory had seemed when he had first heard it propounded. The news of the prisoner's escape, and the—to Don Manuel—sufficient revelation of his real identity, provided incontrovertible proof that the fantastic thing was true.

"He must be recaptured at once!" snapped de Villega. "Every *guardia* in Santa Miranda must seek him without rest day or night. The *peones* must be pressed into the hunt. The State will pay a reward of five thousand *pesos* to the man who brings him to me, alive or dead. As for thee, offal," he added, turning with renewed malevolence upon the prison governor, "if Sancho Quijote, or Benito Mussolini—whatever he calls himself—is not delivered to me in twelve hours I will cast thee into thine own prison to rot there until he is found."

"I will give the orders myself, Excellency," said the governor, glad of an excuse to make his escape, and bowed his way to the door.

He went out backwards, and as he closed the door the Saint

pinioned his arms from behind, and allowed the point of his little knife to prick his throat.

"Make no sound," said the Saint, and lifted the man bodily off his feet.

He carried the governor down the passage, the knife still at his throat, and took him into a room that he had already marked down in his explorations. It was a bedroom. The Saint deposited the man on the floor, sat on his head, and tore a sheet into strips, with which he bound and gagged him securely.

"I will release you as soon as the revolution is over," the Saint promised, with a mocking bow.

Then he walked back to the other room and entered softly, closing the door behind him. De Villega was penning the announcement of the reward, and it was the President who first noticed the intruder and uttered a strangled yap of startlement.

Don Manuel looked up, and loosed an oath. He sprang to his feet, upsetting the inkpot and his chair, as if electric current had suddenly been applied to him.

"Who are you?" he demanded in a cracked voice, though he had guessed the answer.

"You know me best as Benito Mussolini, or Sancho Quijote," said the Saint. "My friends—and enemies—sometimes call me *El Santo*. And I am the father of the revolution."

He lounged lazily against the door, head back, hands resting carefully on his hips. The Saint was himself again, clean and fresh from razor and bath, his hair combed smoothly back to perfection. The Saint had the priceless gift of being able to throw on any old thing and look well in it, but few things could have matched his mood and personality better than the buccaneering touch there was about the attire that had been more or less thrust upon him.

The loose full-sleeved shirt, the flaring trousers, the scarlet sash—the Saint wore these romantic trappings with a marvellous swashbuckling air, lounging there with a reckless and piratical elegance, a smile on his lips. . . .

Seconds passed before the Minister came out of his trance.

"Revolution?"

De Villega echoed the word involuntarily, and the Saint bowed.

"I am the revolution," he said, "and I have just started. For my purpose I arranged that the Army should leave Santa Miranda, so that I should have nothing to deal with but a few officials, yourselves, and a handful of *guardias*. Wonderful as I am, I could not fight an army."

"Fool!" croaked Don Manuel, in a voice that he hardly knew as his own. "The army will return, and then you will be shot."

"Permit me to disagree," said the Saint. "The Army will return, certainly. It will be to find a new Government in power. The Army is the servant of the State, not of one man, nor even of one Government. Of course, on their return, the soldiers would be free to begin a second revolution to overthrow the new Government if they disliked it. But I do not think they will do that, particularly as the new Government is going to increase their pay. Observe the subtle difference. To have attempted to bribe the Army to support a revolution would have been treason, and rightly resented by all patriotic citizens; but to signalise the advent of a new Constitution by a bonus in cash to the Army is an act of grace and generosity, and will be rightly appreciated."

"And the people?" said Don Manuel, as in a dream.

"Will they weep to see you go? I think not. You have crushed them with taxes—we shall liberate them. They could have liberated themselves, but they had not the initiative to begin. Now I give them a lead, and they will follow."

The Saint straightened up off the door. His blue eyes, with a sparkle of mischief in them, glanced from the Minister for the Interior to the President, and back to the Minister for the Interior again. His right hand came off his hip in a commanding gesture.

"*Señores*," he said, "I come for your resignations."

The President came to his feet, bowed, and stood to attention.

"I will write mine at once, *señor*," he said hurriedly. "It is plain that Pasala no longer needs me."

It was the speech of his life, and the Saint swept him a low bow of approval.

"I thank your Excellency," he said mockingly.

"Half-wit!" snarled de Villega over his shoulder. "Let me handle this!"

He thrust the President back and came around the table.

A sword hung at his side, and on the belt of his ceremonial uniform was a revolver holster. He stood before the Saint, one hand on the pommel of his sword, the other fiddling with the little strap which secured the flap of the holster. His dark eyes met Simon Templar's bantering gaze.

"Already the revolution is accomplished?" he asked.

"I have accomplished it," said Templar.

De Villega raised his left hand to stroke his moustache.

"Señor," he said, "all this afternoon we have sat in this room, which overlooks the front courtyard of the palace. Beyond, as you know, is the Calle del Palacio. Yet we have heard no commotion. Is a people that has been newly liberated too full of joy to speak?"

"When the people hear of their liberation," said the Saint, "you will hear their rejoicing."

De Villega's eyes glittered under his black brows.

"And your friends, *señor?*" he pursued. "The other liberators? They have, perhaps, surrounded the palace and overcome the guards without an alarm being raised or a shot fired?"

The Saint laughed.

"Don Manuel," he said, "you do me an injustice. I said I was the father of the revolution. Can a child have two fathers? Alone, Don Manuel, I accomplished it—yet you persist in speaking of my private enterprise as if it were the work of a hundred. Will you not give me the full credit for what I have done?"

De Villega stepped back a pace.

"So," he challenged, "the people does not know. The palace guards do not know. The Army does not know. Will you tell me who *does* know?"

"Our three selves," said the Saint blandly. "Also two friends of mine who organised the war for me. And the governor of the prison, whom I captured on his way to mobilise the *guardias* against me. It is very simple. I intend this to be a bloodless revolution, for I am against unnecessary killing. You will merely resign, appointing a new Government in your places, and leave Pasala at once, never to return again on pain of death."

The holster was now undone, and de Villega's fingers were sliding under the flap.

"And you—alone—demand that?"

"I do," said the Saint, and leapt at de Villega as the revolver flashed from its place.

With one arm he grasped Don Manuel around the waist, pinning his left arm to his side; with his left hand he gripped Don Manuel's right wrist, forcing it back, and twisting.

The President sprang forward, but it was all over in a couple of seconds. The revolver exploded twice, harmlessly, into the floor, and then fell with a clatter as the Saint's grip became too agonising to be borne.

The Saint hurled de Villega from him, into the President's very arms, and as de Villega staggered back his sword grated out of its sheath and remained in the Saint's right hand. The President's revolver was halfway out of its holster when the Saint let him feel the sword at his breast.

"Drop it!" ordered Simon.

The President obeyed.

Templar forced the two men back to the wall at the sword's point. Then he turned quickly, using the sword to fish up the two revolvers from the floor by their trigger guards, and turned again to halt their immediate rally with the guns impaled on his blade.

From below, through the open windows, came the shouting of the sentries, and the sound of running feet thundered in the passage outside the room.

Like lightning the Saint detached the revolvers from his sword, and held them one in each hand. They covered their owners with an equal steadiness of aim.

The two shots that de Villega had fired, though they had hit no one, had done damage enough. They hadn't entered into the Saint's plan of campaign. He had betted on being quick enough to catch de Villega before he could get his hand to his gun in its cumbersome holster—and the Saint, for once, had been a fraction of a second slow on his timing. But the error might yet be repaired.

"You, Excellency, to the windows!" rapped the Saint in a low voice. "You, de Villega, to the door! Reassure the guards, tell them that the President was unloading his revolver when it accidentally exploded. The President will repeat the same thing from the window to the sentries below."

He dodged out of sight behind the door as it burst open, but there was no mistaking the menace of the revolvers which he still focussed on the two men.

The President was already addressing the sentries below. De Villega, with one savagely impotent glance at the unfriendly muzzle that was trained upon him, followed suit, giving the Saint's suggested explanation to the guards who crowded into the doorway.

"You may go," he concluded. "No harm has been done. But remain within call—I may need you shortly."

It required some nerve to add that last remark, in the circumstances, but de Villega thought that the Saint would not betray his presence with a shot if he could possibly help it. He was right. The President came back from the window. The guards withdrew, with apologies for their excited irruption, and the door closed. The Saint slid the bolt into its socket.

"A wise precaution, Don Manuel, to warn the guards that you might need them," he said. "But I do not think it will help you."

He stuck the revolvers into his sash and picked up the sword again. It was a better weapon for controlling two men than his little knife, and much quieter than revolvers.

"Your resignations or your lives, *señores?*" said the Saint briskly. "I will take whichever you prefer to give, but I must have one or the other at once."

De Villega sat down at the table, but did not write. He unbuttoned his coat, fished out a packet of cigarettes, and lighted one, blowing out a great cloud of smoke. Through it he looked at the Saint, and his lips had twisted into a sneering grin.

"I have another thing to offer, *señor,*" he remarked viciously, "which you might prefer to either of the things you have mentioned."

"*Es decir?*" prompted Simon, with a frowning lift of his eyebrows.

De Villega inhaled again with relish, and let the smoke trickle down from his nostrils in two long feathers. There was a glow of taunting triumph in his malignant stare.

"There is the Señorita McAndrew," he said, and the Saint's face suddenly went very meek.

"What of her?"

"It was the Señor Shannet," said de Villega, enjoying his moment, "who first suggested that you were the man behind the war. We did not believe him, but now I see that he is a wise man. He left us over half an hour ago to take her as hostage. You gave me no chance to explain that when the guards entered the room just now. But I told them to remain within call for that reason—so that I could summon them as soon as you surrendered. Now it is my turn to make an offer. Stop this war, and deliver yourself and your accomplices to justice, and I will save the Señorita McAndrew. Otherwise——" Don Manuel shrugged. "Am I answerable for the affections of the Señor Shannet?"

A throaty chuckle of devilish merriment shook him, and he bowed to the motionless Saint with a leering mock humility.

"I, in my turn, await your decision, *señor,*" he said.

## X

The Saint leaned on his sword.

He was cursing himself for the fool he was. Never before in his career had he been guilty of such an appalling lapse. Never would he have believed that he could have been capable of overlooking the probability of such an obvious counter-attack. Now his brain was whirling like the flywheel of a great dynamo, and he was considering, calculating, readjusting, summarising everything in the light of this new twist that de Villega had given to the affair. Yet his face showed nothing of the storm behind it.

"And how do I know that you will keep your bargain?" he asked.

"You do not know," replied de Villega brazenly. "You only know that if you do not agree to my terms the Señor Shannet will certainly take reprisals. I offer you a hope."

So that was the strength of it. And taken by and large, it didn't strike the Saint as a proposition to jump at. It offered him exactly nothing—except the opportunity to go nap on Don Manuel's honour and Shannet's generosity, two bets which no one could have called irresistibly attractive. Also it involved Kelly and Sheridan, who hadn't been consulted. And it meant, in the end, that all three of them would most certainly be executed, whatever de Villega decided to do about Lilla McAndrew, whom Shannet would probably claim, and be given as a reward for his share in suppressing the revolution. No. . . .

Where were Kelly and Sheridan? The Saint was reckoning it out rapidly, taking into consideration the age of Kelly's Ford and the reported abominable state of the roads between Esperanza and Santa Miranda. And checking his calculation over, the Saint could only get one answer, which was that Kelly and Sheridan were due to arrive at any minute. They would learn of the abduction. . . .

"The Señora Kelly?" asked the Saint. "What of her?"

De Villega shrugged.

"She is of no importance."

Yes, Mrs Kelly would be left behind—if she had not been shot. She was middle-aged and stout and past her attractiveness, and no one would have any interest in abducting her. So that Kelly and Sheridan arriving at the bungalow would hear the tale from her.

And then—there was no doubt about it—they would come storming down to the palace, *guardias* and sentries notwithstanding, with cold murder in their hearts.

The Saint came erect, and de Villega looked up expectantly. But there was no sign of surrender in the Saint's poise, and nothing relenting about the way in which he stepped up to the Minister and set the point of the sword at his breast.

"I said I came for your resignations," remarked the Saint with a deadly quietness. "That was no idle talk. Write now, de Villega, or, by the vixen that bore thee, thou diest!"

"Fool! Fool!" Don Manuel raved. "It cannot help you!"

"I take the risk," said the Saint icily. "And do not speak so loud— I might think you were trying to attract the attention of the guards. Write!"

He thrust the sword forward the half of an inch, and de Villega started back with a cry.

"You would murder me?"

"With pleasure," said the Saint. "Write!"

Then there was sudden silence, and everyone was quite still, listening. For from the courtyard below the windows came the rattle of urgent hoofs.

The Saint leapt to the windows. There were three horses held by the sentries. He saw Shannet and two other men dismounting—and saw, being lifted down from Shannet's saddle-bow, Lilla McAndrew with her hands tied.

He could have shouted for joy at the justification of his bold defiance. And yet, if he had thought a little longer, he might have foreseen that the girl would be brought to the palace. She was not the victim of Shannet's privateering but an official hostage. But even if the Saint hadn't foreseen it, there it was, and he could have prayed for nothing better. He saw all the trump cards coming into his hands. . . .

Then he whipped round, in time to frustrate de Villega's stealthy attack, and the Minister's raised arm dropped to his side.

The Saint speared the sword into the floor and slipped the revolvers out of his sash. For the second time he dodged behind the opening door. He saw the girl thrust roughly into the room, and Shannet followed, closing the door behind him.

"Fancy meeting you again, honeybunch," drawled the Saint, and Shannet spun round with an oath.

The Saint leaned against the wall, the Presidential and Ministerial revolvers in his hands. On his lips was a smile so broad as to be almost a laugh, and there was a laugh in his voice.

"Take that hand away from your hip, Shannet, my pet," went on the Saint, in that laughing voice of sheer delight. "I've got you covered—and even if I'm not very used to these toys, I could hardly miss you at this range. . . . That's better. . . . Oh, Shannet, my sweet and beautiful gargoyle, you're a bad boy, frightening that child. Take the cords off her wrists, my angel. . . . No, Señor de Villega, you needn't edge towards that sword. I may want it again myself in a minute. *Gracias!* . . . Is that more comfortable, Lilla, old dear?"

"Oh," cried the girl, "thank God you're here! Where's Archie?"

"On his way, old darling, on his way, as the actress said of the bishop," answered the Saint. "Are you all right?"

She shuddered a little.

"Yes, I'm all right," she said. "Except for the touch of his filthy hands. But I was very frightened. . . ."

"Archie will deal with that when he arrives," said the Saint. "It's his business—he'd never forgive me if I interfered. Come here, my dear, keeping well out of the line of fire, while I deal with the specimens. I'm not the greatest revolver shot in the world, and I want to be sure that it won't matter who I hit."

He steered her to safety in a corner, and turned to Don Manuel.

"When we were interrupted," said the Saint persuasively, "you were writing. The interruption has now been disposed of. Proceed, *Señor!*"

De Villega lurched back to the table, the fight gone out of him. He could never have envisaged such an accumulation and culmination of misfortunes. It was starting to seem to him altogether like a dream, a nightmare rather—but there was nothing ethereal about the revolver that was levelled so steadily at him. The only fantastic part of the whole catastrophe was the man who had engineered it —the Saint himself, in his extraordinary borrowed clothes, and the hell-for-leather light of laughing recklessness in his blue eyes. That was the last bitter pill which De Villega had to swallow. He might perhaps have endured defeat by a man whom he could understand— a cloaked and sinister conspirator with a personality of impressive grimness. But this lunatic who *laughed.* . . . *Que diablo!* It was impossible. . . .

And then from outside drifted a grinding screaming metallic rattle that could only be made by one instrument in the world.

"Quick!" said the Saint. "Slither round behind Master Shannet, Lilla darling, and slip the gat out of his hip pocket. . . . That's right. . . . Now d'you mind sticking up the gang for a sec while I hail the troops? Blaze away if anybody gets funny."

The girl handled Shannet's automatic as if she'd been born with her finger crooked round a trigger, and the Saint, with a nod of approval, crossed over to the window.

Kelly's Ford was drawn up in the courtyard, and both Kelly and Sheridan were there. Kelly was just disposing of a sentry who had ventured to question his right of way.

"Walk right in, souls," the Saint hailed them cheerily. "You're just in time to witness the abdication of the Government."

"Have you seen Lilla?" shouted a frantic Sheridan, and the Saint grinned.

"She's safe here, brother."

The report of an automatic brought him round with a jerk.

With the Saint's back turned, and the Saint's victory now an accomplished fact, Shannet had chanced everything on one mad gamble against the steadiness of the nerve and aim of the girl who for a moment held the situation in her small hands. While Lilla McAndrew's attention was distracted by the irresistible impulse to try to hear what Archie Sheridan was saying he had sidled closer . . . made one wild leaping grab . . . missed. . . .

The Saint stooped over the still figure and made a swift examination. He straightened up with a shrug, picking up his revolvers again as the first of the guards burst into the room.

"Quietly, *amigos*," he urged; and they saw sudden death in each of his hands, and checked.

The next instant the crowd stirred again before the berserk rush of Archie Sheridan, who had heard the shot as he raced up the palace steps. A yard behind him followed Kelly, breaking through like a bull, his red head flaming above the heads of the guards.

"Relax, Archie," said the Saint. "It was Shannet who got it."

But Lilla McAndrew was already in Archie Sheridan's arms.

"Here, Kelly," rapped the Saint. "Let's get this over. Take these guns and keep the guards in order while I dispose of the Government."

Kelly took over the weapons, and the Saint stepped back and wrenched the sword out of the floor. He advanced towards the President and de Villega, who stood paralysed by the table.

"You have written?" he asked pleasantly.

De Villega passed over a piece of paper, and the Saint read it and handed it back.

"You have omitted to nominate your successors," he said. "That will be the Señor Kelly and those whom he appoints to help him. Write again."

"Half a minute," Kelly threw back over his shoulder, with his eyes on the shuffling guards. "I don't fancy being President myself— it's too risky. I'll be Minister for the Interior, and the President can stay on if he behaves himself."

The President bowed.

"I am honoured, *señor*," he assented with alacrity.

"Write accordingly," ordered the Saint, and it was done.

The Saint took the document and addressed the guards.

"By this," he said, "you know that the President dismisses Señor Manuel Concepción de Villega, the Minister for the Interior, and his Government, and appoints the Señor Kelly in his place. To celebrate his appointment, the Señor Kelly will in a few days announce the removal of a number of taxes which have hitherto oppressed you. Now take this paper and cause it to be embodied in a proclamation to the free people of Pasala. Let tomorrow be a public holiday and a day of rejoicing for this reason, and also because it is now proved that there is no war with Maduro. That was a rumour spread by certain malicious persons for their own ends. See that a *radiógrafo* is sent to *Estados Unidos*, explaining that, and saying that they may recall the warship they were sending. You may go, *amigos*."

There was a silence of a few seconds; and then, as the full meaning of the Saint's speech was grasped, the room rang and echoed again to a great crash of *Vivas!*

When Kelly had driven the cheering guards out into the passage and closed the door in their faces, Simon Templar thought of something and had the door opened again to send for the governor of the prison. The man was brought quickly.

"*Señor*," said the Saint. "I apologise for the way I treated you just now. It happened to be necessary. But the revolution is now completed, and you are a free man. I bear you no malice—although I am going to insist that you disinfect your prison."

He explained the circumstances, and the prison governor bowed almost to the floor.

"It is nothing, *ilustrísimo señor*," he said. "But if I had known I would have seen to it that your honour was given better accommodation. Another time, perhaps. . . ."

"God forbid," said the Saint piously.

Then he turned and pointed to the now terrified de Villega.

"Take this man with you," he directed. "He is to leave Pasala by the next boat, and meantime he is to be closely guarded. He will probably attempt either to fight or to bribe for his escape. My answer to that is that if he is not delivered to me when I send for him, your life and the lives of all your warders will answer for it."

"It is understood, *señor*."

Kelly watched the departure of the governor and his prisoner open-mouthed; and when they were gone he turned to the Saint with a blank expression.

"Look here," he said, as if the thought had just struck him— "where's all this fightin' I've been told so much about?"

The Saint smiled.

"There is no fighting," he said. "This has been what I hoped it would be—a bloodless revolution. It was undertaken in the name of a justice which the law could not administer, to ruin a man more than six thousand miles away, back in London, England. He had ruined thousands, but the law could not touch him. This was my method. Your first duty as Minister for the Interior will be to revoke the original oil concession and to make out a fresh one, assigning the rights in perpetuity to Miss McAndrew and her heirs." He laid a hand on Kelly's shoulder. "I'm sorry to give you such a disappointment, son; and if you must have a fight, I'll have a round or two with you myself before dinner. But I had to do it this way. Any other kind of revolution would have meant the sacrifice of many lives, and I didn't really want that."

For a moment Kelly was silent and perplexed before the Saint's sudden seriousness; then he shrugged, and laughed, and took Simon Templar's hand in a huge grip.

"I don't confess to know what yez are talkin' about," he said. "And I don't care. I suppose it's been worth it—if only to see the look on de Villega's ugly face whin yez sent him to prison. And, anyway, a laughin' devil who can run a show like yez have run this one deserves to be allowed to work things his own way."

"Good scout," smiled the Saint. "Was Mrs Kelly all right?"

"A bit scared, but no harm done. It was Lilla she was afraid for. They just tied the missus up in a chair and left her. An' that reminds me—there was a cable waitin' for me up at the bungalow, and I can't make head or tail of it. Maybe it's something to do with you."

Kelly fumbled in his pocket and produced the form. The Saint took it over, and one glance told him that it was meant for him.

"It's from an agent of mine in London," he explained. "He wouldn't have addressed it to Archie or me in case anything had gone wrong and it was intercepted."

He knew the code almost perfectly, and he was able to write the translation in between the lines at once.

*Pops down trumped twelve thousand—*

The Saint wrote:

*POP's fell heavily. Cleared twelve thousand pounds. Campard committed suicide this morning.*

It was signed with the name of Roger Conway.

"Archie!" called the Saint, thoughtfully; and again: "Archie!"

"They sneaked out minutes ago," said Kelly. "She's a sweet girl, that Lilla McAndrew. . . ."

And it was so, until evening.

And at even the Saint went forth and made a tour of a number of disreputable cafés, in each of which he bought much liquor for the clientele. They did not recognise him until he started to sing— a strange and barbarous song that no one could understand. But they recognised it, having heard it sung before, with many others like it, by a certain *peón:*

> *"The bells of Hell go ting-a-ling-a-ling,*
> *For you but not for me;*
> *For me the angels sing-a-ling-a-ling,*
> *They've got the goods for me—"*

To this day you will hear that song sung by the peasants of Santa Miranda. And if you should ask one of them why he sings it, he will answer, with courteous surprise at your ignorance: "That, *señor*, is one of the songs of freedom. . . ."

# THE STORY OF A DEAD MAN

## From WANTED FOR MURDER

---

THE LAST SELECTION *from what you might call this trilogy of the Saint's earliest recorded background will always be interesting to me for the light that it throws on an old proverb that "History repeats itself". Because my own theory is that History, being an entirely involuntary concatenation of events, is by definition incapable of deliberately doing anything. My own careful generalisation would be that history is full of people who have tried to repeat the performances of their predecessors, usually with no greater success.*

*For instance. This story centres, in part, around the desire of a certain man to become officially dead and yet at the same time to remain alive; and the way in which he proposed to achieve this convenient miracle is carefully revealed. He failed. But nevertheless, not long after this story was published, another gentleman attempted to perform the same feat by an identical method. His attempt to repeat History was fully reported by the newspapers of the time. I am obliged to mention this in case any other enterprising individuals should remain at large who still think he had the makings of a good idea. They hanged him.*

# THE STORY OF A DEAD MAN

WHEN LONG HARRY came out of Pentonville Prison, he was not expecting to be welcomed by a cohort of friends. At the worst, he had reckoned an emissary of the Prisoners' Aid Society would be the most he would have to deal with, and consequently the sight of the plump and ponderous Chief Inspector Teal lounging somnolently against a lamp-post a few yards from the prison gates was an unwelcome surprise.

Pulling his hat down over his eyes, Harry tactfully began to stroll in the opposite direction, but Inspector Teal was not so lightly to be deprived of the pleasure of renewing his acquaintance with an old customer.

He hitched himself off his lamp-post, and came up with Long Harry in a few slothful strides that nevertheless managed to convey him over the intervening ground in a surprisingly short space of time.

His hand fell on Harry's shoulder, and the yegg pulled up and faced about uneasily.

"I want you, Harry," said Mr Teal, whose sense of humour was sometimes lacking in good taste.

Harry shuffled his feet.

"You've got nothing on me, Mr Teal," he said defensively.

"I want you, Harry," repeated Mr Teal sleepily, "to come along to the Corner House and have some breakfast with me, and then we'll have a little talk."

Harry said that he had had breakfast, but Mr Teal was not so easily to be put off.

"If you won't eat yourself," he said, "you can watch me—and listen," he added, with unconscious humour.

As he spoke he was gently shepherding Harry back past the prison gates to a diminutive car that was drawn up by the kerb.

They passed down Caledonian Road in silence. Mr Teal had the gift of investing his silences with a peculiarly disturbing quality, and Long Harry became more and more unhappy as the miles ticked over on the speedometer in front of him.

"I suppose," said Harry, breaking a period of almost intolerable suspense as they turned round Park Crescent into Portland Place, "I suppose you aren't thinking I had anything to do with that Regent Street job?"

"I've stopped thinking about that," said Mr Teal, "since I became certain."

"That's like you flatties," complained Harry bitterly. "Let a man do his time and not say a word, and then wait for him outside the prison to shop him for another stretch."

Mr Teal said nothing. They whizzed down Regent Street in another spell of silence.

"It isn't even a fair charge," said Harry presently with an injured air. "I've got a beautiful alibi for you."

"You always have," said Mr Teal, without resentment. "I've never known you disappoint me yet."

They sat over bacon and eggs in Coventry Street, and Inspector Teal then condescended to relieve some of Harry's apprehensions by explaining the reason for his hospitality.

"I want you," said Mr Teal, in his sleepy way, "to tell me a little story about a man named Connell. I've got an idea he's a particular friend of yours."

The other's face twisted up in a vicious grin.

"Connell," snarled Long Harry, "is a——"

"Yes?" prompted Mr Teal drowsily.

Harry's clenched fist opened slowly. His vicious grin became cunning, then mask-like.

"Connell," said Harry softly, "is a man I've met occasionally. I can't tell you more about him than that, Mr Teal."

The detective sighed.

"Sure you can't?"

Harry shook his head.

"You know I'm always ready to help you when I can, Mr Teal," he said speciously, "but I don't know anything about Connell."

Mr Teal looked sceptical.

"Except," said Harry slowly, "that I've a good idea he was the squealer who shopped me for the Bayswater joke."

"You let me down over Bayswater," said Mr Teal reproachfully. "I never thought you carried a cosh around with you."

"Nor do I," said Harry. "Listen!"

He leant forward across the table.

"You and me, Mr Teal," he said, "have met pretty often—on business, as you might say. Now, you know I'm a respectable burglar. You've never caught me with a cosh, let alone a gun, yet. You've put me away six times, and I don't mind admitting now that I asked for the whole half dozen, but I swear to you I never went near Bayswater that night."

"You ought to have told that to the Court," said Mr Teal.

"Look here," persisted Harry with charming simplicity. "You remember pulling me in, don't you? Well, had I got an alibi? Did I say anything about an alibi? You know I didn't. Now, I ask you, Mr Teal, have you ever known me to be pulled in for a job of work that I really did and me not have an alibi ready?"

Mr Teal's eyes were half closed, and he appeared to be taking no notice. That pose of lazy boredom was his one affectation.

"The whole thing was a frame-up from start to finish," repeated Harry, "and you ought to know it, Mr Teal. I never used a cosh in my life, and I never did a porch job, anyway. And the man might have died, from what the papers said. Then I'd have been hanged. Maybe I was meant to be hanged. But Connell——"

Mr Teal's eyes suddenly opened very wide.

"What are you going to do to Connell?" he asked.

Harry relaxed.

"Well, when I see him," he said, "maybe I'll stand him a drink, and maybe I won't. Who knows?"

"And when I take you again," said Mr Teal, "maybe you'll get a lifer, and maybe you'll hang. Who knows about that, either?"

It was an unsatisfactory interview from all points of view, and Mr Teal, who had dragged himself out of bed at half-past five that morning in order to bring it about, was pardonably annoyed.

He got back to his room at Scotland Yard about half-past nine, and his assistant found him in an unpleasant mood.

"I've been thnking," began the recently-promoted Sergeant Barrow, and Mr Teal cut him short with a ferocious glare.

"Why?" demanded Mr Teal unkindly. "I'm sure it hurts you, and you know I've always told you to take care of yourself."

"I've been thinking about the Camberwell Post Office hold-up," insisted the younger man aggrievedly. "Now couldn't that man Horring have been in it?"

"He could," agreed Mr Teal carefully, "if they hadn't hanged him at Wandsworth the week before. Go away and rest. You'll be getting brain fever if you go on thinking like this."

After that, Mr Teal felt better.

"And on your way down," he called after the retreating sergeant as the door closed, "tell Sergeant Jones I want him."

There is a special department at Scotland Yard whose sole function is to indulge its curiosity, and the facts which it brings to light are strange and various. Some of them are gleaned from the reports of patrolling constables, who are instructed to note down any unusual happenings which they observe on their beats. Others are gleaned by painstaking subterranean investigation.

No plain van draws up outside a house at night and proceeds to discharge its cargo without the fact being reported; no man moves suddenly from a bed-sitting-room in Bermondsey to a service flat in Jermyn Street without arousing the interest of this inquisitive department; no man becomes a regular frequenter of the hotels and restaurants in the West End which are shared as a meeting ground by London society, foreign millionaires, crooks both home-bred and imported, and that curious fraternity which without coming into conflict with the law, contrives to live in luxury by its wits and the generosity of its relatives without this prying department interesting itself in the subject.

Of this department, Sergeant Jones was an esteemed ornament. He spent his life in a maze of card indexes, turning over the disjointed and apparently insignificant reports which came in to him from time to time, sorting the wheat from the chaff, filing away accredited information, and requesting the further investigation of those facts which seemed to him to require it.

Sometimes the threads he followed led nowhere. Sometimes, by devious means, they were linked up with other threads, which in their turn tangled up again with yet more threads. And then, perhaps, a house would be surrounded, a couple of detectives would enter, and in a few moments some very surprised men would be hustled unostentatiously into a waiting taxi and removed to a place where they would have leisure to wonder how the seemingly undetectable had been detected.

"Sit down, Jones," said Mr Teal, settling himself comfortably in the big swivel chair behind his desk and closing his eyes, "and tell me all about Vanney's."

Sergeant Jones sat down. He was a long lanky man, with sandy hair and a large nose.

"Directors," said Sergeant Jones, "as follows: President and managing director, James Arthur Vanney, 48, of 52 Half Moon Street; secretary, Sebastian Tombs, Esquire, of no fixed address; director, Malcolm Standish, 34, Solicitor, of Lincoln's Inn."

"Do we know anything about these men?"

"Not much. Standish we know. He's behind half the criminal cases that are defended at the Old Bailey—a lot more than his name appears in. If any big crook gets landed he sends for Standish at once. We've never had anything on him, but I shouldn't be surprised if he'd made a tidy pile out of some of the cases he's worked on. Vanney built that new house at the bottom of Half Moon Street about nine months ago. Two cars—a Rolls and a Daimler. Four servants. Does himself pretty well on the whole."

"Where was he before he moved into Half Moon Street?"

"He stayed at the Savoy while the house was being built. His address was registered there as Melbourne, Victoria. Someone commissioned the architect and got the building job in hand a couple of months before Vanney arrived. . . . That man Tombs is a bloke I'd like to know a lot more about."

"And so should I," said Teal.

He fingered his chin thoughtfully.

"Staff?" he queried.

"Very small. Girl secretary, name of Pamela Marlowe, and two clerks. Pamela Marlowe was Stenning's ward."

Mr Teal nodded faintly to signify that the interview was at an end, and Sergeant Jones rose.

He was leaving the room when a man brought in a small parcel.

"One moment," murmured Mr Teal, and the sergeant stopped by the door.

Teal examined the packet carefully, and then held it to his ear. Then he blinked, and the ghost of a smile crossed his face.

"How surprisingly unoriginal," remarked Mr Teal mildly.

Sergeant Jones came back to his desk, and Mr Teal held out the packet to him. Jones took it doubtfully.

"Walk that round to the Explosives Department," said Teal, "and mind you don't drop it. You can also spend your spare time praying that it doesn't go off before you get there!"

## II

Vanney's Ltd, who were vaguely described on the glass panel of their door as "Agents", occupied a suite of offices in a new block of buildings opposite Charing Cross Station.

There were four rooms looking out on to the Strand. A private corridor ran the length of the suite, and each room opened separately on to it, while a system of communicating doors permitted access to any room from any of the other rooms without entering the passage. The first room was a waiting-room, in the second room worked two clerks, and in the third were Tombs and Miss Marlowe. The fourth was the sanctum of James Arthur Vanney himself, a thick-set man of medium height, who actually looked short by reason of his exceptional breadth of shoulder. He was dark and bearded, sparing of speech, and gruff in manner.

Chief Inspector Teal knocked on the door marked "Inquiries" one afternoon, and was told by the clerk who opened it that Mr Vanney was busy.

"I'll wait," said Mr Teal philosophically, and the clerk appeared to be nonplussed.

The door communicating the clerks' room with the secretary's office was open. Through it Mr Teal perceived a familiar back. He flowed irresistibly past the clerk, passed through the communicating door, and tapped Simon Templar's shoulder.

"When did you change your name to Tombs?" asked Mr Teal drowsily.

"Quite recently," said the Saint unabashed. "It seemed a jolly sort of name. Didn't the clerk tell you that Mr Vanney was engaged?"

Teal nodded.

"He did," he admitted, "and I said I'd wait."

"Mr Vanney," persisted the Saint, "will be engaged all the afternoon."

"I've got a lot of time to spare," said Teal calmly, "and when I get bored with waiting you can come and talk to me."

"Mr Vanney," continued the Saint, pointedly, "will not be able to see you until tomorrow morning."

Teal extracted from his pocket a small packet done up in pink paper. From it he took a smaller packet, from which he took a thin wafer of chewing gum. With his jaws moving rhythmically, he cast a sleepily speculative eye about the room.

"I can doss down in a corner," he said. "Or have you a camp bed?"

Simon Templar inspected a row of buttons on his desk, selected one, and pressed it.

Mr Teal masticated in silence until a knock on the door answered the bell.

"In," said the Saint briskly.

The door opened, and a man in a plain blue serge suit and a bowler hat stood framed in the aperture.

"George," said the Saint, in the same brisk tone, "show this gentleman the way out."

Mr Teal shifted his gum round so as to give the other side of his face its full share of exercise.

"Suppose," he suggested languidly, "that I just had a word with you in private first?"

The Saint shrugged.

"I can give you two minutes exactly," he said. "You can wait outside the door, George. Miss Marlowe, would you mind?"

Mr Teal lounged into a chair.

"Nice girl that," he remarked.

"Very," agreed the Saint briefly. "And now let's hear the bright brisk business. What has fetched you to this wilderness, old watermelon?"

Teal stretched his arms lazily.

"I was interested," he said. "A name like Sebastian Tombs seemed too good to be true, and when I saw you—well, I was just more interested than ever."

"That must have been frightfully jolly for you," agreed the Saint carefully. "May one ask why?"

Teal closed his eyes, but his jaws continued to maltreat Spearmint with monotonous regularity.

"Somehow," he said, "whenever I find you off your usual beat, I have an idea there's a catch in it. What's the idea this time?"

"I have reformed," said the Saint speciously. "Overwhelmed with the burden of my sins, and gloomily conscious of many wasted years, I have decided to go out into the great wide world and make good. These are paths of righteousness, Teal, but I can't expect you to believe that."

"Then you won't be disappointed," said Teal languidly. "Now can I see your boss?"

"I'm afraid not," said the Saint. "I've told you he's engaged."

Teal looked across at the opposite communicating door. The upper panel was of frosted glass, and across this was painted the word "Private".

"Does he always see his visitors in the dark?" asked Teal gently.

"Always," said the Saint blandly. "It's one of his many peculiarities."

Mr Teal's eyes were half closed.

"And does he," pursued Mr Teal, in the same tired voice, "always hang his hat and coat up in the clerks' room? I can see your hat and coat hanging up in the corner there, and there were three hats and coats in the room I came through."

"That," said the Saint fluently, "is another of his eccentricities. He says he hates to have his hat and coat hanging up in his own room."

Mr Teal nodded, and then he moved.

It has already been mentioned that for such a large and slothful man he could, when he so desired, cover ground with a surprising turn of speed.

He had flung open the communicating door marked "Private" before the Saint could stop him, and the lights clicked up under his thumb as Simon reached his side.

The room was empty.

It was sparsely but comfortably furnished, with a big knee-hole desk set crosswise in the corner by the window, a safe in the opposite corner, and a filing cabinet against one wall. There were two armchairs upholstered in leather, and a plain wooden armchair behind the desk. Facing the communicating door was a fireplace, and on either side of this was a tall cupboard built into the wall. There was no sign of Vanney.

Teal leaned back against the jamb of the door, looking at the Saint's blank face and chewing unemotionally.

"And," said Mr Teal, without changing the bored tone of his voice, "does Mr Vanney automatically vanish, together with his visitor, when this door is opened?"

Simon put his hands in his pockets and settled himself comfortably in the doorway. He looked quizzically at the detective.

"I've never known him to do it before," he replied calmly. "But great men are always slightly erratic in their habits. It will be an interesting little problem for you to take home with you."

Mr Teal removed a speck of dust from his bowler hat.

"On second thoughts," he said, "I don't think I'll spend the night here. Bye-bye, Saint. See you later, I expect."

"I'm afraid so," said Simon affably.

Mr Teal opened the door to find the porter standing patiently outside.

"You may go, George," said Teal. "I'll find my own way out."

He was sauntering down the corridor when a thought struck him, and he returned. He opened the door a few inches without the formality of knocking, and poked his head in.

Simon Templar was writing at the desk, and the girl was tapping the typewriter in the corner.

"Goodbye, old fruit," said the Saint pleasantly, without looking up.

"When Mr Vanney comes back," drawled the imperturbable Mr Teal, "you might tell him, with my compliments, that if he makes any more childish attempts to kill me I shall be seriously annoyed."

He closed the door again and resumed his leisurely progress towards the stairs, humming gently to himself.

Mr Teal was sometimes unable to overcome a weakness for playing the magazine detective.

### III

Simon Templar put the finishing touches to the letter he was drafting. Then, settling himself back in his chair, he reached out a long arm to the neat row of bell-pushes which occupied one corner of his desk. Selecting one with a thoughtful air, he pressed it. The small brass plate beside the knob was engraved with the word "Secretary", and the bell rang in the opposite corner of the same room, over Pamela Marlowe's head. The outsider would have failed to see the point of this arrangement, but the Saint had not been in business long enough to get tired of playing with the mechanical gadgets provided in all up-to-date offices for the amusement of the staff.

Simon lighted a cigarette and gazed reflectively at the ceiling.

"Take a letter," he said. "This is to Stanforth and Watson: Dear Sirs,—With reference to our telephone conversation this morning. Stop. Something seems to be eating you."

Pamela Marlowe looked up from her pad in surprise.

"Do you want me to put that down?" she asked.

"No," replied the Saint, taking his eyes off the ceiling. "The remark was addressed to you."

He was regarding her keenly, and after a few seconds' silence she looked away.

"You may tell me all," he remarked gently. "I am a Grand Master of the Order of Father Confessors."

She met his eyes again, and the question with which she took advantage of his invitation did not come as a surprise to him.

"Who was that man who came in just now?"

"That," said the Saint, "was the worthy Chief Inspector Claud Eustace Teal, of the Criminal Investigation Department, New Scotland Yard. He has a prying disposition, and he isn't anything like the fool he looks. I grant you that would be difficult."

The girl hesitated, fidgeting with her pencil. But Simon, unruffled himself, made no attempt to fluster her.

"Mr Tombs," she said at length, "I wasn't trying to hear the conversation that went on after you sent me out of the room, but the partition wall is very thin."

"It's these jerry-building methods," sighed the Saint. "I'll dictate a letter to the *Times* about it in a moment."

The girl's lips tightened a little.

"I couldn't help hearing what Mr Teal said."

Simon said nothing.

He, who should by rights have been the one to show embarrassment, registered nothing of the kind.

"You didn't deny his charges," said the girl.

"Naturally not," said the Saint. "George Washington was an ancestor of mine, and I cannot tell a lie."

Pamela Marlowe had heard of the Saint—she would have been an amazing woman if she had not. The Saint realised exactly what was in her mind, but the thought failed to disturb him. He was mildly amused.

"What's the worry?" he enquired.

"Are you really the Saint?"

"I am. Did you really think I went through life permanently attached by the ear to a name like Sebastian Tombs?"

"Well," said the girl bluntly, "I shall hate doing it, but doesn't it occur to you that it's my duty to say something to Mr Vanney about it? That is, if you can't give me some sort of explanation."

Simon smiled without mockery.

"Of course it is," he agreed cheerfully. "And I should like to say that I appreciate the nobility of your impulse. I shall draw Mr Vanney's attention to it. But as for the other matter, I'm afraid you won't be able to tell him anything that he doesn't know. The thought that I am immovably parked in his office is the bane of his life. Try it on him tomorrow morning, if you don't believe me."

He dictated a number of letters, waited while she typed them, and took them into Mr Vanney's private office. He was back in a few moments with the sheaf duly signed.

"You can go as soon as you have addressed them," he said. "George will take them down to the post."

She ventured to be inquisitive.

"Why do we need a special porter for this office?" she asked.

"One should always," said the Saint impressively, "surround one-self with all the evidences of prosperity that one can afford. It creates a good impression. George will have a nice new uniform with brass buttons tomorrow, and I shall expect to see an immediate jump in our turnover."

It was an invariable rule at Vanney's that Mr "Tombs" was the last to leave the office. On that particular evening, however, Pamela Marlowe, with her hat and coat on, appeared to be uncertain whether she should take him at his word.

"I've told you you can go," said the Saint, without looking up from the letter he was perusing.

She made a demur.

"Are you sure Mr Vanney won't want me again?"

"Mr Vanney," said the Saint carefully, "never wants you. You know that perfectly well."

It was true. All instructions to the office staff were given by Mr "Tombs", and he dictated all the letters that were sent out, and opened all that came in. The rest of the staff were never allowed to pass through the door marked "Private".

"I've told you that I shall not want you any more this evening," said the Saint, "and you may take that as official. Mr Vanney has already left."

She stared.

"He hasn't come through for his hat and coat," she objected.

"He left by his private entrance," Simon answered shortly, "without a hat and coat. He has just joined the Ancient Order of Kangaroos, and one of their rules is that no member is allowed to take his hat and coat home with him on Friday."

There was nothing for her but to leave without further argu-ment, but the incident found its place in her memory beside a number of other extraordinary things which she had noticed during the few months that she had worked under Simon Templar.

Mr "Tombs" was in every way an ideal employer. His manner, without being brusque, was at all times irreproachably impersonal, but she had never been able to understand his mentality. Whenever she ventured to comment on any unusual happening, he was never at a loss for an explanation, but the reasons he gave so glibly would have been an insult to the intelligence of an imbecile.

There had been a time when she had wondered if he fancied himself as a wag and was expecting her to laugh, but he made the most outrageous statements without smiling, and if he showed any emotion at all it was one of concealed delight at her annoyed perplexity.

She found another enigma to interpret when she arrived at the office the following Monday; for the Saint, with his coat off, was supervising the finishing touches which were being put by two workmen to a curious erection which had appeared at the far end of the private corridor.

Simon greeted her in his usual affable manner, and invited her to admire it.

"This is George's new home," he said.

It was, in fact, no more than a partition which turned into a sort of cubicle the blind end of the passage beyond the door that opened into Vanney's private room. It would have been nothing but an ordinary janitor's box but for an unusual feature in its design. The partition reached all the way to the ceiling, and there were only two small windows—one in the partition itself, and one in the door which the workmen were at that moment engaged in putting in position. Furthermore, each window was obscured by a row of steel bars set close together.

Coming closer, she made another surprising discovery.

"But why is it lined with steel?" she asked in amazement.

"Because," said the Saint, "a half-inch deal board is not much protection against a bullet. We should hate to lose our one and only George."

The girl was silent, but Simon was perfectly at his ease.

"Observe, too, the strategic position," he murmured, with the enthusiasm of an artist. "No one can reach George without having to cover the whole length of the suite, either through the offices or down the corridor. Consequently it'll be his own fault if he doesn't hear them coming. Besides, we've got another little safety device. I'll show you if you wait here a moment."

He went down the corridor, and as he got near the door a low burring noise came to her ears. Staring blankly about her, she eventually located its source in a small metal box screwed to the wall inside the cubicle.

Simon passed on to the door, and the buzzing stopped. He turned, and it recommenced; then he came back down the corridor, and it stopped again.

"What is it?" she asked. "A burglar alarm?"

"The very latest," said the Saint. "Come and have a look."

He led her down the passage, and when they were within a yard of the door the low buzzing made itself heard again. She stopped and gazed around puzzledly, but she could see nothing.

"I have them all over my own home," he explained. "It's the best idea of its kind in the world. It's worked by a ray that shines across the corridor on to a selenium cell. It's invisible, but if you get in its path the buzzer gives tongue. It's impossible to put it out of action until it's too late, because only Sebastian Tombs"—the Saint shuddered involuntarily—"and the electrician who fitted it know exactly where it is."

He was amused at her bewilderment.

"Don't you think it's rather neat?" he asked.

"It seems a lot of trouble to take over a porter."

The Saint smiled.

"George," he said virtuously, "is a member of Vanney's just as much as you or I. Isn't it the duty of the firm to see that he is thoroughly protected against the dangers of his position?"

In her astonishment she forgot the lesson which experience should have taught her.

"But why should George be in any danger?" she said, and Simon Templar's face instantly assumed its gravest expression.

"Haven't you read about all these armed robberies?" he demanded severely. "Haven't you ever heard of the Black Hand? And do you mean to say that I never told you that the Union of Porters, Commissionaires, Caretakers, Undertakers, and Glue Refiners have threatened to do George in for allowing us to put two more than the regulation number of buttons on his uniform?"

She turned away in despair, and went into the office.

The Saint followed her, and resumed his coat. Then he leaned back in his chair, put his feet on the desk, and pressed the bell marked "Secretary".

"Take a letter to the *Times*," he said. "To the Editor of the

*Times.* Sir,—The scamping of work at present practised by the building trade is a disgrace. Stop. In the house which I have recently taken, the walls are so thin that a nail which I drove into the wall last night in order to hang a picture was distinctly felt by the occupants of the next room. Stop. Consequently, my wife has been compelled to take her meals off the mantelpiece ever since, with the result that our domestic arrangements have been seriously disorganised. Stop. I am, etcetera, Lieut-Colonel, Retired. And just remember, Miss Marlowe, that George is one of the most important people in this office, and if anybody happened to shoot at him successfully the firm would probably go into liquidation, and you and I would be looking for new jobs."

## IV

The memory of Mr Teal's visit had occupied a prominent part of Pamela Marlowe's thoughts ever since the afternoon when the Saint had so shamelessly acknowledged the truth of that lethargic detective's accusations. But when Simon arrived one morning and told her that he had arranged for her to carry the tale to Vanney, she felt a paradoxical reluctance to go to her employer with a charge against his manager's honesty, even while she welcomed the opportunity of testing the truth of his statements that Vanney knew the whole story of his misdeeds.

Simon Templar, however, appeared to have no doubts about what the outcome of the interview would be.

"Tell him everything you heard," he encouraged, when the bell rang from Mr Vanney's office to summon her. "He will be interested."

She took the Saint at his word, but it was a profitless conversation.

Vanney listened attentively to her story, but when she had finished she could have sworn that he was smiling behind his beard. His voice, however, was quite serious.

"I appreciate your high sense of duty, Miss Marlowe," he said, "but what—er—Mr Tombs told you is quite correct. I know everything about him, and in spite of that he has my complete confidence."

He had a stiff manner of speaking, and appeared to think each sentence out carefully before he uttered it. He did not once look directly at her, but kept his eyes fixed on a point in space a foot or so away from her left shoulder.

"I didn't wish to do Mr Tombs any harm," she felt compelled to explain. "But I had to remember that you were the one who was employing me."

"I quite understand," said Vanney.

He continued to gaze past her in silence for some seconds, stroking his beard. Then he said:

"Did you know that your late guardian's last request to me was that, if anything happened to him, I should look after you?"

"But you were in Australia."

"I know," said Vanney, rather testily. "He wrote to me."

The girl nodded.

"I see. But I never knew much about him, and I never heard him speak of any of his friends. My father knew him a long time ago—they were boys together, but they hadn't met for over twenty years. Just before father died, he happened to meet Mr Stenning again, quite by accident; and since I had no other relatives living, and father and Mr Stenning had been such close friends before they lost touch with each other, it was fairly natural that he should appoint Mr Stenning my guardian. But I only saw Mr Stenning three times, and that was when I was quite young. He discharged all his duties through his solicitors."

"He often mentioned your name to me when he wrote," said Vanney. "I believe that, behind the scenes, he took a great interest in you."

He began to fidget with a pencil on his desk, and she could not help noticing his hands. They were rough and ill-kept, and not at all the hands that one would have associated with a millionaire—for Vanney was reputed to be no less.

He appeared suddenly to become aware of their defects, for he dropped the pencil and hid his hands in his pockets.

"I had a very rough life in Australia before I made my fortune," he volunteered. "And I fear that, as guardian, I should be of very little use to you. Now, of course, you are old enough not to need looking after. But if you would honour me with your company at dinner one evening, Miss Marlowe, I should appreciate the compliment."

She hesitated.

"If you want me to——"

"You don't seem very keen," he said.

She had to pause to think of a reply.

"I hardly go out at all," she said at length, and was conscious of the flimsiness of the excuse as soon as she had uttered it.

But Vanney did not appear to be at all put out. He pulled a book towards him and began to turn the pages.

"Very well, Miss Marlowe," he said, with a return to the gruffness of tone which had softened for a moment. "That will be all, then. You may go back to your work."

She returned to the outer room feeling vaguely uncomfortable. She knew that her refusal of Vanney's invitation had not been an example of perfect tact, and the realisation was not a congenial one. There was no logical reason that she could see why she should have been so perverse, and she was annoyed with herself for having given way so readily to an unaccountable feeling of revulsion.

The Saint was drawing on his blotting-pad a portrait of his employer which would, if it had been published in a newspaper, have provided more than sufficient grounds for a libel action.

"You are subdued," he remarked, without taking his eyes off his work. "Therefore I deduce that you have been unwillingly forced to admit that I'm more truthful by nature than you believed."

She smiled, but he was not looking at her.

"I owe you an apology," she said. "You warned me that I was making a fool of myself, but I refused to be convinced."

"Your apology is accepted," said the Saint amiably.

He picked up a two-colour pencil and added a roseate hue to Mr Vanney's nose, while she transcribed a letter.

"But," said the Saint, "if you're thinking that one day I shall be revealed as the brilliant and noble detective who masquerades as a criminal, caring nothing for his own reputation and matrimonial prospects, in order to nab the crook of crooks, it is my duty to warn you that nothing so romantic will happen. I am a bold bad man, and I love it. And the fact that you have one of the most adorable mouths I have ever seen will never alter that."

He said this without the least change of tone, so that it was fully a minute before she realised the meaning of the words which closed his speech. When the point dawned upon her, she stopped tapping the typewriter and stared at him.

The Saint seemed blissfully unaware that he had in any way departed from his usual style of conversation. While she watched him in amazement, he drew a dissipated-looking wrinkle under Vanney's left eye with the blue end of his pencil, and then laid it down and gazed at the ceiling with an air of furious concentration.

She did not know what to say, and so said nothing. This was not difficult, for he did not appear to be expecting her to make any comment. After a short period of scowling rumination, he picked up his pencil again and continued drawing.

Pamela gazed hopelessly at a blank sheet of paper. The situation was impossible, but the Saint gave no sign that he perceived any incongruity in it.

"You are still subdued, Pamela," he murmured, pushing the blotter aside. "I can't imagine that to hear my views on your mouth would affect you so deeply, so I am left to conclude that Vanney has asked you to meet him in a social sort of way."

"I don't think it's any business of yours, Mr Tombs," she began, and then he looked up at her.

"Since the villain has been unmasked," drawled the Saint, "I think you can forget that name. I only chose it in the hope that one day it would annoy Claud Eustace, and the longer I live with it the less I like it."

"Very well—Mr Templar."

"Simon," murmured the Saint, "is even more soothing to my ears." The girl frowned.

"Did he or did he not?" asked the Saint, returning to the argument.

She flushed resentfully at his insistence.

"What if he did?" countered a stubborn Pamela.

Simon fingered his chin.

"I was afraid he would," he said. "The morals of the modern employer are appalling. You might remind me to dictate a letter to the *Times* about it. But I'll just ask Mr Vanney not to annoy you any more."

To her astonishment, he rose at once from his desk and went into the next office. This time she had no compunction about eavesdropping. But strain her ears as she might, she could make nothing of the faint almost inaudible murmur of voices.

In a few minutes the Saint returned, and his normally unwrinkled brow wore a frown that was not one of concentration.

"Mr Vanney is inclined to be obstinate," he said. "I hope I've convinced him of the error of his ways, but if it occurs again you will let me know."

Thereafter he ignored her existence until lunch time, but when she had put on her hat she found him holding her coat for her—a courtesy which he had never offered before.

"Pamela," he said, "will you put me in the same category as Vanney if I ask you to lunch with me?"

Pamela looked at him, met the full brilliance of the Saintly smile, and was lost.

"No—I don't think so."

"Then we'll go and beat up the Carlton," said the Saint cheerfully; and it was so.

Sergeant Jones, who was loitering inconspicuously on the corner of the block, saw them come out. He followed them to the Carlton, and two hours later followed them back.

Inspector Teal, to whom the most trivial details were always a matter of the most tremendously absorbing interest, had posted him there to report on the habits of the clients and staff of Vanney's Ltd; and Sergeant Jones had begun to feel that he had a personal grievance against Simon Templar, for on the previous five days Mr Jones had sacrificed his own midday meal in the hope of getting a chance to observe the Saint at lunch, and had been disappointed.

"He's either been dieting to keep his figure, or he's been on hunger strike," Mr Teal was told that night. "Anyhow, this is the first time he's been out for a bite during the day since I started tailing him."

Inspector Teal blinked once; but inwardly he was chalking up the Saint's mysterious fast among the many other peculiar facts which were catalogued in his mind against the firm of Vanney's.

## V

On a certain morning a grocer in South London was found lying, shot through the heart, behind his counter, when the assistant came to open up the shop in the morning, with the till broken open and the previous three days' takings missing. The man in charge of the case, before he allowed anything to be moved, sent for the police photographers. The pictures they took were developed and printed in a few hours; and these, together with the inspector's own copious notes, were sent immediately to that department of Scotland Yard known as the Records Office, where are catalogued in one gigantic card index all the known forms, variations, and trimmings of crime, with cross-references to the men who are known to practise them.

The usual scientific process of elimination then began. The extra heavy sentence which is always received by a criminal who uses firearms in his work means that comparatively few burglars go armed. From the list of these men were eliminated those whose known methods of entering a house did not correspond with the method used in that case. The list was reduced again by removing the names of those who without a serious divergence from their old habits—a rare phenomenon among habitual criminals—would have solved the problem of the locked till in a way other than that in which it had been solved. The list diminished steadily as the names it contained were in turn tested by other characteristics of the crime in question.

Even with these precise methods, several names are frequently left over for further scrutiny, but in this instance the accumulated evidence pointed with the most convincing certainty to one man.

"You mentioned his name to me only the other day," said the man from the Records Office. "So I thought you would be interested."

"I am," said Mr Teal. "But I'd be still more interested if you could tell me where he is."

It was in a pessimistic spirit that he telephoned an inquiry through to the inspector in charge of F Division, and therefore he was not disappointed when it proved fruitless.

"The last time anything was seen or heard of Connell," F Division informed him concisely, "was in July, two years ago."

Mr Teal, remembering his breakfast of a fortnight ago, took his hat and coat and went for a walk.

He ran his victim to earth in a public house near Victoria Station, and took the next place at the bar.

"This is a pleasant surprise, Harry," said Mr Teal untruthfully, for he had drawn blank at several coverts before he found his fox. "What'll you have?"

"A bottle of champagne with you, Mr Teal," said Long Harry.

"Two bitters, please, Miss," said Mr Teal.

He picked up his tankard and nodded towards a vacant table in a corner.

"Suppose we get out of the crowd, and have a little talk," he suggested, and Long Harry knew of old that when Mr Teal made such a request it was useless to refuse.

He followed the portly detective to the secluded spot he had indicated, and they sat down.

"Now tell me about Connell," said Mr Teal.

Long Harry scowled.

"I told you once, I don't know anything about him."

"But he did a job in Battersea last night," said Mr Teal. "I thought you'd have heard—it's in the lunch editions."

Long Harry shook his head.

"I don't know anything about it, Mr Teal," he said.

"Now, I thought you would," said Teal dreamily. "The lunch editions didn't say Connell did it, but I was expecting you to come along and tell me that. Either Connell did it, or someone who knew his methods inside out arranged it so that everything would point to Connell."

Harry grinned.

"If you're thinking I pulled that job to frame Connell, you're right up the spout. I've got an alibi."

The torpescent Mr Teal felt in his waistcoat pocket for a fresh bar of chewing gum.

"Then," he remarked pensively, "it seems as if you *must* have done it."

"But this," said Harry, "is a copper-bottomed alibi. I spent last night in Marlborough Street Police Station. I'd been entertaining some friends, and we'd had what you might call a sticky evening. It took three policemen to get me there."

Mr Teal raised a reproving eyebrow.

"Drunk, I suppose," he murmured.

"All three of them," said Harry.

The detective ruminated in silence for some moments, and then he said:

"Do you get drunk easily, Harry?"

"I can knock back a tankful and not show it," Harry bragged.

"Entertaining friends, were you?" said Teal slumbrously. "Then you must have come into some easy money. I know how fond you are of work, and you haven't been out of stir long enough to earn that much honestly."

"I got a remittance," said Harry glibly. "An uncle of mine who went out to Australia years ago, suddenly remembered his poor persecuted nephew in the old country, and sent me a tenner."

Mr Teal went back to Scotland Yard very little wiser than he had been when he left it.

That afternoon an idea struck him. He walked up the Embankment to Charing Cross, and he was standing by a tobacco kiosk when Pamela Marlowe left the offices of Vanney's Ltd, and crossed the road to the Strand Tube Station.

"Excuse me, Miss," said Teal, catching her up at the entrance to the subway.

It was not the first time she had been spoken to by a stranger, and she would have hurried on; but something in the businesslike tone of his address stopped her, and she looked round.

She saw a big red-faced sleepy-eyed man of considerable girth wearing a rather noisy tweed suit, with a soft felt hat tilted to the back of his head.

"I am Inspector Teal, of Scotland Yard," said the same, "and you might be able to help me a lot, Miss Marlowe, if you'd just step into that tea den with me and have a chat."

Over a cup of tea, at his request, she repeated the history of her association with Stenning and Vanney, in much the same way as she had told it to Vanney himself. Mr Teal appeared to doze during the recital, but as soon as she had finished he was ready with a question.

"How did you get your job at Vanney's?"

"Mr Vanney wrote to me off his own bat. He knew Mr Stenning, and he says that Mr Stenning had often spoken of me."

"What were you doing before that?"

"Nothing. Father was always pretty well off, and he left me everything he had."

"And something went wrong?"

She nodded.

"Most of the money was in Claravox Gramophones. Father put all his eggs in that basket just before he died. The shares were at about 450, but the promised dividends were colossal." She smiled ruefully. "If you remember, the fraud was shown up two years ago, when Stenning died and the company went smash."

"I remember," said Teal. "Claravox Gramophones was one of Stenning's companies. I guess that man must have held the dud company record for this country."

He drank some tea, and cogitated with his eyes closed; and his next query was a surprising one.

"Does the Saint ever make love to you?"

"No," she replied at once, and wondered how she came to lie so spontaneously.

Teal, however, seemed to have been anticipating that answer.

"He wouldn't," he said. "The Saint's a clean crook. But what about Vanney?"

"I've only seen him once, and then he asked me to have dinner with him."

"Is that so?" Teal opened one eye. "Did you go?"

She shook her head.

"It was only the other day. I put him off, and he hasn't mentioned it since."

With that he seemed to have come to the end of his intended interrogation, and she took advantage of his silence to make an inquiry of her own.

"What did you mean when you said that the Saint was a clean crook?" she asked.

"Well," said Mr Teal judiciously, "he's a crook, all right—you'll know that if you've ever read a newspaper. He doesn't make any bones about it. The reason he's at large is because on the few occasions when he's left any evidence behind him that could be used in court, the injured parties have refused to kick. The Saint has a way of knowing too much about them. He went off the rails once, and then squared that up by stopping a war, confound him; and at the moment anyone who said he was not a respectable citizen could be soaked with good and heavy damages for slander. To give the devil his due, most of the men he's trodden on have been pretty undesirable specimens, but that doesn't make him an honest man."

"Why do you think he does it?"

"The Lord knows," said Teal wearily. "All I can tell you is that if I've got any grey hairs, he gave them to me. Of course he's made plenty of money out of it—the men he's gone after have usually had a good deal of boodle on them, a lot of which seems to drift eventually into the Saint's own bank balance."

She was astonished at this revelation.

"Then why does he work at Vanney's?"

"If you could answer that question, Miss Marlowe," said Teal, "you'd save my mind a lot of hard wear. All I know is that I smell trouble wherever the Saint's hanging around."

The implication did not make itself plain to her at once; but when she had grasped it, she stopped with her cup half way to her lips, and stared.

"Do you mean Vanney's isn't straight?" she asked.

"I've a good idea," said Teal, "that Vanney's is one of the crookedest shows in the history of commerce. If Vanney's is straight, I'm going to ask the Commissioner to call in all the rulers in Scotland Yard, and supply the clerical department with corkscrews."

He gazed at her in his drowsily placid way while she digested this startling piece of information, and his air of heavy-lidded weariness did not prevent him taking in every detail of her appearance. She was pretty—Mr Teal, who by no stretch of imagination could have been called a connoisseur of feminine beauty, would have been blind if he had not recognised that fact. Nice eyes and mouth. A trim figure, and well-chosen clothes that suited her to perfection. Mr

Teal thought that there would have been some excuse for the Saint, anyway.

He thought of the Saint. The Saint, with his gay devil-may-care face, his dancing blue eyes and reckless smile, would have found no difficulty in waltzing into any woman's heart. True, Teal knew that the Saint was theoretically attached to a certain Patricia Holm; but Teal had never thought that the Saint was a man to confuse fidelity with fun. Maybe there would have been some excuse for Pamela Marlowe.

"You seem to be rather interested in Templar," murmured Mr Teal. "Are you in love with him, by any chance?"

"No," she replied promptly. "Whatever made you ask that?"

"It just occurred to me," said the detective vaguely.

After a few minutes' more desultory conversation he left her.

Those were turbulent days for her under their superficial calm, and she was beginning to feel the strain. Consequently it was a most welcome relief for her when, after dinner, the girl who occupied the next room in the house where she lived came in and suggested a visit to the movies.

They went by bus to Piccadilly, and walked up Regent Street.

As they passed the back entrance of the Piccadilly Hotel, two men in evening dress came out, and one of them hailed a passing taxi. They stepped in and were driven away.

One of the men she had recognised at once, for it was none other than Simon Templar. His companion had been a big heavy-featured man with a small military moustache, whose face seemed curiously familiar.

It required some minutes of concentration before she could place him, but when she had done so her involuntary gasp of amazement startled her companion.

It was not surprising that she had not been able to identify him at once, for the last time she had seen him he had been wearing a purple uniform decorated with buttons and braid of gold, and he answered to the name of George.

## VI

Pamela walked on with her brain in a ferment. She felt strangely disinclined to embark on a lengthy explanation of what had startled her, and the other girl, after some futile attempts to draw her, relapsed into an offended silence.

It seemed that she was destined to become more and more lost each day in the network of mystery of which Vanney's was the centre, and no added complication seemed to lead nearer to a solution.

What was the closely guarded secret of Vanney's, and what part was Simon Templar playing in it? Everything she had seen or heard pointed to the secret being a sinister one; and yet, however suspicious a character Simon Templar might be, he had one of the least sinister personalities that she had ever met. But why did so many irregular things mark the conduct of the office which was under his supervision, and why, to cap it all, had he been dining at the Piccadilly with the porter—George?

Pamela's brain seethed with unanswerable questions for the rest of the evening, and the entertainment, which should have been a means of forgetting the perplexities which had worried her for days, was spoilt for her; but her adventures were not yet finished for that night.

She got home to find a note on the hall table informing her that a man had rung her up twice while she had been out. While she was reading it, the telephone bell rang again.

She went to the instrument with an instinctive certainty that the call was for her, and she was right.

"I am speaking for Mr Tombs," said a masculine voice. "An important deal has been concluded this evening, and since the other party is leaving for the Continent early tomorrow morning, Mr Tombs wishes you to come round at once and make out the necessary papers."

"But——"

"Mr Tombs asks me to say that he is very sorry to trouble you at this hour, but he must ask you to come immediately. A closed car is waiting for you at the corner of the street. Please come at once."

Before she could reply, a click from the receiver told her that the man at the other end of the line had rung off.

Pamela put the telephone down slowly, biting her lip. In one sense there was nothing very extraordinary about the request. The circumstances were plausible, and it was not unusual for important business negotiations to be concluded over dinner, although such a thing had never happened before while she had been at Vanney's. And Chief Inspector Teal had said that Simon Templar was a clean crook. She might easily have left without further deliberation, but she did not.

There were one or two things which she could not understand, and they made her pause. First, the message which awaited her when she got in told her that she had been called at 9.30 and at 10.30. If it was so important that papers should be made out without delay, would they have waited so long for her? Another stenographer should have been obtainable; and, besides, the Saint was perfectly capable of working the typewriter efficiently himself—she had seen him do so more than once. Secondly, when she had last seen him, he had been with George; and whatever the reason for that intimacy, it was not likely that the janitor would be present when business was being discussed. And then, what was the reason for the car? Apparently it had been sent much earlier in the evening, so that its arrival would coincide with the first attempt to get her on the telephone, and yet there was no reason for Simon Templar to have suspected a sudden dearth of taxis in Kensington. Finally, why had he not spoken to her himself?

Making up her mind, she picked up the telephone book and found Templar's number. She called it, and his voice answered her almost immediately.

"Yes?"

"It's Pamela speaking, Mr Templar. Did you ring up just now?"

"Certainly not," said the Saint.

She told him about the message she had received, and he whistled.

"You can take it from me, it was a fake," he said. "I don't know who sent it, but I'll try to find out. You say a car is supposed to be waiting for you at the corner?"

"Yes."

"Is it still there?"

"I'll go and see."

Her room was in the front, on the first floor, and she ran quickly up the stairs. Crossing to the window, she looked down, disturbing the curtains as little as possible. There was a car drawn up by the kerb two doors away—a racy-looking saloon.

"It's still there," she said, returning to the telephone.

"Good," said Simon briskly. "Now, you run along off to bed, Pamela, old dear, and forget it. And if you get any more messages like that, give yourself the benefit of the doubt and don't make a move until you've confirmed them. Incidentally, I don't know how you go to the office in the mornings, but I should stick to the tube or bus if I were you. Funny things have happened to taxis before now. Good night, child."

She went upstairs, but she did not undress at once. Instead, she put on a heavy coat, opened the window a little at the bottom, and sat down beside it with a book. She read inattentively, with one eye on the car in the street below.

Ten minutes later, a sports coupé droned round into the street, passed the waiting car, and pulled in to the pavement directly under her window. A man stepped out, and stood for a moment lighting a cigarette, and she recognised the Saint.

He sauntered up to the other car and opened the door.

"Marmaduke," said the Saint clearly, "you're a bad boy. Go right home, and don't do it again."

The driver's reply was inaudible, but she heard Simon speak again, and there was a hard metallic note in his voice.

"You lie," said the Saint. "You are afraid of me, because you know that if I get annoyed there isn't anything in the world that'll stop me showing it—unpleasantly. Do what you're told."

There was a muttered colloquy which she couldn't hear, and then Simon closed the door and stepped back.

He watched the saloon out of sight, and then walked back to his own car.

He stood beside it, scanning the windows above him, and Pamela leaned out.

"It's all right, old darling," called the Saint cheerfully. "You won't be disturbed again. Good night, for the second time."

He climbed into his car and drove off, and she closed the window.

The next morning he seemed to have forgotten the incident, and when she thanked him for disposing of the mysterious driver he appeared to have to concentrate intensely before he could place the reference.

"Oh, that!" he said at length. "Do you know you've broken a record?"

She showed her bewilderment, and he smiled.

"If I put you in a book," he said, "you'd be the first heroine in the history of thick-ear fiction who has not cantered blithely into the first trap that was set for her. Tell me how you did it."

She told him, ending up with the information that she had seen him leaving the Piccadilly with George, but he did not seem at all upset by this discovery.

"George and I are great friends," he said airily. "But perhaps you didn't know that I was a practical Socialist?"

"But he was in evening dress!"

Simon raised his eyebrows.

"Why not?" he demanded. "The only difference was that mine was paid for, whereas so far George has only been able to cough up the first instalment on his. The hire-purchase system is really a fine gift to democracy. George will own that suit in three years, and the dicky and cuffs will be his very own in a couple of months. Who are we to discourage George's efforts to better himself?"

Presently he asked:

"Have you seen Teal lately?"

"He spoke to me in the street the other day, when I was going home."

"What did he talk about?"

"Nothing in particular," she said. "He told me one or two things about you."

"I call myself something in particular," said the Saint, brightening, "even if you don't. What did he say?"

"Oh, things."

Simon looked at her.

"And do you wish to give notice?" he asked.

"I don't think so."

"Good," said the Saint. "For those kind words I'll be more gentle with Teal when I see him again."

That afternoon there was a caller, and Simon frowned thoughtfully over the cheaply printed card which the clerk brought in. "Mr Harold Garrot," it said.

He went through to the waiting-room, and a sallow lantern-jawed man, with shaggy eyebrows and a blue chin, slowly uncoiled his six feet six inches of lanky length from a chair.

"Sit down, Harry," said the Saint affably, "and shoot us the dope in your own time. Also, you might whisper the important passages, because the walls in this office are very thin."

Long Harry sat down, and put his hands on his knees.

"Mr Templar," he said, "you know who I'm looking for."

"I don't," said the Saint.

"Connell," explained Harry tersely.

Simon frowned.

"Is there a catch in this?" he demanded. "Am I supposed to say: 'Who is Connell?'—whereupon you say: 'Connellady eat asparagus without dripping the melted butter down her neck?'—or something soft like that? Because if so I'll buy it—but let's get it over quick."

Long Harry leaned forward.

"Templar," he said, "you know me, and I know you, and we both know Connell. But did you know that I'd just come out of stir?"

"I read in the papers a couple of years ago that you'd just gone in," said the Saint. "How's the old place looking?"

But Harry was not feeling conversational.

"Connell put me there," he said. "I never did that Bayswater job. Connell shopped me, and I'm looking for Connell."

Simon rose.

"Well," he said briefly, "I'm afraid I can't help you. Nobody's seen Connell for two years. Good afternoon."

He held out his hand, but Long Harry ignored it.

"Next time you see Connell," said Mr Garrot, rising, "you can tell him I'm laying for him."

"Good afternoon," said the Saint again, and opened the door. "Call in any time you're passing, but don't stay long."

He returned to his desk with a greater feeling of enthusiasm for his job than he had felt for several days, for the return of Long Harry seemed to him to presage the beginning of troublous times for the firm of Vanney's Ltd; and, in Simon Templar's opinion, that was all to the good.

## VII

"Talking of disappearances, Mr Teal," said Sergeant Barrow— "I've been thinking."

Chief Inspector Teal fixed his subordinate with a basilisk eye.

"Not again?" he drawled with heavy sarcasm.

"What's more," said Barrow, "I've been talking to Jones and the Records Office, and I've got on to something that might interest you."

Teal waited.

"About the time that Connell disappeared," said Barrow earnestly, "Red Mulligan also vanished. The last thing we heard of Red, he was supposed to be dying of pleurisy. Red was the man who worked the Finchley Bank job. He and Long Harry used to run together, and they shared a room in Deptford. Connell made a trio when it suited him. Well, Connell disappears, and a few days after that we stop hearing anything about Red. I went down to

Deptford and made a few inquiries, but all they could tell me was that Harry gave out a story that Red had got better and gone out to Australia. Since when, nobody's seen or heard of him. Now, does a man who's been given up for dead get better as quickly as that, and would he jump right off his bed into a steamer, and shoot off without saying a word to anyone? It's not as if there was anything against him at that time—he had a clean sheet."

Teal nodded.

"That's worth thinking about," he conceded.

But it was not Inspector Teal's practice to make his thought processes public, and he switched off almost immediately on to a new line.

"Go out into the wide world, Barrow," he said, "and find me an Australian."

After some search an Australian was found, and Teal took him out, bought him beer, and invited a geography lesson. Then he bought the Australian more beer, and left him.

He went to Vanney's, and the Saint saw him at once.

"Mr Vanney is engaged," said Simon, "but all my time is yours. What can I do for you today?"

"I'm looking for a man named Connell," said Teal.

"Everybody seems to be doing it," sighed the Saint. "Only yesterday we had a man in looking for him."

"Long Harry?" asked Teal, and Simon nodded.

"It's surprising how popular a man can become all of a sudden."

"Connell's wanted for the Battersea murder," said Teal.

Clearly the Saint was surprised at this item of news, but his surprise did not make him any more helpful.

"Connell is the mystery man of the twentieth century," he said. "Sorry, Teal, but you've come to the wrong shop. We broke off our partnership with Maskelyne's years ago."

"There's another thing," said Teal. "We've got a man in for a bit of work in Curzon Street, and he's made a confession that might put us on to a man we've been looking for for years. I won't go into details, but I will tell you that I'm temporarily stuck, and you might be able to help me."

"Anything within reason, Claud Eustace," said the Saint.

Teal winced.

"The point is," he said, "that this case links up with one in Australia. The trouble is, we haven't got the name of the man who was robbed, and I'm wondering if Mr Vanney could save me the trouble of cabling out to Australia for it. I believe he spent some years in Melbourne."

"That is so."

"Then he might know the name. He's one of the richest men in Melbourne, and I'm told he's got the swellest house in the place. The man I've got couldn't remember the name, but he thinks it began with an 'S'. He remembers that it's a big white stone building at the top of Collins Street, about five minutes from Brighton Beach. The family used to dash down to the sea for a dip every morning before breakfast, and it was while they were out on one of those early swimming parties that the jewels were taken."

The Saint looked up doubtfully.

"It's some time since Mr Vanney was in Melbourne," he said.

"He couldn't help knowing the place," said Teal persuasively. "Collins Street is one of the big thoroughfares, and everybody knows Brighton Beach, and this man's home was a show feature of the city."

The Saint shrugged.

"I'll ask him," he said, "but I doubt if he can help you. Shall I write and let you know what he says?"

"I can get a reply telegraphed from Melbourne quicker than that," said Teal. "Couldn't you ask him now?"

"I'll see," said the Saint, and went.

He was back in two minutes.

"Mr Vanney is very sorry, but he can't remember the name of the man. He knows the house, of course, but he thinks that the man's name began with an 'M'."

"Thanks," said Teal, and heaved his vast bulk out of the chair. "Sorry to have troubled you."

"Sorry to have been troubled," said Simon Templar genially.

Teal stopped by the door.

"By the way," he said, "why have you gone off your feed lately? Are you in love?"

The Saint smiled appreciatively.

"That was clever of you, Teal," he admitted. "I didn't find out till a couple of days ago that you were watching the place. No, I don't have luncheon these days."

"Why?" asked Teal.

"Because," said the Saint fluently, "it is Lent. In Lent, I give up luncheon, lumbago, lion-hunting, and liquorice."

"I," said Teal, "give up lorgnettes, leeks, leprosy, lynching, lamentation, lavender, and life preservers."

It was the first time for many months that Mr Teal had held his own with the Saint in a verbal encounter, and that, in the auspicious circumstances, put him in very good humour.

He returned to Scotland Yard, and sent again for Sergeant Barrow.

"Did you look out all the papers connected with the Stenning case, as I told you?" he asked.

Barrow pointed to a bundle recently placed on Teal's desk, but Teal preferred to cut his work down to a minimum. If he had told the Saint that he gave up labour throughout the year, irrespective of Lent, whenever possible, he would have been very near the truth.

He leaned back, clasped his hands in an attitude of prayer, closed his eyes, and said:

"Have you studied the case?"

Sergeant Barrow intimated that he had done so.

"Tell me about it," said Teal.

Stenning's death had caused a considerable sensation at the time. His name was well known in the City, and the derogatory rumours which circulated persistently among the cognoscenti were not printed in the newspapers, which were restrained by the law of libel, and therefore did not reach the majority of the public. It was not until after Stenning's death that all the facts of his nefarious career were made public, and then there was a panic among the small investors.

Stenning was clever. For years he had sailed perilously near the wind, and had found it a profitable procedure. But with the passing of time, the encouraging recollection of past successes, and the temptation to increase his income still further by risking sailing manœuvres closer and closer to the breeze, had led him to form companies of increasing instability. He had ended up by organising and directing a project which for the first time in his career was flagrantly fraudulent. The result had been to raise his conjectured profits to the seven-figure mark, although at his death his estate was valued at no more than £10,000.

"No man," said Sergeant Barrow, "ever died at a more convenient time."

Stenning had passed over with all his sins when his last and most ambitious scheme was tottering on the dizzy pinnacle of success. Ultimate discovery was inevitable—though whether Stenning realised that, and was banking on being able to leave the country before a warrant was issued for his arrest, would never be known. Certainly, drunk with confidence, he had ended up by overreaching himself; but then he had died. As Sergeant Barrow remarked, he couldn't have timed his death for a more suitable moment.

One night he had set out from London in an open car, accompanied only by his chauffeur, to keep a business appointment at Bristol. According to the evidence at the inquest, the chauffeur, Arthur Wylie, had attempted to take a corner too fast on a lonely stretch of road between Basingstoke and Andover. The car had skidded and overturned. The chauffeur was flung clear, but Stenning had been pinned underneath the wreckage, and before the chauffeur could go to his assistance the car had burst into flames, so that it was impossible to approach it. The car was reduced to a heap of twisted scrap-iron, and of Stenning there remained nothing but a corpse charred beyond recognition, and identified only by a ring, a watch, and a bunch of keys. The chauffeur pleaded inexperience, and it was found that he had only held a driving licence for six months.

A verdict of accidental death was returned, and Stenning was buried in dishonour, for upon his death the full story of all his shady transactions was made public. But of the millions he was reputed to have amassed in the course of his career as a swindler no trace could be discovered.

"That's the story," said Sergeant Barrow. "But what's it got to do with Connell?"

"Nothing, and at the same time everything," answered Mr Teal enigmatically. "And now, if you will listen carefully, I'll tell you a little joke."

Sergeant Barrow produced a smile.

"The joke," said Mr Teal, "is about a man who says that he lived several years in Australia, and who gives Melbourne as his last address. I asked him if he could identify a house at the top of Collins Street, five minutes from Brighton Beach, and I told him how the people who owned the house used to run down to the sea for a bathe before breakfast."

Sergeant Barrow's forehead puckered.

"I'm very sorry, Mr Teal," he said, "but I don't see it."

"Suppose," said Teal dreamily, "that I told you that I'd got a beautiful house in Kensington Gardens overlooking the Embankment. What would you say then?"

"I should say you were a liar, Mr Teal," said Sergeant Barrow diffidently.

Chief Inspector Teal seemed to smile in his sleep.

"I said nothing so insulting," he murmured. "In fact, I said nothing at all. But since the Australian you found gave me his word that Brighton Beach was at least ten miles away from the top of Collins Street, Melbourne, I think I was justified in thinking a lot."

## VIII

"Take a letter," said the Saint. "To the Editor of the *Times*. Sir,— The impudent presumption of the modern employer is a menace to the morals of the community. Stop. The other day, I was applying for the post of secretary to an American business man who is opening a branch in London. Stop. Finding my qualifications and references satisfactory, he then asked me how much I wanted. Stop. 'Four pounds a week,' I said. Stop. 'With pleasure,' he replied. Stop. 'Certainly not,' I retorted. Stop. Can nothing be done about this? Stop. I am, etcetera, Harassed Stenographer. I wonder why they never print my letters?" he added.

"Because," said Pamela Marlowe calmly, "I never send them."

Simon regarded her seriously.

"This is very like insubordination," he said. "However, I suppose you know best. Let's change the subject. Have you got any more complaints to make against the firm?"

"I did remember something the other day," she admitted.

"Let's hear it."

"What did Mr Teal mean by talking about Mr Vanney making childish attempts to kill him?" she asked, and Simon put down his pen and leaned back comfortably.

"Owing to the recent boom in detective fiction," he explained elaborately, "the public have come to regard it as essential that their detectives should lead dangerous lives, in imminent peril of crafty assassination. To meet the popular demand, the proprietors of the leading newspapers have been compelled to organise private squads of thugs, who at intervals attempt the life of a well-known detective and thereby provide headlines for the front page. The detectives, of course, being public servants, take all this in good part; but they do insist on a certain standard of efficiency about the murders, and when the attempt is below par they feel annoyed. Naturally, any self-respecting detective would object to being killed in any of the crude old-fashioned ways."

Pamela Marlowe went back to her table, slammed back the type-writer carriage, rattled in a sheet of paper, and began to pound away with unnecessary violence.

Simon Templar signed a letter with a flourish, blotted it, and flicked it into the tray on his desk. Then he leaned back, lighted a cigarette, and proceeded to smoke meditatively.

"Pamela," he said presently, "you seem to be annoyed."

"I am," she said.

Simon took his feet off the table suddenly and smiled. It has already been mentioned that he had a most engaging smile. He left his chair and came and stood beside her.

"Pamela," he said, holding out his hand, "let's call it a day."

"Very well, Mr Templar," said Pamela, and went on with her work.

Simon looked at the hand she had studiously ignored, sighed, and returned to his desk.

After that he did no more work, and spent his idle moments with his feet on the table, smoking innumerable cigarettes and staring at the ceiling with a frown indicative of furious cerebration.

He had lunch that day with two friends, and the conversation was not particularly inspiring. It was not until the end of the meal that he chose to liven things up.

Then he pushed away his plate, lighted a cigarette, and blew out a long stream of smoke.

"Boys," he said, "we have fortified ourselves with an excellent lunch. Our friend Connell has demonstrated a hidden talent for cheffery which has been a most delightful surprise; and the brandy is on the sideboard in case any of you want bracing up another notch. Help yourselves if you think you need it, because I've got a shock for you."

He paused, inhaling comfortably.

Connell accepted the suggestion, but the other man did not move.

"The first point," said the Saint, settling himself, "is that now is the time for all bad men and blue to realise that this party is liable to break up without notice."

The other two said nothing. Clearly the Saint had only voiced their own thoughts.

"The second point," Simon went on, "is that after all the trouble we've taken, we should go down to history as a set of prize pikers if we beat it now. The boodle should all be in within a week; and if we can only keep our nerve and hang on, we've got a sporting chance of scooping the kitty. The pool isn't as large as it might have been, but that's not our fault. We're being rushed on the last lap, and we've got to make the best of it."

He blew two smoke rings and watched them float upwards.

"Maybe you haven't realised how short our time's getting," he said. "Teal's on to us—that's a cert. He caught us all nicely on the hop the other day over that Melbourne inquiry. I had to let it go through because if I'd tried to stall him off it'd only have made him hotter and it wouldn't have made any difference in the long run. It was only a matter of turning a suspicion into a certainty. Teal knows now that Vanney's a fake, as far as his Australian career is concerned anyway, but that's not a crime in itself. But there are one or two other things."

The Saint stood up. He had taken over the chairmanship of the meeting quite naturally.

"There's been some funny stuff about Connell and Long Harry, and it's new on me. Harry was shopped for busting a house in Bayswater. Anyway, Harry said he was shopped, and he said it in a way that makes me want to believe him. He's just out of Pentonville, and he thinks Connell shopped him, and he's looking for Connell. And Teal told me the other day that Connell was wanted for a job in Battersea. Now, I know Connell didn't do that job. Therefore Connell's been framed, too. Now, what's the point of all this framing business?"

He looked straight at Connell, and Connell growled.

"Harry must have shopped me," he said.

"Get that idea right out of your head, son," advised the Saint. "Teal knew Harry thought you shopped him in Bayswater, and the first thing he'd think of would be that Harry might have tried to return the compliment and shop you. Teal must have had something to make him quite certain that Harry didn't do the Battersea job, or else he'd have had Harry inside in a brace of shakes."

Simon canted up his cigarette between his lips, and set his hands deep in his trouser pockets.

"Even that," he remarked, "is no particular affair of mine. I just put it up to you to think over in your spare time. But the last two points are personal. First of all, this business of trying to bump off Teal has got to stop. I don't know how it was arranged, but Teal said it had been tried, and Teal doesn't bluff that way. I should particularly object to Teal being bumped off. If Teal passed on to his harp, I should have nothing left to live for. Get that. If Teal makes any more complaints of that sort, Simon Templar goes out of this partnership at once."

The other two said nothing, but the Saint had not been expecting a reply. He passed on.

"Finally," he said, "any monkeying about with Miss Marlowe will also stop. I've let you off once, James Arthur Vanney; but I don't know if I made it quite plain then that the next time it happens you will not be let off. That's all."

The bearded man came to his feet slowly.

"Are you running this show by yourself?" he asked.

"At the moment—and in this matter—yes," said the Saint.

James Arthur Vanney turned to the third member of the party.

"And what have you got to say?" he demanded.

"I agree with Templar. It's too dangerous."

The bearded man's fist came down on the table with a crash.

"And I say," he blustered, "that if either of you interfere with my private dealings with that girl, I'll quit the show!"

The third man got to his feet also.

"And if you quit the show," he said quietly, "I might have a little tale to tell Inspector Teal about the mysterious Mr Vanney."

The bearded man looked round, savage-eyed.

"If it comes to telling tales," he said. "I guess I could tell as many as anyone. You wouldn't dare risk it."

Simon flicked his cigarette into the fireplace.

"Nor would you dare risk it, my man," he said smoothly. "Think it over, and while you're thinking just remember that it isn't only old fat Teal you've got to be afraid of. I might get you first."

The Saint's tone was perfectly quiet, but he never took his gaze off the other's face, and the bearded man saw murder in his eyes.

## IX

Mr Teal had discovered long ago that he was the plaything of a peculiar destiny. Whenever he was engaged on a big case, when once the preliminary trifling and ferreting about was done, things had a habit with him of moving with well-oiled precision and alarming swiftness. Mr Teal, in his leisure moments, attributed to this fact his ponderous and somnolent disposition—for, he pointed out, nobody less stolidly constituted could have stood the strain.

It was so with the Vanney case.

There came a day when Mr Teal felt that he had disposed of every detail of the preliminary investigation, and there was nothing left for him to do but to sit down and wait for the other side to make a move which would provide him with a way out of this temporary *impasse*.

He said as much to the Chief Commissioner, Sir Brodie Smethurst, and the Assistant Commissioner, Mr William Kennedy, at a private conference which lasted until the small hours of the morning; and they agreed with him, for the Criminal Investigation Department is jealous of its reputation. Evidence upon which a layman would act without hesitation is sifted and contemplated with a suspicious and cautious eye, for Scotland Yard prefers to bide its time and take no action until the possibility of failure has been brought down to an irreducible minimum. The net is spread, and it is spread so effectively that only a genius could find a way out of it. There have been geniuses in the history of crime, but they are rare, and the police routine is not designed to cope with them.

"I think I've got Vanney's where I want them," said Teal. "If I have, they're safe anyway. I'd rather not risk making a fool of myself and the Department by acting before I've got all the threads in my hands and I can afford to lay a thousand to one on getting my conviction."

"What's their graft at the moment?" asked Kennedy, and Chief Inspector Teal produced several typewritten sheets of paper which he handed over for perusal.

"That's a confidential report from Stanforth and Watson," he said. "Stanforth and Watson are handling a lot of Vanney's business. They'd had their doubts about it for some time, and when I started making inquiries they wanted to chuck it up altogether. I asked them to carry on to help us, and promised them we'd see that everything was all right for them when it came to the showdown. Eventually they agreed. You will find all the particulars here—it's the old bucket-shop game, but done more brilliantly than it's been done for years. Stenning was the last expert we had, and this is in the old tradition. But this time he's come back with some new trimmings on the old game. He's not going after the chickenfeed—the mug punters with a few pounds to throw away here and there. He's got a graft that's specially made up to attract the big men—the men who are nearly as crooked as he is himself. Wads of money have come in to him from every corner of Europe."

"Is it like the Saint to be mixed up with a game like that?" asked Smethurst, and Teal nodded.

"It's just about his mark. The technique may be Stenning, but the basic idea is pure Saint. The only thing that's puzzling me is why the Saint should have bothered to go in with Stenning at all, instead of carrying the whole thing through on his own."

The Chief Commissioner looked up from the report.

"It's very reminiscent of Stenning," he agreed.

Teal nodded.

"It's Stenning to the life," he said.

"He died right on his cue, that man," put in Kennedy.

"He did," said Teal grimly. "It suited some people I could mention—down to the ground. I've got a feeling that if Stenning came to life again it'd mean a lot of trouble for the firm of Vanney."

He left the Commissioner's house at Regent's Park as the clocks were striking three, and drove away in his miniature car towards his own modest lodgings near Victoria.

The grotesqueness of the association of his mammoth bulk with that microscopic automobile had never struck him, but a more practical argument against it was forced upon his notice ten minutes later.

Piccadilly at that hour was almost deserted, and Mr Teal, in defiance of all speed limits, betrayed his satisfaction with the way the Vanney case was going by allowing the lightness of his heart to manifest itself in the heaviness of his foot on the accelerator. He was doing nearly thirtyfive miles an hour when he came level with the Ritz, but even so a big limousine purred up level and passed him effortlessly.

The detective had been guilty of allowing his thoughts to wander, and he was brought rudely back to earth by a sudden vision of the big car steering in to the kerb directly across his front wings.

Faced with the alternative of crashing into the side of the car in front, Teal wrenched the steering round to the left, forgetting that he had no more than two feet of road on that side in which to manœuvre. He realised his mistake as he saw the columns which carry the front of the hotel over the pavement to the edge of the road leaping towards him. He tried to swing the car round again; but it was too late, and in an instant the near front wheel touched the kerb and the steering wheel was wrenched out of his hand. The car piled itself up against the stone wall with a crash.

Shakily, Teal picked himself up out of the road, where the force of the collision had hurled him. By some miracle he was unhurt, though his car was a wreck. The car which had caused the accident was vanishing in the direction of Hyde Park Corner; but the tail light was out, and it was impossible to see the number.

He saw his car removed, with difficulty, to a nearby garage, and went home in a taxi. It was not the first time that an attempt had been made on his life, and he was inclined to take these things philosophically. But on this occasion he was annoyed, for the accident, and the consequent necessary arrangements for the disposal of the ruins, had deprived him of two hours' sleep.

The next morning, however, found him in a good temper; for his escape of the night before seemed to him, by all precedent, to mean that the case was entering on its last hectic stages; and he was almost cordial to the longsuffering Sergeant Barrow.

"I think most of the facts about Vanney's are taped out now," said Teal. "I've made a list of them in chronological order, and the list spells something to me."

He took a small notebook from his waistcoat pocket, marked a place with his thumb, and handed it over.

"Take a look at that."

Sergeant Barrow read the neatly tabulated entry:

*1928 July.*    *Connell and Mulligan disappeared.*
*1928 August.*  *Stenning killed.*
*1929 April.*   *House commissioned for Vanney.*
*1929 June.*    *Vanney arrived from Melbourne, took possession of house, and opened the firm of Vanney.*

"You seem to connect Vanney up with Stenning," remarked Barrow, when he had finished, and Inspector Teal closed his eyes and smiled beatifically.

"I didn't do that," he replied. "Stenning did it himself."

The next development came some hours later.

Teal had returned to his office after dinner, and he was still working at ten o'clock, when a messenger entered.

"There's a question through from C Division," said the man. "Connell's been seen in Soho tonight, and they want to know whether they're to pull him in or tail him, or what."

"Tail him till I arrive," said Teal briskly. "I've got an idea."

He spent twenty minutes in another room, and when he emerged the change in his appearance was amazing. The modern detective does not rely on such crude disguises as false beards. Instead, he pins his faith to the creation of atmosphere. In a certain room at New

Scotland Yard is kept a file of photographs of representative men of different trades, and the minutest details of their habits and characteristics are chronicled.

Teal, suiting his disguise to the framework on which he had to build, had adopted the character of a shady racecourse hanger-on. He changed his sober-blue serge suit for a loud check, hung a massive watch chain across his middle, selected spats, and put them on over a pair of pointed yellowish shoes. On each hand he put a ring, and he fixed a diamond pin in the wrong part of a flashy tie. To his face he did little—a skilful darkening of the eyebrows, a broadening of the face by the insertion in the mouth of rubber pads designed for that purpose, and the attachment of a bristly moustache, was sufficient.

Regretfully he discarded his chewing gum, and put four cigars in a pocket of his waistcoat. He took a bowler hat of the wrong kind, a pair of lemon-coloured gloves, and a silver-knobbed ebony walking-stick, and inspected the ensemble in a full-length mirror. Certainly he was transformed.

At Marlborough Street Police Station he was told that the last report from the men who were keeping track of Connell had placed him in a public house in Shaftesbury Avenue. Arriving there, Teal was met by a detective who told him that their man had moved on to a night club.

The other detective was lounging against the side of a taxicab outside, talking to the driver. The sign he gave Teal would have been unnoticed by a casual observer, but it was enough. Teal went in. He had no difficulty in this, for in his pocket was a collection of membership cards which would have gained him admittance to any night club in London.

He saw his man as soon as he entered the room and established himself in a corner a few tables away.

Sipping the drink which was brought to him, he watched Connell covertly.

Connell was there without any attempt at disguise. Gathered together at his table were three or four men whose appearances were decidedly against them. Two of them Teal recognised. There was the usual leavening of "hostesses".

The party was a hilarious one, and Connell was leading every outburst of merriment. Every drink was on him—one round had hardly arrived before he was shouting for another—and he paid for them from a huge roll of Bank of England notes.

"Drink up!" he shouted at intervals. "I'm on a good thing, and this is my night out."

Teal watched for an hour, and when the party quietened down into a sodden stupor he judged that it was his turn to take a hand.

Taking a pencil and an envelope from his pocket, he scribbled a note: "If you want to make some more easy money, don't say anything to anybody, but follow me out of here."

"Slip that to the gentleman over there," said Teal to a passing waiter, and pointed out Connell.

Connell read the note, and Teal caught his eye. Then the detective rose and walked towards the exit.

Connell caught him up in the street.

"What's this?" he demanded thickly, brandishing the envelope.

Teal took it from him.

"I want you to do a job for me," he said. "There's a place just up the road where we can talk without being disturbed. It's worth a hundred to you. Are you on?"

Connell swayed, and steadied himself.

"Let's hear," he said, and Teal took his arm and walked him up the road.

In half an hour Connell was back at the club calling for more drinks, but Teal did not return. He went back to Scotland Yard, changed into his ordinary clothes, and went home to bed.

He retailed the encounter to Sergeant Barrow the next morning.

"I asked him if he could drive a car, and he said he could. Then I asked him if he could do tricks with one, and he asked me what I meant. I told him I'd got a down on a man and I wanted him messed up in an accidental sort of way. 'This man's given his chauffeur notice,' I said, 'and I can get you the job, references and all, in any name you like. If you're a fool, you'll land yourself for dangerous driving; but if you're clever, maybe you can get away with it and draw the hundred I'm offering.' He was in a boastful mood, and he said he could make a car eat out of his hand and turn somersaults just when he wanted it to. I arranged to meet him at the same place in two days' time with the money, and that was that."

"And?" prompted Sergeant Barrow.

"And," said Mr Teal, with languid satisfaction, "I think that tells me all I want to know about the later history of Mulligan; and how Stenning managed to die so successfully."

Altogether it was a successful twentyfour hours for Mr Teal; for a few minutes later the man he had set to tail Connell home arrived with his report, and another mystery was well on its way to solution.

Mr Teal now had a very good idea why the Saint had been going out to lunch so infrequently, and this further progress increased his conviction that things would shortly commence to hum.

## X

At twelve o'clock on a certain morning, Simon Templar made a decision.

He came to this decision at the end of twentyfour hours' unbroken deliberation. In the office he had been moody, going about his work with his usual efficiency, but with the air of devoting to it no more attention than was absolutely necessary, while all the spare energy of his mind was simultaneously devoted to this far more important thing of which he said nothing. When he was not working, he sat back in his chair, scowling darkly about him.

Pamela Marlowe diagnosed these symptoms as the proof of a misspent night before; but in this she was wrong, for the night before did not occur until the night after. The Saint had gone back to the luxuriously converted garage in Upper Berkeley Mews where he made his home, and had gone to bed before midnight like a good boy.

The decision was finally made at twelve o'clock, and with the removal of uncertainty and the arrival of a definite plan of campaign he brightened perceptibly. His pencil went flying across the room into a corner, the blotting-paper was screwed up into a ball and hurled into the wastepaper basket with the gesture of a challenger throwing down the gauntlet, and his feet returned to their usual position on top of the desk.

"I've got it," he said triumphantly.

"Badly, I should say," agreed Pamela, but he refused to be suppressed.

"Since lunchtime yesterday," he explained solemnly, "I have been tormented by visions of helpless orphans struggling to make their way in the world, with no mother to spank them and no father to borrow fivers from. I think something ought to be done about it. Don't you?"

"Are you going to start an orphanage?" she asked.

The Saint stroked his chin.

"Not exactly," he replied gravely. "I'm starting a fund for distressed orphans, and the fund will be used to help deserving cases to end their days in the luxury to which the hardships of their early years have entitled them. I am an orphan," he added absently.

Clearly he was bursting with some big scheme, but he was too intent upon it to waste time elaborating any more fantastic explanations.

He plumped down in his chair, and rang the bell marked "Secretary".

"Take a letter," he said. "This is to Rolands and Battersby, 240 Threadneedle Street. Dear Sirs,—With reference to your advertisement of a thousand-ton ocean-going motor-cruiser, in the current issue of *Yachting*, I'll buy the darned thing at the price mentioned. Paragraph. I understand that the said hooker is at present lying in Southampton Water. Stop. You will kindly rake up a crew, shove them on board, and tell them to shoot the old tub along to Gravesend. Stop. This must be done immediately, as I am likely to be leaving on short notice. Stop. Communicate these instructions to Southampton by telephone, and drum it into the fat heads of the big stiffs at the other end of the line that the barnacled barge aforesaid has got to arrive at Gravesend within fortyeight hours of your receipt of this letter. Yours faithfully. Turn that into respectable business English, and type it on plain paper. Vanney's," he said, "will shortly know me no more. Observe my tears."

"Are you serious?" she asked.

"I was never more serious in my life," answered the Saint.

"You're leaving Vanney's?"

The Saint smiled.

"Certainly there's going to be a break in the partnership," he said. "But whether I shall leave Vanney's or Vanney's will leave me remains to be seen."

Business had been getting brisker every day, and that afternoon established a new record. Simon spent the whole of his time in a whirl of letters, telegrams, and telephone conversations, and he had no leisure in which to give vent to the high spirits which otherwise he would have enjoyed indulging.

He was not sorry to leave the office that night, for work was a thing in which he was accustomed to indulge spasmodically, and with the sole object of reaping sufficient profit from it to render further work unnecessary for a considerable period.

With a number of late nights behind him, and the prospect of tiring days ahead, he had intended to go to bed early that night; but unfortunately for that plan, when he was half undressed, he was smitten with an idea. With the Saint, to conceive an idea and to put it into execution were things so closely consecutive as to be almost simultaneous. He sighed, dressed again, and went out.

The next morning, however, he showed no trace of tiredness as he ran up the stairs to the office.

He was always the first to arrive, as only Vanney and himself and one other man held keys, and the other two were invariably late. He was feeling cheerful that morning, as he let himself in, but the gay humming died swiftly on his lips as he endeavoured to extract the key from the lock.

He twisted, pulled, and wrenched, and eventually it came away. Then he looked at the lock and discovered the reason for the jam. It was a Yale, and it took him no more than ten seconds' expert investigation to see and appreciate how neatly it had been broken.

He went quickly through the offices—waiting-room, clerks' room, and his own room. The communicating doors were all open. He might have left them like that himself, but one door was open which he had never by any chance forgotten to close, and that was the door between his own office and the room marked "Private".

He passed quickly through, and what he saw made him pull up suddenly with his face gone strangely stern.

Facing him, on either side of the fireplace, were two tall cupboards, which, as has been mentioned, were kept locked. Presumably they were used for storing the private files of the company. But since nobody except himself and his partners ever entered the room, the question was never a subject for curiosity and comment. Now both the cupboards had been roughly broken open, and the doors sagged wide, showing their interiors.

One was empty. The intruder, whoever he was, had drawn blank with his first guess. The other was also empty; but instead of the wooden back which one might have expected to see there was clearly visible the raw brick work of the wall, and this had been broken away so that there was a large gap through which a man could easily pass. On the other side of this gap was a curtain, which had been drawn aside, and through the hole in the wall could be seen a room.

The Saint stood still for a long time. Then he took out his cigarette-case, and very slowly and calmly selected and lighted a cigarette. With this in his mouth he strolled forward, pushed through the doors of the right-hand cupboard, ducked through the aperture in the wall, and came out into the room beyond. It was furnished as

a sitting-room, with a safe in one corner and a writing-desk in another. The safe had been smashed by an expert, and its heavy door
stood wide open—a battered and drunken-looking apology for a
door. Papers were strewn about the floor. The writing-desk was in
a similar state of disrepair; every drawer had been forced, and the
contents were scattered over it, around it, and across the carpet.

   After what he had already seen, these catastrophes were of minor
importance, and even the litter failed to exasperate his tidy instincts.
Moving very slowly and deliberately, he examined the rest of the
flat, and found that no part of it which might constitute a hiding-
place had been overlooked.

   The Saint smiled faintly, but it was not because he was amused.

   He went back into Vanney's office, pulled the cupboard doors to,
and returned to his own room, closing the door marked "Private"
carefully behind him.

   When Pamela Marlowe arrived he was comfortably blowing
smoke rings, and no one would have known from his expression what
a jar he had received.

   She sat down, and it was some time before he became aware that
she was expecting him to do something. He pulled himself together
with an effort.

   "Oh, yes, the letters," he murmured, and swept the pile before him
neatly into a drawer. "I've already opened those, and there's nothing
to attend to yet."

   He played a tattoo on the desk with a pencil.

   "By the way," he said casually, "I'm giving you a week's notice,
though the necessity for your services may cease to exist before
then."

   It was some moments before she could recover from her surprise.

   "Why?" she stammered. "Isn't my work satisfactory?"

   "Perfectly, sweetheart," he said. "But the firm you work for isn't.
Later on in the day I shall be giving myself notice, so you needn't
think you are the only victim. You will receive three months' salary
in lieu of however much longer notice you thought you were entitled to, and a further three months' salary instead of a reference.
The procedure may seem strange to you, but it is dictated by my
wishes for your welfare. You could have a reference if you wanted
one, but it would be quite useless. The money I spoke of has already
been paid into your bank account, and you will receive confirmation of that from them as soon as the cheque has been passed
through."

"But surely," said Pamela blankly, "six months' salary isn't necessary in lieu of notice and a reference?"

"The firm of Vanney," answered the Saint, "although eccentric to the point of being crooked, has a reputation for generosity to maintain. I have just started to give it that reputation, and you are the first beneficiary."

She hesitated.

"It's very kind of you," she said at length. "But since the money has already been paid over, you must have known that this was going to happen."

"I did," he replied. "But I wasn't sure exactly when. I discovered this morning that it was going to happen today."

Pamela looked straight at him.

"Simon," she said, "since I'm leaving Vanney's, and this looks like being the last eccentricity I shall have to puzzle over, is it any use asking you to give me the real reason for it?"

The Saint stood up. He was quite serious.

"I'm sorry," he said. "I've stopped playing the fool from this moment. So I'll just say that it's impossible to answer your question today. Tomorrow, perhaps. . . ."

The last words were spoken almost in a whisper, and he was standing quite still with his head bent slightly forward, as though listening.

"One moment," he said, and went quickly into Vanney's office.

"George," said the Saint quickly, to the porter, "yours not to reason why, yours but to promptly fly. In English, pull out of here right away. You also, my king beaver"—this to Vanney. "Go away and sit down and open your hearts to each other. And wait till I come back—it will be within two hours."

He returned to his own office, taking no notice of Pamela; jerked his hat down from the rack, and went out.

A taxi took him to Upper Berkeley Mews. It was there that Teal found him an hour later. There was a half-filled suitcase on the table, and the Saint, having admitted the detective, returned unconcernedly to the task of trying to close the lid of a trunk that was already crammed to bursting point. A selection of clothes was laid out on the bed, and every chair in the room was similarly loaded.

Teal surveyed the disorder thoughtfully.

"Where are you going, Saint?" he inquired.

"Where am I going, old dear? Well, that isn't decided yet. I may be going abroad, or I may not—it just depends how things turn out."

## XI

Teal did not seem surprised.

"That's what I came to see you about," he remarked. "I suppose there's no chance of your putting in a bit of King's Evidence?"

"Teal," said the Saint, "surely you know me better than that!"

The detective sighed.

"Unfortunately, I do," he said. "But I was told to try it."

He picked up his hat.

"There are some men who say 'No'," he observed, "and you wonder whether they mean 'Yes'. You don't say yes or no, but one always knows what you mean. Sorry to have troubled you."

"The last man who said that to me," remarked the Saint reminiscently, "is one of the only two possible starters for the Great Burglary Sweepstakes. Tell me, do you boys ever indulge in what you might call judicially sanctioned crime?"

"Not that I know of."

"I just wondered," said the Saint. "Now I know. It must have been Harry."

Teal put down his hat again. If he had not been so obviously incapable of such contortions, one would have said that he pricked up his ears.

"Harry?" he repeated.

"The same. But if you think you're going to get anything out of me before you've got me in the dock, you may have another guess free. Good morning, Claud—and don't forget to close the door as you go out."

Obediently, Teal went to the door.

"By the way," he said from the threshold, "you were working late at the office last night, Saint."

"I was," said Simon, folding a dinner-jacket. "What about it?"

"I made some inquiries, and I found that the rule in those offices is that everyone must be out of them by eight o'clock."

"True," said the Saint. "But since Mr Vanney owns not only the offices, but the whole block of flats as well, and since he made that rule, I think one may say that he and his staff are allowed to break it. Goodbye."

"See you again soon," said Teal, and went.

The two hours which the gentlemen known as George and the King Beaver had been told to wait had expired to the minute when

Simon Templar returned. He knew that he had been followed from Upper Berkeley Mews back to the office, but he was not bothering about such trifling troubles.

He walked quickly down the corridor and turned into his own room.

It was empty.

With a grim foreboding, the Saint swung round on his heel and flung open the door leading into the clerks' room.

"Anybody seen or heard of Miss Marlowe?" he observed.

They had not.

"You're an idle pair, and you know it," Simon rapped back. "Don't waste your breath telling me you were so busy working you couldn't hear anything, because I shan't believe it. She couldn't have left the office without your hearing the door close. Have you heard her go out?"

They had not.

"Right," said the Saint violently, and closed the door with a contrasting gentleness.

He went through into Vanney's room, closing the door behind him, passed through the cupboard and the wall beyond, and entered the flat. There was only one man there.

"Stenning," said the Saint, "I want to know where Pamela Marlowe is, and I want to know it quick!"

"Miss Marlowe?" repeated the big man blankly.

"You heard me the first time," snapped the Saint.

"I don't know anything about her."

Simon put his hands in his pockets.

"You're a liar and a dog, Stenning, my pal," he said. "But I'll settle that account later. Where's your partner in crime?"

The Saint looked round the room.

"He was here when I left you," he said. "He can't have gone without your knowing—unless you weren't here yourself. Which is it?"

Stenning rose.

"I left him," he said.

"I told you to stay here."

"And I chose to leave. Have you got anything to say?"

"A mouthful," said the Saint, "but that'll wait. Where did you go?"

"I went out to buy a bottle of whisky, if you want to know."

Simon's glance fell on the table.

"I see. Well, we'll come to that in due course. I'm only putting it off because I think that when I've finished my interview with you, you'll be more disposed to tell me all the things I want to know about Connell."

He flung some papers on the table.

"Take a look at those," he said.

Stenning looked.

"A cheque for twenty thousand pounds, which only needs your signature to make it worth that amount, payable to Miss Pamela Marlowe. That is the sum of twelve thousand pounds which you swindled off her father, plus a sum of interest which, I grant you, is extortionate, but which you will pay all the same. A receipt for that sum, signed by Miss Marlowe. I know it'll pass in a court of law, because I forged the signature myself. You may keep it as a souvenir. Also, there's a cheque for fifty thousand pounds, payable to myself, for which I am afraid I omitted to provide a receipt. I'll address it to you on Dartmoor, if you think you'd like something to remember me by."

Stenning's mouth twisted.

"And how do you think you're going to make me sign?"

"Moral persuasion," said the Saint. "Reinforced, if necessary, by physical. Take your pen and follow the dotted lines."

Stenning laughed.

"You're mad," he said.

"Absolutely," agreed the Saint cordially. "Sign, please."

Stenning sneered.

"I refuse."

"Right," said the Saint. "If you maintain your refusal, I shall be compelled to inflict divers unpleasant forms of physical violence on your person. But before I start I'll tell you something. Anything I can do to you may not make you sign. But if my methods of persuasion fail to convince you, I have one argument up my sleeve. Do what you're told, and I'll fade out of the picture and say nothing. Without my assistance the firm of Vanney will probably be seriously handicapped, but I can't help that. I'll get out, and nothing will be said. But don't sign, and the firm of Vanney will be shown up within an hour. Teal's on to you already, but if he's got to make his own way he can't get going in time to stop your getaway—if you're quick enough. But if I help him, there'll be a nasty cold cell waiting for you, Stenning."

Stenning sat down. He seemed to be enjoying the joke.

"Templar," he said, "that one's too old for me. I know the game as well as you do, and I tell you it won't work. There are two things to stop you squealing. One is that if you squeal you'll be in the same boat with the rest of us. The other is that even if you squeal, that won't make me sign."

"Granted," said the Saint. "There are two answers to that. One is that I planned this little meeting, and everything is plotted out on my timetable to the last minute. Within one hour Teal could have all the evidence he needs, and I can be away and out on the high seas. Can you say the same?"

Stenning made no answer.

"The second," said the Saint, "is that even if putting you away for at least ten years' penal servitude won't make you pay Miss Marlowe back that money, it'll be the least I can do for her by way of compensation. I'll do it cheerfully—don't make any mistake about that, Beautiful."

The other showed his teeth.

"You rat!" he snarled.

"Your name," said the Saint calmly, "is Mug. It is my distressing duty to have to tell you that you've been had. Your leg has been pulled to such an extent that if you wanted to pose for your portrait with one foot in the grave and the other kicking the cobwebs off the roof of the Chrysler Building, it would have to be a damned deep grave." The Saint smiled with a beautifully cherubic magnificence.

Stenning sat quite still.

"You seem," said the Saint, "to have thought that I'd change my habits for your especial benefit. And that was your gravest error. It wasn't so very long ago, when I was travelling round the wilds of South America, that I met Arthur Wylie. A good soul, but talkative when he had absorbed the best part of a bottle of whisky. That's how I learnt all about your fake death. Wylie told me how Connell and Long Harry raked up Red Mulligan for you—who, most fortunately for your purposes, had just decided to die, and who, still more considerately, had contrived to end up his useless days with much the same build as yourself. I came back with your dossiers all locked up in the trunk marked 'Not Wanted On Voyage'—and then you had to let me in. And I know everything that's happened in this firm since I joined it. Long Harry's sphere of usefulness passed over, but he was dangerous. He didn't know much, but he might have guessed a lot. You framed him for a job in Bayswater, but it wasn't your fault that the man didn't die and so put Harry out of the way for ever. Connell stayed in the partnership, but he was always a danger. Because he's a mug, it took him some time to realise how important he was. But you know as well as I do that he was starting to realise that he held the whip hand; and what's more, he had started to put the screw on, feeling his way. You disposed of that—by fixing him for a job in Battersea. That time you made no mistake about the murder. After that, I expect you felt safer, because if Connell started to get any more uppish you would have a very good way of putting him back in his place."

Stenning remained motionless in his chair, hunched up. His face had gone pale; and in that set pallid mask his eyes glowed with hate. The Saint, lounging against the table, went on speaking in the same calm level tones.

"You were clever," he admitted. "You even realised that since Harry was out and was known to be looking for Connell, Harry might be pulled in by mistake for the Battersea job. Knowing your man, you sent Harry money, and, as you expected, he got very tight on it, and was arrested, thereby establishing his alibi beyond all dispute. In fact, the whole show was a really brilliant piece of work, but you went off the rails badly when you began to think you were sitting pretty with the Saint playing a hand in the game. Did you really think I'd changed my habits so much, dear heart, as to want to share the profits in any swindle with anyone—particularly with a flop-eared simoleon-toad like you? Now sign!"

"You're a fool!" said Stenning harshly. "Even if you made me sign, I could still stop the cheque."

"You couldn't," said the Saint. "Being a thoughtful sort of bird, I shall take care to put you in a place where you won't have a chance of stopping it until it has been paid."

"And even then," said Stenning, "I could recover the money, because my signature was obtained under duress."

The Saint smiled beatifically.

"You'll have a job proving it," he murmured. "In any case, it won't be necessary, because you're going to sign that cheque voluntarily."

"Am I?"

"You certainly are," said the Saint. "Because if you don't sign it voluntarily, I shall now proceed to beat you up."

Stenning came to his feet again.

"You're going to beat me up, are you?"

"I am," drawled Simon, with a certain enthusiasm. "And it will be no ordinary beating up. I'm an expert in the beating-up game, and I may mention that the mercy of a knockout does not figure in my programme until—oh, well beyond the thirtieth round. It will be painful for you, and I'm afraid your face will be rather crudely damaged; but unfortunately I haven't any more subtle instruments of torture than my fists."

Stenning came round the table, and the Saint, who was unarmed but prepared for a display of armoury, divined the next move in the game before Stenning's hand had reached his hip pocket. The toe of his right shoe caught the big man on the wrist as the automatic came into sight, and the force of the kick was shattering.

The Saint fell to the floor a second after the gun, and his legs, flailing round in a scissors motion, knocked Stenning's feet from under him. Stenning went down with a crash, but Simon was up again in an instant with the automatic in his hand. He slipped it into his hip pocket, and shed his coat as Stenning scrambled up again.

"The show devolves on me now—what?" he murmured. "That wrist of yours won't help you a lot."

The next instant Stenning was upon him.

It was not a pretty fight to watch, nor would any boxing referee have allowed it to continue for more than three seconds. Simon Templar was giving at least three stone away, and he was not prepared to take chances. The encounter lasted nine minutes by the clock, and at the end of that period Stenning went to the floor for the eleventh time and stayed there.

"Up, Jenkins!" encouraged the Saint. "You're not nearly out yet, so it's no good shamming. The only Queensberry rule we haven't broken yet is the one which forbids rolling about on the floor fighting, but if you don't come up again quickly I'll break that rule too."

Stenning came to a sitting position.

"I'll sign," he gasped.

The Saint took him by the collar, yanked him to his feet, and pushed him into a chair.

"Here's your pen, and here are the cheques," he said briskly. "Get on with it, because I'm in a hurry. And mind you don't drip blood all over them, because the bank might ask questions."

## XII

Simon examined the signatures, folded the cheques carefully, and put them in his pocket. His hair was tousled and his shirt torn, but he was breathing quite regularly. He felt ready to begin again at any time, and in spirits he was completely unruffled.

"While I think of it, there's one thing more. Take your pen and write as I dictate. 'I, James Arthur Vanney, formerly known as Stenning, hereby confess——' "

"I refuse! You damned double-crosser——"

"I don't," said the Saint, "want any more unpleasantness. But if you're going to be obstinate——"

He took a step forward, and Stenning, seeing the look on his face, drew a clean sheet of paper hurriedly towards him.

The Saint dictated, and Stenning wrote; and when the confession was completed and signed, the Saint read it through carefully and stowed it away in his wallet.

"Now for Connell," he remarked. "Where is he, Stenning?"

The limp mess at the table buried its pulped face in its hands.

"You may as well know now—he's with Miss Marlowe."

"And where's that?"

"Downstairs. There are vaults under the building that I never told you about. The only way into them is from this flat. I had a private lift put in—I was going to use the cellars to hide in if the police got on to us and there was no time to make a bolt for it. Connell was putting the screw on—he said he must have the girl, and I helped him take her. They're down there now."

Simon took the automatic from his pocket, and thumbed back the safety catch.

"If anything's happened to her," he said, "you're certainly going to collect a bullet, my pet. Where is this lift?"

Stenning gestured weakly towards the wall.

"Press the panel next to that picture," he said.

Simon did so. The panel slipped back a fraction of an inch at his touch, and he waited. For a few moments it seemed as if nothing was going to happen. There was no sound, but then a piece of panelling swung open with a click, and in front of him was a small lift. He stepped in, and the panelling closed behind him automatically.

In the wall of the lift were two switches. He tried one without result, but when he clicked over the other, the lift began to move downwards.

Presently it stopped. In front of him was a gap in the shaft, hardly distinguishable in the darkness. He stepped out, and then he was able to see better.

A tunnel ran to the left and right of him. The paving, walls, and ceiling were of stone, and the passage lost itself in darkness at either end. But a little way down to his right there was a space in the wall from which a faint light came. That must have been a branch tunnel, and since light came from it it seemed as if his search would not have to be a long one. He began to creep towards it, moving as silently as possible over the flags, but he had hardly taken two steps before a low hum from behind him made him swing round. He saw the lift by which he had just descended commencing to move upwards, and for an instant he weighed up in his mind the possibility of reaching it and checking its ascent; but the idea was no sooner formulated than it was discarded. That was Stenning, of course— he should have knocked him out completely, or tied him up—but it was too late to think of that now. For a moment again he thought of retracing his steps and waiting for Stenning to arrive, but before he could figure out the pros and cons of that scheme it was driven out of his head by a scream that shrilled and echoed hollowly down the passage.

He leapt towards the turning from which the light came. Another shorter tunnel stretched before him, dimly lighted by two flickering gas jets. At the end it appeared to open into a room so brightly lighted that at that point the gas jets must have given place to electricity. He could see a chair and the end of a table—nothing else—but it was the only place from which the scream could have come.

Simon Templar was inside the room in a matter of seconds.

Pamela Marlowe was there, and so was Connell. Connell was holding her in his great arms. Pamela was struggling, but she was a child in Connell's terrific embrace. The Saint never took in more than the bare details of the scene. His hand gripped Connell's collar and literally bounced the man off his feet.

"Connell, my lad," said the Saint pleasantly, "that will be all from you."

Connell's fist came up like lightning; but Simon was even quicker, and the big man went sprawling against the wall from a mule-kick of a punch that carried every ounce of the Saint's weight and strength behind it.

Connell reeled, and nearly fell. Then he came catapulting back to reply, like a jack-in-the-box. The Saint sidestepped coolly, and landed an uppercut that started at his knees and travelled skywards with detonating force to impact smashingly on the point of Connell's jaw; and Connell went down like a log.

"The conventional situation at last, Pamela," said the Saint sadly, and he was just in time to catch her with his arm as she staggered.

In those few merry moments he had forgotten everything else, and he was brought back to reality with a jar that sent a stream of cold air whistling down his spine.

The sound was slight—no more than a subdued rattle that told of a lock being turned home. But the Saint heard it and whipped round—a few seconds too late.

What had been an unguarded way out back into the tunnel was now barred by a solid iron gate, and on the other side of the gate was Stenning—Stenning leaning weakly against the wall, with his face mashed to a jelly and his coat spattered with blood, but Stenning vindictive and triumphant.

"Now will you squeal, Templar?" he croaked.

The Saint made no answer.

The nearest gas jet was directly over Stenning's head. Stenning reached up one hand, and the flame was extinguished. A faint hissing sound could be heard.

"Do you know what I've done, Templar?" asked Stenning shrilly.

The Saint's left arm was round the girl. With his right hand he was fumbling behind him.

But Stenning was taking no notice. Forcing his tortured body to obedience by the exercise of a tremendous effort of will, he was reeling back down the corridor, lurching from side to side like a drunken man, keeping himself erect half the time by resting against the wall, but dragging himself, somehow, to the other end of the corridor and the second gas jet. He reached it.

"Shall I tell you what I've done, Saint?" Stenning's voice came booming hollowly down the tunnel, and as he spoke his hand went up and found the tap he sought.

Simon knew then that the man was mad.

The last gas jet went out, and the hissing sound became louder. The only light in the corridor now was that which came from the electric bulb in the room in which Simon and the girl were imprisoned.

"I have turned on the gas," said Stenning.

And he laughed—a harsh, strident, demoniacal laugh. He was still laughing when the Saint shot him dead.

"The late lamented," murmured the Saint calmly.

After the shot the silence that followed was so unbroken that Simon could hear his own breathing. Stenning would never speak again, and Connell was out for a long time.

Slowly the Saint returned Stenning's automatic to his hip pocket. It was no use now. One glance at the massive lock on the barred gate, which went from the floor to the top of the tunnel arch, told him that any attempt to shoot away the fastening would be wasted. Besides, with the gas continuing to escape, even the flash from a pistol would be enough to blow them all up.

He felt quite unperturbed. A tight corner like that never bothered him in his life, though he knew how thin his chances were.

He had thought that the girl had fainted, but he saw that her eyes were open. Even so, he did not let go of her.

"Sorry about this, old dear," said the Saint quietly.

She nodded.

"I understand," she said.

"They took you when I was away, of course," he said. "Something seems to have gone wrong with this conventional situation. Remind me to write to the *Times* about it when we get out."

He told her of the cheques he had made Stenning sign, and took one of them out of his pocket to show her.

"It may be of some use to your heirs and legatees—if you've made a will," he said cheerfully.

She looked up at him steady-eyed; and it was not only that he was holding her, but she was holding on to him. At that moment it seemed the most natural thing to do.

"Is there no hope?" she asked; and the gaiety of the old reckless Saintly smile was as swift and natural as ever.

"There's always hope," said the Saint. "Somehow or other I'm the most unsuccessful corpse that ever lived. Listen. I'd planned out everything I was going to do today. I wrote a complete account of everything I knew about Vanney—or Stenning, as he really was—and what I proposed to do about him, and left it at a District Messenger office addressed to Teal. They were to send it straight round to him at one o'clock, unless I cancelled the order by telephone. The motor boat is at Gravesend as I ordered it, and by one o'clock, if anything unforeseen had gone wrong, I should have been miles away. What we've got to consider is whether we're likely to last long enough to give Teal time to get on the job. The gas will spread; it'll have to fill all the cellars. I don't know how big they are, but it will creep up all the same."

There was a long silence, and then the Saint said:

"Since the situation is working out in such a cheerful way, I think we ought to make the best of it."

"Perhaps you're right," she said.

"In these matters, I am invariably right," said the Saint; and he kissed her.

Presently she seemed to grow heavier in his arms. He was stronger himself, and his mind was still clear, but his eyes felt strangely heavy, and his chest was starting to ache with the labour of trying to extract some life-giving oxygen from that poisoned air. There was a rushing as of many waters in his ears, and it seemed as if a thousand trip-hammers were pounding on his brain.

He wondered if she was already gone, but then she spoke. It was no more than a whisper, but her voice seemed to come from a tremendous distance.

"Goodbye, Saint," she said.

The Saint laughed softly.

"Tell 'em to save a harp for me," he said, and kissed her again.

He was starting to feel very weak, and the room was swaying dizzily before his eyes. He leant against the wall, but he still held her with the last of his strength. It seemed to be getting dark, and he knew that he could not last much longer.

## XIII

"There's a man to see you, sir," said Sergeant Barrow, entering the room.

Teal looked at the card, and read the note that accompanied it.

"Send him up," he said.

He started a fresh piece of chewing gum, and waited as though asleep. He remained in that attitude when the visitor was shown in, for his party manners were not his strong point.

"Go right ahead," said Teal, without opening his eyes.

The man sat down.

"The circumstances are rather peculiar," he explained. "At about eleven o'clock this morning a rather bulky letter was deposited at one of our branches, addressed to you, with instructions that it was to be delivered at one o'clock unless the order was cancelled by telephone. It seemed a rather extraordinary proceeding to me at the time, especially as the address on the envelope told me that it was likely to be a message with some bearing on your professional activities. So after thinking it over, and taking the opinion of our head office by telephone, I decided that it was my duty to come round and see you at once."

"Have you the letter with you?" asked Teal.

"Naturally, I brought it along."

Teal stretched out his hand.

"Let's have a look at it," he suggested.

He had to open his eyes to read the address, and then he was suddenly galvanised into life. He sat up with a violence that made his chair, solid as it was, creak protestingly.

"The Saint!" he muttered. "I'd know that writing in a million."

"I hope I did right," ventured the stranger.

"You did one of the best things you're ever likely to do in your life," said Teal, as he pressed a bell on his desk.

"Barrow," said Teal, as his subordinate entered, "take this gentleman away, fill him up with whatever he likes to drink, and thank him as profusely as you know how. I'm going to be busy."

Left alone again, he sat down and ripped open the envelope. He read, and he read quickly, and in five minutes he was leaping down the stone stairs in the direction of that wing of Scotland Yard which constitutes Cannon Row Police Station.

"Every man you've got, armed and at the double!" rapped Teal.

And the sergeant in charge was so astonished at this display of energy and hustle on the part of his normally drowsy superior officer that the order was obeyed in what must have come close to record time.

At about half-past twelve, the keen observer might have noticed a number of burly men in plain clothes unostentatiously taking up positions round the block in which Vanney's stood. Teal circumnavigated the block himself, and made certain that every possible exit was watched. Then he went in alone.

A clerk met him in the waiting-room, but Teal had pushed past him before his business could be questioned. He went through the clerks' room, into Simon Templar's office, took in the emptiness of it at a glance, and went straight across to the door marked "Private". His hand was on the gun in his pocket as he walked in.

"Ah!" said Teal.

One cupboard was still open as the Saint had left it, and Teal could see through into the disorder of the room beyond. He went forward cautiously, and squeezed through the hole in the wall.

There was a man in the room, and Teal had him in an iron grip before the other could be quite sure what was happening.

"I'll take you for a start, Harry," said Teal. "Now tell me what you've done with the rest of the gang, and tell me quick!"

Long Harry straightened up.

"I've been in this place all day," he said. "I bust in. I don't mind telling you that now. I was looking for Connell, or something that would tell me where he was, but I couldn't find him. So I waited. I hid in the bathroom. Templar came in early in the morning, saw the mess, and looked round, but he never saw me. Then Connell arrived, but he wasn't alone, and I didn't dare start anything with witnesses. I heard them talking. Then, presently, after Templar had been in and spoken to them, Connell and the other man went out into the office and grabbed a girl who works in there. They had a blanket over her head, so I couldn't see who it was, but I was watching round the corner of the door and I saw Connell take her down."

"Down where?" snapped Teal.

"I'll tell you in a moment. Connell took her down, but the other man stayed here, and I didn't dare follow. Then Templar came in, and there was a fight. He knocked the other man out, and made him tell where Connell had taken the girl, and he went after her. Presently the other man followed. I waited, hoping Connell would come back alone. Then I heard something like a shot."

"Can't you get to the point?" snarled Teal. "Where did they go?"

"There," said Harry, and pointed.

Teal stared.

"I can't see anything."

"I'll show you," said Harry.

He went across and pressed a panel, as the Saint had done. Presently a larger piece of the panelling opened, and the lift was revealed.

Teal put his head inside, and stepped back quickly.

"Gas," he muttered. "For the love of mud, don't strike a match!"

He came back into the room and stood over Long Harry, who, taking the situation philosophically, had sat down comfortably in a chair to await removal to his home from home.

"Harry," said Teal, "would you like to improve your chances of getting off with a light sentence?"

"Tell me how, Mr Teal!" replied Harry with alacrity.

"Go down out of here any way you like—there are busies at every door. Send them up after me, and tell them I've gone down in that lift. There's been something funny going on with all that gas about, and if you only heard one shot it means someone's likely to be in trouble. Now jump!"

Long Harry jumped.

Teal went into the bathroom, soaked his handkerchief under the tap, and tied it over his nose and mouth. Then he went back and entered the lift.

The door closed automatically behind him, and he was fortunate enough to find the right switch at his first attempt. The lift started to go down. With every yard of the descent the smell of gas, even through his wet handkerchief, grew worse, and Teal knew that he would not be able to live for long in that atmosphere. But he was a man without fear.

Presently the lift stopped, and he stepped out. He saw a faint light coming from the branch tunnel, and hurried towards it. At the end was a lighted room, and in one corner he could see the Saint sagging against the wall with Pamela Marlowe in his arms. With the fumes already starting to make their presence felt, Teal hurried forward.

He tried the iron gate, but it was immovable.

"Saint!" he roared.

The Saint's eyes half-opened dazedly, but Teal knew that he could see nothing.

"Saint!" he bellowed again. "Where's the key?"

Simon's chest heaved, and Teal had to strain his ears to catch the reply. It came, with a fearful effort.

"Stenning's pocket——"

Teal went stumbling back down the corridor towards the inert figure that he had nearly tripped over on his first journey. He bent down and fumbled with the man's pockets. The gas lay more heavily near the ground, and Teal wondered if he could hold out. But he found the bunch of keys, straightened up, and went staggering back down the tunnel. Somehow he found the lock. The gate opened. He was in time to catch the girl as the Saint fell.

By this time his heart was pounding furiously, and his head seemed to weigh a ton. Few men could have remained conscious and active for so long, but Chief Inspector Teal was a giant in strength.

He picked the girl up as if she were a feather, and fireman's-lifted her on to his shoulder. He bent down again, and got an arm round the Saint. Carrying the girl, and dragging the Saint behind him, he began the terrible journey back along the tunnel to the lift.

It was like a nightmare. At every step he seemed to grow weaker, and it was only by a superhuman effort of grim determination that he was able to move at all. He never knew how he accomplished the journey with his double load; but after what seemed an eternity of ineffective struggling he found the lift in front of him.

It would only hold two at a time. He dragged the girl in, and pressed the switch. The lift crept upwards.

At the end of a thousand years the bare wall of the lift turned into panelling, and the panelling sprang open in front of him; and Teal fell out of the lift into the arms of two of his men.

"Get her to a doctor," he gasped, and somehow reached the bathroom. He felt sick and weak and giddy, but he soaked his handkerchief again, replaced it, and went back to the lift. They tried to stop him, and then he was savage.

"The Saint's down there," he said, "and I owe him something. Let me go!"

This time the journey was not so difficult, for his short relief in the purer air of the room above had revived him a little, but there was a limit even to his endurance. He remembered dragging the Saint into the lift; he remembered pressing the button that started them on their upward journey; he remembered the beginning of the ascent. Then everything went black.

When he opened his eyes again he was in bed. Looking to right and left, he saw a row of beds in which other men lay motionless. The room was almost in darkness, but in the dim twilight he saw nurses moving about, and a man in a white jacket was bending over the next cot. At the side of his own bed a nurse was sitting reading, but she looked up as soon as he moved.

"I gather I'm not going to die," drawled Teal. But this time he spoke drowsily because he really felt drowsy.

The nurse smiled.

"You'll be back at work in a couple of days," she said cheerfully.

Teal sighed comfortably, and rolled over. As he did so, the doctor moved away from the next bed, and Teal saw who the patient was.

"How are you, Saint?" said Teal.

"I'm fine," said the Saint. "Sorry, old dear."

"Remind me to arrest you when you're better," said Teal, and went to sleep.

## XIV

Four days later, Mr Teal, a trifle pale but otherwise his old self, rang the bell of No 7 Upper Berkeley Mews, and the Saint answered the door himself.

"Why, it's old Claud Eustace," said the Saint. "Come right in."

Teal came in.

"Say when," murmured Simon.

Teal said when.

"Cheerio," said the Saint.

"Cheerio," said Teal.

"By the way," said the Saint, "I believe you saved my life, and all that sort of thing. God bless you, damn your eyes!"

For the first time in his life Mr Teal looked embarrassed, but he shook the hand which the Saint offered.

"And before I arrest you," said Teal presently, "why haven't you tried to jump for it on that boat you've got lying at Gravesend?"

"It didn't happen to be necessary," said the Saint. "I have a little story signed by the late James Arthur himself to show you. Take a look at it, and get ready to laugh."

Teal sat down and unwrapped a fresh packet of his favourite sweetmeat.

"This is our one consolation for having lost America," he remarked. "Let's see this confession."

The Saint passed over the paper. Teal read it through, and glowered.

"When did you write this?" he inquired.

"I didn't write it. Our one and only James Arthur wrote it. It'll stand any test. Sorry, but it's perfectly authentic."

"You haven't by any chance got his signed permission to shoot him, have you?" asked the detective sardonically.

"Self defence, old dear. Self defence. Want to have it argued out in court?"

Teal sighed.

"And how's Connell?" asked the Saint.

"Enjoying a tropical climate, I should say," replied Teal dispassionately. "They got him up later, when the firemen had arrived with gas masks, but he was one of the deadest men I've ever seen."

The Saint lighted a cigarette.

"He was Vanney, of course," he said. "And at the same time he wasn't. It would have been too risky to let Stenning interview people that he had probably done business with before, although he had grown a moustache and made one or two little alterations to his face. But dressed up in livery, as George—a mere porter—nobody ever noticed him. There was a door opening right out of the private office to the passage, only a yard from his cubicle. When I went through to speak to Vanney, I really went further through, and spoke to George. When Vanney had to interview people I got my instructions from Stenning, and conducted most of the interview myself. Connell simply said 'Yes' and 'No' as I tipped him the wink."

Teal nodded.

"I guessed all that," he said.

"I don't suppose you'd have spotted us so soon if we had been able to keep Connell in order. He looked great in a false beard, but he started getting uppish. He had to have money, and wanted more and more. We tried to keep him indoors in case he got tight and spilled the beans, but he got away the other night."

"I found him," said Teal. "He told me a lot that I wanted to know. It was clever the way he and Stenning arranged for that chauffeur to drive him and the body of Red Mulligan, recently deceased, into the country at night, upset the car, and have Wylie to swear that it was Stenning who had been killed. In fact, it was all very clever, but it wasn't good enough."

"It was good enough for me," said the Saint cheerfully.

"And what have you got out of it?"

"An untarnished reputation, and a glorious escape from the name of Tombs. You can have no idea how tired I was getting of that name."

There was a silence, during which Teal ruminated in a certain atmosphere of gloom.

He rose ponderously to his feet at last.

"Well," he said, "you seem to have done it again."

"I'm always doing it," said the Saint modestly.

They walked together to the door, but on the threshold Teal stopped and gave birth to the expression of his greatest worry.

"Saint," he said, "when you were locked up down in that cellar with Miss Marlowe——"

"Yes?"

"Wasn't it—er—um— Well, you know, I've only seen that sort of thing on the movies, but when I arrived you were—er——"

"Teal," said the Saint, "you're a naughty old man. Go home and read the *News of the World*."

And he closed the door gently, and left the detective blinking at a polished brass knocker of very doubtful respectability.

# THE UNBLEMISHED BOOTLEGGER

## From The Brighter Buccaneer

---

WHAT IS NOW CALLED *the Prohibition Era in the United States —sometimes, I suspect, in the sentimentally reminiscent tone of voice that is meant to make you think of "old unhappy far-off things and battles long ago"—probably gave rise to more stories per square second than any comparable epoch in history. It was not to be expected that such an intense concentration of stirring events would have left Simon Templar's life altogether untouched. But because most of the stories that stem from this period are fundamentally so much alike, I choose this story of the Saint because it is so different. And also, I must admit, because I myself saw it develop from the beginning.*

*In the first pages of the story there is quoted a letter "which had been passed on to the Saint by a chance acquaintance".*

*On reading it over now, I realise that this phrase was nothing but a convenient trick designed to eliminate a longer explanation for which at the time I didn't think I could spare the space.*

*But I remember very clearly what really happened. The place was Juan-les-Pins; the time, a sultry summer afternoon. I was paddling idly around a lake-smooth Mediterranean, in a canoe, with the man who can claim as much credit as anyone else for the fact that I have been bullied into recording so many chapters of the Saint Saga.*

*He said, among various other things: "By the way, just before I left London, a fellow showed me a letter that the Saint ought to have a look at. . . ."*

*Because by occupation this man is an editor; and ever since the first Saint story he has never stopped pestering me to dig into my memory for more stories of the Saint. In fact, as you see, he will go so far as to try to imitate them. But the disgraceful thing about this case is that after it was all over—he didn't get the story. By that time I was in the middle of a series for another editor, in which this one somehow became included.*

*You might think that he could never have forgiven me for a thing like that. But he did. Possibly he had to. For in due course he himself had a lapse, which I have been able to hold over him ever since.*

*Obviously I can't give his real name here. But that story was told in the book* Getaway; *and in it I gave him the name of "Monty Hayward".*

# THE UNBLEMISHED BOOTLEGGER

MR MELFORD CROON considered himself a very prosperous man. The brass plate outside his unassuming suite of offices in Gray's Inn Road described him somewhat vaguely as a "Financial Consultant"; and while it is true that the gilt-edged moguls of the City had never been known to seek his advice, there is no doubt that he flourished exceedingly.

Out of Mr Croon's fertile financial genius emerged, for example, the great Tin Salvage Trust. In circulars, advertisements, and statements to the Press, Mr Croon raised his literary hands in horror at the appalling waste of tin that was going on day by day throughout the country. "Tins," of course, as understood in the ordinary domestic vocabulary to mean the sepulchres of Heinz's 57 Varieties, the Crosse & Blackwell vegetable garden, or the Chef soup kitchen, are made of thin sheet iron with the most economical possible plating of genuine tin; but nevertheless (Mr Croon pointed out) *tin was used*. And what happened to it? *It was thrown away*. The dustman removed it along with the other contents of the dustbin, and the municipal incinerators burnt it. And tin was a precious metal—not quite so valuable as gold and platinum, but not very far behind silver. Mr Croon invited his readers to think of it. Hundreds of thousands of pounds being poured into dustbins and incinerators every day of the week from every kitchen in the land. Individually worthless "tins" which in the accumulation represented an enormous potential wealth.

The great Tin Salvage Trust was formed with a capital of nearly a quarter of a million to deal with the problem. Barrows would collect "tins" from door to door. Rag-and-bone men would lend their services. A vast refining and smelting plant would be built to recover the pure tin. Enormous dividends would be paid. The sub-scribers would grow rich overnight.

The subscribers did not grow rich overnight; but that was not Mr Croon's fault. The Official Receiver reluctantly had to admit it, when the Trust went into liquidation eighteen months after it was formed. The regrettable capriciousness of fortune discovered and enlarged a fatal leak in the scheme; without quite knowing how it all happened, a couple of dazed promoters found themselves listen-ing to sentences of penal servitude; and the creditors were glad to accept one shilling in the pound. Mr Croon was overcome with grief—he said so in public—but he could not possibly be blamed for the failure. He had no connection whatever with the Trust, except as Financial Consultant—a post for which he received a merely nominal salary. It was all very sad.

In similar circumstances, Mr Croon was overcome with grief at the failures of the great Rubber Waste Products Corporation, the Iron Workers' Benevolent Guild, the Small Investors' Cooperative Bank, and the Universal Albion Film Company. He had a hard and unprofitable life; and if his mansion flat in Hampstead, his Rolls Royce, his shoot in Scotland, his racing stud, and his house in Mar-low helped to console him, it is quite certain that he needed them.

"A very suitable specimen for us to study," said Simon Templar.

The latest product of Mr Croon's indomitable inventiveness was spread out on his knee. It took the form of a very artistically type-written letter, which had been passed on to the Saint by a chance acquaintance.

*Dear Sir,*

*As you cannot fail to be aware, a state of Prohibition exists at present in the United States of America. This has led to a highly profitable trade in the for-bidden alcoholic drinks between countries not so affected and the United States.*

*A considerable difference of opinion exists as to whether this traffic is morally justified. There can be no question, however, that from the standpoint of this country it cannot be legally attacked; nor that the profits, in proportion to the risk, are exceptionally attractive.*

*If you should desire further information on the subject, I shall be pleased to supply it at the above address.*

Yours faithfully,

MELFORD CROON.

Simon Templar called on Mr Croon one morning by appointment; and the name he gave was not his own. He found Mr Croon to be a portly and rather pale-faced man, with the flowing iron-grey mane of an impresario; and the information he gave—after a few particularly shrewd inquiries about his visitor's status and occupation—was very much what the Saint had expected.

"A friend of mine," said Mr Croon—he never claimed personally to be the author of the schemes on which he gave Financial Consultations—"a friend of mine is interested in sending a cargo of wines and spirits to America. Naturally, the expenses are somewhat heavy. He has to charter a ship, engage a crew, purchase the cargo, and arrange to dispose of it on the other side. While he would prefer to find the whole of the money—and, of course, reap all the reward—he is unfortunately left short of about two thousand pounds."

"I see," said the Saint.

He saw much more than Mr Croon told him, but he did not say so.

"This two thousand pounds," said Mr Croon, "represents about one-fifth of the cost of the trip, and in order to complete his arrangements my friend is prepared to offer a quarter of his profits to anyone who will go into partnership with him. As he expects to make at least ten thousand pounds, you will see that there are not many speculations which offer such a liberal return."

If there was one rôle which Simon Templar could play better than any other, it was that of the kind of man whom financial consultants of every size and species dream that they may meet one day before they die. Mr Croon's heart warmed towards him as Simon laid on the touches of his self-created character with a master's brush.

"A very charming man," thought the Saint, as he paused on the pavement outside the building which housed Mr Croon's offices.

Since at various stages of the interview Mr Croon's effusive bonhomie had fairly bubbled with invitations to lunch with Mr Croon, dine with Mr Croon, shoot with Mr Croon, watch Mr Croon's horses win at Goodwood with Mr Croon and spend week-ends with Mr Croon at Mr Croon's house on the river, the character which Simon Templar had been playing might have thought that the line of the Saint's lips was unduly cynical; but Simon was only thinking of his own mission in life.

He stood there with his walking-stick swinging gently in his fingers, gazing at the very commonplace street scene with thoughtful blue eyes, and became aware that a young man with the physique of a pugilist was standing at his shoulder. Simon waited.

"Have you been to see Croon?" demanded the young man suddenly.

Simon looked round with a slight smile.

"Why ask?" he murmured. "You were outside Croon's room when I came out, and you followed me down the stairs."

"I just wondered."

The young man had a pleasantly ugly face with crinkly grey eyes that would have liked to be friendly; but he was very plainly nervous.

"Are you interested in bootlegging?" asked the Saint; and the young man stared at him grimly.

"Listen. I don't know if you're trying to be funny, but I'm not. I'm probably going to be arrested this afternoon. In the last month I've lost about five thousand pounds in Croon's schemes—and the money wasn't mine to lose. You can think what you like. I went up there to bash his face in before they get me, and I'm going back now for that same reason. But I saw you come out, and you didn't look like a crook. I thought I'd give you a word of warning. You can take it or leave it. Goodbye."

He turned off abruptly into the building, but Simon reached out and caught him by the elbow.

"Why not come and have some lunch first?" he suggested. "And let Croon have his. It'll be so much more fun punching him in the stomach when it's full of food."

He waved away the young man's objections and excuses without listening to them, hailed a taxi, and bundled him in. It was the kind of opportunity that the Saint lived for, and he would have had his way if he was compelled to kidnap his guest for the occasion. They lunched at a quiet restaurant in Soho; and in the persuasive warmth of half a litre of Chianti and the Saint's irresistible personality the young man told him what he knew of Mr Melford Croon.

"I suppose I was a complete idiot—that's all. I met Croon through a man I used to see in the place where I always had lunch. It didn't occur to me that it was all a put-up job, and I thought Croon was all right. I was fed to the teeth with sitting about in an office copying figures from one book to another, and Croon's stunts looked like a way out. I put three thousand quid into his Universal Albion Film Company: it was only on paper, and the way Croon talked about it made me think I'd never really be called on for the money. They were going to rent the World Features studio at Teddington—the place is still on the market. When the Universal Albion went smash I had to find the money, and the only way I could get it was to borrow it out of the firm. Croon put the idea into my head, but—Oh, hell! It's easy enough to see how things have happened after the damage is done."

He had borrowed another two thousand pounds—without the cashier's knowledge—in the hope of retrieving the first loss. It had gone into a cargo of liquor destined for the thirsty States. Six weeks later Mr Croon broke the news to him that the coastal patrols had captured the ship.

"And that's what'll happen to any other fool who puts money into Croon's bootlegging," said the young man bitterly. "He'll be told that the ship's sunk, or captured, or caught fire, or grown wings and flown away. He'll never see his money back. My God—to think of *that* slimy swab trying to be a bootlegger! Why, he told me once that the very sight of a ship made him feel sick, and he wouldn't cross the Channel for a thousand pounds."

"What are you going to do about it?" asked the Saint, and the young man shrugged.

"Go back and try to make him wish he'd never been born—as I told you. They're having an audit today at the office, and they can't help finding out what I've done. I stayed away—said I was ill. That's all there is to do."

Simon took out his cheque-book and wrote a cheque for five thousand pounds.

"Whom shall I make it payable to?" he inquired, and his guest's eyes widened.

"My name's Peter Quentin. But I don't want any of your damned——"

"My dear chap, I shouldn't dream of offering you charity." Simon blotted the pink slip and scaled it across the table. "This little chat has been worth every penny of it. Besides, you don't want to go to penal servitude at your age. It isn't healthy. Now be a good fellow and dash back to your office—square things up as well as you can——"

The young man was staring at the name which was scribbled in the bottom right-hand corner of the paper.

"Is that name Simon Templar?"

The Saint nodded.

"You see, I shall get it all back," he said.

He went home with two definite conclusions as the result of his day's work and expenses: first, that Mr Melford Croon was in every way as undesirable a citizen as he had thought, and second, that Mr Melford Croon's contribution to the funds of righteousness was

long overdue. Mr Croon's account was, in fact, exactly five thousand pounds overdrawn; and that state of affairs could not be allowed to continue.

Nevertheless, it took the Saint twentyfour hours of intensive
thought to devise a poetic retribution; and when the solution came
to him it was so simple that he had to laugh.

Mr Croon went down to his house on the river for the weekend.
He invariably spent his weekends there in the summer, driving out
of London on the Friday evening and refreshing himself from his
labours with three happy days of rural peace. Mr Croon had an
unexpected appetite for simple beauty and the works of nature: he
was rarely so contented as when he was lying out in a deck-chair
and spotless white flannels, directing his gardener's efforts at the
flowerbeds, or sipping an iced whisky and soda on his balcony
while he watched supple young athletes propelling punts up and
down the stream.

This weekend was intended to be no exception to his usual
custom. He arrived at Marlow in time for dinner, and prepared for
an early night in anticipation of the tireless revels of a mixed company of his friends who were due to join him the next day. It was
scarcely eleven o'clock when he dismissed his servant and mixed
himself a final drink before going to bed.

He heard the front door bell ring, and rose from his armchair
grudgingly. He had no idea who could be calling on him at that
hour; and when he had opened the door and found that there was
no one visible outside he was even more annoyed.

He returned to the sitting-room, and gulped down the remainder
of his nightcap without noticing the bitter tang that had not been
there when he poured it out. The taste came into his mouth after
the liquid had been swallowed, and he grimaced. He started to walk
towards the door, and the room spun round. He felt himself falling
helplessly before he could cry out.

When he woke up, his first impression was that he had been
buried alive. He was lying on a hard narrow surface, with one
shoulder squeezed up against a wall on his left, and the ceiling
seemed to be only a few inches above his head. Then his sight
cleared a little, and he made out that he was in a bunk in a tiny un-
ventilated compartment lighted by a single circular window. He
struggled up on one elbow, and groaned. His head was one reeling
whirligig of aches, and he felt horribly sick.

Painfully he forced his mind back to his last period of consciousness. He remembered pouring out that last whisky and soda—the ring at the front door—the bitter taste in the glass. . . . Then nothing but an infinity of empty blackness. . . . How long had he been unconscious? A day? Two days? A week? He had no means of telling.

With agonising effort he dragged himself off the bunk and staggered across the floor. It reared and swayed sickeningly under him, so that he could hardly keep his balance. His stomach was somersaulting nauseatingly inside him. Somehow he got over to the one round window: the pane was frosted over, but outside he could hear the splash of water and the shriek of wind. The explanation dawned on him dully—he was in a ship!

Mr Croon's knees gave way under him, and he sank moaning to the floor. A spasm of sickness left him gasping in a clammy sweat. The air was stiflingly close, and there was a smell of oil in it which made it almost unbreathable. Stupidly, unbelievingly, he felt the floor vibrating to the distant rhythm of the engines. A ship! He'd been drugged—kidnapped—shanghaied! Even while he tried to convince himself that it could not be true, the floor heaved up again with the awful deliberateness of a seventh wave; and Mr Croon heaved up with it. . . .

He never knew how he managed to crawl to the door between the paroxysms of torment that racked him with every movement of the vessel. After what seemed like hours he reached it, and found strength to try the handle. The door failed to budge. It was locked. He was a prisoner—and he was going to die. If he could have opened the door he would have crawled up to the deck and thrown himself into the sea. It would have been better than dying of that dreadful nausea that racked his whole body and made his head swim as if it were being spun round on the axle of a dynamo.

He rolled on the floor and sobbed with helpless misery. In another hour of that weather he'd be dead. If he could have found a weapon he would have killed himself. He had never been able to stand the slightest movement of the water—and now he was a prisoner in a ship that must have been riding one of the worst storms in the history of navigation. The hopelessness of his position made him scream suddenly—scream like a trapped hare—before the ship slumped suckingly down into the trough of another seventh wave and left his stomach on the crest of it.

Minutes later—it seemed like centuries—a key turned in the locked door, and a man came in. Through the bilious yellow mists that swirled over his eyes, Mr Croon saw that he was tall and wiry, with a salt-tanned face and farsighted twinkling blue eyes. His double-breasted jacket carried lines of dingy gold braid, and he balanced himself easily against the rolling of the vessel.

"Why, Mr Croon—what's the matter?"

"I'm sick," sobbed Croon, and proceeded to prove it.

The officer picked him up and laid him on the bunk.

"Bless you, sir, this isn't anything to speak of. Just a bit of a blow —and quite a gentle one for the Atlantic."

Croon gasped feebly.

"Did you say the Atlantic?"

"Yes, sir. The Atlantic is the ocean we are on now, sir, and it'll be the same ocean all the way to Boston."

"I can't go to Boston," said Croon pathetically. "I'm going to die."

The officer pulled out a pipe and stuffed it with black tobacco. A cloud of rank smoke added itself to the smell of oil that was contributing to Croon's wretchedness.

"Lord, sir, you're not going to die!" said the officer cheerfully. "People who aren't used to it often get like this for the first two or three days. Though I must say, sir, you've taken a long time to wake up. I've never known a man be so long sleeping it off. That must have been a very good farewell party you had, sir."

"Damn you!" groaned the sick man weakly. "I wasn't drunk—I was drugged!"

The officer's mouth fell open.

"Drugged, Mr Croon?"

"Yes, drugged!" The ship rolled on its beam ends, and Croon gave himself up for a full minute to his anguish. "Oh, don't argue about it! Take me home!"

"Well, sir, I'm afraid that's——"

"Fetch me the captain!"

"I am the captain, sir. Captain Bourne. You seem to have forgotten, sir. This is the *Christabel Jane*, eighteen hours out of Liverpool with a cargo of spirits for the United States. We don't usually take passengers, sir, but seeing that you were a friend of the owner, and you wanted to make the trip, why, of course we found you a berth."

Croon buried his face in his hands.

He had no more questions to ask. The main details of the conspiracy were plain enough. One of his victims had turned on him for revenge—or perhaps several of them had banded together for the purpose. He had been threatened often before. And somehow his terror of the sea had become known. It was poetic justice—to shanghai him on board a bootlegging ship and force him to take the journey of which he had cheated their investments.

"How much will you take to turn back?" he asked; and Captain Bourne shook his head.

"You still don't seem to understand, sir. There's ten thousand pounds' worth of spirits on board—at least, they'll be worth ten thousand pounds if we get them across safely—and I'd lose my job if I——"

"Damn your job!" said Melford Croon.

With trembling fingers he pulled out a cheque-book and fountain pen. He scrawled a cheque for fifteen thousand pounds and held it out.

"Here you are, I'll buy your cargo. Give the owner his money and keep the change. Keep the cargo. I'll buy your whole damned ship. But take me back. D'you understand? *Take me back*——"

The ship lurched under him again, and he choked. When the convulsion was over the captain had gone.

Presently a white-coated steward entered with a cup of steaming beef tea. Croon looked at it and shuddered.

"Take it away," he wailed.

"The Captain sent me with it, sir," explained the steward. "You must try to drink it, sir. It's the best thing in the world for the way you're feeling. Really, sir, you'll feel quite different after you've had it."

Croon put out a white flabby hand. He managed to take a gulp of the hot soup; then another. It had a slightly bitter taste which seemed familiar. The cabin swam round him again, more dizzily than before, and his eyes closed in merciful drowsiness.

\*          \*          \*          \*          \*

He opened them in his own bedroom. His servant was drawing back the curtains, and the sun was streaming in at the windows.

The memory of his nightmare made him feel sick again, and he clenched his teeth and swallowed desperately. But the floor underneath was quite steady. And then he remembered something else, and struggled up in bed with an effort which threatened to overpower him with renewed nausea.

"Give me my cheque-book," he rasped. "Quick—out of my coat pocket——"

He opened it frantically, and stared at a blank counterfoil with his face growing haggard.

"What's today?" he asked.

"This is Saturday, sir," answered the surprised valet.

"What time?"

"Eleven o'clock, sir. You said I wasn't to call you——"

But Mr Melford Croon was clawing for the telephone at his bedside. In a few seconds he was through to his bank in London. They told him that his cheque had been cashed at ten.

Mr Croon lay back on the pillows and tried to think out how it could have been done.

He even went so far as to tell his incredible story to Scotland Yard, though he was not by nature inclined to attract the attention of the police. A methodical search was made in Lloyd's Register, but no mention of a ship called the *Christabel Jane* could be found.

Which was not surprising; for the *Christabel Jane* was the name temporarily bestowed by Simon Templar on a dilapidated Thames tug which had wallowed very convincingly for a few hours in the gigantic tank at the World Features studio at Teddington for the filming of storm scenes at sea, which would undoubtedly have been a great asset to Mr Croon's Universal Albion Film Company if the negotiations for the lease had been successful.

# THE APPALLING POLITICIAN

## From The Brighter Buccaneer

---

It is not too easy *at first sight to visualise a character so active and extraverted as Simon Templar in the somewhat abstract and dreamy setting of a story of pure detection. All the same, it is equally difficult to conceive a life so busily concerned with every possible variation on the theme of Crime which had never contained any such problems. As a matter of fact, the Saint has so far had two of them, of which this was the first. (The second, which I called* The Noble Sportsman, *can be found in the book* Boodle.)

*I only have one other explanation to add to this story.*

*It has been suggested to me on more than one occasion that the broadcast speech of the Politician, with which the story opens, is an excessively farcical exaggeration. Solely in self defence, I take this opportunity to plead Not Guilty. I wrote the quotation down practically verbatim, altering only the occasion and the sport referred to. I only regret that I cannot substantiate this defence with the name of the actual speechmaker. One reason, of course, which prevents me from doing so is that this speech was really grafted on to the Politician in the story, and should not be taken to mean that there is any other similarity whatever between the Speechmaker and the Appalling Politician of this piece. I used it simply because, as an artist, I felt that such a deathless gem of statesmanlike oratory should not be allowed to perish from the earth.*

*And the other reason is that, for all I know, before this book is out of print, the gentleman who made the speech might easily be Prime Minister of Great Britain. And how could he frighten Hitler and Mussolini if they could dig a speech like that out of his past?*

# THE APPALLING POLITICIAN

"BADMINTON," boomed the frog-like voice of Sir Joseph Whipple-thwaite, speaking from the annual dinner of the British Badminton Society, "is an excellent means of acquiring and retaining that fitness of body which is so necessary to all of us in these strenuous times. We politicians have to keep fit, the same as everyone else. And many of us—as I do myself—retain that fitness by playing badminton. Badminton," he boomed, "is a game which pre-eminently requires physical fitness—a thing which we politicians also require. I myself could scarcely be expected to carry on my work at the Ministry of International Trade if I were not physically fit. And badminton is the game by which I keep myself fit to carry out my duties as a politician. Of course I shall never play as well as you people do; but we politicians can only try to do our best in the intervals between our other duties. Badminton," boomed the frog-like voice tirelessly, "is a game which makes you fit and keeps you fit; and we politicians——"

Simon Templar groaned aloud, and hurled himself at the radio somewhat hysterically. At odd times during the past year he had accidentally switched on to Sir Joseph Whipplethwaite speaking at the annual dinners of the North British Lacrosse League, the British Bowling Association, the Southern Chess Congress, the International Ice Skating Association, the Royal Toxophilite Society, and the British Squash Racquets Association; and he could have recited Sir Joseph Whipplethwaite's speech from memory, with all its infinite variations. In that mellow oak-beamed country pub, where he had gone to spend a restful weekend, the reminder of that appalling politician was more than he could bear.

"It's positively incredible," he said, returning limply to his beer. "Pat, I'll swear that if you put that into a story as an illustration of the depths of imbecility that can be reached by a man who's considered fit to govern this purblind country, you'd simply raise a shriek of derisive laughter. And yet you've heard it with your own ears—half a dozen times. You've heard him playing every game under the sun in his after-dinner speeches, and mixing it fifty-fifty with his god-like status as a politician. And that—*that*—that blathering oaf is a member of His Majesty's Cabinet and one of the men on whom the British Empire's fate depends. O God, O Ottawa!"

Words failed him, and he buried his face wrathfully in his tankard.

But he was not destined to forget Sir Joseph Whipplethwaite that weekend or ever again; for early on the Monday morning a portly man with a round red face and an unrepentant bowler hat walked into the hotel, and Simon recognised him with some astonishment.

"Claud Eustace himself, by the Great White Spat of Professor Clarence Skinner!" he cried. "What brings my little ray of sunshine here?"

Chief Inspector Claud Eustace Teal looked at him suspiciously. "I might ask the same question."

"I'm recuperating," said the Saint blandly, "from many months of honest toil. There are times when I have to get away from London just to forget what petrol fumes and soot smell like. Come and have a drink."

Teal handed his bag to the boots and chewed on his gum continuously.

"What I'm wanting just now is some breakfast—I've been on the go since five o'clock this morning without anything to eat."

"That suits me just as well," murmured the Saint, taking the detective's arm and steering him towards the dining-room. "I see you're staying. Has some sinister local newsagent been selling newspapers after eight o'clock?"

They sat down in the deserted room, and Teal ordered himself a large plate of porridge. Then his sleepily cherubic blue eyes gazed at the Saint again, not so suspiciously as before, but rather regretfully.

"There are times when I wish you were an honest man, Saint," he said; and Simon raised his eyebrows a fraction.

"There's something on your mind, Claud," he said. "May I know it?"

Mr Teal pondered while his porridge was set before him, and dug a spoon into it thoughtfully.

"Have you heard of Sir Joseph Whipplethwaite?"

Simon stared at him; and then he covered his eyes.

"Have I not!" he articulated tremulously. He flung out a hand. "'Badminton'," he boomed, "'is the game that has made we politicians what we are. Without badminton, we politicians——'"

"I see you have heard of him. Did you know he lived near here?"

Simon shook his head. He knew that Sir Joseph Whipplethwaite had acquired the recently-created portfolio of the Minister of International Trade, and had gathered from broadcast utterances that Sir Joseph considered Whipplethwaite an ideal man for the job; but he had not felt moved to investigate the matter further. His energetic life was far too full to allow him time to trace the career of every pinhead who exercised his jaw in the Houses of Parliament at the longsuffering taxpayer's expense.

"His house is only about a mile away—a big modern place with four or five acres of garden. And whatever you like to think about him yourself, the fact remains that he has fairly important work to do. Things go through his office that it's sometimes important to keep absolutely secret until the proper time comes to publish them."

Simon Templar had never been called slow.

"Good Lord, Teal—is this a stolen treaty business?"

The detective nodded slowly.

"That sounds a little sensational, but it's about the truth of it. The draft of our commercial agreement with the Argentine is going before the House tomorrow, and Whipplethwaite brought it down here on Saturday night late to work on it—he has the pleasure of introducing it for the Government. I don't know much about it myself, except that it's to do with tariffs, and some people could make a lot of money out of knowing the text of it in advance."

"And it's been stolen?"

"On Sunday afternoon."

Simon reached thoughtfully for his cigarette case.

"Teal, why are you telling me this?"

"I don't really know," said the detective, looking at him soberly.

"When you walked in and found me here, I suppose you thought I was the man."

"No—I didn't think that. A thing like that is hardly in your line, is it?"

"It isn't. So why bring me in?"

"I don't really know," repeated the detective stubbornly, watching his empty porridge plate being replaced by one of bacon and eggs. "In fact, if you wanted to lose me my job you could go right out and sell the story to a newspaper. They'd pay you well for it."

The Saint tilted back his chair and blew a succession of smoke-rings towards the ceiling. Those very clear and challenging blue eyes rested almost lazily on the detective's somnolent pink half-moon of a face.

"I get you, Claud," he said seriously, "and for once the greatest criminal brain of this generation shall be at the disposal of the Law. Shoot me the whole works."

"I can do more than that," said Teal, with a certain relief. "I'll show you the scene presently. Whipplethwaite's gone to London for a conference with the Prime Minister."

The detective finished his breakfast, and refused a cigarette. After a few minutes they set out to walk to Whipplethwaite's house, where Teal had already spent several hours of fruitless searching for clues after a special police car had brought him down from London. Teal, having given his outline of the barest facts, had become taciturn; and Simon made no attempt to force the pace. He appreciated the compliment of the detective's confidence—although perhaps it was only one of many occasions on which those two epic antagonists had been silent in a momentary recognition of the impossible friendship that might have been just as epic if their destinies had lain in different paths. Those were the brief interludes when a truce was possible between them; and the hint of a sigh in Teal's silent ruminations might have been taken to indicate that he wished the truce could have been extended indefinitely.

In the same silence they turned in between the somewhat pompous concrete gate-pillars that gave entrance to the grounds of Sir Joseph Whipplethwaite's country seat. From there, a gravelled carriage drive led them in a semi-circular curve through a rough densely-grown plantation and brought them rather suddenly into sight of the house, which was invisible from the road. A uniformed local constable was patrolling in front of the door: he saluted as he saw Teal, and looked at the Saint inquiringly. Teal, however, was uncommunicative. He stood aside for the Saint to pass, and ushered him personally through the front door—a performance which, from the village constable's point of view, was sufficient introduction to one who could scarcely have been less than an Assistant Commissioner.

The house was not only modern, as Teal had described it—it was almost prophetic. From the outside, it looked at the first glance like the result of some close in-breeding between an aquarium, a wedding cake, and a super cinema. It was large, white, and square, with enormous areas of window and erratic balconies which looked as if they had been transferred bodily from the façade of an Atlantic liner. Inside, it was remarkably light and airy, with a certain ascetic barrenness of furnishing that made it seem too studiously sanitary to be comfortable, like a hospital ward. Teal led the way down a long wide white hall, and opened a door at the end. Simon found himself in a room that needed no introduction as Sir Joseph's study. Every wall had long book-shelves let into its depth in the modern style, and there was a glass-topped desk with a steel-framed chair behind it; the upper reaches of the walls were plastered with an assortment of racquets, bats, skis, skates, and illuminated addresses that looked oddly incongruous.

"Is this architecture Joseph's idea?" asked the Saint.

"I think it's his wife's," said Teal. "She's very progressive."

It certainly looked like a place in which any self-respecting mystery should have died of exhaustion looking for a suitable place to happen. The safe in which the treaty had reposed was the one touch about it that showed any trace of fantasy, for it was sunk in flush with the wall and covered by a mirror which, when it was opened, proved to be the door of the safe itself, and the keyhole was concealed in a decorative scroll of white metal worked into the frame of the glass which slid aside in cunningly-fashioned grooves to disclose it. Teal demonstrated its working; and the Saint was interested.

"The burglars don't seem to have damaged it much," he remarked, and Teal gave him a glance that seemed curiously lethargic.

"They haven't damaged it at all," he said. "If you go over it with a magnifying glass you won't find a trace of its having been tampered with."

"How many keys?"

"Two. Whipplethwaite wears one on his watch-chain, and the other is at his bank in London."

For the first time that day two thin hairlines of puzzlement cut vertically down between the Saint's level brows. They were the only outward signs of a wild idea, an intuition too ludicrous even to hint at, that flickered through his mind at the tone of the detective's voice.

"Whipplethwaite went to church on Sunday morning," said Teal, with an expressionless face, "and worked over the treaty when he came back. He took it in to lunch with him; and then he locked it up in the safe and went upstairs to his room to rest. He was rather taken up with the importance of secrecy, and he had demanded two guards from the local police. One of them was at the front door, where we came in. The other was outside here."

Teal walked towards the tall windows which filled nearly the whole of one wall of the room. Right in the centre of these windows, on the stone-flagged terrace outside, the back of a seated man loomed against the light like a statuette in a glass case. Simon had noticed him as soon as they entered the room: he appeared to be painting a scene of the landscape, and as they went through the windows and came out behind him Simon observed that the canvas on his easel was covered with brightly-coloured daubs of paint in various abstruse geometrical shapes. He looked up at the sound of their footsteps, gave the Saint a casual nod, and bowed politely to the detective.

"Well, sir," he said, with a trace of mockery, "how are the investigations going?"

"We're doing the best we can," said Teal vaguely, and turned to Simon. "This is Mr Spencer Vallance, who was painting exactly where you see him now when the robbery took place. Down there" —he pointed to a grass tennis court which was cut bodily, like a great step, out of the fairly steep slope below them—"those same four people you see were playing. They're the finalists of the South of England Junior Championships, and they're staying here as Whipplethwaite's guests for a week. The other constable on guard was supposed to be patrolling the back of the house—we're at the back here, now—and at the time when the burglary was committed he was about three-quarters of the way down this slope, with his back to the house, watching the game. In fact, the scene you see is almost exactly the same as it was at half-past three yesterday afternoon."

Simon nodded, and glanced again at Mr Vallance, who had resumed his interrupted task of painting a neat blue border round a green isosceles triangle on a short brown stalk that was presumably intended to represent a poplar in the foreground. The Art of Mr Spencer Vallance was so perfectly appropriate to his background that it gave one a sense of shock. One felt that such a preposterous aptness outraged one's canons of that human inconsistency which we have come to accept as normal: it was like seeing a commissionaire in Arab costume outside a restaurant called "The Oasis," and discovering that he really was a genuine Arab. Vallance's picture was exactly like the house behind it: scientific, hygienic, and quite inhuman. Simon spent a few seconds trying to coordinate the masses of colour on the canvas with the scene before his eyes, which was particularly human and charming. To left and right of him, strips of untouched plantation which were probably continuations of the spinney through which they had approached the house flanked the grounds right down beyond the tennis court to the banks of a stream; while beyond the stream the land rose again up a long curve of hill crowned with a dark sprawl of woods.

"There are two poplars there, Mr Vallance," Simon ventured to point out, when he had got his bearings on the picture; and the artist turned to him with an exasperated glare.

"My dear sir, what people like you want isn't an artist—it's a photographer. There are millions of blades of grass on that lawn, and you'd like me to draw every one of them. What I paint," said Spencer Vallance magnificently, "is the Impression of Poplar. The Soul of all Poplars is expressed in this picture, if you had the eyes to see it."

Mr Vallance himself was the very antithesis of his art, being a small straggly man with straggly hair and a thin straggly beard. His clothes hung about him shapelessly; but his scrawny frame was obviously capable of so much superb indignation under criticism that Simon thought it best to accept the rebuke in all humility. And then Chief Inspector Teal took the Saint's arm and urged him firmly down the slope away from temptation.

"I'd better tell you what happened from our point of view," said the detective. "At twenty minutes to four the constable who was out here turned round and started to walk back towards the house. He had then been watching the tennis for about a quarter of an hour; and you might remember that all this time both the back and the front of the house had been covered, and nothing smaller than a field-mouse could have come through the plantation at the sides without making a noise that would certainly have attracted attention. The constable noticed that Vallance was not at his easel, and the windows of Whipplethwaite's study behind were open—he couldn't remember if they had been open before. Of course he thought nothing of that—I don't think I mentioned that Vallance is also staying here as a guest. Then, just as the constable reached the top of the slope, Vallance came staggering out of the study, holding his head and bellowing that he'd been sandbagged. He was working at his painting, it appeared, when he was hit on the head from behind and stunned; and he remembered nothing more until he woke up on the floor of the study. The constable found a sandbag lying on the terrace just behind Vallance's stool. He went into the study and found the safe wide open. The theory, of course, would be that the robber dragged Vallance inside so that his body would not attract attention if the constable looked round."

Teal's voice was as detached and expressionless as if he had been making his statement in court; but once again that uncanny premonition flashed through the Saint's mind, rising ridiculously from that odd-sounding subjunctive in the detective's last sentence. Simon lighted a cigarette.

"I gather that Vallance is Lady Whipplethwaite's guest," he said presently; and Teal was only slightly surprised.

"That is correct. How did you know?"

"His art fits in too perfectly with the house—and you said she was very progressive. I suppose he's been investigated?"

"This is Lady Whipplethwaite's statement," he said, taking out a notebook. "I'll read it to you."

" 'I first met Mr Vallance in Brisbane fifteen years ago. He fell in love with me and wanted to marry me, but I refused him. For five years after that he continued to pester me, although I did my best to get rid of him. When I became engaged to Sir Joseph he was insanely jealous. There was never anything between us that could have given him the slightest grounds for imagining that he had a claim on me. For a few years after I was married he continued to write and implore me to leave Sir Joseph and run away with him, but I did not answer his letters. Six months ago he wrote to me again in London, apologising humbly for the past and begging me to forgive him and meet him again, as he said he was completely cured of his absurd infatuation. I met him with my husband's consent, and he told me that he had been studying art in Paris and was getting quite a name among the Moderns. I liked his pictures, and when he begged me to let him paint me a picture of our house to give me I asked him down to stay, although Sir Joseph was very much against it. Sir Joseph has never liked him. They have had several heated arguments while he has been staying with us.' "

Teal closed the notebook and put it away.

"As soon as the theft was discovered," he said, "Sir Joseph wanted me to arrest Vallance at once, and I had a job to make him see that we couldn't possibly do that without any evidence."

They had reached a rustic seat at the end of the tennis court. Teal rested his weight on it gingerly, and produced a fresh packet of chewing gum.

"Our problem," he said, gazing intently at the tennis players, "is to find out how the man who opened the safe got in here—and got out again."

Simon nodded quietly.

"The tennis players would hardly make any difference," he remarked. "They'd be so intent on their game that they wouldn't notice anything else."

"And yet," said Teal, "the man who did it had to pass the constable in front or the constable at the back—and either of them should have seen him."

"It sounds impossible," said the Saint; and the man beside him put a slip of gum in his mouth and masticated stolidly.

"It does," he said, without moving a muscle; and at that moment the fantastic idea that had been creeping round the Saint's mind sprang into incredulous life.

"Good God! Teal—you don't mean——"

"I don't mean anything," said Teal in the same toneless voice. "I can't possibly tell you any more than I've told you already. If I mentioned that Whipplethwaite was badly hit in the Doncaster Steel Company's crash three months ago—that a Cabinet Minister's salary may be a large one, but you need a lot more than that to keep up the style that the Whipplethwaites like to live in—I should only be mentioning things that have nothing to do with the case. If I said that the man who could open that safe without damaging it in any way would be a miracle worker, I'd only be theorising."

Simon's cigarette had gone out, but he did not notice it.

"And I suppose," he said, in a slightly strained voice—"just taking an entirely mythical case—I suppose that if the details of that treaty got about, the Powers would know that there'd been a leakage? I mean, if there were only one man through whom the leakage could have occurred, he'd have to cover himself by staging some set of circumstances that would account for it without hurting his reputation?"

"I suppose so," agreed Teal formally. "Unfortunately there's no Third Degree in this country, and when you get into high places you have to walk very carefully. Sometimes we're set almost impossible tasks. My orders are to avoid a scandal at any cost."

The Saint sat quietly, taking in the full significance of that astounding revelation that was so much more momentous for having been made without any direct statement. And, as he looked up at the house in a kind of breathlessness, he visualised the scene. There was no space for secret passages in such an edifice as that; but for reasons known only to the architect a sun balcony on the first floor, built over the study, was linked with the ground by two flying buttresses on either side of it that angled down on either side of the study windows like gigantic staircases of three-foot steps. He could see the podgy figure of Sir Joseph Whipplethwaite creeping out with exaggerated caution, like a rhinoceros walking on tiptoe, and surveying the scene below. He saw the man clambering down the steps of the flying buttress, one by one, hampered by the sandbag clutched in one hand . . . saw him creeping up behind the unconscious artist . . . striking that single clumsy blow. With a scapegoat whom he disliked so heartily ready to be accused, why should he think he ran any risk? . . .

"I know what you think of our abilities at the Yard," Teal was saying, in the same passionless way. "But we do get ideas sometimes. What you don't make allowances for is the fact that in our position we can't act on nothing more substantial than a brilliant idea, like detectives do in stories." He was chewing monotonously, with his cherubic blue eyes fixed expressionlessly on the flying white ball on the court. "I think that if the treaty could somehow be recovered and put back where it was taken from, the guilty man would have to confess. An adventurer in a story, I suppose, might kidnap the suspected person and force him to say where it was hidden; but we can't do that. If anything like that happened in real life, and the kidnapper was caught, he'd be for it. By the way, Whipplethwaite will be driving back from London this evening. He has a green Rolls Royce, number XZ 9919. . . . I expect you've had enough of this, haven't you?"

The detective stood up; and for the first time in a long while he looked at the Saint again. Simon had rarely seen those baby blue eyes so utterly sleepy and impassive.

"Yes—it's about time for my morning tankard of ale," he murmured easily.

They strolled slowly back to the house.

"That's Joseph's room—the one with the balcony—is it?" he asked idly, and Teal nodded.

"Yes. That's where he was lying down."

"Does he suffer from indigestion?"

The detective flashed a glance at him.

"I don't know. Why?"

"I should like to know," said the Saint.

Back in the house, he asked to be shown the dining-room. On the sideboard he discovered a round cardboard box carefully labelled —after the supererogatory habit of chemists—"*The Pills*". Underneath was the inscription: "*Two to be taken with water after each meal, as required*".

He examined the tablets, and smiled gently to himself.

"Now could I see the bathroom?"

A very mystified Mr Teal rang for the butler, and they were shown upstairs. The bathroom was one of those magnificent halls of coloured marble and chromium plate which the most modern people find necessary for the preservation of their personal cleanliness; but Simon was interested only in the cupboard over the washbasin. It contained an imposing array of bottles, which Simon surveyed with some awe. Sir Joseph was apparently something of a hypochondriac.

Simon read the labels one by one, and nodded.

"Is he shortsighted?"

"He wears glasses," said the detective.

"Splendid," murmured Simon, and went back to the hotel to supervise the refuelling of his car without relieving Teal's curiosity.

At six o'clock that evening a very frightened man, who had undergone one of the slickest feats of abduction with violence that he could ever have imagined, and who had been very efficiently gagged, bound, blindfolded, and carried across country by the masked bandit who was responsible, sat with his back to a tree where he had been roughly propped up in a deep glade of the New Forest and watched the movements of his captor with goggling eyes. The Saint had kindled a small crisp fire of dry twigs, and he was feeding more wood to it and blowing into it with the dexterity of long experience, nursing it up into a solid cone of fierce red heat. Down there in the hollow where they were, the branches of the encircling trees filtered away the lingering twilight until it was almost as dark as midnight; but the glow of the fire showed up the Saint's masked face in macabre shadings of red and black as he worked over it, like the face of a pantomime devil illuminated on a darkened stage. The Saint's voice, however, was far from devilish—it was almost affectionate.

"You don't seem to realise, brother," he said, "that stealing secret treaties is quite a serious business, even when they're the daft sort of treaties that We Politicians amuse ourselves with. And it's very wrong of you to think that you can shift the blame for your crimes on to that unfortunate ass whom you dislike so much. So you're going to tell me just where you put that treaty, and then there'll be no more nonsense about it."

The prisoner's eyes looked as if they might pop out of his head at any moment, and strangled grunts came through the gag as he struggled with the ropes that bound his arms to his sides; but the Saint was unmoved. The fire had been heaped up to his complete satisfaction.

"Our friend Mr Teal," continued the Saint, in the same oracular vein, as he began to unlace the captive's shoes, "has been heard to complain about there being no Third Degree in this country. Now that's obviously ridiculous, because you can see for yourself that there is a Third Degree, and I'm It. Our first experiment is the perfect cure for those who suffer from cold feet. I'll show it to you now —unless you'd rather talk voluntarily?"

The prisoner shook his head vigorously, and emitted further strangled grunts which the Saint rightly interpreted as a refusal. Simon sighed, and hauled the man up closer to the fire.

"Very well, brother. There's no compulsion at all. Any statement you like to make will be made of your own free will." He drew one of the man's bared feet closer to his little fire. "If you change your mind," he remarked genially, "you need only make one of those eloquent guggling noises of yours, and I expect I shall understand."

It was only five minutes before the required guggling noise came through the gag; but after the gag had been taken out it was another five minutes before the red-faced prisoner's speech became coherent enough to be useful.

Simon left him there, and met Teal in the hotel at half-past seven.

"The treaty is pushed under the carpet in Whipplethwaite's study," he said; and the detective's pose of mountainous sleepiness failed him for once in his life.

"As near as that?" he ejaculated. "Good Lord!"

The Saint nodded.

"I don't think you'll have to worry your heads about whether you'll prosecute," he said. "The man's mentally deficient—I thought so from the beginning. And my special treatment hasn't improved his balance a lot. . . . As a general rule, problems in detection bore me stiff—it's so much more entertaining to commit the crime yourself—but this one had its interesting points. A man who could hate a harmless ass like that enough to try and ruin him in such an elaborate way is a bit of a museum specimen. You know, Claud, I've been thinking about those brilliant ideas you say you policemen get sometimes; it strikes me that the only thing you want——"

"Tell me about it when I come back," said Teal, looking at his watch. "I'd better see Whipplethwaite at once and get it over."

"Give him my love," drawled the Saint, dipping his nose into the pint of beer which the detective had bought for him. "He'll get his satisfaction all right when you arrest Vallance."

The detective stood stock still and stared at him with an owl-like face.

"Arrest *who?*" he stammered.

"Mr Spencer Vallance—the bloke who put insomnia tablets in Whipplethwaite's dyspepsia companion at lunch time, nipped up to Whipplethwaite's room for the key, opened the safe, replaced key, and then staggered out of the study bellowing that he'd been sandbagged. The bloke I've just been having words with," said the Saint.

Teal leaned back rather limply against the bar.

"Good Lord alive, Templar——"

"You meant well, Claud," said the Saint kindly. "And it was quite easy really. The only difficult part was that insomnia-tablet business; but I figured that the culprit might want to make quite sure that Joseph would be sleeping soundly when he buzzed up for the key, and the method was just an idea of mine. Then I saw that Joseph's insomnia dope was white, while his indigestion muck was light grey, and I guessed he must have been shortsighted to fall for the change-over. When I looked up at the house it was quite obvious that if anyone could climb down that flying buttress, someone else could just as easily climb up. That's why I was going to say something about your brilliant police ideas."

He patted the detective consolingly on the back.

"Policemen are swell so long as they plod along in their methodical way and sort out facts—they catch people that way quite often. But directly they get on to a really puzzling case, and for some reason it strikes them that they ought to be Great Detectives just for once—then they fall down with the gooseberries. I've noticed those symptoms of detectivosis in you before, Claud. You ought to keep a tighter hand on yourself."

"How long have you known it wasn't Whipplethwaite?" asked Teal.

"Oh, for months," said the Saint calmly. "But when your elephantine hints conjured up the vision of Joseph creeping stealthily down from the balcony upon his foe, couldn't you see a sort of grisly grotesqueness about it? I could. To stage a crime so that another man would naturally be suspected requires a certain warped efficiency of brain. To think for a moment that Joseph could have produced a scheme like that was the sort of brilliant idea that only a policeman in your condition would get. How on earth could Joseph have worked all that out? He's only a politician."

# THE MILLION POUND DAY

## From THE SAINT VS. SCOTLAND YARD

---

NOT VERY LONG AGO *I received a letter from a faithful follower of this series who had just discovered, it seemed with some distress, that the Saint was getting older.*

*"In* Meet the Tiger," *she wrote, "you say that the Saint is 26, and in one of the latest books he has aged to 35, and at that rate Patricia must be somewhere around 27 or 29, and that is not a nice age for a heroine. She should always be about 20, and the Saint should remain 26. They shouldn't age, because what are you going to do when the Saint gets about 40 and Patricia is nearly 30?"*

*This is not at all an easy question to answer, even apart from its slightly frantic arithmetic. It was, incidentally, a mild shock to an old gaffer like myself to learn that such comparatively adolescent years as the early thirties were regarded in some quarters as coming perilously close to the borders of senile decay.*

*Well, I thought, let us pretend that Patricia is 30 (she is ageing a little slower than the Saint, of course, skipping a birthday here and there with a feminine agility which my correspondent, being of the same sex, tactfully takes for granted). She will be, I tried to think, almost an Old Hag. But the only conclusion that this led to was that I myself must have quite a weakness for the company of Old Hags; which couldn't possibly be the right answer.*

*So the best I could do was to point out, as a matter of inexorable mathematics, that since all of the Saint's adventures have taken a definite period of time to happen, and since several of them had already called on him for a good deal of ground work before the points at which I began to chronicle them, and since I hoped that there were many other adventures yet to come, any such Peter Pan chronology as she suggested would ultimately lead to a transparent absurdity.*

*My own conception is diametrically opposite. I have never been able to see why a fictional character should not grow up, mature, and develop, the same as anyone else. The same, if you like, as his biographer. The only adequate reason is that—so far as I know—no other fictional character in modern times has survived a sufficient number of stories spread over a sufficient number of years for these changes to be clearly observable. I must confess that a lot of my own selfish pleasure in the Saint has been in watching him grow up.*

*The book from which this story is taken,* **The Holy Terror**, *will always be one of my favourites. Perhaps I have done better since, at times; but not so much better that I am ashamed of the comparison. I am not so sure about the seven that went before it. For this was the first book in which I really felt that I had been able to bring him into three dimensions. It may have been in the nick of time; for I also feel that this was when the Saint himself took a long stride towards his own future.*

# THE MILLION POUND DAY

THE SCREAM PEALED OUT at such point-blank range, and was strangled so swiftly and suddenly, that Simon Templar opened his eyes and wondered for a moment whether he had dreamed it.

The darkness inside the car was impenetrable; and outside, through the thin mist that a light frost had etched upon the windows, he could distinguish nothing but the dull shadows of a few trees silhouetted against the flat pallor of the sky. A glance at the luminous dial of his wrist watch showed that it was a quarter to five: he had slept barely two hours.

A weekend visit to some friends who lived on the remote margin of Cornwall, about thirteen inches from Land's End, had terminated a little more than seven hours earlier, when the Saint, feeling slightly limp after three days in the company of two young souls who were convalescing from a recent honeymoon, had pulled out his car to make the best of a clear night road back to London. A few miles beyond Basingstoke he had backed into a side lane for a cigarette, a sandwich, and a nap. The cigarette and the sandwich he had had; but the nap should have lasted until the hands of his watch met at six-thirty and the sky was white and clear with the morning—he had fixed that time for himself, and had known that his eyes would not open one minute later.

And they hadn't. But they shouldn't have opened one minute earlier, either. . . . And the Saint sat for a second or two without moving, straining his ears into the stillness for the faintest whisper of sound that might answer the question in his mind, and driving his memory backwards into those last blank moments of sleep to recall the sound that had woken him.

And then, with a quick stealthy movement, he turned the handle of the door and slipped out into the road.

Before that, he had realised that that scream could never have been shaped in his imagination. The sheer shrieking horror of it still rang between his eardrums and his brain: the hideous high-pitched sob on which it had died seemed still to be quivering on the air. And the muffled patter of running feet which had reached him as he listened had served only to confirm what he already knew.

He stood in the shadow of the car with the cold damp smell of the dawn in his nostrils, and heard the footsteps coming closer. They were coming towards him down the main road—now that he was outside the car, they tapped into his brain with an unmistakable clearness. He heard them so distinctly, in the utter silence that lay all around, that he felt he could almost see the man who made them. And he knew that that was the man who had screamed. The same stark terror that had gone shuddering through the very core of the scream was beating out the wild tattoo of those running feet— the same stomach-sinking dread translated into terms of muscular reaction. For the feet were not running as a man ordinarily runs. They were kicking, blinding, stumbling, hammering along in the mad muscle-binding heart-bursting flight of a man whose reason has tottered and cracked before a vision of all the tortures of the Pit. . . .

Simon felt the hairs on the nape of his neck prickling. In another instant he could hear the gasping agony of the man's breathing, but he stayed waiting where he was. He had moved a little way from the car, and now he was crouched right by the corner of the lane, less than a yard from the road, completely hidden in the blackness under the hedge.

The most elementary process of deduction told him that no man would run like that unless the terror that drove him on was close upon his heels—and no man would have screamed like that unless he had felt cold upon his shoulder the clutching hand of an intolerable doom. Therefore the Saint waited.

And then the man reached the corner of the lane.

Simon got one glimpse of him—a man of middle height and build, coatless, with his head back and his fists working. Under the feebly lightening sky his face showed thin and hollow-cheeked, pointed at the chin by a small peaked beard, the eyes starting from their sockets.

He was done in—finished. He must have been finished two hundred yards back. But as he reached the corner the ultimate end came. His feet blundered again, and he plunged as if a trip-wire had caught him across the knees. And then it must have been the last instinct of the hunted animal that made him turn and reel round into the little lane; and the Saint's strong arms caught him as he fell.

The man stared up into the Saint's face. His lips tried to shape a word, but the breath whistled voicelessly in his throat. And then his eyes closed and his body went limp, and Simon lowered him gently to the ground.

The Saint straightened up again, and vanished once more in the gloom. The slow bleaching of the sky seemed only to intensify the blackness that sheltered him, while beyond the shadows a faint light was beginning to pick out the details of the road. And Simon heard the coming of the second man.

The footfalls were so soft that he was not surprised that he had not heard them before. At the moment when he picked them up they could only have been a few yards away, and to anyone less keen of hearing they would still have been inaudible. But the Saint heard them—heard the long-striding ghostly sureness of them padding over the macadam—and a second tingle of eerie understanding crawled over his scalp and glissaded down his spine like a needle-spray of ice-cold water. For the feet that made those sounds were human, but the feet were bare. . . .

And the man turned the corner.

Simon saw him as clearly as he had seen the first—more clearly.

He stood huge and straight in the opening of the lane, gazing ahead into the darkness. The wan light in the sky fell evenly across the broad black primitive-featured face, and stippled glistening silver high-lights on the gigantic ebony limbs. Except for a loosely knotted loin-cloth he was naked, and the gleaming surfaces of his tremendous chest shifted rhythmically to the mighty movements of his breathing. And the third and last thrill of comprehension slithered clammily into the small of the Saint's back as he saw all these things —as he saw the savage ruthlessness of purpose behind the mere physical presence of that magnificent brute-man, sensed the primeval lust of cruelty in the parting of the thick lips and the glitter of the eyes. Almost he seemed to smell the sickly stench of rotting jungles seeping its fetid breath into the clean cold air of that English dawn, swelling in hot stifling waves about the figure of the pursuing beast that had taken the continents and the centuries in its bare-foot loping stride.

And while Simon watched, fascinated, the eyes of the negro fell on the sprawling figure that lay in the middle of the lane, and he stepped forward with the snarl of a beast rumbling in his throat.

And it was then that the Saint, with an effort which was as much physical as mental, tore from his mind the steely tentacles of the hypnotic spell that had held him paralysed for those few seconds—and also moved.

"Good morning," spoke the Saint politely, but that was the last polite speech he made that day. No one who had ever heard him talk had any illusions about the Saint's opinion of Simon Templar's physical prowess, and no one who had ever seen him fight had ever seriously questioned the accuracy of those opinions; but this was the kind of occasion on which the Saint knew that the paths of glory lead but to the grave. Which may help to explain why, after that single preliminary concession to the requirements of his manual of etiquette, he heaved the volume over the horizon and proceeded to lapse from grace in no uncertain manner.

After all, that encyclopædia of all the social virtues, though it had some cheering and helpful suggestions to offer on the subject of addressing letters to archdeacons, placing Grand Lamas in the correct relation of precedence to Herzegovinian Grossherzöge, and declining invitations to open bazaars in aid of Homes for Ichthyotic Vulcanisers' Mates, had never even envisaged such a situation as that which was then up for inspection; and the Saint figured that the rules allowed him a free hand.

The negro, crouching in the attitude in which the Saint's gentle voice had frozen him, was straining his eyes into the darkness. And out of that darkness, like a human cannonball, the Saint came at him.

He came in a weird kind of twisting leap that shot him out of the obscurity with no less startling a suddenness than if he had at that instant materialised out of the fourth dimension. And the negro simply had no time to do anything about it. For that suddenness was positively the only intangible quality about the movement. It had, for instance, a very tangible momentum, which must have been one of the most painfully concrete things that the victim of it had ever encountered. That momentum started from the five toes of the Saint's left foot; it rippled up his left calf, surged up his left thigh, and gathered to itself a final wave of power from the big muscles of his hips. And then, in that twisting action of his body, it was swung on into another channel: it travelled down the tautening fibres of his right leg, gathering new force in every inch of its progress, and came right out at the end of his shoe with all the smashing violence of a ten-ton stream of water cramped down into the finest nozzle of a garden hose. And at the very instant when every molecule of shattering velocity and weight was concentrated in the point of that right shoe, the point impacted precisely in the geometrical centre of the negro's stomach.

If there had been a football at that point of impact, a rag of shredded leather might reasonably have been expected to come to earth somewhere north of the Aberdeen Providential Society Buildings. And the effect upon the human target, colossus though it was, was just as devastating, even if a trifle less spectacular.

Simon heard the juicy *whuck!* of his shoe making contact, and saw the man travel three feet backwards as if he had been caught in the full fairway of a high-speed hydraulic battering-ram. The wheezy *phe-e-ew* of electrically emptied lungs merged into the synchronised sound effects, and ended in a little grunting cough. And then the negro seemed to dissolve on to the roadway like a statue of sculptured butter caught in the blast of a superheated furnace. . . .

Simon jerked open one of the rear doors of the car, picked the bearded man lightly off the ground, heaved him in upon the cushions, and slammed the door again.

Five seconds later he was behind the wheel, and the self-starter was whirring over the cold engine.

The headlights carved a blazing chunk of luminance out of the dimness as he touched a switch, and he saw the negro bucking up on to his hands and knees. He let in the clutch, and the car jerked away with a spluttering exhaust. One running-board rustled in the long grass of the banking as he lashed through the narrow gap; and then he was spinning round into the wide main road.

Ten yards ahead, in the full beam of the headlights, a uniformed constable tumbled off his bicycle and ran to the middle of the road with outstretched hands; and the Saint almost gasped.

Instantaneously he realised that the scream which had woken him must have been audible for some considerable distance—the policeman's attitude could not more clearly have indicated a curiosity which the Saint was at that moment instinctively disinclined to meet.

He eased up, and the constable guilelessly felt round to the side of the car.

And then the Saint revved up his engine, let in the clutch with a bang and went roaring on through the dawn with the policeman's shout tattered to futile fragments in the wind behind him.

## II

It was full daylight when he turned into Upper Berkeley Mews and stopped before his own front door, and the door opened even before he had switched off the engine.

"Hullo, boy!" said Patricia. "I wasn't expecting you for another hour."

"Neither was I," said the Saint.

He kissed her lightly on the lips, and stood there with his cap tilted rakishly to the back of his head and his leather coat swinging back from wide square shoulders, peeling off his gloves and smiling one of his most cryptic smiles.

"I've brought you a new pet," he said.

He twitched open the door behind him, and she peered puzzledly into the back of the car. The passenger was still unconscious, lolling back like a limp mummy in the travelling rug which the Saint had tucked round him, his white face turned blankly to the roof.

"But—who is he?"

"I haven't the faintest idea," said the Saint blandly. "But for the purposes of convenient reference I have christened him Beppo. His shirt has a Milan tab on it—Sherlock Holmes himself could deduce no more. And up to the present, he hasn't been sufficiently compos to offer any information."

Patricia Holm looked into his face, and saw the battle glint in his eye and a ghost of Saintliness flickering in the corners of his smile, and tilted her sweet fair head.

"Have you been in some more trouble?"

"It was rather a one-sided affair," said the Saint modestly. "Sambo never had a break—and I didn't mean him to have one, either. But the Queensberry Rules were strictly observed. There was no hitting below belts, which were worn loosely around the ankles——"

"Who's this you're talking about now?"

"Again, we are without information. But again for the purposes of convenient reference, you may call him His Beatitude the Negro Spiritual. And now listen."

Simon took her shoulders and swung her round.

"Somewhere between Basingstoke and Wintney," he said, "there's a gay game being played that's going to interest us a lot. And I came into it as a perfectly innocent party, for once in my life—but I haven't got time to tell you about it now. The big point at the moment is that a cop who arrived two minutes too late to be useful got my number. With Beppo in the back, I couldn't stop to hold converse with him, and you can bet he's jumped to the worst conclusions. In which he's damned right, but not in the way he thinks he is. There was a phone box twenty yards away, and unless the Negro Spiritual strangled him first he's referred my number to London most of an hour ago, and Teal will be snorting down a hot scent as soon as they can get him out of bed. Now, all you've got to know is this: I've just arrived and I'm in my bath. Tell the glad news to anyone who rings up and anyone who calls; and if it's a call, hang a towel out of the window."

"But where are you going?"

"The Berkeley—to park the patient. I just dropped in to give you your cue." Simon Templar drew the end of a cigarette red, and snapped his lighter shut again. "And I'll be right back," he said, and wormed in behind the wheel.

A matter of seconds later the big car was in Berkeley Street, and he was pushing through the revolving doors of the hotel.

"Friend of mine had a bit of a car smash," he rapped at a sleepy reception clerk. "I wanna room for him now, and a doctor at eleven. Will you send a coupla men out to carry him in? Car at the door."

"One four eight," said the clerk, without batting an eyelid.

Simon saw the unconscious man carried upstairs, shot half-crowns into the hands of the men who performed the transportation, and closed the door on them.

Then he whipped from his pocket a thin nickelled case which he had brought from a pocket in the car. He snapped the neck of a small glass phial and drew up the colourless fluid it contained into the barrel of a hypodermic syringe. His latest protégé was still sleeping the sleep of sheer exhaustion, but Simon had no guarantee of how long that sleep would last. He proceeded to provide that guarantee himself, stabbing the needle into a limp arm and pressing home the plunger until the complete dose had been administered.

Then he closed and locked the door behind him and went quickly down the stairs.

Below, the reception clerk stopped him.

"What name shall I register, sir?"

"Teal," said the Saint, with a wry flick of humour. "Mr C E Teal. He'll sign your book later."

"Yes, sir. . . . Er—has Mr Teal no luggage, sir?"

"Nope." A new ten-pound note drifted down to the desk. "On account," said the Saint. "And see that that doctor's waiting here for me at eleven, or I'll take the roof off your hotel and crown you with it."

He pulled his cap sideways and went back to his car. As he turned into Upper Berkeley Mews for the second time, he saw that his first homecoming had only just been soon enough. But that did not surprise him, for he had figured out his chances on that schedule almost to a second. A warning blink of white from an upper window caught his expectant eye at once, and he locked the wheel hard over and pulled up broadside on across the mews. In a flash he was out of his seat unlocking a pair of garage doors right at the street end of the Mews, and in another second or two the car was hissing back into that garage with the cut-out firmly closed.

The Saint, without advertising the fact, had recently become the owner of one complete side of Upper Berkeley Mews, and he was in process of making some interesting structural alterations to that block of real estate of which the London County Council had not been informed and about which the District Surveyor had not even been consulted. The great work was not yet by any means completed, but even now it was capable of serving part of its purposes.

Simon went up a ladder into the bare empty room above. In one corner, a hole had been roughly knocked through the wall; he went through it into another similar room, and on the far side of this was another hole in a wall; thus he passed in quick succession through numbers 1, 3, and 5, until the last plunge through the last hole and a curtain beyond it brought him into No 7 and his own bedroom.

His tie was already off and his shirt unbuttoned by that time, and he tore off the rest of his clothes in little more than the time it took him to stroll through to the bathroom. And the bath was already full—filled long ago by Patricia.

"Thinks of everything!" sighed the Saint, with a wide grin of pure delight.

He slid into the bath like an otter, head and all, and came out of it almost in the same movement with a mighty splash, tweaking the plug out of the waste pipe as he did so. In another couple of seconds he was hauling himself into an enormously woolly blue bathrobe and grabbing a towel . . . and he went paddling down the stairs with his feet kicking about in a pair of gorgeously dilapidated moc-

casins, humming the hum of a man with a copper-plated liver and
not one solitary little baby sin upon his conscience.

And thus he rolled into the sitting-room.

"Sorry to have kept you waiting, old dear," he murmured; and
Chief Inspector Claud Eustace Teal rose from an armchair and surveyed him heavily.

"Good morning," said Mr Teal.

"Beautiful, isn't it?" agreed the Saint affably. Patricia was smoking a cigarette in another chair. She should, according to the book
of etiquette, have been beguiling the visitor's wait with some viva-
cious topical chatter; but the Saint, who was sensitive to atmosphere,
had perceived nothing but a glutinously expanding silence as he
entered the room. The perception failed to disturb him. He lifted
the silver cover from a plate of bacon and eggs, and sniffed appreciatively. "You don't mind if I eat, do you, Claud?" he murmured.

The detective swallowed. If he had never been required to interview the Saint on business he could have enjoyed a tolerably placid
life. He was not by nature an excitable man, but these interviews
never seemed to take the course which he intended them to take.

"Where were you last night?" he blurted.

"In Cornwall," said the Saint. "Charming county—full of area.
Know it?"

"What time did you leave?"

"Nine-fifty-two pip."

"Did anybody see you go?"

"Everyone who had stayed the course observed my departure,"
said the Saint carefully. "A few of the male population had retired
hurt a little earlier, and others were still enthusiastic but already
blind. Apart from seven who had been ruled out earlier in the week
by an epidemic of measles——"

"And where were you between ten and five minutes to five this
morning?"

"I was on my way."

"Were you anywhere near Wintney?"

"That would be about it."

"Notice anything peculiar around there?"

Simon wrinkled his brow.

"I recall the scene distinctly. It was the hour before the dawn.
The sleeping earth, still spellbound by the magic of the night, lay
quiet beneath the paling skies. Over the peaceful scene brooded the

expectant hush of all the mornings since the beginning of these days. The whole world, like a bride listening for the footfall of her lover, or a breakfast sausage hoping against hope——"

The movement with which Teal clamped a battered piece of spearmint between his molars was one of sheer ferocity.

"Now listen," he snarled. "Near Wintney, between ten and five minutes to five this morning, a Hirondel with your number-plates on it was called on to stop by a police officer—and it drove straight past him!"

Simon nodded.

"Sure, that was me," he said innocently. "I was in a hurry. D'you mean I'm going to be summonsed?"

"I mean more than that. Shortly before you came past, the con-stable heard a scream——"

Simon nodded again.

"Sure, I heard it too. Weird noises owls make sometimes. Did he want me to hold his hand?"

"That was no owl screaming——"

"Yeah? You were there as well, were you?"

"I've got the constable's telephoned report——"

"You can find a use for it." The Saint opened his mouth, inserted egg, bacon, and buttered toast in suitable proportions, and stood up. "And now *you* listen, Claud Eustace." He tapped the detec-tive's stomach with his forefinger. "Have you got a warrant to come round and cross-examine me at this ungodly hour of the morning—or any other hour, for that matter?"

"It's part of my duty——"

"It's part of the blunt end of the pig of the aunt of the gardener. Let that pass for a minute. Is there one single crime that even your pop-eyed imagination can think of to charge me with? There is not. But we understand the functioning of your so-called brain. Some loutish cop thought he heard someone scream in Hampshire this morning, and because I happened to be passing through the same county you think I must have had something to do with it. If somebody tells you that a dud shilling has been found in a slot machine in Blackpool, the first thing you want to know is whether I was within a hundred miles of the spot within six months of the event. A drowned man is fished out of the ocean at Boston, and if you hear a rumour that I was staying beside the same ocean at Biarritz two years before——"

"I never——"

"You invariably. And now get another earful. You haven't a search-warrant, but we'll excuse that. Would you like to go upstairs and run through my wardrobe and see if you can find any blood-stains on my clothes? Because you're welcome. Would you like to push into the garage and take a look at my car and see if you can find a body under the back seat? Shove on. Make yourself absolutely at home. But digest this first." Again that dictatorial forefinger impressed its point on the preliminary concavity of the detective's waistcoat. "Make that search—accept my invitation—and if you can't find anything to justify it, you're going to wish your father had died a bachelor, which he may have done for all I know. You're becoming a nuisance, Claud, and I'm telling you that this is where you get off. Give me the small half of less than a quarter of a break, and I'm going to roast the hell out of you. I'm going to send you up to the sky on one big balloon; and when you come down you're not going to bounce—you're going to spread yourself out so flat that a short-sighted man will not be able to see you sideways. Got it?"

Teal gulped.

His cherubic countenance took on a slightly redder tinge, and he shuffled his feet like a truant schoolboy. But that, to do him justice, was the only childish thing about his attitude, and it was beyond Teal's power to control. For he gazed deep into the dancing, mocking, challenging blue eyes of the Saint standing there before him, lean and reckless and debonair even in that preposterous bathrobe outfit; and he understood the issue exactly.

And Chief Inspector Claud Eustace Teal nodded.

"Of course," he grunted, "if that's the way you take it, there's nothing more to be said."

"There isn't," agreed the Saint concisely. "And if there was, I'd say it."

He picked up the detective's bowler hat, dusted it with his towel, and handed it over. Teal accepted it, looked at it, and sighed. And he was still sighing when the Saint took him by the arm and ushered him politely but firmly to the door.

### III

"And if that," remarked the Saint, blithely returning to his interrupted breakfast, "doesn't shake up Claud Eustace from the Anzora downwards, nothing short of an earthquake will."

Patricia lighted another cigarette.

"So long as you didn't overdo it," she said. *"Qui s'excuse, s'accuse——"*

"And *honi soit qui mal y pense*," said the Saint cheerfully. "No, old sweetheart—that outburst had been on its way for a long while. We've been seeing a great deal too much of Claud Eustace lately, and I have a feeling that the Teal-baiting season is just getting into full swing."

"But what *is* the story about Beppo?"

Simon embarked upon his second egg.

"Oh, yes! Well, Beppo. . . ."

He told her what he knew, and it is worth noting that she believed him. The recital, with necessary comment and decoration, ran out with the toast and marmalade; and at the end of it she knew as much as he did, which was not much.

"But in a little while we're going to know a whole lot more," he said.

He smoked a couple of cigarettes, glanced over the headlines of a newspaper, and went upstairs again. For several minutes he swung a pair of heavy Indian clubs with cheerful vigour; then a shave, a second and longer immersion in the bath with savon and vox humana accompaniment, and he felt ready to punch holes in three distinct and different heavyweights. None of which being available, he selected a fresh outfit of clothes, dressed himself with leisurely care, and descended once more upon the sitting-room looking like one consolidated ray of sunshine.

"Cocktail at the Bruton at a quarter to one," he murmured, and drifted out again.

By that time, which was 10.44 precisely, if that matters a damn to anyone, the floating population of Upper Berkeley Mews had increased by one conspicuous unit; but that did not surprise the Saint. Such things had happened before; they were part of the inevitable paraphernalia of the attacks of virulent detectivosis which periodically afflicted the ponderous lucubrations of Chief Inspector Teal; and after the brief but comprehensive exchange of pleasantries earlier that morning, Simon Templar would have been more disappointed than otherwise if he had seen no symptoms of a fresh outbreak of the disease.

Simon was not perturbed. . . . He raised his hat politely to the sleuth, was cut dead, and remained unperturbed. . . . And he sauntered imperturbably westwards through the smaller streets of Mayfair until, in one of the very smallest streets, he was able to collar the one and only visible taxi, in which he drove away, fluttering his handkerchief out of the window, and leaving a fuming plainclothes man standing on the kerb glaring frantically around for another cab in which to continue the chase—and finding none.

At the Dover Street corner of Piccadilly, he paid off the driver and strolled back to the Piccadilly entrance of the Berkeley. It still wanted a few minutes to eleven, but the reception clerk, spurred on perhaps by the Saint's departing purposefulness, had a doctor already waiting for him.

Simon conducted the move to the patient's room himself, and had his first shock when he helped to remove the man's shirt.

He looked at what he saw in silence for some seconds; and then the doctor, who had also looked, turned to him with his ruddy face gone a shade paler.

"I was told that your friend had had an accident," he said bluntly, and the Saint nodded.

"Something unpleasant has certainly happened to him. Will you go on with your examination?"

He lighted a cigarette and went over to the window, where he stood gazing thoughtfully down into Berkeley Street until the doctor rejoined him.

"Your friend seems to have been given an injection of scopolamine and morphia—you have probably heard of 'twilight sleep'. His other injuries you've seen for yourself—I haven't found any more."

The Saint nodded.

"I gave him the injection myself. He should be waking up soon—he had rather less than one-hundredth of a grain of scopolamine. Will you want to move him to a nursing home?"

"I don't think that will be necessary, unless he wishes it himself, Mr——"

"Travers."

"Mr Travers. He should have a nurse, of course——"

"I can get one."

The doctor inclined his head.

Then he removed his pince-nez and looked the Saint directly in the eyes.

"I presume you know how your friend received his injuries?" he said.

"I can guess." The Saint flicked a short cylinder of ash from his cigarette. "I should say that he had been beaten with a rawhide whip, and that persuasion by hot irons had also been applied."

The doctor put his fingertips together and blinked.

"You must admit, Mr Travers, that the circumstances are—er—somewhat unusual."

"You could say all that twice, and no one would accuse you of exaggerating," assented the Saint, with conviction. "But if that fact is bothering your professional conscience, I can only say that I'm as much in the dark as you are. The accident story was just to satisfy the birds below. As a matter of fact, I found our friend lying by the roadside in the small hours of this morning, and I sort of took charge. Doubtless the mystery will be cleared up in due course."

"Naturally, you have communicated with the police."

"I've already interviewed one detective, and I'm sure he's doing everything he can," said the Saint veraciously. He opened the door, and propelled the doctor decisively along the corridor. "Will you want to see the patient again today?"

"I hardly think it will be necessary, Mr Travers. His dressings should be changed tonight—the nurse will see to that. I'll come in tomorrow morning——"

"Thanks very much. I shall expect you at the same time. Good-bye."

Simon shook the doctor warmly by the hand, swept him briskly into the waiting elevator, and watched him sink downwards out of view.

Then he went back to the room, poured out a glass of water, and sat down in a chair by the bedside. The patient was sleeping easily; and Simon, after a glance at his watch, prepared to await the natural working-off of the drug.

A quarter of an hour later he was extinguishing a cigarette when the patient stirred and groaned. A thin hand crawled up to the bare throat, and the man's head rolled sideways with his eyelids flickering. As Simon bent over him a husky whisper of a word came through the relaxed lips.

"*Aqua. . . .*"

"Sure thing, brother." Simon propped up the man's head and put the glass to his mouth.

"*Mille grazie.*"

"*Prego.*"

Presently the man sank back again. And then his eyes opened, and focused on the Saint.

For a number of seconds there was not the faintest glimmer of understanding in the eyes: they stared at and through their object like the eyes of a blind man. And then, slowly, they widened into round pools of shuddering horror, and the Italian shrank away with a thin cry rattling in his throat.

Simon gripped his hand and smiled.

"*Non tema. Sono un amico.*"

It was some time before he was able to calm the man into a dully incredulous quietness; but he won belief before he had finished, and at last the Italian sank back again among the pillows and was silent.

Simon mopped his brow and fished out his cigarette-case.

And then the man spoke again, still weakly, but in a different voice.

"*Quanti ne abbiamo quest'oggi?*"

"*E il due ottobre.*"

There was a pause.

"*Vuol favorire di dirmi il suo nome?*"

"Templar—Simon Templar."

There was another pause. And then the man rolled over and looked at the Saint again. And he spoke in almost perfect English.

"I have heard of you. You were called——"

"Many things. But that was a long time ago."

"How did you find me?"

"Well—I rather think that you found me."

The Italian passed a hand across his eyes.

"I remember now. I was running. I fell down. Someone caught me. . . ." Suddenly he clutched the Saint's wrist. "Did you see—*him?*"

"Your gentleman friend?" murmured Simon lightly. "Sure I did. He also saw me, but not soon enough. Yes, we certainly met."

The grip of the trembling fingers loosened slowly, and the man lay still, breathing jerkily through his nose.

"*Voglia scusarmi,*" he said at length. "*Mi vergogno.*"

"*Non ne val la pena.*"

"It is as if I had awoken from a terrible dream. Even now——" The Italian looked down at the bandages that swathed the whole of the upper part of his body, and shivered uncontrollably. "Did you put on these?" he asked.

"No—a doctor did that."

The man looked round the room.

"And this——"

"This is the Berkeley Hotel, London."

The Italian nodded. He swallowed painfully, and Simon refilled his glass and passed it back. Another silence fell, which grew so long that the Saint wondered if his patient had fallen asleep again. He rose stealthily to his feet, and the Italian roused and caught his sleeve.

"Wait." The words came quite quietly and sanely. "I must talk to you."

"Sure." Simon smiled down at the man. "But do you want to do it now? Hadn't you better rest for a bit—maybe have something to eat——"

The Italian shook his head.

"Afterwards. Will you sit down again?"

And Simon Templar sat down.

And he listened, almost without movement, while the minute hand of his watch voyaged unobserved once round the dial. He listened in a perfect trance of concentration, while the short precise sentences of the Italian's story slid into the atmosphere and built themselves up into a shape that he had never even dreamed of.

It was past one o'clock when he walked slowly down the stairs with the inside story of one of the most stupendous crimes in history whirling round in his brain like the armature of a high-powered dynamo.

Wrapped up in the rumination of what he had heard, he passed out like a sleepwalker into Berkeley Street. And it so happened that in his abstraction he almost cannoned into a man who was at that moment walking down towards Piccadilly. Simon stepped aside with a muttered apology, absentmindedly registering a kind of panoramic impression of a brilliantly purple suit, lemon-coloured gloves, a gold-mounted cane, a lavender shirt, spotted tie, and——

Just for an instant the Saint's gaze rested on the man's face. And then they were past each other, without a flicker of recognition, without the batting of an eyelid. But the Saint knew . . .

He knew that that savagely arrogant face, like a mask of black marble, was like no other black face that he had ever seen in his life before that morning. And he knew, with the same certainty, that the eyes in the black face had recognised him in the same moment as he had recognised them—and with no more betrayal of their knowledge. And as he wandered up into Berkeley Square, and the portals of the Bruton Club received him, he knew, though he had not looked back, that the black eyes were still behind him, and had seen where he went.

## IV

But the smile with which the Saint greeted Patricia was as gay and carefree a smile as she had ever seen.

"I should like," said the Saint, sinking into an armchair, "three large double Martinis in a big glass. Just to line my stomach. After which, I shall be able to deal respectfully with a thirst which can only be satisfactorily slaked by two gallons of bitter beer."

"You will have one Martini, and then we'll have some lunch," said Patricia; and the Saint sighed.

"You have no soul," he complained.

Patricia put her magazine under the table.

"What's new, boy?" she asked.

"About Beppo? . . . Well, a whole heap of things are new about Beppo. I can tell you this, for instance: Beppo is no smaller a guy than the Duke of Fortezza, and he is the acting President of the Bank of Italy."

"He's what?"

"He's the acting President of the Bank of Italy—and that's not the half of it. Pat, old girl, I told you at the start that there was some gay game being played, and, by the Lord, it's as gay a game as we may ever find!" Simon signed the chit on the waiter's tray with a flourish and settled back again, surveying his drink dreamily. "Remember reading in some paper recently that the Bank of Italy was preparing to put out an entirely new and original line of paper currency?" he asked.

"I saw something about it."

"It was so. The contract was placed with Crosby Dorman, one of our own biggest printing firms—they do the thin cash and postal issues of half a dozen odd little countries. Beppo put the deal through. A while ago he brought over the plates and gave the order, and one week back he came on his second trip to take delivery of three million pounds' worth of coloured paper in a tin-lined box."

"And then?"

"I'll tell you what then. One whole extra million pounds' worth of mazuma is ordered, and that printing goes into a separate box. Ordered on official notepaper, too, with Beppo's own signature in the south-east corner. And meanwhile Beppo is indisposed. The first crate of spondulix departs in the golden galleon without him, completely surrounded by soldiers, secret service agents, and general detectives, all armed to the teeth and beyond. Another of those nice letters apologises for Beppo's absence, and instructs the guard to carry on; a third letter explains the circumstances, ditto and ditto, to the Bank——"

Patricia sat up.

"And the box is empty?"

"The box is packed tight under a hydraulic press, stiff to the sealing-wax with the genuine articles as per invoice."

"But——"

"But obviously. That box had got to go through. The new issue had to spread itself out. It's been on the market three days already. And the ground bait is now laid for the big haul—the second box, containing approximately one million hundred-lire bills convertible into equivalent sterling on sight. And the whole board of the Bank of Italy, the complete staff of cashiers, office boys, and outside porters, the entire vigilance society of soldiers, secret service agents, and general detectives, all armed to the teeth and beyond, are as innocent of the existence of that million as the unborn daughter of the Caliph's washerwoman."

The girl looked at him with startled eyes.

"And do you mean Beppo was in this?"

"Does it seem that way?" Simon Templar swivelled round towards her with one eyebrow inquisitorially cocked and a long wisp of smoke trailing through his lips. "I wish you could have seen him. . . . Sure he's in it. They turned him over to the Negro Spiritual, and let that big black swine pet him till he signed. If I told you what they'd done to him you wouldn't be in such a hurry for your lunch." For a moment the Saint's lips thinned fractionally. "He's just shot to pieces, and when you see him you'll know why. Sure, that bunch are like brothers to Beppo!"

Patricia sat in a thoughtful silence, and the Saint emptied his glass.

Then she said: "Who are this bunch?"

Simon slithered his cigarette round to the corner of his mouth.

"Well, the actual bunch are mostly miscellaneous, as you might say," he answered. "But the big noise seems to be a bird named Kuzela, whom we haven't met before, but whom I'm going to meet damned soon."

"And this money——"

"Is being delivered to Kuzela's men today." The Saint glanced at his watch. "Has been by now. And within twentyfour hours parcels of it will be burning the sky over to his agents in Paris, Amsterdam and Brussels. Within the week it will be gravitating back to him through the same channels—big bouncing wads of it, translated into authentic wads of francs, guilders and so forth—while one million perfectly genuine hundred-lire bills whose numbers were never in the catalogue are drifting home to a Bank of Italy that will be wondering whether the whole world is falling to pieces round its ears. . . . Do you get me, Pat?"

The clear blue eyes rested on her face with the twist of mocking hell-for-leather delight that she knew so well, and she asked her next question almost mechanically.

"Is it your party?"

"It is, old Pat. And not a question asked. No living soul must ever know—there'd be a panic on the international exchanges if a word of it leaked out. But every single one of those extra million bills has got to be taken by the hand and led gently back to Beppo's tender care—and the man who's going to do it is ready for his lunch."

And lunch it was without further comment, for the Saint was like that. . . . But about his latest meeting with the Negro Spiritual he did not find it necessary to say anything at all—for, again, the Saint was that way. . . . And after lunch, when Patricia was ordering coffee in the lounge, yet another incident which the Saint was inclined to regard as strictly private and personal clicked into its appointed socket in the energetic history of that day.

Simon had gone out to telephone a modest tenner on a horse for the 3.30, and he was on his way back through the hall when a porter stopped him.

"Excuse me, sir, but did you come from the Berkeley?"

The Saint fetched his right foot up alongside his left and lowered his brows one millimetre.

"Yeah—I have been in there this morning."

"A coloured gentleman brought these for you, sir. He said he saw you drop them as you came out of the hotel, but he lost you in the crowd while he was picking them up. And then, as he was walking through Lansdowne Passage, he happened to look up and see you at one of the windows, so he brought them in. From the description he gave me it seemed as if it must have been you, sir——"

"Oh, it was certainly me."

The Saint, who had never owned a pair of lemon-coloured gloves in his life, accepted the specimens gingerly, folded them, and slipped them into his pocket.

"Funny coincidence, sir, wasn't it?" said the porter chattily. "Him happening to pass by, and you happening to be in the window at that time."

"Quite remarkable," agreed the Saint gravely, recalling the care he had taken to avoid all windows; and, turning back, he retired rapidly to a remote sanctuary.

There he unfolded the gloves in an empty wash-basin, contriving to work them cautiously inside out with his fountain pen in one hand and his propelling pencil in the other.

He had not the vaguest idea what kind of creeping West African frightfulness might be waiting for him in those citron-hued misdemeanours, but he was certainly a trifle surprised when he saw what fell out of the first glove that he tackled.

It was simply a thin splinter of wood, pointed at both ends, and stained with some dark stain.

For a moment or two he looked at it expressionlessly.

Then he picked it up between two matches and stowed it carefully in his cigarette-case.

He turned his attention to the second glove, and extracted from it a soiled scrap of paper. He read:

*If you will come to 85 Vandermeer Avenue, Hampstead, at midnight tonight, we may be able to reach some mutually satisfactory agreement. Otherwise, I fear that the consequences of your interference may be infinitely regrettable.*

K.

Simon Templar held the message at arm's length, well up to the light, and gazed at it wall-eyed.

"And whales do so lay eggs," he articulated at last, when he could find a voice sufficiently impregnated with emotion.

And then he laughed and went back to Patricia.

"If Monday's Child comes home, you shall have a new hat," he said, and the girl smiled.

"What else happens before that?" she asked.

"We go on a little tour," said the Saint.

They left the Club together, and boarded a taxi that had just been paid off at the door.

"Piccadilly Hotel," said the Saint.

He settled back, lighting a cigarette.

"I shook off Teal's man by Method One," he explained. "You are now going to see a demonstration of Method Two. If you can go on studying under my supervision, all the shadowers you will ever meet will mean nothing to you. . . . The present performance may be a waste of energy"—he glanced back through the rear window—"or it may not. But the wise man is permanently suspicious."

They reached the Piccadilly entrance of the hotel in a few minutes, and the Saint opened the door. The exact fare, plus bonus, was ready in the Saint's hand, and he dropped it in the driver's palm and followed Patricia across the pavement—without any appearance of haste, but very briskly. As he reached the doors, he saw in one glass panel the reflection of another taxi pulling in to the kerb behind him.

"This way."

He steered the girl swiftly through the main hall, swung her through a short passage, across another hall, and up some steps, and brought her out through another door into Regent Street. A break in the traffic let them straight through to the taxi rank in the middle of the road.

"Berkeley Hotel," said the Saint.

He lounged deep in his corner and grinned at her.

"Method Two is not for use on a trained sleuth who knows you know he's after you," he murmured. "Other times, it's the whelk's knee-cap." He took her bag from her hands, slipped out the little mirror, and used it for a periscope to survey the south side pavement as they drove away. "This is one of those whens," he said complacently.

"Then why are you going to the Berkeley?"

"Because you are the nurse who is going to look after Beppo. His number is 148, and 149 is already booked for you. Incidentally, you might remember that he's registered in the name of Teal—C. E. Teal. I'll pack a bag and bring it along to you later; but once you're inside the Berkeley Arms you've got to stay put so long as it's daylight. The doctor's name is Branson and mine is Travers, and if anyone else applies for admission you will shoot him through the binder and ring for the bellhop to remove the body."

"But what will you be doing?"

"I am the proud possessor of a Clue, and I'm going to be very busy tying a knot in its tail. Also I have an ambition to be humorous, and that will mean that I've got to push round to a shop I wot of and purchase one of those mechanical jokes that are said to create roars of laughter. I've been remembering my younger days, and they've brought back to me the very thing I need. . . . And here we are."

The cab had stopped at its destination, and they got out. Patricia hesitated in the doorway.

"When will you be back?" she asked.

"I shall be along for dinner about eight," said the Saint. "Meanwhile, you'll be able to get acquainted with Beppo. Really, you'll find him quite human. Prattle gently to him, and he'll eat out of your hand. When he's stronger, you might even be allowed to sing to him—I'll ask the doctor about that tomorrow. . . . So long, lass!"

And the Saint was gone.

And he did exactly what he had said he was going to do. He went to a shop in Regent Street and bought a little toy and took it back with him to Upper Berkeley Mews; and a certain alteration which he made to its inner functionings kept him busy for some time and afforded him considerable amusement.

For he had not the slightest doubt that there was going to be fun and games before the next dawn. The incident of those lemon-coloured gloves was a distinct encouragement. It showed a certain thoroughness on the part of the opposition, and that sort of thing always gave the Saint great pleasure.

"If one glove doesn't work, the other is expected to oblige," he figured it out, as he popped studs into a snowy white dress shirt. "And it would be a pity to disappoint anyone."

He elaborated this latter idea to Patricia Holm when he rejoined her at the Berkeley, having shaken off his official watcher again by Method Three. Before he left he told her nearly everything.

"At midnight, all the dreams of the ungodly are coming true," he said. "Picture to yourself the scene. It will be the witching hour. The menace of dark deeds will veil the stars. And up the heights of Hampstead will come toiling the pitiful figure of the unsuspecting victim, with his bleary eyes bulging and his mouth hanging open and the green moss sprouting behind his ears; and that will be Little Boy. . . ."

## V

Some men enjoy trouble; others just as definitely don't. And there are some who enjoy dreaming about the things they would do if they only dared—but they need not concern us.

Simon Templar came into Category A—straight and slick, with his name in a panel all to itself, and a full stop just where it hit hardest.

For there is a price ticket on everything that puts a whizz into life, and adventure follows the rule. It's distressing, but there you are. If there was no competition, everything would be quite all right. If you could be certain that you were the strongest man in the world, the most quick-witted, the most cunning, the most keen-sighted, the most vigilant, and simultaneously the possessor of the one and only lethal weapon in the whole wide universe, there wouldn't be much difficulty about it. You would just step out of your hutch and hammer the first thing that came along.

But it doesn't always pan out like that in practice. When you try the medicine on the dog, you are apt to discover some violent re-actions which were not arranged for in the prescription. And then, when the guns give tongue and a spot of fur begins to fly, you are liable to arrive at the sudden and soul-shattering realisation that a couple of ounces of lead travelling with a given velocity will make precisely as deep an impression on your anatomical system as they will on that of the next man.

Which monumental fact the Saint had thoroughly digested a few days after mastering his alphabet. And the effect it had registered upon his unweaned peace of mind had been so near to absolute zero that a hairline could not have been drawn between them—neither on the day of the discovery nor on any subsequent day in all his life.

In theory . . .

In theory, of course, he allowed the artillery to pop, and the fur to become volatile, without permitting a single lock of his own sleek dark hair to aberrate from the patent-leather discipline in which he disposed it; and thereby he became the Saint. But it is perfectly possible to appreciate and acknowledge the penetrating unpleasant-ness of high-velocity lead, and forthwith to adopt a debonairly philosophical attitude towards the same, without being in a tearing hurry to offer your own carcass for the purposes of practical demonstration; this also the Saint did, and by doing it with meticulous attention contrived to be spoken of in the present tense for many years longer than the most optimistic insurance broker would have backed him to achieve.

All of which has not a little to do with 85 Vandermeer Avenue, Hampstead.

Down this road strolled the Saint, his hands deep in the pockets of knife-edged trousers, the crook of his walking-stick hooked over his left wrist, and slanting sidelong over his right eye a filibustering black felt hat which alone was something very like a breach of the peace. A little song rollicked on his lips, and was inaudible two yards away. And as he walked, his lazy eyes absorbed every interesting item of the scenery.

> *"Aspidistra, little herb,*
> *Do you think it silly*
> *When the botaniser's blurb*
> *Links you with the lily?"*

Up in one window of the house, he caught the almost imperceptible sway of a shifting curtain, and knew that his approach had already been observed. "But it is nice," thought the Saint, "to be expected." And he sauntered on.

> *"Up above your window-ledge*
> *Streatham stars are gleaming:*
> *Aspidistra, little veg,*
> *Does your soul go dreaming?"*

A low iron gate opened from the road. He pushed it wide with his foot, and went up the steps to the porch. Beside the door was a bell-push set in a panel of polished brass tracery.

The Saint's fingers moved towards it . . . and travelled back again. He stooped and examined the filigree more closely, and a little smile lightened his face.

Then he cuddled himself into the extreme houseward corner of the porch, held his hat over the panel, and pressed the button with the ferrule of his stick. He heard a faint hiss, and turned his hat back to the light of a street lamp. A stained splinter of wood quivered in the white satin lining of the crown; and the Saint's smile became blindingly seraphic as he reached into a side pocket of his jacket for a pair of tweezers. . . .

And then the door was opening slowly.

Deep in his angle of shadow, he watched the strip of yellow light widening across the porch and down the short flagged passage to the gate. The silhouette of a man loomed into it and stood motionless for a while behind the threshold.

Then it stepped out into full view—a big heavy-shouldered close-cropped man, with thick bunched fists hanging loosely at his sides. He peered outwards down the shaft of light, and then to right and left, his battered face creasing to the strain of probing the darkness on either side. The Saint's white shirt-front caught his eye, and he licked his lips and spoke like an automaton.

"Comin' in?"

"Behind you, brother," said the Saint.

He stepped across the light, taking the bruiser by the elbows and spinning him adroitly around. They entered the house in the order of his own arrangement, and Simon kicked the door shut behind him.

There was no machine-gun at the far end of the hall, as he had half expected; but the Saint was unashamed.

"Windy?" sneered the bruiser, as the Saint released him; and Simon smiled.

"Never since taking sodamint," he murmured. "Where do we go from here?"

The bruiser glanced sideways, jerking his head.

"Upstairs."

"Oh, yeah?"

Simon slanted a cigarette into his mouth and followed the glance. His eyes weaved up the banisters and down the separate steps of the stairway.

"After you again," he drawled. "Just to be certain."

The bruiser led the way, and Simon followed discreetly. They arrived in procession at the upper landing, where a second bruiser, a trifle shorter than the first, but even heavier of shoulder, lounged beside an open door with an unlighted stump of a cigar in his mouth.

The second man gestured with his lower jaw and the cigar.

"In there."

"Thanks," said the Saint.

He paused for a moment in the doorway and surveyed the room, one hand ostentatiously remaining in the pocket of his coat.

Facing him, in the centre of the rich brown carpet, was a broad flat-topped desk. It harmonised with the solid simplicity of the bookcases that broke the panelling of the bare walls, and with the long austere lines of the velvet hangings that covered the windows— even, perhaps, with the squat square materialism of the safe that stood in a corner behind it. And on the far side of the desk sat the man whom the Saint had come to see, leaning forward out of a straight-backed oak chair.

Simon moved forward, and the two bruisers closed the door and ranged themselves on either side of him.

"Good evening, Kuzela," said the Saint.

"Good evening, Mr Templar." The man behind the desk moved one white hand. "Sit down."

Simon looked at the chair that had been placed ready for him.

Then he turned, and took one of the bruisers by the lapels of his coat. He shot the man into the chair, bounced him up and down a couple of times, swung him from side to side, and yanked him out again.

"Just to make *quite* certain," said the Saint sweetly. He beamed upon the glowering pugilist, felt his biceps, and patted him encouragingly on the shoulder. "You'll be a big man when you grow up, Cuthbert," he said affably.

Then he moved the chair a yard to one side and sat in it himself.

"I'm sure you will excuse all these formalities," he remarked conversationally. "I have to be so careful these days. The most extraordinary things happen to me. Only the other day, a large spotted hypotenuse, overtaking on the wrong side——"

"I have already observed that you possess a well-developed instinct of self-preservation, Mr Templar," said Kuzela suavely.

He clasped his well-kept hands on the blotter before him, and studied the Saint interestedly.

Simon returned the compliment.

He saw a man in healthy middle age, broadshouldered and strongly built. A high firmly modelled forehead rose into a receding setting of clipped iron-grey hair. With his square jaw and slightly aquiline nose, he might have posed for a symbolical portrait of any successful business man. Only his eyes might have betrayed the imposture. Pale blue, deep-set, and unwinking, they levelled themselves upon the object of their scrutiny in a feline stare of utter ruthlessness. . . . And the Saint looked into the eyes and laughed.

"You certainly win on the exchange," he said; and a slight frown came between the other's eyebrows.

"If you would explain——?"

"I'm good-looking," said the Saint easily, and centred his tie with elegance.

Kuzela leaned back.

"Your name is known to me, of course; but I think this is the first time we have had the pleasure of meeting."

"This is certainly the first time you've had the pleasure of meeting me," said the Saint carefully.

"Even now, the responsibility is yours. You have elected to interfere with my affairs——"

Simon shook his head sympathetically.

"It's most distressing, isn't it?" he murmured. "And your most strenuous efforts up to date have failed to dispose of the interference. Even when you sent me a pair of gloves that would have given a rhinoceros a headache to look at, I survived the shock. It must be fate, old dear."

Kuzela pulled himself forward again.

"You are an enterprising young man," he said quietly. "An unusually enterprising young man. There are not many men living who could have overcome Ngano, even by the method which you adopted. The mere fact that you were able to enter this house is another testimony to your foresight—or your good luck."

"My foresight," said the Saint modestly.

"You moved your chair before you sat down—and that again showed remarkable intelligence. If you had sat where I intended you to sit, it would have been possible for me, by a slight movement of my foot, to send a bullet through the centre of your body."

"So I guessed."

"Since you arrived, your hand has been in your pocket several times. I presume you are armed——"

Simon Templar inspected the fingernails of his two hands.

"If I had been born the day before yesterday," he observed mildly, "you'd find out everything you wanted to know in approximately two minutes."

"Again, a man of your reputation would not have communicated with the police——"

"But he would take great care of himself." The Saint's eyes met Kuzela's steadily. "I'll talk or fight, Kuzela, just as you like. Which is it to be?"

"You are prepared to deal?"

"Within limits—yes."

Kuzela drummed his knuckles together.

"On what terms?"

"They might be—one hundred thousand pounds."

Kuzela shrugged.

"If you came here in a week's time——"

"I should be very pleased to have a drink with you," said the Saint pointedly.

"Suppose," said Kuzela, "I gave you a cheque which you could cash tomorrow morning——"

"Or suppose," said the Saint calmly, "you gave me some cash with which to buy jujubes on my way home."

Kuzela looked at him with a kind of admiration.

"Rumour has not lied about you, Mr Templar," he said. "I imagine you will have no objection to receiving this sum in—er—foreign currency?"

"None whatever," said the Saint blandly.

The other stood up, taking a little key from his waistcoat pocket. And the Saint, who for the moment had been looking at the delicately painted shade of the lamp that stood on one side of the desk, which was the sole dim illumination of the room, slewed round with a sudden start.

He knew that there was going to be a catch somewhere—that, with a man of Kuzela's type, a man who had sent those gloves and who had devised that extremely ingenious bell-push on the front door, a coup could never be quite so easy. How that last catch was going to be worked he had no idea; nor was he inclined to wait and learn it. In his own way, he had done as much as he had hoped to do; and, all things considered——

"Let me see that key!" he exclaimed.

Kuzela turned puzzledly.

"Really, Mr Templar——"

"Let me see it!" repeated the Saint excitedly.

He reached over the desk and took the key out of Kuzela's hands. For a second he gazed at it; and then he raised his eyes again with a dancing devil of mischief glinting out of their blueness.

"Sorry I must be going, souls," he said; and with one smashing sweep of his arm he sent the lamp flying off the desk and plunged the room into inky blackness.

## VI

The phrase is neither original nor copyright, and may be performed in public without fee or licence. It remains, however, an excellent way of describing that particular phenomenon.

With the extinction of the single source of luminance, the darkness came down in all the drenching suddenness of an unleashed cataract of Stygian gloom. For an instant, it seemed to blot out not only the sense of sight, but also every other active faculty; and a frozen throbbing stillness settled between the four walls. And in that stillness the Saint sank down without a sound upon his toes and the the tips of his fingers. . . .

He knew his bearings to the $n$th part of a degree, and he travelled to his destination with the noiseless precision of a cat. Around him he could hear the sounds of tensely restrained breathing, and the slithering caress of wary feet creeping over the carpet. Then behind him, came the vibration of a violent movement, the thud of a heavy blow, a curse, a scuffle, a crashing fall, and a shrill yelp of startled anguish . . . and the Saint grinned gently.

"I got 'im," proclaimed a triumphant voice, out of the dark void. "Strike a light, Bill."

Through an undercurrent of muffled yammering sizzled the crisp kindling of a match. It was held in the hand of Kuzela himself, and by its light the two bruisers glared at each other, their reddened stares of hate aimed upwards and downwards respectively. And before the match went out the opinions of the foundation member found fervid utterance.

"You perishing bleeder," he said, in accents that literally wobbled with earnestness.

"Peep-bo," said the Saint, and heard the contortionist effects blasphemously disentangling themselves as he closed the door behind him.

A bullet splintered a panel two inches east of his neck as he shifted briskly westwards. The next door stood invitingly ajar: he went through it as the other door reopened, slammed it behind him, and turned the key.

In a few strides he was across the room and flinging up the window. He squirmed over the sill like an eel, curved his fingers over the edge and hung at the full stretch of his arms. A foot below the level of his eyes there was a narrow stone ledge running along the side of the building: he transferred himself to it, and worked rapidly along to the nearest corner. As he rounded it, he looked down into the road, twenty feet below, and saw a car standing by the kerb.

Another window came over his head. He reached up, got a grip of the sill, and levered his elbows above the sill level with a skilful kick and an acrobatic twist of his body. From there he was able to make a grab for the top of the lower sash. . . . And in another moment he was standing upright on the sill, pushing the upper sash cautiously downwards.

A murmur of dumbfounded voices drifted to his ears.

"Where the 'ell can 'e 'ave gorn to?"

"Think 'e jumped for it?"

"Jumped for it, yer silly fat-'ead? . . ."

And then the Saint lowered himself cat-footed to the carpet on the safe side of the curtains in the room he had recently left.

Through a narrow gap in the hangings he could see Kuzela replacing the shattered bulb of the table lamp by the light of a match. The man's white efficient hands were perfectly steady; his face was without expression. He accomplished his task with the tremorless tranquillity of a patient middle-aged gentleman whom no slight accident could seriously annoy—tested the switch. . . .

And then, as the room lighted up again, he raised his eyes to the convex mirror panel on the opposite wall, and had one distorted glimpse of the figure behind him. . . .

Then the Saint took him by the neck.

Fingers like bands of steel paralysed his larynx and choked back into his chest the cry he would have uttered. He fought like a maniac; but though his strength was above the average, he was as helpless as a puppet in that relentless grip. And almost affectionately Simon Templar's thumbs sidled round to their mark—the deadly pressure on the carotid arteries which is to crude ordinary throttling what foil play is to sabre work. . . .

It was all over in a few seconds. And Kuzela was lying limply spreadeagled across the desk, and Simon Templar was fitting his key into the lock of the safe.

The plungers pistoned smoothly back, and the heavy door swung open. And the Saint sat back on his heels and gazed in rapture at what he saw.

Five small leather attaché cases stood in a neat row before his eyes. It was superb—splendiferous—it was just five times infinitely more than he had ever seriously dared to hope. That one hundred million lire were lying around somewhere in London he had been as sure as a man can be of anything—Kuzela would never have wasted time transporting his booty from the departure centre to the country house where the Duke of Fortezza had been kept—but that the most extempore bluff should have led him promptly and faultlessly to the hiding-place of all that merry mazuma was almost too good to be true. And for a few precious seconds the Saint stared entranced at the vision that his everlasting preposterous luck had ladled out for his delight. . . .

And then he was swiftly hauling the valises out on to the floor.

He did not even have to attempt to open one of them. He knew. . . .

Rapidly he ranged the bags in a happy little line across the carpet. He picked up his stick; and he was adjusting his hat at its most effective angle when the two men who had pursued him returned through the door. But there was a wicked little automatic pivoting round in his free hand, and the two men noticed it in time.

"Restrain your enthusiasm, boys," said the Saint. "We're going on a journey. Pick up your luggage, and let's be moving."

He transferred one of the bags to his left hand, and his gun continued to conduct the orchestra. And under its gentle supervision the two men obeyed his orders. The delirious progress of events during the past couple of minutes had been a shade too much for their ivorine uptakes: their faces wore two uniformly blank expressions of pained bewilderment, vaguely reminiscent of the registers of a pair of precocious goldfish photographed immediately after signing their first talking picture contract. Even the power of protest had temporarily drained out of their vocal organs. They picked up two bags apiece, and suffered themselves to be shepherded out of the room in the same bovine vacuity of acquiescence.

In the hall, Simon halted the fatigue party for a moment.

"Before we pass out into the night," he said, "I want you to be quite clear about one thing. Those bags you're carrying, as you may or may not know, are each supposed to contain the equivalent of two hundred thousand pounds in ready money; and I want you to know that anything you might be prepared to do to keep all those spondulix for yourselves is just so much tadpole-gizzard beside what I'm prepared to do to prise it off you. So you should think a long while before you do anything rash. I am the greatest gun artist in the world," said the Saint persuasively, but with a singular lack of honesty, "and I'm warning you here and now that at the first sign I see of any undue enterprise I shall shoot each of you through the middle of the eleventh spinal vertebra, counting from the bottom. Move on, my children."

The procession moved on.

It went down the porch steps and through the iron wicket gate to the road; and the Saint brought up the rear with his right hand in his pocket. The comedy was played without witnesses: at that hour Vandermeer Avenue, a quiet backwater even at the height of the day, was absolutely deserted. A sum total of four lighted windows was visible along the whole length of the thoroughfare, and those were too far away to provide the slightest inconvenience in any conceivable circumstances. Hampstead was being good that night. . . .

The car which Simon had observed on his prowl round the exterior of the house was parked right opposite the gate—which was where he had expected it to be. As the two men paused outside the gate, waiting for further instructions, a door of the car opened, and a slim supple figure decanted itself lightly on to the sidewalk. Patricia. . . . She came forward with her swinging long-limbed stride.

"OK, Simon?"

"OK, lass."

"Gee, boy, I'm glad to see you!"

"And I you. And the whole Wild West show was just a sitting rabbit, believe it or believe it not." The Saint's hand touched her arm. "Get back behind the wheel, Pat, start her up, and be ready to pull out so soon as the boodle's on board. It isn't every day we ferry a cool million across London, and I don't see why the honour of being the pilot shouldn't be your share of the act."

"Right-ho. . . ."

The girl disappeared, and Simon opened another door.

He watched the cases being stowed one by one in the back of the car, and the forefinger of his right hand curled tensely over the trigger of his gun. He had meant every word of his threat to the two men who were doing the job; and they must have known it, for they carried out his orders with commendable alacrity.

And yet Simon felt a faint electric tingle of uneasiness fanning up his back and into the roots of his hair like the march of a thousand ghostly needle-points. He could not have described it in any other way, and he was as much at a loss to account for it as if the simile had been the actual fact. It was sheer blind instinct, a seventh sense born of a hundred breathless adventures, that touched him with that single thrill of insufficient warning—and left it at that. And for once in his life he ignored the danger sign. He heard the whine of the self-starter, followed by the low-pitched powerful pulsing of the eight cleanly balanced cylinders, and saw the door closed upon the last of the bags; and he turned smiling to the two bruisers. He pointed.

"If you keep straight on down that road," he said, "it ought to land you up somewhere near Birmingham—if you travel far enough. You might make that your next stop."

One of the men took a pace towards him.

"You just listen a minute——"

"To what?" asked the Saint politely.

"I'm tellin' yer——"

THE MILLION POUND DAY

"A bad habit," said the Saint disapprovingly. "You must try and break yourself of that. And now I'm sorry, but I can't stop. I hope you'll wash the back of your neck, see that your socks are aired, say your prayers every night, and get your face lifted at the first opportunity. . . . Now push your ears back, my cherubs, and let your feet chase each other."

His right hand moved significantly in his pocket, and there was an instant's perilous silence. And then the man who had spoken jerked his head at the other.

"Come on," he said.

The two men turned and lurched slowly away, looking back over their shoulders.

And the Saint put one foot on the running-board.

And somewhere, far away, he heard the sound of his own head being hit. It was as extraordinary an experience as any that had ever happened to him. Patricia was looking ahead down the road, while her hand eased the gears quietly into mesh; and the Saint himself had not heard the slightest movement that might have put him on his guard. And the premonitory crawling of his nerves which he had felt a few seconds earlier had performed what it considered to be its duty, and had subsided. . . . He could have believed that the whole thing was an incredibly vivid hallucination—but for the sickening sharp stab of sudden agony that plunged through his brain like a spurt of molten metal and paralysed every milligram of strength in his body.

A great white light swelled up and exploded before his eyes; and after it came a wave of whirling blackness shot with rocketing flashes of dizzy dazzling colour, and the blackness was filled with a thin high singing note that drilled into his eardrums. His knees seemed to melt away beneath him. . . .

And then, from somewhere above the vast dark gulf into which he was sinking, he heard Patricia's voice cry out.

"*Simon!*"

The word seemed to spell itself into his dulled brain letter by letter, as if his mind read it off a slowly uncoiling scroll. But it touched a nerve centre that roused him for one fractional instant of time to fight back titanically against the numbing oblivion that was swallowing him up.

He knew that his eyes were open, but all he could see was one blurred segment of her face, as he might have seen her picture in a badly focused fade-out that had gone askew. And to that isolated scrap of vision in the overwhelming blackness he found the blessed strength to croak two words:

"Drive on."

And then a second surge of darkness welled up around him and blotted out every sight and sound, and he fell away into the infinite black void.

## VII

"So even your arrangements can break down, Templar—when your accomplice fails you," Kuzela remarked silkily. "My enterprising young friend, when you are older you will realise that it is always a mistake to rely upon a woman. I have never employed a woman myself for that reason."

"I'll bet that broke her heart," said the Saint.

Once again he sat in Kuzela's study, with his head still throbbing painfully from the crashing welt it had received, and a lump on the back of it feeling as if it were growing out of his skull like a great auk's egg. His hair was slightly disarranged, and the straps on his wrists prevented him from rearranging it effectively; but the Saintly smile had not lost one iota of its charm.

"It remains, however, to decide whether you are going to be permitted to profit by this experience—whether you are going to live long enough to do so. Perhaps it has not occurred to you that you may have come to the end of your promising career," continued the man on the other side of the desk dispassionately; and the Saint sighed.

"What, not again?" he pleaded brokenly, and Kuzela frowned.

"I do not understand you."

"Only a few months ago I was listening to those very words," explained the Saint. "Alas, poor Wilfred! And he meant it, too. 'Wilf, old polecat,' I said, 'don't you realise that I can't be killed before page three hundred and twenty?' He didn't believe me. And he died. They put a rope round his neck and dropped him through a hole in the floor, and the consequences to his figure were very startling. Up to the base of the neck he was not so thin—but oh, boy, from then on. . . . It was awfully sad."

And Simon Templar beamed around upon the congregation—upon Kuzela, and upon the two bruisers who loafed about the room, and upon the negro who stood behind his chair. And the negro he indicated with a nod.

"One of your little pets?" he inquired; and Kuzela's lips moved in the fraction of a smile.

"It was fortunate that Ngano heard some of the noise," he said. "He came out of the house just in time."

"To soak me over the head from behind?" drawled the Saint genially. "Doubtless, old dear. But apart from that——"

"Your accomplice escaped, with my property. True. But, my dear Templar, need that prove to be a tragedy? We have your own invaluable self still with us—and you, I am quite sure, know not only where the lady has gone, but also where you have hidden a gentleman whom I should very much like to have restored to me."

Simon raised languid eyebrows.

"When I was the Wallachian Vice-Consul at Pfaffenhausen," he said pleasantly, "our diplomacy was governed by a picturesque little Pomeranian poem, which begins:

*"Der Steiss des Elephanten*
*Ist nicht, ist nicht so klein.*

If you get the idea——"

Kuzela nodded without animosity. His deliberate ruthless white hands trimmed the end of a cigar.

"You must not think that I am unused to hearing remarks like that, Templar," he said equably. "In fact, I remember listening to a precisely similar speech from our friend the Duke of Fortezza. And yet——" He paused to blow a few minute flakes of tobacco leaf from the shining top of the desk, and then his pale bland eyes flicked up again to the Saint's face. . . . "The Duke of Fortezza changed his mind," he said.

Simon blinked.

"Do you know," he said enthusiastically, "there's one of the great songs of the century there! I can just feel it. Something like this:

*"The Duke of Fortezza*
*Quite frequently gets a*
*Nimpulse to go blithering off on the blind,*
*But the Duchess starts bimbling*
*And wambling and wimbling*
*And threatens to wallop his ducal behind;*
*And her Ladyship's threats are*
*So fierce that he sweats a*
*Nd just sobs as he pets her*
*With tearful regrets—Ah!*
*The Duke of Fortezza*
*Is changing his mind.*

We could polish up the idea a lot if we had time, but you must admit that for an impromptu effort——"

"You underrate my own sense of humour, Templar." Unemotionally Kuzela inspected the even reddening of the tip of his cigar, and waved his match slowly in the air till it went out. "But do you know another mistake which you also make?"

"I haven't the foggiest notion," said the Saint cheerfully.

"You underrate my sense of proportion."

The Saint smiled.

"In many ways," he murmured, "you remind me of the late Mr Garniman. I wonder how you'll get on together?"

The other straightened up suddenly in his chair. For a moment the mask of amiable self-possession fell from him.

"I shall be interested to bandy words with you later—if you survive, my friend." He spoke without raising his voice; but two little specks of red burned in the cores of his eyes, and a shimmering marrow of vitriolitic savagery edged up through his unalteringly level intonation. "For the present, our time is short, and you have already wasted more than your due allowance. But I think you understand me." Once again, a smooth evanescent trickle of honey glossed over the bitingly measured syllables. "Come now, my dear young friend, it would be a pity for us to quarrel. We have crossed swords, and you have lost. Let us reach an amicable armistice. You have only to give me a little information; and then, as soon as I have verified it, and have finished my work—say after seven days, during which time you would stay with me as an honoured guest—you would be as free as air. We would shake hands and go our ways." Kuzela smiled, and picked up a pencil. "Now firstly: where has your accomplice gone?"

"Naturally she drove straight to Buckingham Palace," said the Saint.

Kuzela continued to smile.

"But you are suspicious. Possibly you think that some harm might befall her, and perhaps you would be unwilling to accept my assurance that she will be as safe as yourself. Well, it is a human suspicion after all, and I can understand it. But suppose we ask you another question. . . . Where is the Duke of Fortezza?" Kuzela drew a small memorandum block towards him, and poised his pencil with engaging expectancy. "Come, come! That is not a very difficult question to answer, is it? He is nothing to you—a man whom you met a few hours ago for the first time. If, say, you had never met him, and you had read in your newspaper that some fatal accident had overtaken him, you would not have been in the least disturbed. And if it is a decision between his temporary inconvenience and your own promising young life. . . ." Kuzela shrugged. "I have no wish to use threats. But you, with your experience and imagination, must know that death does not always come easily. And very recently you did something which has mortally offended the invaluable Ngano. It would distress me to have to deliver you into his keeping. . . . Now, now, let us make up our minds quickly. What have you done with the Duke?"

Simon dropped his chin and looked upwards across the desk.

"Nothing that I should be ashamed to tell my mother," he said winningly; and the other's eyes narrowed slowly.

"Do I, after all, understand you to refuse to tell me?"

The Saint crossed his left ankle over on to his right knee.

"You know, laddie," he remarked, "you should be in the movies, really you should. As the strong silent man you'd be simply great, if you were a bit stronger and didn't talk so much."

For some seconds Kuzela looked at him.

Then he threw down his pencil and pushed away the pad.

"Very well," he said.

He snapped his fingers without turning his head, and one of the two bruisers came to his side. Kuzela spoke without giving the man a glance.

"Yelver, you will bring round the car. We shall require it very shortly."

The man nodded and went out; and Kuzela clasped his hands again on the desk before him.

"And you, Templar, will tell us where we are going," he said, and Simon raised his head.

His eyes gazed full and clear into Kuzela's face, bright with the reckless light of their indomitable mockery, and a sardonically Saintly smile curved the corners of his mouth.

"You're going to hell, old dear," he said coolly; and then the negro dragged him up out of his chair.

Simon went meekly down the stairs with the negro gripping his arm and the second bruiser following behind; and his brain was weighing up the exterior circumstances with lightning accuracy.

Patricia had got away—that was the first and greatest thing. He praised the Lord who had inspired her with the sober farsightedness and clearness of head not to attempt any futile heroism. There was nothing she could have done, and mercifully she'd had the sense to see it. . . . But having got away, what would be her next move?

"Claud Eustace, presumably," thought the Saint; and a wry little twist roved across his lips, for he had always been the most incorrigible optimist in the world.

So he reached the hall, and there he was turned round and hustled along towards the back of the house. As he went, he stole a glance at his wrist watch. . . . Patricia must have been gone for the best part of an hour, and that would have been more than long enough for Teal to get busy. Half of that time would have been sufficient to get Teal on the phone from the nearest call-box and have the house surrounded by enough men to wipe up a brigade—if anything of that sort were going to be done. And not a sign of any such developments had interrupted the playing of the piece. . . .

Down from the kitchen a flight of steps ran to the cellar; and as the Saint was led down them he had a vivid appreciation of another similarity between that adventure and a concluding episode in the history of the late Mr Garniman.* The subterranean prospects in each case had been decidedly uninviting; and now the Saint held his fire and wondered what treat was going to be offered him this time.

The cigar-chewing escort stopped at the foot of the steps, and the Saint was led on alone into a small bare room. From the threshold, the negro flung him forward into a far corner, and turned to lock the door behind him. He put the key in his pocket, took off his coat, and rolled up his sleeves; and all the time his dark blazing eyes were riveted upon the Saint.

And then he picked up a great leather whip from the floor, and his thick lips curled back from his teeth in a ghastly grin.

"You will not talk, no?" he said.

He swung his arm; and the long lash whistled and crackled through the air, and snaked over the Saint's shoulders like the recoiling snap of an overstrained hawser.

## VIII

Simon reeled away in a slash of agony that ate into his chest as if a thin jet of boiling acid had been sprayed across his back.

And he went mad.

Never, otherwise, could he have accomplished what he did. For

*In *The Saint vs. Scotland Yard.*

one blinding instant, which branded itself on his optic nerves with such an eye-aching clarity that it might have stood for an eternity of frozen stillness, he saw everything there was to see in that little room. He saw the stained grey walls and ceiling and the dusty paving underfoot; he saw the locked door; he saw the towering figure of the gigantic hate-vengeful negro before him, and the cyclopean muscles swelling and rippling under the thin texture of the lavender silk shirt; and he saw himself. Just for that instant he saw those things as he had never seen anything before, with every thought of everything else and every other living soul in the world wiped from his mind like chalk marks smeared from a smooth board. . . .

And then a red fog bellied up before his eyes and the stillness seemed to burst inwards like the smithereening of a great glass vacuum.

He felt nothing more—in that white heat of berserk fury, the sense of pain was simply blotted out. He dodged round the room by instinct, ducking and swerving mechanically, and scarcely knew when he succeeded and when he failed.

And at his wrists he felt nothing at all.

The buckle of the strap was out of reach of his teeth, but he twisted his hands inwards, one over the other, tightening up the leather with all his strength, till his muscles ached with the strain. He saw the edges of the strap biting into his skin, and the flesh swelling whitely up on either side; the pain of that alone should have stopped him, but there was no such thing. . . . And he stood still and twisted once again, with a concentrated passion of power that writhed over the whole of his upper body like the stirring of a volcano; and the leather broke before his eyes like a strip of tissue paper. . . .

And the Saint laughed.

The whip sang around again, and he leapt in underneath it and caught it as it fell. And what he had intuitively expected happened. The negro jerked at it savagely—and Simon Templar did not resist. But he kept his hold fast, and allowed all the vicious energy of that jerk to merge flowingly into his own unchecked rush; and it catapulted him to his mark like a stone from a sling. His right fist sogged full and square into the negro's throat with a force that jarred the Saint's own shoulder, and Simon found the whip hanging free in his hand.

He stepped back and watched the grin melting out of the contorted black face. The negro's chest heaved up to the encompass-

ing of a great groaning breath, but the shattering mule-power of
that pent-up super-auxiliated swipe in the gullet had stunned his
thyro-arytenoids as effectively as if a bullet had gone through them.
His mouth worked wildly, but he could produce nothing more
than an inaudible whisper. And the Saint laughed again, gathering
up the whip.

"The boys will be expecting some music," he said, very gently.
"And you are going to provide it."

Then the negro sprang at him like a tiger.

That one single punch which had reversed the situation would
have sent any living European swooning off into hours of tortured
helplessness, but in this case the Saint had never expected any such
result from it. It had done all that he had ever hoped that it would
do—obliterated the negro's speaking voice, and given the Saint himself the advantage of the one unwieldy weapon in the room. And
with the red mists of unholy rage still swilling across his vision,
Simon Templar went grimly into the fight of his life.

He sidestepped the negro's first maniac charge as smoothly and
easily as a practised pedestrian evading a two-horse dray, and as he
swerved he brought the whip cracking round in a stroke that split
the lavender silk shirt as crisply as if a razor had been scored across it.

The negro fetched up against the far wall with an animal scream,
spun round, and sprang at him again. And again the Saint swayed
lightly aside, and made the whip lick venomously home with a report like a gunshot. . . .

He knew that that was the only earthly hope he had—to keep his
opponent tearing blindly through a hazing madness of pain and fury
that would scatter every idea of scientific fighting to the four winds.
There were six feet eight inches of the negro, most of three hundred
pounds of pitiless clawing blood-mad primitive malignity caged up
with Simon Templar within those blank, damp-blotched walls; and
Simon knew, with a quiet cold certainty, that if once those six feet
eight inches, those three hundred odd pounds of bone and muscle,
resolved themselves into the same weight and size of logical crafty
fighting precision, there was no man in the world who could have
stood two minutes against them. And the Saint quietly and relentlessly crimped down his own strength and speed and fighting madness into the one narrow channel that would give him a fighting
chance.

It was a duel between brute strength and animal ferocity on the
one hand, and on the other hand the lithe swiftness and lightning

eye of the trickiest fighting man alive—a duel with no referee, in which no foul was barred. Tirelessly the Saint went round the room, flitting airily beyond, around, even under the massive arms that grappled for him, bobbing and swooping and turning, up on his toes and supple as a dancer, as elusive as a drop of quicksilver on a plate; and always the tapered leather thong in his hand was whirling and hissing like an angry fer-de-lance, striking and coiling and striking again with a bitter deadliness of aim. Once the negro grabbed at the whip and found it, and the Saint broke his hold with a kick to the elbow that opened the man's fingers as if the tendons had been cut; once the Saint's foot slipped and he battered his way out of a closing trap in a desperate flurry of rib-creaking body blows that made even the negro stagger for a sufficient moment; and the fight went on.

It went on till the negro's half-naked torso shone with a streaming lather of sweat and blood, and a sudden kicking lurch in his step shot into Simon's taut-strung brain the wild knowledge that the fight was won.

And for the first time the Saint stood his ground, with his back to one wall, holding the negro at bay by the flailing sweep of the lash alone.

Then Simon pressed forward, and the negro went back. . . .

The Saint drove him into the opposite corner and beat him whimpering to his knees. And then, as the man spilled forward on to his face, Simon leapt in and got an ankle hold.

"Get your hands right up behind your back," he rasped incisively, "or I'll twist the leg off you!"

He applied his leverage vigorously, and the man obeyed him with a yelp. Simon locked the ankle with his knee and bent his weight over it. With quick deft fingers he knotted the tail of the whip round the negro's wrists, and passed the stock over one shoulder round the neck, and back over the other shoulder into a slip-knot. A draught of air gulped noisily into the negro's straining lungs, and Simon gave the noose a yank.

"One word from you, and you graze in the Green Pastures," he stated pungently, and heard the lungful choke sibilantly out again. "And get this," said the Saint, with no increase of friendliness: "if you move the half of an inch in that hog-tie, you'll bowstring your own sweet self. That's all."

He fished the key of the door out of the negro's pocket and stood up, breathing deeply.

He himself was starting to look as if he had recently taken a warm shower-bath in his clothes; and now that the anæsthetic red mists were thinning out, a large part of his back was beginning to stiffen itself up into an identical acreage of ache; but he was not yet ready to sit down and be sorry about such minor discomforts. With the key snapping over in the lock, he brushed the hair back off his forehead and opened the door; and the cigar-chewer at the foot of the steps crawled upright like a slow-motion picture, with his jaw sagging nervelessly and his eyes popping from their orbits, gazing at the Saint as he might have gaped at his own ghost. . . .

Smiling, and without any haste, Simon walked towards him.

And the man stood there staring at him, watching him come on, numbed with a bone-chilling superstitious terror. It was not until the Saint was within two yards of him that a sobbing little wail gurgled in his throat and he reached feebly round to his hip pocket.

And of the rest of the entertainment he knew little. He knew that a grip about which there was nothing ghostly seized upon his right wrist before he had time to draw, while another metallic clutch closed round his knees; he knew that the weight came suddenly off his feet; and then he seemed to go floating ethereally through space. Somewhere in the course of that flight an astonishingly hard quantity of concrete impinged upon his skull, but it did not seem an important incident. His soul went bimbering on, way out into the land of blissful dreams. . . .

And the Saint went on up the steps.

He was halfway up when a bell jangled somewhere overhead, and he checked involuntarily. And then a tiny skew-eyed grin skimmed over his lips.

"Claud Eustace for the hell of it," he murmured, and went upwards very softly.

Right up by the door at the top of the stairs he stopped again and listened. He heard slow and watchful footsteps going down the hall, followed by the rattle of a latch and the cautious whine of slowly turning hinges. And then he heard the most perplexing thing of all, which was nothing more or less than an expansive and omnipotent silence.

The Saint put up one hand and gently scratched his ear, with a puzzled crease chiselling in between his eyebrows. He was prepared to hear almost anything else but that. And he didn't. The silence continued for some time, and then the front door closed again and the footsteps started back solo on the return journey.

And then, in the very opposite direction, the creak of a window-sash sliding up made him blink.

Someone was wriggling stealthily over the sill. With his ear glued to a panel of the door, he could visualise every movement as clearly as if he could have seen it. He heard the faint patter of the intruder's weight coming on to the floor, and the equally faint sound of footsteps creeping over the linoleum. They connected up in his mind with the footsteps of the man who had gone to the door like the other part of a duet. Then the second set of footsteps died away, and there was only the sound of the man returning from the hall. Another door opened. . . . And then a voice uttered a corrosively quiet command.

"Keep still!"

Simon almost fell down the steps. And then he windmilled dazedly back to his balance and hugged himself.

"Oh, Pat!" he breathed. "Mightn't I have known it? And you ring the bell to draw the fire, and sprint round and come in the back way. . . . Oh, you little treasure!"

Grinning a great wide grin, he listened to the dialogue.

"Put your hands right up. . . . That's fine. . . . And now, where's Kuzela?"

Silence.

"Where is Kuzela?"

A shifting of feet, and then the grudging answer:

"Upstairs."

"Lead on, sweetheart."

The sounds of reluctant movement. . . .

And the whole of Simon Templar's inside squirmed with ecstasy at the pure poetic Saintliness of the technique. Not for a thousand million pounds would he have butted in just then—not one second before Kuzela himself had also had time to appreciate the full ripe beauty of the situation. He heard the footsteps travelling again: they came right past his door and went on into the hall, and the Saint pointed his toes in a few movements of an improvised cachucha.

And then, after a due pause, he opened the door and followed on.

He gave the others time to reach the upper landing, and then he went whisking up the first flight. Peeping round the banisters, he was just in time to get a sight of Patricia disappearing into Kuzela's study. Then the door slammed behind her, and the Saint raced on up and halted outside it.

While after the answering of the dud front door call there had certainly been a silence, the stillness to which he listened now made all previous efforts in noiselessness sound like an artillery barrage. Against that background of devastating blankness, the clatter of a distant passing truck seemed to shake the earth, and the hoot of its klaxon sounded like the Last Trump.

And then Patricia spoke again, quite calmly, but with a lethal clearness that was hedged around on every side with the menace of every manner of murder.

"Where is the Saint?" she asked.

And upon those words Simon Templar figured that he had his cue.

He turned the handle soundlessly and pushed the door wide open.

Patricia's back was towards him. A little further on to one side the second bruiser stood by with his hands high in the air. And behind the desk sat Kuzela, with his face still frozen in an expression of dumb incredulous stupefaction. . . . And as the door swung back, and the Saint advanced gracefully into the limelight, the eyes of the two men revolved and centred on him, and dilated slowly into petrified staring orbs of something near to panic.

"Good morning," said the Saint.

Patricia half-turned. She could not help herself—the expressions on the faces of the two men in front of her were far too transparently heart-felt to leave her with any mistrust that they were part of a ruse to put her off her guard.

But the result of her movement was the same; for as she turned her eyes away, the smallest part in the cast had his moment. He awoke out of his groping comatosity, saw his chance, and grabbed it with both fists.

The automatic was wrested violently out of the girl's hands, and she was thrown stumbling back into the Saint's arms. And the Saint's gentle smile never altered.

He passed Patricia to one side, and cocked a derisive eye at the gun that was turned against him. And with no more heed for it than that, he continued on towards the desk.

"So nice to see you again," he said.

## IX

Kuzela rose lingeringly to his feet.

There was a perceptible pause before he gained control of the faculty of speech. The two consecutive smacks that had been jolted

into the very roots of his being within the space of the last forty
seconds would have tottered the equilibrium of any man—of any
man except, perhaps, the Saint himself. . . . But the Saint was not
at all disturbed. He waited in a genteel silence, while the other
schooled the flabby startlement out of his face and dragged up his
mouth into an answering smile.

"My dear young friend!"

The voice, when Kuzela found it, had the same svelte timbre as
before, and Simon bowed a mocking compliment to the other's
nerve.

"My dear old comrade!" he murmured, open-armed.

"You have saved us the trouble of fetching you, Templar," Kuzela said blandly. "But where is Ngano?"

"The Negro Spiritual?" The Saint aligned his eyebrows banter-
ingly. "I'm afraid he—er—met with a slight accident."

"Ah!"

"No—not exactly. I don't think he's quite dead yet, though he
may easily have strangled himself by this time. But he hasn't enjoyed
himself. I think, if the circumstances had been reversed, he would
have talked," said the Saint, with a glacial inclemency of quietness.

Kuzela stroked his chin.

"That is unfortunate," he said.

And then he smiled.

"But it is not fatal, my friend," he purred. "The lady has already
solved one problem for us herself. And now that she is here, I am
sure you would do anything rather than expose her to the slightest
danger. So let us return to our previous conversation at once. Perhaps the lady will tell us herself where she went to when she drove
away from here?"

Simon put his hands in his pockets.

"Why, yes," he said good-humouredly. "I should think she
would."

The girl looked at him as if she could not quite believe her ears.
And Simon met her puzzled gaze with blue eyes of such a blinding
Saintly innocence that even she could read no enticement to decep-
tion in them.

"Do you mean that?" she asked.

"Of course," said the Saint. "There are one or two things I
shouldn't mind knowing myself."

Patricia put a hand to her head.

"If you want to know—when I left here I drove straight to——"

"Buckingham Palace," drawled the Saint. "And then?"

"I had the bags taken up to Beppo's room, and I saw him myself. He was quite wide awake and sensible. I told him I was coming back here to get you out, and said that if I wasn't back by four o'clock, or one of us hadn't rung him up, he was to get in touch with Teal. I gave him Teal's private number. He didn't want me to go at all, but I insisted. That's all there is to tell. I picked up a puncture on the second trip out here, and that held me up a bit——"

"But who cares about that?" said the Saint.

He turned back to the desk.

The man with the gun stood less than a yard away on his right front; but the Saint, ignoring his very existence, leaned a little forward and looked from the distance of another yard into the face of Kuzela. The loose poise of his body somehow centred attention even while it disarmed suspicion. But the mockery had gone out of his eyes.

"You heard?" he asked.

Kuzela nodded. His mouth went up at one corner.

"But I still see no reason for alarm, my friend," he said, in that wheedling voice of slow malevolence. "After all, there is still time for much to happen. Before your friend Mr Teal arrives——"

"Before my friend Chief Inspector Teal arrives with a squad of policemen in a plain van I shall be a long way from here," said the Saint.

Kuzela started.

"So you have invoked the police?" he snapped. And then again he recovered himself. "But that is your affair. By the time they arrive, as you say, you will have left here. But where do you think you will have gone?"

"Home, James," said the Saint.

He took one hand out of his pocket to straighten his coat, and smiled without mirth.

"Fortunately, the argument between us can be settled tonight," he said, "which will save me having to stage any reunions. Your black torturer has been dealt with. I have given him a dose of his own medicine which will, I think, put him in hospital for several weeks. But you remain. You are, after all, the man who gave Ngano his orders. I have seen what you did to the Duke of Fortezza, and I know what you wanted to have done with me. . . . I hope you will get on with Wilfred."

"And what do you think you are going to do to me?" asked
Kuzela throatily; and Simon held him with his eyes.

"I'm going to kill you, Kuzela," he said simply.

"Ah! And how will you do that?"

Simon's fingers dipped into his pocket. They came out with an
ordinary matchbox, and he laid it on the desk.

"That is the answer to all questions," he said.

Kuzela stared down at the box. It sat there in the middle of his
clean white blotter, yellow and oblong and angular, as commonplace a thing as any man could see on his desk—and the mystery of
it seemed to leer up at him malignantly. He picked it up and shook
it: it weighed light in his hand, and his mind balked at the idea that
it could conceal any engine of destruction. And the Saint's manner
of presenting it had been void of the most minute scintilla of excitement—and still was. He eyed Kuzela quizzically.

"Why not open it?" he suggested.

Kuzela looked at him blankly. And then, with a sudden impatience, he jabbed his thumb at the little sliding drawer. . . .

In a dead silence, the box fell through the air and flopped half-
open on the desk.

"What does this mean?" asked Kuzela, almost in a whisper.

"It means that you have four minutes to live," said the Saint.

Kuzela held up his hand and stared at it.

In the centre of the ball of his right thumb a little globule of
blood was swelling up in the pinky-white of the surrounding skin.
He gazed stupidly from it to the match-box and back again. In
imagination, he felt a second time the asp-like prick that had bitten
into his thumb as he moved the drawer of the box—and understood.
"The answer to all questions. . . ."

He stood there as powerless to move as a man in a nightmare,
and watched the infinitely slow distension of the tiny crimson sphere
under his eyes, his face going ashen with the knowledge of inescapable doom. The drop of blood hypnotised him, filled his vision
till he could see nothing else but the microscopic reflections glistening over the surface of it—until all at once it seemed to grow magi-
cally into a coruscating red vesicle of enormous size, thrusting in
upon him, bearing him down, filling the whole universe with the
menace of its smothering scarlet magnitude. A roaring of mighty
waters seethed up about his ears. . . .

The others saw him brace himself on his feet as if to resist falling;
and he remained quite still, with his eyes fixing and going dim. And

then he took one step sideways, swayed, and crumpled down on to the floor with his limbs twitching convulsively and his chest labouring. . . .

Quite calmly and casually the Saint put out a hand and clasped it on the gun wrist of the man who stood beside him.

The man seemed to come alive out of a dream. And without any noticeable interregnum of full consciousness, he seemed to pass right on into another kind of dream—the transition being effected by the contingence upon the point of his jaw of a tearing uppercut that started well below the Saint's waistline and consummated every erg of its weight and velocity at the most vital angle of the victim's face. With the results aforementioned. He went down in a heap and lay very still, even as his companion had done a little earlier; and Simon picked up the gun.

"Which finishes that," said the Saint, and found Patricia looking down again at Kuzela.

"What happened to him?" she asked, a trifle unsteadily.

"More or less what he tried to make happen to me. Ever come across those trick match-boxes that shoot a needle into you when you try to open them? I bought one last afternoon, and replaced the needle with something that was sent to me along with the message you know about. And I don't know that we shall want it again."

He took the little box of death over to the fireplace, dropped it in the grate, and raked the glowing embers over it. Then he took up his hat and stick, which he saw lying in a chair, and glanced around for the last time. Only Kuzela's fingers were twitching now, and a wet froth gleamed on his lips and dribbled down one cheek. . . . Simon put an arm round the girl's shoulders.

"I guess we can be going," he said, and led her out of the room.

It was in the hall that the expression on the face of a clock caught his eye and pulled him up with a jerk.

"What time did you say Beppo was going to get in touch with Teal?" he inquired.

"Four o'clock." Patricia followed his gaze, and then looked at her wrist. "That clock must be fast——"

"Or else you've stopped," said the Saint pithily. He turned back his sleeve and inspected his own watch. "And stopped you have, old darling. It's thirtythree minutes after four now—and to give Claud Eustace even a chance to think that he pulled me out of a mess would break my heart. Not to include another reason why he mustn't find us here. Where did you leave the car?"

"Just one block away."

"This is where we make greyhounds look lazy," said the Saint, and opened the front door.

They were at the gates when Simon saw the lights of a car slowing up and swinging in to the kerb on his left. Right in front of him, Kuzela's car was parked; and the Saint knew clairvoyantly that that was their only chance.

He caught Patricia's arm and flipped up the collar of her coat.

"Jump to it," he crisped.

He scudded round to the driving seat, and the girl tumbled in beside him as he let in the clutch. He shot right past the police car with his head well down and his shoulders hunched. A tattered shout reached him as he went by; and then he was bucking off down a side street with the car heeling over on two wheels as he crammed it round the corner. The police car would have to be turned right round in a narrow road before it could get after him, and he knew he was well away. He dodged hectically southeast, and kept hard at it till he was sure he had left any pursuit far behind.

Somewhere in the northern hinterlands of the Tottenham Court Road he stopped the car and made some hurried repairs to his appearance with the aid of the driving mirror, and ended up looking distinctly more presentable than he had been when they left Hampstead. He looked so presentable in fact, that they abandoned the car on that spot, and walked boldly on until they met a taxi, which took them to Berkeley Square.

"For the night isn't nearly over yet," said the Saint, as they walked down Upper Berkeley Mews together after the taxi had chugged off out of sight.

It was one of those foolproof prophecies which always delighted his sense of the slickness of things by the brisk promptness with which they fulfilled themselves. He had hardly closed the door of his house when the telephone bell began to ring, and he went to answer the call with a feeling of large and unalloyed contentment.

"Hullo-o? . . . Speaking. . . . That's which? . . . Teal? . . . Well, blow me, Claud Eustace, this is very late for you to be out! Does your grandmother allow you—— What? . . . What have I been doing tonight? I've been drinking beer with Beppo. . . . No, not a leper—BEPPO B for bdellium, E for eiderdown, P for psychology, P for pneumonia, O for a muse of fire that would ascend the brightest heaven of . . . I beg your pardon? . . . You were called up and told I was in trouble? . . . Someone's been pulling your leg;

Claud. I'm at peace with the world. . . . Whassat? . . . Why, sure. I was just going to bed, but I guess I can stay up a few minutes longer. Will you be bringing your own gum? . . . Right-ho. . . ."

He listened for a moment longer; and then he hung up the receiver and turned to Pat.

"Claud's coming right along," he said gleefully, and the laughter was lilting in his voice. "We're not to try to get away, because he'll have an armed guard at every sea and airport in the British Isles ten minutes after he gets here and finds we've done a bunk. Which will be tremendous fun for all concerned. . . . And now, get through to Beppo as fast as you can spin the dial, old sweetheart, while I sprint upstairs and change my shirt—for there's going to be a great day!"

## X

Chief Inspector Claud Eustace Teal fixed his pudgy hands in the belt of his overcoat, and levelled his unfriendly gaze on the superbly elegant young man who lounged against the table in front of him.

"So that message I had was a fake, was it?" he snarled.

"It must have been, Claud."

Teal nodded fatly.

"Perhaps it was," he said. "But I went to the address it gave me—and what do you think I found?"

"The Shah of Persia playing ludo," hazarded Simon Templar, intelligently; and the detective glowered.

"In the cellar I found a nigger tied up with the whip that had beaten half the hide off his back. Outside, there was a white man with a fractured skull—he's gone to hospital as well. In a room upstairs was another man laid out with a broken jaw, and a fourth man in the same room—dead."

The Saint raised his eyebrows.

"But, my dear old sturgeon!" he protested reasonably—"what on earth do you think I am? A sort of human earthquake?"

"Both the nigger and the man with the broken jaw," Teal continued stonily, "gave me a description of the man responsible, and it fits you like a glove. The man with the broken jaw also added the description of a woman who couldn't be distinguished apart from Miss Holm."

"Then we obviously have doubles, Claud."

"He also heard the woman say: 'Where is the Saint?'"

Simon frowned.

"That's certainly odd," he admitted. "Where did you say this was?"

"You know darned well where it was! And I'll tell you some more. Just as I got there in the police car, a man and a woman dashed out of the house and got away. And who do you suppose they looked like?"

"The same doubles, obviously," said the Saint with great brilliance.

"And just one block away from that house we found a blue saloon Lagonda, which the two people I saw would have got away in if they'd had time to reach it. The number of it was ZX1257. Is that the number of your car?"

The Saint sat up.

"Claud, you're a blessing in disguise! That certainly is my car—and I was thinking I'd lost her! Pinched outside the May Fair only yesterday afternoon, she was, in broad daylight. I was meaning to ring up Vine Street before, but what with one thing and another——"

Teal drew a deep breath—and then he exploded.

"Now would you like to know what I think of your defence?" he blurted out, in a boiling gust of righteous wrath. And he went on without waiting for encouragement. "I think it's the most weak-kneed tangle of moonshine I've ever had to listen to in my life. I think it's so drivelling that if any jury will listen to it for ten minutes, I'll walk right out of the court and have myself certified. I've got two men who'll swear to you on their dying oaths, and another one to put beside them if he recovers, and I know what I saw myself and what the men who were with me saw; and I think everything you've got to say is so maudlin that I'm going to take you straight back to Scotland Yard with me and have it put in writing before we lock you up. I think I've landed you at last, Mr Saint, and after what you said to me this morning I'm damned glad I've done it."

The Saint took out his cigarette-case and flopped off the table into an armchair, sprawling one leg comfortably over the arm.

"Well, that does express your point of view quite clearly," he conceded. He lighted a cigarette, and looked up brightly. "Claud, you're getting almost fluent in your old age. But you've got to mind you don't let your new-found eloquence run away with you."

"Oh, have I?" The detective took the bait right down into his œsophagus, and clinched his teeth on the line. "Very well. Then

while all these extraordinary things were being done by your double
—while half a dozen sober men were seeing you and listening to
you and being beaten up by you and getting messages from you—
maybe you'll tell me what you were doing and who else knows
it besides yourself?"

Simon inhaled luxuriously, and smiled.

"Why, sure. As I told you over the phone, I was drinking beer
with Beppo."

"And who's he?"

"The Duke of Fortezza."

"Oh, yes?" Teal grew sarcastic. "And where was the King of
Spain and the Prime Minister of Jugo-Slavia?"

"Blowed if I know," said the Saint ingenuously. "But there were
some other distinguished people present. The Count of Montalano,
and Prince Marco d'Ombria, and the Italian Ambassador——"

"The Italian *what?*"

"Ambassador. You know. Gent with top hat and spats."

"And where was this?"

"At the Italian embassy. It was just a little private party, but it
went on for a long time. We started about midnight, and didn't
break up till half-past four—I hadn't been home two minutes when
you phoned."

Teal almost choked.

"What sort of bluff are you trying to pull on me now?" he demanded. "Have you got hold of the idea that I've gone dotty? Are
you sitting there believing that I'll soak up that story, along with
everything else you've told me, and just go home and ask no questions?" Teal snorted savagely. "You must have gone daft!" he
blared.

The Saint came slowly out of his chair. He posed himself before
the detective, feet astraddle, his left hand on his hip, loose-limbed
and smiling and dangerous; and the long dictatorial forefinger which
Teal had seen and hated before drove a straight and peremptory line
into the third button of the detective's waistcoat.

"And now you listen to me again, Claud," said the Saint waspily.
"Do you know what you're letting yourself in for?"

"Do I know what I'm——"

"Do you know what you're letting yourself in for? You burst
into my house and make wild accusations against me. You shout at
me, you bully me, you tell me I'm either lying or dippy, and you
threaten to arrest me. I'm very sensitive, Claud," said the Saint, "and

you hurt me. You hurt me so much that I've a damned good mind to let you run me in—and then, when you'd put the rope right round your own neck and drawn it up as tight as it'd go, I'd pull down such a shemozzle around your bat ears that you'd want nothing more in life than to hand in your resignation and get away to some forgotten corner of the earth where they've never seen a newspaper. That's what's coming your way so fast that you're going to have to jump like a kangaroo to get from under it. It's only because I'm of a godly and forgiving disposition," said the Saint virtuously, "that I'm giving you a chance to save your skin. I'm going to let you verify my alibi before you arrest me, instead of having it fed into you with a stomach-pump afterwards; and then you are going to apologise to me and go home," said the Saint.

He picked up a telephone directory, found a place, and thrust the book under Teal's oscillating eyes.

"There's the number," he said. "Mayfair three two three O. Check it up for yourself now, and save yourself the trouble of telling me I'm just ringing up an accomplice."

He left the detective blinking at the volume, and went to the telephone.

Teal read off the number, put down the book, and pulled at his collar.

Once again the situation had passed out of his control. He gazed at the Saint purply, and the beginnings of a despondent weariness pouched up under his eyes. It was starting to be borne in upon him, with a preposterous certitude, that he had just been listening to something more than bluff. And the irony of it made him want to burst into tears. It was unfair. It was brutal. It outraged every canon of logic and justice. He knew his case was watertight, knew that against the evidence he could put into a witness-box there could simply be no human way of escape—he would have sworn to it on the rack, and would have gone to his death still swearing it. And he knew that it wasn't going to work.

Through a haze of almost homicidal futility, he heard the Saint speaking.

"Oh, is that you, Signor Ravelli? . . . Simon Templar speaking. Listen: there's some weird eruption going on in the brains of Scotland Yard. Some crime or other was committed somewhere tonight, and for some blithering reason they seem to think I was mixed up in it. I'm sorry to have to stop you on your way to bed, but a fat policeman has just barged in here——"

"Give me that telephone!" snarled Teal.

He snatched the instrument away and rammed the receiver up against his ear.

"Hullo!" he barked. "This is Chief Inspector Teal, Criminal Investigation Department, speaking. I have every reason to believe that this man Templar was concerned in a murder which took place in Hampstead shortly after four o'clock this morning. He's tried to tell me some cock-and-bull story about . . . What? . . . But damn it— . . . I beg your pardon, sir, but I definitely know . . . From twelve o'clock till half-past four? . . . But . . . But . . . But, oh hell, I. . . . No, sir, I said . . . But he . . . *Who?* . . ."

The diaphragm of the receiver clacked and chattered, and Teal's red face sagged sickly.

And then:

"All right, sir. Thank you very much, sir," he said in a strangled voice, and slammed the microphone back on its bracket.

The Saint smoothed his hair.

"We might get on to Beppo next," he suggested hopefully. "He's staying at the Berkeley. Then you can have a word with Prince d'Ombria——"

"Can I?" Teal had eaten wormwood, and his voice was thick and raw with the bitterness of it. "Well, I haven't got time. I know when I'm licked. I know where I am when half a dozen princes and ambassadors will go into the witness-box and swear that you're chasing them round the equator at the very moment when I know that I'm talking to you here in this room. I don't even ask how you worked it. I expect you rang up the President of the United States and got him to fix it for you. But I'll be seeing you another time—don't you worry."

He hitched his coat round, and grabbed up his hat.

"Bye-bye," sang the Saint.

"And you remember this," Teal gulped out. "I'm not through with you yet. You're not going to sit back on your laurels. You wouldn't. And that's what's going to be the finish of you. You'll be up to something else soon enough—and maybe you won't have the entire Italian Diplomatic Service primed to lie you out of it next time. From this minute, you're not even going to blow your nose without I know it. I'll have you watched closer than the Crown Jewels, and the next mistake you make is going to be the last."

"Cheerio, dear heart," said the Saint, and heard the vicious bang of the front door before he sank back into his chair in hysterics of helpless laughter.

But the epilogue of that story was not written until some weeks later, when a registered packet bearing an Italian postmark was delivered at No 7 Upper Berkeley Mews.

Simon opened it after breakfast.

First came a smaller envelope, which contained a draft on the Bank of Italy for a sum whose proportions made even Simon Templar blink.

And then he took out a small shagreen case, and turned it over curiously. He pressed his thumbnail into the little spring catch, and the lid flew up and left him staring.

Patricia put a hand on his shoulder.

"What is it?" she asked, and the Saint looked at her.

"It's the medallion of the Order of the Annunziata—and I think we shall both have to have new hats on this," he said.

# THE DEATH PENALTY

## From THE SAINT AND MR TEAL

MOST OF THIS STORY *takes place in the Scilly Isles; and as you might expect, it is partly the result of a stay which I myself made one summer in that half-forgotten little archipelago off the western tip of Cornwall.*

*Some of the things I felt about the place are written into the story. The attempt may have fallen far short of what I intended, and I think it was rather rapidly obscured by the exigencies of an unusually melodramatic plot; but I hope that the lovable and friendly islanders whom I knew there will understand from a few lines what I was trying to say.*

*I have never been back there. But I am happily reminded of that one visit on every Atlantic crossing. Before then, when I saw the first blink of Bishop's Light far down on the dark horizon, it was merely the first landfall of the Old World and a promise that we should be in England in the morning. But now I remember that Bishop's Rock is only one of the farthest outposts of the Scilly Isles, and I have a sentimental feeling that the light is flashing especially for my benefit, because friends have come out to meet me.*

*But this was not the final reason that made me choose this—I must be candid—not very distinguished story to be reprinted here. It was because, when I read it over to consider it for inclusion in this volume, it brought back one other glimpse that I had of the Scilly Isles.*

*It was on a westbound trip, that time. They swam out of a grey and hazy dawn, closer than I had ever seen them before on an ocean crossing. The morning mists parted like a drawn veil, and there were the islands suddenly, grey humps of rock breaking the calm of a leaden sea. I could identify them all,* as if I saw them on a chart: I fancied that I could even pick out different places in St Mary's where I had been. They fell behind very quickly, and then only the empty Atlantic was ahead of us. But it seemed less empty for that last passing of familiar scenes.

I shall never see the Scilly Isles in exactly that way again. For that was on the first flight to New York of the late Zeppelin "Hindenburg".

# THE DEATH PENALTY

THEY HANGED GALBRAITH STRIDE at eight o'clock on the morning of the 22nd of November.

They came in and strapped his hands together, and led him out to the narrow whitewashed shed that was to be his last glimpse of the world—walking very fast, like a man who has made up his mind to see an unpleasant appointment through as quickly as possible. They stood him on the chalked T in the centre of the trap, and drew the white cap down over his bald head and his pale frightened eyes, till the only feature of his face that could be seen was the thin twitching mouth under his little grey moustache. They settled the rope round his neck, with the knot just under his left ear; and the executioner stepped back to the lever that would send him into eternity.

They asked him if he had anything to say before he paid the extreme penalty of the law, and the tip of his tongue slipped once over those twitching lips.

"Get it over," he said; and with that they dropped him.

All this was after many other things had happened, and a lady had thanked the Saint for assistance.

## II

Laura Berwick came into the Saint's life unasked, uninvited, and unintroduced; which was what one might have expected of her. She had brown hair, brown eyes, and a chin that was afraid of no dragons —not even of an outlaw so notorious and unpopular as Simon Templar. And as far as the Saint was concerned, any girl with her face and figure could have come into his life unasked, uninvited, and unintroduced every day of the week, and he would have had nothing but praise for the beneficence of a Providence that provided surprises of such quality. He was able to frame that appraisement of her physical perfections within a bare few minutes of meeting her for the first time—which in this case happens to be a far more respectable statement than it sounds.

Simon Templar had left London. The wanderlust that would never let him be still for long had filled him again with dreams of wild adventurous voyaging after an exceptionally short rest in the city that was as near home to him as anywhere else in the world. Partly because his rest had been so extraordinarily unrestful. In a very few months, London had loaded down his life with such a plentiful supply of excitement that he had made up his mind to take wing again promptly, before the standard of lawlessness and unrest depreciated. The house that he had chosen when he first returned was still in the hands of interior decorators who were struggling to repair the damage that can only be done by a powerful bomb exploded in a small room, and after viewing the progress of their efforts he had decided to terminate his lease and take up residence at the Dorchester for the remainder of his stay. An expensive luxury, but one which he considered he had earned. Or, if he hadn't earned it, he would doubtless contrive to do so before he left. . . . And then—since this was in that memorable year when the sun shone upon England—the thermometer hopped back on top of the ninety mark, and after two days of it the Saint tore off his coat and tie and went forth into the West End swearing a quiet sirocco of wrath whose repercussions were recorded at Kew.

"Civilisation be damned," said the Saint, in one of his few lucid moments. "I saw an English Gentleman in Piccadilly yesterday. With great daring he had removed his coat, waistcoat, collar, and tie, and he was walking about in a flannel shirt and a hideous pair of braces striped with his old school colours. Under the neck of his shirt and the roll-up of his sleeves you could see the edges of his abominable woollen vest. I refuse to discuss in detail the occult reasonings which may have made him ever put on the superfluous garments that he was carrying over his arm. But when you consider the abysmal chasms of imbecility personified in that perspiring oaf, and then realise that he was only a pale pink renegade—that a real English Gentleman and Public School Man would have died before he removed a single garment—then you know that the next deluge is long overdue."

He had a lot more to say, much of which would have made certain seaside Borough Councillors who spend most of their time deliberating on the minimum length of sleeve that may without peril to the public morality be permitted on bathing costumes foam at the mouth with indignation. He said it all very forcefully, using much of the language which by similarly coherent standards is judged to be harmless to an audience of three thousand men, women, and children congregated in a theatre, but definitely corrupting to the same audience if they happen to be congregated in a cinema. Also he travelled as fast and as far as he possibly could on the strength of it, which perhaps has more to do with this story.

The Scilly Islands are not quite at the end of the world; but Simon Templar went there because a letter came to him which quite innocently told him something that he could scarcely ignore.

"We have about the usual number of visitors for the time of year," wrote Mr Smithson Smith. "They disappear just as they always do, and St Mary's still seems uncrowded . . . The *Scillonian* went aground in a fog the other day, but they got her off quite safely at high tide . . . They caught some Frenchmen picking up their pots inside the three-mile limit on Sunday, and fined them £80 . . . There are a couple of fine yachts anchored over at Tresco—one of them belongs to an Egyptian, a man called Abdul Osman. I've been wondering if he's the man I heard about once when I was in Assuan. . . ."

There were six pages of local gossip and general reminiscence, of the kind that Mr Smithson Smith felt moved to write about three times a year. They had met in a dispute about a camel many years ago outside Ismailia; and the Saint, who was no letter-writer, responded at equally vague intervals. But the name of Abdul Osman was not strange to him, and he had no doubts about its associations.

There was a glint in his eye when he had finished reading.

"We're going to the Isles of Scilly, where the puffins go to breed," he said poetically; and Patricia Holm looked at him with an air of caution.

"I'm not a puffin," she said.

"Nevertheless, we'll go," said the Saint.

It may sound flippant to say that if Simon Templar had not shared some of the dim instincts of the puffin, Laura Berwick would undoubtedly have been drowned; but that is nothing but the truth.

She was sailing much too close to the wind—quite literally. Simon Templar saw it from the beginning, and had wondered whether it was pure daring or sheer foolishness. He was perched up on a comparatively smooth ledge of rock, sunning himself in a sublime vacancy of relaxation, and thinking of nothing in particular. The cool waters of the Atlantic were swishing and gurgling among the boulders a dozen feet below him, countering the pale brazen blue of the sky with a translucent intensity of colour that was as rich as anything in the Mediterranean: he had bathed in them for a few minutes, feeling the sticky heat of his walk dissolving under their icy impact with a gratitude that touched the foundations of utter physical contentment: then he had climbed up to his chosen ledge to let the sun dry his body. He wondered lazily whether the RSPCA would have its views about the corruptive influence of his costume on the morals of a score of seagulls that were squabbling raucously over a scrap of food that had been left in a rocky pool by the falling tide; and he wondered also, with the same peaceful laziness, what strange discontent it was that had made Man of his own free will turn his back on the life that was always his, and take himself with his futile insatiable ambitions to the stifling cities from which the escape to his own inheritance seemed so fantastic and impossible. And out of lazily half-closed eyes he watched the white sailing dinghy dancing over the swell. Too close to the wind—much too close. . . .

It all happened in a flash, with the suddenness that every experienced yachtsman knows and labours to avoid. The breeze was baffling, switching around six points of the compass in strong gusts that scraped little raw patches of white foam off the tops of the ponderous rollers. The girl stood up and tried to reach something forward, steadying the tiller with one hand as she leaned away from it. The wind shifted round another point and blew a vicious puff at the flapping canvas, and the mainsail swung across with a sharp crack. The boom seemed to catch the girl on the side of the head, and she went over the side with a splash.

Simon stood up, watching for her to come up and swim back to the boat; but she didn't rise again.

It was not a particularly sensational rescue, as rescues go. The dinghy was only about thirty yards from the shore, and the Saint was a fast swimmer. He found her in a few moments, and towed her after the boat. The fitful breeze had broken down short-windedly, and it was fairly easy. Simon was able to haul her on board and slacken the sheet before it blew again; then the girl moved, coughing and choking, and the Saint slipped hurriedly over the side again.

She rubbed the side of her head tenderly; and then she opened her eyes and saw his tanned face smiling down at her, with a pair of brown forearms braced over the gunwale.

"What happened?" she asked dizzily.

"You jibed," answered a dispassionate Saint. "A bad show—and not to be encouraged in a real wind."

It was obvious that the power of resenting criticism had been temporarily bumped and soaked out of her—an indicative symptom which might profitably be remembered by harassed husbands who take their spouses for holidays by the sea.

"Where did you come from?"

"Off a rock," said the Saint.

She coughed, and choked again with a grimace.

"Excuse me if I spit," she said.

The Saint excused her. She did it to windward, which was not too successful. Simon regarded her sadly.

"You're new to this, aren't you?" he said mildly.

"You've got to begin sometime," she said defiantly. "I've had a few lessons from one of the men, and I thought I'd like to try it by myself. Nobody was using the dinghy, so I just took it."

"There's only one policeman in the Scilly Isles," murmured Simon, "so if you lie low you may get away with it."

"Oh, I didn't steal it. It belongs to the yacht."

Simon raised his eyebrows.

"Have you got a yacht?"

"My stepfather has. The *Claudette*. We're lying over at Tresco."

The line of black-etched eyebrows seemed to harden fractionally.

"Near Abdul Osman's?"

"Why—how did you know?"

"Sort of bush telegraph," said the Saint. "It's amazing how the news travels in these wild parts."

It was during some of this conversation that he was able to review the artistic proportions of her body; for she was dressed in nothing more than a bathing costume in the modern style, consisting largely of entrances for the priceless ultra-violet ray.

"Are you determined to stay where you are?" she inquired presently; and the Saint smiled.

"Not permanently," he said. "But my bathing costume is even more modern than yours. You interrupted a lovely sunbath *à l'allemande*. However, if you like to stay here for a minute I'll swim back and fetch some clothes."

He slid down into the water without waiting for his suggestion to be accepted, and made for the shore again, cutting a clean line through the water and leaving a wake behind. He returned on his

back, one hand holding a bundle of shirt, trousers, and shoes, high
and dry in the air.

"I was born without shame," he said, heaving the bundle over the
stern. "But if you feel bashful you can go forward and talk to the
fish while I use your towel."

"I suppose you saved my life," said the girl, staring with intense
concentration at a completely empty horizon, while the boat rocked
under her as he pulled himself on board.

"There is no charge," said the Saint.

He towelled himself rapidly, and pulled on his trousers; then he
set himself to bring the dinghy round and trim her on a straight
course back towards Tresco. The girl turned round and watched
his easy manœuvres enviously. It was done with an effortless confidence that seemed no trouble at all; and he settled himself at the
tiller and smiled at her again out of that rather reckless brown face.
She saw challenging blue eyes gleaming with a ready mockery, wiry
muscles that rippled under a skin like brown satin; sensed a personality that had no respect for polite conventions. She knew that
the hint of antagonism that had infected her was due to nothing but
her own feeling of foolishness, and knew that he knew she knew.

"I shan't tell," he said, and his words fitted in with her thoughts
so uncannily that for a moment longer she had to continue looking
at him.

"My stepfather might want to know where I picked you up,"
she said.

"That's true," Simon admitted, and said no more until he had run
the dinghy neatly alongside the rather excessively magnificent-
looking yacht that was riding in the New Grimsby channel.

He made the boat fast to the gangway, and helped the girl out.
One of the hands had noticed their arrival, and there was a middle-
aged gentleman in white flannels waiting for them on the deck. He
wore a yachting cap and a blue reefer jacket with a vague air of
uneasiness, as if at every moment he was expecting some rude urchin
to utter shrill comments on his pretensions to the uniform.

"Where have you been, Laura?" he demanded unnecessarily.

"Out in the dinghy," said the girl, no less unnecessarily, but with
a certain impish satisfaction.

The man looked round at the Saint with a kind of restrained
impatience, as though his presence had been imposed as a deliberate
obstacle to the development of some plain speaking that was definitely called for.

"This hero has just saved my life," said Laura, also looking at the Saint. "Hero, this is my stepfather, Mr Stride."

"Ha!" said Mr Stride, intelligently. "Hum!"

His eyes absorbed the Saint's appearance dubiously—they were small eyes, rather surprisingly sharp when they looked at you. Simon was still only wearing his shirt in a haphazard way—he had flung it carelessly over his shoulders and knotted the sleeves loosely under his chin—and he looked quite disreputable and quite happy about it. Mr Stride groped hesitantly for his notecase.

"I got knocked overboard," said the girl. "I did something silly with the sails, and the boom hit me on the head——"

"It might have happened to anyone," said the Saint airily—he had never blushed over a lie in his life. "A sudden squall can make a lot of trouble for any boat, and you get plenty of them around here."

"Ha," said Mr Stride. His sharp eyes ran once up the Saint's lean poiseful length, thoughtfully; but at the sound of the Saint's voice he had let go his wallet as if it had grown red-hot in his fingers. "Ha," said Mr Stride. He tugged at his grey moustache. "Very lucky that you saw the accident, Mr——"

Simon elegantly ignored the invitation to supply his name.

"We were just going to have lunch, Mr——" said Stride, dangling the bait again. "Won't you stay?"

"That's awfully kind of you," murmured the Saint, and thought that Mr Stride would have been more cordial if he had refused.

He proceeded to put on his shirt, with a calm indifference to his host's emotions that would have been boorish if it had been a shade less transparently innocent; and as he did so he was glancing over the other ships that were anchored within a hundred yards of the *Claudette*. There were a couple of French fishing smacks, broad-beamed sea boats, with high bows and low sterns, held idly into the wind by their great rust-red sails. Beyond them was a superb 200-ton Diesel yacht with a sweet line of clipper bow: Simon could read the name painted there—*Luxor*. Beside the wheelhouse Simon could see a man focusing a pair of binoculars, and he knew that it was the *Claudette* that was the object of his attention.

"A lovely boat," said Stride, purringly.

"Lovely," agreed the Saint. "You have to be a very successful man to own a ship like that—or even a ship like yours, Mr Stride."

The other shot one of his surprisingly sharp glances at the unruffled young man beside him.

"Hum," he assented mechanically; but he was spared the neces-

sity of finding some suitable amplification of his answer by the
arrival of a white-coated steward with a tray of glasses, followed
by what appeared to be the remainder of his guests.

These consisted of a pleasant-faced youngster of about twentyfive with a diligently suppressed crinkle in his fair hair, and a sleek
and saturnine man of indeterminate age whose coat fitted very
tightly to his waist and whose hair waved unashamed in faultless
undulations that Nature unaided could scarcely have made so symmetrical. The fair-haired youngster's name was Toby Halidom, and
his solicitude for Laura Berwick's complete recovery from the effects
of her adventure seemed to account satisfactorily for the engagement ring which appeared on her finger when she had powdered her
nose and changed for lunch. The sleek and saturnine one was introduced as Mr Almido, private secretary to Mr Stride; he spoke little,
and when he did so it was with a lisping accent that was certainly
no more English than his clothes.

Mr Stride swallowed his cocktail in silence, and led the way below
almost abruptly. His lack of festive geniality, remarkable in a man
whose stepdaughter had so recently been saved from a watery grave,
continued for fully half the meal; but the Saint was unabashed. And
then, just as surprisingly for anyone who had begun to accept his
taciturnity, he began to thaw. He thawed so much that by the time
the dessert was placed on the table he was inquiring into the Saint's
plans with something approaching affability.

"Are you staying long?" he asked.

"Until I'm tired of absorbing Vitamin D, probably," said the
Saint. "I have no plans."

"I always thought the South of France was the favourite resort
of sunbathers," remarked Mr Stride, with a show of interest in which
only an ear that was listening for it could have discerned the veiled
point. "I think, if that were my object, I should be inclined to go
there rather than risk the uncertainties of the British climate. I'm sure
that would be wiser."

"Ah, but even there they make you wear some clothes," said the
Saint ingenuously. "It always annoys me to see myself in my bath
looking as if I was wearing a ridiculous pair of transparent white
pants. Here I can find a nice piece of coast all to myself, and acquire
the same beautiful colour all over."

Mr Toby Halidom, who was wearing an Old Harrovian tie,
looked faintly shocked; but Mr Stride was unmoved.

He accompanied Simon on to the deck, with Laura Berwick,

when the Saint excused himself as soon as coffee had been served. One of the men, he said, would take Mr Hum Ha back to St Mary's in the motor dinghy; and while the boat was being brought round Simon glanced across again to the *Luxor*. A seaman was standing on the deck, looking towards them, and as Simon came into view the man turned and spoke through a hatch to someone below. A moment later the man who had watched the Saint before came up the companion and adjusted his binoculars again.

"I hope we shall see some more of you," said Mr Stride, standing by the gangway. "Come and pay us a call whenever you like."

"I should love to," murmured the Saint, just as politely; and then, with such a smooth transition that the effect of it was like a gunshot, he said: "I didn't know Abdul Osman was shortsighted."

Galbraith Stride went white, as if the blood had been drained from his face by a vacuum pump.

"Do you know Mr Osman?" he asked, with an effort.

"Fairly well," said the Saint casually. "I branded him on both cheeks five years ago, and it must have cost him no end of money in plastic surgeons to put his face right again. If anyone had done that to me I shouldn't have to look at him twice through the field-glasses to be sure who it was."

"Very interesting," said Galbraith Stride slowly. "Very interesting." He held out his hand. "Well, good-bye, Mr—er—hum."

"Templar," said the Saint. "Simon Templar. And thanks so much for the lunch."

He shook the proffered hand cordially and went down to the boat; and he was so happy that he wanted to sing to himself all the way back to St Mary's.

### III

"If," said Patricia Holm, "that was supposed to be another of your famous Exercises in Tact——"

"But what else could it have been?" protested the Saint. "If I hadn't used extraordinary tact, I shouldn't have been invited to lunch; and that would have meant I'd have missed a display of caviare, lobster mayonnaise, and dry champagne that no man with a decent respect for his stomach could resist—not to mention a first-hand knowledge of the geography of Stride's boat——"

"And by dinner-time," said Patricia, "she'll be fifty miles away, with the *Luxor* racing her."

Simon shook his head.

"Not if I know Abdul Osman. The surgeons may have refreshened his face, but there are scars inside him that he will never forget . . . I should have had to scrape an acquaintance with Laura some time, and that accident made it so beautifully easy."

"I thought we were coming here for a holiday," said Patricia; and the Saint grinned, and went in search of Mr Smithson Smith.

Mr Smithson Smith was then the manager of Tregarthen's, which is one of the three hotels with which the island of St Mary's is provided. Simon Templar, whose taste in hotels could be satisfied by nothing less lavish than palaces like the Dorchester, failing which he usually plunged to the opposite extreme, had declined an invitation to stay there, and had billeted himself in a house in the village, where he had a private sitting-room thrown in with the best of home-cooked meals for a weekly charge that would have maintained him in an attic at the Dorchester for about five minutes. At Tregarthen's, however, he could stay himself with draught Bass drawn from the wood, and this was one of the things of which he felt in need.

The other thing was a few more details of local gossip, with which Mr Smithson Smith might also be able to provide him.

It was then half-past three in the afternoon; but by a notable oversight on the part of the efficient legislators who framed that unforgettable Defence of the Realm Act which has for so long been Britain's bulwark against the horrors of an invasion of foreign tourists, the Scilly Islands were omitted from the broad embrace of that protection, and it is still lawful to drink beer at almost any hour at which a man can reasonably raise a thirst. As Simon entered the long glass-fronted verandah overlooking the bay, he naturally expected to find it packed to suffocation with sodden islanders wallowing in the decadent excesses from which a beneficent Government had not been thoughtful enough to protect them; but such (as the unspeakable newspapers say, in what they apparently believe to be the English language) was not the case. In fact, the only occupant of the bar was Mr Smithson Smith himself, who was making out bills beside an open window.

"Why—good afternoon, Templar. What can I do for you?"

"A pint of beer," murmured the Saint, sinking into a chair. "Possibly, if my thirst holds, two pints. And one for yourself if you feel like it."

Mr Smithson Smith disappeared into his serving cubicle, and re-

turned with a brimming glass. He excused himself from joining in
the performance.

"I'd rather leave it till the evening, if you don't mind," he said
with a smile. "What have you been doing today?"

He was a thin mild-mannered man with sandy-grey hair, a tiny
moustache, and an extraordinary gentle voice; and it was a strange
thing that he was only one of many men in those islands who were
more familiar with the romantic cities of the East than they were
with the capital of their own country. Simon had been struck by
that odd fact on his first call at Tregarthen's, and subsequent visits
had confirmed it. There, on those lonely clusters of rock breaking
out of the sea forty miles from Land's End, where you would expect
to find men who had seen scarcely anything of the world outside·
the other rocky islands around their own homes, you found instead
simple men whose turns of reminiscence recalled the streets of
Damascus and Baghdad by their names. And whenever reminiscence
turned that way, Mr Smithson Smith would call on his own memories with a faraway look in his eyes, and the same faraway sound in
that very gentle voice, as if his dreams saw the deserts of Arabia
more vividly than the blue bay beyond his windows. "I mind a time
when I was in Capernaum . . ."–Simon had heard him say it, and
felt that for that man at least all the best days lay in the past. It was
the War, of course, that had picked men out of every sleepy hamlet
in England and hurled them into the familiarity of strange sights and
places as well as the flaming shadows of death, and in the end sent
some of them back to those same sleepy hamlets to remember; but
there was in that quiet man a mystic sensitiveness, a tenseness of
poetry struggling rather puzzledly for the expression he could not
give it, that made his memories more dreamy with a quaint kind
of reverence than most others.

"I've been over by Tresco," said the Saint, lifting his face presently from the beer.

"Oh. Did you see those yachts—are they still there?"

Simon nodded.

"As a matter of fact, I managed to scrounge lunch on one of
them."

"Was it Abdul Osman's?"

"No—Galbraith Stride's. I saw Osman's, though. It's a long way
for him to come all the way over here."

He knew that the other would need the least possible encouragement to delve into the past; and his expectations were founded on

the soundest psychology. Mr Smithson Smith sat down and accepted a cigarette.

"I think I said in my letter that I thought I'd heard his name before. I was thinking about it only yesterday, and the story came back to me. He hasn't visited St Mary's—at least, if he has, I don't think I've seen him—but I should know this Abdul Osman if he was the same man, because he was branded on both cheeks."

The Saint's eyebrows rose in innocent surprise.

"Really?"

The other nodded.

"It's quite a story—you could almost put it in a book. An Englishman did it—at least, the rumour said he was an Englishman, although they never caught him. This Abdul Osman was supposed to have a monopoly of various unpleasant things in the East—brothels and gambling dens and drug trafficking, all that sort of thing. I don't know if it was true, but that was what they told me. He had a fine house in Cairo, anyway, so he must have made plenty of money out of it. I remember what happened distinctly. It was a local sensation at the time . . . I hope I'm not boring you?"

Mr Smithson Smith was oddly afraid of being boring, as if he felt that any mundane restlessness in his audience would break the fragile glamour of those wonderful things he could remember.

"Not a bit," said the Saint. "What happened?"

"Well, apparently this Abdul Osman disappeared one night. He was supposed to be driving back to Cairo from Alexandria, just himself and his chauffeur. It was a beautiful car he had, I've often seen it driving past Shepheard's Hotel. Well, he didn't arrive when they were expecting him; and as the time went on, and he was three or four hours late and hadn't sent any message to say what had held him up, his household became anxious and went out to look for him. They drove all the way to Alexandria without seeing him, but when they got there they were told by the place where he'd been staying that he'd left about eight hours previously. Then they went to the police, and there was another search. No trace of him was found."

A couple of young men in white open shirts and flannel trousers came in and sat down. Mr Smithson Smith excused himself to go and take their order, and while he was filling it the Saint lighted a cigarette and glanced at them disinterestedly. They were quiet, very respectable young men; but their faces were sallow and the arms exposed by their rolled-up sleeves were white above the elbows.

"Well," said Mr Smithson Smith, returning to his chair, "they searched for him half the night, but he seemed to have vanished into thin air. Of course, it wasn't easy to make a thorough search in the dark, so in the morning they tried again. And then they found him. His car was on the road—they found tracks that showed it had been driven off quite a long way into the desert, and brought back again; and out in the desert where it had been turned round there was the remains of a fire. The chauffeur was just recovering consciousness —he'd been knocked on the head and tied up and gagged—and Abdul Osman was in the back of the car with his brand on both his cheeks. Whoever did it had burnt it in almost to the bone with a red-hot iron—it was an Arabic word, and it meant just what this man was."

"Stout piece of work," murmured the Saint, pushing his glass forward for replenishment.

"Probably it was." Mr Smithson Smith provided another pint of beer, and resumed his seat. "And the only clue they had was a sort of drawing that had been painted on the sides of Osman's beautiful car—the paint was still wet when they found it. It was a sort of figure made out of straight lines, with a round head, like you see kids drawing on walls, only this one had a circle on top like the haloes in those mediæval church pictures. I've often wondered what it was meant to be. It couldn't have been a picture of Abdul Osman, because he had no right to a halo. Perhaps it was meant for a picture of the man who did it."

"It sounds possible," murmured the Saint.

One of the respectable young men rose and left the bar: idly, Simon watched him going slowly down the sloping path to the gate.

"Yes," said Mr Smithson Smith thoughtfully . . . "I mind another time when I heard of him. This was in Beirut. A friend of mine met a girl there in a dance place—it was the sort of dance place that wouldn't be allowed at all in England. She told him a story about Abdul Osman—I don't think I should like to repeat the details to anyone, but if it was true he couldn't be painted any blacker than he is. As a matter of fact, I did tell this story to a man I met on a boat going across to Marseilles, who had just retired from the Egyptian police, and he said it was probably true. It was——"

"Hullo," said the Saint. "Bloke seems to have fallen down."

The respectable young man who had gone out had stumbled as he stepped down to the road, and at that moment he was sprawled in the dust just beyond the gate. He was clutching one ankle, and his face was turned back towards the verandah with a twisted expression of agony.

Mr Smithson Smith looked out, then round to the respectable young man's companion.

"Your friend seems to have hurt himself," he said. "It looks as if he has sprained his ankle."

The respectable young man came over to the table and also looked out.

"I'll go and see," he said.

Simon watched him go, inhaling speculatively.

"Staying in the hotel?" he queried.

"Yes," said Mr Smithson Smith, with his eyes on the developments below. "They're staying here."

"Have they been here long?"

The question was put with perfect casualness.

"About a fortnight," said Mr Smithson Smith. "I don't know much about them. They're out most of the day—I think they go bathing, but by the look of the basket they take with them you'd think they needed towels enough to dry a regiment."

"They aren't very sunburnt," said the Saint softly, almost as if he was speaking to himself.

He picked up his glass mechanically—and put it down again. The young man with the injured ankle was coming back, limping painfully and leaning on his companion's arm.

"Silly thing to do, wasn't it?" he said; and Mr Smithson Smith nodded with some concern.

"Would you like me to get you a doctor?"

The young man shook his head.

"I'll just go and bathe it with cold water and rest it for a bit. I don't think it's anything serious."

The three-legged party went on through into the hotel premises; and Simon sat down again and lighted another cigarette. Mr Smithson Smith's gentle voice was continuing his interrupted anecdote, but the Saint scarcely heard a word. The narrative formed no more than a vague undercurrent of sound in his senses, a restful background to his working thoughts. In a life like the Saint's, a man's existence is prolonged from day to day by nothing but that ceaseless vigilance, that unsleeping activity of a system of question marks in the mind which are never satisfied with the obvious explanations that pass though the torpid consciousness of the average man. To him, anything out of the ordinary was a red light of possible danger, never to be dismissed as mere harmless eccentricity: nine times out of ten the alarm might be proved false, but it could never be ignored. And it seemed odd that two very respectable young men should have attracted attention by carrying an outsize basket of towels; odd, too, that after bathing every day for a fortnight they should still have the soft white bodies of men who have not been free of the muffling protection of clothes for many years . . . And then the Saint's probing suspicions came to a head in a sudden flash of inspiration, and he pulled himself swiftly out of his chair. He was across the bar in a flash, over to the closed door through which the two respectable young men had disappeared; and Mr Smithson Smith, startled to silence by his abrupt movement, noticed in an eerie moment of perplexity that the Saint's feet made no sound as they swung over the floor. It was like the charge of a leopard in its smooth powerful noiselessness; and then Simon Templar had his hand on the handle of the door, jerking it open, and the young man who had assisted the injured one stumbled and almost fell into the room.

"Come in, brother," said the Saint heartily. "Come in and have a drink."

The young man's face went red, and his mouth opened in a weak grin.

"I—I'm sorry," he stammered. "I must have tripped or something——"

A thin smile cut into the corners of the Saint's mouth.

"Sure you must, brother."

"I'll—I'll have a whisky and soda."

"You'll have beer!"

The Saint caught up his own glass from the table and thrust it out. He was only a yard from the other, on his toes, indefinably dangerous.

"Drink this," he said; and the young man went white.

"I—I don't——"

Simon's free fist caught him on the mouth and knocked him backwards.

"I'll have the police on you for this," blustered the other; and the Saint smiled again.

"Go get him. And don't be too lavish with your plurals, because there is only one. But ask Abdul what he thinks of the idea first, or you may find yourself unpopular. Now amscray—and if you value your beauty, don't damage my beer again!"

He seized the respectable young man by the ear and propelled him deftly and vigorously out of the bar; then he turned back to face the outraged stare of Mr Smithson Smith. The course of events had been so violently sudden and incomprehensible that the manager had been pardonably nonplussed; but by this point at least his path of duty seemed unmistakable.

"Why—really, Templar!" he said, with his quiet voice shaking. "You can't behave like that here. I shall have to apologise to my guest. I'm afraid you'll have to leave this bar——"

Simon took his arm calmly, and pointed.

A fly was crawling down the inside of the half-emptied glass of beer which he had just replaced on the table. It was quite unhurried about the journey, after the impudent fashion of flies: perhaps its thirst was of no great dimensions, or perhaps it had been reared in scrupulously well-mannered circumstances. It moved downwards in little short runs, pausing once to wash its hands and once to rub its feet together, in a genteel ecstasy of anticipation. Mr Smithson Smith's eye followed it because it was the only moving object in the direction which the Saint had indicated, and there seemed to be nothing else to look at.

Even so, it seemed an extremely trivial spectacle, and he moved his arm restlessly in the Saint's grasp. But Simon Templar continued to point at it, and there was something dynamic about the immobility of that extended finger. Mr Smithson Smith watched, and saw the fly reach the level of the beer. It looked around cautiously, and lowered its proboscis delicately into the liquid. For two or three seconds after that it was motionless. And then, without any kind of struggle, it pitched over in a limp somersault and floated quietly on its back, with its legs stretched stiffly upwards. . . .

## IV

Mr Smithson Smith blinked, and wiped his forehead. His arm relaxed slowly, as if it required a conscious effort to loosen the involuntary contraction of his muscles. He had no idea why the miniature drama that he had seen enacted should have had such an effect on him. It might have been the utter stillness in which it was played out, the unexplanatory silence of the man beside him—anything. But it seemed as if for the last few seconds he had forgotten to breathe, and when it was finished he expanded his chest with an inaudible sigh.

Then the Saint spoke; and his voice jarred the other's ears by sheer contrast with the silence.

"Don't tell me your beer's as potent as all that!"

The manager stared at him.

"Do you mean—do you mean it was drugged?"

"No less, and possibly even some more. We'll soon see." With unruffled calm, the Saint fished out the fly with a match-stick and laid it in an ashtray to cool off. "But I don't somehow think it was sudden death—that would probably be considered too good for me."

"But—but—damn it!" Mr Smithson Smith felt queerly shaken under his instinctive incredulity. "You can't tell me that Mr Trape——"

"Is that his name?" The Saint was as cool as an ice-pack. "I can't tell you much about him, but I can tell you that. My dear chap"— he put his hand on the manager's shoulder for a moment—"can you be expected to guarantee the morals of everyone who stays at your hotel? Can you demand a budget of references from anyone who asks for a room? Of course you can't. You have to take them at their face value, and so long as they behave themselves while they're here you aren't expected to ask them whether their fingerprints are registered at Scotland Yard. No—they just had to find somewhere to stay, and you were unlucky."

The manager frowned.

"If what you say is true, Templar, I shall have to ask for their room," he said; and the Saint had to laugh.

"You've got your room now, old lad. But whether they've left money to pay the bill is another matter."

He sat on the table with a glance at the fly, which was still sunken in its coma. He found it difficult to think it could be dead—although, of course, a drug that a man would survive might be fatal to an insect. But his summary of Abdul Osman's character didn't fit in with such a clean conclusion. The hot irons that had scored their insult on the Egyptian's face would call for something much more messy in the way of vengeance—Abdul Osman would not forget, nor would he be so easily satisfied when his chance came. Then why the drug? And why, anyway, the very presence of those two respectable young men, who on Smithson Smith's own statement had been staying at the hotel for the past fortnight? It seemed improbable that Abdul Osman claimed any of the gifts of necromantic clairvoyance which popular novelists attribute to the "mysterious East". And yet . . .

All at once he recognized a slim figure in wide blue trousers walking up from the harbour towards the hotel, and waved to it joyfully out of the window. He was in a state of puzzlement in which he wanted to think aloud, and he could not have hoped for a better audience. But it struck him, while he was waiting for her to arrive, that it was a remarkable thing that he had not seen the two respectable young men making their way hastily towards the harbour, even as he had seen her coming in the opposite direction.

"Look here, Templar," began Mr Smithson Smith worriedly; but the Saint interrupted him with a smile of seraphic blindness.

"Excuse me—I'll be back in a sec."

He went out and met Patricia at the gate.

"What about a spot of tea, boy?" she suggested; and then the electric gaiety of him opened her eyes, and she stopped.

"Sit down here—this is a conference, but since we aren't politicians we can't fix a date for it next year on the other side of the world." The Saint pulled open the gate, seated himself on the step, and drew her down beside him. "Pat, a very respectable-looking young man, name of Trape, has just put a sleeping-draught in my beer."

"Good Lord—you haven't drunk it, have you?"

The Saint laughed.

"I certainly haven't. In fact, I punched the face of Mr Trape, just to learn him, and kicked him out of the bar—to the pardonable indignation of our friend Mr Smith. But I think he's beginning to understand—probably more than I wanted him to. I dropped a line about Abdul Osman while interviewing Mr Trape that must have made Smith think a bit . . . I'll tell you how it happened. I was having my drink, and these two harmless-looking birds strolled in. They ordered lemonade, or something; and then one of them went out. He walked down the path, tripped on this very spot where we're sitting, and appeared to sprain his ankle. I saw it happen, and Smith called his pal over to the window. That was when he did it, of course. He wanted an excuse to come over to our table, with both of us looking outside, so he could slip in the dope. That's what the whole plant was for—and damned well done it was, too. I didn't see it at all until the injured warrior had been helped back to the hotel and away to his room, and then only because I'm naturally suspicious. I'll tell you the things that struck me as odd later—never mind them now. But all at once it dawned on me that there *was* something in my beer that hadn't been there when I started it, and also that Mr Trape might be listening outside the door to see what happened. I opened the door, and there he was—so I pushed his teeth in. Episode over."

"But what was the idea?"

"That's just what I want to get—and I want it quick." He was speaking so rapidly that it wasn't easy for her to pick the facts and deductions out of that vital rush of vivid sentences. "I want to reconstruct what might have happened if I'd drunk the beer. Make holes in it anywhere you can."

"Go ahead."

"Right. I drink the beer. I appear to go groggy. Smith registers alarm. Trape hears, and walks innocently in—probably requesting brandy for wounded comrade. Apparently I've fainted. Cold water, keys, feathers, smelling-salts—all tried and found wanting. Smith departs to summon doctor, leaving me with Trape. Whereupon I'm rushed out of the place——"

"But what happens when Smith comes back?"

"Exactly . . . No, that's easy enough. Trape returns to bewildered Smith, explains that I revived and pushed off. Maybe I saw a man I had to talk to about a dog, or anything like that. Apologies, thanks, and so forth . . . Well, where do they take me? Answer: the *Luxor*, of course—Abdul was watching me through fieldglasses all the time I was on Stride's deck. That's all right till——"

"But there are holes everywhere!" she protested. "Suppose anyone saw him carrying you away?"

The Saint's keen blue eyes flicked round the scene.

"Abdul's a clever man—he doesn't forget much. There's a donkey and jingle two yards away, isn't there? And probably Trape hired it for the occasion. He could also have a sack—and I become cold potatoes. Down to the harbour—into a boat—there'd be no hurry. Once he had me in the cart he could leave me there for hours if it was good dope. And even when I was missing for good, his alibi would hold water. I don't say there was no risk, but it could have been done. And Abdul would be the man to do it. What I want to know is what the scheme is now that I haven't drunk the beer. Those two birds have been here a fortnight, so they were put here for some other job. Have they finished that job, and are they free to get away? I expect they'd have to consult Abdul, and Abdul wouldn't approve of bungling. I haven't seen them come out of the hotel, though I expect they could work round the back of the town——"

He was still trying to frame his thoughts aloud, but actually the thread of them was racing away ahead of his voice. And a new light dawned on him at the same moment. His fingers clamped on Patricia's wrist.

"Organisation—that's what it is! Gee, I'm as slow as a village concert today!"

In another second he was on his feet and sprinting back to the bar. He entered it from the path as Mr Smithson Smith came in at the other end.

"What have you decided to do about all this unpleasantness?" asked the Saint; and the manager put his hands on his hips.

"Well, I've just seen the young fellow with the sprained ankle——"

The Saint's smile was fast and thin.

"I thought you would. And if you hadn't gone to see him, he'd have sent for you. Meanwhile the most extraordinary things go on happening to my beer. First a sleeping-draught—then it grows legs!"

Mr Smithson Smith looked down at the table rather blankly. The fly still reclined in the ash-tray, oblivious of all excitement in its rigid stupor; but the glass of beer from which oblivion had overtaken it was gone.

"Someone may have been in here and moved it," began Mr Smithson Smith hazily, and Simon showed his teeth.

"Someone *has* been here and moved it—you can write that down in the family Bible. That sprained ankle was good enough for another stall. Did you go up and see the bloke off your own bat?"

"As a matter of fact, he asked me to go up——"

"And naturally you had to go. Organisation, that's what it is. What did he say?"

"He said that his friend had told him what happened, and he couldn't understand it. He wanted to know if I should be asking them to leave."

"Did you say anything about doped beer?"

"No."

"Or flies?"

"No."

"Then that lets you out," said the Saint, with some relief. "If they think you don't know anything they won't worry about you. What did you say?"

"I said I should have to consider the matter."

"That," said the Saint grimly, "will be all right so long as you don't consider it too deeply."

Mr Smithson Smith looked at him. The events he had witnessed, and that rattle of cross-examination, had left that gentle-voiced man utterly bewildered without shifting the foundations of his practical standpoint.

"Look here, Templar," he said directly. "I don't know what you or these two young men are playing at, but I'm in a responsible position. I can't take any risks with this hotel. Unless one of you can give me a satisfactory explanation, I think I shall have to tell the Sergeant as much as I know, and leave him to deal with it."

Simon pondered for a moment; and then he nodded.

"That's obviously your duty, and I think it would be better from every point of view if you did it. May I go up to Trape's room and see if he'll speak to me? I don't know if he'll accept an apology, but if he did it might save a little scandal."

He knew that he was taking rather an unfair advantage, but the idea was one that he had to follow. The bait was tempting; and Mr Smithson Smith, with the interests of his employers at heart and no conception of the depths of duplicity to which Simon Templar could sink when it was necessary, could scarcely refuse it. Simon obtained permission, and the number of the room which the two respectable-looking young men were sharing, and went upstairs with as much consolation as he could derive from the knowledge that if his plan went through successfully the victims would be most unlikely to complain to the management. If he were caught in the act, of course, he would find himself ten times more unpopular with the controlling powers of that respectable hotel than he was already; but the Saint had an unshakable faith in his guardian angels.

He knocked on the door, and went in with the forefinger of his right hand prodding out the shape of his trousers pocket in an ostentatious untruth. Both the respectable-looking young men were there.

"Put your hands up, and don't even think of shouting," he said genially. "You'd only give the chambermaids hysterics."

For a moment the two young men were speechless.

"Sorry to arrive so late, boys," Simon went on in the same friendly tone. "I should have been here long ago, but your organization was so slick it took me a little while to catch up with it. I congratulate you on getting rid of the evidence of that doped beer so smartly. We gather that you haven't yet told Abdul about our mutual misunderstanding. I guess you were wise—he wouldn't have been very sympathetic, and you had lots of time to take a second shot at me."

Their faces gave him confirmation. And then Mr Trape, who was nearest, brought himself a couple of paces nearer, with his head twisted viciously on one side.

"Why not, Templar?" he said. "You wouldn't dare to shoot here."

"Maybe you're right, Eric," admitted the Saint, with astonishing meekness, and removed his hand from his empty pocket. "But then it mightn't be necessary—considering the evidence you've got on your ceiling."

He glanced upwards as he spoke; and Mr Trape would not have been human if he had not followed that compelling gaze. He also glanced upwards, and in so doing he arranged his chin at an angle that could not have been posed better. Simon's fist shot up to the inviting mark, and impacted with a crisp click. . . .

The Saint had been long enough in the game to know that even a modest two to one is bigger odds than any sane man takes on for his health, and at that moment he was feeling more hurried than heroic. Mr Trape was sinking limply towards the carpet before his companion realized that he was left to carry the banner alone, and by that time it was a bit late for realizations. The second respectable-looking young man was only beginning to scramble up off the bed when the Saint's flying leap caught him irresistibly round the shoulders and hurled his face mufflingly back into the pillow; then Simon aimed his fist in a scientifically merciless jolt to the nape of the exposed neck.

The Saint returned coolly to the floor, and smoothed his hair. The second respectable-looking young man would not recover from the effects of that blow for several minutes; but it was the aggressive Mr Trape whom Simon selected automatically for his experiment. There was a large gunny sack and a coil of manila under the bed—Simon could not have deduced the plans for his own transportation better if he had been in the know from the beginning like any storybook detective—and in a few seconds he had Mr Trape inside the sack and the sack fastened. Then he went to the window and looked out. It was only a short drop to a small garden at the rear of the hotel, which was built on a steep slope; and Simon dumped Mr Trape over the sill unceremoniously. That was the greatest risk he took, but a searching glance round before he did it revealed a landscape apparently bare of watchers. Then he followed himself, and went back to Patricia.

"Let's exercise the donkey," he said.

The ensacked Mr Trape was loaded into the cart, and they were moving placidly down towards the harbour, before Patricia asked the inevitable question.

"I'm giving Abdul a visitor," said the Saint cheerfully. "He's expecting one, and why should he be disappointed? If you want another reason, write it down as my everlasting love of exasperating the ungodly. I have no other mission in life . . . You'd better stay back here—I'm banking on the sea gang not knowing the land operators, but they'd certainly ask questions about you."

The girl fell back, and Simon led the donkey out on to the jetty. For a very brief space he wondered if he would be able to locate the tender that awaited him; and then he saw a glistening white speedboat moored by some steps running down to the water. Its crew was dark-complexioned and swarthy, and to remove all doubt it flew a red burgee with the name *Luxor* woven into it.

Simon hitched the sack on to his shoulder, and walked brazenly down the steps.

"Here he is," he said.

Not one of the crew raised an eyebrow. Simon lowered his burden into the boat, saw the engine started, and went back along the causeway in an anguish of noiseless laughter.

## V

It had been a simple gesture of a kind that Simon Templar could never resist, and it gave him exactly the same unfathomably primitive satisfaction that an urchin derives from putting his thumb to his nose and extending his fingers outwards. It was a moral catharsis that touched the well-springs of all unsophisticated human bliss. And if he could have witnessed the reception of his jest his pleasure would have been almost too ecstatic to be borne.

Abdul Osman himself came out on deck to supervise the hoisting up of the sack, and the leer on his face did not improve his beauty. Mr Trape was beginning to recover by that time, and the sack was squirming vigorously to an accompaniment of hoarse grunts and indistinguishable words.

"He must have a head of iron, that Englishman," muttered Osman. "He should have slept for many hours."

The thought crossed his mind that a man with a constitution like that would stand much torture, and his mouth watered at the prospect. He lifted his foot and kicked the sack cold-bloodedly, and it yelped at each thump of his shoe.

"Before you die you shall have much more to shout for," said Osman gloatingly. "Take him to the saloon."

Rough hands dragged the sack below, and Abdul Osman followed. Then it was cut open, and the storm broke.

Osman, it must be admitted, had never been considered even attractively ugly. He was a short pot-bellied man with a fat sallow face and black hair that covered his head in tight curls. Out of his own hearing, it was said that much of his family tree was as black as his hair, and certainly he had a squat nose and a yellowish tinge in the whites of his pig-like eyes that supported the theory. A closely-clipped black moustache curved in a broad arch over his thick pouting lips and gave his face, even in repose, an expression of sensual bestiality that was nauseating.

And his rage at the sight of Mr Trape emerging from the sack put him right out of comparison with anything human. His face resembled nothing so much as the fat end of a bloated and malignant slug. His eyes almost disappeared in the rolls of unhealthy-looking fat that creased down on them. Clearly marked circles of bright red sprang up and burned on his cheeks, plainly revealing the edges of the skin-grafting operations that had obliterated the Saint's brands; the rest of his jowl was blotched yellow and grey. And out of his distorted mouth flowed a stream of shrill profanity that was horrible to hear.

Nor was his wrath purely vocal. He kicked Trape again, and kicked and tore at the men who had carried in the sack until they fled from the room. And then, with the most lasting and concentrated malignance, he kicked his secretary, who had played no part in the proceedings at all.

But that was nothing unusual. Mr Clements was there to be kicked. He was kicked whenever anything went wrong, and just as impartially when everything went right. Abdul Osman kicked him, cuffed him, and spat in his face; and his secretary cringed. There was something hideous about his quivering submission.

For Clements was a white man. His hair was almost ash-blonde, his shrinking eyes grey.

"Swine!" Osman hissed.

His sunken eyes glittered with the vindictive pleasure that soothed his senses whenever he heaped humiliations on that cowering travesty of a man. Even in that paroxysm of fury the sensation was like balm to his uncontrolled nerves—perhaps it was the very thing that finally turned the tide of his unleashed savagery and began to restore him to reason. For that crawling servile thing that had once been a man was the most permanently soothing monument to Abdul

Osman's vanity in the world. Simon Templar, as a helpless prisoner, might supplant him; but until the day came when Osman could look down and spit in the face of that ultimate triumph the degradation of Clements reigned as his supreme achievement.

Less hastily, ten times more malignantly, Osman reached out a hand, grasped his secretary by the nose, and forced him to his knees. He stared at him contemptuously for a moment; then he put a foot in his face and sprawled him over.

"Get up, pig."

Clements obeyed.

"Look at me."

The white man raised his eyes slowly. Abdul Osman saw the red sparks of futile hate glowing in their depths like hot embers, and laughed.

"You know that I always have my revenge, don't you?" His almost perfect English had a sibilant accent, as if a snake had spoken. "How unfortunate it was that my misguided parents should have sent me to an English school! Unpleasant for me, perhaps; but how much more enduringly regrettable for you! I was a dirty nigger then, wasn't I? And it seemed so humorous to you to humiliate me. I trust you look back on those days with satisfaction, Clements?"

The man did not answer.

"It was such a pity that you began to try the needle, and then found you couldn't live without it. And then that you committed that indiscretion which finally put you at my mercy . . . You were so strong and healthy once, weren't you?—so proud and brave! You would never have let me strike you. You would have struck me yourself, like this."

His flat hand smacked the other's face from side to side—once, twice.

"You would like to strike me again, wouldn't you? But then there is always the certainty that you would have to bare your back to my little whip. It's wonderful how hunger for the needle, and the entertainment of my little whip, have curbed your spirits." He was playing with the man now, drugging his disordered vanity again with the sadistic repetition of a scene that he had played hundreds of times and never tired of. "Pah! I've crushed you so much that now you haven't even the courage to kill yourself and end your misery. You're mine, body and soul—the idol of the school fawning on the dirty nigger. Doesn't that reflection please you, Clements?" He was watching the silent man with a shrewdness in his slow malevolence.

"You'll be wanting the needle again about now, won't you! I've a good mind to keep you waiting. It will amuse you to have to come crawling round my feet, licking my shoes, pleading, weeping, slobbering—won't it, Clements?"

The secretary licked his lips. It looked for a moment as if at last the smouldering fires in him would flare up to some reply, and Osman waited for it hopefully. And then came voices and footsteps on the deck over their heads, feet clattering down the companion, and the door was opened by a smart-uniformed Arab seaman to admit a visitor.

It was Galbraith Stride.

"Did you get him?" he demanded huskily.

There were beads of perspiration on his face, and not all of them were due to the heat of the day. Osman's puffy lips curled at the sight of him.

"No, I didn't," he said shortly. "A fool bungled it. I have no time for fools."

Stride mopped his forehead.

"It's on my nerves, Osman. He's been on the *Claudette*, admitted who he was—who knows what he'll do next? I tell you——"

"You may tell me all you want to in a few minutes," said Osman suavely. "I have some business to attend to first—if you will excuse me." He turned to the seaman. "Ali, send Trape to me."

The Arab touched his forehead and disappeared, and Osman elbowed his secretary aside and helped himself from an inlaid brass cigarette box on the table. All his self-possession had returned, and somehow his heavy tranquillity was more inhuman than his raving anger.

Presently the Arab came back with Trape. Osman gazed at him unwinkingly for some seconds, and then he spoke.

"I have no time for fools," he repeated.

Young Harry Trape was sullen and frightened. The ways of violence were not new to him—he had been in prison three times, and once they would have flogged him with a nine-thonged lash if the doctors had not said he was too weak to endure the punishment. Young Harry had a grievance: he had not only been knocked out by the Saint and tied up in a stuffy sack, but he had been viciously kicked both unknowingly and knowingly by the man he had tried to serve, and he felt he had much to complain about. He had come to the saloon prepared to complain, but the snake-like impassiveness of the unblinking stare that fastened on his face held him mute and strangely terrified.

"You are a fool, Trape," said Osman, almost benevolently, "and I don't think I require your services any longer. Ali will take you back to St Mary's in the speedboat. You will give up your room at Tregarthen's, make a parcel of all the cocaine you have and post it to the usual address, and then you will take yourself, your friend, and your luggage back to the speedboat, which will take you both to Penzance immediately. Your money will be waiting for you in London. You may go."

"Yes, sir," said Trape throatily.

He left the saloon quickly. The seaman was about to follow him, but Osman stayed him with a gesture.

"It will not really be necessary to go to Penzance, Ali," he remarked deliberately; and the man nodded and went out.

Stride's bloodshot eyes stared at the Egyptian.

"My God—you're a coldblooded devil!" he half-gasped.

Osman chuckled wheezily.

"Oh, no, not coldblooded, my dear Stride! You ought to know that. Far from it. But a dead fool is a safe fool, and I believe in safety first. But not coldblooded. There are times when my flesh burns like fire—have I not told you?"

Galbraith Stride shuddered in spite of himself, for he knew what Osman meant.

"I came to see you about that," he said jerkily.

"Ah! You have decided?"

Stride nodded. He sat down at the table, helped himself with nervous fingers from the inlaid cigarette box. The secretary stood by, ignored by both.

It was a strange venue for a peace conference, but that was what it was—and it explained also the terror which had come to Galbraith Stride that afternoon on the sunny deck of his yacht, the terror that had looked at him out of two cold reckless eyes that were as blue as the sea. Each of those two men was a power in an underground world of ugly happenings, though in their personal contact there was no question about which was the dominating personality. Even as Abdul Osman's tentacles of vice reached from Shanghai to Constantinople, so did Galbraith Stride's stretch from London south to the borders of the Adriatic and out west across the ocean to Rio.

Looking at Abdul Osman, one could build about him just such a mastery, but there was nothing about Galbraith Stride to show the truth. And yet it was true. Somehow, out of the restless cunning that evolved from the cowardice of his ineffectual physique, Stride had built up that subterranean kingdom and held it together, unknown to his stepdaughter, unknown to the police, unknown even to the princelings of his noisome empire, who communicated with him only through that silent Ramon Almido who passed as Stride's secretary. And thus, with the growth of both their dominions, it had come to a conference that must leave one of them supreme. Abdul Osman's insatiable lust for power dictated it, for Stride would have been content with his own boundaries. And with it, in the first meeting between them, had come to Abdul Osman the knowledge that he was Stride's master, that he need not be generous in treating for terms. The spectacle of Stride's uneasiness was another sop to Osman's pride.

"What a different conclusion there might have been if we had not both simultaneously thought of depositing the same letters with our solicitors!" said Osman reflectively. "To think that if either of us died suddenly there would be left instructions to the police to investigate carefully the alibi of the other! Quite a dramatic handicap, isn't it?"

Stride licked his lips.

"That's the only part of the bargain you've kept," he said. "Why, I've just heard you admit that your men have been landing cocaine here."

"I took the liberty of assuming our agreement to be a foregone conclusion," said Osman smoothly. Then his voice took on a harsher tone. "Stride, there's only one way out for you. For the last two years my agents have been steadily accumulating evidence against you—evidence which would prove absorbing reading to your good friends at Scotland Yard. That is the possibility for which you were not prepared, and it's too late now for you to think of laying the same trap for me. In another month that evidence can be brought to the point where it would certainly send you to prison for the rest of your life. You see, it was so much easier for me than for the police—they did not know whom to suspect, whereas I knew, and only had to prove it."

Stride had heard that before, and he did not take much notice.

"And so," continued Osman, "I make you the very fine offer of your liberty; and in return for that you retire from business and I marry Miss Laura."

Stride started up.

"That's not what you said!" he blurted. "You said if I—if I gave you Laura—you'd retire from Turkey and——"

"I changed my mind," said Osman calmly. "Why should I give? I was foolish. I hold all the cards. I am tired of arguing. As soon as this Simon Templar is on board I wish to leave—the year is getting late, and I can't stand your winters. Why should I make concessions?" He spat—straight to the priceless carpet, an inch from his visitor's polished shoes. "Stride, you were a fool to meet me yourself. If you had dealt with me through your clever Mr Almido I might have had some respect for you. You are not sufficiently important to look at—it shows me too plainly which of us is going to get his own way."

He spoke curtly, and, oddly enough for him, with a lack of apparent conceit that made his speech deadly in its emphasis. And Stride knew that Osman spoke only the truth. Yet, even then, if certain things had not happened. . . .

"You are afraid of the Saint, Stride," said Osman, reading the other's thoughts. "You are more afraid of him perhaps than you are of prison. You did not know that he knew you, but now that you know you want nothing more than to run away and hide in some place where he can't find you. Well, you can go. I shouldn't stand in your way, my dear Stride."

The other did not answer. Something had broken in the core of his resistance—a thing which only a psychologist who knew the workings of his mind, and the almost superstitious fear which the name of the Saint could still drive into many consciences, could have understood. He sat huddled in a kind of collapse; and Osman looked at him and chuckled again.

"I shall expect a note to tell me that you agree by ten o'clock to-night. You will send it across by hand—and who could be better employed to deliver it than Miss Laura?"

Galbraith Stride stood up and went out without a word.

## VI

Simon Templar saw Young Harry Trape and his companion carrying their suitcases down to the quay and thought they were trying to catch the *Scillonian*, which was scheduled to sail for the mainland at 4.15. He watched their descent rather wistfully from the hillside where he was walking, for it was his impression that they had got off much too lightly. He was not to know that Abdul

Osman had himself decided to dispense with their existence according to the laws of a strictly oriental code by which the penalty of failure was death; but if he had known, the situation would have appealed to his sense of humour even more than the memory of his recent treatment of Young Harry.

At the same time, their departure solved at least one problem, for it definitely relieved Mr Smithson Smith of further anxiety about the good name of his hotel.

It was past six o'clock when Simon came back to the village, for the solution of the mystery of an overloaded basket of towels had suddenly dawned on him, and he had set out to visit a few likely spots on the coast in the hope of finding further evidence. He had failed in that, but he remained convinced that his surmise was right.

"It was an ingenious method of smuggling dope," he told Patricia. "Nobody's thinking about anything like that here—if they see a strange ship loafing around their only suspicion is that it may be another French poacher setting lobster-pots in forbidden waters, and if the boat looked ritzy enough they simply wouldn't think at all. The sea party would dump sacks of it somewhere among the rocks, and the Heavenly Twins would fetch it home bit by bit in their basket without attracting any attention. Then they pack it in a suitcase and take it over to Penzance with their other stuff, and there isn't even a Customs officer to ask if they've got a bottle of scent. Which is probably what they're doing now—I wish we could have arranged a sticky farewell for them."

He had been much too far away to think of an attempt to intercept the evacuation, and the idea of telegraphing a warning to the chief of police at Penzance did not appeal to him. Simon Templar had no high idea of policemen, particularly provincial ones. And as a matter of fact his mind was taken up with a graver decision than the fate of two unimportant intermediaries.

He walked along from the lifeboat station with the details of his plan filling themselves out in his imagination; and they were just about to turn into Holgate's, the hotel at the other end of the town, when his ruminations were interrupted by a figure in uniform that appeared in his path.

"I've been looking for you, sir," said the Law.

The Law on the Scilly Islands was represented by one Sergeant Hancock, a pensioner of the Coldstream Guards, who must have found his rank a very empty honour, for there were no common constables to salute him. In times of need he could call upon a force of eight specials recruited from among the islanders, but in normal times he had nothing to make him swollen-headed about his position. Nor did he show any signs of ever having suffered from a swollen head—a fact which made him one of the very few officers of the Law whom Simon had ever been able to regard as even human. Possibly there was something in the air of the Islands, that same something which makes the native islanders themselves the most friendly and hospitable people one could hope to meet, which had mellowed the character of an exsergeant-major to the man who had become not only the head, but also the personal body and complete set of limbs, of the Scilly Islands Police; but certainly the Saint liked him. Simon had drunk beer with him, borrowed his fishing-line and fished with it, and exchanged so many affable salutes with him that the acquaintance was in danger of becoming a historic one in the Saint's life.

"What is it, Sergeant?" asked the Saint cheerfully. "Have I been dropping banana-peel in the streets or pulling faces at the mayor?"

"No, it's nothing like that. I want to know what's been going on up at Tregarthen's."

"Mr Smith has seen you, has he?"

"Yes, he came down and told me about it. I went to have a talk with those two young men, but they'd just paid their bill and gone. Then I came looking for you."

Simon offered a cigarette.

"What did Smith tell you?"

"Well, sir, he told me that you were having a drink in the bar, and one of those fellows put dope in your beer, and you punched his nose. Then one of them came down and threw the beer away, so there was no evidence, except a fly that Smith couldn't find. And Smith said you said something about Abdul Osman, which he said he thought might be a man who has a yacht over by Tresco."

The Sergeant's pleasant face was puzzledly serious, as well it might be. Such things simply did not happen on his well-conducted island.

Simon lighted his cigarette and thought for a moment. Abdul Osman was too big a fish for the net of a police force consisting of one man, and the only result of any interference from that official quarter would most likely be the unhappy decease of a highly amiable sergeant—a curiosity whom Simon definitely felt should be preserved for the Nation. Also he recalled a story that the Sergeant had told him on their first meeting—a story so hilariously incredible that it surpassed any novelist's wildest flights of fantasy.

A previous holder of the office once arrested a man and took him to the village lock-up, only to find that he hadn't the keys of the lock-up with him.

"Stay here while I get my keys," said the worthy upholder of the Law sternly; and that was the last they saw of their criminal.

While Simon did not doubt for a moment that Sergeant Hancock would be incapable of such a magnificent performance as that, his faith did not extend to the ability of a village lock-up to keep Abdul Osman inside and his shipload of satellites out.

"That's very nearly what happened, Sergeant," he said easily. "I think their idea was to rob the hotel and get away on the boat that afternoon. Smith wasn't drinking, so they couldn't drug him; but with me out of the way they'd have been two to one, and he wouldn't have stood much chance. They'd been staying in the hotel for a fortnight to get the lie of the land. I just happened to notice what they'd done to my beer."

"But what was that about Abdul Osman?"

"I think Smith can't have heard that properly. He was telling me some story about a man of that name, and it must have been on his mind. When I punched this bloke's face he threatened to call the police, and what I said was: 'Ask your pal what he thinks of the idea first.' Smith must have thought I said 'Ask Abdul'."

The Sergeant's face was gloomy.

"And you just punched his nose and let him get away! Why, if you'd only got hold of me——"

"But Smith did get hold of you."

"Oh, yes, he got hold of me after they'd gone. I had to go and see a man over at the other end of the island about paying his rates, and Smith couldn't find me till it was too late. I can't be everywhere at once."

The Saint grinned sympathetically.

"Never mind. Come in here and drown it in drink."

"Well, sir, I don't mind if I do have just one. I don't think I'm supposed to be on duty just this minute."

They went into the bar and found the barman enjoying his evening shave—a peculiarity of his which the Saint had observed before, and which struck Simon as being very nearly the perfect illustration for a philosophy of the Futility of Effort.

They carried their drinks over to the window at the bottom end of the bar, which looked across the harbour. The local boats were

coming in to their moorings one by one, with their cargoes of holiday fishing parties. Simon studied them as they came in with a
speculative eye.

"Whose boat's that—just coming in?" he asked; and the Sergeant
looked out.

"What, that nearest one? That's Harry Barrett's. He's a good boat-
man if you want to go out for the day."

"No—the other one—just coming round the end of Rat island."

The Sergeant screwed up his eyes.

"I don't know that one, sir." He turned round. "John, what's the
name of that boat out there by the pier?"

The barman came down and looked out.

"That? That one's Lame Frankie's boat—the *Puffin*. Built her himself, he did."

Simon watched the boat all the way in to her mooring, and
marked its position accurately in his memory. He discarded the idea
of Barrett's trim-looking yawl reluctantly—he was likely to have his
hands full while he was using the craft he proposed to borrow, and
the *Puffin*, though she was too broad in the beam for her length,
judged by classic standards of design, looked a trifle more comfortable as a single-hander for a busy man. And, in making his
choice, he noted down the name of Lame Frankie for a highly
anonymous reward; for the Saint's illicitly contracted obligations
were never left unpaid.

But none of his intentions just then were public property. He
held up to the light a glass of gin-and-It of astounding size for which
he had been charged the sum of ninepence, and sighed.

"How I shall ever be able to bring myself to pay one and six for
a drink about one-eighth the size of this in London again, is more
than I know," he murmured contentedly, and improved the shining
hour by drinking it down rapidly and calling for another.

He strolled back with Patricia to their modest supper as it was
beginning to grow dark. Their meal was just being put on the
table.

"You poach a wonderful egg, Mrs Nance," he remarked approvingly, and sank into his chair as the door closed behind that excellent
landlady. "Pat, darling, you must wish me *bon appétit* because I've
got a lot to do on these vitamins."

She had not liked to question him before, but now she gazed at
him resignedly.

"We were going away for a holiday," she reminded him.

"I know," said the Saint. "And we still are—away to the south, where there's sunshine and good wine and tomorrow is also a day. But we came by this roundabout way on a hunch, and the hunch was right. There is still a little work for us to do."

He finished his plate without speaking again, poured himself out a cup of coffee, and lighted a cigarette. Then he said:

"There's more nonsense talked about capital punishment than anything else, and the sentimentalists who organize petitions for the reprieve of every murderer who's ever sentenced are probably less pernicious than the more conventional humanitarians. Murder, in England anyway, is the most accidental of crimes. A human life is such a fragile thing, it's so easily snuffed out; and dozens of respectable men, without a thought of crime in their heads, have lost control of themselves for one second, and have woken up afterwards to the numbing and irrevocable realization that they have committed murder, and the penalty is death. There are deliberate murders; but there are other crimes no less deliberate and no less damning. The drug trafficker, the white slaver, the blackmailer—not one of them could ever plead that he acted in uncontrollable passion, or gave way to an instant's temptation, or did it because his wife and children were starving. All of those crimes are too deliberate—need too much capital, too much premeditation, too long to work through from beginning to end. And each of them wrecks human lives less mercifully than a sudden bullet. Why should the death penalty stop where it does? . . . That is justice as we have chosen to see it; and even now I believe that the old days were worth while."

He sat and smoked until it was quite dark; and, being the man he was, no detail of the future weighed on his mind. He scribbled industriously on a writing-pad, with occasional pauses for thought; and presently Patricia came round behind him to see what he had written.

At the top of the sheet he had roughly pinned the scrap of a report torn from the *Daily Telegraph*, and panelled it in characteristic slashes of blue pencil.

". . . He saw his friend in difficulties," said the Coroner, "and although he could not swim himself he went to his assistance. *He did what any Englishman would have done. . . .*"

The blue pencil had scored thickly under the last sentence. And underneath it the Saint was writing:

FLOREAT HARROVIA!

When Adam fell, because of Eve,
   Upon that dreadful day,
He did not own up loud and strong,
And take his licking with a song,
   In our good English way:
He had so little chivalry,
He said "The woman tempted me,"
   And tried to hide away.

(CHORUS)    *But in the blaze of brighter days*
        *Britannia yet shall rule,*
       *While English Sportsmen worship God*
       *And bend their bottoms to the rod*
        *For the Honour of the School!*

When Joshua strafed Jericho
   (NB—another Jew)
He did not risk his precious gore
Or take a sporting chance in war
   As English soldiers do:
He marched his bandsmen round the walls
And knocked it down with bugle calls—
   A trick that is tabu.

(CHORUS)

When Roland, at the gates of Spain,
   Died beside Oliver,
He must have found it rather hard
To stand his ground and keep the guard,
   Being a foreigner:
So we can only think he went
There by some kind of accident,
   Or as an arbiter.

(CHORUS)

When Louis faced the guillotine,
   That calm the people saw
Flinched to a sickly pallor when
He knew he was an alien,
   A Breed without the Law;
Where one of truly British phlegm,
Of course, would have leapt down at them
   And socked them on the jaw.

(CHORUS)

"Is all that necessary?" asked Patricia with a smile.
"Of course it is," said the Saint. "Because I've got an appointment

with one kind of excrescence, must I forget all the others? God in Heaven, while there's still a supply of smug fools for me to tear in pieces I shall have everything to live for . . . There are about five hundred and fifty more verses to that song, embracing everything from the massacre of Garigliano, down through Christopher Columbus and Marco Polo to the last Czar of Russia, which I may write some day. I think it will end like this——"

He wrote again, rapidly:

> But in our stately tolerance
>     We condescend to see
> That heroes whose names end in *vitch*
> Are striving to be something which
>     We know they cannot be,
> But, sweating hard, they make a good
> Attempt to do what Britons would
>     Achieve instinctively.

> (CHORUS)   *So let's give praise through all our days,*
>         *Again and yet again,*
>     *That we do not eat sauerkraut,*
>     *That some storks knew their way about,*
>         *And made us Englishmen!*

"I can never finish my best songs—my gorge rises too rapidly," said the Saint; and then he looked at his watch, and stood up, stretching himself with his gay smile. "Pat, I must be going. Wish me luck."

She kissed him quickly; and then he was gone, with the cavalier wave of his hand that she knew so well. All the old ageless Saint went with him, that fighting troubadour who he chose to be, who could always find time to turn aside in an adventure to shape one of those wild satires that came from him with such a biting sincerity. In some way he left her happier for that touch of typical bravado.

Her emotion was not shared by Galbraith Stride.

Something had come into the life of that successful man that he felt curiously impotent to fight against, something that had stricken him with a more savage shock because it was the one thing that he had never prepared himself for. It had the inexorable march of a machine. It left him unable to think clearly, with a sense of physical helplessness as if he had been worn down overnight by a fierce fever, struggling with the foreknowledge of defeat against a kind of paralysis of panic. And that thing was the name of the Saint.

He was a silent man at dinner that night. He knew that Abdul

Osman had crushed and beaten him with an ease that seemed fantastically ridiculous, and the knowledge hypnotised him into a sort of horrible nightmare. And yet at the same time he knew that he might still have been fighting, calling on all the resources of guile and duplicity that had brought him to the power that was being stripped from him, if it had not been for the words that had stunned his ears early that afternoon. He was that strange psychological freak, a criminal possessed of an imagination that amounted almost to mania; and when Osman had told him that the Saint was still at large an overstrained bulwark on the borders of his reason seemed to have crashed inwards. He was still fighting for all he could hope to save from the disaster, but it was a dumb stubborn fight without vitality.

He sent for Laura Berwick at nine o'clock. Her slender young body looked particularly beautiful in the black evening gown she was wearing; in some way its cool sweetness was framed in that sombre setting with an effect that was pulse-quickeningly radiant from the contrast. To do him justice, Galbraith Stride felt a momentary twinge of remorse as he saw her.

"My dear, I want you to take a note over to Mr Osman. It's rather important, and I'd feel relieved if you delivered it yourself."

He had been drinking, but the whisky that reeked on his breath had thickened his voice without making him drunk. It served the purpose of nipping that twinge of remorse in the bud, before he had time to forget his own danger.

"Couldn't one of the crew go?" she asked in some surprise.

"I'm afraid there are reasons why they can't," he said. "They—er—hum—I may be able to explain later. A matter of business. It's vitally important——"

"But what about Mr Almido?"

"Mr Almido," said Stride, "is a fool. Between ourselves, I don't trust him. Some funny things have been happening to my accounts lately. No, my dear, you must do this for me. I'd go myself, only—I—I'm not feeling very well. You can take the motorboat."

He was staring at her with the fixed and glassy eyes of semi-intoxication—she could see that—but there was something besides alcohol in his stare that frightened her. His excuses for requiring her to go over in person seemed absurd; and yet it seemed equally absurd to imagine that there could be anything serious behind them. She was fond of him, in a purely conventional way—chiefly because he was the only relative she had had since she was six years old. She knew nothing of his business; but in his remotely fussy way he had been kind to her.

"All right—I'll go for you. When do you want it done?"

"At once." He pressed a sealed envelope into her hand, and she felt that his own hand was hot and sticky. "Run along right away, will you?"

"Right-ho," she said; and wondered, as she went to the door, why her own words rang in her ears without a trace of the artificial cheerfulness that she had tried to put into them.

She left him sitting at the table, squinting after her with the same glazed stare; and went up on deck to find Toby Halidom.

"Daddy wants me to go over to the *Luxor* and deliver a note," she said, and he was naturally perplexed.

"Why shouldn't one of the crew go—or that Dago secretary with the Marcel wave?"

"I don't know, Toby." Out under the stars, the vague impressions she had received in the saloon seemed even more absurd. "He was rather funny about it, but he seemed to want it particularly badly, so I said I'd go."

"Probably suffering from an attack of liver," hazarded Toby heartily. "All the same, he ought to know better than to ask you to pay calls on a reptile like that at this hour of the night. I'd better come with you, old thing—I don't like you to go and see that ugly nigger alone."

It was not Toby Halidom's fault that he had been brought up to that inscrutable system of English thought in which all coloured men are niggers unless they happen also to be county cricketers; but on this occasion at least his apprehensions were destined to be fully justified. They had both met Abdul Osman once before during their stay, and Laura knew that her fiancé had shared her instinctive revulsion. She felt relieved that he had spontaneously offered to go with her.

"I'd be glad if you would come, Toby."

Galbraith Stride heard the motorboat chugging away from the side, and listened to it till the sound died away. Then he went over and pressed a bell in the panelling. It was answered by the saturnine Mr Almido.

"We shall be leaving at ten," he said; and his secretary was pardonably surprised.

"Why, sir, I thought——"

"Never mind what you thought," said Stride thickly. "Tell the captain."

Almido retired; and Stride got up and began to pace the saloon. The die was cast. He had abdicated to Abdul Osman. He had saved his liberty—perhaps he could even save himself from the Saint. The reaction was starting to take hold of him like a powerful drug, spurring him with a febrile exhilaration and scouring an unnatural brightness into the glaze of his eyes. He had no compunction about what he had done. Laura Berwick was not his own flesh and blood —that would have been his only excuse, if he had bothered to make any. The thought of her fate had ceased to trouble him. It counted for nothing beside his own safety. For a brief space he even regretted the feebleness of his surrender—wondered if a card like Laura could not have been played to far better effect. . . .

It was only another twist in the imponderable thread that had begun to weave itself when the boom of the *Claudette's* dinghy had swung over against Laura Berwick's head that morning; but the twist was a short one. For Fate, masking behind the name which Galbraith Stride feared more than any other name in the world, had taken a full hand in the game that night.

There were two doors into the saloon. One of them opened into a microscopic vestibule, from which a broad companion gave access to the deck and an alleyway led out to other cabins and the crew's quarters forward; the other opened into Stride's own stateroom. In his restless pacing of the saloon, Stride had his back turned to the second door when he heard a sharp swish and thud behind him. He jerked round, raw-nerved and startled; and then he saw what had caused the sound, and his heart missed a beat.

Standing straight out from the polished woodwork of the door was a long thin-bladed knife with a hilt of exquisitely carved ivory, still quivering from the force of the impact that had driven it home.

His lungs seemed to freeze achingly against the walls of his chest, and a parching dryness came into his throat that filled him with a presentment that if he released the scream which was struggling for outlet just below his wishbone it could only have materialised as a thin croaking whisper. The hand that dragged the automatic from his pocket was shaking so much that he almost dropped it. The sudden appearance of that quivering knife was uncanny, supernatural. The opposite door had been closed all the time, for he had been pacing towards it when the thing happened; the ports and skylight also were fastened. From the angle at which it had driven into the door it should have flashed past his face, barely missing him as he walked; but he had not seen it.

If he had been in any state in which he could think coherently, he might have hit on the explanation in a few moments; but he was not in that state. It never occurred to him that the door behind him might have been opened, the knife driven home, and the door rapidly and silently closed again, with just that very object of misleading his attention which it had achieved.

Which was indubitably very foolish of Mr Galbraith Stride.

Filled with the foreboding that a second attack would almost instantly follow the first unsuccessful one, trembling in the grip of a cold funk that turned his belly to water, he backed slowly and shakily towards the door where the knife had struck, facing in the direction from which he believed the danger threatened. Curiously enough, his only idea was that Abdul Osman had decided to take no chances on his regretting his bargain, and had sent one of his men stealthily to eliminate that possibility. If he had thought of anything else, it is possible that the scream which he ached to utter would not have been suppressed.

Back . . . back . . . three paces, four paces. . . . And then suddenly he saw the bulkheads on each side of him, and realized with an eerie thrill of horror that he was actually passing through them —that the door which should have come up against his back had been opened noiselessly behind him, and he was stepping backwards over the threshold.

He opened his mouth to cry out, turning his head as he did so; but the cry rattled voicelessly in his throat. A brown shirt-sleeved arm whipped round his neck from behind and strangled him in the crook of its elbow, while fingers like bars of steel fastened on his wrist just behind the gun. His head was dragged back so that he looked up into the inverted vision of twin blue eyes that were as clear and cold as frozen ultramarines; and then the intruder's mouth spoke against his ear.

"Come and pay calls with me, Galbraith," he heard; and then he fainted.

## VII

Abdul Osman had also been drinking, but with him it had been almost a festive rite. He had put on a dinner suit, with a red tarboosh; and his broad soft stomach, swelling out under the sloping expanse of a snowy shirtfront, gave him the appearance of a flabby pyramid walking about on legs, as if a bloated frog had been dressed up in European clothes. His wide sallow face was freshly shaved, and had a slightly greasy look around the chin. Although he wore Western clothes cut by the best tailors in London, the saloon of his yacht, in which he was walking about, was decorated entirely in the Oriental style, which was the only one in which he felt truly comfortable. The rugs on the floor were Bokhara and Shiraz, virtually priceless; the tables ebony inlaid with mother-of-pearl; the couches low, covered with dark silk brocades, heavily strewn with cushions. Even the prosaic portholes were framed with embroidered hangings and barred with iron grilles so that they should not clash with the atmosphere, and the dim concealed lights left corners full of shadows. Osman, in his dinner-jacket and white starched shirt-front, fitted into those surroundings with a paradoxical effect, like an ardent nudist clinging to his straw hat and *pince-nez;* but he was incapable of perceiving the incongruity.

He was preening himself before a mirror, a half-emptied glass in one hand, the other smoothing an imperceptible crease out of his bow tie, a thin oval cigarette smouldering between his lips, when he heard the approaching sputter of a motor launch. He listened in immobile expectancy, and heard the engine cut off and the sound of voices. Then the Arab seaman, Ali, knocked on the door and opened it, and Laura Berwick stood in the entrance.

Abdul Osman saw her in the mirror, from which he had not moved; and for a second or two he did not stir. His veins raced with the sudden concrete knowledge of triumph. Cold-blooded? The corners of his mouth lifted fractionally, wrinkling up his eyes. At their very first meeting, the formal touch of her hand had filled him with a hunger like raging furnaces: now, seeing her gloriously modelled face and shoulders standing out brilliantly pale in the dark doorway, his heart pounded molten flame through his body.

He turned slowly, spreading out one arm in a grandiose gesture.

"So you have come—my beautiful white rose!"

Laura Berwick smiled hesitantly. The room was full of the peculiarly dry choky scent of sandalwood. Everything in her recoiled in disgust from its ornately exotic gloom. It seemed unhealthy, suffocating, heavy with an aura of horribly secret indulgence, like the slack puffy body of the man who was feeding his eyes on her. She was glad that Toby had come with her—his clear-cut Spartan cleanness was like an antiseptic.

"Mr Stride asked me to bring a note over to you," she said.

He held out his hand, without taking his eyes from her face. Unhurriedly he ripped open the envelope—it contained nothing but a blank sheet of paper. Deliberately he tore it into four pieces, and laid them on a table.

"Perhaps," he said, "it was more important that a note should bring you over to me."

Then for the first time he saw Toby Halidom, and his face changed.

"What are you doing here?" he inquired coldly.

The young man was faintly taken aback.

"I just buzzed over with Miss Berwick," he said. "Thought she might like some company, and all that."

"You may go."

There was an acid drawling incisiveness in Osman's voice that was too dispassionate to be rude. It staggered Halidom with the half-sensed menace of it.

"I asked Mr Halidom to come with me," said Laura, striving to keep a sudden breathlessness out of her voice. "We shall be going back together."

"Did—er—your stepfather suggest that arrangement?"

"No. Toby just thought he'd come."

"Really!" Osman laughed softly, an almost inaudible chuckle that made the girl shiver unaccountably. "Really!" He turned away, a movement that came after his temporary motionlessness with a force that was subtly sinister. "Really!" The joke seemed to amuse him. He strolled away down the room, the cigarette smouldering between his fingers, and turned again at a place where the dim lights left him almost in darkness. The cigarette-end glowed like a hot ruby against the grey smudge of his shirtfront in the gloom—they could not see his thick fingers touching bells that had men always waiting to answer them. "How very romantic, my dear Halidom! The perfect knight-errant!"

Toby Halidom flushed dully at the sneer. Something in the atmosphere of the interview was getting under his skin, in spite of the healthy unimaginativeness of his instincts.

"Well, Laura, let's be getting along," he said, and heard the note of strain in his own assumed heartiness.

Osman's ghostly chuckle whispered again out of the shadows, but he said nothing. Halidom turned abruptly to the door, opened it, and stopped dead. There were three of Osman's crew outside, crowded impassively across the opening.

Toby faced the Egyptian with clenched fists.

"What's the idea, Osman?" he demanded bluntly.

Abdul moved an inch or two from his position, so that his broad fleshy face stood out like a disembodied mask of evil under one of the rose-shaded light globes.

"The idea, Hamilton, is that Laura is staying here with me—and you are not."

"You lousy nigger——"

Halidom leapt at the mask like a young tiger-cat, but he was stopped short in less than a foot. Sinewy brown arms caught his arms from behind, twisted and pinioned them expertly.

Osman stepped forward slowly.

"Did you say something, Halidom?"

"I called you a lousy nigger," retorted Toby defiantly. "You heard me all right. Shall I say it again?"

"Do."

Osman's voice was sleek, but his hands were shaking. His face had gone a dead white, save only for the scarred red circles on his cheeks. Toby swallowed, and flung up his head.

"You foul slimy——"

Osman's fist smacked the last word back into his teeth.

"If you had remembered your manners, Halidom, your fate might have been very different," he said; and it was obvious that he was only controlling himself momentarily, by an effort of will that brought beads of perspiration on to the whiteness of his forehead. "But that is one word you cannot use. There was another man who used it many years ago—perhaps you would like to see him?"

He spoke to Ali purringly, in Arabic, and the man disappeared. Halidom was struggling like a maniac.

"You can't get away with this, you ugly swine——"

"No?"

Osman struck him again; and then, after a moment's pause, deliberately spat in his face. Laura cried out and flung herself forward, but one of the men caught her instantly. Osman sauntered over to her and tilted up her chin in his bloated hands.

"You're a spitfire too, are you, my dear? That makes it all the more interesting. I'm good at taming spitfires. In a moment I'll show you one of my tamed ones. You shall see me tame Halidom in the same way—and you too."

He looked round as the seaman returned with his secretary. Clements was in a pitiful state—Osman had withheld the needle from him all that day, as he had threatened to do, and the slavering creature that tottered into the room made even Halidom's blood run cold.

The man fell on his knees at Osman's feet, slobbering and moaning unintelligibly; and Osman caught him by the hair and dragged him upright.

"Do you see this, Halidom? This is a man who used to call me a dirty nigger. Once upon a time he was just like you—strong, straight, insolent. He feared nothing, and despised me because I wasn't another stupid Englishman like himself. But then, one day, someone introduced him to the needle—the little prick that brings so much courage and cleverness for a while. Have you ever tried it, Halidom? You haven't even thought of it. You've been too busy playing cricket and being called a fine fellow because you could play it well. But you will try it. Oh, no, not voluntarily, perhaps—but the effects will be just the same. You will feel big, strong, clever, a fine fellow, until the drug wears off, and then you will feel very tired. Then I shall give you some more, and again you will feel fine and big and strong. And so we shall go on; you will want a little more each time, but I shall give you just the right amount, until"—in a sudden spasm of savagery he shook Clements by the handful of hair that he was still holding—"until you are bigger and stronger than ever—a finer fellow than you have ever been—like this thing here!"

He thrust the man away; but Clements was back as soon as he had recovered his balance, clutching Osman's hand, kissing it, fawning over it in a trembling abjectness that was nauseating.

"That will be pleasant for you, Halidom, won't it?"

Toby was staring at Clements with an incredulous loathing that turned his stomach sick.

"You filthy swine——"

"I have found, Halidom," said Osman, staring at him steadily, "that the needle is an excellent help for taming your kind. But my little whip also does its share—especially in the beginning, when there are moments of open rebellion. Would you like to see that as well?"

He touched a concealed spring, and a section of the panelling sprang open. Clements darted forward as he saw it, but Osman pushed the enfeebled body away easily with one hand and sent it sprawling. Inside the cupboard that was disclosed they could see a couple of hypodermic syringes set in gleaming nickelled racks, with a row of tiny glass phials beside them; but Osman left those alone. He took out a short leather whip, so thick at the base that it was difficult to see where it joined the handle, and tapering to a point in which there was a thin hard point.

"An excellent instrument," Osman said, "which has helped to drive a proper sense of respect into the man you see."

He ran the lash through his fingers thoughtfully, gazing down at the grovelling creature by his feet. Something in the sight of that last triumph of his, that living completeness of humiliation, seemed to snap the thread of his gloating self-control. With his thick lips twisting back wolfishly, he leapt at Halidom and slashed twice at his face; then he turned and dragged Clements up again, holding him pinned against the wall with a hand grasping his throat.

"Look at them, Clements!" he screamed. "Look at them!" He forced the man's livid face round towards Toby and Laura. "Can you see them—or are you too hungry for the needle? They're white —white—the colour you were so proud of! And you're not ashamed, are you? I've thrashed you often enough before my blacks—you're used to that—but how do you like your own people to see what you've sunk to? Look at them, I tell you. A white man and a white girl—staring at you—despising you—and even that doesn't give you enough self-respect to stand up for yourself. Bah!"

He stepped back and sent the whip hissing about the man's thin shoulders; and then he came close to Halidom again.

"And that," he said hoarsely—"that is what you will be like, Halidom."

His mouth was drooling at the corners, his fingers twitching with the intensity of his passion. Toby looked him in the eyes.

"You'll never get away with this," he said, as quietly as he could. "Stride knows we're here, and as soon as he gets worried about Laura——"

Abdul Osman laughed harshly.

"My dear Halidom, you're mistaken. Stride sent Laura to me—to stay! He did not send you, but I imagine your disappearance will be a relief to him—if you had been left on his hands he might not have known what to do with you. By this time he is making his preparations to leave."

"I don't believe it!" cried the girl. "Toby—it can't be true—he's lying——"

Osman looked at her.

"It doesn't matter to me what you believe," he said silkily. "Doubtless you will be convinced in course of time."

"It's a lie!" she protested again, but a chill fear had closed on her heart. "He'll go straight to the police——"

"The police?" Osman's sinister chuckle whispered through the room. "They would be delighted to see him. You little fool! Didn't you know where his money came from? Didn't you know that all his life he's done nothing but trade in women and drugs—that I hold enough evidence to send him to prison for twenty years? You, my dear Laura, are the price of his liberty: you and—er—his retirement from business. A price that he was glad to offer, and that I was very happy to accept."

She could not think properly, could not comprehend the whole hideous significance of what he was saying. She could not believe it; and yet, from the manner in which he said it, either it must be true or he must be mad. And neither alternative opened out a gleam of hope. But she remembered the strangeness that she had seen in Galbraith Stride's eyes when he insisted that she must deliver his message herself, and she was frozen with dread before that unspeakable explanation.

Beside her, Toby Halidom was struggling again in a blind fury of helplessness; and Osman looked at him again.

"I shall commence your treatment very soon, my friend," he said; and then he spoke again to Ali. "Take him away and bind him carefully—I shall ring when I wish to see him again."

Almost before he could speak Halidom was hustled out of the room, with the girl's wild pitiful cry ringing in his ears. Rough brown hands forced him down a dark alleyway, tightened ropes round his wrists and ankles, and hurled him into an evil-smelling unlighted cabin. He heard the door locked on the outside, and was alone with a despair such as he had never dreamed of in his life, a despair haunted with visions that verged on sheer shrieking madness. There was only one hope left for him—a hope so small that it was almost worse than no hope at all. They had not troubled to search him, and there was a penknife in his pocket. If he could reach that, saw at the ropes on his wrists . . . then there would still be the locked door, and a hostile crew to break through unarmed . . . But he was trying to get at that knife, with strange futile tears burning under his eyelids.

Laura Berwick thought that her reason would break. The last of the swarthy seamen had released her and gone out with Toby—

there was no one in the saloon but herself and Abdul Osman, and that ghastly relic of a man cowering in a corner and watching Osman's movements with blubbering hate-filled eyes. Osman did not even seem to be aware of his existence—perhaps he had grown so used to having that thing of his own creation with him that he took no more notice of him than if he had been a dog; or perhaps in the foul depths of his mind there was some spawning idea of heaping humiliation on humiliation both for the girl and his beaten slave. He edged towards her unsteadily, his glittering eyes leering with unutterable things, and she retreated from him as she would have done before a snake, until her back was to the wall and she could retreat no further.

"Come to me, beautiful white rose!"

His arms reached out for her. She tried to slip sideways away from their clawing grasp, keeping her eyes out of sheer terror from looking full into that puffed lecherous face; but he caught her arm and held it with a strength greater than her own. She was drawn irresistibly into his hot embrace—she felt the horrible softness of his paunch against her firm young flesh, and shuddered until mists swam before her eyes. She could not possibly endure it much longer. Her senses reeled, and she seemed to have lost all her strength. . . .

And then, as his greedy lips found her face, her brain went out at last into merciful blackness; and she heard the shot that struck him down only as a dim part of her dream.

## VIII

Simon Templar slammed the door of the glory hole forward, twisted the key, and snapped it off short in the lock. He heard a babel of shouts and jabbering in heathen tongues break out behind it, and grinned gently. So far as he had been able to discover in a lightning reconnaissance, practically the whole of Osman's crew was congregated up there in the fo'c'sle: he had already battened down the hatch over their heads, and it would take them nothing less than an hour to break out.

It was the moment for a speed of action that could be outdistanced by nothing less nimble than a Morality Squad discovering new vices to suppress—that speed of decision and performance in which the Saint had no equal. With the stillness of the ship still freshly bruised by the sharp thud of that single shot, it was a time when committee meetings and general philosophy had to take second place.

He raced down the alleyway towards the second door under which he had seen a strip of light; it was thrown open as he reached it, and an olive-skinned man in uniform, with his shirt unbuttoned, stared into his face from a range of twelve inches. In the cabin behind him, two others, apparently fellow officers, were frozen statuesquely around a table littered with cards. Just for the sharp-etched half of a second there was an utter immobility; and then Simon's fist crashed into the man's face and sent him staggering. In another second that door also was locked, and the key broken.

Simon had located only one other danger point, and that was a few steps further down the passage. As he opened the door he saw that it was the galley, and the explanation of the light he had seen was provided by a coal-black Kano boy who was placidly peeling potatoes and humming one of his own weird melodies. The song died away in an abrupt minor as the Kano boy looked up at him with rolling eyes: Simon saluted him cheerily, and turned the third key on the safe side of the door.

Then he went aft to the saloon; and as he went he saw another door hanging drunkenly open on its mutilated hinges.

Toby Halidom was pillowing Laura's head on one arm, babbling silly incoherent things to her. His other hand covered the doorway with the automatic that had killed Osman, and for one second Simon felt nearer death than he cared to stand at any time.

"Put that down, you ass," he said; and then Toby recognized him, and lowered the gun slowly.

"What are you doing here?"

"Getting you out of trouble," said the Saint briskly. "You needn't worry—the crew won't be interfering yet. I've just locked them up to keep them out of mischief."

His gaze swept comprehensively around the room—over the body of Abdul Osman, who lay stretched out on his back, half underneath a table that he had clutched at and brought down with him in his fall, with a slowly widening red stain on his white shirtfront; over the unconscious figure of Galbraith Stride; over the enslaved secretary, Clements, who sat without movement on one of the couches, his face hidden in his hands, with an empty hypodermic syringe lying where it had fallen on the dark tapestry beside him. . . . He reached out and took the automatic from Halidom's unresisting fingers.

"I don't care if I hang for it!" said the young man hysterically. "He deserved everything he got."

Simon's eyebrows went up through one slow half-centimetre.

"If *you* hang for it?" he repeated.

"Yes. They can do what they like. I killed him—the swine. I shot him——"

The Saint's smile, that quirk of the lips which could be so gay, so reckless, so mocking, so debonair, so icily insolent, so maddeningly seraphic, as his mood willed it, touched his mouth and eyes with a rare gentleness that transformed him. A strange look, almost of tenderness, touched the chiselled lines of that mad buccaneering face.

"Hang you, Toby?" he said softly. "I don't think they'll do that."

The young man scarcely heard him. For at that moment Laura's eyes opened, full of the horror of her last moment of consciousness, and saw the face of the young man bending over her with a queer little choking sob.

"Toby!"

She clung to him, raising herself against his shoulder, still wild-eyed with lingering nightmares; and then she shrank back as she saw Abdul Osman.

"Toby! Did you——"

"It's all right, darling," said Halidom huskily. "He won't trouble us again."

Then the Saint's hands touched each of their shoulders.

"I don't think you need to stay here," he said quietly.

He led them out on to the deck, out into the night air that was cool and fresh with the enduring sweetness of the sea. The motorboat in which they had come was still moored at the bottom of the gangway; but now the *Puffin* was made fast behind it, with its spread sails stirring like the wings of a grey ghost against the dark water. Between them they helped the girl down to the motorboat; and Simon sat on the half-deck and gazed aft to the seats where the other two had settled themselves. A match flared at the end of his cigarette.

"Will you try and listen to me?" he said, in the same quiet tone. "I know what you've been through tonight, because I was listening most of the time. There were some things I had to know before I moved—and then, when the time came for me to interfere, there wasn't much for me to do. I did what I could, and no one will stop you going back to the *Claudette*."

The hand with the cigarette moved towards the *Luxor's* side in a faint gesture.

"A man was killed there tonight. I've never seen any good reason for buttering up a bad name just because it's a dead one. As Toby said, he deserved everything he got—maybe more. He was a man whose money had been wrung farthing by farthing out of the ruin and degradation of more human lives than either of you can imagine. He was a man who'll leave the world a little cleaner for being dead.

"But in the eyes of the law he was murdered. In the eyes of the law he was a citizen who had every right to live, who could have called for policemen paid for by other citizens to protect him if he'd ever been threatened, who would have been guiltless for ever in the eyes of the law until his crimes could have been proved according to the niggling rules of evidence to twelve bamboozled half-wits by a parade of blathering lawyers. And the man who killed him will be sentenced to death according to the law.

"That man was Galbraith Stride."

They were staring at him, intent and motionless.

"I know what you thought, Toby," said the Saint. "You burst into the saloon with murder in your heart, and saw Osman dead, and Laura with the gun close to her hand. You could only think for the moment that she had done it, and you made a rather foolish and rather splendid confession to me with some wild idea of shielding her. If I had any medals hung around me I'd give you one. But you certainly weren't in your right mind, because it never occurred to you to ask what Stride was doing there, or where Laura found the gun."

"Laura, I don't want to make it any harder for you, but there is one thing you must know. Every word that Osman told you was true. Galbraith Stride himself was just such a man as Osman. He has never been such a power for evil, perhaps; but that's only because he wasn't big enough. He was certainly no better. Their trades were the same, and they met here to divide their kingdoms. Osman won the division because he was just a shade more unscrupulous, and Stride sent you to him in accordance with their bargain.

"You might like to think that Stride repented at the last moment and came over to try and save you; but I'm afraid even that isn't true. He killed Osman for a much more sordid reason, which the police will hear about in due time."

Even in the darkness he could see their eyes fixed on him. It was Laura Berwick who spoke for them both.

"Who are you?" she asked; and Simon was silent only for a second.

"I am Simon Templar, known as the Saint—you may have heard of me. I am my own law, and I have sentenced many men who were lesser pestilences than Abdul Osman or Galbraith Stride . . . Oh, I know what you're thinking. The police will also think it for a little while. I did come here tonight to kill Abdul Osman, but I wasn't quick enough."

He stood up, and swung himself lightly back on to the gangway. His deft fingers cast off the painter and tossed it into the boat; and without another word he went up to the deck and down again to the saloon.

* * * * * * *

They sentenced Galbraith Stride for the murder of Abdul Osman on the first day of November, just over a month after these events that have been recorded, after a trial that lasted four days.

One of the documents that played a considerable part in bringing the jury to their verdict was a sealed letter that was produced by a London solicitor at the inquest. It was addressed in Abdul Osman's own heavy sprawling calligraphy: *"To the Coroner: to be handed to him in the event of my death in suspicious circumstances within the next three months."*

Inside was a comprehensive survey of Galbraith Stride's illicit activities that made the police open their eyes. It was typewritten; but the concluding paragraph was in Osman's own handwriting.

*This is written in the expectation of a meeting between Stride and myself at which our respective spheres of influence are to be agreed on and mutually limited. If any "accident" should happen to me during this conference, therefore, the man responsible will certainly be Galbraith Stride, whom I should only expect to violate our truce as he has violated every other bargain he has ever made.*

(Signed) ABDUL OSMAN.

The defence made a valiant effort to save their case by making great play with the fact that the notorious Simon Templar was not only in the district, but was actually on board the *Luxor* when the murder was committed; but the judge promptly suppressed all questions that were not directly concerned with the circumstances of the murder.

"The police," he said, "have charged Galbraith Stride with the murder, and I cannot have alternative murderers dragged in at this stage of the proceedings. We are here to decide whether the prisoner, Galbraith Stride, is guilty or not guilty; and if he should eventually be found not guilty it will be open to the police to bring charges against such other persons as they think fit."

There was also, somewhat inconsistently, an attempt on the part of the defence to represent their client as a repentant hero hastening to rescue his stepdaughter from her fate. The case for the prosecution lasted two days, and this happened when the Crown's position was rapidly becoming unassailable. And then Clements was called, and that finished it.

He was a very different man from the whimpering wreck who had suffered all the indignities that Osman's warped brain could think of to heap upon him. From the moment of Osman's death he had become free of the supplies of cocaine that were stocked in that concealed cupboard in the saloon: he had used them liberally to maintain himself in the normal state that he would never be able to return to again without the help of drugs, keeping their existence secret until the case was transferred to the mainland and he could secure proper treatment. But there was no treatment that could give him back the flame of life; and so the police surgeon told him.

"Honestly, Clements, if I'd been told that a man could develop the resistance to the stuff that you've got, so that he would require the doses that you require to keep him normal, without killing himself, I shouldn't have believed it. You must have had the constitution of an ox before you started that—that——"

"Folly?" queried Clements, with a flicker of expression passing over his wasted features. "Yes, I used to be pretty strong, once."

"There's no cure for what you've got," said the doctor bluntly; for he was still a young man, an old Rugger blue, and some of the things that he saw in his practice hurt him.

But Clements only smiled. He knew that the poisons they were pumping into him six times a day to keep him human would kill him within a matter of weeks, but he could not have lasted much longer anyway. And he had one thing to finish before he died.

He went into the witness-box steady-nerved, with his head erect and the sparkle of cocaine in his eyes. The needle that the young doctor had rammed into his arm half an hour before had done that; but that was not in evidence. They knew he was a cocaine addict, of course—he told them the whole story of his association with Abdul Osman, without sparing himself. The defence remembered this when their turn came to crossexamine.

"In view of these sufferings which you endured at the hands of the dead man," counsel put it to him, "didn't you ever feel you would like to kill him?"

"Often," said Clements calmly. "But that would have cut off my supplies of the drug."

"Wouldn't it be quite conceivable, then," counsel continued, persuasively, "that if you *had* killed him you would be particularly anxious to keep yourself out of the hands of the police at any cost?"

Just for that moment the witness's eyes flashed.

"You'd better ask the doctor," he said. "He'll tell you that I shall probably be dead in a couple of months anyway. Why should I waste my last days of life coming here to tell you lies? It would make no difference to me if you sentenced me to death today."

Counsel consulted his notes.

"You had never met Galbraith Stride before?"

"Never."

Then came the attempt to represent the killing as an act in the defence of a girl's honour.

"I have told the court already," said Clements, with that terribly patient calm of a man for whom time has no more meaning, which somehow set him apart from the reproof that would immediately have descended upon any ordinary witness who attempted to make a speech from the box, "that nothing of the sort was suggested. Miss Berwick had fainted; and during the time that she was being attacked I was only occupied with taking advantage of the confusion to get at Osman's supply of cocaine. I cannot make any excuses for that—no one who has been spared that craving can understand how it overrules all other considerations until it has been satisfied. Deprived of it, I was not a man—I was a hungry animal. I went to the cabinet and gave myself an injection, and sat down to allow the drug time to take effect. When I looked up, Galbraith Stride was there. He had a pistol in his hand, and he appeared to have been drinking. He said: 'Wait a minute, Osman. She's worth more than that. I'm damned if I'll let you have her and get rid of me as well. You can make another choice. If you take her, we'll divide things differently.' Osman flew into a rage and tried to hit him. Stride fired, and Osman fell. I thought Stride was going to fire again, and I caught hold of the nearest weapon I could find—a brass vase—and hit him with it. I hadn't much strength, but luckily it struck him on the chin and knocked him out."

"And it was you who went over to St Mary's and informed Sergeant Hancock what had happened?"

"Yes."

"On your own initiative?"

"Entirely."

"I suggest that Templar said: 'Look here, Osman's dead, and there's no need for us to get into trouble. Let's go over to Sergeant Hancock and tell him that Stride did it.' "

"That is absurd."

"You remember the statement that Stride made to Sergeant Hancock when he was arrested?"

"Fairly well."

"You will recall, perhaps, that Stride described how he was attacked in his cabin on the *Claudette* by this man Templar, and that significant mention of a knife that was alleged to have been thrown into a door. Did you hear Sergeant Hancock give evidence that he examined the door in the saloon of the *Claudette*, and found the mark of a knife having been driven deeply into it?"

"Yes."

"How would you account for that?"

"If you ask me, I should say that a man like Stride might well have foreseen the possibility of accidents, and he could easily have prepared that mark to substantiate his story in case of trouble."

It was on this point that the greatest weakness of the case for the prosecution seemed to rest. Simon Templar was recalled before the end, and his evidence re-examined.

"You have admitted that you went out to the *Luxor* on the night in question with the intention of assaulting Osman?"

"I've never denied it," said the Saint.

"Why, if you were so anxious to take the law into your own hands, did you confine your attentions to the deceased?"

"Because I'd heard of him, and I hadn't heard of Stride. Mr Smithson Smith told me about Osman—that's already been given in evidence."

"And you," said counsel, with deliberate irony, "were immediately filled with such a passion for justice that you couldn't sleep until you had thrashed this monster that Osman was represented to you to be?"

"I thought it would be rather a rag," said the Saint, with a perfectly straight face.

"It has been suggested that you were the man who branded Osman five years ago—was that also intended to be rather a rag?"

"I never met the man before in my life."

"You have heard Galbraith Stride say that you told him that you had done that?"

"He must be dotty," said the Saint—a reply that earned him a three-minute lecture from the learned judge.

In his closing speech, the counsel for the Crown suggested that the difficulty might not be so great as it appeared.

"In this case," he said, "the only discrepancies which you need to take into consideration are those between the evidence given by Mr Clements and Mr Templar, and the story told by the prisoner. It is my submission to you that the defence has in no way succeeded in shaking the credibility of those two witnesses; and when you remember, in discarding the evidence of the prisoner, that it is not supported by any other witness at any point, and that the only alternative to discarding it as the fantastic story of a man lying desperately to save his neck is to regard all the stories of all the other witnesses as nothing short of a deliberate conspiracy to send an innocent man to the gallows—then, ladies and gentlemen of the jury, in my humble submission, there is only one conclusion at which any reasonable person can arrive."

The jury was away for three hours; but to the reporters in the crowded press seats it was a foregone conclusion. The fingerprints of Galbraith Stride had been found on the gun, and that seemed to clinch it.

So they found him guilty, as we know; and the warders had to hold him up when the judge put on the black cap.

## IX

Three weeks later an early post brought Toby Halidom a letter.

He was awake to receive it; for during that night the story as it concerned him had dragged through its last intolerable lap. It was the end of three weeks of dreadful waiting—three weeks in which the lines of strain that had marked themselves on the face he loved had been etched in indelible lines of acid on his own memory. It was not that either of them bore any more affection for the man who had made his infamous bargain with Abdul Osman, and who was now awaiting the final irrevocable summons of the Law; Galbraith Stride had placed himself beyond that; but they had known him personally, eaten at his table, seen him walking and talking as a human being of the same race as themselves instead of the impersonal deformed specimen in a glass case which the criminologists were already making of him, and they would not have been human themselves if that period of waiting for the relentless march of the Law had not preyed on their waking and sleeping hours like an intermittent nightmare. And that night had been the last and worst of all.

At midnight Toby had seen Laura sent to bed by a kindly doctor with a draught which would send her the sleep that could not have come naturally; and he had gone back to his bachelor apartment to get what rest he could. All her sufferings had been his by sympathy: he had seen her stared at in the court by goggle-eyed vampires with no better use for their time than to regale themselves with the free entertainment provided for them by her ordeal—had read with a new-found disgust the sensational journalism that was inevitably splurged on the case, and seen press photographers descending on her like a pack of hounds every time she left the court. He had knocked down one who was too importunate, and it had given him some relief. But the rest of it had remained; and it had been made no easier by the sudden inaccessibility of the one man who might have been able to help him. Simon Templar had been as elusive as a phantom; a couple of days after the case, Chief Inspector Teal, who came down with a watching brief, told him that the Saint had gone abroad.

Toby had slept fitfully until six o'clock, and had woken up unrested. He got up and brewed himself a cup of tea, and paced restlessly up and down his tiny sitting-room. The clatter of the postman's knock on his front door was a kind of relief: anything that would serve to distract his mind for a few minutes was welcome.

He went out and found that single letter. It bore a Spanish stamp, and was postmarked from Barcelona.

*My dear Toby:*

*I know you've been thinking some hard things about me since I became so obstinately impossible to lay hands on during the trial of Galbraith Stride. Will you understand that I only did what I thought was best, and what I think in the future you also will see was the best thing for you both?*

*You will remember that at our last meeting, after the police court proceedings, you told me what was on your mind, and I could only give you the vaguest possible comfort. I didn't want to try you too highly then; because not all of us are born to be self-appointed judges and executioners, and what you didn't know you couldn't possibly be tempted to reveal. We agreed that it would be better if you knew nothing until it was all over; and that Laura must never know.*

*Well, that time has nearly come; and it has been brought much nearer by a cable I had this morning, which removes the last reason I might have had for keeping silent. Clements is dead.*

*And he, Toby, was the man who killed Abdul Osman.*

*I know all the things you've been thinking. That confession you made in the saloon, when you told me that you had done it, wasn't quite such a foolish thing as I tried to make you believe; and perhaps you never did wholly believe it. Perhaps even now there are moments when you wonder . . . You couldn't ask her, of course. Well, that's one shadow I can take away from your young lives.*

*And then there were other times when you thought I'd done it myself. Toby, old lad, you may have gathered some idea of my views on the Englishman and Public School Man legend; but here's where I make an everlasting exception in your case. You rose to something much bigger then—something that makes me sorry you'll always have that Public School background behind you in your ordinary life, and go on to become a highly respected county magistrate, chairman of the golf club, and member of the Athenæum. But even though it wasn't necessary, I think a hell of a lot of the loyalty that kept you from breathing a word of it when they were grilling you in the box.*

*You figured to yourself that it was Galbraith Stride who sold Laura and I who saved her; and therefore even if I perjured myself to hell you had a debt to me that would never let you speak. And now, Toby, you've got to show yourself just as big a man to the memory of that poor devil who died the other day.*

*This is exactly what happened.*

*I arrived on the Claudette just as you and Laura were pushing off from the other side. I heard your boat buzzing away, and thought nothing of it at the time. I was after Galbraith Stride and Abdul Osman at the same time. You know all about me, and all the things I've done in the name of what I think is justice. I had decided that both Osman and Stride were far too foul to live any longer. I've killed men before, many of them—it didn't mean anything like the same thing to me as it would have to you. I meant to carry the pair of them off on the Puffin, rope them together with half a ton of lead for ballast, and drop them quietly into the sea away off beyond Round Island where there's forty fathoms of water and they could swing there on the tides till the lobsters had finished with them. There'd have been no bungling about it, no fuss; and I'd have had a peach of an alibi waiting back on St Mary's for me if there hadn't been other things doing that night which upset all my plans.*

*I hauled Stride up on to the Luxor, and whizzed over the ship to locate the crew so I'd know where to expect trouble coming from if there was any. Then I headed for the saloon, lifted the skylight half an inch to look in, and saw all the jamboree going on. Toby, I simply had to stay watching. Call it morbid fascination or what you like, there were things going on down there that I had to know more about. I heard most of it—and remember that I could have butted in at any time things started looking too rough. I might have spared you some of the things that happened, but my professional curiosity had to see the scene through as far as I dared let it go.*

*Osman was telling the truth about Stride's bargain—I could tell that at once. You remember that the torn note they found in the saloon, the one Laura was sent over with, was just a blank sheet of paper? Wasn't that proof enough? You saw it later; but I was looking down right over Osman's shoulder, and I saw it the minute he opened it.*

*You know what happened up to the time you were taken out of the saloon.*

Then Abdul started trying his sheik stuff on Laura, as you've been told. The only other person there was Clements—the man Abdul forgot—the man everyone always forgot. And Clements, crazed with the need for the drug that Abdul had broken him in to—he had been kept without it all day, as he told me afterwards, just for one of those spiteful whims of torture that Abdul's pleasant imagination was always producing—Clements' only idea was to take advantage of the confusion and help himself from the cupboard where the stuff was kept. I could see him stumbling towards it like a madman; and it seemed that that was the cue for me to butt in at last.

I'd started out unarmed—recent notoriety has made me rather cautious about running the risk of letting anyone catch me within miles of a gun—but Stride had an automatic when I captured him, and I'd shoved it away in a hip pocket that wasn't designed for a quick draw, after considering for some moments whether I should pitch it into the sea. I wanted it badly then, and I was trying to get hold of it with one hand while I held the skylight propped up with the other, when Clements pulled his big scene.

He'd got his hands into the cupboard, and there was an automatic there. He touched it, actually picked it up—heaven knows why. And then he looked round. Laura had just fainted, and Abdul was clawing at her.

I told you that I was my own judge and jury; but there are some things which even I will not presume to judge. You may say that Clements had every reason to hate Osman, that even he might know that Osman's death, whatever it cost him, would mean the end of a slavery that was worse than any hangman. You may say that Osman's demonstration on him that night, before your eyes, fanned his hate to a furnace that even the fear of being deprived of his drug could not quell. Or perhaps, Toby, you may like to think that even in that broken wreck of a man that Osman had made of him there was a lingering spark of the man that Clements had been before, a spark that had been awakened into a faint flame of new courage by that last brutal humiliation which you saw, a spark that even in his hopeless soul could feel the shame of that final outrage which he had been left to witness. You will think what you like; and so shall I. I shall only tell you what I saw.

Clements turned round, with the gun. His face was under the light, and it had a look—I can't say of hate or rage—a look of sudden peace that was almost glorious. He stepped up to Abdul Osman and shot him through the heart, and stood quite still and watched him fall. And then he dropped the gun—it just happened to fall near Laura, that's all—and went back to the cupboard. And I should like to say that he didn't stagger back like a starving animal, as he had gone there at first: he went quite slowly, quite quietly, though I could see that every one of his nerves was a white-hot wire of agony with his hunger for that poison.

Well, it seemed as if the inquest was the next thing, and I didn't want it to be held on any of us at the same time, with that heathen crew roused by the shot. I dashed round and locked them up pronto, after heaving the skylight wide open and dumping Galbraith bodily in to get him out of the way—he was still sleeping peacefully from the clout I'd given him on the jaw, and wasn't likely to make any trouble for some time.

I took you and Laura down to your motorboat and left you—by the way, you must be a pretty hefty bird when you're roused, for the hinges of that door you'd bust open looked as if they'd been through an earthquake. I still *had to go on thinking at a speed that nearly gave me brain fever, because when you've got to work out alibis that weren't prepared in advance in less than sixty seconds there isn't much time for writing poetry. I hashed up everything I told you in the boat straight out of my head, without coffee or ice compresses; and then I left you and went back to the saloon to try and stage it to look true.*

*Even on the spur of the moment, you see, I'd made up my mind that Clements wasn't going to swing for what he'd done if I could possibly avoid it. Abdul had asked for it, and Abdul had got what was coming to him anyhow. Clements had simply paid off a debt of ten years of living death; and, Toby, after all, it had been Clements who actually saved your girl. I'd seen that look on his face when he shot Osman, that look which I can't hope ever to describe to you, and which I'd rather leave out of this story and leave for you to see in your own heart if you can. There seemed to be a much more suitable victim ready to hand: Galbraith Stride, who had also had it coming to him that night. The only question was whether Clements could be pulled together sufficiently to catch on.*

*The dope had taken effect when I got back to him, and he was more or less normal. Also he was very calm. He used practically your own words.*

*"They can hang me if they like," he said. "It doesn't matter much."*

*I took him by the shoulders; and believe it or not, he could look me in the eye.*

*"They're not hanging you," I said. "They're going to hang Galbraith Stride."*

*"I don't mind what happens," said Clements. "I'm not sorry to have killed Osman. Do you see me? I'm only one man that he's ruined. There were thousands of others. I've seen them. You haven't been through it, and you don't know what it means."*

*"Perhaps I do," I said. "But Galbraith Stride is only another like him."*

*And I told him that I had meant to kill Stride as well that night, and who I was. Then he caught on.*

*"I haven't long to live anyway," he said. "But I should like to see this work finished."*

*He wanted to shoot Stride then and there where he lay and take the rap for the two of them, but I told him there was a better way. It didn't seem to mean much to him; but somehow I wanted to be able to think that that poor devil was going to see out the rest of his life decently, in the freedom that he hadn't known for ten years. I talked to him for twenty minutes, working out the story we were to tell; and he took it in quickly enough. Then the crew burst down the door of the glory hole and came yelling down to the saloon; and it was lucky for me Clements could swing a good line of Arabic oratory and tell 'em the facts as we'd agreed on them.*

*And so we told our stories as you heard them; and Galbraith Stride will hang on the day you get this.*

*I've no excuses to make to you. Deliberately and with infinite malice aforethought I arranged to frame your stepfather-in-law-to-be to the gallows; and nothing that can ever happen can make me sorry for what I did. That was a just thing as I have always seen justice, and as I shall see it all my life, according to a law that is bigger than all your man-made laws. But you have been taught to respect those man-made laws; so this letter will help to set your conscience free. You guessed some of it, of course; and you're free now to say as much of it as you like. Clements is beyond your justice, but Chief Inspector Teal would like nothing better than a chance to send his sleuths trailing after me with extradition warrants overflowing from their pockets. They wouldn't catch me, of course, but they could have lots of harmless fun trying.*

*If you're interested in anything that Clements thought, after what I've told you, you might like to know the last thing I heard from him. It came to me in a letter, which he must have written when he knew that the sands had almost run out. There was just one line.*

"Go on and prosper."

*Not a very Public School sentiment, Toby, you may think. Rather more melodramatic than any English Gentleman should have been. But he had come back from depths that I hope you'll never see—from which, even if I hadn't been on board that night, he would still have saved you. You will judge him and decide what to do according to what you think of that farewell. It is only right that you should make your own choice.*

*If that choice is what I think it will be, we may meet again.*

*Ever yours,*
SIMON TEMPLAR.

Toby Halidom lighted a cigarette and read the letter through again, word by word. In some way it lifted a terrible load from his mind, brought him a great breath of relief in the fullness of knowledge that it gave him. And as he read there was a queer little smile on his lips that any Headmaster of Harrow would have been surprised to see. . . .

He put the letter in the empty grate, set a match to it, and watched the sheets flare and curl and blacken. "*Go on and prosper.*" . . . And then, with a heart that felt suddenly light and clear, he went to the open window and leaned on the sill, looking out into the blue-grey lightening of that morning of the 22nd of November. Somewhere a clock was striking the hour of eight.

# THE SIMON TEMPLAR FOUNDATION

## From THE MISFORTUNES OF MR TEAL

---

EVERY HERO *of a continued series that I can think of has had a stooge. Sherlock Holmes had his Watson, Raffles had his Bunny, and their army of modern imitations is much too numerous to catalog. Nor am I even sure that Watson and Bunny are entitled to be cited as the originators of a fashion; for I seem to remember that Sancho Panza was stooging for Don Quixote a few centuries before either of those gentlemen were thought of.*

*Since it is not too easy to believe that so many writers, who in various other ways have exhibited positive symptoms of originality, should by some strange coincidence have accidentally imitated each other in this one respect with such remarkable unanimity, I am forced to wonder whether this whole idea of stoogeship or stoogery may not betray the functioning of some fundamental law which none of them was consciously aware of, some cosmic canon to which all heroes of crime stories are subject, whether they like it or not. It is much too glib to argue that the slow-wittedness, jitteriness, and conventionality which seem to be the common denominators of these stooges provide a perfect contrast with which to show off the brilliance, the audacity, and the dazzling personalities of their heroes. I am hard to convince, for instance, that Mr A J Raffles, with a nice jail sentence waiting for him at the first mistake, would have persistently entrusted his fate to a man like Bunny for no better reason than that it made it easier for Mr E W Hornung to write stories about him.*

*Now I suppose this is no place for developing theories, and so I am just passing that one on to anybody who wants to play with it. I can, however, contribute one item of solid fact towards a study of the subject.*

*The Saint started his literary career, and cheerfully sailed through eleven volumes of it, without any Sancho Panza. It is true that he was introduced in the first book with a slightly eccentric servant named Orace, who as a matter of fact is still with him; but Orace was never prominent enough to be called a stooge in this sense. It is also true that during several of his earlier adventures in London the Saint was assisted by a small set of amiable young men, some of whom he still mobilises occasionally. But one of them was killed, and all the others got married off when their turn came and at least partially retired from active service, without in any way crippling the Saint's progress.*

*The story ahead of you, therefore, can only be a belated but inexorable fulfilment of this form of destiny which I was suggesting. For in it was introduced a character who has been with the Saint ever since, and whom it seems impossible for the Saint ever again to be permanently without.*

*I hereby cross my heart and swear that I never deliberately created him and manœuvred him into this rôle. He arrived exactly as he is shown arriving here, without any premeditation whatsoever. He grew on to the Saint exactly as you can see him growing. And directly the story was published, there was a public yell for more of him.*

*The yell was unnecessary. By the time it became audible, he was already in the middle of another of the Saint's adventures. The encore led automatically to a third appearance. After that, there was nothing more to yell about. It was obvious, and accepted as obvious, that he was a fixture. He is so obviously a fixture still, that the circumstances of his introduction may already be growing a little dim in memory. That is why I knew that this collection of stories simply had to include the first published appearance of our friend Mr Hoppy Uniatz.*

# THE SIMON TEMPLAR FOUNDATION

---

THERE WAS NOTHING UNUSUAL about the fact that when Simon Templar landed in England he was expecting trouble. Trouble was his chosen vocation; the last ten years of his life had held enough of it to satisfy a couple of dozen ordinary men for three or four lifetimes, and it would have been surprising if after so many hectic events he had contemplated a future of rustic quietude, enlivened by nothing more thrilling than wild gambles on the laying abilities of leghorns. But it was perhaps more unusual that the particular trouble which he was expecting on this occasion could not be blamed on any fault of his.

He came down the gangway of the *Transylvania* with a light step in the summer sunlight, with a soft grey hat canted rakishly over one eye, and a raincoat slung carelessly over his shoulder. There was death in his pocket and peril of an even deadlier kind under his arm; but he faced the Customs officer across his well-labelled luggage with an easy smile, and ran a humorous glance down the list of dutiable and prohibited articles presented for his inspection.

"Yes," he said, "I'm carrying large quantities of silk, perfume, wines, spirits, tobacco, cut flowers, watches, embroidery, eggs, typewriters, and explosives. I also have some opium and a couple of howitzers——"

"You don't have to be funny about it, anyway," grunted the official, and scrawled the cryptic hieroglyphics that passed him through with his two guns into England.

He sauntered on through the bleak echoing shed, waving casual adieus to his acquaintances of the voyage. An American banker from Ohio, who had lost three thousand dollars to him over the poker-table, buttonholed him without malice.

"See you look me up next time you're in Wapakoneta," he said.

"I won't forget," Simon answered gravely.

355

There was a girl with raven hair and deep grey eyes. She was very good to look upon, and Simon had sat out with her on the boat deck under the moon.

"Perhaps you'll be coming to Sacramento one day," she said.

"Maybe I will," he said with a quick smile; and the deep grey eyes followed him rather wistfully out of sight.

Other eyes followed the tall lean figure as it swung by, and carried their own pictures of the brown fighting face and the smile that touched the strong reckless mouth and gay blue eyes. They belonged to a Miss Gertrude Tinwiddle, who had been seasick all the way over, and who would never have been taken on to the boat deck anyhow.

"Who is that man?" she asked.

"His name is Templar," said her neighbour, who knew everything. "And you mark my words, there's something queer about him. I shouldn't be surprised if he was a sort of gangster."

"He looks like a—a sort of cavalier," said Miss Tinwiddle timidly.

"Pish!" said her companion testily, and returned to the grim task of trying to convince a cynical Customs officer that twentyfour silk dresses would have been a beggarly allowance even for a weekend traveller.

At the end of the shed, Detective-Sergeant Harry Jepson, of the Southampton CID, said to Police Constable Ernest Potts:

"You see the tall fellow in the grey tweeds coming this way? Handsome devil, isn't he? Well, you'd better remember that face."

"Who is he?" asked Police Constable Potts.

"That," said Sergeant Jepson, "is Mr Simon Templar, alias the Saint; and you aren't likely to see a smarter crook than him in your time. At least, I hope not. He's committed every blooming crime there is from murder downwards, and he'll tell you so himself, but nobody's ever been able to hang a thing on him. And to look at him you'd think he had a conscience like a newborn babe."

In which utterance Detective-Sergeant Harry Jepson was as close to eternal truth as he was ever likely to get; for the Saint had never been sure that he had a conscience at all, but if he had one there was certainly nothing on it. He looked the two officers shamelessly in the eye as he approached, and as he strolled past them his right hand waved a quizzical salute that had no regard whatever for the affronted majesty of the law.

"D'you ever hear of such blooming sauce?" demanded Mr Jepson indignantly.

But Simon Templar, who was called the Saint, neither heard nor cared. He stood on the railroad platform, tapping a cigarette on a thin platinum case, and panned a thoughtful and quietly vigilant eye along the whole length of the train. He was expecting somebody to meet him, but he knew that it would not be anyone whose welcome would be friendly; and he had the additional disadvantage of not even being able to guess what the welcomer might look like. The Saint's vocation was trouble, but he had contrived to stay alive for thirtytwo years only because of an unceasing devotion to the business of divining where the trouble would come from, and meeting it on his toes.

"Wantcher luggidge in the van, sir?" asked the porter who was wheeling his barrow.

The Saint's gaze travelled round to measure up two suitcases and a wardrobe trunk.

"I think so, George," he murmured. "I shouldn't be able to run very far with that load, should I?"

He took over his small overnight bag, and saw the rest of his impedimenta registered through to his apartment on Piccadilly. He was still carrying the black book under his arm, and it occurred to him that there were more convenient forms of camouflage for it than the slung raincoat by which it was temporarily hidden. He paused at the bookstall and glanced over the volumes of fiction offered for the entertainment of the traveller. In the circumstances, his choice had to be dictated by size rather than subject-matter.

"I'll take this," he said brazenly and the assistant's eyes bulged slightly as he paid over three half-crowns for a copy of an opus entitled *Her Wedding Secret*.

A signpost adjoining the bookstall invited gentlemen to enter and make themselves at home, and the Saint drifted through with his purchase. No other gentlemen were availing themselves of the Southern Railway's hospitality at the time, and it was the work of a moment to slip the intriguing jacket from the volume he had just bought and transfer it to the black book from under his arm, where it fitted quite comfortably. He pitched the unknown lady's wedding secret dexterously through the skylight, and went out again with the newly-jacketed black book conspicuously flaunted in his hand—no one who had been watching him would have had any reason to suspect that there had been any change in the contents of that artistically suggestive wrapper.

There were several minutes left before the train was due to leave, and the Saint strolled unhurriedly along the platform with his bag, as though selecting a carriage. If the welcomer or welcomers that he expected were there, he wanted to help them in every possible way. He covered the whole length of the train before he turned back, and then made his choice of an empty smoker. Pushing his suitcase up on to the rack and dumping his raincoat and book on a corner seat, he leaned out of the window and slid another idly thoughtful glance over the scene.

A military-looking man of about fortyfive, with a strongly aquiline nose and a black guardee moustache, came slowly down the platform. He passed the window without looking round, walked on a little way, and turned. He stood there for a while, teetering toe to heel and gazing vacantly over the gallery of posters plastered on the opposite wall; then he came back past the Saint's window again, circumnavigated a farewell party congregated outside the next carriage, and did the same thing on the other side.

The Saint's cool blue eyes never once looked directly at him; his brown keen-cut face never changed its expression from one of languid patience, but he had seen every movement of the military-looking man's manœuvres. And Simon Templar knew, beyond a shadow of doubt, that this was at least one of the welcomers whom he had been expecting.

Along the train came a bustle of belated activity, the banging of doors, the scream of the guard's whistle. Simon remained in his window, finishing his cigarette, and saw the military-looking man climbing into an adjoining compartment. The engine let out a hiss of steam, and the platform began to slip back under his eyes.

Simon dropped his cigarette and settled back into his corner. He turned the pages of the black book in its new wrapper, refreshing his memory. The action was more automatic than deliberate, only different in degree from a nervous person's gesture in twiddling his thumbs while waiting on tenterhooks for some anticipated event to happen. The Saint already knew almost every line of that amazing volume by heart—he had had plenty of time to study it from cover to cover on the voyage over. The odds were about fifty to one that the military-looking man was mentioned somewhere in its pages; but it was rather difficult to decide, out of the available names, which one he was most likely to bear.

The conductor came round and collected tickets; and then fifteen minutes passed before the door of the Saint's compartment slid back again. Simon closed his book and looked up with exactly the conventional nuance of irritated curiosity which darkens the distinguished features of the railroad passenger who has contrived to secure a compartment to himself and who finds his privacy illegitimately invaded at the last moment; but the military-looking man put his back to the door and stared at him with a grimness that was by no means conventional.

"Come on," he said grimly. "Give me that book!"

"What, this?" said the Saint in innocent surprise, raising *Her Wedding Secret*. "You're welcome to it when I've finished, brother, but I hardly think it's in your line. I've only got to the part where she discovers that the man she has married is a barbarian lover——"

The intruder pushed the unoffending volume roughly aside.

"I don't mean that," he said shortly. "You know perfectly well what book I mean."

"I'm afraid I don't," said the Saint.

"And you know perfectly well," continued the intruder, "what I'm going to do to you if I don't get it."

Simon shook his head.

"I can't guess that one either," he remarked mildly. "What is it—slap my wrist and tell me to stand in the corner?"

The man's mouth was working under his moustache. He came further into the compartment, past the Saint, and jerked a small automatic from his pocket. It was an almost pathetically amateurish movement—Simon could have forestalled it easily, but he wanted to see how far the other would go.

"Very well," grated the man. "I'll have to take it myself. Put 'em up!"

"Up what?" asked the Saint, doing his best to understand.

"Put your hands up. And don't think of any more of that funny stuff, or you'll be sorry for it."

Simon put his hands up lazily. His bag was on the rack directly over his head, and the handle was within an inch of his fingers.

"I suppose the keepers will be along to collect you in a minute, old fruit?" he drawled. "Or do you fancy yourself as a sort of highwayman?"

"Now listen, you," came the snarling answer. "I'm going to allow you five seconds to give me that book. If I haven't got it in that time, I'm going to shoot. I'll start counting now. One . . . two . . ."

There was a crazy red glare in the intruder's eyes, and although the gun was shaking unsteadily, something told Simon that he had permitted the melodrama to go far enough.

"You know all the rules, don't you, brother?" he said gently; and his fingers grasped the handle of his bag and hurled it full into the other's face.

The man reeled back with the force of the impact, and went crashing against the outside door. It flew open under his weight; and the Saint's blue eyes turned to sudden ice as he realised that it could not have been properly latched when he got in. For one awful instant the man's fingers clawed at the frame; and then with a choking gasp he was gone, and there was only the drab streaked wall of the cutting roaring by the door. . . .

Simon's hand reached up instinctively towards the communication cord. And then it drew back.

The intruder, whoever he was, had asked for it: he had taken his own chances. And although Simon Templar had only done what was justified in self-defence, he knew his own reputation at Scotland Yard too well to believe for a moment that it would be a brief and simple task to impress that fact upon the suspicious hostility of the CID. To stop the train would achieve nothing more helpful than his own immediate arrest; and of all the things which might happen to him while he had that black book in his possession, an interlude behind bars in Brixton Prison was the least exhilarating.

He caught the swinging door and closed it again, and then restored his suitcase to the rack. The unknown casualty's gun had gone out with him—there was no other evidence that he had ever entered the compartment.

The Saint lighted a cigarette and sat down again, listening to the rhythmic thrum and rattle of the wheels pounding over the metals towards London. There was nothing unusual about the fact that he was expecting trouble when he returned to Europe, or even about the fact that a fair sample of that trouble should have greeted him within such a short time of setting foot in England.

But it was perhaps more unusual that the particular trouble he was expecting could not be blamed on any fault of his. And the queerest thing of all was that everything should hinge around the black book on his knee which was the legacy of Rayt Marius—the strangest and deadliest gift that any man ever received.

## II

He was one of the first passengers to alight from the train at Waterloo, with his raincoat slung over his shoulder and the book in his hand; but he did not take the first available taxi. He allowed six to go by him, and boarded the seventh after taking a good look at it.

"Hyde Park Corner," he directed it clearly, and watched the traffic out of the rear window as they drove away.

Another taxi swung in behind them, and he noted the number. Five minutes later he looked back again, and it was still there. Simon pressed the button of the telephone.

"Turn right round at Hyde Park Corner and go back the way we've come," he said.

He waited a short time after his instructions had been carried out, and looked back for the third time. The other taxi was plugging patiently along three yards behind, and the Saint's teeth gleamed in a thin smile. Coincidence of destination was one thing, but coincidence of such a radical change of direction as he had ordered his driver to carry out was quite another matter.

"Now we'll go through the Green Park and up St James's Street," he said through the telephone. The driver was so moved that he opened the door an inch and performed incredible contortions to yell back through it.

"Wot is this?" he demanded. "A game of 'ide-and-seek?'"

"You have no idea," said the Saint.

The apartment he was heading for was on the north side of Piccadilly, overlooking the Green Park. It was only one of many addresses that he had had at various times, to several of which he still owned the keys; but it was the one which had been prepared for his return, and he had no intentions of being prevented from going there. The only question was how the shadowing party was to be shaken off.

As they ran up St James's Street he looked at the meter and counted off the necessary change to pay the fare with a substantial tip. When the next traffic light reddened against them he stretched a long arm through the window and thrust the money into the driver's hand.

"I shall be leaving you any minute now, Alphonse," he said. "But don't let that stop you. Keep right on your way, and don't look back till you get to Hyde Park Corner. And have a bob on Samovar for the Derby."

He had the door on the latch as they passed the Ritz, and his steel-blue eyes were watching the traffic intently. Three buses were taking on passengers at the stop just west of the hotel, and as they went past the leader was edging out into the stream. Simon looked back and saw it cut out close behind him, baulking the following taxi; and that was his chance. In a flash he was out of his cab, dropping nimbly to the road, and the red side of the bus thundered by a couple of inches from his shoulder. It hid him perfectly from whoever was trailing him in the other cab, which was trying to pass the obstruction and catch up again; and he stood on the sidewalk and watched the whole futile procession trundling away westwards with a relentless zeal that brought an irresponsible twinkle of sheer urchin mischief into his eyes.

A few minutes later he was sauntering into his apartment building and nodding cheerily to the janitor.

"Anybody called while I've been away, Sam?" he asked, as if he had only been away for a weekend.

Sam Outrell's beam of delight gave way to a troubled gravity. He looked furtively about him.

"There was two detectives here the other day, sir," he said.

The Saint frowned at him thoughtfully for a moment. Although Sam Outrell was nominally employed by the management of the building, he was on Simon Templar's private payroll as well; but no stipend could have bought the look of almost dog-like devotion with which he waited anxiously for the Saint's reaction. Simon looked up at him again and smiled.

"I expect they were the birds I hired to try and find a collarstud that went down the wastepipe," he said, and went whistling on his way to the lift.

He let himself into his apartment noiselessly. There were sounds of someone moving about in the living-room, and he only stopped to throw his hat and coat on to a chair before he went through and opened the second door.

"Hullo, Pat," he said softly. "I thought you'd be here."

Across the room, a tall slender girl with fair golden hair gazed at him with eyes as blue as his own. There was the grace of a pagan goddess in the way she stood, caught in surprise as she was by the sound of his voice, and the reward of all journeys in the quiver of her red lips.

"So you have come back," she said.

"After many adventures," said the Saint, and took her into his arms.

She turned away presently, keeping his arm round her, and showed him the table.

"I got in a bottle of your favourite sherry," she said rather breathlessly, "in case you came."

"In case?" said the Saint.

"Well, after you wired me not to meet you at Southampton——"

He laughed, a quiet lilt of laughter that had rung in her memory for many weeks.

"Darling, that was because I was expecting another deputation of welcome at the same time, and it might have spoilt the fun for both of us. The deputation was there, too—but you shall hear about that presently."

He filled the two glasses which stood beside the bottle and carried one of them over to an armchair. Over the rim of his glass he regarded her, freshening the portrait which he had carried with him ever since he went away. So much had happened to him, so many things had touched him and passed on into the illimitable emptiness of time, but not one line of her had changed. She was the same as she had been on the day when he first met her, the same as she had been through all the lawless adventures that they had shared since she threw in her lot irrevocably with his. She looked at him in the same way.

"You're older," she said quietly.

He smiled.

"I haven't been on a picnic."

"And there's something about you that tells me you aren't on a picnic even now."

He sipped the golden nectar from his glass and delved for a cigarette. When she said that he was older she could not have pointed to a grey hair or a new line on his face to prove her statement. And at that moment she felt that the clock might well have been put back five years. The fine sunburnt devil-may-care face, the face of a born outlaw, was in some subtle way more keenly etched than ever by the indefinable inward light that came to it when trouble loomed up in his buccaneering path. She knew him so well that the lazy quirk of the unscrupulous freebooter's mouth told a story of its own, and even the whimsical smile that lurked in his eyes could not deceive her.

"It isn't my fault if you develop these psychic powers, old sweetheart," he said.

"It's your fault if you can't even stay out of trouble for a week now and again," she said, and sat on the arm of his chair.

He shook his head, and took one of her hands.

"I tried to, Pat, but it just wasn't meant to happen. A wicked ogre with a black guardee moustache hopped through a window and said 'Boo!' and my halo blew off. If I wanted to, I could blame it all on you."

"How?"

"For just managing to catch me in Boston before I sailed, with that parcel you forwarded!"

Patricia Holm puckered her sweet brow.

"Parcel? . . . Oh, I think I remember it. A thing about the size of a book—it came from Monte Carlo, didn't it?"

"It came from Monte Carlo," said the Saint carefully, "and it was certainly about the size of a book. In fact, it was a book. It was the most amazing book I've ever read—maybe the most amazing book that was ever written. There it is!"

He pointed to the volume which he had put down on the table, and she stared at it and then back at him in utter perplexity.

"*Her Wedding Secret?*" she said. "Have you gone mad, or have I?"

"Neither of us," said the Saint. "But you wouldn't believe how many other people are mad about it."

She looked at him in bewildered exasperation. He was standing up again, a debonair wide-shouldered figure against the sunlight that streamed in through the big windows and lengthened the evening shadows of the trees in the Green Park. She felt the spell of his daredevil delight as irresistible as it had always been, the absurd glamour which could even take half the sting from his moments of infuriating mysteriousness. He smiled, and his hands went to her shoulders.

"Listen, Pat," he said. "That book is a present from an old friend, and he knew what he was doing when he sent it to me. When I show it to you, you'll see that it's the most devilishly clever revenge that ever came out of a human brain. But before we go any further, I want you to know that there's more power in that book for the man who's got it than anyone else in England has today, and for that very reason——"

The sharp trill of the telephone bell cut him off. He looked at the instrument for a moment, and then lifted the receiver.

"Hullo," he said.

"This is Outrell, sir," said an agitated voice. "Those two detectives I told you about—they've just bin here again. They're on their way up to you now, sir."

Simon gazed dreamily at the ceiling for a second or two, and his fingertips played a gently syncopated tattoo on the side table.

"Okay, Sam," he said. "I'll give them your love."

He replaced the instrument and stood with his hand on it, looking at Patricia. His level blue eyes were mocking and enigmatic, but this time at least she knew enough of his system to read beyond them.

"Hadn't you better hide the book?" she said.

"It is hidden," he answered, touching the gaudy wrapper. "And we may as well have a look at these sleuths."

The ringing of another bell put a short stop to further discussion, and with a last smile at her he went out to open the door. The trouble was coming thick and fast, and there were tiny chisellings at the corners of his mouth to offset the quiet amusement in his eyes. But he only stopped long enough in the little hall to transfer the automatic from his hip pocket to a pocket in his raincoat, and then he opened the door wide with a face of seraphic tranquillity.

Two men in dark suits stood on the mat outside. Both of them wore bowler hats; neither of them carried sticks or gloves.

"Mr Simon Templar?" queried one of them, in a voice of astounding refinement.

Simon nodded, and they moved determinedly through the door with a concerted solidity which would certainly have obstructed any attempt he might have made to slam it in their faces.

"I am Inspector Nassen," said the genteel spokesman, "and I have a warrant to search your flat."

"Bless my soul!" ejaculated the Saint, with his juiciest lisp. "So you're one of our new public school policemen. How perfectly sweet!"

The other's lips tightened.

"We'll start with searching you," he said shortly.

His hands ran over the Saint's pockets in a few efficient movements which were sufficient to assure him that Simon had no lethal weapon on his person. The Saint restrained a natural impulse to smack him on the nose, and smiled instead.

"This is a great game, Snowdrop, isn't it?" he said. "Personally I'm broadminded, but if you did these things to a lady she might misunderstand you."

Nassen's pale face flushed wrathfully, and an unholy gleam came into the Saint's eye. Of all the detectives who ought never to have called upon him, one who was so easily baited was booked for a rough passage before he ever set out.

"We'll go over the flat now," he said.

Simon led them into the living-room and calmly set about refilling his sherry glass.

"Pat," he explained casually, "these are two little fairies who just popped through the keyhole. They seem to want to search the place and see if it's all cleany-weeny. Shall we let them get on with it?"

"I suppose so," said Patricia tolerantly. "Did they wipe their tootsy-wootsies before they came in?"

"I'm afraid not," said the Saint. "You see, they aren't very well-bred little fairies. But when you have a beautiful Oxford accent you aren't supposed to need manners as well. You should just hear Snowdrop talking. Sounds as if all his teeth were loose. . . ."

He went on in the same vein throughout the search, with an inexhaustible resource of wicked glee, and it was two very red and spluttering men who faced him after they had ransacked every room under the running commentary with which he enlivened their tour.

"Get your hat," Nassen said. "You're coming along with us."

Simon put down his glass—they were back in the living-room then.

"On what charge, Snowdrop?" he inquired.

"The charge is being in possession of information contrary to the Official Secrets Act."

"It sounds a mouthful," Simon admitted. "Shall I pack my powder-puff as well, or will you be able to lend me one?"

"Get your hat!" Nassen choked out in a shaking voice.

The Saint put a cigarette between his lips and stroked a thumb over the cog of his lighter. He looked at Patricia through the first feather of smoke, returning the lighter to his pocket, and the careless twinkle in his eyes might or might not have been an integral part of the smile that flitted across his brown face.

"It looks as if we shall have to finish our talk later, old darling," he murmured. "Snowdrop is in a hurry. Save some sherry for me, will you—I shan't be long."

Almost incredulously, but with a sudden leap of uncomprehending fear, she watched him saunter serenely from the room, and through the open door she saw him pick up his raincoat from the hall chair and pause to adjust his soft hat to its correct piratical angle before he went out. Long after he had gone, she was still trying to make herself believe that she had seen Simon Templar, the man who had tantalised all the forces of law and order in the world

for more years than any of them liked to be reminded of, arrested
as easily as that.

## III

Riding in a taxi between the two detectives, the Saint looked at
his watch and saw that he had been in England less than four hours;
and he had to admit that the pace was fairly rapid even by his exact-
ing standards. One whiskered holdup merchant, an unidentified
shadower in a taxi, and two public school detectives, worked out at
a reasonably hectic average for the time involved; but Simon knew
that that was only a preliminary sample of the kind of attention he
could expect while he remained the holder of *Her Wedding Secret*.
On either side of him, Nassen and the other sleuth licked their
sores in silence. Whether they were completely satisfied with the
course of events so far is not known, nor does the chronicler feel
that posterity will greatly care. Simon thought kindly of other possible ways of adding to their martyrdom; but before he had made
his final choice of the various forms of torment at his disposal the
taxi was stopped by a traffic light at the corner of St James's Street,
and the Saint looked through the window from a range of less than
two yards full into the chubby red face and sleepy eyes of the man
without whom none of his adventures were really complete.
Before either of the other two could stop him, he had slung himself forward and loosed a delightful yell through the open window.
"Claud Eustace, by the bedsocks of Dr Barnardo!" cried the Saint
joyfully.
The man's drowsy optics revolved towards the source of the
sound, and, having located it, widened with indescribable eloquence.
For a second or two he actually stopped chewing on his gum. His
jaws seized up, and his portly bowler-hatted figure halted statuesquely.
There were cogent and fundamental reasons for the tableau—reasons which were carved in imperishable letters across the sluggish
coagulation of emotions which Chief Inspector Claud Eustace Teal
himself would have been much too diffident to call his soul. They
were reasons which went way back through the detective's life to
those almost unimaginably distant blissful days before anyone in
England had ever heard of the Saint—the days when a policeman's
lot had been a reasonably happy one, moving through well-ordered
grooves to a stolid and methodical percentage of success, and there
had been no such incalculable filibuster sweeping at intervals into

the peaceful scene to tie all averages in knots and ride such rings round the wrath and vengeance of Scotland Yard as had never been ridden before. They were reasons which could have been counted one by one on Mr Teal's grey hairs; and all of them surged out of his memory in a solid phalanx at such moments as that, when the Saint returned to England after an all too brief absence, and Mr Teal saw him in London again and knew that the tale was no nearer its end than it had ever been.

All these things came back to burden Mr Teal's overloaded heart in that moment's motionless stare; and then with a sigh he stepped to the window of the taxicab and faced his future stoically.

"Hullo," he said.

The Saint's eyebrows went up in a rising slant of mockery.

"Claud!" he protested. "Is that kind? I ask you, is that a brotherly welcome? Anyone might think you weren't pleased to see me."

"I'm not," said Mr Teal dourly. "But I shall have to see you."

The Saint smiled.

"Hop in," he invited hospitably. "We're going your way."

Teal shook his head—that is the simplest way of describing the movement, but it was such a perfunctory gesture that it simply looked as if he had thought of making it and had subsequently decided that he was too tired.

"Thanks," he said. "I've got another job to do just now. And you seem to be in good company." His baby blue eyes, restored to their habitual affectation of sleepiness, moved over the two embarrassed men who flanked the Saint. "You know who you're with, boys," he told them. "Watch him."

"Pardon me," said the Saint hastily. "I forgot to do the honours. This specimen on my left is Snowdrop, the Rose of Peckham——"

"All right," said Teal grimly. "I know them. And I'll bet they're going to wish they'd never known you—if they haven't begun wishing it already." The traffic light was at green again, and the hooting of impatient drivers held up behind made the detective step back from the window. "I'll see you later," he said, and waved the taxi on.

The Saint grinned and settled back again as the cab turned south towards the Park. That chance encounter had set the triumphal capstone on his homecoming: it was the last familiar chord of the old opening chorus, his guarantee that the old days had finally come back in all their glory. The one jarring note was in the sinister implications of Teal's parting speech. Ever frank and open, the Saint sought to compare opinions on the subject.

"It sounds," he murmured, "almost as if Claud Eustace had something on his mind. Didn't it sound that way to you, Snowdrop?"

Nassen was wiping his forehead with a large white handkerchief; and he seemed deaf to the advance. His genteel sensitive soul had been bruised, and he had lost the spirit of such candid camaraderie. He put his handkerchief away and slipped an automatic from his pocket. Simon felt the muzzle probe into his ribs, and glanced down at it with one satirical eyebrow raised.

"You know, you could kill someone with that," he said reprovingly.

"I wish it could be you," said the Rose of Peckham in a tone of passionate earnestness, and relapsed into morbid silence.

Simon chuckled and lighted another cigarette. The gun in his own raincoat pocket rested comfortingly across his thigh, but he saw no need to advertise his own armoury. He watched their route with patient interest—they emerged at Parliament Square, but instead of turning down to the Embankment they circled the Square and went back up Victoria Street.

"I suppose you know this isn't the way to Scotland Yard, Snowdrop?" he remarked helpfully.

"This is the way you're going first," Nassen told him.

The Saint shrugged. They turned quickly off Victoria Street, and pulled up shortly afterwards outside a house in one of those almost stupefyingly sombre and respectable squares in the district known to its residents as Belgravia but to the vulgar public, less pretentiously, as Pimlico. Nassen's colleague got out and went up the steps to ring the bell, and the Saint followed under the unnecessarily aggressive propulsion of Nassen's gun.

The door was opened by one of the most magnificently majestic butlers that the Saint had ever seen. He seemed to be expecting them, for he stood aside immediately, and the Saint was led quickly through the hall into a spacious library on the ground floor.

"I will inform his lordship of your arrival," said the butler, and left them there.

Simon Templar, who had been taking in his surroundings with untroubled interest, turned round as the door closed.

"You ought to have told me we were going to visit a lord, Snowdrop," he said reproachfully. "I'd have put on my Old Etonian suspenders and washed my neck. I know you washed your neck today, because I can see the line where you left off."

Nassen tugged at his lower lip and simmered audibly, but his woes had passed beyond the remedy of repartee. And he was still smouldering pinkly when Lord Iveldown came in.

Lord Iveldown's name will not go down to history in the company of Gladstone, Disraeli, or the Earl of Chatham. Probably it will not go down to history at all. He was a minor statesman whose work had never been done in the public eye, which was at least a negative blessing for a public eye which has far too much to put up with already. In plain language, which tradition forbids any statesman to use, he was one of those permanent Government officials who do actually run the country while the more publicised politicians are talking about it. He was a big man inclined to paunchiness, with thin grey hair and pince-nez and the aura of stupendous pomposity by which the permanent Government official may instantly be recognised anywhere; and the Saint, whose portrait gallery of excrescences left very little ground uncovered, recognised him at once.

He came in polishing his pince-nez, and took up a position with his back to the fireplace.

"Sit down, Mr Templar," he said brusquely, and turned to Nassen. "I take it that you failed to find what you were looking for?"

The detective nodded.

"We turned the place inside out, your lordship, but there wasn't a sign of it. He might have sewn it up inside a mattress or in the upholstery of a chair, but I don't think he would have had time."

"Quite," muttered Lord Iveldown. "Quite." He took off his pince-nez, polished them again, and looked at the Saint. "This is a serious matter, Mr Templar," he said. "Very serious."

"Apparently," agreed the Saint blandly. "Apparently."

Lord Iveldown cleared his throat, and wagged his head once or twice.

"That is why I have been obliged to adopt extraordinary measures to deal with it," he said.

"Such as sending along a couple of fake detectives to turn my rooms inside out?" suggested the Saint languidly.

Lord Iveldown started, peered down at him, and coughed.

"Ah-hum," he said. "You knew they were—ah—fakes?"

"My good ass," said the Saint, lounging more snugly in his armchair, "I knew that the Metropolitan Police had lowered itself a lot by enlisting public school men and what not, but I couldn't quite believe that it had sunk so low as to make inspectors out of herbaceous borders like Snowdrop over there. Besides, I'm never arrested by ordinary inspectors—Chief Inspector Teal himself always comes to see me."

"Then why did you allow Nassen to bring you here?"

"Because I figured I might as well take a gander at you and hear what you had to say. The gander," Simon admitted frankly, "is not quite the greatest thrill I've had since I met Dietrich."

Lord Iveldown cleared his throat again and expanded his stomach, clasping his hands behind his back under his coat-tails and rocking slightly in the manner of a schoolmaster preparing to deal with a grave breach of the public school code.

"Mr Templar," he said heavily, "this is a serious matter. A very serious matter. A matter, I might say, of the utmost gravity. You have in your possession a volume which contains certain—ah—statements and—ah—suggestions concerning me—statements and suggestions which, I need scarcely add, are wholly without foundation——"

"As, for instance," said the Saint gently, "the statement or suggestion that when you were Under-Secretary of State for War you placed an order for thirty thousand Lewis guns with a firm whose tender was sixty per cent higher than any other, and enlarged your own bank balance immediately afterwards."

"Gross and damnable falsehoods," persisted Lord Iveldown more loudly.

"As, for instance," said the Saint, even more gently, "the gross and damnable falsehood that you accepted on behalf of the Government a consignment of one million gasmasks which technical experts had already condemned in the strongest languages as worse than useless——"

"Foul and calumnious imputations," boomed Lord Iveldown in a trembling voice, "which can easily be refuted, but which if published would nevertheless to some degree smirch a name which hitherto has not been without honour in the annals of this nation. It was only for that reason, and not because I feared that my public and private life could not stand the light of any inquiry whatever that might be directed into it, that I consented to—ah—grant you this interview."

Simon nodded.

"Since your synthetic detectives had failed to steal that book from me," he murmured, "it was—ah—remarkably gracious of you."

His sardonic blue eyes, levelled over the shaft of a cigarette that slanted from between his lips like the barrel of a gun, bored into

Lord Iveldown with a light of cold appraisal which made the noble-man shift his feet awkwardly.

"It was an extraordinary situation," repeated his Lordship in a resonant voice, "which necessitated extraordinary measures." He cleared his throat, adjusted his pince-nez, and rocked on his heels again. "Mr Templar," he said, "let us not beat about the bush any longer. For purely personal reasons—merely, you understand, be-cause I desire to keep my name free from common gossip—I desire to suppress these base insinuations which happen to have come into your possession; and for that reason I have accorded you this per-sonal interview in order to ascertain what—ah—value you would place on this volume."

"That's rather nice of you," said the Saint guardedly.

"If, for example," said Lord Iveldown throatily, "a settlement of, shall we say—ah—two thousand pounds——"

He broke off at that point because suddenly the Saint had begun to laugh. It was a very quiet, very self-contained laugh—a laugh that somehow made the blood in Lord Iveldown's hardened arteries run colder as he heard it. If there was any humour in the laugh, it did not reach the Saint's eyes.

"If you'd mentioned two hundred thousand," said the Saint coolly, "you would have been right on my figure."

There was a long terrific silence in which the mere rustle of a coat-sleeve would have sounded like the crash of doom. Many sec-onds went by before Lord Iveldown's dry cough broke the stillness like a rattle of musketry.

"How much did you say?" he articulated hoarsely.

"I said two hundred thousand pounds."

Those arctic blue eyes had never shifted from Lord Iveldown's faintly empurpled face. Their glacial gaze seemed to go through him with the cold sting of a rapier blade—seemed to strip away all his bulwarks of pomposity like tissue, and hold the naked soul of the man quivering on the point like a grub on a pin.

"But that," said Lord Iveldown tremblingly—"that's impossible! That's blackmail!"

"I'm afraid it is," said the Saint.

"You sit there, before witnesses——"

"Before all the witnesses you like to bring in. I don't want you to miss the idea, your lordship. Witnesses don't make any difference. In any ordinary case—yes. If I were only threatening to advertise your illicit love affairs, or anything like that, you could bring me to justice and your own name would quite rightly be suppressed. But in a case like this even the Chief Commissioner couldn't guarantee you immunity. This isn't just ordinary naughtiness. This is high treason."

Simon tapped the ash from his cigarette and blew a smoke-ring towards the ceiling; and once again his relentless eyes went back to Lord Iveldown's face. Nassen and the other detective, staring at the Saint in sullen silence, felt as if an icy wind blew through the room and goose-fleshed their skin in spite of the warmth of the evening. The bantering buffoon who had goaded them to the verge of apoplexy had vanished as though he had never existed, and another man spoke with the same voice.

"The book you're talking about," said the Saint, in the same level dispassionate tones, "is a legacy to me, as you know, from Rayt Marius. And you know what made him a millionaire. His money was made from war and the instruments of war. All those amazing millions—the millions out of which you and others like you were paid, Lord Iveldown—were the wages of death and destruction and wholesale murder. They were coined out of blood and dishonour and famine, and the agony of peaceful nations. Men—and women and children, too—were killed and tortured and maimed to find that money—the money out of which you were paid, Lord Iveldown."

Lord Iveldown licked his lips, and opened his mouth to speak. But that clear ruthless voice went on, cleaving like a sword through his futile attempt at expostulation.

"Since I have that book, I had to find a use for it. And I think my idea is a good one. I am organising the Simon Templar Foundation, which will be started with a capital of one million pounds— of which your contribution will be a fifth. The Foundation will be devoted to the care and comfort of men maimed and crippled in war, to helping the wives and children of men killed in war, and to the endowment of any cause which has a chance of doing something to promote peace in the future. You must agree that the retribution is just."

Iveldown's bluff had gone. He seemed to have shrunk, and he was not teetering pompously on the hearth any more. His blotched face was working, and his small eyes had lost all their dominance—they were the mean shifty eyes of a man who was horribly afraid.

"You're mad!" he said, and his voice cracked. "I can't listen to anything like that. I won't listen to it! You'll change your tune before you leave here, by God! Nassen——"

The two detectives started forward, roused abruptly from their trance; and in the eyes of the Rose of Peckham particularly Simon saw the dawn of a sudden vengeful joy. He smiled, and moved his raincoat a little to uncover the gun in his hand.

"Not just now, Snowdrop," he said smoothly, and the two men stopped. "I have a date, and you've kept me too long already. A little later, I think, you'll get your chance." His gaze roved back to Lord Iveldown's sickly features, on which the fear was curdling to a terrible impotent malevolence; and the Saintly smile touched his lips again for a moment. "I shall expect that two hundred thousand pounds by Saturday midnight," he said. "I haven't the least doubt that you'll do your best to kill me before then, but I'm equally sure that you won't succeed. And I think you will pay your share. . . ."

## IV

Simon Templar was not a light sleeper, by the ordinary definition. Neither was he a heavy one. He slept like a cat, with the complete and perfect relaxation of a wild animal, but with the same wild animal's gift of rousing into instant wakefulness at the slightest sound which might require investigation. A howling thunderstorm would not have made him stir, but the stealthy slither of a cautiously opened drawer brought him out of a dreamless untroubled slumber into tingling consciousness.

The first outward sign of awakening touched nothing more than his eyelids—it was a trick he had learned many years ago, and it had saved his life more than once. His body remained still and passive, and even a man standing close beside his bed could have detected no change in the regular rate of his breathing. He lay staring into the dark, with his ears strained to pick up and locate the next infinitesimal repetition of the noise which had awoken him.

After a few seconds he heard it again, a sound of the identical quality but from a different source—the faint scuff of a rubber sole moving over the carpet in his living-room. The actual volume of sound was hardly greater than a mouse might have made, but it brought him out of bed in a swift writhing movement that made no sound in response.

And thereafter the blackness of the bedroom swallowed him up like a ghost. His bare feet crossed the floor without the faintest whisper of disturbance, and his fingers closed on the door-knob as surely as if he could have seen it. He turned the knob without a rattle, and moved noiselessly across the hall.

The door of the living-room was ajar—he could see the blackness ahead of him broken by a vague nimbus of light that glowed from the gap and shifted its position erratically. He came up to the door softly, and looked in.

The silhouette of a man showed against the darkened beam of an electric torch with the aid of which he was silently and systematically going through the contents of the desk; and the Saint showed his teeth for a moment as he sidled through the doorway and closed the door soundlessly behind him. His fingers found the switch beside the door, and he spoke at the same time.

"Good morrow, Algernon," he murmured.

The man swung round in the sudden blaze of light. At the very moment when he started to turn Simon saw the gun in his hand, and thanked his immortal deities that he had not removed his fingers too promptly from the switch. In a split second he had clicked the lever up again, and the darkness fell again with blinding intensity after that one dazzling instant of luminance.

The Saint's voice floated once more out of the darkness.

"So you pack a rod, do you, Algernon? You must know that rods aren't allowed in this respectable city. I shall have to speak to you severely about that presently, Algernon—really I shall. . . ."

The beam of the intruder's torch stabbed out again, printing a white circle of light on the door; but Simon was not inside the circle. The Saint had no rooted fear of being coldbloodedly shot down in that apartment—the chances of a clean getaway for the shooter were too remote—but he had a very sound knowledge of what a startled burglar, amateur or professional, may do in a moment of panic; and what had been visible of the intruder's masked face as he spun round had not been tender or sentimental.

Simon heard the man's heavy breathing as the ray of the flashlight moved to left and right of the door and then began with a wilder haste to dance over the other quarters of the room. For the space of about half a minute it was a game of deadly hide-and-seek; the door appeared to be unguarded, but something told the intruder that he would be walking into a trap if he attempted to make a dash for liberty that way. At the end of that time his nerve broke and he plunged desperately for the only visible path of escape, and in so doing found that his suspicions had been almost clairvoyantly accurate.

A weight of teak-like bone and muscle landed on his back with a cat-like spring; steel fingers fastened on his gun hand, and another equally strong hand closed round his throat, driving him remorse-lessly to the floor. They wrestled voicelessly on the ground, but not for long. Simon got the gun away without a single shot being fired, and flung himself clear of his opponent with an acrobatic twist of his body. Then he found his way to the switch and turned on the lights again.

The burglar looked up at him from the floor, breathing painfully; and Simon permitted the muzzle of the captured gun to settle into a steady aim on the centre of the man's tightly tailored torso.

"You look miserable, Algernon," he remarked affably. "But you couldn't expect to have all the fun to yourself, could you? Come on, my lad—take that old sock off your head and let's see how your face is put together."

The man did not answer or obey, and Simon stepped forward and whipped off the mask with a deft flick of his hand.

Having done which, he remained absolutely motionless for several ticks of the clock.

And then, softly, helplessly, he started to laugh.

"Suffering snakes," he wailed. "If it isn't good old Hoppy Uniatz!"

"Fer cryin' out loud," gasped Mr Uniatz. "If it ain't de Saint!"

"You haven't forgotten that time when you took a dive through the window of Rudy's joint on Mott Street?"

"Say, an' dat night you shoot up Angie Paletta an' Russ Kovari on Amsterdam Avenue?"

"And you got crowned with a chair and locked in the attic—you remember that?"

Mr Uniatz fingered his neck gingerly, as though the aches in it brought back memories.

"Say," he protested aggrievedly, "whaddaya t'ink I got for a memory—a sieve?" He beamed again, reminiscently; and then an-other thought overcast his homely features with a shadow of retro-spective alarm. "An' I might of killed you!" he said in an awed voice.

The Saint smiled.

"If I'd known it was you, I mightn't have thought this gun was quite so funny," he admitted. "Well, well, well, Hoppy—this is a long way from little old New York. What brings you here?"

Mr Uniatz scrambled up from the floor, and scratched his head.

"Well, boss," he said, "t'ings never were de same after prohibition went out, over dere. I bummed around fer a while, but I couldn't get in de money. Den I hoid dey was room fer guys like me to start up in London, so I come over. But hell, boss, dese Limeys dunno what it's all about, fer God's sake. Why, I asks one mob over here what about gettin' a coupla typewriters, an' dey t'ink I'm nuts."

Mr Uniatz frowned for a moment, as if the incapability of the English criminal to appreciate the sovereign uses of machine-guns was still preying on his mind. "I guess I must of been given a bum steer," he said.

Simon nodded sympathetically, and strolled across to the table for a cigarette. He had known Hoppy Uniatz many years ago as a seventh-rate gunman of the classical Bowery breed, and had never been able to regard him with the same distaste as he viewed other hoodlums of the same species. Hoppy's outstanding charm was a skull of almost phenomenal thickness, which, while it had protected his brain from fatal injury on several occasions, had by its disproportionate density of bone left so little space for the development of grey matter that he had been doomed from the beginning to linger in the very lowest ranks even of that unintellectual profession; but at the same time it lent to Hoppy's character a magnificent simplicity which the Saint found irresistible. Simon could understand that Hoppy might easily have been lured across the Atlantic by exaggerated rumours of an outbreak of armed banditry in London; but that was not all he wanted to know.

"My heart bleeds for you, Hoppy," he murmured. "But what made you think I had anything worth stealing?"

"Well, boss," explained Mr Uniatz apologetically, "it's like dis. I get interdooced to a guy who knows anudder guy who's bein' blackmailed, an' dis guy wants me to get back whatever it is he's bein' blackmailed wit' an' maybe bump off de guy who's got it. So I'm told to rent an apartment here, an' I got de one next door to you—it's a swell apartment, wit' a bathroom an' everyt'ing. Dat's how I'm able to come in de building wit'out de janitor stoppin' me an' askin' who I wanna see."

Simon blew out a thoughtful streamer of smoke—he had overlooked that method of slipping through his defences.

"Didn't they tell you my name?" he asked.

"Sure. But all dey tell me is it's a Mr Templar. When I hear it, I feel somehow I oughta remember de name," said Mr Uniatz, generously forgetting the indignation with which he had received a recent aspersion on his memory, "but I never knew it was you. Honest, Saint, if I'd of known it was you, it'd of been ixnay on de job, for mine. Ya wouldn't believe anyt'ing else, woujja, boss?"

The Saint shook his head.

"You know, Hoppy," he said slowly, "I don't think I would."

An idea was germinating in his mind—one of those sublimely fantastic ideas that sometimes came to him, an idea whose gorgeous simplicity, even in embryo, brought the ghost of a truly Saintly smile back to his lips. He forgot his interrupted beauty sleep.

"Could you do with a drink, old man?" he asked.

Hoppy Uniatz allowed the breath to hiss between his teeth, and a light of childlike beatitude irradiated his face.

"Boss," he replied, "what couldn't I do wit' a drink?"

Simon refrained from suggesting any answers to the conundrum. He poured out a liberal measure, and saved his soda-water. Mr Uniatz took the glass, sniffed it, and sucked his saliva for a moment of disciplined anticipation.

"Don't get me wrong, boss," he said earnestly. "Dose t'ings I said about Limeys wasn't meant poisonal. I ain't never t'ought about you as a Limey. You've been in New York, an' you know what it's all about. I know we had some arguments over dere, but over on dis side it don't seem de same. Say, I been so lonesome here it makes me feel kinda mushy just to have a little fight like we had just now wit' a guy like you, who knows what a Roscoe's for. I wish you an' me could of teamed up before, boss."

The Saint had helped himself to a more modest dose of whisky. He stretched himself out on the davenport, and waved Mr Uniatz to an armchair.

"Maybe it's not too late even now, Hoppy," he said; and he had much more to talk about, which kept him out of bed for another two hours.

## V

Chief Inspector Teal arrived while the Saint was finishing a belated breakfast. Simon Templar's breakfasts were usually belated, for he had never been able to appreciate the spiritual rewards of early rising; but on this particular morning the lateness was not entirely his fault. He had already been interrupted twice during the meal, and the bell which heralded the third interruption made him finally abandon a cup of coffee which had abandoned all pretension to being even lukewarm.

"Mr Teal is here, sir," said Sam Outrell's voice on the telephone; and the Saint sighed.

"Okay, Sam. Send him up." He replaced the microphone and turned back to Mr Uniatz, who was engulfing quantities of toast with concentrated gusto. "I'm afraid you've got to blow again, Hoppy," he said. "I'll see you later."

Mr Uniatz rose wearily. He had been shot out of the Saint's apartment to make room for other visitors so often that morning that he had grave fears for his digestion. There was one slice of toast left for which even his gargantuan mouth was temporarily unable to find room. In order to eliminate any further risks of having his meal disturbed, he put the slice in his pocket and went out obediently; and he was the first thing that Teal saw when Simon opened the door.

"Hi, Claud," said Mr Uniatz amiably, and drifted on towards the sanctity of his own quarters.

"Who the deuce is that?" demanded the startled detective, staring after Hoppy's retreating rear.

The Saint smiled.

"A friend of mine," he said. "Come along in, Claud, and make yourself uncomfortable. This is just like old times."

Mr Teal turned round slowly and advanced into the apartment. The momentary human surprise which Hoppy's greeting had given him faded rather quickly out of his rubicund features. The poise of his plump body as he came to rest in the living-room, the phlegmatic dourness of his round pink face under its unfashionable bowler hat, was exactly like old times. It was Chief Inspector Teal paying an official call: Chief Inspector Teal, with the grim recollection of many such calls haunting his mind, trundling doggedly out once again to take up his hopeless duel with the smiling young freebooter before him. The sum of a score of interviews like that drummed through his head, the memory of a seemingly endless sequence of failures and the bitter presentiment of many more to come was in his brain; but there was no hint of weakness or evasion in the somnolent eyes that rested on the Saint's brown face.

"Well," he said, "I told you I'd be coming to see you."

Simon nodded pleasantly.

"It was nice of you to make it so soon, Claud," he murmured. "And what do you think is going to win the Derby?"

He knew as well as the Chief Commissioner himself that Mr Teal would never have called on him to enjoy small talk and racing gossip; but it was not his business to make the first move. A faint smile of humorous challenge stayed on his lips, and under the light of that smile Teal rummaged in his pockets and pulled out a folded sheet of paper.

"Do you know anything about that?" he asked.

Simon took the sheet and flattened it out. It was his own note-heading, and there was certainly no surprise for him in the words which were written on it; but he read the document through obligingly.

*The Rt Hon Leo Farwill*
*384 Hanover Square*
*London W 1*

*Dear Sir:*

*As you have probably been informed, I have in my possession a volume of unique international interest in which your own distinguished name happens to be mentioned.*

*I have decided to sell this volume, in sections, for the benefit of the Simon Templar Foundation, which I am founding. This foundation will exist for the purpose of giving financial and other assistance to the needy families of men who were killed or deprived of their livelihood in the last war, to the care of the incurably crippled wounded, and to the endowment of any approved cause which is working to prevent a repetition of that outbreak of criminal insanity.*

*The price to you, of the section in which your name appears, is £200,000; and, knowing your interest in literature, I am sure you will decide that the price is reasonable—particularly as the Simon Templar Foundation will in its small way work towards the promise of "a land fit for heroes to live in" with which you once urged men to military service, death, and disablement, and which circumstances (always, of course, beyond your control) have since made you unable to fulfil.*

*In expecting your cheque to reach me before next Saturday midnight, I am, I feel sure, my dear honourable Leo, only anticipating your own natural urgent desire to benefit such a deserving charity.*

*Yours faithfully,*

SIMON TEMPLAR.

"Very lucid and attractive, I think," said the Saint politely. "What about it?"

Teal took the letter back from him.

"It's signed with your name, isn't it?" he asked.

"Certainly," said the Saint.

"And it's in your handwriting?"

"Beyond a doubt."

"So that it looks very much as if you wrote it."

Simon nodded.

"That Sherlock Holmes brain of yours goes straight to the point, Claud," he said. "Faced with such keen deductive evidence, I can't deceive you. I did write it."

Teal folded the letter again and put it back in his pocket. His mouth settled into a relentless line. With any other man than the one who faced him, he would have reckoned the interview practically over; but he had crossed swords with the Saint too often ever to believe that of any interview—had seen too many deadly thrusts picked up like the clumsy lunges of an amateur on the rapier-like brilliance of the Saint's brain, and tossed aside with a smile that was more deadly than any riposte. But the thrust had to be made.

"I suppose you know that's blackmail," Teal said flatly.

The Saint frowned slightly.

"Demanding money with menaces?" he asked.

"If you want the technical charge," Teal said stubbornly, "yes."

And it came—the cool flick of the rapier that carried his point wide and aimless.

"Where," asked the Saint puzzledly, "are the menaces?"

Teal swallowed an obstruction in his throat. The game was beginning all over again—the futile hammering of his best blades on a stone wall that was as impalpable as ether, the foredoomed pursuit of the brigand who was easier to locate than any other lawbreaker in London, and who was more elusive than a will-o'-the-wisp even when he was most visible in the flesh. All the wrath that curdled his milk of human kindness was back in the detective at that moment, all the righteous anger against the injustice of his fate; but he had to keep it bottled up in his straining chest.

"The menaces are in the letter," he said bluntly.

Simon stroked his chin in a rendering of ingenious perplexity that acted on Teal's blood-pressure like a dose of strychnine.

"I may be prejudiced," he remarked, "but I didn't see them. It seemed a very respectable appeal to me, except for a certain unconventional famili..rity at the end, where Leo's Christian name was used—but these are free and easy days. Otherwise I thought it was a model of restrained and touching eloquence. I have a book, of which it occurs to me that Leo might like to buy the section in which his name appears—you know what publicity-hounds most of these politicians are. Therefore I offer to sell it to him, which I'm sure must be strictly legal."

"Mr Farwill's statement," retorted Teal, "is that the part of the book you're referring to is nothing but a collection of libellous lies."

Simon raised his eyebrows.

"He must have a guilty conscience," he murmured. "But you can't put me in jail for that. I didn't say anything in my letter to give him that impression. I defy you to find one threat, one word of abuse, one questionable insinuation. The whole epistle," Simon said modestly, "is couched in the most flattering and even obsequious terms. In expecting his cheque to reach me before next Saturday midnight, I am, I feel sure, only anticipating his own natural urgent desire to benefit such a deserving charity. Leo may have turned out to be not quite the eager philanthropist I took him for," said the Saint regretfully, "but I still hope he'll see the light of godliness in the end; and I don't see what you've got to do with it, Claud."

Mr Teal gulped in a breath that hurt him as it went down his windpipe.

"Oh, you don't, don't you?" he bit out.

"I'm afraid I don't, Claud," said the Saint. "Leo may have been caught in a hysterical moment, but other blokes have had the identical letter without feeling that way about it. Look at this."

He picked up a slip of tinted paper from beside the coffee-pot, and held it out so that the detective could read the words. It was a cheque on the City & Continental Bank, dated that day, and it was made out for two hundred thousand pounds.

"Sir Barclay Edingham came here at half-past nine to give me that—he was in such a hurry to do his share. Major-General Sir Humbolt Quipp blew in at half-past ten—he grumbled and thundered a bit about the price, but he's gone away again to think it over, and I'm sure he'll pay in the end. The other contributors will be coming through in the next day or two, and I wouldn't mind betting that Leo will be one of them as soon as he comes out of his tantrum. You ought to have another talk with him, Claud—it might help him to see the path of duty."

"Never you mind what I ought to do," Teal said hotly. His baby blue eyes, with all the sleepiness knocked out of them, were goggling like young balloons at the cheque which Simon was dangling under his nose, as if his brain had flatly refused to believe their message and they had swollen to twice their normal size with proper indignation at the insult. With a genuine physical effort he averted them from the astounding figures. "Sir Barclay Edingham gave you that?" he repeated incredulously.

Simon inclined his head.

"And he was glad to. Sir Barclay Edingham has a very keen appreciation of literature. The pages I sold him are now his most treasured possession, and you couldn't buy them off him for twice as much as he gave me."

He folded the cheque carefully and put it away in his wallet; and the detective straightened up.

"Where is this book?" he demanded.

The Saint's eyebrows shifted again fractionally. It was a gesture that Teal knew better than any other of the Saint's bar one, and that almost imperceptible change of alignments carried more meaning than a thousand words of description could convey.

"It's in England," he answered.

"That's good," said Teal grimly, "because I want to see it."

The Saint picked up a cigarette, spun it into the air, and caught it in his mouth without moving his head. He snapped a flame from his lighter and blew out a long feather of smoke.

"Do you?" he murmured interestedly.

"Yes, I do!" barked the detective. "And I mean to see it before I go. I mayn't be much of a critic, but I'll soon find out whether this literary work is worth two hundred thousand pounds a chapter. I'll get my own ideas about whether it's libellous. Now, are you going to show me that book or am I going to look for it?"

"Where's your search-warrant?" inquired Simon imperturbably.

Teal gritted his teeth.

"I don't need a search-warrant. You're a suspected person——"

"Only in your wicked suspicious mind, Claud. And I'm telling you that you do need a search-warrant. Or, if you're going to take my home apart without one, you need three or four strong men with you. Because if you do try to do it yourself, I shall pick you up by the scruff of your neck and the seat of your pants and throw you over the Ritz, and there's no magistrate in England who could give you a comeback!"

The Saint was smiling; but Mr Teal had no illusions about that smile. It was not a smile of simple-hearted bonhomie and good will towards policemen. It was a smile that could have been worn by no one but that lean dangerous privateer who was never more dangerous than when he smiled.

And Mr Teal knew that he hadn't got a leg to stand on. The Saint had tied him in a knot again. There were no menaces, no threats of any kind, in the letter with which the Honourable Leo Farwill had gone to Scotland Yard—it was a pleasant polite epistle with no unlawful insinuations whatsoever, and any fairly clever advocate could have convinced a normally half-witted jury that the suspicions attached to it arose from nothing but the notorious Simon Templar's signature at the end. And without a definite charge of blackmail, there were no grounds at all for demanding an inspection of the literary work on which the whole case hinged.

Mr Teal knew all these things as well as anyone—and knew also that in spite of the strictly legal appearances no man had ever given the Saint two hundred thousand pounds except as the reward of some devilish and unlawful cunning that had been born in that gay unscrupulous brain. He knew all these things as well as he knew his own birthday; but they did not cheer him. And Simon Templar's forefinger went out and tapped him on the stomach in the Saintly gesture that Mr Teal knew and hated best of all.

"You're too full of naughty ideas and uncharitable thoughts these days," said the Saint. "I was hoping that after I'd been away for a bit you might have got over them; but it seems as if you haven't. You're having one of your relapses into detectivosis, Claud; and it offends me. You stand there with your great stomach wobbling——"

"It doesn't wobble!" yapped the detective furiously.

"It wobbles when I poke it with my finger," said the Saint coldly, and proceeded to demonstrate.

Teal struck his hand aside.

"Now listen," he brayed. "You may be able to twist the law around to suit yourself for a while——"

"I can twist the law around to suit myself as long as I like," said the Saint cheerfully; "and when I fall down on it, it will be soon enough for you to come and see me again. Now you've completely spoiled my breakfast; and I've got an important appointment in ten minutes, so I can't stop to play with you any more. Drop in again next time you wake up, and I'll have some more to say to you."

Chief Inspector Teal settled his bowler hat. The wrath and righteous indignation were steaming together under his waistcoat; but with a terrific effort he recovered his pose of torpid weariness.

"I'll have some more to say to you," he replied curtly, "and it'll keep you out of trouble for several years."

"Let me know when you're ready," murmured the Saint, and opened the door for him with old-world courtesy.

A couple of minutes later, with his wide-brimmed felt hat tipped challengingly over his right eye, he was knocking at the door of the adjoining apartment.

"Come along, Hoppy," he said. "We've left it late enough already—and I can't afford to miss this date."

Mr Uniatz put down a bottle of Vat 69 regretfully and took up his hat. They left the building by the entrance in Stratton Street; and as they came out on to the pavement a shabby and ancient touring car pulled away from the kerb and went past. Simon felt as if a gust of wind plucked at his swashbuckling headgear and carried it spinning: the crack that went with the gust of wind might have been only one of the many backfires that a big city hears every hour.

## VI

Simon collected his hat and dusted it thoughtfully. The bullet-hole made a neat puncture in the centre of the crown—the only mistake in the aim had been the elevation.

The attack surprised him seriously. He had allowed himself to believe that during his possession of *Her Wedding Secret* his life at least was safer than it had ever been—that while the opposition would go to any lengths to obtain that classic work, they would be extraordinarily solicitous about his own bodily health. He turned to Mr Uniatz, and had a sudden spasm of alarm when he saw that enterprising warrior standing out on the edge of the sidewalk with an automatic waving towards the retreating car. Simon made a grab at the gun and whipped it under his coat.

"You everlasting fathead!" he said. "Where the blazes do you think you are?"

Mr Uniatz scratched his head and looked around him.

"I t'ink we're in Stratton Street, boss," he said anxiously. "Ain't dat right? I can't seem to find my way around dis town. Why ja grab de Betsy off me?—I could of plugged dat guy easy."

The Saint sighed. By some miracle the street had been practically deserted, and no one appeared to have noticed the brief flourish of gangland armaments.

"Because if you'd plugged that guy you'd have had us both in the hoosegow before you knew what had happened, you poor sap," he said tersely, and slipped the lethal weapon cautiously back into its owner's pocket. "Now keep that Betsy of yours buttoned up until I tell you to let it out—and try to remember which side of the Atlantic you're on, will you?"

They walked round to the garage where Simon kept his car, with Mr Uniatz preserving a silence of injured perplexity. The ways of the old world were strange to him; and his brain had never been geared to lightning adaptability. If one guy would take a shot at another guy and get away with it, but the other guy couldn't take a shot back at the first guy without being clapped in the hoosegow, what the hell sort of a country was this England, for God's sake? There was just no percentage in trying to hold down a racket in those parts, reflected Hoppy Uniatz, and laboured over the subtleties of this sociological observation for twenty minutes, while Simon Templar whisked the huge purring Hirondel through the traffic to the southwest.

Simon had a different problem to ponder, and he was inclined to share it.

"Tell me, Hoppy," he said. "Suppose a bloke had some papers that he was blackmailing you with—papers that would be the end of you if they ever came out. Suppose he'd got your signed confession to a murder, or something like that. What would you do about it?"

Mr Uniatz rubbed his nose.

"Dat's easy, boss. I'd bump de guy off, sure."

"I'm afraid you would," said the Saint. "But suppose you did bump him off—those papers would still be around somewhere, and you wouldn't know who was going to get hold of them next."

This had not occurred to Mr Uniatz. He frowned gloomily for a while; and then he brightened again as the solution struck him like a ray of sunshine.

"Why, boss," he said, "I know what I'd do. After I'd bumped him off, I'd look for de papers."

"And where would you look for them?" asked the Saint.

"In de guy's pocket," said Mr Uniatz promptly.

"And suppose they weren't there?"

Hoppy sighed. The corrugations of worried thought returned to his brow. Thinking had never been his greatest talent—it was one of the very few things that were capable of hurting his head.

Simon shot the Hirondel between a lorry and an omnibus with the breadth of a finger to spare on either side, and tried to assist.

"I mean, Hoppy," he said, "you might have thought: 'Suppose I bump this guy off. Suppose he isn't carrying the papers in his pocket. Well, when a guy's bumped off, one of the first things the cops want to know is who did it. And one of the ways of finding that out is to find out who might have had reason to do it. And one of the ways of finding that out is to go through his letters and anything else like that that you can get hold of.' So if you'd thought it all out, Hoppy, you might have decided that if you bumped him off the cops might get hold of those papers, and that wouldn't be too healthy for you."

Mr Uniatz ruminated over this point for two or three miles, and finally he shrugged.

"I dunno," he said. "It looks like we better not bump off dis guy, at dat. Whadda you t'ink, boss?"

Simon realised that he would have to be content with his own surmises, which were somewhat disturbing. He had been prepared to bank heavily on his immunity from death, if not from organised discomfort, so long as the ungodly were in doubt about the concurrent fate of *Her Wedding Secret;* but the recent episode was a considerable discouragement to his faith. Leaving aside the possibility that Lord Iveldown had gone completely and recklessly berserk, it meant that the ungodly were developing either a satanic cunning or a denseness of cranium equalled only by that of Hoppy Uniatz.

He made a rough summary of the opposition. They had been five in number originally, and it was only to be expected that out of those five a solid percentage would have been non-resisters. Sir Barclay Edingham had paid. Major-General Sir Humbolt Quipp would pay. The active dissenters consisted of Lord Iveldown, who had already declared his hand, a certain Mr Neville Yorkland, MP, with whom the Saint was going to have an interview, and perhaps the Honourable Leo Farwill, who might jump either way. But none of these three gentlemen, undesirable citizens though they might be, could lightly be accused of excessive denseness of cranium. Neither, as a matter of fact, had the Saint been prepared to credit them with talents of satanic cunning; but on that score it was dawning on him that he might do well to maintain an open mind.

The inevitable triangle possessed a third corner—if anything so nearly spherical could be described as a corner—in the rotund shape of Chief Inspector Claud Eustace Teal. Whatever his other errors may have been, Simon Templar was not guilty of kidding himself that he had finally and eternally disposed of that menace in the brief *tête-à-tête* they had enjoyed that morning.

The Saint, it must be confessed, had sometimes been guilty of deceiving Chief Inspector Teal. He had not always unbosomed all his secrets as Mr Teal would have liked him to. At times, even, he had deliberately and grievously misled that persistent enforcer of the Law—a breach of the public school code which all English gentlemen will undoubtedly deplore.

He had misled Mr Teal that morning when telling him that he had an appointment in ten minutes. As a matter of fact, the Saint's appointment was not until that evening, and he had merely been promising himself an idle day in the country on the way, with which he did not propose to allow Scotland Yard to interfere. It was a casual and almost pointless untruth; but he might have thought more about it if he had foreseen its results.

Mr Teal brooded all day over his problem. In the course of the afternoon he had a second interview with the Honourable Leo Farwill; and that estimable politician's reaction to his report, far from consoling him, made him still more uneasy.

Later that evening he saw the Assistant Commissioner.

"There's something darned funny going on, sir," he summarised his conclusions tentatively.

The Assistant Commissioner sniffed. He had a sniff which annoyed Mr Teal almost as much as Simon Templar's irreverently prodding forefinger.

"I, in my humble way, had reached the same conclusion," said the Commissioner sarcastically. "Has Farwill said any more?"

"He was just wooden," said Teal. "That's what I don't like about it. If he'd gone off the deep end, ranted about the inefficiency of the police and the questions he was going to ask in Parliament—all the usual stuff, you know—I'd have felt happier about it. That was what I was expecting him to do, but he didn't do it. He seemed to go back into a sort of shell."

"You mean you got the impression that he was rather regretting having gone to the police with that letter?"

Teal nodded.

"It did seem like that. I've seen it happen before, when the Saint's on a job. The fellow may kick up a fuss at first, but pretty soon he shuts down like a clam. Either he pays, or he tries to deal with the Saint on his own. He doesn't ask us to interfere again."

"And yet you haven't the faintest idea why solid and respectable people—public men like Farwill, for instance—crumple up like frightened babies just because this man writes them a letter," remarked the Assistant Commissioner acidly.

The detective twiddled a button on his coat.

"I have got the faintest idea, sir," he said redly. "I've got more than a faint idea. I *know* why they do it. I know why they're doing it now. It's blackmail."

"Do you know, I really believe you've solved the mystery," said the Commissioner, with a mildness that singed the air.

"If I've done that, I've done more than anyone else in this building," retorted Teal heatedly. "But there are plenty of people sitting in their offices criticising me who couldn't have got half as far as I have, even if that isn't saying much." He glared at his chief stubbornly, while all the accumulated wrath and resentment of a score of such conferences rose up recklessly in his breast and strangled his voice for a moment. "Everybody knows that it's some kind of blackmail, but that doesn't help. We can't prove it. When I produced that letter, Templar simply laughed at me. And he was right. There wasn't a line of blackmail in it—except to anyone who knew what was in the book he mentions."

"Which you failed to find out," said the Commissioner.

"Which I failed to find out," agreed Teal feverishly, "because I'm not a miracle worker. I never said I was."

The Assistant Commissioner picked up his pen.

"Do you want a search-warrant—is that what all these hysterics are about?" he inquired icily.

Teal gulped.

"Yes, I want a search-warrant!" he exploded defiantly. "I know what it means. The Saint'll probably get around that somehow. When I get there, the book will have disappeared, or it'll turn out to be a copy of *Fairy Tales for Little Children*, or something. And Edingham and Quipp will get up and swear it was never anything else." Goaded beyond endurance though he was, the detective checked for an instant at the horrific potentialities of his prophecy; but he plunged on blindly. "I've seen things like that happen before, too. I've seen the Saint turn a cast-iron conviction into a cast-iron alibi in ten seconds. I'm ready to see it happen again. I'm ready to see him give the newspapers a story that'll make them laugh themselves sick for two months at my expense. But I'll take that search-warrant!"

"I'll see that you have it in half an hour," said the Assistant Commissioner coldly. "We will discuss your other remarks on the basis of what you do with it."

"Thank you, sir," said Chief Inspector Teal, and left the room with the comfortless knowledge that the last word on that subject was a long way from having been said.


# VII

"Gents," announced Mr Uniatz, from a chest swelling with proper pride, "dis here is my pal Mr Orconi. Dey calls him Pete de Blood. He's de guy youse guys is lookin' for. He'll fix t'ings. . . ."

From that moment, with those classic words, the immortal gorgeousness of the situation was established for all time. Simon Templar had been in many queer spots before, had cheerfully allowed his destiny to be spun giddy in almost every conceivable whirlpool of adventure, but never before had he entered such a portentous conclave to solemnly discuss the manner in which he should assassinate himself; and the sheer ecstatic pulchritude of the idea was prancing balmily through his insides in a harebrained saraband which only a delirious sense of humour like the Saint's could have appreciated to the full.

He stood with his hands in his pockets, surveying the two other members of the conference with very clear blue eyes, and allowing the beatific fruitiness of the scheme which Mr Uniatz had made possible to squirm rapturously through his system.

"Pleased to meet ya," he drawled, with a perfect gangster intonation that had been learned in more perilous and unsavoury surroundings than a fireproof airconditioned movie theatre.

Mr Neville Yorkland, MP, fidgeted with his tie and looked vaguely about the room. He was a broad tubby little man, who looked something like a cross between a gentleman farmer and a dilettante artist —an incongruous *soufflé* of opposites, with a mane of long untidy hair crowning a vintage-port complexion.

"Well," he said jerkily, "let's sit down. Get to business. Don't want to waste any time."

The Honourable Leo Farwill nodded. He was as broad as Yorkland, but longer; and he was not fussy. His black brows and heavy black moustache were of almost identical shape and dimensions, so that his face had a curiously unfinished symmetry, as if its other features had been fitted quite carelessly into the decisive framework of those three arcs of hair.

"An excellent idea," he boomed. "Excellent. Perhaps we might have a drink as well. Mr—ah—Orconi——"

"Call me Pete," suggested the Saint affably, "and let's see your liquor."

They sat, rather symbolically, on opposite sides of the long table in Farwill's library. Hoppy Uniatz gravitated naturally to the Saint's elbow, while Yorkland pulled up a chair beside Farwill.

The Honourable Leo poured sherry into four glasses from a crystal decanter.

"Mr—er—Uniatz gives us to understand that you are what is known as a—ah—gunman, Mr Orconi."

"Pete," said the Saint, sipping his drink.

"Ah—Pete," Farwill corrected himself, with visible distaste.

Simon nodded gently.

"I guess that's right," he said. "If there's anyone horning in on your racket, you've come to the guy who can stop him."

"Sure," echoed Hoppy Uniatz, grasping his opportunity and swallowing it in one gulp. "We'll fix him."

Farwill beamed laboriously, and produced a box of cigars.

"I presume that Mr Uniatz has already acquainted you with the basic motives of our proposition," he said.

"Hoppy told me what you wanted—if that's what you mean," said the Saint succinctly, stripping the band from his selected Corona. "This guy Templar has something on you, an' you want him taken off."

"That—ah—might be a crude method of expressing it," rumbled the Honourable Leo. "However, it is unnecessary to go into the diplomatic niceties of the dilemma. I will content myself with suggesting to you that the situation is one of, I might almost say, national moment."

"Tremendous issues involved," muttered Mr Neville Yorkland helpfully. "World-wide catastrophe. The greatest caution is called for. Tact. Secrecy. Emergency measures."

"Exactly," concluded Farwill. "Emergency measures. The ordinary avenues are closed to us by the exigencies of the crisis. You would, in fact, find yourself in the position of an unofficial secret service agent—taking your own risks, fighting your own battles, knowing that in the event of failure you will be disowned by your employers. The situation, in short, calls for a man who is able to take care of himself, who is prepared to endanger his life for a reasonable reward, who—who——"

"I get it," said the Saint blandly. "This guy Templar has something on you, an' you want him taken off."

Farwill compressed his lips.

"At this stage of developments, I feel called upon neither to confirm that statement nor repudiate it," he said with the fluency of many years in Parliament. "The points at issue are, first, whether you are a suitable man for the mission——"

"Nuts," said the Saint tersely. "You want a guy like me, an' I'm the guy you want. When do you cut the cackle an' come to the hosses?"

The Honourable Leo glanced despairingly at Yorkland, as if appealing to the Speaker on a point of order. Yorkland twiddled his thumbs.

"Should be all right," he mumbled. "Looks the type. Vouched for by Mr Uniatz. Been to America myself. Can't pick and choose. Got to decide."

"Ah, yes," admitted Farwill despondently, as if the very idea violated all his dearest principles. "We have got to decide." He inflated his chest again for the only outlet of oratory that was left to him. "Well, Mr Orconi—ah—Pete, you are doubtless familiar with the general outline of the engagement. This book, of which Mr Uniatz must have told you, must be recovered—whether by guile or force is immaterial. Nothing must be permitted to obstruct a successful consummation of the undertaking. If, in the course of your work, it should prove necessary to effect physical injuries upon this man Templar, or even to—er—expedite his decease, humanitarian considerations must not influence our firmness. Now, I would suggest that a fee of two hundred pounds——"

Simon straightened up in his chair and laughed rudely.

"Say, whaddaya think I'm lookin' for?" he demanded. "Chicken-feed?"

The Honourable Leo drew further breath for eloquence, and the argument was on. It would scarcely be profitable to record it in detail. It went on for a long time, conducted on the Parliamentary side in rounded periods which strayed abstractedly to every other subject on earth except the one in hand and nearly sent the Saint to sleep. But Simon Templar had a serene determination of his own which could even survive the soporific flatulence of Farwill's long-winded verbiage; he was in no hurry, and he was still enjoying himself hugely. Hoppy Uniatz, endowed with a less vivid appreciation of the simple jests of life, did actually fall into a doze.

At long last a fee of two thousand pounds was agreed on; and the Saint helped himself to a fifth glass of sherry.

"Okay, boys," he murmured. "We'll get that guy."

"Sure," echoed Mr Uniatz, rousing with a snort. "We'll get him."

Yorkland shuffled about on the edge of his seat, buttoned and unbuttoned his coat, and got up.

"Very well," he stuttered. "That's settled. Glad it's all fixed up. Now I must get back to town. Late already. Important meetings." His restless eyes glanced at the other member of his side. "Count on me for my share, Farwill."

The Honourable Leo nodded.

"Certainly," he reverberated. "Certainly. You may leave it to me to arrange the details." He drew the sherry decanter towards him and replaced the stopper unobtrusively but firmly. "I think we owe a vote of thanks to Mr Uniatz for the—er—introduction."

Simon Templar surveyed him dispassionately over a second corona.

"You owe more than that, fella," he said.

Farwill coughed.

"I thought the—er—honorarium was payable when the commission had been—ah—executed."

"Half of it is," agreed the Saint pleasantly. "The first half is payable now. I done business with politicians before. You make so many promises in your job, you can't expect to remember 'em all."

"Sure," seconded Hoppy Uniatz heartily. "Cash wit' order is de rule in dis foim."

Farwill drew out his wallet grudgingly; but it was stocked with a supply of currency which indicated that some such demand had not been unforeseen. He counted out a number of banknotes with reluctant deliberation; and Yorkland watched the proceeding with a hint of hollowness in his round face.

"Well," he said with a sigh, "that's done. Send you a cheque tonight, Farwill. Thanks. Really must be off now. Excuse me. Goodbye."

He shook hands all round, with the limp perfunctory grip of the professional handshaker, and puttered out of the room; and they heard his car scrunching away down the drive.

The Saint smiled to himself, and raked in the money. He counted it into two piles, pushed one towards Hoppy Uniatz, and folded the other into his pocket. There were five hundred pounds in his own share—it was a small enough sum as the Saint rated boodle, but there were circumstances in which he could take a fiver with just as much pleasure as he would have taken five thousand. It was not always the amount of swag, it was the twists of the game by which it was collected; and beyond all doubt the twist by which that five hundred had been pulled in ranked high in the scale of pure imponderable delights. On such an occasion even a purely nominal allowance of loot was its own reward; but still the Saint had not achieved everything that had been in his mind when he set out on that soul-satisfying jag.

One other riddle had been working in his brain ever since he left his apartment that morning, and he led up to it with studied casualness.

"The job's as good as done, Leo," he said.

"Sure," echoed the faithful Mr Uniatz. "De guy is dead an' buried."

"Excellent," responded Farwill formally. "Ah—excellent."

He had almost got the decanter away when Simon reached it with a long arm. Farwill winced, and averted his eyes.

"This ain't such bad stuff, Leo," the Saint commented kindly, emptying his glass and refilling it rapidly. He spilt an inch of ash from his cigar onto the carpet, and cocked one foot on to the polished table with a callous disregard for his host's feelings which he felt would go well with the imaginary character of Pete de Blood, and which soothed his own sleepless sense of mischief at the same time. "About this guy Templar," he said. "Suppose I do have to rub him out?"

"Rub him out?" repeated Farwill dubiously. "Ah—yes, yes. Suppose you have to kill him." His eyes shifted for a moment with the hunted look of the politician who scents an attempt to commit him to a definite statement. "Well, naturally it is understood that you will look after yourself."

"Aw, shucks," said the Saint scornfully. "I can look after myself. That ain't what I mean. I mean, suppose he was rubbed out, then there wouldn't be any way to find out where the book was, an' the cops might get it."

Farwill finally collared the decanter and transported it in an absentminded way to the cellaret, which he locked with the same preoccupied air. He turned round and clasped his hands under his coat-tails.

"From our point of view, the problem might be simplified," he said.

The Saint rolled his cigar steadily between his finger and thumb. The question with which he had taxed the imagination of Mr Uniatz had been propounded again where it might find a more positive reply; but the Saint's face showed no trace of his eagerness for a solution. He tipped the dialogue over the brink of elucidation with a simple impassive monosyllable.

"How?"

"The Saint has a—ah—confederate," said Farwill, looking at the ceiling. "A young lady. We understand that she shares his confidence in all his—ah—enterprises. We may therefore assume that she is cognisant of the whereabouts of the volume in question. If the Saint were—ah—removed, therefore," Farwill suggested impersonally, "one would probably have a more—ah—tractable person with whom to deal."

A flake of ash broke from the Saint's cigar and trickled a dusty trail down his coat; but his eyes did not waver.

"I get you," he said.

The simplicity of the argument hit him between the eyes with such a force that almost staggered him. Now that it had been put forward, he couldn't understand how he had failed to see it himself from the beginning. It was so completely and brutally logical. The Saint was tough: everyone knew it, everyone admitted it. And he held the whip hand. But he could be—ah—removed; and the whip would pass into the hands of one lone girl. Undoubtedly, the problem might be simplified. It would be reduced to an elementary variant of an old game of which the grim potentialities were still capable of sending a cold trickle down his spine. He should have seen it at once. His hat hung in the hall with a bullet-punched ventilation through the crown which was an enduring testimony that the opposition had neither gone berserk nor sunk into the depths of imbecility: without even charting the pinnacles of satanic cunning, they had merely grasped at the elusive obvious—which he himself had been too wooden-headed to see.

"That's a great idea," said the Saint softly. "So after we've rubbed out this guy Templar, we go after his moll."

"Ah—yes," assented Farwill, staring into the opposite corner as if he were not answering the question at all. "If that should prove necessary—ah—yes."

"Sure," chirped Mr Uniatz brightly, anticipating his cue. "We'll fix de goil."

The Saint silenced him with a sudden lift of ice-blue eyes. His voice became even softer, but the change was too subtle for Farwill to notice it.

"Who thought of that great idea?" he asked.

"It was jointly agreed," said the Honourable Leo evasively. "In such a crisis, with such issues at stake, one cannot be sentimental. The proposition was received with unanimous approval. As a matter of fact, I understand that an abortive attempt has already been made in that direction—I should perhaps have explained that there is another member of our—er—coalition who was unfortunately unable to be present at our recent discussion. I expect him to arrive at any moment, as he is anxious to make your acquaintance. He is a gentleman who has already done valuable independent work towards this—ah—consummation which we all desire."

The Saint's eyebrows dropped one slow and gentle quarter-inch over his steady eyes.

"Who is he?"

Farwill's mouth opened for another elaborate paragraph; but before he had voiced his preliminary "Ah" the headlights of a car swept across the drawn blinds and the gravel scraped again outside the windows. Footsteps and voices sounded in the hall, and the library door opened to admit the form of the Honourable Leo's butler.

"Lord Iveldown," he announced.

## VIII

Simon Templar's cigar had gone out. He put it down carefully in an ashtray, and took out his cigarette-case. It stands as a matter of record that at that moment he did not bat an eyelid, though he knew that the showdown had arrived.

"Delighted to see you, Iveldown," the Honourable Leo was exclaiming. "Yorkland was unfortunately unable to stay. However, you are not too late to make the acquaintance of our new—ah—agents. Mr Orconi . . ."

Farwill's voice trailed hesitantly away. It began to dawn on him that his full-throated flow of oratory was not carrying his audience with him. Something, it seemed, was remarkably wrong.

Standing in front of the door which had closed behind the retiring butler, Lord Iveldown and Mr Nassen were staring open-mouthed at the Saint with the aspect of a comedy unison dance team arrested in mid-flight. The rigidity of their postures, the sag of their lower jaws, the glazed bulging of their eyes, and the suffusion of red in their complexions, were so ludicrously identical that they might have been reflections of each other. They looked like two peas who had fallen out of their pod and were still trying to realise what had hit them; and the Honourable Leo looked from them to the Saint and back again with a frown of utter bewilderment.

"Whatever is the matter?" he demanded, startled into uttering one of the shortest sentences of his life; and at the sound of his question Lord Iveldown came slowly and painfully out of his paralysis.

He turned, blinking through his pince-nez.

"Is that—that—the American gunman you told me about?" he queried awfully.

"That is what I have been—ah—given to understand," said Farwill, recovering himself. "We are indebted to Mr Uniatz for the introduction. I am informed that he has had an extensive career in the underworld of—ah—Pittsburg. Do you imply that you are already acquainted?"

His lordship swallowed.

"You bumptious blathering ass!" he said.

Simon Templar uncoiled himself from his chair with a genial smile. The spectacle of two politicians preparing to speak their minds candidly to one another was so rare and beautiful that it grieved him to interrupt; but he had his own part to play. It had been no great effort to deny himself the batting of an eyelid up to that point—the impulse to bat eyelids simply had not arisen to require suppressing. Coming immediately on the heels of Leo Farwill's revelation, he was not sorry to see Lord Iveldown.

"What ho, Snowdrop," he murmured cordially. "Greetings, your noble lordship."

Farwill gathered himself together.

"So you are already acquainted," he rumbled with an effort of heartiness. "I thought——"

"Do you know who that is?" Iveldown asked dreadfully.

Some appalling intuition made Farwill shake his head; and the Saint smiled encouragingly.

"You tell him, Ivelswivel," he urged. "Relieve the suspense."

"That's the Saint himself!" exploded Iveldown.

There are times when even this talented chronicler's genius stalls before the task of describing adequately the reactions of Simon Templar's victims. Farwill's knees drooped and his face took on a greenish tinge; but in amplification of those simple facts a whole volume might be written in which bombshells, earthquakes, dynamite, mule-kicks, and other symbols of devastating violence would reel through a kaleidoscope of similes that would still amount to nothing but an anæmic ghost of the sight which rejoiced Simon Templar's eyes. And the Saint smiled again, and lighted his cigarette.

"Of course we know each other," he said. "Leo and I were just talking about you, your lordship. I gather that you're not the only bird who suggested bumping me off so that you'd only have Patricia Holm to deal with, but your little pal Snowdrop was the bloke who tried it on this morning, and wrecked a perfectly good hat with his rotten shooting. I shall have to add a fiver on to your account for that, brother; but the other part of your brilliant idea isn't so easily dealt with."

Farwill's face was turning from green to grey.

"I seem to have made a mistake," he said flabbily.

"A pardonable error," said the Saint generously. "After all, Hoppy Uniatz didn't exactly give you an even break. But you didn't make half such a big mistake as Comrade Iveldown over there——"

Out of the corner of his eye he saw Nassen make a slight movement, and his hand had flashed to his pocket before he remembered that he had set out to enjoy his joke with so much confidence that he had not even gone heeled. But even if there had been a gun there, he would have been too late. Nassen had a hand in his coat pocket already; and there was a protuberance under the cloth whose shape Simon knew only too well.

He looked round and saw the reason for it. The ponderous thought processes of Hoppy Uniatz had at last reduced the situation to terms which he could understand. In his slow but methodical way, Mr Uniatz had sifted through the dialogue and action, and arrived at the conclusion that something had gone amiss. Instinct had made him go for his gun; but the armchair in which he was ensconced had impeded his agility on the draw, and Nassen had forestalled him. He sat with his right hand still tangled in his pocket, glaring at the lanky stillness of Iveldown's private detective with self-disgust written all over his face.

"I'm sorry, boss," he growled plaintively. "De guy beat me to it."

"Never mind," said the Saint. "It's my fault."

Iveldown came forward, with his mouth twitching.

"The mistake could have been worse," he said. "At least we have the Saint. Where is Yorkland?"

Farwill chewed his lower lip.

"I believe he could be intercepted. When he first arrived, he told me that he had meant to call on Lady Bredon at Camberley on his way down, but he had not had time. He intimated that he would do so on his way back——"

"Telephone there," snapped Iveldown.

He strode about the room, rubbing his hands together under his coat-tails, while Farwill made the call. He looked at the Saint frequently, but not once did he meet Simon's eyes. Simon Templar never made the mistake of attributing that avoidance of his gaze to fear: at that moment, Iveldown had less to fear than he had ever had before. Watching him with inscrutable blue eyes, the Saint knew that he was looking at a weak pompous egotistical man whom fear had turned into a jackal at bay.

"What message shall I leave?" asked Farwill, with his hand over the transmitter.

"Tell them to tell him—we've caught our man," said Iveldown.

The Saint blew a smoke-ring.

"You seem very sure about that, brother," he remarked. "But Snowdrop doesn't look too happy about that gun. He looks as if he was afraid that it might go off—and do you realise, Snowdrop, that if it did go off it'd burn a hole in your beautiful Sunday suit, and Daddy would have to smack you?"

Nassen looked at him whitely.

"Leave him to me," he said. "I'll make him talk."

Simon laughed shortly.

"You might do it if you're a ventriloquist," he said contemptuously. "Otherwise you'd be doing good business if you took a tin cent for your chance. Get wise to yourself, Snowdrop. You've lost your place in the campaign. You aren't dealing with a girl yet. You're talking to a man—if you've any idea what that means."

Lord Iveldown stood aside, with his head bowed in thought, as if he scarcely heard what was going on. And then suddenly he raised his eyes and looked at the Saint again for the first time in a long while; and, meeting his gaze, Simon Templar read there the confirmation of his thoughts. His fate lay in the hands of a creature more ruthless, more vindictive, more incalculable than any professional killer—a weak man, shorn of his armour of pomposity, fighting under the spur of fear.

"The mistake could have been worse," Iveldown repeated.

"You ought to be thinking about other things," said the Saint quietly. "This is Friday evening; and the sun isn't standing still. By midnight tomorrow I have to receive your contribution to the Simon Templar Foundation—and yours also, Leo. And I'm telling you again that whatever you do and whatever Snowdrop threatens, wherever I am myself and whether I'm alive or dead, unless I've received your cheques by that time Chief Inspector Teal will get something that at this moment he wants more than anything else you could offer him. He'll get a chance to read the book which I wouldn't let him see this morning."

"But meanwhile we still have you here," said Lord Iveldown, with an equal quietness that contrasted strangely with the nervous flickers that jerked across his mottled face. He turned to his host. "Farwill, we must go to London at once. Miss Holm will be—ah—concerned to hear the news."

"She has a great sense of humour," said the Saint metallically, but his voice sounded oddly in his own ears.

Iveldown shrugged.

"That remains to be seen. I believe that it will be comparatively easy to induce her to listen to reason," he said thoughtfully; and the Saint's blood went cold.

"She wouldn't even listen to you," he said, and knew that he lied.

Lord Iveldown must have known it too, for he paid no attention. He turned away without answering, gathering his party like a schoolmaster rallying a flock of boys.

"Nassen, you will remain here and guard these two. When Mr Yorkland arrives, explain the developments to him, and let him do what he thinks best. . . . Farwill, you must find some pretext to dismiss your servants for the night. It will avoid difficulties if Nassen is compelled to exercise force. We will leave the front door open so that Yorkland can walk in. . . ."

"Mind you don't catch cold," said the Saint in farewell.

He smoked his cigarette through, and listened to the hum of Lord Iveldown's car going down the drive and fading away into the early night.

Not for a moment since Iveldown walked into the room had he minimised his danger. Admittedly it is easier to be distantly responsible for the deaths of ten thousand unknown men than to directly order the killing of one; yet Simon knew that Lord Iveldown, who had done the first many years ago, had in the last two days slipped over a borderline of desperation to the place where he would be capable of the second. The fussiness, the pretentious speech, the tatters of pomposity which still clung to him and made him outwardly ridiculous, made no difference. He would kill like a sententious ass; but still he would kill. And something told the Saint that the Rose of Peckham would not be unwilling to do the job at his orders.

He lighted another cigarette and paced the room with the smooth nerveless silence of a cat. It was queer, he thought, how quickly and easily, with so little melodrama, an adventurer's jest could fall under the shadow of death; and he knew how utterly false to human psychology were the ranting bullying villains who committed the murders in pictures and plays. Murder was so rarely done like that. It was done by heavy grandiose flabby frightened men—like Lord Iveldown or the Honourable Leo Farwill or Mr Neville Yorkland MP. And it made no difference that Simon Templar, who had often visualised himself being murdered, had a futile angry objection to being murdered by pettifogging excrescences of that type.

They would have no more compunction in dealing with Patricia. Perhaps less.

That was the thought which gnawed endlessly at his mind, infinitely more than any consideration of his own danger. The smooth nerveless silence of his own walking was achieved only by a grim effort of will. His muscles strained against it; a savage helplessness tore at his nerves while the minutes went by. Farwill and Iveldown had seventyfive miles to go; and with every minute his hope of overtaking them, even with his car and brilliant driving, was becoming more and more forlorn.

He glanced at Hoppy Uniatz. Mr Uniatz was sitting hunched in his chair, his fists clenched, glowering at Nassen with steady unblinking malevolence. In Hoppy's philosophy, there could be only one outcome to what had happened and his own failure on the draw. There was no point in revolving schemes of escape; the chance to put them into practice was never given. The only question to be answered was—how long? His wooden nerves warping under the strain of the long silence, he asked it.

"Well," he growled, "when do we go for dis ride?"

"I'll tell you when the time comes," said Nassen.

The Saint pitched away his cigarette and lighted yet another. Nassen was alone. There were two of them; and nobody had thought to take Hoppy's gun away. If Hoppy could only get a second chance to draw—if Nassen's nerves could be played on, skilfully and relentlessly, until it became a question of which side could outlast the other . . .

"What does it feel like to be monarch of all you survey, Snowdrop?" he asked. "Doesn't it make your little heart go pit-a-pat? I mean suppose Hoppy and I suddenly decided we didn't love you any more, and we both jumped up together and slapped you?"

"You better try," said Nassen. "I'd be glad of the excuse."

He spoke with a cold stolidity that made the Saint stop breathing for a moment. Not until then, perhaps, had he admitted to himself how hopeless was the idea which had crossed his mind—hopeless, at least, to achieve any results in time for it to be worth the effort.

He halted in front of Nassen, gazing at him over the gun between them. So there was only one way left. Nassen could not possibly miss him; but he might be held long enough to give Hoppy Uniatz a chance. And after that, Hoppy would have to carry the flag. . . .

"You know that would be murder, don't you, Snowdrop?" he said slowly, without a flinch of fear in his bleak watchful eyes.

"Would it?" said Nassen mincingly. "For all anyone would ever know, you're a couple of armed burglars caught red-handed. Your record at Scotland Yard will do the rest. Don't forget whose house this is——"

He broke off.

Another pair of headlights had flashed across the windows; and a car, frantically braked, skidded on the gravel outside. A bell rang in the depths of the house; the knocker hammered impatiently; then came the slight creak of the front door opening. Every movement of the man outside could be pictured from the sounds. The unlatched door moved when he plied the knocker; he looked at it for a moment in indecision—took the first hesitant step into the hall—hurried on. . . .

Nassen was listening too. And suddenly the Saint realised that the chance he had never looked for, the chance he had never thought of, had been given him. Nassen's attention was distracted—he, too, had been momentarily fascinated by the imaginary picture that could be deducted from the sequence of sounds. But he recovered less quickly than the Saint. And Simon's fist had already been clenched for a desperate blow when the interruption came.

The Saint launched it.

Snowdrop, the Rose of Peckham, was never very clear in his mind about what happened. He was not by nature addicted to physical violence of the cruder sort; and no experience of that kind had ever come his way before to give him a standard of comparison. He saw a bony fist a few inches from his face, travelling towards him with appalling speed; and his mouth opened. The fist shut it again for him, impacting on the point of his chin with a crack that seemed to jar his brain against the roof of his skull. And beyond that there was nothing but a great darkness filled with the hum of many dynamos. . . .

Simon caught him by the coat lapels and eased him silently to the floor, gathering up the automatic as he did so. And then the door burst open and the rounded rabbit features of Mr Neville Yorkland looked into the room.

"Hullo," he stuttered. "What's happened? Got Lord Iveldown's message. Said he'd caught our man." His weak blinking eyes travelled all over the room and came to rest on the prostrate form of the slumbering Nassen. He pursed his lips. "Oh. I see. Is this——"

The Saint straightened up; and a slow godless gleam came into his blue gaze.

"That's the guy," he said, in the accents of Pete de Blood. "Hoppy an' me was just waitin' to see ya before we scram. We gotta get on to London—Lord Iveldown wants us there."


## IX

Patricia Holm was waiting for the Saint when the telephone bell rang to announce the penultimate round of that adventure.

"It's that detective again, miss," said Sam Outrell hoarsely. "Mr Teal. An' he's got another detective with him. They wouldn't wait for me to ask if they could go up."

The girl's heart missed a beat; and then she answered quite quietly:

"All right, Sam. Thanks. Tell Mr Templar as soon as you see him —if they haven't gone before he comes in."

She put down the receiver, and picked up the cigarette which she had been about to light. She looked about the room while she put a match to it—her hand was steady, but her breath was coming a little faster. She had walked with Simon Templar in the ways of lawlessness too long to be flung into panic; but she knew that she was on trial. The Saint had not come back, and he had sent no message: his habits had always been too erratic for a thing like that to frighten her, but this time she was left to hold the fort alone, with no idea of what he had done or was doing or what his plans might be. The only thing she could be sure of was that Chief Inspector Teal had not arrived for the second time that day, bringing another detective with him, on a purely social call.

The book, *Her Wedding Secret*, lay on the table. Patricia picked it up. She had to think—to think quickly and calmly, building up deduction and prophecy and action, as the Saint himself would have done. Simon had left the book there. He had not troubled to move it when Nassen came. But Teal—Teal and another man . . . The bell of the apartment rang while she was still trying to reach a conclusion. There was an open bookcase beside the fireplace, and with a sudden tightening of her lips she thrust the book in among the row of novels on the bottom shelf. She had no time to do anything more; but she was desperately conscious of the inadequacy of what she had done.

Chief Inspector Teal did not know it. He looked across the threshold with affectedly weary eyes at the slim startling beauty of the girl who, even to his phlegmatic unimpressionable mind, was more like a legendary princess than any other woman he had ever seen; who for reasons not utterly beyond his understanding had chosen to give up the whole world that she might have queened to become the companion in outlawry of a prince of buccaneers; and he saw in her blue eyes, so amazingly like the Saint's own, the same light of flickering steel with which Simon Templar had greeted him so many times.

"Good evening, Miss Holm," he said sleepily. "I think you know me; and this is Sergeant Barrow. We have a warrant to search this apartment."

He held out the paper; and she glanced at it and handed it back.

"Mr Templar isn't in," she said coolly. "Hadn't you better call back later?"

"I don't think so," said Mr Teal, and walked past her into the hall.

She closed the door and followed the two detectives into the living-room. Mr Teal took off his bowler hat and put it on the table—it was the only concession he made to her presence.

"We may as well start here," he said to Barrow. "Go over the usual places first."

"Would you like to borrow the vacuum cleaner," inquired Patricia sweetly, "or will you just use your heads?"

"We'll manage," said Teal dourly.

He was more keyed up than he would have cared to admit. The Assistant Commissioner's parting speech still rang in his ears; the resentment of many other similar interviews rang carillons through his brain. He was a man of whom Fate had demanded many martyrdoms. In doing his duty he had to expose himself to the stinging shafts of Saintly irreverence, and afterwards he had to listen to the acidulated comments of the Assistant Commissioner; and there were days when he wondered whether it was worth it. Sometimes he wished that he had never been a policeman.

Patricia stood around and watched the progress of the search with a trip-hammer working under her ribs and a sinking sensation in her stomach. And in a frightful hopeless way she realised that it was not going to fail. It was not a hurried haphazard ransacking of drawers and cupboards like Nassen and his colleague had conducted. It was thorough, systematic, scientific, ordered along the rigid lines of a training that had reduced hiding places to a tabulated catalogue. It would not glance at the cover of a book and pass on. . . .

She knew that even before Barrow came to the bookcase and began to pull out the books one by one, opening them and flicking over the pages without looking at the titles. . . .

What would the Saint have done?

Patricia didn't know. Her face was calm, almost unnaturally calm; but the trip-hammer under her ribs was driving her into the clutches of a maddening helplessness that had to be fought off with all her will power. There was an automatic in the bedroom: if she could only put over some excuse to reach it. . . . But the Saint would never have done that. Teal had his warrant. He was within his rights. Violence of any kind would achieve nothing—nothing except to aggravate the crash when it came.

Barrow had reached the second row of books. He was halfway through it. He had finished it. The first two shelves were stripped, and the books were heaped up untidily on the floor. He was going on to the third.

*What would the Saint have done?*

If only he could arrive! If only the door would open, and she could see him again, smiling and unaccountable and debonair, grasping the situation with one sweep of lazy blue eyes and finding the riposte at once! It would be something wild and unexpected, something swift and dancing like sunlight on open water, that would turn everything upside down in a flash and leave him mocking in command with his forefinger driving gaily and unanswerably into Teal's swelling waistcoat; she knew that, but she could not think what it would be. She only knew that he had never been at a loss—that somehow, madly, magnificently, he could always retrieve the lost battle and snatch victory from under the very scythe of defeat.

Barrow was down to the third shelf.

On the table were the bottle of beer and the glass which she had set out ready for him—the glass over which his eyes should have been twinkling while he harried the two detectives with his remorseless wit. Her hands went out and took up the bottle and the opener, as she would have done for the Saint if he had walked in.

"Would you care for a drink?" she asked huskily.

"No, thank you, Miss Holm," said Teal politely, without looking at her.

She had the opener fitted on the crown cap. The bottle opened with a soft hiss before she fully realised that she had done it. She tried to picture the Saint standing on the other side of the table— to make herself play the scene as he would have played it.

"Excuse me if I have one," she said.

The full glass was in her hand. She sipped it. She had never cared for beer, and involuntarily she grimaced. . . .

Teal heard a gasp and a crash behind him, and whirled round. He saw the glass in splinters on the table, the beer flowing across the top and pattering down on to the carpet, the girl clutching her throat and swaying where she stood, with wide horrified eyes.

"What's the matter?" he snapped.

She shook her head, and swallowed painfully before she spoke.

"It . . . burns," she got out in a whisper. "Inside. . . . Must have been something in it. . . . Meant for . . . Simon. . . ."

Then her knees crumpled and she went down.

Teal went to her with surprising speed. She was writhing horribly, and her breath hissed sobbingly through her clenched teeth. She tried to speak again, but she could not form the words.

Teal picked her up and laid her on the chesterfield.

"Get on the phone," he snarled at Barrow with unnatural harshness. "Don't stand there gaping. Get an ambulance."

He looked about him awkwardly. Water—that was the first thing. Dilute the poison—whatever it was. With a sudden setting of his lips he lumbered out of the room.

Patricia saw him go.

Sergeant Barrow was at the telephone, his back towards her. And the bookcase was within a yard of her. Writhing as she was, the sound of one movement more or less would not be noticed. There was no need for stealth—only for speed.

She rolled over and snatched *Her Wedding Secret* from its place in the bottom shelf. Barrow had been too practical—too methodical. He had not looked at titles. With a swift movement she lifted the first three volumes of one of the inspected piles which he had stacked on the floor, and thrust the book underneath. . . .

"Thank you," said Teal's drowsy voice.

He was standing in the doorway with a grim gleam of triumph in his eyes; and he had not even got a glass of water in his hand. She realised that he had never gone for one. He had thought too fast.

Barrow was gaping at him stupidly.

"You can cancel that call," said Teal shortly.

Patricia sat up and watched him cross the room and pick the book out of the pile. The trip-hammer under her ribs had stopped work abruptly; and she knew the fatalistic quiet of ultimate defeat. She had played and lost. There was no more to do.

Mr Teal opened the book with hands that were not quite steady. The realisation of success made him fumble nervously—it was a symptom which amazed himself. He learned then that he had never really hoped to succeed; that the memory of infinite failures had instilled a subconscious presentiment that he never could succeed. Even with the book in his hands, he could not quite believe that the miracle had happened.

It was in manuscript—he saw that in a moment. Manuscript written in a minute pinched hand that crowded an astonishing mass of words on to the page. Methodically he turned to the beginning.

The first page was in the form of a letter.

> *Villa Philomène*
> *Nice*
> *AM*

*My dear Mr Templar:*

*It is some time now since we last met, but I have no fear that you will have forgotten the encounter.\* Lest it should have slipped my mind at that time, let me immediately pay you the tribute of saying that you are the only man in the world who has successfully frustrated my major plans on two occasions, and who has successfully circumvented my best efforts to exterminate him.*

*It is for this reason that, being advised that I have not many more months to live, I am sending you this small token of esteem in the shape of the first volume of my memoirs.*

*In my vocation of controller of munition factories, and consequently as the natural creator of a demand for their products, I have had occasion to deal with other Englishmen, fortunately in a more amicable manner than you would permit me to deal with you. In this volume, which deals with certain of my negotiations in England before and during the last World War, you will find detailed and fully documented accounts of a few notable cases in which prominent countrymen of yours failed to view my activities with that violent and unbusinesslike distaste which you yourself have more than once expressed to me.*

*The gift has, of course, a further object than that of diminishing any insular prejudices you may have.*

*At the same time as this book is sent to you, there will be sent, to the gentlemen most conspicuously mentioned in these notes, letters which will inform them into whose hands the book has fallen. After reading it yourself, you will see that this cannot fail to cause them great perturbation.*

\*See *The Last Hero* and *The Avenging Saint*.

*Nevertheless, while it would be simple for you to allay their alarm and assure your own safety from molestation, I cannot foresee that a man such as I recall you to be would so tamely surrender such a unique opportunity to apply moral pressure towards the righting of what you consider to be wrongs.*

*I therefore hope to leave behind me the makings of a most diverting contest which my experiments in international diplomacy may have excelled in dimension but can scarcely have excelled in quality. And you will understand, I am sure, my dear Mr Templar that I can hardly be blamed for sincerely trusting that these gentlemen, or their agents, will succeed where I have failed.*

*Very truly yours,*

RAYT MARIUS.

Teal read the letter through, and looked up with an incredulous half-puzzled frown. Then, without speaking, he began to read it through again. Patricia stood up with a little sigh, straightened her dress, and began to comb out her hair. Sergeant Barrow shifted from one foot to the other, and compared his watch with the clock on the mantelpiece—it would be the fourth consecutive night that he had been late home for dinner, and his wife could scarcely be blamed for beginning to view his explanations with suspicion.

Mr Teal was halfway through his second reading when the telephone rang. He hesitated for a moment, and then nodded to the girl.

"You can answer it," he said.

Patricia took up the instrument.

"There are two gentlemen here to see you, miss," said Sam Outrell. "Lord Iveldown and Mr Farwill."

"Send them up," she said recklessly.

She had no idea why those two should have called to see her, but she was also beyond caring.

"Lord Iveldown and the Home Secretary are on their way," she told Teal, as she put down the telephone. "You're holding quite a gathering here, aren't you?"

The detective blinked at her dubiously. He was unable to accept her statement at its face value, and he was unable for the moment to discover either an insulting witticism or the opening of another trap in it. He returned to his reading with only half his mind on it; and he had just finished when the buzz of the doorbell took her from the room.

He closed the book and changed his position so that he could see the hall.

". . . so unceremoniously, Miss Holm," Lord Iveldown was saying as he entered the room. "But the matter is urgent—most urgent."

He stopped as he saw Teal. "And private," he added. "I did not know that you were entertaining."

"It must have been kept a secret," said the girl ironically.

She moved aside to shut the door; and as she did so Mr Teal and the Honourable Leo Farwill saw each other at the same time. There was a moment's dead silence; and then Farwill coughed.

"Ah—Inspector," he said heavily. "I hope we are not—ah—disturbing you."

"No, sir," said Teal, looking at him curiously. He added: "I think you'll be glad to know, sir, that as far as I can see we've got all the evidence we need."

Farwill's hand went to his moustache. His face had gone puffy and grey, and there was a dry hoarseness in his voice.

"Ah—evidence," he repeated. "Ah—quite. Quite. Ah—evidence. That book——"

"Have you read it?" asked Iveldown raspingly.

"Only the first page, my lord," said Teal. "The first page is a letter—it's rather involved, but I think the book will turn out to be the one we were looking for."

His heavy-lidded china-blue eyes were fixed on the Home Secretary perplexedly and with a trace of subconscious hostility. There was a kind of gritty strain in the atmosphere which he could not understand; and, not understanding it, it bothered him. His second reading of the letter had definitely been distracted, and he had not yet clearly sorted its meaning out of the elaborate and unfamiliar phrases in which it was worded. He only knew that he held triumph in his hands, and that for some unaccountable reason the Honourable Leo Farwill, who had first put him on the trail, was not sharing his elation.

"Let me see the book," said Farwill.

More or less hypnotised, Teal allowed it to be taken out of his hand; and when it was gone a kind of wild superstitious fear that was beyond logic made him breathe faster, as if the book had actually dissolved into thin air between his fingers.

Farwill opened the book at the first page and read the letter.

"Ah—quite," he said shortwindedly. "Quite. Quite."

"Mr Farwill was going to say," put in Lord Iveldown, "that we came down here for a special purpose, hoping to intercept you, Inspector. Critical international developments——"

"Exactly," boomed Farwill throatily. "The matter is vital. I might almost say—ah—vital." He tucked the book firmly under his arm.

"You will permit me to take complete charge of this affair, Inspector. I shall have to ask you to accompany Lord Iveldown and myself to Scotland Yard immediately, where I shall explain to the Chief Commissioner the reasons of State which obviously cannot be gone into here—— Ah—and your own assiduous efforts, even if misdirected, will be suitably recognised——"

The gentle click of a latch behind him made everyone spin round at once; and Patricia gave a little choking cry.

"Well, well, well!" breathed the smiling man who stood just inside the door. "That's great stuff, Leo—but how on earth do you manage to remember all those words without notes?"

It was the Saint.

## X

He stood with his hands in his pockets and a freshly lighted cigarette tilting between his lips, with his hair blown awry by the sixty miles an hour he had averaged, and the sparkle of the wind in his eyes; and Hoppy Uniatz stood beside him. According to their different knowledge, the others stared at him with various emotions registering on their dials; and the Saint smiled at them all impartially and came on in.

"Hullo, Pat," he murmured. "I didn't know you'd asked the YMCA to move in. Why didn't you tell me?" His keen blue eyes, missing nothing, came to rest on the gaudily covered volume that Farwill was clutching under his arm. "So you've taken up literature at last, Leo," he said. "I always thought you would."

To say that Farwill and Iveldown were looking at him as if they had seen a ghost would be a trite understatement. They were goggling at him as if he had been the consolidated incarnation of all the spooks and banshees that ever howled through a maniac's nightmare. Their prosperous paunches were caving in like rubber balloons punctured with a sharp instrument; and it seemed as though all the inflation that escaped from their abdomens was going straight into their eyeballs. There was a sick blotchy pallor in their faces which suggested that they had been mentally spirited away on to the deck of a ship that was wallowing through all the screaming furies of the Horn.

It was Farwill who first found his voice. It was not much of a voice—it was more like the croak of a strangling frog—but it produced words.

"Inspector," it said, "arrest that man."

Teal's somnolent eyes opened a little, and there was a gleam of tentative exhilaration in them. So, after all, it seemed as if he had been mistaken. He was not to be cheated of his triumph. His luck had turned.

"I was going to," he said, and started forward.

"On what charge?" asked the Saint.

"The same charge," said Teal inexorably. "Blackmail."

The Saint nodded.

"I see," he said, and shrugged his shoulders. "Oh, well—no game can go on forever, and we've had lots of fun." His gaze watched the advancing detective with a hint of wicked banter in it that belied the rueful resignation of his features; but Teal did not see that at once. "It'll be a sensational case," said the Saint. "Let me give you an idea."

And without warning, with a flow of movements too swift to follow, he took a couple of paces sideways and aimed a punch at what was left of the Honourable Leo's prosperous corporation. Farwill instinctively jerked up his hands; and with a quick smile Simon turned the feint into a deft reach of his hand that caught *Her Wedding Secret* as it fell.

Barrow and Teal plunged towards him simultaneously; and the Saint moved rapidly back—past the automatic that had appeared like magic in the hand of Mr Uniatz who this time had not been artificially obstructed on the draw.

"Stay back, youse guys!" barked Hoppy, in a voice quivering with exultation at his achievement; and involuntarily the two detectives checked.

The two politicians, equally involuntarily taking the lead in any popular movement, went further. They went back as far as the confines of the room would allow them.

"You know your duty, Inspector," said the Home Secretary tremblingly. "I order you to arrest those men!"

"Don't order a good man to commit suicide," said the Saint curtly. "Nobody's going to get hurt—if you'll all behave yourselves for a few minutes. I'm the bloke who's being arrested, and I want to enjoy it. Readings by the Public Prosecutor of extracts from this book will be the high spot of the trial, and I want to have a rehearsal."

He turned the pages and quickly found a place.

"Now here's a juicy bit that'll whet your appetites," he remarked. "It must have something to do with the reasons of State which you were burbling about, Leo. '*On May 15th I dined again with Farwill, then Secretary of State for War. He was inclined to agree with me about the potentialities of the Aix-la-Chapelle incident for increasing the friction between France and Germany; and on my increasing my original offer to fifty thousand pounds he agreed to place before the Cabinet——'"*

"Stop!" shouted Farwill shrilly. "It's a lie!"

The Saint closed his book and put it down; and very slowly the smile returned to his lips.

"I shouldn't be so melodramatic as that," he said easily. "But of course it's a joke. I suppose it's really gone a bit too far."

There was another long silence; and then Lord Iveldown cleared his throat.

"Of course," he said in a cracked voice. "A joke."

"A joke," repeated Farwill hollowly. "Ah—of course."

Simon flicked his cigarette through the open window, and a rumble of traffic went by in the sudden quiet.

"And not, I'm afraid," he murmured, "in the best of taste."

His eyes strayed back to the staring gaze of Chief Inspector Teal.

Of all those persons present, Mr Teal did not seem the most happy. It would be inaccurate to say that he realised exactly what was going on. He didn't. But something told him that there was a catch in it. Somewhere in the undercurrents of that scene, he knew, there was something phony—something that was preparing to gyp him of his triumph at the very moment of victory. He had only the dimmest idea of how it was being worked; but he had seen it happen too many times before to mistake the symptoms.

"What the heck is this joke?" he demanded.

"Leo will tell you," said the Saint.

Farwill licked his lips.

"I—ah—the joke was so—ah—silly that I—ah. . . . Well, Inspector, when Mr Templar approached us with the offer of this—ah—literary work, and—ah—knowing his, if I may say so, notorious—ah—character, I—ah—that is, we—thought that it would be humorous to play a slight—ah—practical joke on him, with your—ah—unwitting assistance. Ah——"

"Whereas, of course, you meant to buy it all the time," Simon prompted him gently.

"Ah—yes," said the Honourable Leo chokingly. "Buy it. Ah—of course."

"At once," said Lord Iveldown quaveringly, taking out his cheque-book.

"Ah—naturally," moaned the Honourable Leo, feeling for his pen. "At once."

"Two hundred thousand pounds, was it not, Mr Templar?" said Lord Iveldown.

The Saint shook his head.

"The price has gone up a bit," he said. "It'll cost you two hundred and fifty thousand now—I need a new hat, and the Simon Templar Foundation isn't intended to pay for that."

With his head swimming and the blood drumming in his ears, Chief Inspector Claud Eustace Teal watched the cheques being made out and blotted and handed over. He would never really know how the trick was turned. He only knew that Simon Templar was back; and anything could happen. . . .

The parting words with which the Saint shepherded the gathering out of the door did nothing to enlighten him.

"By the way, Leo," said the Saint, "you must remember to tell Neville to send on his share. If you toddle straight back home you'll find him waiting for you. He's standing guard over the Rose of Peckham with a great big gun—and for some reason or other he thinks Snowdrop is me."

"Sir Humbolt Quipp came in and left a cheque," said Patricia Holm uncertainly.

Simon took it and added it to his collection. He fanned out the four precious scraps of paper and brought the Honourable Leo Farwill's contribution to the top. Then he removed this one from the others and gazed at it for a long time with a rather rueful frown.

"I'm afraid we let Leo off too lightly," he said. "When I begin to think what a splendiferous orgy of Teal-baiting we could have had with the Home Secretary permanently under our thumb, I almost wonder whether the Simon Templar Foundation is worth it."

But later on he brightened.

"It would have made life damned dull," he said.

# THE UNFORTUNATE FINANCIER

## From THE SAINT INTERVENES

---

IT WILL HAVE BEEN NOTICED *by the connoisseur that the Saint stories of the older vintages contained considerably more physical violence than most of the later brews. I don't mean by this that there are conspicuously fewer citizens at large whose principal ambition is to inflict upon the Saint some grave form of bodily damage. Nor do I mean that, when these citizens attempt to gratify such hearty yearnings, the Saint has lost any of his gusto for the pop of guns or the exhilarating impact of a well-placed poke on the proboscis. Such healthy joys as those can never lose their charm. But I do mean that he has meanwhile been developing an appreciation for other, perhaps even more artistically satisfying, methods of making miserable the lives of the Ungodly.*

*As an example of this more ethereal technique I am offering the following story, which gave me more childish pleasure than I can modestly talk about.*

# THE UNFORTUNATE FINANCIER

"The secret of success," said Simon Templar profoundly, "is never to do anything by halves. If you try to touch someone for a tenner, you probably get snubbed; but if you put on a silk hat and a false stomach and go into the City to raise a million-pound loan, people fall over each other in the rush to hand you blank cheques. The wretched little thief who pinches a handful of silver spoons gets shoved into clink through a perfect orgy of congratulations to the police and the magistrates, but the bird who diddles the public of a few hundred thousands by legal methods gets a knighthood. A sound buccaneering business has to be run on the same principles."

While he could not have claimed any earthshaking originality for the theme of his sermon, Simon Templar was in the perhaps rarer position of being able to claim that he practised what he preached. He had been doing it for so long, with so much diligence and devotion, that the name of the Saint had passed into the Valhalla of all great names: it had become a household word, even as the name of Miss Amelia Bloomer, an earlier crusader, was absorbed into the tongue that Shakespeare did not live long enough to speak—but in a more romantic context. And if there were many more sharks in the broad lagoons of technically legal righteousness who knew him better by his chosen *nom de guerre* than by his real name, and who would not even have recognized him had they passed him in the street, that minor degree of anonymity was an asset in the Saint's profession which more than compensated him for the concurrent gaps in his publicity.

Mr Wallington Titus Oates was another gentleman who did nothing by halves.

He was a large red-faced man who looked exactly like a City

alderman or a master butcher, with a beefy solidity about him which disarmed suspicion. It was preposterous, his victims thought, in the early and expensive stages of their ignorance, that such an obvious rough diamond, such a jovial hail-fellow-well-met, such an almost startlingly lifelike incarnation of the cartoonist's figure of John Bull, could be a practitioner of cunning and deceit. Even about his rather unusual names he was delightfully frank. If he had been an American he would certainly have called himself Wallington T Oates, and the "T" would have been shrouded in a mystery that might have embraced anything from Thomas to Tamerlane. In the more reserved manner of the Englishman, who does not have a Christian name until you have known him for twentyfive years, he might without exciting extraordinary curiosity have been known simply as W T Oates. But he was not. His cards were printed W Titus Oates; and he was not even insistent on the preliminary "W". He was, in fact, best pleased to be known as plain Titus Oates, and would chortle heartily over his chances of tracing a pedigree back to the notorious inventor of the Popish Plot who was whipped from Aldgate to Newgate and from Newgate to Tyburn some three hundred years ago.

But apart from the fact that some people would have given much to apply the same discouraging treatment to Mr Wallington Titus Oates, he had little else in common with his putative ancestor. For although the better-known Titus Oates stood in the pillory outside the Royal Exchange before his dolorous tour, it is not recorded that he was interested in the dealings within; whereas the present Stock Exchange was Mr Wallington Titus Oates's happy hunting ground.

If there was anything that W Titus Oates understood from A to whatever letters can be invented after Z, it was the manipulation of shares. Bulls and bears were his domestic pets. Mergers and debentures were his bedfellows. It might almost be said that he danced contangos in his sleep. And it was all very profitable—so profitable that Mr Oates possessed not only three Rolls-Royces but also a liberal allowance of pocket-money to spend on the collection of postage stamps which was his joy and relaxation.

This is not to be taken to mean that Mr Oates was known in the City as a narrow evader of the law. He was, on the contrary, a highly respected and influential man; for it is one of the sublime subtleties of the laws of England that whilst the manipulation of the form of racehorses is a hideous crime, to be rewarded with expulsion from the most boring clubs and other forms of condign punishment, the manipulation of share values is a noble and righteous occupation by which the large entrance fees to such clubs may commendably be obtained, provided that the method of juggling is genteel and smooth. Mr Oates's form as a juggler was notably genteel and smooth; and the ambition of certain citizens to whip Mr Oates at a cart's tail from Aldgate to Newgate was based not so much on the knowledge of any actual fraud as on the fact that the small investments which represented their life savings had on occasion been skittled down the market in the course of Mr Oates's important operations, which every right-thinking person will agree was a very unsporting and un-British attitude to take.

The elementary principles of share manipulation are, of course, simplicity itself. If large blocks of a certain share are thrown on the market from various quarters, the word goes round that the stock is bad, the small investor takes fright and dashes in to cut his losses, thereby making matters worse, and the price of the share falls according to the first law of supply and demand. If, on the other hand, there is heavy buying in a certain share, the word goes round that it is a "good thing," the small speculator jumps in for a quick profit, adding his weight to the snowball, and the price goes up according to the same law. This is the foundation system on which all speculative operators work; but Mr Oates had his own ways of accelerating these reactions.

"Nobody can say that Titus Oates ain't an honest man," he used to say to the very exclusive circle of confederates who shared his confidence and a reasonable proportion of his profits. "P'raps I am a bit smarter than some of the others, but that's their funeral. You don't know what tricks they get up to behind the scenes, but nobody knows what tricks I get up to, either. It's all in the day's work."

He was thinking along the same lines on a certain morning, while he waited for his associates to arrive for the conference at which the final details of the manœuvre on which he was working at that time would be decided. It was the biggest manipulation he had attempted so far, and it involved a trick that sailed much closer to the wind than anything he had done before; but it has already been explained that he was not a man who did things by halves. The economic depression which had bogged down the market for many months past, and the resultant steadfast refusal of stocks to soar appreciably, however stimulated by legitimate and near-legitimate means, had been very bad for his business as well as others. Now, envisaging the first symptoms of an upturn, he was preparing to cash in on it to an extent that would compensate for many months of failure; and with so much lost ground to make up he had no time for half measures. Yet he knew that there were a few tense days ahead of him.

A discreet knock on his door, heralding the end of thought and the beginning of action, was almost a relief. His new secretary entered in answer to his curt summons, and his eyes rested on her slim figure for a moment with unalloyed pleasure—she was a remarkably beautiful girl with natural honey-golden hair and entrancing blue eyes which in Mr Oates's dreams had sometimes been known to gaze with Dietrichesque yearning upon his unattractive person.

"Mr Hammel and Mr Costello are here," she said.

Mr Oates nodded.

"Bring them in, my dear." He rummaged thoughtfully through his pockets and produced a crumpled five-pound note, which he pushed towards her. "And buy yourself some silk stockings when you go out to lunch—just as a little gift from me. You've been a good gal. Some night next week, when I'm not working so hard, we might have dinner together, eh?"

"Thank you, Mr Oates," she said softly, and left him with a sweet smile which started strange wrigglings within him.

When they had dinner together he would make her call him Titus, he thought, and rubbed his hands over the romantic prospect. But before that happy night he had much to do; and the entrance of Hammel and Costello brought him back to the stern consideration of how that dinner and many others, with silk stockings and orchids to match, were to be paid for.

Mr Jules Hammel was a small rotund gentleman whose rimless spectacles gave him a benign and owlish appearance, like somebody's very juvenile uncle. Mr Abe Costello was longer and much more cadaverous, and he wore a pencil-line of hair across his upper lip with a certain undercurrent of self-consciousness which might have made one think that he went about in the constant embarrassing fear of being mistaken for Clark Gable. Actually their resemblance to any such harmless characters was illusory—they were nearly as cunning as Mr Oates himself, and not even a trifle less unscrupulous.

"Well, boys," said Mr Oates, breaking the ice jovially, "I found another good thing last night."

"Buy or sell?" asked Costello alertly.

"Buy," said Mr Oates. "I bought it. As far as I can find out, there are about a dozen in the world. The issue was corrected the day after it came out."

Hammel helped himself to a cigar and frowned puzzledly.

"What is this?"

"A German 5-pfennig with the *Befreiungstag* overprint inverted and spelt with a P instead of a B," explained Mr Oates. "That's a stamp you could get a hundred pounds for any day."

His guests exchanged tolerant glances. While they lighted their Partagas they allowed Mr Oates to expatiate on the beauties of his acquisition with all the extravagant zeal of the rabid collector; but as soon as the smokes were going Costello recalled the meeting to its agenda.

"Well," he said casually, "Midorients are down to 25."

"24," said Mr Oates. "I rang up my brokers just before you came in and told them to sell another block. They'll be down to 23 or 22 after lunch. We've shifted them pretty well."

"When do we start buying?" asked Hammel.

"At 22. And you'll have to do it quickly. The wires are being sent off at lunch-time tomorrow, and the news will be in the papers before the Exchange closes."

Mr Oates paced the floor steadily, marshalling the facts of the situation from an audience which was already conversant with them.

The Midorient Company owned large and unproductive concessions in Mesopotamia. Many years ago its fields had flowed with seemingly inexhaustible quantities of oil of excellent quality, and the stock had paid its original holders several thousand times over. But suddenly, on account of those abstruse and unpredictable geological causes to which such things are subject, the supply had petered out. Frenzied boring had failed to produce results. The output had dropped to a paltry few hundred barrels which sufficed to pay dividends of two percent on the stock—no more, and, as a slight tempering of the wind to the shorn stockholders, no less. The shares had adjusted their market value accordingly. Boring had continued ever since, without showing any improvement; and indeed the shares had depreciated still further during the past fortnight as a result of persistent rumours that even the small output which had for a long while saved the stock from becoming entirely derelict was drying up—rumours which, as omniscient chroniclers of these events, we are able to trace back to the ingenious agency of Mr Titus Oates.

This was sufficient to send the moribund stock down to the price at which Messrs Oates, Costello, and Hammel desired to buy it. The boom on which they would make their profit called for more organisation, and involved the slight deception on which Mr Oates was basing his gamble.

Travelling in Mesopotamia at that moment there was an English tourist named Ischolskov, and it is a matter of importance that he was there entirely at Mr Oates's instigation and expense. During his visit he had contrived to learn the names of the correspondents of the important newspapers and news agencies in that region, and at the appointed time it would be his duty to send off similarly worded cablegrams, signed with the names of these correspondents, which would report to London that the Midorient Company's engineers had struck oil again—had, in fact, tapped a gigantic gusher of petroleum that would make the first phenomenal output of the Midorient Oil Fields look like the dribbling of a baby on its bib.

"Let's see," said Mr Oates. "This is Tuesday. We buy today and tomorrow morning at 22 or even less. The shares'll start to go up tomorrow afternoon. They'll go up more on Thursday. By Friday morning they ought to be around 45—they might even go to 50. They'll hang fire there. The first boom will be over, and people will be waiting for more information."

"What about the directors?" queried Hammel.

"They'll get a wire too, of course, signed by the manager on the spot. And don't forget that I'm a director. Every penny I have is tied up in that company—it's my company, lock, stock, and barrel. They'll call a special meeting, and I'll know exactly what they're doing about it. Of course they'll cable the manager for more details, but I can arrange to see that his reply won't get through to them before Friday lunch."

Costello fingered his wispy moustache.

"And we sell out on Friday morning," he said.

Mr Oates nodded emphatically.

"We do more than sell out. We sell ourselves short, and unload twice as much stock as we're holding. The story'll get all over England over the weekend, and when the Exchange opens on Monday morning the shares'll be two a penny. We make our profit both ways."

"It's a big risk," said Hammel seriously.

"Well, I'm taking it for you, ain't I?" said Mr Oates. "All you have to do is to help me spread the buying and selling about, so it don't look too much like a one-man deal. I'm standing to take all the knocks. But it can't go wrong. I've used Ischolskov before—I've got too much on him for him to try and doublecross me, and besides he's getting paid plenty. My being on the Midorient board makes it watertight. I'm taken in the same as the rest of 'em, and I'm hit as hard as they are. You're doing all the buying and selling from now on—there won't be a single deal in my name that anyone can prove against me. And whatever happens, don't sell till I give you the wire. I'll be the first to know when the crash is coming, and we'll hold out till the last moment."

They talked for an hour longer, after which they went out to a belated but celebratory lunch.

Mr Oates left his office early that afternoon, and therefore he did not even think of the movements of his new secretary when she went home. But if he had been privileged to observe them, he would have been very little the wiser; for Mr Oates was one of the numerous people who knew the Saint only by name, and if he had seen the sinewy sunburned young man who met her at Piccadilly Circus and bore her off for a cocktail he might have suffered a pang of jealousy, but he would have had no cause for alarm.

"We must have an Old Fashioned, Pat," said the Saint, when they were settled in Oddenino's. "The occasion calls for one. There's a wicked look in your eye that tells me you have some news. Have you sown a few more wild Oates?"

"Must you?" she protested weakly.

"Shall we get him an owl?" Simon suggested.

"What for?" asked Patricia unguardedly.

"It would be rather nice," said the Saint reflectively, "to get Titus an owl."

Patricia Holm shuddered.

Over the cocktails and stuffed olives, however, she relented.

"It's started," she said. "Hammel and Costello had a long conference with him this morning. I suppose they finished it after lunch, but I'd heard enough before they went out."

She told him every detail of the discussion that had taken place in Mr Titus Oates's private office, and Simon Templar smiled approvingly as he listened. Taken in conjunction with what he already knew, the summaries of various other conversations which she had reported to him, it left him with the whole structure of the conspiracy clearly catalogued in his mind.

"You must remember to take that microphone out of his office first thing in the morning," he remarked. "It might spoil things if Titus came across it, and I don't think you'll need to listen any more. . . . Here, where did you get that from?"

"From sowing my wild Oates," said Patricia angelically, as the waitress departed with a five-pound note on her tray.

Simon Templar regarded her admiringly.

"Darling," he said at length, "there are no limits to your virtues. If you're as rich as that, you can not only buy me another Old Fashioned but you can take me to dinner at the Barcelona as well."

On the way to the restaurant he bought an *Evening Standard* and opened it at the table.

"Midorients closed at 21," he said. "It looks as if we shall have to name a ward in our Old Age Home for Retired Burglars after Comrade Oates."

"How much shall we make if we buy and sell with him?" asked the girl.

The Saint smiled.

"I'm afraid we should lose a lot of money," he said. "You see, Titus isn't going to sell."

She stared at him, mystified; and he closed the menu and laughed at her silently.

"Did you by any chance hear Titus boasting about a stamp he bought for his collection last night?" he asked, and she nodded. "Well, old darling, I'm the bird who sold it to him. I never thought I should sink to philatelism even in my dotage, but in this case it seemed the best way to work. Titus is already convinced that I'm the greatest stamp-sleuth in captivity, and when he hears about the twopenny blue Mauritius I've discovered for him he will be fairly purring through the town. I don't see any reason why our Mr Oates should go unpublished for his sins and make a fortune out of this low swindle. He collects stamps, but I've got an even better hobby. I collect queer friends." The Saint was lighting a cigarette, and his blue eyes danced over the match. "Now listen carefully while I tell you the next move."

Mr Wallington Titus Oates was gloating fruitily over the closing prices on the Friday evening when his telephone bell rang.

He had reason to gloat. The news story provided by the cable-grams of Mr Ischolshov had been so admirably worded that it had hit the front page of every afternoon edition the previous day; and a jumpy market had done the rest. The results exceeded his most optimistic estimates. On the Wednesday night Midorients had closed at 32, and dealings in the street had taken them up to 34. They opened on Thursday morning at 38, and went to 50 before noon. One lunch edition ran a special topical article on fortunes made in oil, the sun shone brilliantly, England declared for 537 for six wickets in the first Test, all the brokers and jobbers felt happy, and Midorients finally went to 61 at the close. Moreover, in the evening paper which Mr Oates was reading there could not be found a breath of suspicion directed against the news which had caused the boom. The Midorient directors had issued a statement declaring that they were awaiting further details, that their manager on the spot was a reliable man not given to hysterical exaggerations, and that for the moment they were satisfied that prosperity had returned to an oil field which, they pointed out, had merely been suffering a temporary setback. Mr Oates had had much to do with the wording of the statement himself; and if it erred somewhat on the side of optimism, the error could not by any stretch of imagination have been described as criminal misrepresentation.

And when Mr Oates picked up his receiver and heard what it had to say, his cup was filled to overflowing.

"I've got you that twopenny blue," said a voice which he recognised. "It's a peach! It must be one of the most perfect specimens in existence—and it'll cost you nine hundred quid."

Mr Oates gripped the receiver, and his eyes lighted up with the unearthly fire which illumines the stare of the collector when he sees a coveted trophy within his grasp. It was, in its way, a no less starkly primitive manifestation than the dilating nostrils of a bloodhound hot on the scent.

"Where is it?" barked Mr Oates, in the baying voice of the same hound. "When can I see it? Can you bring it round? Have you got it yourself? Where is it?"

"Well, that's the snag, Mr Oates," said the Saint apologetically. "The owner won't let it go. He won't even let it out of his safe until it's paid for. He says he's got to have a cheque in his pocket before he'll let me take it away. He's a crotchety old bird, and I think he's afraid I might light a cigarette with it or something."

Mr Oates fairly quivered with suppressed emotion.

"Well, where does he live?" he yelped. "I'll settle him. I'll go round and see him at once. What's his name? What's the address?"

"His name is Dr Jethero," Simon answered methodically, "and he lives at 105 Matlock Gardens, Notting Hill. I think you'll catch him there—I've only just left him, and he said nothing about going out."

"Doctor Jethero—105—Matlock—Gardens, Notting—Hill," re-peated Mr Oates, reaching for a message pad and scribbling frantically.

"By the way," said the Saint, "I said he was crotchety, but you may think he's just potty. He's got some sort of a bee in his bonnet about people trying to get in and steal his stamp, and he told me that if you want to call and see him you've got to give a password."

"A password?" bleated Mr Oates.

"Yes. I told him that everybody knew Titus Oates, but ap-parently that wasn't good enough for him. If you go there you've got to say 'I was whipped from Aldgate to Newgate and from New-gate to Tyburn.' Can you remember that?"

"Of course," said Mr Oates indignantly. "I know all about that. Titus Oates was an ancestor of mine. Come and see me in the morn-ing, my dear boy—I'll have a present waiting for you. Goodbye."

Mr Oates slammed back the receiver and leapt up as if unleashed. Dithering with ecstasy and excitement, he stuffed his note of the address into his pocket, grabbed a cheque-book, and dashed out into the night.

The taxi ride to his destination seemed interminable, and when he got there he was in such a state of expectant rapture that he flung the driver a pound note and scurried up the steps without waiting for change. The house was one of those unwieldy Victorian edifices with which the west of London is encumbered against all hopes of modern development; and in the dim street lighting he did not even notice that all the windows were barred, nor would he have been likely to speculate upon the reasons for that peculiar feature if he had noticed it.

The door was opened by a white-coated man, and Mr Oates almost bowled him over as he dashed past him into the hall.

"I want Dr Jethero," he bayed. "I'm Titus Oates!"

The man closed the door and looked at him curiously.

"Mr Titus Oates, sir."

"Yes!" roared the financier impatiently. "Titus Oates. Tell him I was whipped from Aldgate to Newgate, and from Newgate to Tyburn. And hurry up!"

The man nodded perfunctorily, and edged past him at a cautious distance of which Mr Oates was too wrought up to see the implica-tions.

"Yes, sir. Will you wait in here a moment, sir?"

Mr Oates was ushered into a barely furnished distempered room and left there. With an effort he fussed himself down to a superficial calm—he was Titus Oates, a power in the City, and he must conduct himself accordingly. Dr Jethero might misunderstand a blundering excitement. If he was crotchety, and perhaps even potty, he must be handled with tact. Mr Oates strode up and down the room, working off his overflow of excitement. There was a faint characteristic flavour of iodoform in the air, but Mr Oates did not even notice that.

Footsteps sounded along the hall, and the door opened again. This time it admitted a grey-bearded man who also wore a white coat. His keen spectacled eyes examined the financier calmly. Mr Oates mustered all his self-control.

"I am Titus Oates," he said with simple dignity.

The grey-bearded man nodded.

"You wanted to see me?" he said; and Mr Oates recalled his instructions again.

"Titus Oates," he repeated gravely. "I was whipped from Aldgate to Newgate, and from Newgate to Tyburn."

Dr Jethero studied him for a moment longer, and glanced towards the door, where the white-coated attendant was waiting unobtrusively—Mr Oates had not even noticed the oddity of that.

"Yes, yes," he said soothingly. "And you were pilloried in Palace Yard, weren't you?"

"That's right," said Mr Oates eagerly. "And outside the Royal Exchange. They put me in prison for life, but they let me out at the Revolution and gave me my pension back."

Dr Jethero made clucking noises with his tongue.

"I see. A very unfortunate business. Would you mind coming this way, Mr Oates?"

He led the way up the stairs, and Mr Oates followed him blissfully. The whole rigmarole seemed very childish, but if it pleased Dr Jethero Mr Oates was prepared to go to any lengths to humour him. The white-coated attendant followed Mr Oates. Dr Jethero opened the door of a room on the second floor, and stood aside for Mr Oates to pass in. The door had a barred grille in its upper panels through which the interior of the room could be observed from the outside, an eccentricity which Mr Oates was still ready to accept as being in keeping with the character of his host.

It was the interior of the room into which he was shown that began to place an excessive strain on his adaptability. It was without furnishings of any kind, unless the thick kind of mattress in one corner could be called furnishings, and the walls and floor were finished in some extraordinary style of decoration which made them look like quilted upholstery.

Mr Oates looked about him, and turned puzzledly to his host.

"Well," he said, "where's the stamp?"

"What stamp?" asked Dr Jethero.

Mr Oates's laboriously achieved restraint was wearing thin again.

"Don't you understand? I'm Titus Oates. I was whipped from Aldgate to Newgate, and from Newgate to Tyburn. Didn't you hear what I said?"

"Yes, yes, yes," murmured the doctor peaceably. "You're Titus Oates. You stood in the pillory and they pelted you with rotten eggs."

"Well," said Mr Oates, "what about the stamp?"

Dr Jethero cleared his throat.

"Just a minute, Mr Oates. Suppose we go into that presently. Would you mind taking off your coat and shoes?"

Mr Oates gaped at him.

"This is going too far," he protested. "I'm Titus Oates. Everybody knows Titus Oates. You remember—the Popish Plot——"

"Mr Oates," said the doctor sternly, "will you take off your coat and shoes?"

The white-coated attendant was advancing stealthily towards him, and a sudden vague fear seized on the financier. Now he began to see the reason for the man's extraordinary behaviour. He was not crotchety. He was potty. He was worse—he must be a raving homicidal lunatic. Heaven knew what he would be doing next. A wild desire to be away from number 105 Matlock Gardens gripped Mr Oates—a desire that could not even be quelled by the urge to possess a twopenny blue Mauritius in perfect preservation.

"Never mind," said Mr Oates liberally. "I'm not really interested. I don't collect stamps at all. I'm just Titus Oates. Everyone knows me. I'm sure you'll excuse me—I have an appointment——"

He was edging towards the door, but Dr Jethero stood in the way.

"Nobody's going to hurt you, Mr Oates," he said; and then he caught the desperate gleam in Mr Oates's eye, and signed quickly to the attendant.

Mr Oates was seized suddenly from behind in a deft grip. Overcome with terror, he struggled like a maniac, and he was a big man; but he was helpless in the expert hands that held him. He was tripped and flung to the floor, and pinioned there with practised skill. Through whirling mists of horror he saw the doctor coming towards him with a hypodermic syringe, and he was still yelling feebly about the Popish Plot when the needle stabbed into his arm. . . .

Dr Jethero went downstairs and rang up a number which he had been given.

"I've got your uncle, Mr Tombs," he announced. "He gave us a bit of trouble, but he's quite safe now."

Simon Templar, who had found the name of Tombs a convenient alias before, grinned invisibly into the transmitter.

"That's splendid. Did he give you a lot of trouble?"

"He was inclined to be violent, but we managed to give him an injection, and when he wakes up he'll be in a strait-jacket. He's really a most interesting case," said the doctor with professional enthusiasm. "Quite apart from the delusion that he is Titus Oates, he seems to have some extraordinary hallucination about a stamp. Had you noticed that before?"

"I hadn't," said the Saint. "You may be able to find out some more about that. Keep him under observation, doctor, and call me again on Monday morning."

He rang off and turned gleefully to Patricia Holm, who was waiting at his elbow.

"Titus is in safe hands," he said. "And now I've got a call of my own to make."

"Who to?" she asked.

He showed her a scrap of paper on which he had jotted down the words of what appeared to be a telegram.

*Amazing discovery stop have reason to believe boom may be based on genuine possibilities stop do not on any account sell without hearing from me.*

"Dicky Tremayne's in Paris, and he'll send it for me," said the Saint. "A copy goes to Abe Costello and Jules Hammel tonight—I just want to make sure that they follow Titus down the drain. By the way, we shall clear about twenty thousand if Midorients are still at 61 when they open again tomorrow morning."

"But are you sure Jethero won't get into trouble?" she said.

Simon Templar nodded.

"Somehow I feel that Titus will prefer to keep his mouth shut after I've had a little chat with him on Monday," he said; and it is a matter of history that he was absolutely right.

# THE SLEEPLESS KNIGHT

## From THE SAINT INTERVENES

---

QUITE NATURALLY, *it seems to me, concurrently with the broadening conception of poetic justice which we were just discussing, there has been a shifting of the Saint's chief interest from common crime towards deeper waters.*

*That is not to say that the time-honoured themes of embezzlement, drug trafficking, blackmail, burglary, and the Blunt Instrument no longer amuse him. Far from it. But there is a measurable waning of the naïve exuberance which once found such simple villainies the completely satisfying and unsurpassable objectives of a buccaneer's attention. He has come to be aware of larger issues, of a lurking background of bigger and beastlier dragons.*

*This story deals with what you might call a transitional or intermediate size of dragon, and may therefore be read just as beneficially by students of evolution as by missionaries, bartenders, grocers, actuaries, and manufacturers of patent corset fastenings—a most happy state of affairs, in my opinion.*

# THE SLEEPLESS KNIGHT

IF A GREAT MANY NEWSPAPER CUTTINGS and references to newspapers find their way into these chronicles, it is simply because most of the interesting things that happen find their way into newspapers, and it is in these ephemeral sheets that the earnest seeker after unrighteousness will find many clues to his quest.

Simon Templar read newspapers only because he found collected in them the triumphs and anxieties and sins and misfortunes and ugly tyrannies which were going on around him, as well as the results of races in which chosen horses carried samples of his large supply of shirts; not because he cared anything about the posturings of Transatlantic fliers or the flatulence of international conferences. And it was solely through reading a newspaper that he became aware of the existence of Sir Melvin Flager.

It was an unpleasant case; and the news item may as well be quoted in full.

### JUDGE CENSURES TRANSPORT COMPANY

Driver's four hours' sleep a week

#### "MODERN SLAVERY"

*—Mr Justice Goldie.*

SCATHING criticisms of the treatment of drivers by a road transport company were made by Mr Justice Goldie during the trial of Albert Johnson, a lorry driver, at Guildford Assizes yesterday.

Johnson was charged with manslaughter following the death of a cyclist whom he knocked down and fatally injured near Albury on March 28th.

Johnson did not deny that he was driving to the danger of the public, but pleaded that his condition was due to circumstances beyond his control.

Police witnesses gave evidence that the lorry driven by Johnson was proceeding in an erratic manner down a fairly wide road at about 30 miles an hour. There was a cyclist in front of it, travelling in the same direction, and a private car coming towards it.

Swerving to make way for the private car, in what the witness described as "an unnecessarily exaggerated manner," the lorry struck the cyclist and caused fatal injuries.

The police surgeon who subsequently examined Johnson described him as being "apparently intoxicated, although there were no signs of alcohol on his breath."

"I was not drunk," said Johnson, giving evidence on his own behalf. "I was simply tired out. We are sent out on long journeys and forced to complete them at an average speed of over 30 miles an hour, including stops for food and rest.

"Most of our work is done at night, but we are frequently compelled to make long day journeys as well.

"During the week when the accident occurred, I had only had four hours' sleep.

"It is no good protesting, because the company can always find plenty of unemployed drivers to take our places."

Other employees of the Flager Road Transport Company, which employs Johnson, corroborated his statement.

"This is nothing more or less than modern slavery," said Mr Justice Goldie, directing the jury to return a verdict of Not Guilty.

"It is not Johnson, but Sir Melvin Flager, the managing director of the company, who ought to be in the dock.

"You have only to put yourselves in the position of having gone for a week on four hours' sleep, with the added strain of driving a heavy truck throughout that time, to be satisfied that no culpable recklessness of Johnson's was responsible for this tragedy.

"I would like to see it made a criminal offence for employers to impose such inhuman conditions on their employees."

Sir Melvin Flager was not unnaturally displeased by this judicial comment; but he might have been infinitely more perturbed if he had known of the Saint's interest in the case.

Certain readers of these chronicles may have reached the impression that Simon Templar's motives were purely selfish and mercenary, but they would be doing him an injustice. Undoubtedly his exploits were frequently profitable; and the Saint himself would have been the first to admit that he was not a brigand for his health; but there were many times when only a very small percentage of his profits remained in his own pocket, and many occasions when he embarked on an episode of lawlessness with no thought of profit for himself at all.

The unpleasantness of Sir Melvin Flager gave him some hours of quite altruistic thought and effort.

"Actually," he said, "there's only one completely satisfactory way to deal with a tumour like that. And that is to sink him in a barrel of oil and light a fire underneath."

"The Law doesn't allow you to do that," said Peter Quentin pensively.

"Very unfortunately, it doesn't," Simon admitted with genuine regret. "All the same, I used to do that sort of thing without the sanction of the Law, which is too busy catching publicans selling a glass of beer after hours to do anything about serious misdemeanours, anyway. . . . But I'm afraid you're right, Peter—I'm much too notorious a character these days, and Chief Inspector Claud Eustace Teal isn't the bosom pal he was. We shall have to gang warily; but nevertheless, we shall certainly have to gang."

Peter nodded approvingly. Strangely enough, he had once possessed a thoroughly respectable reverence for the Law; but several months of association with the Saint had worked irreparable damage to that bourgeois inhibition.

"You can count me in," he said; and the Saint clapped him on the back.

"I knew it without asking you, you old sinner," he said contentedly. "Keep this next weekend free for me, brother, if you really feel that way—and if you want to be specially helpful you can push out this afternoon with a false beard tied round your ears and try and rent a large garage from which yells of pain cannot be heard outside."

"Is that all?" Peter asked suspiciously. "What's your share going to be—backing losers at Hurst Park?"

The Saint shook his head.

"Winners," he said firmly. "I always back winners. But I'm going to be busy myself. I want to get hold of a Gadget. I saw it at a motor show once, but it may take me a couple of days to find out where I can buy one."

As a matter of fact it took him thirtysix hours and entailed a good deal of travelling and expense. Peter Quentin found and rented the garage which the Saint had demanded a little more quickly; but the task was easier and he was used to Simon Templar's eccentric commissions.

"I'm getting so expert at this sort of thing, I believe I could find you a three-humped camel overnight if you wanted it," Peter said modestly, when he returned to announce success.

Simon grinned.

The mechanical details of his scheme were not completed until the

Friday afternoon, but he added every hour and penny spent to the private account which he had with Sir Melvin Flager, of which the slave-driving knight was blissfully in ignorance.

It is barely possible that there may survive a handful of simple unsophisticated souls who would assume that since Mr Justice Goldie's candid criticisms had been pronounced in open court and printed in every newspaper of importance, Sir Melvin Flager had been hiding his head in shame, shunned by his erstwhile friends and treated with deferential contempt even by his second footman. To these unfledged innocents we extend our kindly sympathy, and merely point out that nothing of the sort had happened. Sir Melvin Flager, of course, did not move in the very Highest Society, for an uncle of his on his mother's side still kept and served in a fried-fish shop near the Elephant and Castle; but the society in which he did move did not ostracise him. Once the first statement-seeking swarm of reporters had been dispersed, he wined and dined and diverted himself and ran his business exactly the same as he had done before; for the business and social worlds have always found it remarkably easy to forgive the trespasses of a man whose prices and entertainments are respectively cheaper and better than others.

On that Friday night Sir Melvin Flager entertained a small party to dinner, and took them on to a revue afterwards. Conscience had never troubled him personally; and his guests were perfectly happy to see a good show without worrying about such sordid trifles as how the money that paid for their seats was earned. His well-laden lorries roared through the night with red-eyed men at the wheel to add to his fortune; and Sir Melvin Flager sat in his well-upholstered seat and roared with carefree laughter at the antics of the comedian, forgetting all about his business until nearly the end of the first act, when a programme girl handed him a sealed envelope.

Flager slit it open and read the note.

*One of our trucks has had another accident. Two killed. Afraid it may be bad for us if this comes out so soon after the last one. May be able to square it, but must see you first. Will wait in your car during the interval.*

It was in his business manager's handwriting, and it was signed with his business manager's name.

Sir Melvin Flager tore the note into small pieces and dumped it in the ashtray before him. There was a certain forced quality about his laughter for the next five minutes; and as soon as the curtain came down he excused himself to his guests and walked down the line of cars parked in a side street adjoining the theatre. He found his own limousine, and peered in at the back.

"You there, Nyson?" he growled.

"Yes, sir."

Flager grunted, and opened the door. It was rather dark inside the car, and he could only just make out the shape of the man who sat there.

"I'll fire every damned driver I've got tomorrow," he swore, as he climbed in. "What the devil do they think I put them on the road for—to go to sleep? This may be serious."

"You've no idea how serious it's going to be, brother," said the man beside him.

But the voice was not the voice of Mr Nyson, and the mode of address was not that which Sir Melvin Flager encouraged from his executives. For a moment the managing director of the Flager Road Transport Company did not move; and then he leaned sideways to stare more closely at his companion. His eyes were growing accustomed to the dark, but the movement did not help him at all, for with a sudden shock of fear he saw that the man's features were completely covered by a thin gauzy veil which stretched from his hat-brim down to his coat collar.

"Who the hell are you?" rasped Flager uncertainly.

"On the whole, I think it would be better for you not to know," said the Saint calmly.

Another man had climbed into the driver's seat, and the car vibrated almost imperceptibly as the engine started up. But this second man, although he wore a chauffeur's peaked cap, had a silhouette that in no way resembled that of the chauffeur whom Sir Melvin Flager employed.

Under his touch the car began to edge out of the line; and as he saw the movement Flager came back to life. In the stress of the moment he was unable to form a very clear idea of what was happening, but instinct told him that it was nothing to which he wanted to lend his tender person.

"Well, you won't kidnap me!" he shouted, and lashed out wildly at the veiled face of the man beside him.

Which was the last thing he knew about for the next half-hour, for his desperate swing was still far from its mark when a fist like a ball of iron struck him cleanly on the point of the jaw and lifted him back on to the cushions in a dreamless slumber.

When he woke up, his first impulse was to clasp his hands to his painfully singing head; but when he tried to carry it out his wrists refused to move—they felt as if they were anchored to some solid object. Blinking open his eyes, he looked down at them. They were handcuffed to what appeared to be the steering wheel of a car.

In another second the memory of what had happened to him before he fell asleep returned. He began to struggle frantically, but his body also refused to respond, and he saw that a broad leather strap like the safety belt of an aeroplane had been passed round his waist and fastened in front of his abdomen, locking him securely to his seat. Wildly he looked about him, and discovered that he was actually sitting in the driving seat of a lorry. He could see the bonnet in front of him, and, beyond it, a kind of white screen which seemed vaguely familiar.

The feeling that he had been plunged into some fantastic nightmare seized him, and he let out a stifled yell of fright.

"That won't help you," said a cool voice at his side; and Flager jerked his head round to see the veiled face of the unknown man who had sat at his side in the car.

"Damn you!" he raved. "What have you done to me?"

He was a large fleshy man, with one of those meaty faces which look as if their owner had at some time invited God to strike him pink, and had found his prayer instantaneously answered. Simon Templar, who did not like large fleshy men with fleshy pink faces, smiled under his mask.

"So far we haven't done very much," he said. "But we're going to do plenty."

The quietness of his voice struck Flager with a sudden chill, and instinctively he huddled inside his clothes. Something else struck him as unusual even as he did so, and in another moment he realised what it was. Above the waist, he had no clothes on at all—the whole of his soft white torso was exposed to the inclemency of the air.

The Saint smiled again.

"Start the machine, Peter," he ordered; and Flager saw that the chauffeur who had driven the car was also there, and that he was similarly masked.

A switch clicked over, and darkness descended on the garage. Then a second switch clicked, and the white screen in front of the truck's bonnet lighted up with a low whirring sound. Bewildered but afraid, Flager looked up and saw a free moving picture show.

The picture was of a road at night, and it unrolled towards him as if it had been photographed from behind the headlights of a car that was rushing over it. From time to time, corners, crossroads, and the lights of other traffic proceeding in both directions swept up towards him—the illusion that he was driving the lorry in which he sat over that road was almost perfect.

"What's this for?" he croaked.

"You're taking the place of one of your own drivers for the weekend," answered the Saint. "We should have preferred to do it out on the road under normal working conditions, but I'm afraid you would have made too much noise. This is the best substitute we were able to arrange, and I think it'll work all right. Do you know what it is?"

Flager shook his head.

"I don't care what it is! Listen here, you——"

"It's a gadget for testing people's ability to drive," said the Saint smoothly. "When I turn another switch, the steering wheel you have there will be synchronised with the film. You will then be driving over the road yourself. So long as you keep on the road and don't try to run into the other traffic, everything will be all right. But directly you make a movement that would have taken you off the road or crashed you into another car—or a cyclist, brother—the film will stop for a moment, a red light will light up on top of the screen, and I shall wake you up like this."

Something swished through the air, and a broad stinging piece of leather which felt like a razor strop fell resoundingly across Sir Melvin's well-padded shoulders.

Flager gave a yelp of anguish; and the Saint laughed softly.

"We'll start right away," he said. "You know the rules and you know the penalties—the rules are only the same as your own employees have to obey, and the penalties are really much less severe. Wake up, Flager—you're off!"

The third switch snapped into place, and Flager grabbed blindly at the steering wheel. Almost at once the picture faltered, and a red light glowed on top of the screen.

*Smack!* came the leather strap across his shoulders.

"Damn you!" bellowed Flager. "What are you doing this for?"

"Partly for fun," said the Saint. "Look out—you're going to hit that car!"

Flager did hit it, and the strop whistled through the darkness and curled over his back. His shriek tortured the echoes; but Simon was without mercy.

"You'll be in the ditch in a minute," he said. "No. . . . Here comes a corner. . . . Watch it! . . . Nicely round, brother, nicely round. Now mind you don't run into the back of this cart—you've got plenty of room to pass. . . . Stick to it. . . . Don't hit the cyclist. . . . You're going to hit him. . . . Mind the fence—you're heading straight for it—look out. . . . Look out!"

The strap whacked down again with a strong and willing arm behind it as the red light sprang up again.

Squealing like a stuck pig, Sir Melvin Flager tore the lorry back on to its course.

"How long are you keeping this up for?" he sobbed.

"Until Monday morning," said the Saint calmly. "And I wish it could be a month. I've never seen a more responsive posterior than you have. Mind the cyclist."

"But you're making me drive too fast!" Flager almost screamed. "Can't you slow the machine up a bit?"

"We have to average over thirty miles an hour," answered the Saint remorselessly. "Look out!"

Sir Melvin Flager passed into a nightmare that was worse than anything he had thought of when he first opened his eyes. The mechanical device which he was strapped to was not quite the same as the cars he was used to; and Simon Templar himself would have been ready to admit that it might be more difficult to drive. Time after time the relentless leather lashed across his shoulderblades, and each time it made contact he let loose a howl of pain which in itself was a reward to his tormentors.

After a while he began to master the steering, and long periods went by when the red light scarcely showed at all. As these intervals of immunity lengthened, Flager shrugged his aching back and began to pluck up courage. These lunatics who had kidnapped him, whoever they were, had taken a mean advantage of him at the start. They had fastened him to an unfamiliar machine and promptly proceeded to shoot it through space at forty miles an hour: naturally he had made mistakes. But that could not go on for ever. He had got the hang of it at last, and the rest of it seemed more or less plain sailing. He even had leisure to ponder sadistically on what their fate would be when they let him go and the police caught them, as they undoubtedly would be caught. He seemed to remember that the cat-o'-nine-tails was the punishment invariably meted out by the Law for crimes of violence. Well, flogging him with that leather strap was a crime of violence. He brooded savagely over various tales he had heard of the horrors of that punishment. . . .

*Whack!*

The red light had glowed, and the strap had swung home again. Flager pulled himself together with a curse. It was no good getting careless now that he had mastered the machine. But he was beginning to feel tired. His eyes were starting to ache a little with the strain of keeping themselves glued watchfully to the cinematograph screen ahead. The interminable unwinding of that senseless road, the whirr of the unseen projector, the physical effort of manipulating the heavy steering wheel, the deadly monotony of the task, combined with the heavy dinner he had eaten and a long sequence of other dinners behind it to produce a sensation of increasing drowsiness. But the unwinding of the road never slackened speed, and the leather strap never failed to find its mark every time his weary attention caused him to make a mistake.

"You're getting careless about your corners," the Saint warned him tirelessly. "You'll be in the ditch at the next one. Look out!"

The flickering screen swelled up and swam in his vision. There was nothing in the world—nothing but that endlessly winding road uncoiling out of the darkness, the lights of other traffic that leapt up from it, the red light above the screen, and the smack of the leather strap across his shoulders. His brain seemed to be spinning round like a top inside his head when at last, amazingly, the screen went black and the other bulbs in the garage lighted up.

"You can go to sleep now," said the Saint.

Sir Melvin Flager was incapable of asking questions. A medieval prisoner would have been no more capable of asking questions of a man who released him from the rack. With a groan he slumped back in his seat and fell asleep.

It seemed as if he had scarcely closed his eyes when he was roused again by someone shaking him. He looked up blearily and saw the strange chauffeur leaning over him.

"Wake up," said Peter Quentin. "It's five o'clock on Saturday morning, and you've got a lot more miles to cover."

Flager had no breath to dispute the date. The garage lights had gone out again, and the road was starting to wind out of the cinematograph screen again.

"But you told me I could sleep!" he moaned.

"You get thirtyfive minutes every night," Peter told him pitilessly. "That averages four hours a week, and that's as much as you allowed Albert Johnson. Look out!"

Twice again Flager was allowed to sleep, for exactly thirtyfive minutes; four times he watched his two veiled tormentors change places, a fresh man taking up the task while the other laid down on a very comfortable bed which had been made up in one corner and slept serenely. Every three hours he had five minutes' rest and a glass of water, every six hours he had ten minutes' rest, a cup of coffee, and a sandwich. But the instant that those timed five or ten minutes had elapsed, the projector was started up again, the synchronisation switch was thrown over, and he had to go on driving.

Time ceased to have any meaning. When, after his first sleep, he was told that it was only five o'clock Saturday morning, he could have believed that he had been driving for a week; before his ordeal was over, he felt as if he had been at the wheel for seven years. By Saturday night he felt he was going mad; by Sunday morning he thought he was going to die; by Sunday night he was a quivering wreck. The strap fell on his shoulders many times during the last few hours, when the recurrent sting of it was almost the only thing that kept his eyes open; but he was too weary even to cry out. . . .

And then, at the end of what might have been centuries, Monday morning dawned outside; and the Saint looked at his watch and reversed the switches.

"You can go to sleep again now," he said for the last time; but Sir Melvin Flager was asleep almost before the last word was out of his mouth.

Sunken in the coma of utter exhaustion, Flager did not even feel himself being unstrapped and unhandcuffed from his perch; he did not feel the clothes being replaced on his inflamed back, nor did he even rouse as he was carried into his own car and driven swiftly away.

And then again he was being shaken by the shoulder, woken up. Whimpering, he groped for the steering wheel—and did not find it. The shaking at his shoulder went on.

"All right," he blubbered. "All right. I'm trying to do it. Can't you let me sleep a little—just once. . . ."

"Sir Melvin! Sir Melvin!"

Flager forced open his bloodshot eyes. His hands were free. He was sitting in his own car, which was standing outside his own house. It was his valet who was shaking him.

"Sir Melvin! Try to wake up, sir. Where have you been? Are you ill, sir?"

Flager found strength to move his head from one side to the other.

"No," he said. "I just want to sleep."

And with a deep groan he let his swollen eyelids droop again, and sank back into soothing abysses of delicious rest.

When he woke up again he was in his own bed, in his own bedroom. For a long time he lay without moving, wallowing in the heavenly comfort of the soft mattress and cool linen, savouring the last second of sensual pleasure that could be squeezed out of the most beautiful awakening that he could remember.

"He's coming round," said a low voice at last; and with a sigh Flager opened his eyes.

His bed seemed to be surrounded with an audience such as a seventeenth-century monarch might have beheld at a levee. There was his valet, his secretary, his doctor, a nurse, and a heavy and stolid man of authoritative appearance who held an unmistakable bowler hat. The doctor had a hand on his pulse, and the others stood by expectantly.

"All right, Sir Melvin," said the physician. "You may talk for a little while now, if you want to, but you mustn't excite yourself. This gentleman here is a detective who wants to ask you a few questions."

The man with a bowler hat came nearer.

"What happened to you, Sir Melvin?" he asked.

Flager stared at him for several seconds. Words rose to his lips, but somehow he did not utter them.

"Nothing," he said at length. "I've been away for the weekend, that's all. What the devil's all this fuss about?"

"But your back, Sir Melvin!" protested the doctor. "You look as if you'd had a terrible beating——"

"I had a slight accident," snapped Flager. "And what the devil has it got to do with you, sir, anyway? Who the devil sent for all of you?"

His valet swallowed.

"I did, Sir Melvin," he stammered. "When I couldn't wake you up all day yesterday—and you disappeared from the theatre without a word to anybody, and didn't come back for two days——"

"And why the devil shouldn't I disappear for two days?" barked Flager weakly. "I'll disappear for a month if I feel like it. Do I pay you to pry into my movements? And can't I sleep all day if I want to without waking up to find a lot of quacks and policemen infesting my room like vultures? Get out of my house, the whole damned lot of you! Get out, d'you hear?"

Somebody opened the door, and the congregation drifted out, shaking its heads and muttering, to the accompaniment of continued exhortations in Flager's rasping voice.

His secretary was the last to go, and Flager called him back.

"Get Nyson on the telephone," he ordered. "I'll speak to him myself."

The secretary hesitated for a moment, and then picked up the bedside telephone and dialled the number dubiously.

Flager took the instrument as soon as his manager answered.

"Nyson?" he said. "Get in touch with all our branch depots immediately. From now on, all our drivers will be on a five-hour day, and they get a twenty percent rise as from the date we took them on. Engage as many more men as you need to make up the schedules."

He heard Nyson's incredulous gasp over the line.

"I beg your pardon, Sir Melvin—did you say——"

"Yes, I did!" snarled Flager. "You heard me all right. And after that, you can find out if that cyclist Johnson killed left any dependents. I want to do something for them. . . ."

His voice faded away, and the microphone slipped through his fingers. His secretary looked at him quickly, and saw that his eyes were closed and the hemispherical mound of his abdomen was rising and falling rhythmically.

Sir Melvin Flager was asleep again.

# THE HIGH FENCE

## From The Saint Goes On

I AM RATHER WELL AWARE *that the Saint Saga is somewhat noticeably sprinkled with a large number of allusions to the British Public School, the Public School Man, and the Public School Spirit, and that all of these allusions are so conspicuously devoid of proper reverence that it begins to look as if I might have a complex on the subject. But I had to re-read the next story in our collection, which plays the same tune with more than ordinarily concentrated consistency, to realise that the time might be coming when some astute reader would be liable to pounce on me for an explanation of this violent prejudice.*

*Whereupon I also realised that I should also have to be very cautious in my choice of the explanation I gave, since a study of what I proudly call my fan mail statistics reveals that a large percentage of my most faithful readers are either past or present members of some British Public School.*

*The more deeply I pondered the various horns of this dilemma, the more clearly I saw the fact that there was positively no explanation I could give (since any definitive explanation must, a priori, involve a statement of my own personal opinions on several broad but very ticklish subjects) that would not be doomed to expose me to the undying hatred of just about as many readers as it would deathlessly endear me to. And I therefore hereby give notice that any future questions addressed to me on the subject will be tactfully but ruthlessly ignored.*

*But since on this one occasion something inescapably had to be said about it, I have taken refuge in that sublime genius for equivocation and diplomacy which was so tragically stolen from the world of politics when my first publisher accepted my first novel. I propose, as my last public utterance on the matter (until next time) to tell a very short story which is also scripturally true.*

*This was during one of my last months at one of the Public Schools which we are talking about. The class was devoted to the study of English—a language which, to judge by the curriculum, and the hushed whispers in which it was referred to, became extinct quite early in the nineteenth century. The crucial point was an exercise in composition, on some standard dreary subject, such as* An Appreciation of the Humour of Shakespeare's Clowns.

*Feeling, at the time, somewhat full of oats, I had ventured, for perhaps the first time in my academic career, to kick over the traces of what my British Public School considered to be the inviolable commandments of respectable English prose. I was waggish and disrespectful. I pulled the wisecrack and the long nose. I cannot say that I wrote anything that would have held any interest for the passionate commentator; on the other hand, I am equally sure that nobody else in the class did, either. But I am no less certain—even after so many years—that any editor of any popular publication would have read more than the first paragraph of it; which is more than he would have read of any of the other theses submitted.*

*Returning my opus to me, with many indignant blue-pencillings of my choicest epigrams, and with the lowest marks at his disposal written in the largest figures that there was room for, my instructor peered at me over his spectacles and said severely:*

*"My advice to you, Charteris, is to confine yourself to the subject you are supposed to be studying, and get rid of the idea that you are starting on some sort of literary career of your own."*

# THE HIGH FENCE

ApaRT FROM THE FACT that neither of them was a productive or useful member of the community, Johnny Anworth and Sunny Jim Fasson had very little in common. They did not own allegiance to the same Dear Old School; they had no meeting-ground in a passion for the poems of William Wordsworth, no shared devotion to collecting birds' eggs or the rarer kinds of cheese. But the circumstances in which they ceased to adorn their usual places in the files of Records Office at New Scotland Yard had a connecting link which must be the chronicler's excuse for reciting them in quick succession.

Johnny Anworth entered a jeweller's shop in Bond Street during the Easter holidays of that year, and omitted to pay for what he took out. He entered through the ceiling, from an apartment on the floor above which he had rented temporarily. It was a pretty neat job, for Johnny was a sound worker in his line; but it had his personality written all over it, and Headquarters put out the routine dragnet and in twentyfour hours duly brought him in.

He was taken to Market Street police station, where he was seen by the Divisional Inspector. The awkward part of it from Johnny's point of view was that he had most of the proceeds of his burglary on him when he was caught—at any rate he had all the precious stones, which had been prised out of their settings, carefully packed in a small cardboard box, and done up with brown paper and string. What he had not had time to do was to write an address on the package, and for this reason the DI was very gentle with him.

"You were going to send that stuff to the High Fence, weren't you, Johnny?" he said.

"I dunno wot yer talkin' abaht, guv'nor," answered Johnny me-

447

chanically. "I fahnd the stuff lyin' in the gutter in Leicester Square, an' I did it up to send it to the Lost Property Office."

The Divisional Inspector continued to be gentle.

"You've been in stir six times already," he said, consulting a memorandum on his desk. "If we wanted to be hard on you now, we could have you sent to the Awful Place. You could go to the Moor for seven years, and then have three years' preventive detention waiting for you. On the other hand, if you told us who you were going to send this parcel to, we might forget about those previous convictions and put in a word for you."

Johnny considered this. There is honour among thieves, but it is not designed to resist bad weather.

"Orl right, guv'nor," he said philosophically. "I'll squeal."

This story might have ended there if the station shorthand writer had been available. But he had already gone out to lunch; and the Divisional Inspector was also hungry.

They put Johnny Anworth back in his cell with instructions to order anything he wanted to eat at the DI's expense, and an appointment to make his statement at two o'clock. His lunch, which consisted of roast beef and cabbage, was delivered from a nearby restaurant by an errand-girl who deposited it in the charge-room. Almost as soon as she had gone, after some flirtatious exchanges with the charge-sergeant, it was picked up by the gaoler, who carried it in to Johnny. He was the last man who saw the talented Mr Anworth alive.

The girl had taken the tray from the chef in the kitchen, and no one had stopped her or spoken to her on the way. The chef had had no unusual visitors. The only people in the charge-room when the girl delivered the tray were the gaoler, the charge-sergeant, and Inspector Pryke. And yet, somehow, somewhere on the short journey which Johnny Anworth's last meal had taken, someone had contrived to dope the horseradish sauce with which his plate of roast beef was garnished with enough cyanide to kill a regiment.

The murder was a nine days' wonder which provoked its inevitable quota of headlines, newspaper criticisms, and questions in Parliament. Every inquiry seemed to lead to a dead end. But the Criminal Investigation Department has become phlegmatically accustomed to dead ends; and Chief Inspector Teal was still working methodically on the case, six weeks later, when Mr James Fasson clicked to the tune of five thousand pounds' worth of gems to which he had no legal right whatsoever.

The assets of Sunny Jim Fasson were a smile which made children and hard-boiled business men trust him instinctively, a wardrobe of prosperous-looking clothes, some high class American luggage plastered with a wonderful collection of expensive cosmopolitan labels, enough ready cash to create an impression of affluence at any hotel where he stayed, and a girl friend who posed as his wife, sister, niece, or old widowed mother with equal success and distinction.

On this occasion he stayed at the Magnificent, a hotel which he had not previously honoured with his presence. He was a wealthy American on his honeymoon; and for a few days he and his charming wife were quite happy seeing the sights and making a round of the theatres. One day, however, a small rift appeared in their marital bliss.

"I guess she's feelin' kinda homesick, or something," Sunny Jim confided to a clerk at the inquiry desk. "Whaddaya do when your wife gets moody, son?"

"I don't really know, sir," confessed the clerk, who was not employed to answer that kind of inquiry.

"Y'know, I always think a woman wants some kinda kick outa life when she feels that way," mused Sunny Jim. "Some lil thing that makes her feel good with herself. A noo hat, or a fur coat, or—or a diamond bracelet. . . . That's what she wants!" he cried, recognising divine inspiration when it breathed on him. "A diamond bracelet! Say, what's the best store in this town to buy a diamond bracelet?"

"Peabody's, in Regent Street, are very good, sir," said the clerk, after a moment's thought.

Sunny Jim beamed.

"Ring 'em up and tell 'em to send some of their best diamond bracelets around," he said. "I'll have the man take 'em right up to her room, and she can pick out what she likes. Say, I bet that'll put everything right."

Whether it put everything right or not is a question that the various parties concerned might have answered differently. The hotel was glad enough to oblige such a lavish guest; and Mr Peabody, the jeweller, was so impressed with their brief account of Mr James Fasson that he hurried round in person with six diamond bracelets in his bag. After a short discussion, Mrs Fasson chose the most expensive, a mere trifle valued at a thousand pounds; and Mr Fasson rang for a pageboy to take his cheque for that amount round to the bank to be cashed.

"You must have a drink while you're waitin' for your money," said Sunny Jim, turning to a bottle and a siphon which stood on a side table.

Mr Peabody had a very small drink; and remembered nothing more for another hour, at the end of which time Mr and Mrs Fasson had left the Magnificent for ever, taking all his six diamond bracelets with them. Nor did Mr Peabody's afternoon look any brighter when the bank on which Mr Fasson's cheque had been drawn rang up the hotel to mention that they had never carried an account for anybody of that name.

This episode was the subject of a hurriedly assembled conference in the Assistant Commissioner's room at New Scotland Yard.

The other two men present were Chief Inspector Claud Eustace Teal and Junior Inspector Pryke. Mr Teal, who was responsible for the conference, explained his point of view very briefly.

"Anworth and Fasson used to be fairly well acquainted, and if Anworth was using the High Fence there's a good chance that Fasson will be using him too. I know exactly where I can lay my hands on Sunny Jim, and I want permission to try and get a squeal out of him unofficially."

"What is your objection to having him arrested and questioned in the ordinary way?" asked the Commissioner.

"He'd have to be taken to Market Street, wouldn't he?" meditated Teal aloud. His baby blue eyes hid themselves under studiously sleepy lids. "Well," he said dryly, "because I don't want him murdered."

Junior Inspector Desmond Pryke flushed. He was one of the first graduates of Lord Trenchard's famous Police College, and he usually gave the impression of being very well satisfied with his degree. He was dark, slim, and well-manicured; and the inventor of that classic experiment for turning gentlemen into detectives could certainly have pointed to him as a product who looked nothing like the traditional idea of a policeman. Mr Teal had been heard to thank God that there was no possibility of confusing them, but there were obvious reasons why Mr Teal was irrevocably prejudiced in favour of the old order.

"It's in your manor, Pryke," said the Assistant Commissioner. "What do you think?"

"I don't see what there is to be gained by it," said the other. "If Fasson hasn't been too frightened by the murder of Anworth to talk anyhow——"

"What does Fasson know about the murder of Anworth?" demanded Teal quickly, for the official statements to the Press had contained certain deliberate gaps.

Pryke looked at him.

"I don't suppose he definitely *knows* any more than any other outsider, but it's common gossip in the underworld that Anworth was murdered because he was going to turn informer."

"You look as if you spent a lot of your time picking up gossip from the underworld," retorted Teal sarcastically. He caught the Assistant Commissioner's chilly eye on him, and went on more politely: "In any case, sir, that's only another reason why I don't want to take him to a police station. I want to try and prevent him thinking that any squeal could be traced back to him."

There was some further discussion, through which Teal sat stolidly chewing a worn-out lump of spearmint, with his round pink face set in its habitual mask of weary patience, and eventually gained his point.

"Perhaps you had better take Inspector Pryke with you," suggested the Commissioner, when he gave his permission.

"I should like to, sir," said Mr Teal, with great geniality, "but I don't know whether this can wait long enough for him to go home and change."

Pryke adjusted the set of his coat delicately as he rose. It was undoubtedly part of a resplendent suit, being of a light fawn colour with a mauve overcheck; a very different proposition from Teal's shiny blue serge.

"I didn't know that Police Regulations required you to look like an out-of-work rag and bone man," he said; and Chief Inspector Teal's complexion was tinged with purple all the way to Hyde Park Corner.

He resented having Inspector Pryke thrust upon him, partly because he resented Inspector Pryke and partly because the High Fence had been his own individual assignment ever since Johnny Anworth put his knife and fork into that fatal plate of roast beef six weeks ago. For a lieutenant, when necessity called for one, Mr Teal preferred the morose and angular Sergeant Barrow, who had never been known to speak unless he was spoken to, and who then spoke only to utter some cow-like comment to which nobody with anything better to do need have listened. Chief Inspector Teal had none of the theoretical scientific training in criminology with which the new graduates of the Police College were pumped to offensive overflowing, but he had a background of thirty years' hard-won experience which took the intrusion of manicured theorists uneasily; and at the entrance of the small apartment building in which Sunny Jim Fasson had been located he said so.

"I want you to keep quiet and let me do the talking," was his instruction. "I know how I'm going to tackle Fasson, and I know how to get what I want out of him."

Pryke fingered his MCC tie.

"Like you've always known how to get what you want out of the Saint?" he drawled.

Mr Teal's lips were tightly compressed as he stumped up the narrow stairway. His seemingly interminable failure to get anything that he really wanted out of that cool smiling devil who passed so incongruously under the name of the Saint was a thorn in his side which Inspector Pryke had twisted dextrously before. Whenever Chief Inspector Teal attempted to impress the rising generation of detectives with his superior craftsmanship, that gibe could always be brought up against him, openly or surreptitiously; and Mr Teal was getting so tired of it that it hurt. He wished, viciously, that some of the smart infants who were being pushed up under him could have as much to cope with as he had had in his time.

But Sunny Jim Fasson was quite a different problem from the blue-eyed bantering outlaw who had occupied so much of Mr Teal's time in other days; and he felt a renewal of confidence when he saw Sunny Jim's startled face through the slit of the opening door and wedged his foot expertly in the aperture.

"Don't make a fuss, and nobody's going to hurt you, Sunny," he said.

Sunny Jim, like Johnny Anworth, was also a philosopher in his way. He retreated into the tiny bed-sitting-room without dropping the ash from his cigar.

"What's it about this time, Mr Teal?" he inquired, with the sang-froid of old experience.

He did not even bother to put on his cultivated American accent; which saved him considerable trouble, for he had been born in the Old Kent Road and had learnt all that he knew of America from the movies.

"It needn't be about some diamond bracelets that were stolen from Peabody's—unless you want it to be," said Teal, with equal coldbloodedness.

Sunny Jim raised his eyebrows. The gesture was mechanical.

"I don't know what you mean, Mr Teal."

"Would you know what I meant," replied the detective, with impregnable drowsiness, "if I told you that Peabody has identified your photograph and is quite sure he can identify you; and half the Magnificent Hotel staff are ready to back him up?"

Sunny Jim had no answer to that.

"Mind you," said Teal, carefully unwrapping a fresh slice of chewing gum, "I said that we needn't go into that unless you want to. If you had a little talk with me now, for instance—why, we could settle it all here in this room, and you needn't even come with us to the station. It'd be all over and forgotten—just between ourselves."

When Sunny Jim Fasson was not wearing the well-trained smile from which he had earned his nickname, his face fell into a system of hard-bitten lines which drew an illuminating picture of shrewd and sharp intelligence. Those lines became visible now. So far as Sunny Jim was concerned, Teal's speech needed no amplification; and Sunny Jim was a man who believed in the comfort and security of Mr James Fasson first, last, and in the middle. If Teal had arrived half an hour later he would have been on his way to Ostend, but as things were he recognised his best alternative health resort.

"I'm not too particular what I talk about with an old friend, Mr Teal," he said at length.

"Do you sell your stuff to the High Fence, Sunny?"

Fasson held his cigar under his nose and sniffed the aroma.

"I believe I did hear of him once," he admitted cautiously.

The appearance of bored sleepiness in Chief Inspector Teal's eyes was always deceptive. In the last few seconds they had made a detailed inventory of the contents of the room, and had observed a torn strip of brown paper beside the wastebasket and a three-inch end of string on the carpet under the table.

"You've already got rid of Peabody's diamond bracelets, haven't you?" he said persuasively; and his somnolent eyes went back to Sunny Jim's face and did not shift from it. "All I want to know from you is what address you put on the parcel."

Sunny Jim put his cigar back in his mouth till the end glowed red.

"I did send off a parcel not long ago," he confessed reminiscently. "It was addressed to——"

He never said who it was addressed to.

Mr Teal heard the shot behind him, and saw Sunny Jim's hand jerk to his brow and his head jar with the shock of the bullet. The slam of the door followed, as Teal turned round to it in a blank stupor of incredulity. Pryke, who was nearest, had it open again when his superior reached it; and Teal barged after him in a kind of incandescent gaze, out on to the landing. The sheer fantastic unexpectedness of what had happened had knocked his brain momentarily out of the rhythm of conscious functioning, but he clattered down the stairs on Pryke's heels, and actually overtook him at the door which let them out on to the street.

And having got there, he stopped, with his brain starting work again, overwhelmed by the utter futility of what he was doing.

There was nothing sensational to be seen outside. The road presented the ordinary aspect of a minor thoroughfare in the Shepherd Market area at that time of day. There was an empty car parked on the other side of the road, a man walking by with a brief-bag, two women laden down with parcels puttering in the opposite direction, an errand-boy delivering goods from a tricycle. The commonplace affairs of the district were proceeding uninterrupted, the peace of the neighbourhood was unbroken by so much as a glimpse of any sinister figure with a smoking gun scooting off on the conventional getaway.

Teal's dizzy gaze turned back to his subordinate.

"Did you see him?" he rasped.

"Only his back," said Pryke helplessly. "But I haven't the faintest idea which way he went."

Teal strode across to the errand-boy.

"Did you see a man come rushing out of that building just now?" he barked; and the lad looked at him blankly.

"Wot sort of man, mister?"

"I don't know," said Teal, with a feeling that he was introducing himself as the most majestic lunatic in creation. "He'd have been running hell for leather—you must have noticed him——"

The boy shook his head.

"I ain't seen nobody running abaht, not till you come aht yerself, mister. Wot's the matter—'as 'e pinched something?"

Mr Teal did not enlighten him. Breathing heavily, he rejoined Junior Inspector Pryke.

"We'd better get back upstairs and see what's happened," he said shortly.

But he knew only too well what had happened. The murder of Johnny Anworth had been repeated, in a different guise, under his very nose—and that after he had pleaded so energetically for a chance to guard against it. He did not like to think what ecstatic sarabands of derision must have been dancing themselves silly under the smug exterior of Desmond Pryke. He clumped up the stairs and across the landing again in a dumb paroxysm of futile wrath, and went back into the flat.

And there he halted again, one step inside the room, with his eyes bulging out of their sockets and the last shattered remnants of his traditional pose of sleepiness falling off him like autumn leaves from a tree, staring at what he saw as if he felt that the final vestiges of sanity were reeling away from his overheated mind.

## II

The body of Sunny Jim Fasson was no longer there. That was the brain-staggering fact which Chief Inspector Teal had to assimilate. It had simply ceased to exist. For all the immediate evidence which Teal's reddening gaze could pick up to the contrary, Sunny Jim Fasson might never have lived there, and might never have been interviewed there, and might never have been shot there. The ultimate abysses of interplanetary space could not have been more innocent of any part of Sunny Jim Fasson than that shabby one-room flatlet as Teal saw it then. There could hardly have been much less trace of Sunny Jim if he had never been born.

And instead of that, there was someone else sitting in the chair where the bullet had hit Sunny Jim—a man whose mere recollection was enough to raise Chief Inspector Teal's blood-pressure to apoplectic heights, a man whose appearance on that spot, at that precise catastrophic moment, turned what might have been an ordinary baffling mystery into something that made Mr Teal's voice fail him absolutely for several seconds.

"Stand up, Saint," he got out at last, in a choking gurgle. "I want you!"

The man peeled himself nonchalantly up from the armchair, and managed to convey the impression that he was merely following a course which he had chosen for himself long ago, rather than that he was obeying an order. And Mr Teal glowered at him unblinkingly over every inch of that leisured rise.

To anyone unfamiliar with the dim beginnings and cumulative ramifications of the feud between those two (if anyone so benighted can be imagined to exist in the civilised world) Mr Teal's glower might justifiably have seemed to lack much of the god-like impartiality which ought to smooth the features of a conscientious detective. It was a glower that had no connection with any detached survey of a situation, any abstract weighing of clues and conundrums. It was, to describe it economically, the kind of glower on which eggs can be fried. It was as calorifically biassed and unfriendly as a glower can be.

The Saint didn't seem to notice it. He came upright, a lean wide-shouldered figure in a light grey suit which had a swashbuckling elegance that nothing Inspector Pryke wore would ever have, and met the detective's torrid glare with cool and quizzical blue eyes.

"Hullo, Claud," he murmured. "What are you doing here?"

The detective looked up at him dourly—Teal was not nearly so short as his increasing middle-aged girth made him appear, but he had to look up when the Saint stood beside him.

"I want to know what you're doing here," he retorted.

"I came to pay a call on Sunny Jim," said the Saint calmly. "But he doesn't seem to be here—or did you get here first and knock him off?"

There were times when Mr Teal could exercise an almost super-human restraint.

"I'm hoping to find out who got here first," he said grimly. "Sunny Jim has been murdered."

The Saint raised one eyebrow.

"It sounds awfully exciting," he remarked; and his bantering eyes wandered over to Pryke. "Is this the bloke who did it?"

"This is Junior Inspector Pryke, of C Division," said Mr Teal formally; and the Saint registered ingenuous surprise.

"Is it really?" he murmured. "I didn't know they'd put trousers on the Women Police."

Chief Inspector Teal swallowed hastily; and it is a regrettable fact that a fraction of the inclement ferocity faded momentarily out of his glare. There was no lawful or official reason whatsoever for this tempering of his displeasure, but it was the very first time in his life that he had seen any excuse for the Saint's peculiar sense of humour. He masticated his gum silently for a couple of seconds that gave him time to recover the attitude of mountainous boredom which he was always praying for strength to maintain in the Saint's presence. But his relief was only temporary.

"I suppose you're going to tell me you came to see Fasson just to ask him what he thought about the weather," he said.

"Certainly not," said the Saint blandly. "I wouldn't try to deceive you, Claud. I blew in to see if he knew anything about some diamond bracelets that a bird called Peabody lost this afternoon. I might have pointed out to him that Peabody is very upset about losing those jools. I might have tried to show him the error of his ways, and done my best to persuade him that they ought to be sent back. Or something. But I can't say that I thought of shooting him."

"How did you know he was shot?" Teal cut in.

"My dear fathead, I don't. I merely said that I didn't think of shooting him. Was he shot?"

Teal hesitated for a moment, studying him with that deceptively bovine gaze.

"Yes, he was shot."

"When?"

"Just now."

The bantering blue eyes had an impish twinkle.

"You must have been doing some fast detecting," said the Saint. "Or did somebody tell you?"

Mr Teal frowned at him, shifting his gum from tooth to tooth till he got it lodged behind his wisdoms. His sluggish glance travelled once again over that keen sunburned face, handsome as Lucifer and lighted with an indescribable glimmer of devil-may-care mockery; and he wondered if there would ever be any peace for him so long as he was in the employment of the Law and that amazing buccaneer was on the other side.

For Simon Templar was the incalculable outlaw for whom the routines of criminal investigation had no precedents. He belonged to no watertight classication, followed no rules but his own, fitted into no definite category in the official scheme of things. He was the Saint: a creation of his own, comparable to nothing but himself. From time to time, desperate creatures of that nebulously frontiered stratosphere commonly called "the Underworld" had gone forth vowing unprintable revenge, and had come back empty-handed— when they came back at all. Many times, Chief Inspector Claud Eustace Teal had thought that all his ambitions would be fulfilled if he could see the Saint safely locked away behind the bars of Larkstone Prison—and yet some of his most spectacular coups could never have been made without the Saint's assistance. And in spite of all the wrath that had been directed on him from these diametrically antagonistic quarters, the Saint had still gone on, a terror to the underworld and a thorn in the side of Scotland Yard, a gay crusader in modern dress who returned from his lawless raids with more booty than any adventurer had ever found before him.

And with all these memories freshened in his mind during that slothful survey, almost against his will, Chief Inspector Teal found himself impotent to believe that the High Fence could be merely another alias of the man before him. It was not psychologically possible. Whatever else could be said about him, the Saint was not a man who sat spinning webs and weaving complex but static mysteries. Everything that he did was active: he would go out to break up the web and take his illicit plunder from the man who wove it, but he wouldn't spin . . . And yet there was the evidence of Teal's own flabbergasted senses, there in that room, to be explained away; and Mr Teal had suffered too much at the Saint's hands to feel that there could ever be any comfortable certainty in the wide world when that incorrigible freebooter was around.

He clasped his pudgy hands behind his back and said: "Sunny Jim was shot in this room, less than five minutes ago. Somebody opened the door and shot him while I was talking to him. He was shot just in time to stop him telling me something I very much wanted to hear. And I want to know what you were doing at that time."

The Saint smiled rather mildly.

"Is that an invitation or a threat?" he inquired.

"It's whichever you like to make it," Teal answered grimly. "Sunny Jim didn't shoot himself, and I'm going to find out who did it."

"I'm sure you are, Claud," said the Saint cordially. "You always do find out these things, with that marvellous brain of yours. . . . Have you thought of the High Fence?"

Teal nodded.

"I have."

"What do you know about the High Fence?" demanded Pryke suspiciously.

Simon took out his cigarette-case and looked at him equably.

"This and that. I've been looking for him for some time, you know."

"What do you want with the High Fence, Saint?" asked Mr Teal.

Simon Templar glanced with unwontedly passionless eyes at the chair where Sunny Jim had stopped talking, and smiled with his lips. He lighted a cigarette.

"The High Fence has killed two men," he said. "Wouldn't you like a chance to see him in the dock at the Old Bailey?"

"That isn't all of it," answered the detective stubbornly. "You know as well as I do that the High Fence is supposed to keep a lot of the stuff he buys together, and ship it out of the country in big loads. And they say he keeps a lot of cash in hand as well—for buying."

The glimmer of mockery in the Saint's eyes crisped up into an instant of undiluted wickedness.

"Teal, this is all news to me!"

"You're a liar," said the detective flatly.

He stared at the Saint with all the necessary symptoms of a return of his unfriendly glower, and added: "I know what your game is. You *know* the High Fence; but you don't know what he does with the stuff he's bought, or where he keeps his money. That's all you want to find out before you do anything about putting him in the dock at the Old Bailey on a charge of murder. And when that time comes, you'll buy a new car and pay some more cash into your bank balance. That's all the interest you have in these two men who've been killed."

"I can't get around to feeling that either of them is an irreparable loss," Simon admitted candidly. "But what's all this dramatic lecture leading to?"

"It's leading to this," said Teal relentlessly. "There's a law about what you're doing, and it's called being an accessory after the fact."

Simon aligned both eyebrows. The sheer unblushing impudence of his ingenuousness brought a premonitory tinge of violet into the detective's complexion even before he spoke.

"I suppose you know what you're talking about, Claud," he drawled. "But I don't. And if you want to make that speech again in a court of law, they'll want you to produce a certain amount of proof. It's an old legal custom." Only for the second time in that interview, Simon looked straight at him instead of smiling right through him. "There's a lot of laws about what you're doing; and they're called slander, and defamation of character, and——"

"I don't care what they're called!"

"But you've got to care," said the Saint reasonably. "After all, you're telling me that a bloke's been shot, and that I did it, or I know something about it. Well, let's begin at the beginning. Let's be sure the bloke's dead. Where's his body?"

In spite of certain superficial resemblances, it can be fairly positively stated that Chief Inspector Teal had never, even in some distant incarnation, been a balloon. But if he had been, and the point of a pin had been strategically applied to the most delicate part of his rotundity, it would have had practically the same effect as the Saint's innocently mooted question. Something that had been holding out his chest seemed to deflate, leaving behind it an expanding and exasperating void. He felt as if someone had unscrewed his navel and his stomach had fallen out.

The cigar which had slipped stupidly out of Sunny Jim's mouth when the bullet hit him was lying on the carpet in front of him, tainting the room with an acrid smell of singeing wool. Teal put his foot on it. It was his only concrete assurance that the whole fantastic affair hadn't been a grotesque hallucination—that the overworked brain which had struggled through so many of the Saint's shattering surprises hadn't finally weighed its anchor and gone wallowing off into senile monsoons of delirious delusion. His lips thinned out in an effort of self-control which touched the borders of homicidal fever.

"That's what I want to know," he said. "The body was here when I went out. When I came in again it had disappeared—and you were here instead. And I think you know something about it."

"My dear Claud," Simon protested, "what d'you think I am—a sort of amateur body-snatcher?"

"I think you're a——"

Simon raised his hand.

"Hush," he said, with a nervous glance at Inspector Pryke. "Not before the lady."

Teal gulped.

"I think——"

"The trouble is," said the Saint, "that you don't. Here you are shooting off your mouth about a body, and nobody knows whether it exists. You wonder whether I could have shot Sunny Jim, when you don't even know whether he's dead. You hint at pinching me for being an accessory after the fact, and you can't produce the fact that I'm supposed to be an accessory to."

"I can prove——"

"You can't. You can't prove anything, except your own daftness. You're doing that now. You ask me what's happened to Sunny Jim's body, with the idea that I must have done something with it. But if you can't produce this body, how d'you know it ever was a body?

How d'you know it didn't get up and walk out while you were away? How d'you know any crime's been committed at all?" The Saint's lean forefinger shot out and tapped the detective peremptorily on the waistcoat, just above his watch-chain. "You're going to make a prize idiot of yourself again, Claud, if you aren't very careful; and one of these days I shall be very angry with you. I put up with the hell of a lot of persecution from you——"

"Will you stop that?" barked Mr Teal, jerking his tummy hysterically back from the prodding finger.

The Saint smiled.

"I am stopping it, dear old pumpkin," he pointed out. "I've just told you that my patience is all wore out. I'm not taking any more. Now you go ahead and think out your move. Do you take a chance on running me in for murdering a bloke that nobody can prove was murdered, and stealing a corpse that nobody can prove is a corpse—or do you phone for your photographers and fingerprint fakers and leave me out of it?"

Glowering at him in a supercharged silence that strained against his ribs, Mr Teal thought of all the things he would have liked to do, and realised that he could do none of them. He was tied up in a knot which there was no visible way of unravelling. He had seen similar knots wound round him too often to cherish any illusions on that score—had gorged his spleen too often on the maddeningly confident challenges of that debonair picaroon to hope that any amount of thought could make this one more digestible.

It was airtight and watertight. It was as smooth as the Saint's languid tantalising voice. It located the one unanswerable loophole in the situation, and strolled through it with as much room to spare as an ant going through the Arc de Triomphe. It was exactly the sort of thing that the Saint could always be relied upon to do.

The knowledge soaked down into Mr Teal's interior like a dose of molten lead. The ancient duel was embarking upon the umpteenth round of a series which seemed capable of going on into eternity; and the prospect seemed as hopeless as it had always seemed. If Mr Teal had any formulated idea of hell, it was something exactly like that—an endless succession of insoluble riddles that he had to try to solve, while the Saint's impudent forefinger and the Assistant Commissioner's disparaging sniff worked in alternate relays to goad his thoughts away from the last relics of coherence. And there were moments when he wondered if he had already died without knowing it, and was already paying for his long-forgotten sins.

"You can go for the present," he said smolderingly. "I'll find you again when I want you."

"I'm afraid you will," said the Saint sadly, and adjusted the brim of his hat to the correct piratical angle. "Well, I'll be seein' ya, Claud Eustace. . . ." He turned his vague unspeakably mischievous smile on to Junior Inspector Pryke, who had been standing sulkily mute since he was last noticed. "And you too, Sweet Pea," he said hopefully.

Chief Inspector Claud Eustace Teal watched his departure with malignant gloom. It was discouragingly reminiscent of too many other Saintly exits that Mr Teal had witnessed, and he had a very apathetic interest in the flashlight photography and fingerprint dusting which he had to superintend during the next hour or two.

For those records were made only at the dictation of a system in which Mr Teal was too congenitally rut-sunk to question. There was a fire escape within easy reach of the bathroom window which had more to tell than any number of photographs of an empty chair from which an unproven corpse had disappeared.

Sunny Jim Fasson had been shot at by somebody who had opened the door of the flatlet while Mr Teal was interrogating him, the same somebody who had found means of silencing Johnny Anworth on the verge of an identically similar squeak; after which Fasson had vanished off the face of the earth. And Teal had a seething conviction that the only living man who knew every secret of what had happened was walking free in the Saint's custom-built shoes.

The Assistant Commissioner was very polite.

"But it has possibly failed to occur to you," he commented, "that this is the sort of thing news editors pray for."

"If you remember, sir," Pryke put in smugly, "I was against the idea from the first."

"Quite," said the Commissioner. "Quite." He was a man who had won his appointment largely on the qualification of a distinguished career of pig-sticking and polo-playing with the Indian Army, and he was inclined to sympathise with the officer whom he regarded as a pukka sahib, like himself. "But you went with Mr Teal, and you may know why Templar was not at least arrested on suspicion."

"On suspicion of what?" demanded Teal wildly. "The worst you could prove is that he abetted Fasson's escape; and that means nothing, because Fasson hadn't even been arrested."

Pryke nibbled his thumbnail.

"I believe that if we could account for the Saint, the rest of the mystery would be settled," he said.

"Mr Teal has been trying to account for the Saint for several years," the Assistant Commissioner reminded him acrimoniously.

What Mr Teal wanted to say would have reduced Scotland Yard to a small pool of steaming lava.

## III

Simon Templar sauntered around the corners of a couple of blocks, and presently waited by the kerb while a big grey saloon cruised slowly up towards him. As it came level, he stepped neatly on to the running-board, opened the nearest door, and sank into the seat beside the driver. As if the upholstery on which he deposited his weight had had some direct connection with the accelerator, the car picked up speed again and shot away into the traffic with its engine purring so smoothly that the leap of the speedometer needle seemed an absurd exaggeration.

With her small deft hands on the steering wheel, nosing a way through the traffic stream where no one else but the Saint himself would have seen a way visible, Patricia Holm took her eyes momentarily from the road to glance at him helplessly.

"What on earth," she inquired, "are we playing at?"

The Saint chuckled.

"Is the game puzzling you, old darling?"

"It's doing its best." She took his cigarette away from between his fingers while she thrust the murmuring grey car under the snout of a speeding lorry with the other hand. "You come down this way to see Fasson about some diamonds. You and Hoppy go in to see him. After a while Hoppy comes out with a body; and a long time after that you come out yourself, looking as if you'd just heard the funniest story of your life. Naturally I'm beginning to wonder what we're playing at."

Simon took out his cigarette case and replaced his stolen smoke.

"I suppose you aren't so wide of the mark, with the funny story angle," he admitted. "But I thought Hoppy would have put you on the trail."

He slewed round to cock an eyebrow at the passenger who rode in the back seat; but the passenger gazed back at him with troubled blankness and said: "I dunno what de game is, neider, boss."

Hoppy Uniatz had never been really beautiful even as a child,

and the various contacts which his face had had with blunt instruments since then had not improved it. But it has sometimes been
known for such faces to be lighted with a radiance of spirituality
and intellect in which their battered irregularity of contour is easily
forgotten.

The physiognomy of Mr Uniatz was illuminated by no such light.
Reluctant as Simon Templar always was to disparage such a faithful
friend, he could never honestly claim for Mr Uniatz any of those
intellectual qualities which might have redeemed his other failings.
A man of almost miraculous agility on the draw, of simple and unquestioning loyalties, of heroic appetite, and of a tank-like capacity
for absorbing incredible quantities of every conceivable blend of
alcohol—yes, Mr Uniatz possessed all those virtues. But a strenuous
pursuit of most of the minor rackets of the Bowery had never left
him time to develop the higher faculties of that curious organisation
of reactions which can only apologetically be called his brain. Simon
Templar perceived that Mr Uniatz could not have enlightened anybody. He was in painful search of enlightenment himself.

Simon dropped an arm over the back of the seat and hauled up
another hitherto invisible passenger, on whom Mr Uniatz had been
thoughtlessly resting his feet.

"This is Sunny Jim, Pat," he explained.

"Hoppy did manage to tell me that much," said Patricia Holm
with great patience. "But did you really have to bring him away?"

"Not really," said the Saint candidly, allowing the passenger to
drop back again on to the floor. "But it struck me as being quite
a good idea. You see, Sunny Jim is supposed to be dead."

"How do you know he isn't?"

Simon grinned.

"There might be some argument about it," he conceded. "At any
rate, he's among the Saints."

"But what was it all about?"

The Saint lighted his cigarette and stretched himself out.

"Well, it was this way. Hoppy and I blew up the fire escape, as
arranged, and went in through the bathroom window. When we got
inside, what should we hear but the voice of good old Claud Eustace
Teal, holding converse with Sunny Jim. Apparently Claud was just
on the point of getting a squeak out of him, and I was just getting
down to the keyhole to take a look at the séance and hear what
Sunny had to say, when a gun went off and broke up the party. As
far as I've been able to make out, somebody opened the front door

and took a pot at Sunny Jim at the crucial moment, and Teal went chasing the assassin down the stairs, along with a perfectly twee little policebody from Eton that he had with him."

Simon drew at his cigarette with a reminiscent smile, while the grey car whirled around Piccadilly Circus and plunged down the Haymarket.

"Anyway, Hoppy and I beetled in while they were away, and took a gander at Sunny Jim. And as a matter of fact, he isn't dead; though he's had the narrowest shave that any man ever had, and his head's going to ring carillons when he wakes up. He's been creased as neatly as I've seen it done—the bullet just parted his hair in a new place and knocked him out, but his skull hasn't any holes in it. That's when I had my brilliant idea."

"I was hoping we'd get to that," said the girl.

"But haven't you seen it already?" Simon demanded. "Look at what I've told you! Here's Sunny Jim preparing to squeal, and somebody tries to rub him out. Why? Squealers don't get bumped off, not in this country, just because they may have a little titbit to give away. Sunny Jim must have known something worth knowing; and there he was, sitting in his chair, out to the world, and nobody to get in our way. The bumper-offer can't be sure what's happened to him, and Claud Eustace is probably quite sure he's dead. But nobody knows. . . . Isn't it all pretty obvious?"

"It's getting clearer."

"Of course it is! I tell Hoppy to grab the body and hustle it down the fire escape, out to this car, and pick me up later. And I wait for Claud Eustace and his boy friend. We exchange the compliments of the season, and have lots of fun and games together. And then I walk out. As soon as the next editions are on the streets, the bumper-offer is going to know that his body disappeared while I was around, and he's going to work himself into seven different kinds of cold sweat wondering whether it *is* a body. He may guess that it isn't, and itch to bump me off for what I may have found out from it; but he can't do that because if I got killed he'd never know what had happened to the body and where it might turn up next. Doesn't that make you see the joke?"

Patricia nodded slowly.

"But who," she said, "was the bumper-offer?"

"Who else could it be," asked the Saint, "but our old friend that all the excitement and bubble is about—the High Fence?"

There were adequate grounds for the outbreak of official excitement and bubble which had been provoked by the man who was known only by that unusual name.

A fence, in the argot, is nothing to do with steeplechasing or an enclosure containing sheep. He is the receiver of stolen goods, the capitalist of crime, and incidentally the middleman but for whose functioning larceny in most of its forms would soon die a natural death. He runs less risk than any of the actual stealers, and makes much bigger profits. And very often he takes his cut both ways, making his profit on the receipt of stolen goods and betraying the stealers to a friendly detective at the same time.

The fence is a member of an unchartered union, the only code of which is to pay as little for a purchase as the vendor can be persuaded to accept.

Seven or eight months ago, the invisible tentacles of the CID which spread wider and more delicately than many of its critics would believe, touched on the humour of a man who violated that rule. He bought nothing but metals and precious stones, and paid twice as much for them as any other receiver in London was offering. By contenting himself with a hundred percent profit instead of three hundred percent he could well afford to do it; but it is a curious fact that no other receiver before him had thought of such a scandalously unethical expedient. And through the strange subterranean channels in which such gossip circulates, the word went round that he was "good".

Because of the prices he paid, they called him the High Fence; but nobody knew anything more about him. He had no shop where he conducted his business. Anything that was offered to him for sale had to be sent through the post, to an accommodation address which was changed every week. The address was passed round the limited circle of his clients by word of mouth, and it was impossible to find out who first put it into circulation. Every client had always "heard about it" from another—the trail turned inevitably into a hopeless merry-go-round. Nor was the circle of initiates unrestricted. It was a jealously closed ring of talent which the High Fence picked for himself; and queer things were rumoured to have happened to those who had ventured to spread the good news among their friends without permission. To those who were tempted by circumstances to talk to the CID even queerer things could happen—as we have shown.

The High Fence might never have encountered a serious setback, if there had not been one outlaw in England for whom queer happenings had no terrors, and to whom the scent of booty was the supreme perfume in the breath of life.

"I'm afraid Claud Eustace has a depressingly cynical idea of what I'm up to," said the Saint. "He thinks I know who the High Fence is—in which he's flattering me too much, and I wish he wasn't. And he thinks that all I'm wanting is to find out where this bird keeps his boodle and his cash, so that I can take it off him before he gets pinched."

"In which he's perfectly right."

The Saint sighed.

"I don't know where you get these ideas from," he said in a pained voice. "By the way, are you going anywhere in particular, or are we just sightseeing?"

"I'm waiting for you to tell me."

"Let's go to Abbot's Yard—it's about the only hideout we have left that isn't in Teal's address-book. And I don't think Sunny Jim is going to be too keen on seeing callers for a while."

He relaxed at full length, with his eyes half closed against the smoke curling past them from his cigarette, while she circled Sloane Square and headed west along the King's Road. The soft waves of her fair golden head rippled in the gentle stir of air that came through the windows; her face was as calmly beautiful as if she had been driving them on nothing less innocuous than the commonplace sightseeing tour which he had mentioned. Perhaps she was only calm because even the most adventurous girl, after some years of partnership with such a man, must achieve permanent nonchalance or perish of nervous exhaustion; but one never knew. . . . And in the back of the car, Mr Uniatz and Mr Fasson were both, in their respective ways, silently unconscious.

The car threaded its way more slowly through the clotted congestion of trucks, omnibuses, vans, and drays with which the King's Road is permanently constipated, and turned off abruptly into a narrow side street composed of cottage hovels with freshly painted and utterly dilapidated fronts in approximately equal proportions. It was one of those Chelsea backwaters which are undergoing a gloomy degradation from honest slumdom to synthetic Bohemianism, and the external symptoms of its decay gave it an air of almost pathetic indecision, like a suburban bank manager on a spree in the high spots, who is trying to make up his mind whether to be thoroughly folksy or very dignified, but who is quite certain that he is as sober and important as any of his co-revellers. But in spite of this uninviting aspect, it contained a comfortable studio which the Saint had found useful before; and Simon roused himself cheerfully to open the door beside him as the car stopped.

"I think it's a case for the wheelchair and blanket," he said, after a judicial survey of Sunny Jim.

The transportation of an unconscious captive across a London pavement is not quite such an easy and automatic affair as the credulous reader of fiction may have been deluded to believe; but Simon Templar had had such problems to solve before. On one of the rare occasions on which Mr Uniatz did not find it necessary to delay the proceedings with unnecessary questions, he hopped intelligently out of the car and opened the door of the studio with a key which the Saint threw at him. After a brief absence, he returned with an invalid chair. Simon took the folded blanket from the seat, and between them they wrapped the limp figure of Sunny Jim Fasson tenderly up in it—so tenderly that there was not enough of him left protruding for any stray passerby to recognise. In this woolly cocoon they carried him to the chair, and in the chair wheeled him up the steps and into the house, with all the hushed solicitude of two expectant nephews handling a rich and moribund uncle. And, really, that was all about it.

"There is beer in the pantry," said the Saint, subsiding into a chair in the studio. "But don't let Hoppy see it, or I never shall. Hoppy, you get a sponge of cold water and see if you can bring the patient round."

"He does wake up, once," said Mr Uniatz reminiscently. "In de car. But I club him wit' de end of my Betsy and he goes to sleep again."

Simon gazed after him resignedly, and sipped the glass of Carlsberg which Patricia brought to him. A sense of tact and diplomacy could well be added to the other virtues in which Mr Uniatz was so unfortunately deficient. Hoping to extract information from a man by presenting oneself to him as his saviour and honorary guardian angel, one endeavours to calm the aching brain. One tends the wounds. One murmurs consolation and soothing comfort. One does not, intelligently, greet him on his first return to consciousness by clubbing him with the blunt end of a Betsy. It rather ruled out the potentialities of guile and cunning; but the Saint was equally prepared for the alternative.

He finished his cigarette at leisure while Mr Uniatz applied his belated ministrations; and presently an inaugural groan from the invalid chair brought him up to take over the management of the interview.

"Welcome, stranger," he said genially.

## IV

Sunny Jim Fasson did not seem happy. It is not overstimulating for any man with less solid bone in the head than a Mr Uniatz to first have his skull grazed by a bullet, and then at the first sign of recovery from that ordeal to be slugged over the ear with a gun-butt; and certainly much of the sunshine from which Sunny Jim had once taken his nickname was missing from his countenance. With the damp traces of Hoppy's first-aid practice trickling down his nose and chin, he looked more like a picture of *November Day* than one of *Hail, Smiling Morn*.

It was perhaps discouraging that the first person he saw when he blinked open his eyes was Hoppy Uniatz. He stared at him hazily for a moment, while his memory worked painfully back to its last association with that homely face; and then, remembering all, he half rose from the chair and lashed out with his fist. That was also discouraging, for Mr Uniatz had won his scars in a vocation where the various arts of violence are systematised to the ultimate degree: he hopped aside from the blow with an agility that gave an unexpected meaning to his name, and in another split second he had caught Sunny Jim's wrist and twisted it firmly up behind his back.

He looked round at the Saint with a beam of justifiable pride, like a puppy that has performed its latest trick. If he had had a tail, he would have wagged it.

"Okay, boss?" he queried. "Or do I give him de heat?"

"That remains to be seen," said the Saint imperturbably. He picked up the sponge and weighed it meditatively in his hand. "Is your brain working again, Sunny, or would you like another refresher?"

Fasson glowered at him sullenly, with a hint of fear in his eyes.

"What do you want?" he snarled.

"Personally, I only want a little talk." Simon weighed the sponge again, and dropped it back in the basin. "But Hoppy seems to have other ideas. By the way, have you met Hoppy? This is Mr Uniatz, Jim—a one hundred percent American from Poland."

"I know him," said Fasson viciously. "He hit me over the head with his gun."

"So he tells me," agreed the Saint, with some regret. "Otherwise this little chat of ours might have been much more amicable. But he's quite a tough guy in his way, is Hoppy; and he's got a kind of natural habit of hitting people with his gun—either with one end or the other. Do you know what he means when he talks about giving you the heat?"

Sunny Jim did not answer. Studying that suspicious surly face from which all the artificial sunshine had been removed, Simon realised that the friendly conversazione which he had had in mind at the beginning would have wanted a lot of organising, even without Hoppy's intervening indiscretion.

"Well, he might mean one of two things, Sunny. He might mean taking you for a ride—ferrying you out to some nice secluded spot and dropping you in a ditch with a tummy-full of liver pills. Or he might mean just making himself sort of unpleasant—twisting your arm off, or burning your feet, or some jolly little romp like that. I never know, with Hoppy. He gets such fascinating ideas. Only the other day, he got hold of a fellow he didn't care for and tied him out on an iron bedstead and burnt candles under the springs—the bloke was awfully annoyed about it."

"Who are you?" rasped Fasson shakily.

The Saint smiled.

"Templar is the name, dear old bird. Simon Templar. Of course, there are all sorts of funny rumours about my having another name —people seem to think I'm some sort of desperado called . . . let me see, what is it?"

The fear in Sunny Jim's eyes brightened into a sudden spark of panic.

"I know who you are," he said. "You're the Saint!"

Simon raised his eyebrows innocently.

"The very name I was trying to remember. People think——"

"You're the High Fence!"

Simon shook his head.

"Oh, no. You're wrong about that."

"You're the swine who tried to shoot me just now."

"Wrong again, brother. When I try to shoot people, they don't usually have a chance to be rude to me afterwards. But don't let's talk about unpleasant things like that." The Saint flipped out his cigarette-case and put a smoke between his lips. "Let's be friendly as long as we can. I didn't shoot you, but I happened into your place just after the shooting. I sort of felt that you couldn't be feeling too happy about the way things were going, so I shifted you out of there. But I still think we ought to have a talk."

Fasson's shifty eyes travelled round the room, and came back to the Saint's face. He answered through his teeth.

"I can't tell you anything."

"Perhaps you haven't quite recovered yet," said the Saint persuasively. "After all, you were going to tell Chief Inspector Teal something. By the way, have you met Mr Uniatz? Only the other day——"

"I don't know anything!"

Hoppy Uniatz shuffled his feet. It is improbable that more than two consecutive words of the conversation which has just been recorded had percolated through the protective layers of ivory that encased his brain; but he had a nebulous idea that time was being wasted, and he could not see why.

"Do I give him de heat, boss?" he inquired hopefully.

Simon inhaled thoughtfully; and Mr Uniatz, taking silence for an answer, strengthened his grip. Fasson's face twisted and turned pale.

"Wait a minute!" he gasped shrilly. "You're breaking my arm!"

"That's too bad," said the Saint concernedly. "What does it feel like?"

"You can't do this to me!" shrieked Sunny Jim. "He'd kill me! You know what happened just now——"

"I know," said the Saint coolly. "But there are lots of different ways of dying. Hoppy knows no end of exciting ones, and I've tried to warn you about him. I don't really want to have to let him go ahead with what he's wanting to do, instead of just playing at it as he is now; but if you've absolutely made up your mind. . . ."

Sunny Jim gulped. The sharp agony in his shoulder, where Hoppy Uniatz's powerful leverage was exerting itself, made the other unpleasant possibilities which the Saint had hinted at seem frightfully close at hand; but he could not find a shadow of pity or remorse in the clear blue eyes that were studying him with the dispassionate curiosity of an entomologist watching the wriggling of a captured insect.

"Do you want me to be murdered?" he sobbed.

"I shouldn't weep at your funeral," Simon confessed coldbloodedly. "But I shouldn't look at things so pessimistically, if I were you. We could probably look after you for a bit, if you told us anything worth knowing—we might even get you out of the country and send you away for a holiday in the South of France until the excitement's all over. But you've got to spill what you know first, and I'm waiting for it to dawn on you that you'll either talk voluntarily or else we'll put you through the mangle and wring it out of you."

His voice was casual and almost kindly; but there was something so tireless and inflexible behind it that Sunny Jim shivered. He was no hothouse flower himself; but in the circles where he moved there were stories about the Saint, brought in by men who had met that amazing buccaneer to their misfortune—legends that told of a slim bantering outlaw whose smile was more deadly than any other man's anger, who faced death with a jest and sent men into eternity with his flippant farewell ringing in their ears. . . . The pain in his shoulder sharpened under Hoppy's impatient hands, and he saw that the Saint's dark lawless face was quite impassive, with the trace of an old smile lingering absentmindedly on the reckless lips. . . .

"Damn you!" he whimpered. "I'll talk. . . . But you've got to let me go."

"Tell me something first."

Fasson's breath came in a grating sigh.

"The Kosy Korner—in Holborn——"

Simon blew a couple of smoke-rings, and nodded to Mr Uniatz.

"Okay, Hoppy," he said. "Give him a rest."

Hoppy Uniatz released his grip, and wiped his palms down his trousers. In so far as his gargoyle features were capable of expressing such an emotion, he looked shocked. As one who had himself kept an iron jaw under everything that could be handed to him in the back rooms of more than one station house in his own country, the spectacle of a guy who came apart under a mere preliminary treatment filled him with the same half-incredulous disgust that an English gentleman feels on meeting a cad who is not interested in cricket.

"I guess dese Limeys can't take it, boss," he said, groping through genuine puzzlement to the only possible conclusion.

Sunny Jim glared at him in vengeful silence. His face was white with pain, and his shoulder really felt as if it had been dislocated. He rubbed it tenderly, while Simon recovered his beer and sat on the edge of the table.

"Well?" Simon prompted him gently.

"I don't know anything much. I've told you——"

"Have you traded with the High Fence before?"

"Yes." Sunny Jim sat hunched in his chair, shrugging his shoulder gingerly in an occasional effort to reassure himself that the joints were still articulating. The words dragged reluctantly through his mouth. "That's how I know. I wanted to know who the High Fence was. I sent him some stuff once, and waited outside the address to see who picked it up. I saw who took it. I started to tail him, but then I got picked up by a split, and I lost him while we were talking."

"But?"

"I saw him again the next day, by accident. In this restaurant."

"The Kosy Korner?"

Fasson nodded, and licked his lips.

"Can I have a drink?" he asked hoarsely.

The Saint made a sign to Hoppy, who abandoned his futile attempt to drain nonexistent dregs out of the bottle from which Simon had refilled his glass and left the room. The Saint's cool blue eyes did not leave Sunny Jim's face.

"And what happened there?"

Fasson got out of his chair and limped around the table, rubbing his head dazedly.

"This fellow shoved the packet in the pocket of an overcoat that was hanging on the rail——"

At that moment he was beside the empty bottle which Mr Uniatz had put down; and for once Simon Templar's understanding was a fraction of a second slow. He did not clearly comprehend what was happening until the neck of the bottle was clutched in Sunny Jim's fist, swinging up and spinning away from the hand with vicious speed.

With an instinct that was swifter than any reasoned understanding, he ducked his head and felt the cold graze of the glass stroking past his ear before it splintered on the wall behind him with an explosive smash; but that automatic movement of self-preservation lost him a vital second of time. He rolled off the table and leapt for the door, only to have it slammed in his face; and when he had wrenched it open again Sunny Jim's footsteps were clattering wildly down the second flight of stairs.

Sunny Jim Fasson tore out into the narrow street and started to run down towards the bright lights of the main thoroughfare. He didn't know exactly where he was going, but he knew that his one broad object was to remove himself as quickly as possible from the city where so many deadly things had begun to happen in one evening. Chance had given him one infinitesimal spark of knowledge that he should not have possessed, normal psychology had tempted him to use it in the purchase of his freedom when Chief Inspector Teal had called; but he had not thought of the retribution. Of what had happened since that brain-dulling bullet grazed across his head he preferred not to think; but he had a foggy idea that whichever way he turned in that perilous tangle would lead him into new dangers. He had had one warning that day. To be killed for squealing, to be tortured and perhaps killed for not squealing—he saw nothing but trouble in every prospect that was offered to him, except the one primitive remedy of frantic flight. He stumbled into the King's Road with his chest heaving, and hesitated on the corner in a moment's ghastly indecision. . . . A motorcycle with a particularly noisy exhaust had started up behind him, but he did not think to look round. It seemed to backfire twice in quick succession; and a tearing shattering agony beside which Hoppy Uniatz's third degree was a fleabite crashed into his back and sent him sprawling blindly forward into the gutter. . . .

Simon Templar stood in the half-open doorway and saw the motorcycle whip round the corner and vanish with its engine roaring. He was aware that Hoppy Uniatz was breathing heavily down his neck, making strange grunting noises in an ecstasy of impatience to get past him.

"Lemme go after him an' give him de woiks, boss," he was pleading. "I'll get him, sure."

The Saint's fingers were still curled over the butt of his own gun, which he had not had time to draw.

"You're too late, Hoppy," he said quietly. "He's got the works."

He stepped back into the hall and moved aside to let Mr Uniatz look out. A small crowd was gathering round the spreadeagled shape on the corner, and the wail of a police whistle drifted faintly over the rumble of untroubled traffic. Simon closed the door again.

"So ya had him on de spot," said Mr Uniatz, with proper admiration. "Chees, boss, you got it all on de top storey. Howja know he was gonna take a powder?"

"I didn't," said the Saint evenly, and went back up the stairs to Patricia.

He knew of nobody who would mourn the passing of Sunny Jim for long, and his own regret for the untimely accident was as sincere as anyone's.

"We'll be moving, kid," he said. "Sunny Jim has clocked out."

"Did you shoot him?"

He shook his head.

"That was the mistake Hoppy made. But I hadn't any reason to. There was a bloke waiting outside on a motorbike, and he got him —it may have been the High Fence himself. I thought this address was our own secret, but somebody else seems to have got on to it. So we'll move on." He lighted another cigarette and trickled an airy feather of smoke through his lips, while Hoppy came plodding up to join them; and she saw that his blue eyes were as bright and cold as steel. "We've lost our insurance policy, old dear. But there may be something better than an insurance policy at the Kosy Korner; and I'm going to find out what it is if I eat there till I'm poisoned!"

## V

Of the millions of people who read of the vanishing and double murder of Sunny Jim Fasson at their breakfast tables the next morning—the ingredients of the case were sensational enough to give it a place on the front page of every newspaper that had a front page— a certain Mr Clive Enderby was not the least perturbed.

Nobody who saw him going to his office that morning would have thought it. Nobody who looked at him with a cynical eye would have suspected him of ever being perturbed about anything. Nobody would have suspected him of thinking about anything. Pottering down the steps of his oldfashioned apartment in Ladbroke Grove, he looked like a typical middle-aged British business man.

He was rather thin and long-faced, a little stooped about the shoulders, a little flat about the feet, a little under-exercised about the stomach. These things were not positive characteristics, but rather vague and diffident tendencies: to have been positive about anything would have been bad form, a vulgar demonstration in which only temperamental foreigners (a subhuman species) indulged. He wore a respectable bowler hat, and, although it was clear and warm, a dark overcoat and brown kid gloves, because the calendar had not yet announced the official advent of summer. He rode to Holborn Circus on a bus, ingesting his current opinions on every subject under the sun from the *Morning Post*. No one would have believed that under the crown of that respectable and unemphatic derby he held the key to a riddle that was working Scotland Yard into a lather of exasperation.

From Holborn Circus he walked to Hatton Garden. His office was on the third floor of a sombre building just off that most unhorticultural preserve, where the greatest jewel business in the world is conducted by nondescript men at street corners and over the tables of adjacent cafés and public houses. It consisted of no more than a couple of shabby unpretentious rooms, but a surprising volume of trade in precious stones passed through it. For three hours Mr Enderby was fully occupied, in his slow-moving way, poring over an accumulation of letters and cables from all parts of the world, and dictating stodgy replies to his unattractive secretary, who could have coped efficiently with two hundred and fifty words a minute but in Mr Enderby's employment had never been strained to a higher average than ten.

At a quarter past twelve he had a telephone call.

"Where are you lunching?" asked the voice.

Mr Enderby showed no surprise or puzzlement at being bluntly addressed with such a question by a caller who did not even announce his identity.

"I thought of going to the Kosy Korner again," he said primly.

He had a voice rather like an apologetic frog.

"That'll do," said the receiver, after a moment's thought; and a click terminated the conversation without further ceremony.

Mr Enderby put down the telephone and ponderously finished dictating the letter in which he had been interrupted. He got up, put on his bowler hat and his superfluous overcoat, and went out. On his way through Hatton Garden he stopped and bought two stones from an acquaintance on the pavement, wrapping them in bits of tissue paper and tucking them away in his waistcoat pocket.

The Kosy Korner is one of those glorified tearooms run by impoverished dowagers of stupendous refinement with which the central areas of London are infested. At the time when Mr Enderby arrived there, it was already well filled with an assortment of business men, clerks, stenographers, and shop assistants, all apparently yearning after a spot of Kosiness to stimulate their digestion of that exquisite roast beef and boiled cabbage which has made English cooking famous among gourmets the world over. Mr Enderby filtered through the mob to a groaning coat-rack already laden with the outer garments of other customers, where he parked his bowler hat and overcoat. He sat in a vacant chair and ate his meal as if it were a necessary evil, a dull routine business of stoking his interior with the essential fuel for continued functioning, reading the *Morning Post* between mouthfuls and paying no attention to anyone else in the place. He washed the repast down with a cup of tea, folded his paper, paid his bill, pushed two coppers under the plate, and got up. He took down his hat from the rack and sorted out his overcoat. There was a small parcel in one side pocket, as he felt when he fished out his gloves, which had not been there when he hung up the coat; but even this did not make him register any surprise. He did not even take it out to see what it was.

Back in his office, Mr Enderby spoke to his secretary.

"I had a large order at lunch for some stones to go to America," he said. "They will have to catch the *Oceanic* tomorrow. Will you ring up the insurance company and make the usual arrangements?"

While she was at the telephone, he broke open the parcel from his overcoat pocket and spilled a small handful of diamonds on to his blotter. He looked at them for a moment, and then turned to the safe behind his desk. It was a comparatively new one of the very latest design, a huge gleaming hulk of steel which would have seemed more at home in a bank vault than in that dingy room. He set the two combinations, turned a key in the lock, and swung back the massive door. There was nothing on the shelves but a couple of cheap cardboard boxes. He took them out and tipped their contents on to the blotter also, submerging the first sprinkle of diamonds which he had put down. A solid heaped cone of glittering wealth, diamonds, emeralds, sapphires, and rubies, iridescent with all the colours of the rainbow, winked up at him.

"That will be all right, Mr Enderby," said his secretary. "They're sending a man round right away."

Mr Enderby nodded, and dragged his eyes away from the pile of jewels to glance at the cheap tin clock on the mantelpiece. He was not, as we have seen, very interested in food; but for more years than he could remember he had had a passionate interest in drink. And the hour had not yet struck when such satanic temptations are officially removed from a nation which would otherwise be certain to spend all its afternoons in drunken debauchery.

"I must leave you to pack them up and attend to the formalities, Miss Weagle," he said. "I have—er—another appointment."

Miss Weagle's stoat-like face did not move a single impolite muscle, although she had listened to a similar ritual every working day for the past five years, and knew perfectly well where Mr Enderby's appointment would be kept. She was not even surprised that he should leave such a collection of gems in her care, for the casualness with which diamond traders handle huge fortunes in stones is only incredible to the layman.

"Very well, Mr Enderby. What is the value of the shipment?"

"Twentyseven thousand six hundred and fifty pounds," replied Mr Enderby, after an almost imperceptible deliberation; and he knew his business so well that the most expert and laborious valuation could not have disputed his snap assessment by more than a five-pound note.

He put on his bowler hat and overcoat again, and paddled thirstily out to the streets, mumbling an apology to the red-faced walrus-moustached man whom he had to squeeze past at the top of the narrow stairs; and the walrus-moustached man gazed after him with thoughtful blue eyes which would have seemed incongruously keen and clear if Mr Enderby had noticed them.

The Saint went back across the landing as Mr Enderby's footsteps died away, and knocked on the door of the office.

"I'm from the insurance company," he said, when Miss Weagle had let him in.

"About the jewels?"

"Yes."

With his walrus moustache and air of disillusioned melancholy, he reminded Miss Weagle of her mother.

"You've been quick," she said, making conversation when she ought to have been making love.

"I was out on a job, and I had to ring up the office from just round the corner, so they told me to come along," Simon explained, wiping his whiskers on his sleeve. He had spent three hours putting on that ragged growth, and every hair was so carefully planted that its falsehood could not have been detected at much closer quarters than he was ever likely to get to with Miss Weagle. He glanced at the little heap of gems, which Miss Weagle had been packing into another cardboard box lined with cotton-wool. "Are these them?" he asked.

Miss Weagle admitted coyly that those were them. Simon surveyed them disinterestedly, scratching his chin.

"If you just finish packing them up, miss," he said, "I'll take 'em along now."

"Take them along?" she repeated in surprise.

"Yes, miss. It's new rule. Everything of this kind that we cover has to be examined and sealed in our office, and sent off from there. It's on account of all these insurance frauds they've been having lately."

The illicit passion which Miss Weagle seemed to have been conceiving for him appeared to wane.

"Mr Enderby has been dealing with your firm for a long time," she began with some asperity.

"I know, miss; but the firm can't make one rule for one customer and another for another. It's just a formality as far as you're concerned, but them's my orders. I'm a new man in this district, and I can't afford to take a chance on my own responsibility. I'll give you a receipt for 'em, and they're covered from the moment they leave your hands."

He sat down at the desk and wrote out the receipt on a blank sheet of paper, licking his pencil between every word. The Saint was an incomparable artist in characterisation at any time, but he had rarely practised his art under such a steady tension as he did then, for he had no means of knowing how soon the real insurance company's agent would arrive, or how long Mr Enderby's appointment would keep him. But he completed the performance without a trace of hurry, and watched Miss Weagle tucking a layer of tissue over the last row of jewels.

"The value is twentyseven thousand six hundred and fifty pounds," she said coldly.

"I'll make a note of it, miss," said the Saint, and did so.

She finished packing the box, and he picked it up. He still had to get away with it.

"You doing anything particular next Saturday?" he asked, gazing at her with a hint of wistfulness.

"The idea!" said Miss Weagle haughtily.

"Do you like Greta Garbo?"

This was different.

"Oh," said Miss Weagle.

She wriggled. Simon had rarely witnessed such a revolting spectacle.

"Meet me at Piccadilly Circus at half-past one," he said.

"All right."

Simon stuffed the box into one of the pockets of his sober and unimaginative black suit, and went to the door. From the door, he blew a juicy kiss through the fringe of fungus which overhung his mouth, and departed with a wink that left her giggling kittenishly—and he was out of the building before she even looked at the receipt he had left behind, and discovered that his signature was undecipherable and there was no insurance company whatever mentioned on it. . . .

It was not by any means the most brilliant and dashing robbery that the Saint had ever committed, but it had a pure outrageous perfection of coincidence that atoned for all its shortcomings in the way of gore. And he knew, without the slightest diminution of the scapegrace beatitude that was performing a hilarious massage over his insides, that nothing on earth could have been more scientifically calculated to fan up the flames of vengeance on every side of him than what he had just done.

What he may not have foreseen was the speed with which the inevitable vengeance would move towards him.

Still wearing his deep-sea moustache and melancholy exterior, he walked west to New Oxford Street and entered a business stationer's. He bought a roll of gummed paper tape, with which he made a secure parcel of Mr Enderby's brown cardboard box, and a penny label which he addressed to Joshua Pond, Esq, Poste Restante, Harwich. Then he went to the nearest post-office and entrusted twenty-seven thousand six hundred and fifty pounds to the care of His Majesty's mails.

Two hours later he crossed Piccadilly from the Green Park underground station, and a vision of slim fair-haired loveliness turned round from a shop window as he swung in towards her.

"Were you waiting for somebody?" he asked gravely.

Her eyes, as blue as his own, smiled at him uncertainly.

"I was waiting for a bold bad brigand called the Saint, who doesn't know how to keep out of trouble. Have you seen him?"

"I believe I saw somebody like him sipping a glass of warm milk at a meeting of the World Federation of Encouraging Kindness to Cockroaches," he said solemnly. "Good-looking fellow with a halo. Is that the guy?"

"What else was he doing?"

"He was risking the ruin of his digestion with some of Ye Fine Olde Englishe Cookinge which is more deadly than bullets even if it doesn't taste much different," he said. "But it may have been worth it. There was a parcel shoved into a bloke's overcoat pocket some time when I was sweating through my second pound of water-logged cabbage, just like Sunny Jim said it would be, and I trailed the happy recipient to his lair. I suppose I was rather lucky to be listening outside his door just when he was telling his secretary to get an insurance hound over to inspect the boodle—— By the way, have you ever seen a woman with a face like a stoat and George-Robey eyebrows wriggling seductively? This secretary——"

"Do you mean you——"

"That's just what I do mean, old darling. I toddled straight into the office when this bloke went out, and introduced myself as the insurance hound summoned as aforesaid in Chapter One. And I got out of Hatton Garden with a packet of boodle valued at twenty-seven thousand six hundred and fifty quid, which ought to keep the wolf from the door for another day or two." The glint of changeless mischief in his eyes was its own infinite elaboration of the theme. "But it'll bring a lot of other wolves around that'll want rather more getting rid of; and I expect we can look forward to fun and games."

She nodded.

"They've started," she said soberly. "There's a reception committee waiting for you."

He was quite still for a moment; but the edge of humour in his gaze was altered only to become keener and more subtly dangerous.

"How many?"

"One."

His brows sloped up in a hairline of devil-may-care delight that she knew only too well—a contour of impenitent Saintliness that had made trouble-hunting its profession too long to be disturbed when the trouble came unasked.

"Not poor old Claud Eustace again?" he said.

"No. It's that new fellow—the Trenchard product. I've been waiting here three quarters of an hour to catch you as you came along and tell you. Sam Outrell gave me the wire."

## VI

The Saint was unperturbed. He had removed the walrus moustache which had whiffled so realistically before Miss Weagle, and with it the roseate complexion and melancholy aspect on which it had bloomed with such lifelike aptness. The costume which he had worn on that occasion had also been put away, in the well-stocked wardrobe of another *pied-à-terre* which he rented under another of his multitudinous aliases for precisely those skilful changes of identity. He had left the plodding inconspicuous gait of his character in the same place. In a light grey suit which looked as if it had only that morning been unpacked from the tailor's box, and a soft hat canted impudently over one eye, he had a debonair and disreputable elegance which made the deputation of welcome settle into clammily hostile attention.

"I was waiting for you," said Junior Inspector Pryke damply.

"No one would have thought it," said the Saint, with a casual smile. "Do I look like your fairy godmother?"

Pryke was not amused.

"Shall we go up to your rooms?" he suggested; and Simon's gaze rested on him blandly.

"What for, Desmond?" He leaned one elbow on the desk at his side, and brought the wooden-faced janitor into the party with a shift of his lazy smile. "You can't shock Sam Outrell—he knew me before you ever did. And Miss Holm is quite broadminded, too. By the way, have you met Miss Holm? Pat, this is Miss Desdemona Pryke, the Pride of the YWCA——"

"I'd rather see you alone, if you don't mind," said the detective.

He was beginning to go a trifle white about the mouth; and Simon's eyes marked the symptom with a wicked glitter of unhallowed mischief. It was a glitter that Mr Teal would have recognized only too easily, if he had been there to see it; but for once that long-suffering waistline of the Law was not its victim.

"What for?" Simon repeated, with a puzzled politeness that was about as cosy and reliable as a tent on the edge of a drifting iceberg. "If you've got anything to say to me that this audience can't hear, I'm afraid you're shinning up the wrong leg. I'm not that sort of a girl."

"I know perfectly well what I want to say," retorted Pryke chalkily.

"Then I hope you'll say it," murmured the Saint properly. "Come along, now, Desmond—let's get it over with. Make a clean breast of it—as the bishop said to the actress. Unmask the Public School Soul. What's the matter?"

Pryke's hands clenched spasmodically at his sides.

"Do you know a man called Enderby?"

"Never heard of him," said the Saint unblushingly. "What does he do—bore the holes in spaghetti, or something?"

"At about ten minutes to three this afternoon," said Pryke, with his studiously smooth University accent burring jaggedly at the edges, "a man entered his office, falsely representing himself to be an agent of the Southshire Insurance Company, and took away about twentyseven thousand pounds' worth of precious stones."

Simon raised his eyebrows.

"It sounds like a tough afternoon for Comrade Enderby," he remarked. "But why come and tell me? D'you mean you want me to try and help you recover these jools?"

The antarctic effrontery of his innocence would have left nothing visible in a thermometer but a shrunken globule of congealed quicksilver. It was a demonstration of absolute vacuum in the space used by the normal citizen for storing his conscience that left its audience momentarily speechless. Taking his first ration of that brass-necked Saintliness which had greyed so many of the hairs in Chief Inspector Teal's dwindling crop, Desmond Pryke turned from white to pink, and then back to white again.

"I want to know what you were doing at that time," he said.

"Me?" Simon took out his cigarette-case. "I was at the Plaza, watching a Mickey Mouse. But what on earth has that got to do with poor old Enderby and his jools?"

Suddenly the detective's hand shot out and grabbed him by the wrist.

"*That's* what you've got to do with it. That scar on your forearm. Miss Weagle—Mr Enderby's secretary—saw it on this fake insurance agent's arm when he picked up the parcel of stones. It was part of the description she gave us!"

Simon looked down at his wrist in silence for a moment, the cigarette he had chosen poised forgotten in midair, gazing at the tail of the furrowed scar that showed beyond the edge of his cuff. It was a souvenir he carried from quite a different adventure, and he had usually remembered to keep it covered when he was disguised. He realised that he had under-estimated both the eyesight of Miss Weagle and the resourcefulness of Junior Inspector Pryke; but when he raised his eyes again they were still bantering and untroubled.

"Yes, I've got a scar there—but I expect lots of other people have, too. What else did this Weagle dame say in her description?"

"Nothing that couldn't be covered by a good disguise," said Pryke, with a new note of triumph in his voice. "Now are you coming along quietly?"

"Certainly not," said the Saint.

The detective's eyes narrowed.

"Do you know what happens if you resist a police officer?"

"Surely," said the Saint, supple and lazy. "The police officer gets a thick ear."

Pryke let go his wrist, and shoved his hands into his pockets.

"Do you want me to have you taken away by force?" he asked.

"I shouldn't want you to try anything so silly, Desmond," said the Saint. He put the cigarette between his lips and struck a match with a flick of his thumbnail, without looking at it. "The squad hasn't been hatched yet that could take me away by force without a good deal of commotion; and you know it. You'd get more publicity than a Hollywood divorce—or is that what you're wanting?"

"I'm simply carrying out my orders——"

"Whose orders?"

"That's none of your business," Pryke got out through his teeth.

"I think it is," said the Saint mildly. "After all, I'm the blushing victim of this persecution. Besides, Desmond, I don't believe you. I think you're misguided. You're behind the times. How long have you been here waiting for me?"

"I'm not here to be crossexamined by you," spluttered the detective furiously.

"I'm not crossexamining you, Desmond. I'm trying to lead you into the paths of reason. But you don't have to answer that one if it hurts. How long has this petunia-blossom been here, Sam?"

The janitor glanced mechanically at the clock.

"Since about four o'clock, sir."

"Has it received any message—a telephone call, or anything like that?"

"No, sir."

"Nobody's come in and spoken to it?"

"No, sir."

"In fact, it's just been sitting around here all on its ownsome, like the last rose of summer——"

Junior Inspector Pryke thrust himself up between them, along the desk, till his chest was almost touching the Saint's. His hands were thrust into his pockets so savagely that the coat was stretched down in long creases from his shoulders.

"Will you be quiet?" he blazed quiveringly. "I've stood as much as I can——"

"As the bishop said to the actress."

"Are you coming along with me," fumed the detective, "or am I going to have you dragged out?"

Simon shook his head.

"You miss the idea, Desmond." He tapped the other firmly on the lower chest with his forefinger, and raised his eyebrows. "Hullo," he remarked, "your stomach hasn't got nearly so much bounce in it as dear old Teal's."

"Never mind my stomach!" Pryke almost screamed.

"I don't mind it," said the Saint generously. "I admit I haven't seen it in all its naked loveliness; but in its veiled state, at this distance, there seems to be nothing offensive about it."

The noise that Pryke made can only be likened to that of a kettle coming to the boil.

"I'll hear that another time," he said. "Simon Templar, I am taking you into custody——"

"But I'm trying to show you that that's exactly what you mustn't do, Desmond," said the Saint patiently. "It would be fatal. Here you are, a rising young officer on the threshold of your career, trying to pull a flivver that'll set you back four years' seniority. I can't let you do it. Why don't you curb the excessive zeal, Rosebud, and listen to reason? I can tell you exactly what's happened."

"I can tell you exactly what's going to happen——"

"It was like this," continued the Saint, as if the interruption not merely fell on deaf ears, but had failed miserably in its effort to occur at all. "This guy Enderby was robbed, as you say. Or he thought he was. Or, still more exactly, his secretary thought he was. A bloke calling himself an insurance agent blew into the office, and breezed out again with a parcel of jools. On account of various complications, the secretary was led to believe that this insurance agent was a fake, and the jools had been pinched. Filled with the same misguided zeal that's pulling the buttons of that horrible waistcoat of yours, Desmond, she called the police. Hearing of this, you come puffing round to see me, with your waistcoat bursting with pride and your brain addled with all the uncomplimentary fairytales that Claud Eustace Teal has told you about me."

"Who said so?"

"I did. It's a sort of clairvoyant gift of mine. But you must listen to the rest of it. You come blowing round here, and wait for me from four o'clock onwards. Pepped up with the idea of scoring a solo triumph, you haven't said anything to anyone about your scheme. Consequently you don't know what's happened since you left headquarters. Which is this. Shortly after the secretary female called for the police, Comrade Enderby himself returned to the office, the shemozzle was explained to him, he explained the shemozzle, and the long and the short of it was that the insurance agent was found to be perfectly genuine, the whole misunderstanding was cleared up, the whole false alarm exposed; and it was discovered that there was nothing to arrest anybody for—least of all me."

"What makes you think that?"

Simon took in a lungful of tobacco smoke, and exhaled through his nose with a slight smile. What made him think that? It was obvious. It was the fundamental formula on which fifty percent of his reputation had been built up.

A man was robbed. Ninetyeight times out of a hundred, the fact was never published at all. But if ever, through some misguided agent, or during a spasm of temporary but understandable insanity on the part of the victim himself, the fact happened to be published, that same victim, as soon as he discovered the accident or came to his senses, was the first and most energetic on the field to explain away the problem with which Scotland Yard had been faced—for the simple reason that there would be things much harder to explain away if the robber were ever detected.

And the bereavement of Mr Enderby was so perfectly on all fours with the formula that, with the horns of the dilemma touched in, it would have looked like a purple cow. There was no answer to it. So Mr Enderby had been robbed of some jewels? Well, could he give a description of the jewels, so that if they were recovered . . . How did the Saint know? He smiled, with unusual tolerance.

"Just the same old clairvoyant gift—working overtime for your special benefit, Desmond. But I'll back it for anything you like to bet—even including that perfectly repulsive shirt you're wearing. If you only got wise to yourself, you'd find that nobody wanted me arrested any more; and it'd save both of us no end of trouble. Now, why don't you get on the phone to Headquarters and bring yourself up to date? Let me do it for you; and then you can save your twopence to buy yourself a bar of milk chocolate on the way home. . . ."

He picked up the telephone on the porter's desk, and pushed his forefinger persuasively into the initial V of the Victoria exchange. It was all ancient history to the Saint, an old game which had become almost stereotyped from many playings, even if with this new victim it had the semblance of a new twist to it. It hadn't seriously occurred to him that the routine could be very different.

And then something hard and compact jabbed into his chest, and his eyes shifted over with genuine surprise from the telephone dial. There was a nickel-plated little automatic in Junior Inspector Pryke's hand—the sort of footling ladylike weapon, Simon couldn't help reflecting, which a man with that taste in clothes must inevitably have affected, but none the less capable of unpleasant damage at contact range. His gaze roamed up to the detective's flaming eyes with a flicker of pained protest that for once was wholly spontaneous and tinged with a glitter of urgent curiosity.

"Put that telephone down," said Pryke sizzlingly.

Simon put the telephone down. There was something in the other's rabid glare which told him that disobedience might easily make Pryke do something foolish—of which the Saint had no desire to suffer the physical effects.

"My dear old daffodil," he murmured, "have you stopped to think that that dinky little pop-gun——"

"Never mind what I think," rasped the detective, whose range of repartee seemed to make up in venom what it lacked in variety. "If there's any truth in what you're saying, we can verify it when we get you to the station. But you aren't going to run away until it has been verified. Come along!"

His finger was twitching over the trigger; and the Saint sighed.

He felt rather sorry for Junior Inspector Pryke. While he disliked the man's face, and his voice, and his clothes, and almost everything else about him, he had not actually plumbed such implacable depths of hatred as to wish him to turn himself into a horrible example which would be held up for the disgusted inspection of students of the Police College for the next decade. But it seemed as if this was the only ambition Desmond Pryke had to fulfil, and he had left no stone unturned in his efforts to achieve it. From permitting himself to be lured into an argument on comparative gastrometry to that final howler of pulling a gun to enforce an ordinary arrest, Junior Inspector Pryke had run doggedly through the complete catalogue of Things A Young Policeman Should Not Do; but it was not Simon Templar's fault.

The Saint shrugged.

"Okay, Desmond," he murmured. "If that's the way you feel about it, I can't stop you. I've done my best. But don't come around asking me for a pension when they drum you out of the Force."

He put on his hat, and pulled the brim out to the perfect piratical tilt. There was not a shadow of misgiving in the smile that he gave Patricia, and he saw no reason for there to be a shadow.

"Be seein' ya, keed," he said. "Don't worry—I'll be back for dinner. But I'm afraid Desdemona is going to have a pain in her little tum-tum before then."

He sauntered out unhurriedly into Stratton Street, and himself hailed the nearest taxi. Pryke put away his gun and climbed in after him. The cab turned into Piccadilly with a burden of internal silence that was almost broken by the exuberance of its own one-sided rancour.

Simon's nostrils detected a curious sweet scent in the air he was breathing. Ever the genial optimist, he tried to thaw out the polar obmutescence with a fresh turn of pleasant gossip.

"That perfume you're using, Desmond," he said. "I don't think I've come across it before. What's it called—*Pansy's Promise*? Or is it *Quelques Tantes*?"

"You wait till we get to the station," said the detective, with sweltering monotony. "Perhaps you won't feel so funny then."

"Perhaps I won't," Simon agreed languidly. "And perhaps you won't look so funny."

He yawned. The cab, with all its windows tightly closed, was warm and stuffy; and the conversational limitations of Inspector Pryke were also conducive to slumber.

The Saint closed his eyes. He felt limp and bored, and his brain was starting to wander in a most remarkable and disjointed manner. It was all rather voluptuous and dreamy, like sinking away in some Elysian hop-joint. . . . Suddenly he felt faintly sick.

He sat up, with a tremendous effort. A message was trying to get through to his brain, but it seemed to be muffled in layer after layer of cotton-wool. His chest was labouring, and he could feel his heart pounding at a crazy speed. The face of Junior Inspector Pryke stared back at him through a kind of violet haze. Pryke's chest was heaving also, and his mouth was open: it crossed the Saint's mind that he looked like an agitated fish. . . . Then everything within his blurring vision whirled round like a top, and the blood roared in his ears like a thousand waterfalls. The message that had been trying to break through to him flashed in at last, and he made a convulsive lunge towards the window behind the driver's impassive back; but he never reached it. It seemed as if the bottom fell out of the world, and he went plunging down through fold after fold of numbing silence, down and down through cold green clouds of that curious perfume into an infinity of utter nothingness. . . .

## VII

There was a decanter and three sherry-glasses on the table—and one of the glasses was untouched. They had been set out there more than an hour ago; and the decanter was nearly empty.

Patricia Holm wandered restlessly about the living-room. Her face was quiet and untroubled, but she couldn't relax and sit down. The dark had come down; and the view of the Green Park from the tall windows was hidden by a grey-blue veil in which the yellow specks of the street lamps shone brighter than the stars, and the lights of cars travelling up and down the Mall gleamed like flocks of dawdling comets. She drew the curtains, for something to do, and stole her thirtyseventh glance at the clock. It was a couple of minutes after nine.

"What's happened to him?" she said.

Mr Uniatz shook his head. He stretched out a spade-shaped hand for the decanter and completed his solo conquest of its contents.

"I dunno," he said feebly. "Maybe he couldn't shake de diddo. Dey come dat way, sometimes."

"He's been arrested before," she said. "It's never kept him as long as this. If anything had gone wrong, he ought to have got word through to us somehow."

Mr Uniatz chewed desperately at his poisonous cigar. He wanted to be helpful. As we have already explained, he was not naturally hot on the higher flights of the intellect; but on such an occasion as this he was not the man to shirk his obligations. The deep creases in his rudimentary forehead bore their own witness to the torture he was enduring from these unaccustomed stresses on his brain.

"Maybe he's on his way, right now," he hazarded encouragingly.

Patricia threw herself into a chair. It was another restless movement, rather than an attempt to rest.

"That's not enough, Hoppy." She was thinking aloud, mechanically, more for the anæsthetic effect of actual speech than with any hope of coaxing something useful out of her companion. "If anything's gone wrong, we've got to be ready for it. We've got to pick up our own cue. He'd expect us to find the answer. Suppose he isn't on his way—what has he done?"

"He's got de ice," said Mr Uniatz, vaguely.

"I don't know whether he's got it now. Probably he parked it somewhere on his way here. That's what he'd have done if he was expecting trouble. Sometimes he simply puts things in the mail—sends them to a hotel or a poste restante somewhere, and picks them up later on when it's all clear. Usually they aren't even addressed to his own name."

Hoppy frowned.

"But if dey ain't addressed to his own name," he said, "how does he pick dem up?"

"Well, when he goes to pick them up, he gives the name that they were addressed to," explained Patricia kindly.

Mr Uniatz nodded. He had always been lost in admiration of the Saint's intellectual gifts, and this solution was only one more justification of his faith. Obviously a guy who could work out things like that in his own head had got what it takes.

"But this time we don't know where he's sent them, or what name he addressed them to," she said.

The tentative expression of pleased complacency faded away from Hoppy's face, and the flutings of honest effort crowded themselves once more into the restricted space between his eyebrows and his hair. He was too loyal to give way to the feeling that this was an unnecessary complication, invented simply to make things more difficult for him; but he wished people wouldn't ask him to tackle problems like that. Reaching again for the decanter and finding it empty, he glowered at it plaintively, like a trusted friend who had done him a gratuitous injury.

"So what?" he said, passing the buck with an air of profound reluctance.

"I must know what's happened to him," said Patricia steadily.

She got up and lighted a cigarette. Twice more she paced out the length of the room with her supple boyish stride; and then with a sudden resolution she slipped into the chair by the telephone and dialled Teal's private number.

He was at home. In a few moments his drowsy voice came over the wire.

"Who's that?"

"This is Patricia Holm." Her voice was as cool and careless as the Saint's own. "Haven't you finished with Simon yet? We're waiting for him to join us for dinner, and I'm getting hungry and Hoppy is getting away with all the sherry."

"I don't know what you mean," he answered suspiciously.

"You ought to know, Claud."

He didn't seem to know. She explained. He was silent for so long that she thought she had been cut off; and then his suspicious perplexity came through again in the same lethargic monotone.

"I'll ring you again in a few minutes," he said.

She sat on at the table, smoking her cigarette without enjoyment, playing a noiseless tattoo with her fingertips on the smooth green bakelite of the instrument. Over on the other side of the room, Hoppy Uniatz discovered the untouched glass which had been reserved for the Saint, and drew it cautiously towards him.

In five minutes the telephone bell rang.

"They don't know anything about it at Scotland Yard or Market Street," Teal informed her. "And it's the first I've heard of it myself. Is this another of your family jokes, or what?"

"I'm not joking," said Patricia, and there was a sudden chill in her eyes which would have made the statement superfluous if Teal could have seen her. "Pryke took him away about half-past five. It was a perfectly ridiculous charge, but he wouldn't listen to reason. It couldn't possibly have kept the Saint as long as this."

The wire was silent again for a second or two. She could visualise the detective sucking his chewing gum more plainly than television could have shown him.

"I'll come round and see you," he said.

He was there inside the quarter-hour, with his round harvest-moon face stodgy and disinterested under his shabby pot hat, chewing the same tasteless cud of chicle and listening to the story again. The repetition added nothing to the sum of his knowledge, except that there was no joke involved. When he had heard it through and asked his questions, he called Scotland Yard and Market Street police station again, only to have his inquiries answered by the same blank negatives. Junior Inspector Pryke, apparently, had left Market Street at about a quarter to four, without saying where he was going; and nothing had been heard of him since. Certainly he had not reported in with an arrest anywhere in the Metropolitan area.

Only one thing required no explanation; and he knew that Patricia Holm knew it, by this time, as well as he knew it himself—although her recital had carefully told him nothing more than Simon Templar himself would have done.

"The Saint was after the High Fence," he said bluntly. "He robbed Enderby this afternoon. I know it, and you know it, even if it is quite true that Enderby got on to us shortly after the alarm and swore it was all a mistake. Therefore it's obvious that Enderby is something to do with the High Fence. Maybe we can't prove it; but the High Fence knows his own men. It doesn't take much more to work out what happened."

"I think you're jumping to a lot of conclusions," said Patricia, with Saintly sweetness, and did not deceive him for an instant.

"Perhaps I am," he said stolidly. "But I know what I'd have done if I'd been the High Fence. I'd have heard what had happened as soon as Scotland Yard did; and I'd have watched this place. I'd have seen Pryke come in; and even that mightn't have stopped me. . . . They left here in a taxi, did they? Well, you ought to be able to work it out as well as I can."

"You mean de High Fence puts de arm on him?" asked Mr Uniatz, translating innuendo into an idiom that he could understand.

Teal looked round at him with heavy-lidded eyes in which the perpetual boredom was as flimsy a sham as anyone was likely to see.

"If you know the answers, I expect you'll go to work on them," he said, with a stony significance of which he would have been the first to disclaim all knowledge. "I've got my own job to do. If one of you keeps in touch with this address, I'll let you know if I find out anything."

He left a roomful of equally stony silence behind him, and went out to take a taxi to Scotland Yard.

The High Fence had got the Saint and Junior Inspector Pryke—he had no doubts about that. He knew, although he could never prove it, that his analysis of the situation had been as mathematically accurate as any jigsaw he would ever put together could hope to be. And it was easier to put together than most problems. He would have been happier if his own course of action had been no less clearly indicated; and it disturbed him more than he would have cared to admit to realise that he was far more concerned about the fate of the Saint than he was about the fate of his own smug subordinate.

This secondary concern, however, was settled shortly after ten o'clock, when a police constable observed a pair of feet protruding from a bush on the edge of Wimbledon Common, and used the feet to haul out the body of a man. In the first flush of instinctive optimism, the policeman thought that the body was dead, and pictured himself (with photograph and biographical note) in the headlines of a sensational murder mystery; but closer investigation showed it to be alive, and with medical assistance it was quite easily resuscitated into a healthily profane Junior Inspector of unmistakable Trenchard parentage.

"So the High Fence didn't kill you," said Mr Teal malignantly, when a police car had brought the salvage to Scotland Yard.

"I thought you'd be pleased," retorted Pryke pettishly.

He had a sick headache from the gas which had been pumped into the cab, and he was on the defensive for trouble. Mr Teal did not disappoint him.

"Who told you to arrest the Saint?" he inquired mucilaginously, when Pryke had given his account of the affair.

"I didn't know I had to be told. I heard of the robbery at Enderby's, and there were grounds for believing that the Saint had a hand in it——"

"You know that Enderby has denied that there ever was a robbery, and said it was entirely a misunderstanding?"

"Has he? That's what the Saint told me, but I didn't believe him. I knew nothing about it. I went out as soon as I received the first information, and waited for him at his flat."

"And you had to use a gun to arrest him."

Pryke flushed. He had thought it wiser to say nothing about that.

"He refused to come with me," he said sulkily. "I had to do something, and I didn't want to make a scene."

"It would have made the biggest scene you're ever likely to be in, if you had got him to the station and that gun had been mentioned in the police court," Teal said caustically. "As it is, you'll be on the carpet first thing in the morning. Or will you tell the Assistant Commissioner that all this was my idea, too?"

Pryke scowled, and said nothing.

"Anyhow," Teal wound up, "the Saint has got to be found now. After your performance, he's technically an escaped prisoner. Since it was your arrest, you'd better do something about it."

"What do you suggest?" asked Pryke, with treacherous humility.

Teal, having no answer, glared at him. Everything that could be prescribed for such an emergency had been done already—every alarm issued, every feeler put out, every net spread. If he could have thought of anything more, Chief Inspector Teal would have done it himself. But there was nothing to guide him: even what had been done was a mere firing of routine shots in the dark. The taxi had disappeared, and no one had even noticed its number. Beyond any doubt, the man who had ordered its movements was the same man who had killed Johnny Anworth and Sunny Jim Fasson—who, unless something were done quickly, would be just as likely to kill Simon Templar. A man knew too much, and he died: the logical sequence was quite clearly established, but Teal found no pleasure in following it to its conclusion.

"Since you're so damned independent of orders and regulations," he said, with excessive violence, "you might pay some attention to this man Enderby. I know he swears that the whole thing was a mistake, but I've heard of plenty of those mistakes before. There's no evidence and nothing we can charge him with, but if those stones that were stolen weren't stolen property already, I'll eat my hat. And if Enderby isn't hand in glove with the High Fence, even if he isn't the High Fence himself, I'll eat yours as well."

Pryke shook his head.

"I don't know that I agree. Fasson was shot as he was running out of Abbot's Yard, and when we made a house-to-house inquiry we found out that Templar had a place there under one of his aliases——"

"Well, what about it? I've never believed that the Saint didn't have something to do with it. I don't believe he killed Fasson; but I do believe that he got the body away from the flat where Fasson was shot, and that Fasson wasn't dead. I believe that he made Fasson talk; and that Fasson wasn't really killed until either the Saint let him go, or he ran away. I think Fasson told him something that made him go after Enderby, and——"

Pryke shook his head again, with an increase of confidence and patronising self-satisfaction that made Teal stop short with his gorge rising under the leaven of undutiful thoughts of murder.

"I think you're wrong," he said.

"Oh, I am, am I?" said Mr Teal malevolently. "Well, what's the right answer?"

The smug shaking of Junior Inspector Pryke's head continued until Teal could have kicked him.

"I have a theory of my own," he said, "which I'd like to work on—unless you've got something definite that you want me to do."

"You go ahead and work on it," replied Teal blisteringly. "When I want something definite done, I shan't ask you. In another minute you'll be telling me that the Assistant Commissioner is the High Fence."

The other stood up, smoothing down the points of his waistcoat. In spite of the situation for which he was responsible, his uncrushable superciliousness was reviving outwardly untouched; but Teal saw that underneath it he was hot and simmering.

"That wouldn't be so wild as some of your guesses," he said mysteriously. "I'd like to get the Saint—if anyone can be made a Chief Inspector for failing to catch him, they'd have to make a Superintendent of anyone who did it."

"Make you a Superintendent?" jeered Teal. "With a name like yours?"

"It's a very good name," said his junior tartly. "There was a Pryke at the Battle of Hastings."

"I'll bet he was a damn good cook," snarled Mr Teal.

## VIII

For Simon Templar there was an indefinite period of trackless oblivion, from which he was roused now and again to dream curious dim dreams. Once the movement of the cab stopped, and he heard voices; then a door slammed, and he sunk back into the dark before his impression had more than touched the fringe of consciousness. Once he seemed to be carried over a gravel path: he heard the scrunch of stones, and felt the grip of the hands that were holding him up, but there was no power of movement in his limbs. It was too much trouble to open his eyes, and he fell asleep again almost immediately. Between those momentary stirrings of awareness, which were so dull and nebulous that they did not even stimulate a desire to amplify them, stretched a colourless void of languorous insensibility in which time had no landmarks.

Then there was the feeling of a hard chair under him, a constriction of cords about his wrists and ankles, and a needle that stabbed his forearm. His eyelids felt weighted down almost beyond his power to lift, but when he dragged them up once he could see nothing. He wondered vaguely whether the room was in darkness, or whether he was blind; but he was too apathetic to dwell earnestly on a choice between the alternatives. There was a man who talked softly out of the blackness, in a voice that sounded hazily familiar, asking him a lot of questions. He had an idea that he answered them, without conscious volition and equally without opposition from his will. Afterwards he could never remember what he said.

Presently the interval of half-consciousness seemed to merge back without a borderline into the limitless background of sleep.

When he woke up again his head ached slightly with a kind of empty dizziness, and his stomach felt as if it had been turned inside out and spun round on a flywheel till it was raw and tender. It was an effort to open his eyes, but not such a hopeless and unimportant feat as it had seemed before. Once open, he had more difficulty at first in focussing them. He had an impression of bare grey boards, and his own feet tied together with strands of new rope. The atmosphere was warm and close, and smelt nauseatingly of paint and oil. There was a thrumming vibration under him, coupled with a separate and distinct swaying movement: after a while he picked an irregular splash and gurgle of water out of the background of sound, and induced his eyes to coordinate on a dark circular window framed in tarnished brass.

"So you're waking up for a last look round, are you?" growled a voice somewhere to his left.

Simon nodded. Shifting his gaze gingerly about, he made out more details. There was an unshaded electric bulb socketed into the low ceiling which gave a harsh but sufficient light. He was in the cabin of a boat—a small craft, by the look and motion of it, either a canal tug or a scrap-heap motor cruiser. From the rows of orderly lights that drifted past the portholes on both sides of the cabin, he deduced that they were running down the Thames.

The man who had spoken sat on an old canvas sack spread out on the bare springs of a bunk. He was a thickset prognathous individual with thin reddish hair and a twisted mouth, most unnautically clad in a striped suit, a check cap, and canary-yellow shoes.

"Where are we off to?" Simon asked.

The man chuckled.

"You're going to have a look at some fishes. I don't know whether they'll like you, but they'll be able to go on lookin' at you till they get used to it."

"Is that the High Fence's joke?" inquired Simon sardonically.

"It's the High Fence you're talkin' to."

The Saint regarded him contemptuously.

"Your name is Quincey. I believe I could give you a list of all your convictions. Let me see. Two for robbery with violence, one for carrying firearms without a licence, one for attempted——"

"All right," said Quincey good-humouredly. "I know 'em all myself. But the High Fence and me are like *that*." He locked his thick fingers together symbolically. "We're more or less the same thing. He wouldn't be able to do much without me."

"He mightn't have been able to get Sunny Jim murdered," Simon agreed thoughtfully.

"Yes, I did that. It was pretty neat. I was supposed to be waitin' for both of you, but when Fasson came out an' ran down to King's Road, I was frightened of losin' him, so I had to go without you. Yes, I was ridin' the motorbike. They can't prove it, but I don't mind tellin' you, because you'll never tell anyone else. I killed Sunny Jim—the rat! An' now I'm goin' to feed the great Simon Templar to the fishes. I know a lot of fellers who'd give their right hands to be in my place."

Simon acknowledged the truth of that. The list of men who would have paid drastically for the privilege of using him for ground-bait in the deepest and hungriest stretch of water at their disposal could have been conveniently added up in round dozens. But his brain was still far from clear, and for the moment he could not see the High Fence's object in sending him to that attractive fate so quickly.

"If you feed me to the fishes, you feed them twentyseven thousand six hundred and fifty pounds' worth of stones as well—did you know that, brother?" he asked.

Quincey grinned.

"Oh, no, we don't. We know where those are. They're at the Harwich Post Office, addressed to Mr Joshua Pond. You told us all about that. The High Fence has gone to Harwich to be Mr Pond."

The Saint's eyes hardened into chips of flint. For an instant of actual physical paralysis, he felt exactly as if he had been kicked in the middle. The terse, accurate, effortless, unhesitating throwing back at him of an arrangement which he had not even told Patricia, as if his brain had been flung open and the very words read out of it, had a staggering calamitousness like nothing he had ever experienced before. It had an unearthly inescapable completeness that blasted the foundations from under any thought of bluff, and left him staring at something that looked like a supernatural intervention of Doom itself.

His memory struggled muzzily back over the features of his broken dream. The taxi—he had taken it off the kerb right outside his door, without a thought. Ordinarily he would never have done such a thing; but the very positive presence of trouble in the shape of Junior Inspector Pryke had given him a temporary blind spot to the fact that trouble in another shape could still be waiting for him— and might logically be expected to wait in much the same place.

The sickly sweet perfume which he had accused Pryke of using. Pryke's agitated face, gulping like a fish; and the labour of his own breathing. Gas, of course—pumped into the closed cab by some mechanism under the control of the driver, and quick enough in its action to put them out before they were sufficiently alarmed to break a window. Then the scrunch of gravel, and the grip of hands carrying him. He had been taken somewhere. Probably Pryke had been dumped out somewhere on the route. Unlike Mr Teal, Simon hoped he had not been killed—he would have looked forward to experimenting with further variations on that form of badinage to which Desmond was so alluringly sensitive.

The prick of the needle, and the soft voice that asked him questions out of the darkness. Questions that he couldn't remember, that dragged equally forgotten answers out of a drugged subconsciousness that was too stupefied to lie. . . . Understanding came to him out of that fuddled recollection with stunning clarity. There was nothing supernatural about it—only unexpected erudition and refinement. So much neater and surer than the old-fashioned and conventional systems of torture, which, even when they unlocked a man's mouth, gave no guarantee that he spoke the truth. . . . He could even identify the drug that must have been used.

"Scopolamine?" he said, without any indication on his face of the shocks he had taken to reach that conclusion.

Quincey scratched the back of his ear.

"I think that's the name. The High Fence thought of it. That's what we are—scientific."

Simon glanced steadily at the opposite porthole. Something like a solid black screen cut off the procession of embankment lights, briefly, and slid by. It told him that they had not yet passed under all the bridges; but he found it impossible to identify their whereabouts any more particularly. Seen from the unfamiliar viewpoint of the water, the passing lights formed themselves into no patterns which he could positively recognise; and an occasional glimpse of a neon sign, high up on a building, was no more illuminating, except on the superlative merits of Bovril or Guinness. Somewhere below London Bridge, down past the Pool, probably, he would be dropped quietly over the side. There was a queer quiet inevitability about it, a dispassionate scientific precision, which seemed an incongruous end for such a stormy and impetuous life.

"May I have a cigarette?" he asked.

Quincey hesitated for a moment, and then took out a packet of Players. He put one between the Saint's lips and lighted it for him, and then returned watchfully to his seat on the bunk.

"Thanks," said the Saint.

His wrists were bound together in front of him, so that he was able to use one hand on the cigarette. He was also able to make an inconspicuous test of the efficiency of the knotting. It was well done; and the new cord would swell up tighter as soon as it got wet.

He got a view of his wristwatch, and saw that it was a quarter past ten.

"What day is this?" he said.

"The same day as it's been all the time," answered Quincey. "You didn't think we'd keep you under for a week, did you? The sooner you're out of the way, the better. You've given us too much trouble already."

So it was less than five hours since he had gone to sleep in the taxi. Simon got a perspective on his dream. At that rate, there was a sound chance that the High Fence couldn't have got him to wherever he had been taken, drugged and questioned him, and caught a train out of London in time to reach Harwich before the post-office closed. Therefore he might not be able to collect the package from the Poste Restante before morning. And if the Saint escaped. . . .

Simon realised that he was building some beautiful castles in the air. A dog thrown into the river with a brick tied round its neck would have more or less the same chance of escape as he was offered.

And yet . . . there was a dim preposterous hope struggling in his mind that a miracle might happen—or had happened. Where had he felt the stab of that hypnotic needle? He felt sure that it had been in his right forearm; and there was a vague sort of ache in the same place to confirm the uncertain memory. In that case, was there any reason why his left forearm must have been touched? It was a wildly fantastic hope, an improbable possibility. And yet . . . such unlikely things had happened before, and their not wholly improbable possibility was part of the inspiration behind the more unconventional items of his armoury. It might seem incredible that anyone who knew anything of him could fail to credit him with having something up his sleeve in any emergency; and yet. . . . Smoking his cigarette in long tranquil inhalations, he contrived to press his left forearm unobtrusively against his thigh; and what he felt put the dawn of a grim and far-fetched buoyancy into his heart.

Quincey got up and pressed his face against one of the portholes.

"It's about time for you to be goin'," he said unemotionally.

He hauled out a heavy iron weight from under the bunk, and bent a short length of rope to a ring set in it. The other end of the rope he knotted to the cords that bound the Saint's ankles. Then he tore a strip of canvas from the sack which he had been sitting on, and stood waiting with it.

"Finish that cigarette," he said.

Simon drew a last leisured puff, and dropped it on the floor. He looked Quincey in the eyes.

"I hope you'll ask for fish for your last breakfast, on the day they hang you for this," he said.

"I'll do that for you," said Quincey, knotting the canvas across his mouth in a rough but effective gag. "*When* they hang me. Stand up."

He pulled the Saint across his shoulder in a fireman's lift, picking up the weight in his left hand, and moved slowly across to the narrow steep companion which led up from the cabin. Mounting the steps awkwardly under his burden, he lifted the hatch with his head and climbed up till he could roll the Saint off on to the deck.

The craft was a small and shabby single-cabin motorboat. A man muffled up in a dark overcoat, with a peaked cap pulled down over his eyes until it almost met the top of his turned-up collar, who was apparently the only other member of the crew, stood at the wheel beside the hatch; but he did not look round. Simon wondered if it was Mr Enderby. The numbers of the gang who actually worked in direct contact with the High Fence would certainly be kept down to the irreducible minimum consistent with adequate functioning, and it might well be that by this time he knew all of them. It was not a racket which called for a large staff, given the original idea and the ingenious leader. His one regret was that he had not been able to make the acquaintance of that elusive quantity: it seemed a ridiculously commonplace problem to take out unanswered into eternity, after solving so many mysteries.

Quincey stepped out over him, picked up the weight again, and rolled him like a barrel towards the stern. As he turned over, the Saint saw the rusty counter of a tramp moored in midstream swing by over his head, punctured with an occasional yellow-lighted port. Over on the Surrey side, a freighter was discharging cargo in a floodlit splash of garish flarelight. He heard the rattle and clank of the tackle, the chuffing of steam winches, the intermittent rise of voices across the water. A tug hooted mournfully, feeling its way across the stream.

He lay on the very edge of the counter, with the wake churning and hissing under his side. Quincey bent over him.

"So long, Saint," he said, without vindictiveness; and pushed outwards.

## IX

Simon stocked his lungs to the last cubic millimeter of their capacity, and tensed his muscles involuntarily as he went down. He had a last flash of Quincey's tough freckled face peering after him; and then the black waters closed over his head. The iron weight jerked at his ankles, and he went rolling over and upright into the cold crushing darkness.

Even as he struck the water he was wrenching his wrists round to seize the uttermost fraction of slack from the cords that bound them. The horror of that helpless plunging down to death, roped hand and foot and ballasted with fifty pounds of iron, was a nightmare that he remembered for the rest of his life; but it is a curious fact that while it lasted his mind was uncannily insulated from it. Perhaps he knew that to have let himself realise it fully, to have allowed his thoughts to dwell for any length of time on the stark hopelessness of his position, would have led inevitably to panic.

His mind held with a terrible intensity of concentration on nothing but the essentials of what he had to do. With his hands twisted round till the cords cut into his flesh, he could get the fingers of his right hand a little way up his left sleeve; and under their tips he could feel the curved shape of something that lay just above the left wrist. That was the one slender link that he had with life, the unconventional item of his armoury which the search that must have been made of his clothes had miraculously overlooked: the thin sharp ivory-hilted knife which he carried in a sheath strapped to his forearm, which had saved him from certain death before and might save him once again. Somehow, slowly, clumsily, with infinite patience and agonising caution, he had to work it out and get it in his hand—moving it in split shavings of an inch, lest it should come loose too quickly and slip out of his grasp to lose itself in the black mud of the river bed, and yet not taking so long to shift it that his fingers would go numb and out of control from the cutting off of the circulation by the tightening ropes. His flesh crawled in the grip of that frightful restraint, and his forehead prickled as if the sweat was trying to break out on it even under the cold clutch of the water that was pressing in at his eardrums. He could feel his heart thudding hollowly in the aching tension of his chest, and a deadly blackness seemed to be swelling up in his brain and trying to overwhelm him in a burst of merciful unconsciousness: every nerve in his body shrieked its protest against the inhuman discipline, cried out for release, for action, for the frantic futile struggle that would anæsthetise the anguish just as surely as it would hasten on the end—for any relief and outlet, however suicidal, that would liberate them from the frightful tyranny of his will.

Perhaps it lasted for three minutes, from beginning to end, that nightmare eternity in which he was anchored to the bottom of the Thames, juggling finickily for life itself. If he had not been a trained underwater swimmer, he could never have survived it at all. There was a time when the impulse to let out his precious breath in a sob of sheer despair was almost more than flesh and blood could resist; but his self-control was like iron.

He won out, somehow. Trickling the air from his lungs in jealously niggard rations that were just sufficient to ease the strain on his chest, he worked the hilt of the knife up with his finger and thumb until he could get another finger on it . . . and another . . . and another . . . until the full shaft was clutched in a hand which by that time had practically gone dead. But he was just able to hold it. He forced himself down, bending his knees and reaching forward, until his numbed fingers could feel the taut roughness of the rope by which he was held down to the weight. And then, giving way for the first time in that ghastly ordeal, he slashed at it wildly—slashed again and again, even when his knife met no resistance and he felt himself leaping up through the reluctant waters to the blessed air above. . . .

For a long while he lay floating on the stream, with only his face above the surface, balancing himself with slight movements of his legs and arms, sawing in an ecstasy of leisure through the other ropes on his wrists and ankles, and drinking in the unforgettable glory of the night. Afterwards, he could never remember those moments clearly: they were a space out of his life that was cut off from everything in the past and everything in the future, when he thought of inconsequential things with an incomparably vivid rapture, and saw commonplace things with an exquisite sensuous delight that could not have been put into words. He couldn't even recollect how long it lasted, that voluptuous realisation of the act of living; he only knew that at the end of it he saw the black bulk of a ship looming up towards him with a tiny white crest at her bows, and had to start swimming to save himself from being run down. Somehow the swim brought him close to the north bank of the river, and he cruised idly upstream until he found a flight of stone steps leading up into a narrow alley between two buildings. The alley led into a narrow dingy street, and somewhere along the street he found a taxi which, in an unlikely spot like that, could only have been planted there for his especial service by a guardian angel with a most commendable sense of responsibility.

The driver peered at him keenly in the light of the melancholy street lamp under which the cab was parked.

"You're wet," he said at last, with the same pride of discovery that must have throbbed in Charles Darwin's breast when he gave the fruit of his researches to the world.

"You know, George, I believe you've hit it," said the Saint, in a whisper of admiring awe in which the old unconquerable mockery was beginning to lift itself again. "I thought something was wrong, but I couldn't make out what it was. Do you think I can have been in some water?"

The driver frowned at him suspiciously.

"Are you drunk?" he asked, with disarming frankness; and the Saint shook his head.

"Not yet—but I have a feeling that with very little encouragement I could be. I want to go to Cornwall House, Piccadilly; and I'll pay for any damage I do to your lovely cushions."

Probably it was the tone and manner of what the chauffeur would have described as a toff which dissolved suspicion away into a tolerant appreciation of aristocratic eccentricity, and induced him to accept the fare. At any rate, he accepted it, and even went so far as to oblige Simon with a cigarette.

Lounging back in a corner with the smoke sinking luxuriously into his lungs, the Saint felt his spirits rising with the speed of an irresponsible rocket. The ordeal he had been through, the shadow of death and the strange supreme joy of life after it, slipped back into the annals of memory. To the High Fence, he was dead: he had been dropped off a boat into the lower waters of the Thames with a lump of iron tied to his feet—swallowed up in the bottom ooze and slime of the river, where any secret might well be safe. Both as a proven interferer and a potentially greater menace, he had been re-moved. But before being drowned, he had given up his secret. He had told exactly what he had done with the parcel of precious stones of which Mr Clive Enderby had been bereaved—and the High Fence was going to Harwich to take the name of Joshua Pond in vain. . . . And Simon Templar had an increasingly blissful idea that he was going to be there to witness the performance.

As the cab drew up before Cornwall House he saw a girl and a man coming out, and decanted himself on to the pavement before the taxi had properly reached a standstill.

"Are you looking for some fun, souls?" he murmured. "Because if so, I could use you."

Patricia Holm stared at him for a moment in breathless silence; and then, with an incoherent little cry, she threw herself into his arms.

Mr Uniatz swallowed, and touched the Saint with stubby fingers, as if he were something fragile.

"Howja get wet, boss?" he asked.

Simon grinned, and indicated the interested taxi-driver with a movement of his head.

"George here thinks I must have been in some water," he said. "Give him a quid for the inspiration, will you?—I only had a fiver on me when I went out, but they pinched it."

He led Patricia back into the building with a damp arm round her shoulders, while Hoppy paid off the taxi and rejoined them in the foyer. They rode up in the elevator in an enforced silence; but Patricia was shaking him by the arm as soon as the door of the apartment had closed behind them.

"Where have you been, boy? What's happened?"

"Were you worried?"

"You know that."

He kissed her.

"I guess you must have been. Where were you off to?"

"We were going to call on Enderby." She was still holding herself in the curve of his arm, wet as he was. "It was the only line we had—what you told me outside here, before Pryke took you off."

"I could of made him talk, boss," said Mr Uniatz, in a tone of pardonable disappointment. "After I'd got t'ru wit' him——"

The Saint smiled.

"I suppose he'd 've been lucky to be able to talk. Well, the scheme might still be a good one. . . ." He toyed with the idea for a thoughtful moment; and then he shook his head. "But no—we don't need it now. And there may be something much more useful for you to do. Get me a drink, Pat, if Hoppy's left anything, and I'll tell you."

Half an hour in his sodden clothes had left him chilled and shivery, but a steep tot of whisky would soon put that right. He lay submerged in a hot bath, with the glass balanced on the edge, and told them the story of his adventures through the open door. It was a tale that made Patricia bite her lips towards the end; but for him it was all in the past. When he came through into the living-room again, cheerful and glowing from the massage of a rough towel, with his hair sleekly brushed again and a woolly bathrobe slung round him, lighting a cigarette with steady hands and the old irrepressible laughter on his lips, it was difficult to imagine that barely an hour ago he had fought one of his most terrific fights with death.

"So here we are," he said, with the blue lights crisp and dancing in his eyes. "We don't know who the High Fence is; but we know where he's going, and we know the password he's going to give. It's rather quiet and logical; but we've got him. Just because he's made that one natural mistake. If I were swinging at the bottom of the Pool, as he thinks I am, there wouldn't be a snag in his life. He'd just go to Harwich and recover his boodle; and that would be the end of a spot of very satisfactorily settled bother. But he's going to have a surprise."

"Can we come with you?" said Patricia.

The Saint shook his head.

"I'd like you to. But I can't be everywhere at once, and I shall want someone in London. You mayn't have realised it, but we still have our own bills to pay. The swine knocked a fiver off me when they took me for that ride and I want it back. Teal's going to achieve his ambition and lag the High Fence, and that parcel of jools that's going to give the High Fence away is evidence now; but we've got our Old Age Pensions to think about. Anyone who wants to amuse himself by pumping me up with gas and dope and heaving me into the river has got to pay for his fun. And that's where you two come in."

He told them more of what was in his mind, in terse sparkling sentences, while he dressed. His brain was working at high pressure by that time, throwing ideas together with his own incomparable audacity, building a plan out of a situation that had not yet come to pass, leaving them almost out of breath behind the whirlwind pace of his imagination. And yet, despite the breakneck pace at which he had swept his strategy together, he had no misgivings about it afterwards—not even while he drove his great thundering car recklessly through the night to Harwich, or when he stood outside the post-office in the early morning waiting for the doors to open.

It should be all right. . . . About some things he had a feeling of sublime confidence, a sense of joyous inevitability, that amounted to actual foreknowledge; and he had the same feeling that morning. These things were ordained: they were the rewards of adventure, the deserved corollaries of battle, murder, and—a slight smile touched his lips—the shadow of sudden death. But with all this assurance of foreknowledge, there was still a ghostly pulse of nervous excitement flickering through his spinal cells when the doors opened to let him in—a tingle of deep delight in the infinitely varied twists of the game, which he loved beyond anything else in life.

He went up to the counter and propped his elbows on the flat of the telegraph section. He wanted to send a cable to Umpopo in British Bechuanaland; but before he sent it he wanted to know all about the comparative merits of the various word rates. He was prepared, according to the inducements offered, to consider the relative attractions of Night Letters, Weekend Letters, or Deferreds; and he wanted to know everything there was to know about each. Naturally, this took time. The official behind the grille, although he claimed a sketchy familiarity with the whereabouts of British Bechuanaland, had never heard of Umpopo; which is not surprising, because the Saint had never heard of it either before he set out to invent a difficult place to want to send a cable to. But with that indomitable zeal which is the most striking characteristic of post-office officials, he applied himself diligently to the necessary research, while Simon Templar lighted another cigarette and waited patiently for results.

He was wearing a brown tweed cap of a pattern which would never ordinarily have appealed to him, and a pair of tortoiseshell glasses and a black military moustache completed the job of disguising him sufficiently to be overlooked on a casual glance even by anyone who knew him. As the last man on earth whom the High Fence would be expecting to meet, he was as well hidden as if he had been buried under the floor. . . . The official behind the counter, meanwhile, was getting buried deeper and deeper under a growing mound of reference books.

"I can't seem to find anything about Umpopo," he complained peevishly, from behind his unhelpful barricade. "Are you sure there is a telegraph office there?"

"Oh, yes," said the Saint blandly. "At least," he added, "there's one at Mbungi which is only half a mile away."

The clerk went back through his books in a silence too frightful to describe; and the Saint put his cigarette back between his lips, and then suddenly remained very still.

Another early customer had entered the office. Simon heard his footsteps crossing the floor and passing behind him, but he did not look round at once. The footsteps travelled along to the Poste Restante section, a couple of yards away, and stopped there.

"Have you anything for Pond?"

The soft voice came clearly to Simon's ears, and he lifted his eyes sidelong. The man was leaning on the counter, like himself, so that his back was half turned; but the Saint's heart stopped beating for a moment.

"What is the first name?" asked the clerk, clearing out the contents of one of the pigeonholes behind him.

"Joshua."

Rather slowly and dreamily, the Saint hitched himself up off his elbow and straightened up. Behind his heaped breakwater of reference books the steaming telegraph official was muttering something profane and plaintive; but the Saint never heard it. He saw the cardboard box which he had posted pushed over to its claimant, and moved along the counter without a sound. His hand fell on the man's shoulder.

"Would you like to see a good-looking ghost?" he drawled, with a throb of uncontrollable beatitude in his voice.

The man spun round with a kind of gasp that was almost a sob. It was Junior Inspector Desmond Pryke.

# X

The writer, whose positively Spartan economy of verbage must often have been noted and admired by every cultured student, recoils instinctively from the temptation to embellish the scene with a well-chosen anthology of those apt descriptive adjectives with which his vocabulary is so richly stocked. The pallor of flabbergasted faces, the glinting of wild eyes, the beading of cold perspirations, the trembling of hands, the tingling of spines, the sinking of stomachs, the coming and going of breath in little, short pants—all those facile clichés which might lure less ruggedly disciplined scribes into the pitfall of endeavouring to make every facet of the situation transparent to the most nitwitted reader—none of these things, on this occasion at least, have sufficient enticement to seduce him. His readers, he assures himself, are not nitwits: they are highly gifted and intelligent citizens, of phenomenal perspicacity and acceleration on the uptake. The situation, he feels, stated even in the baldest terms, could hide none of its facets from them.

It hid none of them from Simon Templar, oɪ from Junior Inspector Pryke. But Simon Templar was the first to speak again.

"What are you doing here, Desmond?" he asked gently.

Pryke licked his lips, without answering. And then the question was repeated, but Simon Templar did not repeat it.

Chief Inspector Teal stepped out from behind a screen which cut off the Savings Bank section of the counter, and repeated it. His hands were in the pockets of his unnecessary raincoat, and his movement had the same suggestion of weary and reluctant effort that his movements always had; but there was something in the set of his round plump jaw and the narrowness of his sleepy-lidded eyes which explained beyond any need of words that he had watched the whole brief incident from beginning to end, and had missed none of the reactions which a police officer on legitimate business need not have shown.

"Yes—what are you doing?" he said.

Pryke's head jerked round again, and his face went another shade greyer. For a further interval of thrumming seconds he seemed to be struggling to find his voice; and the Saint smiled.

"I told you the High Fence would be here to collect his boodle, Claud," he said; and looked at Pryke again. "Quincey told me," he said.

"I don't know what you're talking about." Pryke had got some kind of control over his throat but there was a quiver in his breathing which made odd little breaks in the sentence. "I heard that there were some stolen jewels here——"

"Who from?" Teal asked quietly.

"From a man I found on the theory I was working on. You told me I could——"

"What was his name?"

"That's a long story," said Pryke hoarsely. "I met him. . . ."

Probably he knew that the game was over—that the bluff was hopeless except as a play for time. The attack was too overwhelming. Watching him with smiling lips and bleak blue eyes, the Saint knew that there wasn't a man living who could have warded it off—whose brain, under the shock, could yet have moved fast enough to concoct a story, instantaneously and without reflection, that would have stood the light of remorseless investigation which must have been directed into it.

"I met him last night," said Pryke. "I suppose you have some reason——"

Simon nodded.

"We have," he said gently. "We came here to play the grand old parliamentary game of Sitting on the Fence; and it looks as if you are what might be called the sittee."

"You're crazy," said Pryke harshly.

His hand was sliding towards his hip, in a casual movement that should have been merely the conventional search for a cigarette-case; and Simon saw it a fraction of a second late.

He saw the flash of the nickel-plated gun, and the shot blasted his eardrums as he flung himself aside. Pryke swerved frantically, hesitated an instant, and turned his automatic on the broad target of Chief Inspector Teal; but before he could touch the trigger again the Saint's legs had swung round in a flailing scissor sweep that found its marks faultlessly on knee-joint and ankle-bone. Pryke cursed and went down, clean and flat as a dead fish, with a smack that squeezed half the breath out of his body; and the Saint rolled over and held him in an ankle lock while the local men who had been posted outside poured in through the doors.

And that was approximately that.

The Saint continued to lie prostrate on the floor after Pryke had been handcuffed and taken away, letting the profound contentment of the day sink into his soul and make itself gorgeously at home. Misunderstanding his stillness, Mr Teal bent over him with a shadow of alarm on his pink face.

"Are you hurt?" he asked gruffly; and the Saint chuckled.

"Only in my pride." He reached out and retrieved his cigarette, which had parted company with him during the scuffle, and blew the dust off it before replacing it in his mouth. "I'm getting a worm's eye view of life—you might call it an act of penance. If I'd had to make a list of all the people whom I didn't think would ever turn out to be the High Fence, your Queen of the May would have been first on the roll. Well, I suppose Life has these surprises. . . . But it all fits in. Being on duty at Market Street, he wouldn't have had any trouble in poisoning Johnny Anworth's horse-radish; but I'm not sure how he got Sunny Jim——"

"I am," said Teal grimly. "He was standing a little behind me when I was talking to Fasson—between me and the door. He could have shot Fasson from his pocket and slammed the door before I could look round, without taking a tremendous risk. After all, there was no reason for anyone to suspect him. He put it over on all of us." Teal fingered a slip of chewing gum out of his pocket and unwrapped it sourly, for he also had his pride. "I suppose it was you who took Sunny Jim away," he said suddenly.

Simon grinned.

"Teal! Will you always think these unkind thoughts about me?"

The detective sighed. He picked up the evidential package from the counter, opened it, glanced at the gleaming layers of gems, and stuffed it firmly into his pocket. No one knew better than himself what unkind thoughts he would always have to think. But in this case at least the Saint had done him a service, and the accounts seemed to be all square—which was an almost epoch-making dé-nouement. "What are you getting out of this?" he inquired suspiciously.

The Saint rose to his feet with a smile, and brushed his clothes.

"Virtue," he said piously, "is its own reward. Shall we go and look for some breakfast, or must you get on with your job?"

Mr Teal shook his head.

"I must get back to London—there are one or two things to clear up. Pryke's flat will have to be searched. There's still a lot of stolen property to be recovered, and I shouldn't be surprised to find it there—he must have felt so confident of never being suspected that he wouldn't bother about a secret headquarters. Then we shall have to pull in Quincey and Enderby. But I don't expect they'll give us much trouble now." The detective buttoned his coat, and his drowsy eyes went over the Saint's smiling face with the perpetual haze of unassuageable doubt still lingering in them. "I suppose I shall be seeing you again," he said.

"I suppose you will," said the Saint, and watched Teal's stolid portly figure lumbering out into the street before he turned into the nearest telephone booth. He agreed with Mr Teal that Pryke had probably been confident enough to use his own apartment as his headquarters. But Patricia Holm and Hoppy Uniatz were already in London, whereas Mr Teal had to get there; and Simon Templar had his own unorthodox interpretation of the rewards of Virtue.

# THE UNLICENSED VICTUALLERS

## From The Ace Of Knaves

---

WHEN I WAS A BOY (*only a few hundred years ago*) *it was practically one of the immutable laws of life that every right-minded boy was a readymade customer for a story about Smugglers. So this is a story about Smugglers; and I have included it in this compendium on the assumption that none of us has grown very much older, and in the hope that our minds are not much worse than they used to be, if as bad. The Smugglers, of course, are a trifle streamlined and efficient, and they do not have wooden legs or black patches over one eye; but I trust that in all other respects their villainy will be found to be as satisfactory as that of the older models.*

*Aside from that, this story doesn't really seem to need any special introduction.*

*I notice, however, that it does contain one curious interlude which may provoke some comment.*

*The remarkable ability of Mr Hoppy Uniatz to consume alcohol, without visible discomfort, in quantities which would keep any six ordinary citizens in a state of permanent paralysis, has long been a source of amazement not only to the Saint himself but also to several habitual readers of these chronicles. Indeed, certain sceptical persons, who seem to doubt the historical solemnity of these records, have claimed that it is impossible for any human being to assimilate so much embalming fluid without becoming completely mummified—a somewhat ridiculous contention to us, of course, who have been eye-witnesses on so many occasions when Mr Uniatz has demonstrated that it can be done by doing it.*

*Simon Templar, for his part, has seemed to lean towards the theory that with Mr Uniatz's brain in its normally petri-*

*fied condition, any further ossification would scarcely be perceptible. But this theory hardly seems tenable when one stops to consider that there are several nervous reflexes, perhaps unconnected with conscious cerebration, such as lifting a bottle to the mouth or bopping a guy on the coconut, which are normally suspended during complete alcoholic paralysis, but which in the case of Mr Uniatz appear to be immune to interference.*

*Personally, I do not feel qualified to venture an opinion on such a profound physiological puzzle. But by way of additional data for more learned scientists, and also to partly correct those critics who believe that Mr Uniatz has never shown any reaction to his intake of alcohol, I feel bound to draw attention to the curious interlude which I was referring to.*

*There is one point in this story at which, after a longish session with a cargo of contraband tiger's milk, Mr Uniatz, to my mind, indicates that his apparent immunity may be merely a matter of degree. I don't say that he shows signs of getting tight. But there is a slight exuberance, a faint exhilaration, a gentle glow, which might tempt one towards the daring hypothesis that his absorption of alcohol does not affect him simply because he does not drink enough. I don't really know; but there it is.*

# THE UNLICENSED VICTUALLERS

SOMEWHERE among the black hills to the southwest dawned a faint patch of light. It moved and grew, pulsing and brightening, like a palely luminous cloud drifting down from the horizon; and Simon Templar, with his eyes fixed on it, slid his cigarette-case gently out of his pocket.

"Here it comes, Hoppy," he remarked.

Beside him, Hoppy Uniatz followed his gaze and inhaled deeply from his cigar, illuminating a set of features which would probably have caused any imaginative passerby, seeing them spring suddenly out of the darkness, to mistake them for the dial of a particularly malevolent banshee.

"Maybe dey got some liquor on board dis time, boss," he said hopefully. "I could just do wit' a drink now."

Simon frowned at him in the gloom.

"You've got a drink," he said severely. "What happened to that bottle I gave you when we came out?"

Mr Uniatz wriggled uneasily in his seat.

"I dunno, boss. I just tried it, an' it was empty. It's de queerest t'ing . . ." An idea struck him. "Could it of been leakin', woujja t'ink, boss?"

"Either it was, or you will be," said the Saint resignedly.

His eyes were still fixed on the distance, where the nimbus of light was growing still brighter. By this time his expectant ears could hear the noise that came with it, a faraway rattle and rumble that was at first hardly more than a vibration in the air, growing steadily louder in the silence of the night.

He felt for a button on the dashboard, and the momentary whirr of the starter died into the smooth sibilant whisper of a perfectly tuned engine as the great car came to life. They were parked on the heath, just off the edge of the road, in the shadow of a clump of bushes, facing the ghostly aurora that was approaching them from where the hills rose towards the sea. Simon trod on the clutch and pushed the gear lever into first, and heard a subdued click beside him as Mr Uniatz released the safety catch of his automatic.

"Howja know dis is it?" Mr Uniatz said hoarsely, the point having just occurred to him.

"They're just on time." Simon was looking down at the phosphorescent hands of his wrist watch. "Pargo said they'd be leaving at two o'clock. Anyway, we'll be sure of it when Peter gives us the flash."

"Is dat why you send him down de road?"

"Yes, Hoppy. That was the idea."

"To see de truck when it passes him?"

"Exactly."

Mr Uniatz scratched his head, making a noise like wood being sandpapered.

"How does he know it's de right truck?" he asked anxiously.

"By the number plate," Simon explained. "You know—that bit of tin with figures on it."

Mr Uniatz digested his thought for a moment, and relaxed audibly.

"Chees, boss," he said admiringly. "De way you t'ink of every-t'ing!"

A warm glow of relief emanated from him, an almost tangible radiation of good cheer and fortified faith, rather like the fervour which must exude from a true follower of the Prophet when he arrives in Paradise and finds that Allah has indeed placed a number of supremely voluptuous houris at his disposal, exactly as promised in the *Qur'an*. It was a feeling which had become perennially new to Mr Uniatz, ever since the day when he had first discovered the sublime infallibility of the Saint and clutched at it like a straw in the turbulent oceans of Thought in which he had been floundering painfully all his life. That Simon Templar, on one of those odd quixotic impulses which were an essential part of his character, should have encouraged the attachment, was a miracle that Mr Uniatz had never stopped to contemplate: he asked nothing more than to be allowed to stay on as an unquestioning Sancho Panza to this dazzling demigod who could Think of Things with such supernatural ease.

"Dis is like de good old days," Hoppy said contentedly; and the Saint smiled in sympathy.

"It is, isn't it? But I never thought I'd be doing it in England."

Suddenly the haze of light down the road flared up, blazed into blinding clarity as the headlights of the lorry swung round a bend like searchlights. It was still some distance away, but the road ran practically straight for a mile in either direction, and they were parked in the lee of almost the only scrap of cover on the open moor.

Simon held up one hand to shield his eyes against the direct glare. He was not looking at the headlights themselves, but at a point in the darkness a little to the right of them, waiting for the signal that would identify the lorry beyond any doubt. And while he watched, the signal came—four long equal flashes from a powerful electric torch, strong enough for him to see the twinkle of them even with the lorry's headlights shining towards him.

The Saint drew a deep breath.

"Okay," he said. "You know your stuff, Hoppy. And don't use that Betsy of yours unless you have to."

He flicked his lighter and touched it to the end of the cigarette clipped between his lips. The light thrown upwards by his cupped hands brought out his face for an instant in vivid sculpture—the crisp sweep of black hair, the rakeshell lines of cheekbone and jaw, the half-smile on the clean-cut reckless mouth, the glimmer of scapegrace humour in the clear and mocking blue eyes. It was a face that fitted with an almost startling perfection, as faces so seldom do, not only into the mission that had brought him there that night, but also into all the legends about him. It was a face that made it seem easy to understand why he should be called the Saint, and why some people should think of him almost literally like that, while others called him by the same name and thought of him as a devil incarnate. It might have been the face of a highwayman in another age, waiting by the roadside on his black horse for some unsuspecting traveller—only that the power of a hundred horses purred under the bonnet waiting for the touch of his foot, and the travellers he was waiting for were not innocent even if they were unsuspecting.

The flame went out, dropping his face back into the darkness; and as he slipped the lighter back into his pocket he sent the car whirling forward in a short rush, spinning the wheel to swing it at right angles across the road, and stopped it there, with the front wheels a foot from the grass verge on the other side.

"Let's go," said the Saint.

Hoppy Uniatz was already halfway out of the door on his side. This at least was something he understood. To him, the higher flights of philosophy and intellectual attainment might be for ever barred; but in the field of pure action, once the objects of it had been clearly and carefully explained to him in short sentences employing only the four or five hundred words which made up his vocabulary, he had few equals. And the Saint grinned as he disembarked on to the macadam, and melted soundlessly into the night on the opposite side of the road from the one Mr Uniatz had taken.

The driver of the lorry knew nothing of these preparations until his headlights flooded the Saint's car strongly enough to make it plain that the roadway was completely blocked. Instinctively he muttered a curse and trod and hauled on the brakes; and the lorry had groaned to a standstill only a yard from the obstacle before he realised he might have been unwise.

Even so, there was nothing much else that he could have done, unless he had driven blindly on off the road on to the open heath, with the chance of landing himself in a ditch. Belatedly, it dawned on him that even that risk might have been preferable to the risk of stopping behind such a suspicious-looking barricade, and he groped for a pocket in his overalls. But before he could get his gun out the door beside him was open, and another gun levelled at his middle was dimly visible in the reflected light of the headlamps.

"Would you mind stepping outside?" said a pleasant voice; and the driver set his teeth.

"Not on your mucking life——"

He had got that far when a hand grasped him by the front of his clothing. What followed was something that puzzled him intermittently for the rest of his life, and he would brood over it in his leisure hours, trying to reconcile his own personal impressions with the logical possibilities of the world as he had previously known it. But if it had not been so manifestly impossible, he would have said that he seemed to be lifted bodily out of his seat and drawn through the door with such force that he sailed through the air almost to the edge of the road in a graceful parabola comparable to the flight of the cruising flamingo, before a large portion of the county of Dorset rose up and hit him very hard in several places at once.

As he crawled painfully up on to his hands and knees, he saw the performer of this miracle standing over him.

"'Ere," he protested dazedly, "wot's the idear?"

"The idea is that you ought to be a good boy and do what you're told."

The voice was still cool and genial, but there was an undertone of silky earnestness in it which the driver had overlooked before. Staring up in an effort to make out the details of the face from which it came, the driver realised that the reason why it seemed so curiously featureless was that a dark cloth mask covered it from brow to chin; and something inside his chest seemed to turn cold.

Simon took hold of him again and lifted him to his feet; and as he did so a shrill yelp and a thud came from the other side of the lorry.

"That will be your mate going to sleep," said the Saint cheerfully. "Will you have one of our special bedtime stories, or will you just take things quietly?"

His left hand had been sliding imperceptibly over the man's clothing while he spoke, and before the driver knew what was happening the automatic which he carried in his overalls had been whisked away from him. All he saw of it was the glint of metal as it vanished into one of the Saint's pockets, but he clutched at the place where it had been and found nothing there. The Saint's soft laugh purled on his eardrums.

"Come along, sonny boy—let's see what you've got in that beautiful covered wagon."

With that stifling lump of ice swelling under his ribs, the driver felt himself being propelled firmly towards the rear of the van. Simon slipped a tiny flashlight out of his pocket as they went; and as they reached the back of the lorry the masked face of Mr Uniatz swam round from the other side into the bright beam.

"I heard music," said the Saint.

Hoppy nodded.

"Dat was de udder guy. He tries to make a grab at my mask, so I bop him on de spire wit' my Betsy an' he dives."

"That's what I love about you," murmured Simon. "You're so thoughtful. Suppose he'd got your mask off, he might have died of heart failure, and that would be bloody awkward. You ought to keep that face-curtain on all the time—it suits you."

He gave the driver a last gentle push that almost impaled him on the muzzle of Mr Uniatz's ever-ready Betsy, and turned his attention to the rear doors of the van. While he was fumbling with them, footsteps sounded on the road behind him and another flashlight split the darkness and focussed on the lock from over his shoulder.

"What ho," said Peter Quentin.

"Ho kay," said the Saint. "The operation went off without a

hitch, and one of the patients has a bent spine. Keep that light steady a minute, will you?"

Actually it was not a minute, but only a few seconds, before the lock surrendered its share of the unequal contest with a set of deft fingers that could have disposed of the latest type of burglar-proof safe in rather less time than an amateur would have taken to empty a can of asparagus with a patent can-opener. Simon pocketed the instrument he had been using, swung the doors wide, and hauled himself nimbly up into the interior of the van.

"What have we won this time?" Peter asked interestedly.

The Saint's torch was sweeping over the rows of cases stacked up inside.

"Looks like a good night's work, soaks," he answered. "There's quite a load of Bisquit Dubouché, and a spot of Otard . . . a whole raft of Clicquot Veuve . . . Romanée Conti . . . Chambertin. . . . Here's a case of Château Yquem——"

"Is dey any Scotch?" inquired Mr Uniatz practically.

"No, I don't think so. . . . Oh, yes, there are a few cases in the corner. We don't seem to have done too badly."

He switched off his flashlight and returned to spring lightly down to the road and shut the doors again. For a moment he stood gleefully rubbing his hands.

"Bisquit Dubouché," he said. "Clicquot Veuve. Chambertin. Romanée. Conti. Château Yquem. Even Hoppy's Scotch. Think of it, my perishing pirates. Cases and cases of 'em. Hundreds of quids' worth of bee-yutiful drinks. And not one blinkin' bottle of it has paid a penny of duty. Smuggled in under the noses of the blear-eyed coastguards and pot-bellied excise men. Yoicks! And all for our benefit. Do we smuggle? Do we defraud the Revenue? No, no—a thousand times no. We just step in and grab the loot. Have a drink with me, you thugs."

"That's all very well," Peter Quentin objected seriously. "But we went into this hijacking game to try and find out who was the big bug who was running it——"

"And so we shall, Peter. So we shall. And we'll have a drink with him. And a cigar and a set of silk underwear, like we got last time. How are those lace panties wearing, Hoppy?"

Mr Uniatz made a plaintive noise in his throat, and the Saint pulled himself together.

"All right," he said. "Let's be on our way, Peter, you can carry on with the lorry. Park it in the usual place, and we'll be over in the morning and help you unload. Hoppy and I will take this team along and see if we can find out anything from them."

He turned away and led off along the roadside to move his car out of the way. In the blackness beside the truck he almost stumbled over something lying on the ground, and recalled Hoppy's account of his interview with the driver's mate. As he recovered his balance, he switched his torch on again and turned it downwards.

The sprawled figure in grimy overalls lay with its face turned upwards, quite motionless, the mouth slightly open. The upper part of the face was hard to distinguish under the brim of a tweed cap pulled well down over the eyes, but the chin was smooth and white. He could only have been a youngster, Simon realised, and felt a fleeting twinge of pity. He bent down and shook the lad's shoulder.

"How hard did you bop him, Hoppy?" he said thoughtfully.

"I just gave him a little pat on de bean, boss——"

"The trouble is, everybody hasn't got a skull like yours," said the Saint.

He dropped on one knee and pulled down the zipper from the neck of the overalls, feeling inside the youngster's shirt for the reassurance of a heartbeat. And the others heard him let out a soft exclamation.

"What's the matter?" Peter Quentin demanded sharply.

"Well, we certainly won something," said the Saint. "Look."

He took hold of the shabby tweed cap and jerked it off; and the ray of the torch in Peter's hand jumped wildly as a flood of golden hair broke loose to curl around the face of a girl whose sheer loveliness took his breath away.

## II

Mr Uniatz sucked in his breath with a sound like an expiring soda siphon; and Peter Quentin sighed.

"*Nunc dimittis*," he said weakly. "I can't stand any more. The rest of my life would be an anticlimax. I always knew you were the luckiest man on earth, but there are limits. I believe if you trod on a toad it'd turn out to be a fairy princess."

"You ought to see what happens when I tread on a fairy," said the Saint.

Actually his thoughts were chasing far ahead of his words. The miracle had happened—if it was a miracle—and the story went on from there. He was too hardened a traveller in the strange country of adventure to be dumbfounded by any of the unpredictable twists in its trails. But he was wondering, with a tingle of inward exhilaration, where this particular twist was destined to lead.

He turned up the edge of his mask to light another cigarette, and his mind went back over the events that had brought him out that night, not for the first time, to make the raid that had culminated in this surprise. . . . The laden trucks thundering northwards from the coast, filled to capacity with those easily marketable goods on which the English duties were highest—wines and spirits, cigars and cigarettes, silks and embroideries and Paris models. . . . The rumours in the Press, that leaked out in spite of the efforts of the police, of a super-smuggler whose cunning and audacity and efficient organisation were cheating the Revenue of thousands of pounds a week and driving baffled detectives to the verge of nervous breakdowns . . . The gossip in pubs along the coast, and the whispers in certain exclusive circles to which no law-abiding citizen had access . . . The first realisation that he had enough threads in his hands to be irrevocably committed to the adventure—that the grand old days of his outlawry had come back, as they must always go on coming back so long as he lived, when his name could be a holy terror to the police and the ungodly alike, and golden galleons of boodle waited for his joyous buccaneering forays. . . .

And now he was wondering whether he dared to hope that the clue he had been seeking for many weeks had fallen into his hands at last, in the shape of that slim golden beauty in the oil-stained overalls who lay unconscious under his hands.

He went on thinking without interrupting his examination. She was alive, anyway—her pulse was quick but regular, and she was breathing evenly. There was no blood on her head, and her skull seemed to be intact.

"That cap probably helped," he said. "But it only shows you how careful you have to be when you're patting people on the bean, Hoppy."

Mr Uniatz swallowed.

"Chees, boss——"

"It's all right," Peter consoled him. "You wouldn't have missed anything if you had brained her. If there's going to be any more fun, she'll have it."

The Saint straightened up and turned to the driver of the lorry, who was standing woodenly behind him with his ribs aching from

THE UNLICENSED VICTUALLERS

the steady pressure of a Betsy which in spite of Mr Uniatz's chival-
rous distress had never shifted its position.

"Who is she?" Simon asked.

The driver glowered at him sullenly.

"I don't know."

"What happened—did you find her growing on a tree?"

"I was just givin' her a lift."

"Where to?"

"That's none o' your muckin' business."

"Oh, no?" The Saint's voice was amiable and unruffled. "Pretty
lucky she was all dressed up ready to go riding in a lorry, wasn't
it?"

The man tightened his jaw and stood silent, scowling at the Saint
with grim intensity. He was, as a matter of fact, just starting to
experience that incredulity of his own recollections of his recent
flight through the air which has been referred to before: he was a
big man, and he was thinking that he would like to see an attempt
to repeat the performance.

The jar of Hoppy's gun grinding roughly into his side made him
half turn with a darkening glare.

"Dijja hear de boss ask you a question?" inquired Mr Uniatz, with
all the dulcet persuasiveness of a foghorn.

"You ruddy barstard——"

"That'll do," Simon intervened crisply. "And I wouldn't take any
chances with my health if I were you, brother. That Betsy of
Hoppy's would just about blow you in half, and he's rather sensitive
about his family. We'll go on talking to you presently."

He turned to the others.

"I don't know how it strikes any of you bat-eyed brigands," he
said, "but I've got a feeling that this is the best break we've had yet.
After all, a lot of weird things happen in this world of sin, but you
don't usually find girls in overalls riding on smugglers' trucks with
a cargo of contraband stagger soup."

"You do when you hold 'em up," said Peter stoically.

"She didn't know I was going to hold it up, you fathead. So she's
here for some other reason. Well, she might be just a girl friend of
the Menace here, but I don't think it's likely. Take a look at her, and
then look at him. Of course, if she turned out to be blind and deaf
and halfwitted——"

The driver growled viciously, and received another painful prod
from Hoppy Uniatz's gun for his trouble.

"Well, if she isn't?" said Peter.

"Then she's something a hell of a lot more important. She's one of the nobs—or she knows 'em pretty well. It'd fit in, wouldn't it? Remember that last consignment we hijacked? All silk dresses and lace and crêpe-de-chine underwhatsits. I always thought there might be a woman in it; and if this is her——"

"She," said Peter, helpfully.

The Saint laughed.

"The hell with your grammar," he said. "Let's get going—it'd spoil everything if somebody else came scooting over this blasted heath just now."

He turned away and picked the girl up in his arms like a baby—her body was still limp and lifeless, and it would save a certain amount of trouble if she remained in that state for a little while. So long as Hoppy hadn't struck hard enough for her to be unconscious too long. . . .

He put her down in the car, in the seat beside his own, and closed the door. He had left the engine running in case of the need for a quick getaway, and he knew that in waiting so long he had already tempted the Providence that had sent him such a windfall. He straightened up briskly, and strolled to meet the others who were following him.

"This means that we change our plans a bit," he said. "I like my beauty sleep as much as any of you, even if I don't need it so much; but I've got to know where this is getting us before we go to bed. You can follow along with the lorry to the old Barn, Peter, and Hoppy can take it up to town from there while we see if the fairy princess knows any new fairy tales."

Mr Uniatz cleared his throat. It sounded like the wastepipe of a bath regurgitating; but it was meant to be a discreet and tactful noise. Almost the whole of the intervening conversation had been as obscure to him as a recitation from Euripides in the original Greek, but one minor omission stood out in front of him with pellucid clarity. Mr Uniatz was no genius, but he had an unswerving capacity for detail which many more brightly coruscating brains might have envied.

"Boss," he said, compressing philosophical volumes into one irreducible nutshell. "Dis mug."

"I know," said the Saint hurriedly. "I was exaggerating a bit, I'm afraid. It isn't as bad as all that, really. I don't believe anyone would

actually die of heart failure if they saw it. I've looked at it myself
several times——"

"I mean," said Mr Uniatz shyly, emphasising his objective with
another rib-splitting thrust of his Betsy, "dis mug here."

"Oh, him. Well——"

"Do I give him de woiks?" asked Mr Uniatz, condensing into six
crystalline monosyllables the problem which dictators of every age
and clime have taken thousands of words to propound.

Simon shrugged tolerantly.

"If he gets obstreperous, I should say yes," he murmured. "But if
he behaves himself you can put it off for a while. We will have
words with him first. If he can put us wise about whether the sleeping beauty is one of the first strings in this racket——"

"Or even *the* first string," said Peter Quentin thoughtfully.

The Saint put his cigarette to his mouth and drew it to a bright
spark of light. For a few moments he was silent. It was a thought
that had already occurred to him, long before; but he had been content to let the answer produce itself in its own good time. Even
stranger things than that had happened, in the cockeyed world of
which Simon Templar had made himself the uncrowned king; and
when they did occur they were usually the forerunners of even
more trouble than he had set out to ask for, which was plenty. But
complications like that had to take care of themselves.

"Who knows?" said the Saint vaguely. "It might just as well have
been the secretary of the Women's Temperance League, who isn't
nearly so good-looking. On your way, Peter——"

"*Hey!*" bawled Mr Uniatz.

His voice, which could never at any time have rivalled the musical accents of a radio announcer, blared into the middle of the Saint's
words with a bloodcurdling intensity of feeling that made even
Simon Templar's iron nerves wince. For a moment the Saint was
paralysed, while he searched for some sign of the stimulus that was
capable of drawing such a response from Mr Uniatz's phlegmatic
throat.

And then he became aware that Hoppy was staring straight ahead
with a frozen rigidity that was not even conscious of the sensation
it had caused. A little to the Saint's left, the driver of the lorry was
looking in the same direction with a glitter of evil satisfaction in his
small eyes.

Simon swung round the other way, and saw that Peter Quentin
also was gazing past him with the same petrified immobility. And

as the Saint turned round further, he had a feeling of dizzy unreality that made his scalp creep.

As he remembered it, he had only taken a couple of steps away from his car when Peter Quentin and Hoppy Uniatz and the driver of the lorry had met him. But as he turned, he couldn't see the car at all where it should have been. The road all round him looked empty in the dull gleam of their torches, apart from the black bulk of the van which overshadowed them. It was another second before he saw where his car was. It had swung off on to the heath in a wide arc in order to straighten up; and while he watched it it bumped back on to the macadam and went skimming away up the road to the northeast, with no more than a soft flutter of gas from the exhaust to announce its departure.

### III

"One of the things I envy about you," said Peter Quentin, with a certain relish, "is that magnetic power which makes you irresistible to women. Even if they've just been knocked unconscious, the moment they open their eyes and see what's found them——"

"It's a handicap, really," said the Saint good-humouredly. "Their instinct tells them that if they saw much of me they'd do something their mothers wouldn't like, so as often as not they tear themselves reluctantly away."

"I noticed she looked reluctant," said Peter. "She took your car, too—that must have been a wrench."

The Saint grinned philosophically, and tapped a cigarette on his thumbnail. His spirits were too elastic to know the meaning of depression, and the setback had intriguing angles to it which he was broadminded enough to appreciate as an artist.

The lorry, with Peter at the wheel, churned on through West Holme on to the Wareham road; and Simon Templar lounged back on the hard seat beside him, with his feet propped up where the dashboard would have been if the lorry had boasted any such refinements, and considered the situation without malice. In the interior of the van, behind him, Hoppy Uniatz was keeping the original driver under control; and Simon hoped that he wouldn't do too much damage to the cargo. But even allowing for Mr Uniatz's phenomenal capacity, there was enough bottled kale there to save the night's work from being a total loss.

They were clattering through the sleeping streets of Ringwood before Peter Quentin said: "What are you going to do about the car?"

"Report it stolen some time tomorrow. She'll have ditched it by then—it's too hot to hold on to."

"And suppose she reports the lorry first?"

Simon shook his head.

"She won't do that. It'd be too embarrassing if the police happened to catch us. We come out best on the deal, Peter. And on top of that, we've had a good look at her and we'd know her again."

"It ought to be easy," said Peter cheerlessly. "After all, there are only about ten million girls in England, and if we divide the country up between us——"

"We shan't have to go that far. Look at it on the balance of probabilities. If she stays in this game, and we stay in it, it's ten to one that our trails'll cross again."

Peter thought for a moment.

"Now you come to mention it," he said, "the odds are bigger than that. If she's got any sense, she'll find out who you are from the insurance certificate in the car. And then she'll be calling on you with a team of gunmen to ask for her lorry back."

"I had thought of that," said the Saint soberly. "And maybe that's the biggest advantage of all."

"It would save us the trouble of having to find someone to give it to," Peter agreed sympathetically.

But the Saint blew a cloud of smoke at the low roof of the tiny compartment, and said dreamily: "Just look at it strategically, old lad. All the time we've known that there was some big nob, or bunch of nobs, organising this racket—some guy or guys who keep themselves so exclusive that not even their own mob knows who's at the top. They're the boys we're after, for the simple reason that because they've got the brains to run the show in a way that the saps who do the dirty work, like our pal in the back here, haven't got the intelligence to run it, they've also got the brains to see that they get the fattest dividend. We've been messing about for some time, annoying them in small ways like this and trying to get a lead, and all the time we've been trying to keep ourselves under cover. Now I'm just beginning to wonder if that was the smartest game we could have played. In any case, the game's been changed now, whether we like it or not; and I don't know that I'm broken-hearted. Now we're on the range to be shot at, and while that's going on we may get a look at the shooters."

"Who'll still be just the saps who do the dirty work."

"I'm not so sure."

For once, Peter restrained the flippant retort which came automatically to his mind. He knew as well as any man that the Saint had been proved big enough game to being the shyest and most cautious hunters out of hiding. There was something about the almost fabulous stories which had been built up around the character of the Saint that tended to make otherwise careful leaders feel that he was a problem of which the solution could not be safely deputed to less talented underlings.

"All the same," he said, "we were getting along pretty well with Pargo."

"He was still only one of the rank and file—or maybe you might call him a sergeant. It was a bit of luck that we found him driving the first lorry we hijacked, with what I knew about his earlier career of crime;* and he had sense enough to see that it was safer for him to take his chance with us than have himself parked in a sack outside Scotland Yard; but I don't know that he could ever have got a line on the Nobs . . . I made a date to meet him later tonight, by the way—when he rang me up about this lorry-load he said he'd be driving down from town in the small hours and might have some tips, so I thought we'd better get together."

"Tell him to give us a ring when we're going to be bumped off," said Peter. "I'd like to know about it, so I can pay my insurance premium."

The Saint looked at his watch.

"We've got an hour and a half to go before that," he said. "And we may get a squeal out of Hoppy's protégé before then."

His earlier relaxation, in which he had been not so much recovering from a blow as waiting for the inspiration for a fresh attack, had vanished altogether. Peter Quentin could feel the atmosphere about him, more than through anything he said, in the gay surge of vitality that seemed to gather around him like an invisible aura, binding everyone within range in a spell of absurd magic which was beyond reason and was yet humanly impossible to resist; and once again Peter found himself surrendering blindly to that scapegrace wizardry.

"All right," he said, ridiculously. "Let's squeeze the juice out of him and see what we get."

*See *The Misfortunes of Mr Teal.*

Near Stony Cross they had swung off the main road into a narrow track that seemed to plunge into the cloistered depths of the
New Forest, as if it would drift away into the heart of an ancient
and forgotten England where huntsmen in green jerkins might still
leap up to draw their bows at a stag springing from covert; actually
it was a meandering and unkempt road that wandered eventually
into the busy highways that converged on Lyndhurst. Somewhere
along this road Peter Quentin hauled the wheel round and sent them
jolting along an even narrower and deeper-rutted track that looked
like nothing but an enlarged footpath. They lurched round a couple
of sharp turns, groaned up a forbidding incline, and jarred to a sudden stop.

Peter switched out the lights, and the Saint put his feet down and
stretched his cramped limbs.

"We all know about housemaid's knee," he remarked, "but did
you ever hear about truck-driver's pelvis? That's what I've got. If I
were a union man I should go on strike."

He opened the door and lowered himself tenderly to the ground,
massaging the kinks out of his bones.

In front of him, a broad squat mass loomed blackly against the
starlight—the Old Barn, which really had been a derelict thatched
Tudor barn before Peter Quentin found it and transformed its interior into a cosy rural retreat with enough modern conveniences to
compete with any West End apartment. It had the advantage of
being far from any listening and peeping neighbours; and the Saint
had found those assets adequate reason for borrowing it before. In
that secluded bivouac, things could be done and noises could be
made which would set a whole suburb chattering if they happened
in it. . . .

There was an inexorable assurance of those facts implicit in the
resilience of the Saint's stride as he rambled towards the rear of the
van. And as he approached it, in the silence which had followed
the shutting off of the strangling engine, he heard a hoarse voice
raised in wailing melody.

> *"If I had de wings of a nangel,*
> *From dese prison walls I would fly,*
> *I would fly to de arms of my darling,*
> *An' dere I'd be willing to die. . . ."*

Simon unfastened the doors, while the discordant dirge continued
to reverberate from the interior.

*"I wish I had someone to lurve me,*
*Somebody to call me her own,*
*I wish——"*

The Saint's torch splashed its beam into the van, framing the tableau in its circle of brilliance.

Mr Uniatz sat on a pile of cases, leaning back with his legs dangling and looking rather like a great ape on a jungle bough. In his left hand he held his Betsy, and the flashlight gripped between his knees was focused steadily on the lorry driver, who stood scowling on the opposite side of the van. One of the cases was open, and a couple of bottles rolled hollowly on the floor. A third bottle was clutched firmly in Mr Uniatz's hand, and he appeared to have been using it to beat time.

His face expanded in a smile as he screwed up his eyes against the light.

"Hi, boss," he said, winningly.

"Come on out," said the Saint. "Both of you."

The lorry driver shuffled out first; and as he descended Simon caught him deftly by the wrist, twisted his arm up behind his back, and waited a moment for Peter to take over the hold.

He turned round as Hoppy Uniatz lowered himself clumsily to the ground.

"How much have you soaked up?" he inquired patiently.

"I just had two-t'ree sips, boss. I t'ought I'd make sure de booze was jake. Say, dijja know I could yodel? I just loin de trick comin' along here——"

The Saint turned to Peter with a shrug.

"I'm sorry, old son," he said. "It looks as if you'll have to take the truck on, after all. I've never seen Hoppy break down yet, but all the same it might be awkward if he met a policeman."

"Couldn't that wait till tomorrow?"

"I'd rather not risk it. The sooner the truck's cleared and out of the way the better."

"Okay, chief."

"Hoppy," said the Saint restrainedly, "stop that god-awful noise and take your boy friend inside."

Peter handed over the prisoner, and they walked back towards the front of the van. A last plaintive *layee-Ò*, like the sob of a love-sick cat, squealed through the stilly night before Peter climbed back into the driving seat and restarted the engine. Simon helped him to turn the truck round; and then Peter leaned out of the window.

"What happens next?"

"I'll call you in the morning when I know something," Simon answered. "Happy landings!"

He watched the lorry start on its clattering descent of the hill, and then he turned and went towards the house. In the bright spacious living-room the lorry-driver was lolling in a chair under Hoppy's watchful eye. Simon went straight up to him.

"Get up," he said. "I haven't told you to make yourself at home yet. You're here to answer some questions."

## IV

The man looked up from under his heavy brows, without moving. His mouth was clinched up so that his under lip was the only one visible; and his big frame looked lumpy, as if all the muscles in it were knotted. He went on sitting there stolidly and didn't answer.

"Get up," said the Saint quietly.

The man crossed his legs and turned away to gaze into a far corner of the room.

Simon's hand moved quicker than a striking snake. It took hold of the driver and yanked him up on to his feet as if the chair had exploded under him. The man must have been expecting something to happen; but the response he had produced was so swift and unanswerable that for a moment his eyes were blank with stupefaction. Then he drew back his fist.

The Saint didn't stir or flinch. He didn't even seem to take any steps to meet that crudely telegraphed blow. From the slight tilt of his head and the infinitesimal lift of one eyebrow, he might almost have been vaguely amused. But his eyes held mockery rather than amusement—a curious cold glitter of devilish derision that had a bite like steel sword-points. There was something about it that matched the easy and untroubled and yet perfectly balanced way he was standing, something that seemed an essential offshoot of the supple width of his shoulders and the sardonic curve of his lips and the driver's disturbing memory of an apparently incredible incident only a short time before; something that belonged unarguably to the whiplash quality that had crackled under the quietness of his voice when he spoke. . . . And somehow, for no other reasons, the blow didn't materialise. The driver's fist sank stiffly down to his side.

The Saint smiled.

"Have a cigarette," he said genially.

The driver stared at the packet suspiciously.

"Wot's all this abaht?" he demanded.

"Nothing, Algernon. Nothing at all. Hoppy and I are just a couple of humble philosophers looking for pearls of knowledge. By the way, is your name Algernon?"

"Wot's my name got to do with you?"

"It would help us to talk about you, Algernon. We can't just point at you all the time—it looks so rude. And then there's the blonde you didn't introduce us to. We want to know who she was, so we can give the vicar her phone number. What's her name?"

"Wouldn't you like to know?" snarled the driver belligerently.

Simon nodded with unaltered cordiality.

"You're asking as many questions as I am, Algernon," he remarked. "Which isn't what I brought you here for. But I don't mind letting you into the secret. I would like to know all these things. Go on—have a cigarette."

As the man's mouth opened for another retort, the Saint flipped a cigarette neatly into it. The driver choked and snatched it out furiously. The Saint kindled his lighter. He held it out, and his cool blue eyes met the driver's reddening gaze over the flame. There was no hint of a threat in them, no offer of a challenge, nothing but the same lazy glimmer of half-humorous expectancy as they held before; and yet once again they baffled the driver's wrath with a nonchalance that his brain was not capable of understanding. He put the cigarette back into his mouth and bent his head sulkily to accept the light.

Mr Uniatz, reclining in an abandoned attitude on the settee, had been taking advantage of being temporarily relieved of his duties to sluice his parched throat with the contents of the bottle he had brought with him. Now, after having remained for some minutes with his head tilted back and the bottle up-ended towards the ceiling, he came reluctantly to the conclusion that no more liquid was flowing into the desert, and simultaneously returned to a sense of his responsibilities.

"Lemme give him a rub down, boss," he suggested. "He'll come t'ru fast enough."

Simon glanced at him thoughtfully.

"Do you think you could make him talk, Hoppy?"

"Sure I could, boss. I know dese tough guys. All ya gotta do is boin deir feet wit' a candle, an' dey melt. Lookit, I see a box of candles in de kitchen last night——"

Mr Uniatz struggled up from the couch, fired with ambition and a lingering recollection of having seen a case of Vat 69 in the kitchen at the same time; but the Saint put out an arm and checked him.

"Wait a minute, Hoppy."

He turned back to the driver.

"Hoppy's so impulsive," he explained apologetically, "and I don't really want to turn him loose on you. But I've got an appointment in an hour or so, and if we can't get together before then I'll have to leave Hoppy to carry on. And Hoppy has such dreadfully primitive ideas. The last time I had to leave him to ask a fellow a few questions, when I came back I found that he'd got the mincing machine screwed on to our best table and he was feeding the guy's fingers into it. He got the right answers, of course, but it made such a mess of the table."

"I'm not afraid o' you——"

"Of course you aren't, Algernon. And we don't want you to be. But you've got to change your mind about answering questions, because it's getting late."

The man watched him stubbornly; but his fists were tightening and relaxing nervously, and there was a shining dampness of perspiration breaking out on his forehead. His eyes switched around the room and returned to the Saint's face in a desperate search for escape. But there was no hope there of the kind he was looking for. The Saint's manner was light and genial, almost brotherly; it passed over unpleasant alternatives as remote and improbable contingencies that were hardly worth mentioning at all, and yet the idea of unpleasantness didn't seem to disturb it in any way. A blusterer himself, the driver would have answered bluster in its own language; but that dispassionate imperturbability chilled him with an unfamiliar sensation of fear. . . .

And at that moment, with his uncanny genius for keeping his opponents in suspense, the Saint left the last word unsaid and strolled over to sit on the table, leaving the driver nothing but the threat of his own imagination.

"What's your name, Algernon?" he asked mildly.

"Jopley."

The word fell out after a tense pause, as if the man was fighting battles with himself.

"Been driving these trucks for long?"

"Wot's that got——"

"Been driving these trucks for long?"

"I bin drivin' 'em for a bit."

"Do pretty well out of it?"

The driver was silent again for a space, but this time his silence was not due to obstinacy. His frown probed at the Saint distrustfully; but Simon was blowing wisps of smoke at the ceiling.

"I don't do too bad."

"How much is that?"

"Ten quid a week."

"You know, you're quite a character, aren't you?" said the Saint. "There aren't many people who'd let Hoppy singe their tootsies for ten quid a week. How d'you work it out—a pound a toe?"

The man dragged jerkily at his cigarette, without answering. The question was hardly answerable, anyway—it was more of a gentle twitch at the driver's already overstrung nerves, a reminder of those unpleasant possibilities which were really so unthinkable.

"If I were you," said the Saint, with an air of kindly interest, "I'd be looking for another job."

"Wot sort of job?"

"I think it'd be a kind of sideline," said the Saint meditatively. "I'd look round for some nice generous bloke who wouldn't let people toast my feet or anything like that, but who'd just pay me an extra twenty quid a week for answering a few questions now and again. He might even put up fifty quid when I had anything special to tell him, and it wouldn't hurt me a bit."

"It's a waste of money, boss," said Mr Uniatz with conviction. "If de candles don't woik, I got a new one I see in de movies de udder day. You mash de guy's shins wit' a hammer——"

"You won't pay too much attention to him, will you, Algernon?" said the Saint. "He gets a lot of these ideas, you know—it's the way he was brought up. It's not my idea of a spare-time job, though."

The driver shifted himself from one foot to the other. It wasn't his idea of a spare-time job, either—or even a legitimate part of the job he had. He didn't need to have the balance of the alternatives emphasised to him. They were so clean cut that they made the palms of his hands feel clammy. But that lazily frightening, impersonal voice went on:

"Anyway you don't have to make up your mind in a hurry if you don't want to. Hoppy'll keep you company if you don't mind waiting till I come back, so you won't be lonely. It's rather a lonely place otherwise, you know. We were only saying the other day that a bloke could sit here and scream the skies down, and nobody would hear him. Not that you'd have anything to scream about, of course. . . ."

"Wot is this job?" asked the man hoarsely.

Simon flicked the ash from his cigarette, and hid the sparkle of excitement in his eyes.

"Just telling us some of these odd things we want to know."

The man's lips clamped and relaxed spasmodically, and his broad chest moved with the strain of his breathing. He stood with his chin drawn in, and his eyes peered up from under a ledge of sullen shadow.

"Well," he said. "Go on."

"Who was the girl friend?"

"*Why don't you ask her?*"

The voice was soft and musical, startlingly unlike the harsh growl that Simon's ears had been attuned to; and it came from behind him.

The Saint spun round.

She stood in the open doorway, her feet astride with a hint of boyish swagger, still in her soiled overalls, one hand in the trouser pocket, with the yellow curls tumbling around her exquisitely moulded face, a slight smile on her red lips. Her eyes, he discovered, now that he saw them open for the first time, were a dark midnight grey—almost the same shade as the automatic she held steadily levelled at his chest.

For three seconds the Saint stood rigidly spellbound. And then a slow smile touched the corners of his mouth in response.

"Well, darling," he murmured, "what *is* your name?"

# V

"You ought to be a detective, Mr Templar," she said. "I don't have to ask you yours."

"But you have an advantage. We've tried checking up on your lorries, but you always send them out with fake number plates and no other identification, so it's rather difficult. I have to suffer for being honest."

"Or for not being careful," she said. "By the way, will you tell your friend to do something about his hands?"

Simon looked round. Mr Uniatz was still frozen as the interruption had caught him, with his mouth hanging open and his right hand arrested halfway to the armpit holster where his Betsy nestled close to his heart. His eyes welcomed the Saint with an agonised plea for guidance, and Simon took his wrist and put his hand gently down.

"Leave it alone for a minute, Hoppy," he said. "We don't want the lady to start shooting. . . ." His gaze turned back to the girl. "That is, if she can shoot," he added thoughtfully.

"Don't worry," she said calmly. "I can shoot."

The Saint's glance measured the distance.

"It's about six yards," he observed. "And a lot of people have mistaken ideas about how easy it is to pot a moving target with an automatic at six yards."

"Would you like to try me?"

Simon poised his cigarette-end between his forefinger and thumb and flipped it sideways. It struck Hoppy's discarded bottle, over by the settee, with a faint *plunk!* and sent up a tiny fountain of sparks.

"Hit that," he said.

The muzzle of the gun swung away from his body; but it was only for an instant. She fired without seeming to aim, and the automatic was aligned on the Saint's breastbone again before the crash of the explosion had stopped rattling in his ears, but the bottle was spattered in fragments over the carpet.

The Saint nodded to Hoppy.

"She can shoot," he remarked. "She's been practising."

"It's not much use having a gun if you don't."

"You've been reading some good books," said the Saint, and his smile was serene but watchful. "It looks as if you have what is known as the Bulge—for the time being, anyway. So where do we go from here? Would you like us to sing and dance for you? Hoppy's just discovered that he can yodel, and he's dying for an audience."

"I'm afraid we haven't time for that. Jopley——"

The driver came out of his temporary stupor. He thrust himself forward and retrieved his gun from the Saint's pocket, and shuffled crabwise around the room in the direction of the door, keeping well clear of the girl's line of fire. Remembering the stage at which their conversation had been interrupted, the Saint could understand why he had not been so quick to seize his opportunity as might have been expected; and a malicious twinkle came into his gaze.

"What—you don't want him, do you?" he said. "We thought we'd do you a good turn and take him off your hands."

"I came back for him," she said, "so I suppose I do want him."

Simon acknowledged the argument with a slight movement of his head.

"You didn't waste much time about it, either," he said appreciatively. "How did you track him down—by smell?"

"I followed you. I pulled into a side turning in West Holme and waited to see if you'd go that way. Then I just kept behind you. It wasn't difficult."

It didn't sound very difficult, when the trick was explained. The Saint sighed ruefully at the reflection of his own thoughtlessness.

"That's the worst of lorries," he complained. "It's so hard to notice what's behind you. Something ought to be done about it. . . . But I hope you'll take care of Algernon if you're borrowing him. We were just starting to get matey."

"I heard you," she said.

"Yus." Jopley's voice was loud and grating. "Goin' ter burn me feet, that's 'ow they were goin' ter get matey. I've a good mind——"

"You haven't," said the girl evenly. "We'll leave things like that to gentlemen like Mr Templar."

The Saint smiled at her.

"We've got a secondhand rack and some thumbscrews in the cellar, too," he said. "But I prefer boiling people down with onions and a dash of white wine. It makes quite a good clear soup, rather like *madrilène*."

She really did look like something out of a fairy tale, he thought, or like a moment of musical comedy dropped miraculously into the comfortable masculine furnishings of the Old Barn, with the perfect proportions of her slender body triumphing even over that shabby suit of dungarees, and her face framed in its setting of spun gold; but there was nothing illusory about the unfaltering alertness of those dark grey eyes or the experienced handling of the gun she held. The only uncertain thing about her was the smile that lingered about her lips.

She said: "I'm glad you didn't get me here."

"But you're here now," said the Saint. "So couldn't we make up for lost time?"

His hand moved towards his breast pocket, but the two guns that covered him moved more quickly. Simon raised his eyebrows.

"Can't I have a cigarette?"

"Take them out slowly."

Simon took out his case, slowly, as he was ordered, and opened it.

"Can I offer you one?"

"We haven't got time."

"You're not going?"

"I'm afraid we've got to." Her acting was as light and polished as his own. "But you're coming with us."

The Saint was still for a moment, with the flame of his lighter burning without a quiver under the end of his cigarette. He drew the end of the cigarette to a bright red, and extinguished the flame with a measured jet of smoke.

"But what about Algernon?" he said. "Are you sure he won't be jealous?"

"You're not coming as far as that. We've got to get back to your car, and we don't want any trouble. As long as your friend stays here and doesn't interfere, we shan't have any trouble. I just want you to come down and see us off."

"You hear that, Hoppy?" said the Saint. "Any fancy work from you, and I get bumped off."

"That," said the girl grimly, "is the idea."

Simon weighed his prospects realistically. He hadn't exaggerated the solitude of their surroundings: a pitched battle with machine guns at the Old Barn would have caused less local commotion than letting off a handful of squibs in the deepest wastes of the Sahara. There was nothing to neutralise the value of those two automatics by the door, if the fingers on their triggers chose to become dictatorial—and the experience of a lifetime had taught the Saint to be highly conservative about the chances he took in calling a bluff from the wrong side of a gun. Apart from which, he was wondering whether he wanted to make any change in the arrangements. . . .

As if he were trying to find arguments for accepting the bitterness of defeat, his eyes turned a little away from the girl, to a point in space where they would include a glimpse of the face of the lorry driver. He had sown good seed there, he knew, even if he had been balked of the quick harvest he had hoped for . . . And on the outskirts of his vision, removing all doubt, he saw Jopley's sullen features screwed up in a grotesque wink. . . .

"We always see our visitors off the premises," said the Saint virtuously. "Are you sure you won't have one for the road?"

"Not tonight."

Either he was setting new records in immortal imbecility, Simon realised as he led the way down the steep winding lane, or the threads that had baffled him for the past three weeks were on the point of coming into his reach; and some irrational instinct seemed to tell him that it was not the former. He had no inkling then of how gruesomely and from what an unexpected angle his hunch was to be vindicated.

The beam of his own torch, held in the girl's hand, shone steadily on his back as he walked, and cast his elongated shadow in a long oval of light down the track. The decision was taken now—whatever he might have done to turn the tables back in the Old Barn, out there in the empty night with the torchlight against him and two guns at his back there was no trick he could play that would fall far short of attempted suicide.

They came down to the road, and he saw the lights of his car parked a little way past the turning. Jopley got in first, and took the wheel; and then the girl slipped into the seat beside him, still holding the Saint in the centre of the flashlight's ring of luminance. Simon stood by the side of the car and smiled into the light.

"You still haven't told me your name, darling," he said.

"Perhaps that's because I don't want you to know it."

"But how shall I know who it is when you call me up? You are going to call me up, aren't you? I'm in the London telephone directory, and the number here is Lyndhurst double nine six five." He lingered imperceptibly over the figures—but that was for Jopley's benefit. "Sometime when you're not so busy, I'd like to take you out in the moonlight and tell you how beautiful you are."

"There's no moon tonight," she said, "so you'll want the torch to get home with."

The light spun towards him, and he grabbed for it automatically. By the time he had fumbled it into his hands, the lights of the car were vanishing round the next bend in the road.

The Saint made his way slowly back up the hill. So that was that, and his wisdom or folly would be proved one way or the other before long. He grinned faintly at the thought of the expression that would come over Peter Quentin's face when he heard the news. She really would be worth a stroll in the moonlight, too, if they weren't so busy. . . .

*There was someone in the porch by the front door.*

The Saint stopped motionless, with a flitter of impalpable hailstones sweeping up his spine. As he walked, with the torch swinging loosely in his hand, its arc of light had passed over a pair of feet, cutting them out of the darkness at the ankles. The glimpse had only been instantaneous, before the moving splash of light lost it again; but Simon knew that he had not been mistaken. He had switched out the torch instinctively before he grasped the full significance of what he had seen.

After a moment he took three soundless steps to the side and switched the light on again, holding it well away from his body. And for a second time he experienced that ghostly tingle of nerves.

For the man was sitting, not standing, on a low bench in the alcove beside the door, with his hands hanging down by his sides and his body hunched forward so that his face was buried in his knees. But although his features were hidden, there was something about the general appearance of the man that struck Simon with a sudden shock of recognition.

"Pargo!" said the Saint sharply.

The figure did not move; and Simon stepped quickly forward and raised its head. One look was enough to tell him that Ernie Pargo was dead.

## VI

About the manner of his dying Simon preferred not to speculate too profoundly. He had, actually, been strangled by the cord that was still knotted around his throat so tightly that it was almost buried in the flesh of his neck; but other things had happened to him before that.

"I see anudder guy like dis, once," said Mr Uniatz chattily. "He is one of Dutch Kuhlmann's mob, an' de Brooklyn mob takes him over to Bensenhoist one night to ask him who squealed on Ike Izolsky. Well, when dey get t'ru wit' him he is like hamboiger wit'out de onions——"

"You have such fascinating reminiscences, Hoppy," said the Saint. He was laying Pargo's limp body on the settee and arranged the relaxed limbs for the rough examination which he felt had to be made. It was not a pleasant task; and for all the Saint's hardened cynicism it made his mouth set in a stony line as he went on.

In the brightness of the living-room the dead man looked even more ghastly than he had looked outside—and that had been enough to make the darkness around the house suddenly seem to be peopled with ugly shadows, and to make the soft stir of the leaves sound like cackles of ghoulish laughter. The Brooklyn mob could have learnt very little from whoever had worked on Pargo—Simon did not have to ask himself how they had known where to leave his body.

But when had it been done? There was no sign of *rigor mortis*; and Simon thought that he could still detect some warmth under the man's clothes. The body certainly hadn't been in the porch when they first arrived at the Old Barn. It might have been there when he went out only a few minutes ago, but it would have been easy not to notice it when going out of the door and moving away from the house. It seemed impossible that it could have been placed there during the short time he had been away; but he had circled round the building for some minutes to make sure, like a prowling cat, with every nerve and sense pricked for the slightest vestige of any lurking intruder, until he had to admit that it was a hopeless quest. If it had not been done then, it could only have been done while he was talking to Jopley—or while the girl was there talking to him.

Whatever the answers were to those riddles, the happy-go-lucky irrelevance of the adventure had been brought crashing down to earth as if some vital support in it had been knocked away. There was no longer any question of coming in for the fun of the game: Simon Templar was in it now, up to the neck, and as he went further with his investigation of Pargo's mangled body the steel chilled colder in his eyes.

Hoppy Uniatz, however, having possessed himself of a bottle from the kitchen during the Saint's absence, was prepared to enjoy himself.

"Dat's a funny t'ing now, boss," he resumed brightly. "Dey is a dame wit' de Brooklyn mob what is Izolsky's moll, an' she helps de boys woik on dis guy. She tells him funny stories while dey go over him wit' an electric iron. She had class, too, just like dis dame to-night."

The Saint straightened up involuntarily as Hoppy's grisly memoirs hit a mark which he himself had been unconsciously avoiding. Now that the point was brought home to him, his first impulse was to shut it out again; and yet nagging little needle points of incontrovertible logic went on fretting at the opening that had been made.

The timetable made it impossible for her to have deliberately co-operated from the start in dumping the body where he found it. But she might have met the dumping party on their way to the house, and come in to hold him up while they were doing their job. She might have known from the beginning that the dumping was to be done. She might have had the information that had been tortured out of Pargo to lead her there, without the necessity of following the lorry as she said she had done. She might have seen the body in the porch before she let herself in through the unlocked door, and come in unperturbed by it. In any case, as a confessed member of the gang that had done the job, was there any logical reason to presume that she knew nothing about their methods? Unsentimentally, the Saint acknowledged that golden hair and a face like a truant princess were no proof of a sensitive and lovable character. It was a pity, but the world was like that. . . . The expression on his face did not change.

"She must have been a beauty," he murmured absently.

"Sure, boss, she wuz de nuts. She wuz like a real lady. But I never could make de grade wit' dese ritzy dames." Mr Uniatz sighed lugubriously in contemplation of the unappreciativeness of the female sex; and then his gaze reverted to the figure on the couch. "Dis guy," he said, gesturing with his bottle, "is he de guy we're waitin' for tonight?"

The Saint lighted a cigarette and turned away.

"That's right," he said. "Only we don't have to wait any longer."

"De guy from de goil's mob?"

"Yes."

"De guy who drives de foist truck we hijack?"

"Yes."

"De guy who gives us de wire about dat truck tonight?"

"Yes."

"De guy," said Mr Uniatz, making sure of his identification, "what is goin' to find out who is de big shot in dis racket?"

"That was the idea," said the Saint curtly. "But I suppose he found out too much. He won't tell us anything now, I'm afraid."

Mr Uniatz wagged his head.

"Chees," he said sympathetically, "dat's too bad."

For the first time he seemed to visualise the passing of Mr Pargo as a subject for serious regret. He studied the body with a personal interest which had been lacking in him before, and reached for his bottle again to console himself.

Simon drew smoke monotonously into his lungs and breathed it out in slow trailing streamers. Pargo's death was something that was passing into his own background by then. Anger and pity would do nothing now: his troubles were over, whatever they had been. There remained revenge—and that would be taken in due time, inexorably. The Saint was grimly resolved about that. . . . But that was another part of the background, an item in the unalterable facts of existence like the rising of the sun the next morning, too obvious to require dwelling on in the abstract.

Nor was he thinking of the chance that the same rising sun might find him taking no more active share in the proceedings than Pargo was. Certainly the dumping of the body was a proof that his anonymity was gone for ever; but he had taken that risk voluntarily, before he knew about Pargo, when he let the girl and Jopley go. With his almost clairvoyantly accurate understanding of the criminal mind, he wasn't expecting any further demonstrations that night: the body had been left there for an effect, and nothing more would be done until the effect had had time to sink in.

What he was thinking, with a different kind of coldbloodedness from that of Mr Uniatz, was that the passing of Mr Pargo was a setback which it wouldn't be easy to make good. He had, now, the possible cooperation of Jopley; but that would be suspect for some time even if it materialised. The one proved spy he had had in the enemy's camp had been hideously eliminated.

The Saint sat on the edge of the table and stared abstractedly at the body on the settee. If only Pargo could have got through to him, before that happened, with the information which he had paid for at such a price. . . .

Pargo's left arm slid off the edge of the sofa, and his hand flopped on to the carpet so that his limp wrist turned over at a horribly unnatural angle.

Simon went on looking at it, with his face as impassive as a mask of bronze.

"Some guy tells me once," went on Mr Uniatz, seeking a solution, "dat if you look in a guy's eyes what's been moidered . . ."

The Saint seemed suddenly to have become very still, with his cigarette poised half an inch from his lips.

His examination of Pargo had been confined to the body itself and the contents of the pockets. The former had given nothing but confirmation to his first impressions, and the latter had been emptied of everything that might have given him any kind of information. Now, with a queer feeling of breathless incredulity, he was staring at something so obvious that he could hardly understand how he had overlooked it before, so uncannily like a direct answer from the dead that it made the blood race thunderously through his veins.

As the arm had fallen, the sleeve had been dragged back from the grimy shirt-cuff. And on the shirt-cuff itself there were dark marks too distinct and regularly patterned to be entirely grime.

Simon moved forward and lifted the lifeless hand with a sense of dizzy unreality.

He was barely able to decipher the lines of cramped and twisted writing.

*Their onto me Im done for—The stuff comes in Brandy bay His name is LASSER—I had to tell them—if you——*

There was no more than that; and even in the way it was written the Saint could feel the agony of the man scrawling those words with broken and shaking fingers driven by who could tell what delirious impulse of ultimate loneliness.

Simon's voice trailed away as the message trailed away, into a kind of formless silence.

Hoppy Uniatz gaped at him, and then put down his bottle. He crowded over to squint at the writing with his own eyes.

"Say, ain't dat a break?" he demanded pachydermatously. "Now if we knew who dis guy Lasser is——"

"There's one Lasser you ought to know," said the Saint acidly. "He keeps you supplied with your favourite food . . . my God!"

The immensity of the idea he had stumbled over almost rocked him on his feet, and a blaze came into his eyes as he recovered himself.

"Lasser—Lasser's Wine Stores—the biggest liquor chain in the country! It'd be perfect! . . . Wait a minute—I've just remembered. There's a picture of him somewhere——"

He picked up a copy of the *Sporting and Dramatic News* from the table and tore through it in search of the correlation of that flash of random memory. It was on a page of photographs headed *The Atlantic Yacht Club Ball at Grosvenor House*—one of those dreary collections of flashlight snapshots so dear to the peculiar snobbery of the British public. One of the pictures showed a group taken at their table, with a fat bald-headed jolly-faced man on the left. The caption under it ran:

*Among those present: Mr Grant Lasser, Miss Brenda Marlow——*

The Saint had not read any farther. His eyes were frozen on the picture of the girl next to Lasser, for it was also the picture of the girl who had been holding him up half an hour ago.

## VII

"Yes, I checked up on her," said Peter Quentin, sipping his whisky and soda. "She lives in Welbeck Street, and she runs one of those ultra dress shops in Bond Street. You know the kind of thing—an enormous window with nothing in it but a chromium plated whatnot with one evening wrap hanging on it, and no price tickets."

"It all fits in," said the Saint soberly. "That load of dresses and whoosits that we knocked off a fortnight ago—that's where they would have gone. She probably took a trip to Paris herself, and spent a gorgeous week getting them together. What about Lasser?"

"Nothing that isn't public property anyway. But I found out from Lloyd's that he's the owner of a three-hundred-ton steam yacht called the *Valkyrie*. He's also the owner of a house on Gad Cliff, and if you look at the map you'll see that it overlooks Brandy Bay. It's supposed to have been unoccupied and left in charge of a caretaker for about a couple of years, but we don't have to take the caretaker too seriously."

Peter Quentin had been a rather serious young man since the Saint had told him the complete story over the telephone that morning, and curiously enough he had refrained from making any of the obvious gibes which Simon had been fully prepared for. He had arrived late in the afternoon, after what clearly could not have been an idle morning.

The Saint moved up and down the long living-room of the Old Barn for a moment with the silent restlessness and pent-up energy of a caged tiger.

"I've been going over all that we had from Pargo," he said, "and all the things we'd been trying to get sorted out before. And it all seems so simple now that it almost makes you howl."

Peter didn't interrupt him; and the Saint took another turn round the room and went on:

"What we've been up against all the time was that there seemed to be three separate gangs without any connecting link. There was one gang that brought the stuff across the Channel in some sort of ship. That stuff was brought ashore in small boats and handed over to the shore gang, and none of 'em ever saw the ship that brought it in daylight. The ship always had her lights out, and they could never even find the first thing about her. Pargo was one of the shore gang, and I'm beginning to think now that he ought to have known where the stuff was stored; but probably he was holding out on us to get as much money as he could. Anyway, all the rest he knew was that the shore gang drove trucks to London and parked them wherever they'd been told to and went away, and somebody else came along later and picked up the truck and took it wherever it was going. That, presumably, was the third gang—the distributing gang. And none of the three gangs met anywhere except at the top, which we couldn't get near."

"Unless they all met at the same top."

"Of course, I had been thinking of that. But there was no actual proof that it was the same top; and in any case we didn't know where the top was. The point is that every lead petered out as soon as it started to get interesting. It was the perfect setup—three separate outfits doing separate shares in the same job, and none of 'em making any contact with the others except in places that were practically leakproof. And now they all blow up together."

"Off the same fuse," commented Peter economically.

The Saint nodded.

"That's what it means. The top is the same—right the way through. The steamboat of Lasser's—the *Valkyrie*—brings the stuff over the Channel. That's a cinch. A private yacht can go anywhere, and no questions asked. He could keep her in Southampton Water, push off for a weekend cruise, say he was going to Torquay or anywhere, scoot over the Channel, and pick up his cargo. There's probably a fourth gang on the other side, which just collects contraband for some smugglers unknown. And it's only about seventy miles straight across from Cherbourg to Brandy Bay. The *Valkyrie* comes back and sends the stuff ashore, and steams back to Southampton Water, and nobody knows where she's been or bothers to ask. . . . There's a coastguard station at Worbarrow Head and another one on the far side of Kimmeridge Bay; but Brandy Bay is hidden from both of 'em and coastguarding is pretty much of a dead letter these days."

"And the shore gang picks it up——"

"Under the same orders. It wouldn't be too hard for Lasser to organise that. And then it goes out to the great unsuspecting public, nicely mixed up with any amount of genuine duty-paid legitimate liquor, through the central warehouses of Lasser's Wine Stores Limited—who don't know where it came from, any of the guys who handle it, but just take it as part of the day's work. What's that advertising line of theirs?—'Butlers to the Nation.' It's not a bad line either, from the experience I've had of butlers."

Peter lowered the level of his glass an inch further.

"Apart from what goes rustling around the limbs of the aristocracy from the salons of Brenda et Cie," he remarked.

"Apart from that," Simon agreed unemotionally. "But it all works out so beautifully that we ought to have been on to it months ago."

"I should have been," said Peter, "if you hadn't got in the way. And now it's all so simple. You keep on chasing the shore gang and finding bodies on the doorstep, while I sit on Gad Cliff with a telescope every night catching pneumonia and watching for the smuggling gang, and Hoppy puts on some lipstick and ankles up and down Bond Street looking for chiffon brassières with bottles of whisky in them. I don't know what happens about this fourth gang you've invented on the French side, but I suppose you can always find somebody else to keep track of them." Peter drank deeply, and looked around for a refill. "As you said just now, it's so childishly simple that it almost makes you howl."

The Saint regarded him pityingly.

"I've always approved of these birds who want to strangle imbecile children at birth," he said. "And now I think I shall send them a donation. You ineffable fathead—what do these assorted gangs amount to? It doesn't matter if there are four of them or forty. They're only stooges, like poor old Pargo. Knock the kingpin out, and they all fall apart. Take one man in, and they all go for the same ride. All we want is Lasser, and we can call it a day."

"Just like poor old Pargo," said Peter, *sotto voce.* He looked up from manipulating the siphon. "What happened to him, by the way?"

"We took him down to Lymington and borrowed a boat while the tide was going out. If he ever gets washed up again anywhere he'll be another headache for Chief Inspector Teal; but we had to do something with him."

"Probably that's one reason why he was left here," said Peter intelligently.

Simon was kindling the latest cigarette in a chain that had already filled an ashtray. He saw that it was burning evenly and crushed the preceding fag-end into the heap of wreckage.

"That was one obvious motive—bodies being troublesome things to get rid of," he said. "The other, of course, was *pour encourager les autres.* I've been expecting some more direct encouragement all day, but it hasn't materialised yet. I don't suppose it'll be long now, though."

Mr Uniatz, who had been silent for a long time except for intermittent glugging noises produced by the bottle beside him, stirred himself abruptly and consulted his watch with the earnest air of a martyr who realises that he is the next in line for the lions. His intrusion after such a long absence seemed so portentous that both Peter and the Saint turned towards him with what must have been a disconcerting expectancy. Mr Uniatz blinked at them with his nightmare features creased in the grooves of noble self-abnegation.

"Boss," he said, with some embarrassment, "what's de next train to London?"

"Train?" said the Saint blankly.

"Yes, boss. I t'ought you an' Mr Quentin d' be busy, so ya wouldn't wanta drive me dere, an' dey ain't no udder car——"

The Saint studied him anxiously.

"You aren't feeling ill or anything, are you?" he asked. "But you don't have to worry about the ungodly giving us some more encouragement. Peter and I will hold your hand if there's any rough stuff."

"Encouragement?" repeated Mr Uniatz foggily. He shook his head, as one who was suddenly confronted with a hopelessly outlandish twist of thought. "I dunno, boss . . . But ya said I gotta go to Bond Street an' look for braseers wit' bottles in dem. Dat's okay wit' me," said Mr Uniatz, squaring his shoulders heroically, "but if any a dese dames t'ink I'm gettin' fresh——"

Simon readjusted himself hastily to the pace of a less volatile intellect.

"That's all right, Hoppy," he said reassuringly. "We're putting that idea on the shelf for the moment. You just stick around with us and keep your Betsy ready."

Mr Uniatz's eyes lighted tentatively with the dawn of hope.

"You mean I don't gotta go to London?"

"No."

"Or——"

"No."

Hoppy drew a deep breath.

"Chees, boss," he said, speaking from the heart, "dat's great!"

His bottle glugged again expressively.

"We haven't any other ideas," Peter explained dishearteningly, "but that doesn't matter."

The Saint's eyes mocked him with dancing pinpoints of silent laughter. During that day the Saint's cold anger of the night before seemed to have worn off, although the inexorable pith of it was still perceptible in the fine-drawn core of steel that seemed to underlie his outward languor. But now it was masked by something more vital—the mad gay recklessness that came around him like a mantle of sunlight when the hunt was up and the fanfares of adventure were sounding out in the open.

"You're wrong," he said. "We've got a much better idea. I had a telegram this afternoon—it was phoned through from Lyndhurst just before you arrived. I've been saving it up for you." He picked up the scrap of paper on which he had scribbled the message down. "It says: 'Your car will be at the Broken Sword in Tyneham at nine-fifteen tonight.' It isn't signed, and anyhow it wouldn't have mattered much who signed it. It didn't originate from any of these assorted gangs we've been talking about—otherwise why be so very accurate about the time? It means that the Master Mind is taking a hand, just as I prophesied last night, and whatever happens he won't be far away. It's bait, of course; and we're going to bite!"

## VIII

Simon wanted 73 to finish, and the babble of chaff and facetious comment died down through sporadic resurrections as he took over the darts and set his toe on the line. His first dart went in the treble 19; and the stillness lasted a couple of seconds after that before a roar of delight acknowledged the result of the mental arithmetic that had been working itself out in the heads of the onlookers. His second dart brushed the inside wire of the double 8 on the wrong side as it went in; and the hush came down again, more breathless than before. Somebody in a corner bawled a second encouraging calculation, and the Saint smiled. Quite coolly and unhurriedly, as if he had no distracting thought in his mind, he balanced the third dart in his fingers, poised it, and launched it at the board. It struck and stayed there—dead in the centre of the double 4.

A huge burst of laughter and applause crashed through the silence like a breaking wave as he turned away; and his opponent, who had been pushed forward as the local champion, grinned under his grey moustache and said: "Well, zur, the beer's on me."

The Saint shook his head.

"No, it isn't, George. Let's have a round for everybody on me, because I'm going to have to leave you."

He laid a ten-shilling note on the bar and nodded to the landlord as the patrons of the Broken Sword crowded up to moisten their parched throats. He glanced at his watch as he did so, and saw that it showed sixteen minutes after nine. Zero hour had struck while he was taking his stand for those last three darts, but it had made no difference to the steadiness of his hand or the accuracy of his eye.

Even now, it made no difference; and while he gathered up his change he was as much a part of the atmosphere of the small low-ceilinged bar as any of the rough warm-hearted local habitués. . . . But his eyes were on the road outside the narrow leaded windows, where the twilight was folding soft grey veils under the trees; and while he was looking out there she arrived. His ears caught the familiar airy purr of the Hirondel through the clamour around him before it swept into view, and he saw the brightness of her golden hair behind the wheel without surprise as she slowed by. It was curious that he should have been thinking for the last hour in terms of "she"; but he had been expecting nothing else, and in that at least his instinct had been faultless.

The boisterous fellowship of the Broken Sword was swallowed up in abyss as he closed the door of the public bar behind him. As if he had been suddenly transported a thousand miles instead of merely over the breadth of a threshold, he passed into a different world as he faced the quiet road outside—a world where strange and horrible things happened such as the men he had left behind him to their beer would never believe, a world where a man's life hung on the flicker of an eyelid and the splitting of a second, and where there was adventure of a keen corrosive kind such as the simple heroes of mythology had never lived to see. The Saint's eyes swept left and right before he stepped out of the shadow of the porch, but he saw nothing instantly threatening. Even so, he found some comfort in the knowledge that Peter Quentin and Hoppy Uniatz would be covering him from the ambush where he had posted them behind a clump of trees in the field over the way.

But none of that could have been read in his face or in the loose-limbed ease of his body as he sauntered over to the car. He smiled as he came up, and saluted her with that faint mockery that was his fighting armour.

"It's nice of you to bring the old boat back, darling. And she doesn't look as if you'd bent her at all. There aren't many women I'd trust her with, but you can borrow her again any time you want to. Just drop in and help yourself—but of course I don't have to tell you to do that."

The girl was almost as cool as he was—only a hardened campaigner like the Saint would have detected the sharp edges of strain under the delicate contours of her face. She patted the steering wheel with one white-gloved hand.

"She's nice," she said. "The others wanted to run her over a cliff, but I said that would have been a sin. Besides, I had to see you anyway."

"It's something to know I'm worth saving a car for," he murmured.

She studied him with a kind of speculative aloofness.

"I like you by daylight. I thought I should."

He returned her survey with equal frankness. She wore a white linen skirt and a cobwebby white blouse, and the lines of her figure were as delicious as he had thought they would be. It would have been easy, effortless to surrender completely to the blood-quickening enchantment of her physical presence. But between them also was the ghostly presence of Pargo; and a chilling recollection of Pargo's livid distorted face passed before the Saint's eyes as he smiled at her.

"You look pretty good yourself, Brenda," he remarked. "Perhaps it's because that outfit looks a lot more like Bond Street than what you had on last night."

Her poise was momentarily shaken.

"How did you——"

"I'm a detective too," said the Saint gravely. "Only I keep it a secret."

She unlatched the door and swung out her long slender legs. As she was doing so, a sleek black sedan swam round the nearest bend, slowing up, and turned in towards the front of the pub. The Saint's right hand stayed in his coat pocket and his eyes were chips of ice for an instant, before the driver got out unconcernedly as the car stopped and walked across to the entrance of the bar. The Saint could almost have laughed at himself, but not quite: those reactions were too solidly founded on probabilities to be wholly humorous, and he was still waiting for the purpose of their meeting to be revealed.

The girl didn't seem to have noticed anything. She straightened up as her feet touched the road, flawless as a white statue, with the same impenetrable aloofness. She said: "There's your car. Would you like to take it and drive away? A long way away—to the north of Scotland, or Timbuctoo, or anywhere. At least far enough for you to forget that any of this ever happened."

"The world is so small," Simon pointed out unhappily. "Twelve thousand miles is about the farthest you can get from anything, and that's not very far in these days of high-speed transport. Besides, I don't know that I want to forget. We've still got that date for a stroll in the moonlight——"

"I'm not joking," she said impatiently. "And I haven't got much time. The point is—I found out your name last night, but I didn't know who you were. I suppose I haven't been around enough in that kind of society. But the others knew."

"Look at the advantages of a cosmopolitan education," he observed. "There are more things in this cockeyed world than Bond Street——"

The stony earnestness of her face cut him off.

"This is serious," she said. "Can't you see that? If the others had had their way you wouldn't be here now at all. If you'd been anything else but what you are you wouldn't be here. But they've heard of you, and so it doesn't seem so easy to get rid of you in the obvious way. That's why I'm here to talk to you. If you'll leave us alone it'll be worth a hundred pounds a week to you, and you can draw the first hundred pounds this evening."

"That's interesting," said the Saint thoughtfully. "And where are these hundred travel tickets?"

"There'll be a man waiting in a car with a GB plate at the crossroads in East Lulworth at half past ten. He'll be able to talk to you if you want to discuss it."

The Saint took her arm.

"Let's discuss it now," he suggested. "There's some very good beer inside——"

"I can't." She glanced a little to his left. "That other car's waiting for me—the one that just arrived. The man who brought it has gone out at the back of the pub, and he's only waiting a little up the road to see that you don't keep me. It wouldn't be very sensible of you to try, because he can see us from where he is, and if I don't pick him up at once there'll be trouble." Her hand rested on his sleeve for a moment as she disengaged herself. "Why don't you go to Lulworth? It wouldn't hurt you, and it'd be so much easier. After all, what are you doing this for?"

"I might ask what you're doing it for."

"Mostly for fun. And from what they've told me about you, you might just as easily have been on our side. It doesn't do anyone any harm——"

The Saint's smile was as bright as an arctic noon.

"In fact," he said, "you're beginning to make me believe that it really did Pargo a lot of good."

She shrugged.

"You wouldn't have expected us to keep him after we knew he was selling us out to you, would you?" she asked: and the casual way she said it almost took the Saint's breath away.

"Of course not," he answered, after a pause in which his brain whirled stupidly.

The dusk had been deepening very quickly, so that he could not be quite sure of the expression in her eyes as she looked up at him.

"Talk it over with your friends," she said in a quick low voice. "Try to go to Lulworth. I don't want anything else to happen. . . . Goodbye. Here's the key of your car."

Her arm moved, and something tinkled along the road. As his eyes automatically turned to try and follow it, she slipped aside and was out of his reach. The door of the black sedan slammed, its lights went on, and it rushed smoothly past him with the wave of a white glove. By the time he had found his own ignition key in the gloom where she had thrown it, he knew that it was too late to think of trying to follow her.

The Saint's mind was working under pressure as he waited for Peter and Hoppy to join him at the corner of the inn. There was something screwy about that interview—something that made him feel as if part of the foundations of his grasp of the case were slipping away from under him. But for the present his thoughts were too chaotic and nebulous to share with anyone else.

"We've got a date to be shot up at East Lulworth at half past ten," he said cheerfully, and gave them a literal account of the conversation.

"They're making you travel a bit before they kill you," said Peter. "Are you going on with this mad idea of yours?"

"It's the only thing to do if we're sticking to our plan of campaign. We're fish on the rise tonight, and we'll go on rising until we get a line if it——"

He broke off with his hand whipping instinctively to his pocket again as a bicycle whirred out of the shadows towards them at racing speed. The brakes grated as it shot by, and a man almost threw himself off the machine and turned back towards them. A moment later the Saint saw that it was Jopley.

"Thank Gawd I caught yer," he gasped. "I was afride it 'ud be too late. Yer mustn't go ter Lulworth tonight!"

"That's a pity," said the Saint tranquilly. "But I just made a date to go there."

"You can't do it, sir! They'll be wytin' for yer wiv a machine gun. I 'eard 'im givin' the orders, an' 'ow the lidy was ter meet yer 'ere an' tell yer the tile, an' everythink——"

Simon became suddenly alert.

"You heard who giving the orders?" he shot back.

"The boss 'imself it was—'e's at Gad Cliff 'Ouse naow!"

## IX

The Saint's lighter flared in the darkness, catching the exultant glint in his eyes under impudently slanted brows. When the light went out and left only the glow-worm point of his cigarette, it was as if something vital and commanding had been abruptly snatched away, leaving an irreparable void; but out of the void his voice spoke with the gay lilt of approaching climax.

"That's even better," he said. "Then we don't have to go to Lulworth. . . ."

"You must be disappointed," Peter said sympathetically, "after looking forward to being shot up with a machine gun——"

"This is easier," said the Saint. "This is the fish sneaking out of the river a little way downstream and wriggling along the bank to bite the fisherman in the pants. Peter, I have a feeling that this is going to be Comrade Lasser's unlucky day."

"It might just as well have been any other day," Peter objected. "He isn't any unknown quantity. He's in the telephone book. Probably he's in *Who's Who* as well. You could find out everything about him and all his habits, and choose your own time——"

"You couldn't choose any time like this! Just because he *is* supposed to be such a respectable citizen, his pants would be a tough proposition to bite. Can you imagine us trying to hold him up in his own baronial halls, or taking him for a ride from the Athenæum Club? Why, he could call on the whole of Scotland Yard, including Chief Inspector Teal, not to mention the Salvation Army and the Brigade of Guards, to rally round and look after him if we tried anything. But this is different. Now he isn't a pillar of Society and Industry, surrounded by bishops and barons. He's in bad company, with a machine-gun party waiting for us at East Lulworth—and while he's waiting for news from them he's sitting up at Gad Cliff House, on top of the biggest store of contraband that the Revenue never set eyes on. We've got him with the goods on him, and this is where we take our chance!"

Peter Quentin shrugged.

"All right," he said philosophically. "I'd just as soon take my chance at this house as take it with a machine gun. Lead on, damn you."

Mr Uniatz cleared his throat, producing a sound like the eruption of a small volcano. The anxiety that was vexing his system could be felt even if it could not be seen. Ever a stickler for detail once he had assimilated it, Mr Uniatz felt that one important detail was being overlooked in the flood of ideas that had recently been passing over his head.

"Boss," said Mr Uniatz lucidly, "de skoit."

"What about her?" asked the Saint.

"She didn't look to me like she had no bottles in her braseer."

"She hadn't."

"Den why——"

"We're giving her a rest, Hoppy. This is another guy we're going to see."

"Oh, a guy," said Mr Uniatz darkly. "Den how come he's wearin' a——"

"He's funny that way," said the Saint hastily. "Now let's have a look at the lie of the land."

He led the way over to the Hirondel and spread out a large-scale ordnance map under the dashboard light. Gad Cliff House was plainly marked on it, standing in about three acres of ground bordered on one side by the cliff itself, and approached by a narrow lane from the road that ran over the high ground parallel with the coast.

"That's plan enough," said the Saint, after a brief examination of the plan. "But what are the snags?"

He looked round and found Jopley's face at his shoulder, seeming even more sullen and evil in the dim greenish glow of the light. The man shook his head.

"It's 'opeless, that's wot the snag is," he said bluntly. "There's alarms orl rahnd the plice—them invisible rye things. A rabbit couldn't get in wivout settin' 'em orf."

"But you were able to get out."

"Yus, I got aht."

"Well, how did you manage it?"

"I said I 'ad ter go aht an' buy some fags."

"I mean," said the Saint, with the almost supernatural self-control developed through long association with Hoppy Uniatz, "how did you get out through these alarms?"

Jopley said slowly: "I got aht fru the gates."

"And how will you get back?"

"I'll git back the sime wye. The man ooze watchin' there, 'e knows me, an' 'e phones up to the 'ouse an' ses 'oo it is, an' they ses it's orl right, an' 'e opens the gates an' lets me in."

The Saint folded his map.

"Well," he said deliberately, "suppose when this bird had the gates open to let you in, some other blokes who were waiting outside rushed the pair of you, laid him out, and let themselves in—would anyone at the house know what had happened?"

The man thought it out laboriously.

"Not till 'e came to an' told 'em."

"Then——"

"But yer can't git in that wye," Jopley stated flatly. "Not letting me in for it, yer carn't. Wot 'appens when they find aht I done it? Jer fink I wanter git meself bashed over the 'ead an' frown to the muckin' lobsters?"

Simon smiled.

"You don't have to get thrown to the lobsters, Algernon," he said. "I'm rather fond of lobsters, and I wouldn't have that happen for anything. You don't even have to get bashed over the head, except in a friendly way for the sake of appearances. And 'they' don't have to find out anything about it—although I don't think they'll be in a position to do you much damage anyway, when I'm through with them. But if it'll make you any happier, you don't have to be compromised at all. You just happened to be there when we rushed in, and nobody could prove anything different. And it'd be worth a hundred pounds to you—on the nail."

Jopley looked from one face to the other while the idea seemed to establish itself in his mind. For a few seconds the Saint was afraid that fear would still make him refuse, and wondered what other arguments would carry conviction. In mentioning a hundred pounds he had gone to the limits of bribery, and it was more or less an accident that he had as much money as that in his pockets. . . . He held his breath until Jopley answered.

"When do I get this 'undred quid?"

Simon opened his wallet and took out a folded wad of banknotes. Jopley took them in his thick fingers and glanced through them. His heavy sulky eyes turned up again to the Saint's face.

"I don't do nothink else, mind. Yer can rush me along o' the other bloke, an' if yer can git inside that's orl right. But I didn't 'ave nothink ter do wiv it, see?"

"We'll take care of that," said the Saint confidently. "All we want to know is when you're going back, so that we can be ready. And it had better be soon, because the time's getting on. I want to be in that house before the machine-gun squad gets back from Lulworth."

"I can start back naow," said the other grudgingly. "If you drive there in yer car, yer'll 'ave ten minutes before I git there on me bike."

The Saint nodded.

"Okay," he said peacefully. "Then let's go!"

The steady drone of the Hirondel sank through his mind into silence as the long shining car swept up the winding road towards the crest of the downs. Instead of it, as if the words were being spoken again beside his ears, he heard Brenda Marlow's clear unfaltering voice saying "*You wouldn't have expected us to keep him after we knew he was selling us out to you, would you?*" Lasser, Pargo, what had been done to Pargo, and what might be done at Gad Cliff House that night—those other thoughts were a vague jumble that was almost blotted out by the clearness of the words which he was hearing over again in memory. And he could feel again the chill of downright horror that had struck him like an icy wind when he heard them first.

Simon Templar had travelled too far on the iron highways of outlawry to be afflicted with empty sentimentality, and he had been flippant enough about death in his time—even about such ugly death as Pargo's. But about such an utter unrelenting callousness, coming without the flicker of an eyelash from a face like the one he had seen when it was being spoken, there was a quality of epic inhumanity to which even the Saint could not adjust himself. It made her look like something beside which a blend of Messalina and Lucrezia Borgia would have seemed like a playful schoolgirl—and yet he could recall just as clearly the edged contempt in her voice, after she had overheard the lurid bluff he had encouraged Hoppy to put over on Jopley, when she said "We'll leave things like that to gentlemen like Mr Templar." The contradiction fretted at the smooth surface of his reasoning with maddening persistence; and yet the one and only apparent way of reconciling it raised another question which it was too late now to track down to its possible conclusions. . . .

A dull kind of tightness settled over the Saint's nerves as he brought the Hirondel to a stop just beyond the opening of the lane that led to the entrance of Gad Cliff House. He switched off the engine and climbed out without any visible sign of it; but his right hand felt instinctively for the hilt of the sharp throwing-knife strapped to his left forearm under the sleeve, and found it with an odd sense of comfort. At other times when he had made mistakes, that hidden and unlooked for weapon had brought rescue out of defeat; and the touch of it reassured him. He turned to meet the others without a change in his blithe serenity.

"You know what you have to do, boys and girls," he said. "Follow me, and let's make it snappy."

Mr Uniatz coughed, peering at him through the darkness with troubled intensity.

"I dunno, boss," he said anxiously. "I never hoid of dis invisible rye. Is dat what de guy has in de bottles in his——"

"Yes, that's it," said the Saint, with magnificent presence of mind. "You go on an invisible jag on it, and end up by seeing invisible pink elephants. It saves any amount of trouble. Now get hold of your Betsy and shut up, because there may be invisible ears."

The lane ran between almost vertical grass banks topped by stiff thorn hedges, and it was so narrow that a car driven down it would have had no more than a few inches clearance on either side. The car that came up from the road must have been driven by someone who knew his margins with the accuracy of long experience, for it swooped out of the night so swiftly and suddenly that the Saint's hearing had scarcely made him aware of its approach when it was almost on top of them, its headlights turning the lane into a trench of blinding light. Simon had an instant of desperate indecision while he reckoned their chance of scaling the steep hedge-topped banks and realised that they could never do it in time; and then he wheeled to face the danger with his hand leaping to his gun. Hoppy's movement was even quicker but it was still too late. Another light sprang up dazzlingly from behind the gates just ahead of them: they were trapped between the two opposing broadsides of eye-searing brilliance and the two high walls of the lane as if they had been caught in a box, and Simon knew without any possibility of self-deception that they were helplessly at the mercy of the men behind the lights.

"Put your hands up," ordered a new voice from the car; and the Saint acknowledged to himself how completely and beautifully he had been had.

## X

"I might have known you'd be a great organiser, brother," murmured the Saint, as he led the way obediently into the library of Gad Cliff House with his hands held high in the air. "But you were certainly in form tonight."

The compliment was perfectly sincere. When Simon Templar fell into traps he liked them to be good ones, for the sake of his own self-esteem; and the one he had just walked into so docilely struck him as being a highly satisfactory specimen from every point of view.

It was all so neat and simple and psychologically watertight, once you were let into the secret. He had kept his first appointment with Brenda Marlow, as anyone would have known he would. He had been duly suspicious of the second appointment at the crossroads in East Lulworth, as he was meant to be. He had accepted it merely as a confirmation of those suspicions when Jopley arrived with the warning of the machine-gun party—exactly as he was meant to do. And with the memory of the proposition he had made to Jopley the night before still fresh in his mind, the rest of the machinery had run like clockwork. He had been so completely disarmed that even Jopley's well-simulated reluctance to lead him into the very trap he was meant to be led into was almost a superfluous finishing touch. A good trap was something that the Saint could always appreciate with professional interest; but a trap within a trap was a refinement to remember. He had announced himself as being in the market for bait, and verily he had swallowed everything that was offered him.

Simon admitted the fact, and went on from there. They were in the soup, but even if it was good soup it was no place to stay in. He reckoned the odds dispassionately. Their guns had been taken away from them, but his knife had escaped the search. That was the only asset he could find on his own side—that, and whatever his own quickness of thought was worth, which on its recent showing didn't seem to be very much. And yet no one who looked at him would have seen a trace of the grim concentration that was driving his brain on a fierce defiant search for the inspiration that would turn the tables again.

He smiled at Lasser with all the carefree and unruffled ease that only reached its airiest perfection with him when the corner was tightest and the odds were too astronomical to be worth brooding over.

"What does it feel like to be a Master Mind?" he inquired interestedly.

Lasser beamed back at him, with his rich jolly face shining as if it had been freshly scrubbed.

"I've read a lot about you," he said, "so I knew I should have to make a special effort. In fact, I'm not too proud to admit that I've picked up a few tips from the stories I've heard of you. Naturally, when I knew who our distinguished opponent was, I tried not to disappoint him."

"You haven't," said the Saint cordially. "Except that I may have expected a larger deputation of welcome."

His gaze drifted over the assembly with the mildest and most apologetic hint of criticism. Besides Lasser, there was only Jopley and one other man, presumably the gatekeeper—a short thickset individual with a cast in one eye and an unshaven chin that gave him a vicious and sinister aspect which was almost too conventional to be true. There was also Brenda Marlow, who came into the room last and sat on the arm of a chair near the door, watching from the background with an expression that the Saint couldn't quite analyse.

"I think there are enough of us," said Lasser blandly. He turned to Jopley. "You searched them all thoroughly?"

The man grunted an affirmative; and Lasser's glance passed fleetingly over Peter Quentin and Hoppy and glowed on the Saint again.

"You can put your hands down," he said. "It will be more comfortable for you. And sit down, if you want to." He tugged at the lobe of his ear absentmindedly while the Saint turned a chair round and relaxed in it, crossing his legs. "Ah—about this deputation of welcome. Yes. I had thought of giving you more of a show, but I decided not to. You see, I brought you here to talk over some more or less private business, and I thought that the fewer people who knew about it the better. You have rather a persuasive way with you, Mr Templar, so Jopley tells me, and I shouldn't want you to tempt any more of my employees. Will you have a drink?"

"I'd love one," said the Saint graciously; and Lasser turned to the villainous specimen with the unshaven chin.

"Some drinks, Borieff."

Simon took out his cigarette case while Borieff slouched over to a cupboard under one of the bookshelves and brought out a bottle and a siphon.

"You know, this makes me feel quite guilty," he said. "I've had so many drinks with you before, and yet I've never bought you one."

"Two vanloads, isn't it?" Lasser agreed, with his fat bright smile. "And the other van with—um—silks and things in it. Yes. Yes. That's what I brought you here to talk to you about. We shall have to have those vans back, of course, what you haven't actually used of them."

"Hoppy certainly has rather improved the shining hour," Simon admitted. "But there's quite a lot left. What sort of an offer were you thinking of making?"

Lasser shook his head.

"No," he said judiciously. "No, I wasn't thinking of making an offer. I just want them back. I'm afraid you're going to have to tell us where to find them. That's why I arranged for you to come here."

"What's all this," Brenda Marlow asked quietly, "about bringing them here?"

She had been so much in the background that the others seemed to have forgotten her, and when she spoke it was as startling an intrusion as if she had not been there before and had just walked in. Lasser looked round at her, blinking.

"Eh?"

"What's all this," she repeated, in exactly the same quiet voice, "about bringing them here?"

Lasser rubbed his chin.

"Oh, of course," he said. "Bringing them here. Yes. I didn't tell you—I didn't really mean them to meet me at Lulworth. That was just to get them ready for the story Jopley had to tell them. It was all arranged so that they'd be sure to come here, so I suppose I can say we brought them."

"I see," she said innocently. "So you were just using me as a sort of stuffed decoy."

Lasser's broad smile did not waver.

"I shouldn't say that, my dear. No. Not at all. You couldn't have played your part nearly so well if you hadn't believed in it. I was just making it easier for you." He tugged at his ear again for a moment, and then pulled out his watch, consulted it, stuffed it back in his pocket, and rubbed his hands briskly together with an air of breezy decision. "Now, Brenda, it's time you were off. As a matter of fact, I thought you'd have started by this time. Remember you're due in London at one o'clock."

Her shoulders moved slightly.

"I can make it in three hours easily in the new Lagonda," she said slowly. "And since I'm here I'd like to see how you get on."

"But you've got to allow for accidents. If you had a puncture——"

"Do you mean you don't want me to stay?"

The Saint felt an odd thrill of breathlessness. There was a subtle tension in the room that had not been there before, even in spite of the display of artillery which was still in evidence. To the Saint's præternaturally sharpened senses it was perceptible in the darkened sullenness of Jopley, in the harsh rigidity of Borieff, even in the frozen fixity of Lasser's expansive smile.

And there could only be one explanation for it. It meant that he must have been right in the one wild theory which had come to him on the way there when it was too late to probe into it—that Brenda Marlow and her contradictions were accounted for, and that it was no longer necessary to look to Messalina and Lucrezia Borgia for her prototype. It gave the Saint a curious sense of lightness and relief, even though it did nothing to improve his own position. There were worse things than to be at the mercy of men like Lasser and Jopley and Borieff, and in Simon Templar's own inconsequential philosophy to have to think of a girl as he had been thinking of her was one of them.

"I don't mean that at all," Lasser was saying jovially. "No. Of course not. But that—um—envelope has got to be delivered, and this is rather a private matter——"

"Doesn't it concern all of us?"

The Saint raised his glass and drank with a certain deep satisfaction.

"Comrade Lasser has his own views about who's concerned with one thing and another, darling," he explained. "For instance, there was that business about Pargo. I'll bet you he didn't tell you that Pargo was tortured to death and dumped on my——"

Borieff's lunging fist thudded against the side of the Saint's head and sent the glass he was holding spinning away to splinter itself on the edge of a table.

Simon's muscles gathered themselves in spontaneous reaction. And then, as he gazed squarely into the muzzle of Borieff's automatic, they slowly loosened again. Just as slowly, he took out a handkerchief and wiped a few drops of spilt liquid from his coat.

After the sudden crash of shattering glass there was a brief interval of intense silence. And then Lasser spoke, with his eyes creased up to slits in his plump jolly face.

"Tie them up," he said; and as Jopley and Borieff moved to obey the order, the smile that had been only temporarily shaken came back to his wide elastic mouth. "I'm sorry, Templar, but you must have some respect for the position you're in. I can't have you saying things like that. Now for the rest of this interview you'd better confine yourself to speaking when you're spoken to, or I may have to do something you won't like."

Simon looked at the girl.

"You see how touchy he is?" he drawled recklessly. "I don't know how well you know the signs of a guilty conscience——"

Out of the corner of his eye he could see Lasser's forefinger tightening on the trigger of his levelled gun; but there were provocations that could bring the Saint's contempt for such things to the verge of sheer insanity. What might have happened if he had been allowed to go on was something that he could hardly have refused to bow to in cold blood; but before he could say any more the girl stepped forward.

"Leave him alone, Lasser," she said. "I'm interested in this. What did happen to Pargo?"

"We sent him to Canada, of course, as I told you," Lasser replied brusquely. "You surely don't believe any of this fellow's wild accusations?"

Her dark grey eyes went over him with an unexpected mature kind of thoughtfulness.

"I believe what I see," she said. "And I saw Borieff hit him. I think that was a better answer than yours——"

She was opening her bag as she spoke; and Lasser went to meet her suddenly, with a swiftness that was surprising and somehow horrible in a man of his build. His downward-striking fist knocked the bag through her hands; and then he was holding her by the wrists.

"You mustn't interfere in things like this," he said, still smiling. "Of course I don't tell you everything—you wouldn't like it if I did. But we've got to put a stop to Templar's interference, and that isn't your business unless you want to make it so." He looked at the Saint over his shoulder. "You're going to tell me what happened to those three vans—and do you know why you'll tell me the truth!

Because I'm going to take each one of you separately into the next room and ask you questions in my own way, and when you all tell me the same thing I'll know you aren't lying!"

## XI

There were bands of adhesive tape around the Saint's wrists and ankles, and Peter Quentin had been quickly strapped up in the same way at the same time. Now they were working on Hoppy Uniatz, after first depriving him of the whisky bottle which by some irresistible magnetism had gravitated into his hands.

Lasser held the girl until they had finished, and then he pushed her back into an armchair and signed to Borieff to take charge of her. He straightened his coat and picked up her bag and tossed it into her lap, but not before he had transferred a heavy sealed envelope from it to his pocket.

"This is really very tiresome of you, my dear," he said heartily. "Now I shall have to make some other arrangements."

"You certainly will," she retorted. "I wouldn't have any more to do with this business of yours for all the money in the world."

He stood manipulating his ear meditatively for a little while.

"No," he said. "No, of course not. No. But it's your own fault. You didn't have to know any more than was good for you. Naturally you would be—um—sentimental, but you ought to have realised that there are serious things in this business. Well, we'll talk about that presently. Now that you're here, you'll have to be quiet and behave yourself, because we can't waste any more time."

"Be quiet and behave myself while you torture them, I suppose," she said with bitter directness.

"No. Not necessarily. But they've got to answer my questions. It'll only be their own fault if they're obstinate." He shrugged. "Anyhow, you've no choice. If you don't behave yourself, Borieff will have to keep you quiet."

He beamed at her in his stout avuncular way, as if he were insisting on giving her an especially extravagant birthday present.

She looked at Simon with a white face.

"I apologise for what I said to you last night," she said huskily. "If I'd known why you were going to burn Jopley's feet, I'd have stayed and helped you."

"The joke is that we didn't really mean to do it," Simon answered regretfully. "But next time——"

"There won't be no muckin' next time," Jopley stated with savage complacency. "Come on."

He grasped the Saint's arm; but Simon was still looking at the girl.

"Maybe you made a mistake about me," he said. "And I'm glad I was wrong about you. Remind me to make up for it when we take that stroll in the moonlight."

His gaze rested on her a moment longer with all the steadying courage he could send her; and then he turned to Peter.

"I ought to have come alone," he said. "But since we're all here we might as well tell Comrade Lasser what he wants to know."

"What for?" Peter demanded indignantly, as Simon might have known he would. "If you think we give a damn for that fat slob——"

Lasser pointed to the Saint.

"Take him in, Jopley," he said, like a genial host arranging the procession of guests to a dining room.

With an evil grin, Jopley pushed the Saint off his balance and half dragged and half carried him through a door at one end of the room. The room that it opened into was almost bare of furniture and smelt strongly of paraffin—even at that moment the Saint's brow wrinkled with puzzlement as he met the rank powerful odour.

Jopley heaved him up and shoved him roughly into the only chair as Lasser followed them in. The door closed softly behind him—an ancient and massive door of solid oak that settled into place with a faint *fuff* of perfectly fitting joints, seeming to shut out every sound and contact with the outside world. He stood there smiling benevolently at the Saint, smoothing his large hands one over the other.

"I hope we shan't have to hurt you very much," he said. "If you like to tell me at once what happened to those vans, we needn't go any further. But of course I shall take care that your two friends don't have a chance to find out what you've told me, so if they don't tell the same story we shall have to hurt them until they do."

The Saint looked at him and then at Jopley. And as he did so he felt the blood run faster in his veins. For Jopley was sliding his gun away into his pocket.

A flood of strength seemed to surge through the Saint's body like a tidal wave. He could feel the race of it through his muscles, the galvanic awakening of his nerves, the sudden clearing of his brain to crystal brilliance. It was as if his whole being was lifted up in a sublime ecstasy of renewed life. And yet otherwise everything was the same. The corner was just as tight, the prospects just as deadly; but that one action had altered a balance in which the difference between life and death would be weighed. Lasser had already put away his gun. Jopley's gun was going—had gone. It was in his pocket, and his hands were hanging empty at his sides. In that room, with the two of them together against one man bound hand and foot, they had done what any other two men would have done in the confidence of their obvious superiority. And the astronomical hopelessness of the odds had been lessened by the fraction of time that it would take a man to draw a gun from his pocket. . . .

Only the Saint's face betrayed nothing of the fanfares of exultation that were pouring magnificent music through his soul. He moved slightly in his chair, twisting his right hand round as far as he could; and his fingertips touched the hilt of the knife under his sleeve with a thrill that added new harmonies of its own.

"And what happens after we've told you all this?" he asked.

Lasser pursed his lips.

"Well, I'm afraid we shall still have to get rid of you. You know too much, Templar, and we can't risk your being tempted to interfere with us again."

"Do we get sent to Canada too?"

"No, not to Canada. No. I think we shall just leave you here. This place is being burnt down tonight," Lasser explained calmly. "You may have noticed the smell of paraffin. Yes. It's rather antiquated and I want to rebuild it—something modern, you know. It's quite well insured, so I thought it would be a good idea to have a fire. Yes, we'll just have to leave you here with a lighted candle on the floor, and kill two birds with one stone, if you know what I mean."

Simon had his knife in his hand and he was working the point of it under the tapes on his wrists; but for a moment he almost stopped.

"You mean you'd leave us here to be burnt alive?" he said slowly.

"I'm afraid we'd have to. The place is supposed to be unoccupied, you know, and I sent the caretaker away this morning. It'd look as if you were tramps who'd broken in to sleep for the night, and you might have set fire to the house yourselves by accident. So it wouldn't look right if they found bullets in you or anything like that."

Lasser seemed to ponder over his reasoning again, and shook his head with refreshed conviction.

"No, that would never do," he said; and then his sunny smile dawned again. "But don't let's meet our troubles halfway. After all, I've heard that in a real fire people are often suffocated by the smoke before they get burnt at all. But we could hurt you a lot first if you didn't tell us what happened to those vans."

The Saint's hands were free—behind his back, he could move his wrists apart. But even so, he felt as if his stomach was emptied with a kind of sick revulsion. There was no doubt in his mind that Lasser would have done everything he spoke of with such a genial matter-of-factness—would still do it, if the Saint failed in the only gamble he had left. That rich unchangeably beaming smile was a better guarantee of it even than Jopley's lowering vindictiveness. And now the Saint seemed to read through it for the first time into something that explained it, something monstrous and gloating, something that smoothed Lasser's bald glistening forehead into a horrible vacantness of bland anticipation. . . .

"Where are those vans, Templar?" he asked in a silky whisper.

Simon met his gaze with eyes of frosted sapphire.

"They're where you'll never find them," he said deliberately, "you greasy grinning bladder of lard."

Lasser turned his head as if he was pleased.

"Light the candle, Jopley," he said.

He took three steps forward and squatted down in front of the Saint like a great glossy toad. With leisured care he began to unlace the Saint's shoes.

"You shouldn't say things like that," he muttered protestingly. "You're only making it worse for yourself. Now we shall have to hurt you anyway. But of course you'll tell me about the vans. It's only a question of time, you know. Pargo didn't want to talk to me either, but he had to before Borieff had finished."

The Saint looked sideways. Jopley was at the table, fumbling with a box of matches. He was half turned away, intent on a short length of candle stuck in a saucer. The match he had extracted sizzled and flamed suddenly, and at the same moment Simon felt one of his shoes being pulled off.

If anything was to be done it had to be done now—now, while Jopley was concentrating on dabbing the match at the candlewick, and while Lasser's head was bent as he tugged at the other shoe.

The Saint breathed a silent prayer to whatever gods he acknowledged, and brought his hands from behind him.

His clenched right fist drove down like a hammer at the exposed
nape of Lasser's bent neck. On that blow hung the unthinkable issue
of the adventure and the fate of more lives than his own, and the
Saint stocked it with all the pent-up strength that was in him. For
Peter Quentin, and Hoppy Uniatz, and Pargo, and the girl whose
life might be worth no more than theirs now that she also knew
too much, the Saint struck like a blacksmith, knowing that if he
failed to connect completely with one punch he would have no
chance to throw in a second. He felt his fist plug achingly into the
resisting flesh, and Lasser grunted once and lurched limply forward.

Simon caught him with one hand as he slumped on to his knees,
and his other hand dived like a striking snake for the pocket that
sagged with the weight of Lasser's gun.

Jopley looked round, with the candle burning, as the sudden
whirl of movement caught his ear. An almost comically incredulous
expression transfixed his face as he grasped the import of the scene;
but the shock only stopped him for a moment. In the next instant
he was grabbing for his own gun and plunging towards the Saint
at the same time.

Only for an instant. And then he was brought up again, rocking,
as if he had run into an invisible wall, before the round black
muzzle of the automatic in the Saint's hand.

The Saint's smile was seraphically gentle.

"If I have to shoot you, Algernon," he said, "I shall be terribly
disappointed."

The man glared at him in silence, while Lasser's unconscious
body, released from the Saint's grasp, slid down and rolled over on
the floor.

"You can put your hand in your other pocket," Simon went on,
in that soft and terrible voice. "I want the rest of that sticking
plaster. And then we will talk a little more about this Guy Fawkes
party."

## XII

Standing in the shadows outside the library windows, the Saint
studied the scene within. The chairs where Peter and Hoppy and
Brenda Marlow sat were ranged roughly at the three corners of
a square; approximately at the fourth corner stood Borieff, leaning
against the back of an armchair and watching them, with his gun

in his hand and a cigarette drooping from the corner of his mouth. Simon could easily have dropped him where he stood, but that was not what he wanted. He saw that Borieff's back was directly turned to the door through which they had first entered the library, and spent a few seconds more printing estimated distances and angles on his memory. Then he returned silently along the path to the room he had just left.

Jopley, taped hand and foot exactly as the Saint had been a little while ago, glared up at him malevolently from the floor; and in another corner Lasser groaned and stirred uneasily as if he was rousing from a troubled sleep; but that was very near the limit of their power of self-expression. The Saint smiled encouragingly at Jopley as he went by.

"I don't mind if you yell, Algernon," he said kindly. "I should say that door was almost soundproof, but in any case it'd be quite good local colour."

The other seemed to consider whether he should accept the invitation, but while he was still making up his mind the Saint crossed the room to the door opposite the French windows and let himself out into the dark bare hall.

His fingers closed on the knob of the library door and turned it slowly, without the faintest rattle. His only fear then was that the door itself might creak as it opened, but it swung back with ghostly smoothness as far as he needed to step into the room.

Peter Quentin saw him with an instant's delirious amazement, and quickly averted his eyes. The girl saw him, and her face went white with the clutch of wild half-unbelieving hope before she also looked away. She sat with her head bent and her eyes riveted on the toe of one shoe, her fingers locked together in intolerable suspense. The crudely assembled features of Mr Uniatz contracted in a sudden awful spasm that seemed to squeeze his eyes halfway out of their sockets: if he had been anyone else, the observer would have said that he looked as if he had a stomach-ache, but on Mr Uniatz it only looked as if the normal frightfulness of his countenance had been lightly stirred by the ripple of a passing thought. And the Saint moved forward like a stalking leopard until he was so close behind Borieff that he could have bitten him in the neck.

The actual state of Borieff's neck removed the temptation to do this. Instead, his right hand whipped around Borieff's gun wrist like a ring of steel, and he spoke into the man's ear.

"Boo," he said.

The man gasped and whirled round convulsively as if he had been touched with a live wire; but the Saint's grip on his wrist controlled the movement and kept the gun twisted harmlessly up towards the ceiling. At the same time, Simon's left hand pushed forward the automatic he had taken from Lasser until it met Borieff's ribs.

"I should drop that little toy if I were you," he said. "Otherwise I might get nervous."

He increased the torque on Borieff's wrist to emphasise his point, and the man yelped and let go the gun. Simon kicked it towards the girl.

"Just keep him in order for a minute, will you?" he murmured. "If he does anything foolish, mind you hit him in the stomach—it's more painful there."

As she picked up the gun, he pushed Borieff away and took out his knife. With a few quick strokes he had Peter free, and then he turned to Hoppy.

Peter stood up, peeling off the remains of the adhesive tape.

"I'm getting discouraged," he said. "All these years we've been trying to get rid of you, and every time we think you're nicely settled you come back. Won't you ever learn when to die a hero's death and give somebody else a chance with the heroine?"

"I will when I find someone else who'd have a chance," Simon assured him generously.

He straightened up from releasing Mr Uniatz's ankles, and held out the remains of the roll of plaster.

"Make a parcel of Comrade Borieff, will you, Hoppy?" he said. "We don't want him to get restive and hurt himself."

"Okay, boss," said Mr Uniatz willingly. "All I need is just one drink——"

"I'll have mine first," said Peter Quentin, swooping hastily on the bottle, "or else there mightn't be enough to go round."

Simon took the glass away from him as he filled it, and strolled over to the girl.

"Was that date in London very important?" he said. "Or will you come along with us and make it a party?"

She shook her head.

"I was only going for Lasser—I had to meet the Frenchman who supplies him and give him his money."

"My God," said the Saint. "I'd almost forgotten——"

He left her standing there, and disappeared through the communicating door into the next room. In another moment he was back, with the sealed envelope that Lasser had taken from her bag.

"Is this it?"

"Yes."

"I thought it was worth something the first time I saw it," said the Saint, and slit it open with his thumbnail.

When he had counted the thick wad of banknotes that came out of it, his eyebrows were lifted and his eyes were laughing. He added it to the hundred pounds which he had recovered from Jopley, and put it carefully away in his pocket.

"I can see we staged the showdown on the right evening," he said. "This will be some consolation to all of us when we divide it up." His eyes sobered on her again. "Lasser must have trusted you a good deal."

"I suppose he knew that I was that sort of fool," she said bitterly.

"How did you get in with him?"

"I met him through some friends I used to go sailing with, and he seemed to be an awfully good egg. I'd known him for quite some time when he told me what he was doing and said that he needed some help. I knew it was against the law, but I didn't feel as if I was a criminal. You know how it is—we've all smuggled small things through the customs when we've had the chance, and we don't feel as if we'd done anything wicked. I just thought it'd be great fun with a bit of danger to make it more exciting."

"I've wangled things through the customs myself," said the Saint. "But there's a difference between that and making a business of it."

"Oh, I know," she said helplessly. "I was a damn fool, that's all. But I didn't realise . . . I didn't have anything to do with the organisation. I went out in the yacht once or twice, and another boat met us in the Channel and we took things on board, and then we came back here and unloaded it and went away. I went to Paris and bought those dresses and things, but Lasser gave me the money and he was to take half the profits. And I used to meet people and take them messages and things when he didn't want them to know who they were dealing with. I'd never been on one of the lorries before last night, but Lasser wanted two people to go for safety because of the lorries that had disappeared, and there was nobody else available. I know why, now—because Lasser wanted Borieff to help him, and Pargo was being tortured."

'You didn't happen to think that Jopley and Borieff were retired churchwardens, did you?"

"No—I hated them. But Lasser said you had to employ anyone you could get for jobs like theirs, and I didn't think even they could go so far." She shrugged, and her eyes were dark with pain. "Well, it's my own fault. I suppose you'll be handing them over to the police, and you'd better take me with you. I shan't give you any trouble. Whatever happens, I'm glad you beat them."

He shook his head.

"I'm afraid it wouldn't be any good handing them over to the police," he said. "You see, the Law has such pettifogging rules about evidence."

"But——"

"Oh, yes, you could convict them of smuggling and get them about six months each. But that's all."

"Then——"

He smiled.

"Don't worry about it, darling," he said. "Just stay here for a minute, will you?"

He turned to Peter and Hoppy, and indicated Borieff with a faint nod.

"Bring him in," he said, and led the way into the next room.

Jopley was cursing and fighting against his bonds, and Lasser had recovered enough to be writhing too. Simon dragged them over to the fireplace, and went back to tear down the heavy silk cords that drew the long window hangings. He roped the two men expertly together, and when Borieff arrived he added him to the collection. The other end of the rope he knotted to a bar of the iron grate that was set solidly in the brickwork.

Then he closed the door and looked at Peter and Hoppy, and the smile had gone altogether from his face.

"There's just one thing more which you didn't know," he said quietly. "Comrade Lasser told me about it in here. There's supposed to be a fire here tonight—the place is all prepared for it. And after we'd all been worked over like Pargo was—Borieff was the assistant in that, by the way—whatever else happened, however much we told, the idea was to leave us tied up here with a lighted candle burning down to the floor. We were to be got rid of anyway; and according to Lasser we had to be burnt alive so that it would look like an accident."

The Saint's eyes were as cold and passionless as the eyes of a recording angel.

"We are the only jury here," he said. "What is our justice?"

The Hirondel thundered down into the valley and soared up the slope on the other side. Somewhere near the first crest of the Purbeck Hills, Simon stopped the car to take out a cigarette; and through the hushing of the engine his ears caught a familiar gurgling sound that made him look round.

In the back seat, Mr Uniatz detached the bottle from his lips and beamed at him ingratiatingly.

"I find it in de cabinet where dey keep de liquor, boss," he explained. "So I t'ought it'd keep us warm on de way home."

"At least you won't freeze to death," said the Saint philosophically.

He turned the other way as he struck his lighter, and gazed out into the darkness where the hills rose again at the edge of the sea. Somewhere in the black silhouette of them there was a dull red glow, pulsing and brightening, like a palely luminous cloud. The eyes of the girl beside him turned in the same direction.

"It looks like a fire," she said interestedly.

"So it does," said the Saint, and drove on without another backward glance, eastwards, towards Lyndhurst.

# THE AFFAIR OF HOGSBOTHAM

## From Follow The Saint

---

ORIGINALITY IN A WRITER *is generally supposed to be an asset; although on the other side of the argument there is always the old proverb about how there is nothing new under the sun. In my very limited field I have tried to achieve a little originality; I don't know with how much success.*

*Within the rather conventionalised boundaries of the modern crime story, there are actually only a very small and definite number of choices for the central figure, who must be what you might call the focal point of the lens through which the reader is going to inspect the crime. He (or, if you must strain the point, she) can be (a) an observant bystander, (b) a professional policeman, (c) a brilliant amateur, (d) a sort of Saint, or (e) the criminal. But these possibilities are even more reduced in practice. The observant bystander is necessarily negative, and to me an unsatisfactory evasion. The professional policeman, if credibly depicted, would have to be a little dull and stereotyped, for what seems to me to be the obvious reason that no one with an original personality would want to be a professional policeman—or, if he did want to be one, that no police force under the present system would encourage his ambition. The criminal, on the other hand, while his point of view might provide an interesting angle for a single story, cannot survive a series simply because the repetition of his crimes would make him an increasingly objectionable person—Raffles and Arsène Lupin got away with it in a very different age, and are pardoned now through a kind of sentimental purifying, much as we find it convenient to forget that Richard the Lion Heart probably did not take many baths.*

*This brings us down to two alternatives, of which the*

*Brilliant Amateur* is the most commonly chosen. *Perhaps for this reason, the effort of making him original seems to get a little more shortwinded with every incarnation. He is invested with weirder and weirder attributes in a frantic attempt to distinguish him from his continually multiplying host of predecessors. He progresses from violins and cocaine to Gallic gestures and laboured malapropisms, to collections of Chinese porcelain and Egyptian scarabs, to talking like a combination menu and wine list, to quoting Oriental proverbs, to almost anything within the scope of imagination that will distinguish him as if he carried a flag. Without wanting to disparage the excellent stories that are being written by a goodly number of my contemporaries, I still feel sufficiently patriarchal in this business to admit that I sometimes visualise the agony of a new writer sitting down to the task of creating an original hero. Shall he have a glass eye and a forked red beard, and indulge the eccentricity of playing the cornet on the roof of a taxi whilst brooding over his clues? Or shall she be an overweight spinster with a passion for astrology, who can only solve her problems when she is knitting green stockings in a cemetery and being massaged by a one-armed Hindu who quotes Wordsworth with an Icelandic accent? It is getting so difficult to think of anything that hasn't been done before.*

*But these things, of course, are only mannerisms: they do not make a man. They are characteristics, not character. That should be a platitude, but I'm afraid it is forgotten too often.*

*I have done my best to remember it. As I said at the beginning, I have been trying to make a picture of a man. Changing, yes. Developing, I hope. Fantastic, improbable—perhaps. Quite worthless, quite irritating, if you feel that way. Or a slightly cockeyed ideal, if you feel indifferently. It doesn't matter so much, so long as you feel that you would recognise him if you met him tomorrow.*

*And this is the last story in this book.*

*Originality in a story is something else again. I'm not sure whether there are three million million plots, or fundamentally only three. There are different schools of thought on the subject. I do know that after writing more than eighty separate stories about the same character I have left myself wide open to be accused of falling into a formula. The selection of a concluding story was therefore quite a problem. It was a temptation to try to bow out with a parting burst of brilliance, a farewell display of fireworks. But on the other hand I wanted a story that in its own way would summarise them all. So it should have Patricia, and Teal, and Hoppy. And Orace, and Peter Quentin. And boodle. It should have spicings of mayhem and mystery and murder, also of romance; of Teal-baiting; and of the Saint's own outrageous brand of philosophical indignation. All those are here. So you might say that it just looks like a distillation of all the Saint stories—the mixture as before. You may be right, too. I wouldn't know. But you will get no apologies from me, because I'm afraid I still like it.*

# THE AFFAIR OF HOGSBOTHAM

"THERE ARE TIMES," remarked Simon Templar, putting down the evening paper and pouring himself a second glass of Tio Pepe, "when I am on the verge of swearing a great oath never to look at another newspaper as long as I live. Here you have a fascinating world full of all kinds of busy people, being born, falling in love, marrying, dying and being killed, working, starving, fighting, splitting atoms and measuring stars, inventing trick corkscrews and relativity theories, building skyscrapers and suffering hell with toothache. When I buy a newspaper I want to read all about them. I want to know what they're doing and creating and planning and striving for and going to war about—all the exciting vital things that make a picture of a real world and real people's lives. And what do I get?"

"What do you get, Saint?" asked Patricia Holm with a smile.

Simon picked up the newspaper again.

"This is what I get," he said. "I get a guy whose name, believe it or not, is Ebenezer Hogsbotham. Comrade Hogsbotham, having been born with a name like that and a face to match it, if you can believe a newspaper picture, has never had a chance in his life to misbehave, and has therefore naturally developed into one of those guys who feel that they have a mission to protect everyone else from misbehaviour. He has therefore been earnestly studying the subject in order to be able to tell other people how to protect themselves from it. For several weeks, apparently, he has been frequenting the bawdiest theatres and the nudest night clubs, discovering just how much depravity is being put out to ensnare those people who are not so shiningly immune to contamination as himself; as a result of which he has come out hot and strong for a vigorous censorship of all public entertainment. Since Comrade Hogsbotham has carefully promoted himself to be president of the National Society for the Preservation of Public Morals, he hits the front-page headlines while five hundred human beings who get themselves blown to bits by honourable Japanese bombs are only worth a three-line filler on page eleven. And this is the immortal utterance that he hits them with: 'The public has a right to be protected,' he says, 'from displays of suggestiveness and undress which are disgusting to all right-thinking people.' . . . 'Right-thinking people,' of course, only means people who think like Comrade Hogsbotham; but it's one of those crushing and high-sounding phrases that the Hogs-bothams of this world seem to have a monopoly on. Will you excuse me while I vomit?"

Patricia fingered the curls in her soft golden hair and considered him guardedly.

"You can't do anything else about it," she said. "Even you can't alter that sort of thing, so you might as well save your energy."

"I suppose so." The Saint scowled. "But it's just too hopeless to resign yourself to spending the rest of your life watching nine-tenths of the world's population, who've got more than enough serious things to worry about already, being browbeaten into a superstitious respect for the humbug of a handful of yapping crypt-orchid Hogsbothams. I feel that somebody on the other side of the fence ought to climb over and pin his ears back . . . I have a pain in the neck. I should like to do something to demonstrate my un-paralleled immorality. I want to go out and burgle a convent; or borrow a guitar and parade in front of Hogsbotham's house, sing-ing obscene songs in a beery voice."

He took his glass over to the window and stood there looking down over Piccadilly and the Green Park with a faraway dreami-ness in his blue eyes that seemed to be playing with all kinds of electric and reprehensible ideas beyond the humdrum view on which they were actually focused; and Patricia Holm watched him with eyes of the same reckless blue but backed by a sober under-standing. She had known him too long to dismiss such a mood as lightly as any other woman would have dismissed it. Any other man might have voiced the same grumble without danger of any-one else remembering it beyond the next drink; but when the man who was so fantastically called the Saint uttered that kind of un-saintly thought, his undercurrent of seriousness was apt to be trans-lated into a different sort of headline with a frequency that Patricia

needed all her reserves of mental stability to cope with. Some of
the Saint's wildest adventures had started from less sinister openings
than that, and she measured him now with a premonition that she
had not yet heard the last of that random threat. For a whole month
he had done nothing illegal, and in his life thirty days of untarnished
virtue was a long time. She studied the buccaneering lines of his
lean figure, sensed the precariously curbed restlessness under his
lounging ease, and knew that even if no exterior adventure crossed
his path that month of peace would come to spontaneous disrup-
tion. . . .

And then he turned back with a smile that did nothing to
reassure her.

"Well, we shall see," he murmured, and glanced at his watch.
"It's time you were on your way to meet that moribund aunt of
yours. You can make sure she hasn't changed her will, because we
might stir up some excitement by bumping her off."

She made a face at him and stood up.

"What are you going to do tonight?"

"I called Claud Eustace this morning and made a date to take
him out to dinner—maybe he'll know about something exciting
that's going on. And it's time we were on our way too. Are you
ready, Hoppy?"

The rudimentary assortment of features which constituted the
hairless or front elevation of Hoppy Uniatz's head emerged lingeringly from behind the bottle of Caledonian dew with which he had
been making another of his indomitable attempts to assuage the
chronic aridity of his gullet.

"Sure, boss," he said agreeably. "Ain't I always ready? Where
do we meet dis dame we gotta bump off?"

The Saint sighed.

"You'll find out," he said. "Let's go."

Mr Uniatz trotted placidly after him. In Mr Uniatz's mind, a
delicate organ which he had to be careful not to overwork, there
was room for none of the manifestations of philosophical indignation with which Simon Templar was sometimes troubled. By the
time it had found space for the ever-present problems of quench-
ing an insatiable thirst and finding a sufficient supply of lawfully
bumpable targets to keep the rust from forming in the barrel of his
Betsy, it really had room for only one other idea. And that other
permanently comforting and omnipresent notion was composed
entirely of the faith and devotion with which he clung to the in-

tellectual pre-eminence of the Saint. The Saint, Mr Uniatz had long
since realised, with almost religious awe, could Think. To Mr
Uniatz, a man whose rare experiments with Thought had always
given him a dull pain under the hat, this discovery had simplified
life to the point where Paradise itself would have had few advantages to offer, except possibly rivers flowing with Scotch
whisky. He simply did what he was told, and everything came out
all right. Anything the Saint said was okay with him.

It is a lamentable fact that Chief Inspector Claud Eustace Teal
had no such faith to buoy him up. Mr Teal's views were almost
diametrically the reverse of those which gave so much consolation
to Mr Uniatz. To Mr Teal, the Saint was a perennial harbinger of
woe, an everlasting time-bomb planted under his official chair—with
the only difference that when ordinary bombs blew up they were
at least over and done with, whereas the Saint was a bomb with the
supernatural and unfair ability to blow up whenever it wanted to
without in any way impairing its capacity for future explosions.
He had accepted the Saint's invitation to dinner with an easy and
actually unjustified suspicion that there was probably a catch in it,
as there had been in most of his previous encounters with the Saint;
and there was a gleam of something like smugness in his sleepy eyes
as he settled more firmly behind his desk at Scotland Yard and shook
his head with every conventional symptom of regret.

"I'm sorry, Saint," he said. "I ought to have phoned you, but I've
been so busy. I'm going to have to ask you to fix another evening.
We had a bank holdup at Staines today, and I've got to go down
there and take over."

Simon's brows began to rise by an infinitesimal hopeful fraction.

"A bank holdup, Claud? How much did they get away with?"

"About fifteen thousand pounds," Teal said grudgingly. "You
ought to know. It was in the evening papers."

"I do seem to remember seeing something about it tucked away
somewhere," Simon said thoughtfully. "What do you know?"

The detective's mouth closed and tightened up. It was as if he was
already regretting having said so much, even though the information was broadcast on the streets for anyone with a spare penny to
read. But he had seen that tentatively optimistic flicker of the Saint's
mocking eyes too often in the past to ever be able to see it again
without a queasy hollow feeling in the pit of his ample stomach.
He reacted to it with a brusqueness that sprang from a long train
of memories of other occasions when crime had been in the news

and boodle in the wind, and Simon Templar had greeted both promises with the same incorrigibly hopeful glimmer of mischief in his eyes, and that warning had presaged one more nightmare chapter in the apparently endless sequence that had made the name of the Saint the most dreaded word in the vocabulary of the underworld and the source of more grey hairs in Chief Inspector Teal's dwindling crop than any one man had a right to inflict on a conscientious officer of the law.

"If I knew all about it I shouldn't have to go to Staines," he said conclusively. "I'm sorry, but I can't tell you where to go and pick up the money."

"Maybe I could run you down," Simon began temptingly. "Hoppy and I are all on our own this evening, and we were just looking for something useful to do. My car's outside, and it needs some exercise. Besides, I feel clever tonight. All my genius for sleuthing and deduction——"

"I'm sorry," Teal repeated. "There's a police car waiting for me already. I'll have to get along as well as I can without you." He stood up, and held out his hand. A sensitive man might almost have thought that he was in a hurry to avoid an argument. "Give me a ring one day next week, will you? I'll be able to tell you all about it then."

Simon Templar stood on the Embankment outside Scotland Yard and lighted a cigarette with elaborately elegant restraint.

"And that, Hoppy," he explained, "is what is technically known as the Bum's Rush."

He gazed resentfully at the dingy panorama which is the sum total of everything that generations of London architects and County Councils have been able to make out of their river frontages.

"Nobody loves us," he said gloomily. "Patricia forsakes us to be a dutiful niece to a palsied aunt, thereby leaving us exposed to every kind of temptation. We try to surround ourselves with holiness by dining with a detective, and he's too busy to keep the date. We offer to help him and array ourselves on the side of law and order, and he gives us the tax-collector's welcome. His evil mind distrusts our immaculate motives. He is so full of suspicion and uncharitableness that he thinks our only idea is to catch up with his bank holder-uppers before he does and relieve them of their loot for our own benefit. He practically throws us out on our ear, and abandons us to any wicked schemes we can cook up. What are we going to do about it?"

"I dunno, boss." Mr Uniatz shifted from one foot to the other, grimacing with the heroic effort of trying to extract a constructive suggestion from the gummy interior of his skull. He hit upon one at last, with the trepidant amazement of another Newton grasping the law of gravity. "Maybe we could go some place an' get a drink," he suggested breathlessly.

Simon grinned at him and took him by the arm.

"For once in your life," he said, "I believe you've had an inspiration. Let us go to a pub and drown our sorrows."

On the way he bought another evening paper and turned wistfully to the story of the bank holdup; but it gave him very little more than Teal had told him. The bank was a branch of the City & Continental, which handled the accounts of two important factories on the outskirts of the town. That morning the routine consignment of cash in silver and small notes had been brought down from London in a guarded van to meet the weekly payrolls of the two plants; and after it had been placed in the strong-room the van and the guards had departed as usual, although the factory messengers would not call for it until the afternoon. There was no particular secrecy about the arrangements, and the possibility of a holdup of the bank itself had apparently never been taken seriously. During the lunch hour the local police, acting on an anonymous telephone call, had sent a hurried squad to the bank in time to interrupt the holdup; but the bandits had shot their way out, wounding two constables in the process; and approximately fifteen thousand pounds' worth of untraceable small change had vanished with them. Their car had been found abandoned only a few blocks from the bank premises, and there the trail ended; and the Saint knew that it was likely to stay ended there for all the clues contained in the printed story. England was a small country, but it contained plenty of room for two unidentified bank robbers to hide in.

Simon refolded the newspaper and dumped it resignedly on the bar; and as he did so it lay in such a way that the headlines summarising the epochal utterance of Mr Ebenezer Hogsbotham stared up at him with a complacent prominence that added insult to injury.

The Saint stared malevolently back at them; and in the mood which circumstances had helped to thrust upon him their effect had an almost fateful inevitability. No other man on earth would have taken them in just that way; but there never had been another man in history so harebrained as the Saint could be when his rebellious instincts boiled over. The idea that was being born to him grew momentarily in depth and richness. He put down his glass, and went to the telephone booth to consult the directory. The action was rather like the mental tossing of a coin. And it came down heads. Mr Hogsbotham was on the telephone. And accordingly, decisively, his address was in the book. . . .

The fact seemed to leave no further excuse for hesitation. Simon went back to the bar, and his head sang carols with the blitheness of his own insanity.

"Put that poison away, Hoppy," he said. "We're going places."

Mr Uniatz gulped obediently, and looked up with a contented beam.

"Dijja t'ink of sump'n to do, boss?" he asked eagerly.

The Saint nodded. His smile was extravagantly radiant.

"I did. We're going to burgle the house of Hogsbotham."

## · II

It was one of those lunatic ideas that any inmate of an asylum might have conceived, but only Simon Templar could be relied on to carry solemnly into execution. He didn't waste any more time on pondering over it, or even stop to consider any of its legal aspects. He drove his huge cream and red Hirondel snarling over the roads to Chertsey at an average speed that was a crime in itself, and which would probably have given a nervous breakdown to any passenger less impregnably phlegmatic than Mr Uniatz; but he brought it intact to the end of the trip without any elaborations on his original idea or any attempt to produce them. He was simply on his way to effect an unlawful entry into the domicile of Mr Hogsbotham, and there to do something or other that would annoy Mr Hogsbotham greatly and at the same time relieve his own mood of general annoyance; but what that something would be rested entirely with the inspiration of the moment. The only thing he was sure about was that the inspiration would be forthcoming.

The telephone directory had told him that Mr Hogsbotham lived at Chertsey. It also located Mr Hogsbotham's home on Greenleaf Road, which Simon found to be a narrow turning off Chertsey Lane running towards the river on the far side of the town. He drove the Hirondel into a field a hundred yards beyond the turning and left it under the broad shadow of a clump of elms, and returned to Greenleaf Road on foot. And there the telephone directory's information became vague. Following the ancient custom by which the Englishman strives to preserve the sanctity of his castle from strange visitors by refusing to give it a street number, hiding it instead under a name like "Mon Repos", "Sea View", "The Birches", "Dunrovin", "Jusweetu", and other similar whimsies, the demesne of Mr Hogsbotham was apparently known simply as "The Snuggery". Which might have conveyed volumes to a postman schooled in tracking self-effacing citizens to their lairs, but wasn't the hell of a lot of help to any layman who was trying to find the place for the first time on a dark night.

Simon had not walked very far down Greenleaf Road when that fact was brought home to him. Greenleaf Road possessed no street lighting to make navigation easier. It was bordered by hedges of varying heights and densities, behind which lighted windows could sometimes be seen and sometimes not. At intervals, the hedges yawned into gaps from which ran well-kept drives and things that looked like cart-tracks in about equal proportions. Some of the openings had gates, and some hadn't. Some of the gates had names painted on them; and on those which had, the paint varied in antiquity from shining newness to a state of weatherbeaten decomposition which made any name that had ever been there completely illegible. When the Saint realised that they had already passed at least a dozen anonymous entrances, any one of which might have led to the threshold of Mr Hogsbotham's Snuggery, he stopped walking and spoke eloquently on the subject of town planning for a full minute without raising his voice.

He could have gone on for longer than that, warming to his subject as he developed the theme; but farther down the road the wobbling light of a lone bicycle blinked into view, and he stepped out from the side of the road as it came abreast of them and kept his hat down over his eyes and his face averted from the light while he asked the rider if he knew the home of Hogsbotham.

"Yes, sir, it's the fourth 'ouse on yer right the way yer goin'. Yer carn't miss it," said the wanderer cheerfully, with a native's slightly patronising simplicity, and rode on.

The Saint paused to light a cigarette, and resumed his stride. The lines of his face dimly illumined in the glow of smouldering tobacco were sharp with half-humorous anticipation.

"Hogsbotham may be in London investigating some more night clubs," he said. "But you'd better get a handkerchief tied round your neck so you can pull it up over your dial—just in case. We don't want to be recognised, because it would worry Claud Eustace Teal, and he's busy."

He was counting the breaks in the hedges as he walked. He counted three, and stopped at the fourth. A gate that could have closed it stood open, and he turned his pocket flashlight on it cautiously. It was one of the weatherbeaten kind, and the words that had once been painted on it were practically undecipherable, but they looked vaguely as if they might once have stood for "The Snuggery".

Simon killed his torch after that brief glimpse. He dropped his cigarette and trod it out under his foot.

"We seem to have arrived," he said. "Try not to make too much noise, Hoppy, because maybe Hogsbotham isn't deaf."

He drifted on up the drive as if his shoes had been soled with cotton wool. Following behind him, Mr Uniatz's efforts to lighten his tread successfully reduced the total din of their advance to something less than would have been made by a small herd of buffalo; but Simon knew that the average citizen's sense of hearing is mercifully unselective. His own silent movements were more the result of habit than of any conscious care.

The drive curved around a dense mass of laurels, above which the symmetrical spires of cypress silhouetted against the dark sky concealed the house until it loomed suddenly in front of him as if it had risen from the ground. The angles of its roof-line cut a serrated pattern out of the gauzy backcloth of half-hearted stars hung behind it; the rest of the building below that angled line was merely a mass of solid blackness in which one or two knife-edges of yellow light gleaming between drawn curtains seemed to be suspended disjoint-edly in space. But they came from ground-floor windows, and he concluded that Ebenezer Hogsbotham was at home.

He did not decide that Mr Hogsbotham was not only at home, but at home with visitors, until he nearly walked into a black closed car parked in the driveway. The car's lights were out, and he was so intent on trying to establish the topography of the lighted windows that the dull sheen of its coachwork barely caught his eye in time for him to check himself. He steered Hoppy round it, and wondered what sort of guests a man with the name and temperament of Ebenezer Hogsbotham would be likely to entertain.

And then, inside the house, a radio or gramophone began to play.

It occurred to Simon that he might have been unnecessarily pessimistic in suggesting that Mr Hogsbotham might not be deaf.

From the muffled quality of the noise which reached him, it was obvious that the windows of the room in which the instrument was functioning were tightly closed; but even with that obstruction, the volume of sound which boomed out into the night was startling in its quantity. The opus under execution was the *Ride of the Valkyries*, which is admittedly not rated among the most ethereal melodies in the musical pharmacopœia; but even so, it was being produced with a vim which inside the room itself must have been earsplitting. It roared out in a stunning fortissimo that made the Saint put his heels back on the ground and disdain even to moderate his voice.

"This is easy," he said. "We'll just batter the door down and walk in."

He was not quite as blatant as that, but very nearly. He was careful enough to circle the house to the back door; and whether he would actually have battered it down remained an unanswered question, for he had no need to use any violence on it at all. It opened when he touched the handle, and he stepped in as easily as he had entered the garden.

Perhaps it was at that point that he first realised that the unplanned embryo of his adventure was taking a twist which he had never expected of it. It was difficult to pin down the exact moment of mutation, because it gathered force from a series of shocks that superimposed themselves on him with a speed that made the separate phases of the change seem somewhat blurred. And the first two or three of those shocks chased each other into his consciousness directly that unlatched back door swung inwards under the pressure of his hand.

The very fact that the door opened so easily to his exploring touch may have been one of them; but he could take that in his stride. Many householders were inclined to be absent-minded about the uses of locks and bolts. But the following blows were harder to swallow. The door opened to give him a clear view of the kitchen; and that was when the rapid sequence of impacts began to make an impression on his powers of absorption.

To put it bluntly, which is about the only way anything of that kind could be put, the door opened to give him a full view of what appeared to be quite a personable young woman tied to a chair.

There was a subsidiary shock in the realization that she appeared to be personable. Without giving any thought to the subject, Simon had never expected Mr Hogsbotham to have a servant who was personable. He had automatically credited him with a housekeeper who had stringy mouse-coloured hair, a long nose inclined to redness, and a forbidding lipless mouth, a harridan in tight-laced corsets whose egregiously obvious virtue would suffice to strangle any gossip about Mr Hogsbotham's bachelor ménage—Mr Hogsbotham had to be a bachelor, because it was not plausible that any woman, unless moved by a passion which a man of Mr Hogsbotham's desiccated sanctity could never hope to inspire, would consent to adopt a name like Mrs Hogsbotham. The girl in the chair appeared to be moderately young, moderately well-shaped, and moderately inoffensive to look at; although the dishcloth which was knotted across her mouth as a gag made the last quality a little difficult to estimate. Yet she wore a neat housemaid's uniform, and therefore she presumably belonged to Mr Hogsbotham's domestic staff.

That also could be assimilated—with a slightly greater effort. It was her predicament that finally overtaxed his swallowing reflexes. It was possible that there might be some self-abnegating soul in the British Isles who was willing to visit with Mr Hogsbotham; it was possible that Mr Hogsbotham might be deaf; it was possible that he might be careless about locking his back door; it was possible, even, that he might employ a servant who didn't look like the twin sister of a Gorgon; but if he left her tied up and gagged in the kitchen while he entertained his guests with ear-shattering excerpts from Wagner, there was something irregular going on under his sanctimonious roof which Simon Templar wanted to know more about.

He stood staring into the maid's dilated eyes while a galaxy of fantastic queries and surmises skittered across his brain like the grand finale of a firework display. For one long moment he couldn't have moved or spoken if there had been a million-dollar bonus for it.

Mr Uniatz was the one who broke the silence, if any state of affairs that was so numbingly blanketed by the magnified blast of a symphony orchestra could properly be called a silence. He shifted his feet, and his voice grated conspiratorially in the Saint's ear.

"Is dis de old bag, boss?" he inquired with sepulchral sangfroid; and the interruption brought Simon's reeling imagination back to earth.

"What old bag?" he demanded blankly.

"De aunt of Patricia's," said Mr Uniatz, no less blank at even being asked such a question, "who we are goin' to bump off."

The Saint took a firmer grip of material things.

"Does she look like an old bag?" he retorted.

Hoppy inspected the exhibit again, dispassionately.

"No," he admitted. He seemed mystified. Then a solution dawned dazzlingly upon him. "Maybe she has her face lifted, boss," he suggested luminously.

"Or maybe she isn't anybody's aunt," Simon pointed out.

This kind of extravagant speculation was too much for Mr Uniatz. He was unable to gape effectively on account of the handkerchief over his mouth, but the exposed area between the bridge of his nose and the brim of his hat hinted that the rest of his face was gaping.

"And maybe we've run into something," said the Saint.

The rest of his mind was paying no attention to Hoppy's problems. He was not even taking much notice of the maid's panic-stricken eyes as they widened still further in mute terror at the conversation that was passing over her head. He was listening intently to the music that still racketed stridently in his eardrums, three times louder now that he was inside the house. There had been a time in the history of his multitudinous interests when he had had a spell of devotion to grand opera, and his ears were as analytically sensitive as those of a trained musician. And he was realising, with a melodramatic suddenness that prickled the hairs on the nape of his neck, that the multisonous shrillness of the *Ride of the Valkyries* had twice been mingled with a brief high-pitched shriek that Wagner had never written into the score.

His fingers closed for an instant on Hoppy's arm.

"Stay here a minute," he said.

He went on past the trussed housemaid, out of the door on the far side of the kitchen. The screeching fanfares of music battered at him with redoubled savagery as he opened the door and emerged into the cramped over-furnished hall beyond it. Aside from its clutter of fretwork mirror-mountings, spindly umbrella-stands and etceteras, and vapid Victorian chromos, it contained only the lower end of a narrow staircase and three other doors, one of which was the front entrance. Simon had subconsciously observed a serving hatch in the wall on his left as he opened the kitchen door, and on that evidence he automatically attributed the left-hand door in the hallway to the dining-room. He moved towards the right-hand door. And as he reached it the music stopped, in the middle of a bar, as if it had been sheared off with a knife, leaving the whole house stunned with stillness.

The Saint checked on one foot, abruptly conscious even of his breathing in the sudden quiet. He was less than a yard from the door that must have belonged to the living-room. Standing there, he heard the harsh rumble of a thick brutal voice on the other side of the door, dulled in volume but perfectly distinct.

"All right," it said. "That's just a sample. Now will you tell us what you did with that dough, or shall we play some more music?"

## III

Simon lowered his spare foot to the carpet, and bent his leg over it until he was down on one knee. From that position he could peer through the keyhole and get a view of part of the room.

Directly across from him, a thin small weasel-faced man stood over a radiogram beside the fireplace. A cigarette dangled limply from the corner of his mouth, and the eyes that squinted through the smoke drifting past his face were beady and emotionless like a snake's. Simon placed the lean cruel face almost instantly in his encyclopedic mental records of the population of the underworld, and the recognition walloped into his already tottering awareness to register yet another item in the sequence of surprise punches that his phenomenal resilience was trying to stand up to. The weasel-faced man's name was Morris Dolf; and he was certainly no kind of guest for anyone with the reputation of Ebenezer Hogsbotham to entertain.

The Saint's survey slid off him on to the man who sat in front of the fireplace. This was someone whom the Saint did not recognise, and he knew he was not Mr Hogsbotham. He was a man with thin sandy hair and a soft plump face that would have fitted very nicely on somebody's pet rabbit. At the moment it was a very frightened rabbit. The man sat in a stiff-backed chair placed on the hearthrug, and pieces of clothesline had been used to keep him there. His arms had been stretched round behind him and tied at the back of the chair so that his shoulders were hunched slightly forward by the strain. His shirt had been ripped open to the waist, so that his chest was bare; and his skin was very white and insipid, as if it had never seen daylight since he was born. It was so white that two irregular patches of inflammation on it stood out like blotches of dull red paint. His lips were trembling, and his eyes bulged in wild orbs of dread.

"I don't know!" he blubbered. "I tell you, you're making a mistake I don't know anything about it. I haven't got it. Don't burn me again!"

Morris Dolf might not have heard. He stood leaning boredly against the radiogram and didn't move.

Someone else did. It was a third man, whose back was turned to the door. The back was broad and fitted tightly into his coat, so that the material wrinkled at the armpits, and the neck above it was short and thick and reddish, running quickly into close-cropped wiry back hair. The whole rear view had a hard coarse physical ruthlessness that made it unnecessary to see its owner's face to make an immediate summary of his character. It belonged without a shadow of doubt to the thick brutal voice that Simon had heard first—and equally without doubt, it could not possibly have belonged to Mr Ebenezer Hogsbotham.

The same voice spoke again. It said: "Okay, Verdean. But you're the one who made the mistake. You made it when you thought you'd be smart and try to doublecross us. You made it worse when you tried to turn us in to the cops, so we could take the rap for you and leave you nothing to worry about. Now you're going to wish you hadn't been so damn smart."

The broad back moved forward and bent towards the fireplace. The gas fire was burning in the grate, although the evening was warm; and all at once the Saint understood why he had heard through the music those screechy ululations which no orchestral instrument could have produced. The man with the broad back straightened up again, and his powerful hand was holding an ordinary kitchen ladle of which the bowl glowed bright crimson.

"You have it just how you like, rat," he said. "I don't mind how long you hold out. I'm going to enjoy working on you. We're going to burn your body a bit more for a start, and then we'll take your shoes and socks off and put your feet in the fire and see how you like that. You can scream your head off if you want to, but nobody'll hear you over the gramophone . . . Let's have some more of that loud stuff, Morrie."

Morris Dolf turned back to the radiogram, without a flicker of expression, and moved the pick-up arm. The *Ride of the Valkyries* crashed out again with a fearful vigour that would have drowned anything less than the howl of a hurricane; and the broad back shifted towards the man in the chair.

The man in the chair stared in delirious horror from the glowing ladle to the face of the man who held it. His eyes bulged until there were white rims all round the pupils. His quivering lips fluttered into absurd jerky patterns, pouring out frantic pleas and protestations that the music swamped into inaudibility.

Simon Templar removed his eye from the keyhole and loosened the gun under his arm. He had no fanciful ideas about rushing to the rescue of a hapless victim of persecution. In fact, all the more subtle aspects of the victim looked as guilty as hell to him—if not of the actual doublecrossing that seemed to be under discussion, at least of plenty of other reprehensible things. No entirely innocent householder would behave in exactly that way if he were being tortured by a couple of invading thugs. And the whole argument as Simon had overheard it smelled ripely with the rich fragrance of dishonour and dissension among thieves. Which was an odour that had perfumed some of the most joyous hours of the Saint's rapscallion life. By all the portents, he was still a puzzlingly long way from getting within kicking distance of the elusive Mr Hogsbotham; but here under his very nose was a proposition that looked no less diverting and a lot more mysterious; and the Saint had a sublimely happy-go-lucky adaptability to the generous vagaries of Fate. He took his gun clear out of the spring harness where he carried it, and opened the door.

He went in without any stealth, which would have been entirely superfluous. The operatic pandemonium would have made his entrance mouselike if he had ridden in on a capering elephant. He walked almost nonchalantly across the room; and its occupants were so taken up with their own business that he was within a couple of yards of them before any of them noticed that he was there.

Morris Dolf saw him first. His beady eyes swivelled incuriously towards the movement that must have finally caught the fringes of their range of vision, and became petrified into glassy blankness as they fastened on the Saint's tall figure. His jaw dropped so that the cigarette would have fallen out of his mouth if the adhesive dampness of the paper hadn't kept it hanging from his lower lip. He stood as horripilantly still as if a long icy needle had shot up out of the floor and impaled him from sacrum to occiput.

That glazed paralysis lasted for about a breath and a half. And then his right hand whipped towards his pocket.

It was nothing but an involuntary piece of sheer stupidity born out of shock, and the Saint was benevolent enough to treat it that way. He simply lifted the gun in his hand a little, bringing it more prominently into view; and Dolf stopped himself in time.

The man with a beefy neck, in his turn, must have caught some queer impression from Dolf's peculiar movements out of the corner of his eye. He turned and looked at his companion's face, froze for an instant, and then went on turning more quickly, straightening as he did so. He let go the red-hot ladle, and his right hand started to make the same instinctive grab that Dolf had started—and stopped in midair for the same reason. His heavy florid features seemed to bunch into knots of strangulated viciousness as he stood glowering numbly at the Saint's masked face.

Simon stepped sideways, towards the blaring radiogram, and lifted the needle off the record. The nerve-rasping bombardment of sound broke off into blissful silence.

"That's better," he murmured relievedly. "Now we can all talk to each other without giving ourselves laryngitis. When did you discover this passion for expensive music, Morrie?"

Morris Dolf's eye blinked once at the jar of being addressed by name, but he seemed to find it hard to work up an enthusiasm for discussing his cultural development. His tongue slid over his dry lips without forming an answering syllable.

Simon turned to the big florid man. Now that he had seen his face, he had identified him as well.

"Judd Kaskin, I believe?" he drawled, with the delicate suavity of an ambassador of the old régime. "Do you know that you're burning the carpet?"

Kaskin looked at the fallen ladle. He bent and picked it up, rubbing the sole of his shoe over the smouldering patch of rug. Then, as if he suddenly realised that he had done all that in mechanical obedience to a command that the Saint hadn't even troubled to utter directly, he threw it clattering into the fireplace and turned his savage scowl back to the Saint.

"What the hell do you want?" he snarled.

"You know, I was just going to ask you the same question," Simon remarked mildly. "It seemed to me that you were feeling your oats a bit, Judd. I suppose you get that way after doing five years on the Moor. But you haven't been out much more than three months, have you? You shouldn't be in such a hurry to go back."

The big man's eyes gave the same automatic reaction as Dolf's had given to the accuracy of the Saint's information, and hardened again into slits of unyielding suspicion.

"Who the hell are you?" he grated slowly. "You aren't a cop. Take that rag off your face and let's see who you are."

"When I'm ready," said the Saint coolly. "And then you may wish I hadn't. Just now, I'm asking the questions. What is this doublecross you're trying to find out about from Comrade Verdean?"

There was a silence. Morris Dolf's slight expression was fading out again. His mouth closed, and he readjusted his cigarette. Simon knew that behind that silent hollow-cheeked mask a cunning brain was getting back to work.

Kaskin's face, when he wanted to play tricks with it, could put on a ruddy rough-diamond joviality that was convincing enough to deceive most people who did not know too much about his criminal record. But at this moment he was making no effort to put on his stock disguise. His mouth was buttoned up in an ugly down-turned curve.

"Why don't you find out, if you're so wise?"

"I could do that," said the Saint.

He moved on the arc of a circle towards Verdean's chair, keeping Dolf and Kaskin covered all the time. His left hand dipped into his coat pocket and took out a penknife. He opened it one-handed, bracing it against his leg, and felt around to cut the cords from Verdean's wrists and ankles without shifting his eyes for an instant from the two men at the other end of his gun.

"We can go on with the concert," he explained gently. "And I'm sure Comrade Verdean would enjoy having a turn as Master of Ceremonies. Put the spoon back in the fire, Verdean, and let's see how Comrade Kaskin likes his chops broiled."

Verdean stood up slowly, and didn't move any farther. His gaze wavered idiotically over the Saint, as if he was too dazed to make up his mind what he ought to do. He pawed at his burned chest and made helpless whimpering noises in his throat, like a sick child.

Kaskin glanced at him for a moment, and slowly brought his eyes back to the Saint again. At the time, Simon thought that it was Verdean's obvious futility that kindled the stiffening belligerent defiance in Kaskin's stare. There was something almost like tentative domination in it.

Kaskin sneered: "See if he'll do it. He wouldn't have the guts. And *you* can't, while you've got to keep that gun on us. I'm not soft enough to fall for that sort of bluff. You picked the wrong show to butt in on, however you got here. You'd better get out again in a hurry before you get hurt. You'd better put that gun away and go home, and forget you ever came here——"

And another voice said: "Or you can freeze right where you are. Don't try to move, or I'll let you have it."

The Saint froze.

The voice was very close behind him—too close to take any chances with. He could have flattened Kaskin before it could carry out its threat, but that was as far as he would get. The Saint had a cold-blooded way of estimating his chances in any situation; and he was much too interested in life just then to make that kind of trade. He knew now the real reason for Kaskin's sudden gathering of confidence, and why the big man had talked so fast in a strain that couldn't help centring his attention. Kaskin had taken his opportunity well. Not a muscle of his face had betrayed what he was seeing; and his loud bullying voice had effectively covered any slight noise that the girl might have made as she crept up.

The girl. Yes. Simon Templar's most lasting startlement clung to the fact that the voice behind him unmistakably belonged to a girl.

## IV

"Drop that gun," she said, "and be quick about it."

Simon dropped it. His ears were nicely attuned to the depth of meaning behind a voice, and this voice meant what it said. His automatic plunked on the carpet; and Morris Dolf stooped into the scene and snatched it up. Even then, Dolf said nothing. He propped himself back on the radiogram and kept the gun levelled, watching Simon in silence with sinister lizard eyes. He was one of the least talkative men that Simon had ever seen.

"Keep him covered," Kaskin said unnecessarily. "We'll see what he looks like."

He stepped forward and jerked the handkerchief down from the Saint's face.

And then there was a stillness that prolonged itself through a gamut of emotions which would have looked like the most awful kind of ham acting if they had been faithfully recorded on celluloid. Neither Dolf nor Kaskin had ever met the Saint personally; but his photograph had at various times been published in almost every newspaper on earth, and verbal descriptions of him had circulated through underworld channels so often that they must have worn a private groove for themselves. Admittedly there were still considerable numbers of malefactors to whom the Saint was no more than a dreaded name; but Messrs Dolf and Kaskin were not among them.

Recognition came to them slowly, which accounted for the elaborate and long-drawn detail of their changing expressions; but it came with a frightful certainty. Morris Dolf's fleshless visage seemed to grow thinner and meaner, and his fingers twitched hungrily around the butt of Simon's gun. Judd Kaskin's sanguine complexion changed colour for a moment, and then his mouth twisted as though tasting its own venom.

"The Saint!" he said hoarsely.

"I told you you might be sorry," said the Saint.

He smiled at them pleasantly, as if nothing had happened to disturb his poise since he was holding the only weapon in sight. It was a smile that would have tightened a quality of desperation into the vigilance of certain criminals who knew him better than Dolf and Kaskin did. It was the kind of smile that only touched the Saint's lips when the odds against him were most hopeless—and when all the reckless fighting vitality that had written the chapter headings in his charmed saga of adventure was blithely preparing to thumb its nose at them. . . .

Then he turned and looked at the girl.

She was blonde and blue-eyed, with a small face like a very pretty baby doll; but the impression of vapid immaturity was contradicted by her mouth. Her mouth had character—not all of it very good, by conventional standards, but the kind of character that has an upsetting effect on many conventional men. It was a rather large mouth, with a sultry lower lip that seemed to have been fashioned for the express purpose of reviving the maximum amount of the Old Adam in any masculine observer. The rest of her, he noticed, carried out the theme summarised in her mouth. Her light dress moulded itself to her figure with a snugness that vouched for the fragility of her underwear, and the curves that it suggested were stimulating to the worst kind of imagination.

"Angela," said the Saint genially, "you're looking very well for your age. I ought to have remembered that Judd always worked with a woman, but I didn't think he'd have one with him on a job like this. I suppose you were sitting in the car outside, and saw me arrive."

"You know everything, don't you?" Kaskin gibed.

He was recovering from the first shock of finding out whom he had captured; and the return of his self-assurance was an ugly thing.

"Only one thing puzzles me," said the Saint equably. "And that is why they sent you to Dartmoor instead of putting you in the Zoo.

Or did the RSPCA object on behalf of the other animals?"

"You're smart," Kaskin said lividly. His ugliness had a hint of bluster in it that was born of fear—a fear that the legends about the Saint were capable of inspiring even when he was apparently disarmed and helpless. But the ugliness was no less dangerous for that reason. Perhaps it was more dangerous. . . . "You're smart, like Verdean," Kaskin said. "Well, you saw what he got. I'm asking the questions again now, and I'll burn you the same way if you don't answer. And I'll burn you twice as much if you make any more funny answers. Now do your talking, smart guy. How did you get here?"

"I flew in," said the Saint, "with my little wings."

Kaskin drew back his fist.

"Wait a minute," said the girl impatiently. "He had another man with him."

Kaskin almost failed to hear her. His face was contorted with the blind rage into which men of his type are fatally easy to tease. His fist had travelled two inches before he stopped it. The girl's meaning worked itself into his intelligence by visibly slow degrees, as if it had to penetrate layers of gum. He turned his head stiffly.

"What's that?"

"There were two of them. I saw them."

"Then where's the other one?" Kaskin said stupidly.

Simon was asking himself the same question; but he had more data to go on. He had left the kitchen door open, and also left the living-room door open behind him when he came in. The girl had come in through the door without touching it; and she must have entered the house at the front, or she would have met Hoppy before. The chances were, therefore, that Hoppy had heard most of the conversation since the music stopped. But with the living-room door still open, and three of the ungodly in the room facing in different directions, it would be difficult for him to show himself and go into action without increasing the Saint's danger. He must have been standing in the hall by that time, just out of sight around the edge of the doorway, waiting for Simon to make him an opening. At least, Simon hoped he was. He had to gamble on it, for he was never likely to get a better break.

Kaskin swung back on him to repeat the question in a lower key.

"Where's your pal, smart guy?"

"You haven't looked at the window lately, have you?" said the Saint blandly.

At any other time it might not have worked; but this time the ungodly were at a disadvantage because one of their own number had brought up the subject. They had another disadvantage, because they didn't realise until a second later that the room contained more than one window. And their third misfortune was that they all gave way simultaneously to a natural instinct of self-preservation that the Saint's indescribably effortless serenity did everything in its power to encourage. All of them looked different ways at once, while all of them must have assumed that somebody else was continuing to watch the Saint. Which provided a beautiful example of one of those occasions when unanimity is not strength.

Kaskin was nearly between Simon and the girl, and the Saint's swift sidestep perfected the alignment. The Saint's right foot drove at the big man's belt buckle, sent Kaskin staggering back against her. She was caught flat-footed, and started moving too late to dodge him. They collided with a thump; but Kaskin's momentum was too great to be completely absorbed by the impact. They reeled back together, Kaskin's flailing arms nullifying the girl's desperate effort to regain her balance. The small nickelled automatic waved wildly in her hand.

Simon didn't wait to see how the waltz worked out. He had only a matter of split seconds to play with, and they had to be crowded ones. He was pivoting on his left foot, with his right leg still in the air, even as Kaskin started caroming backwards from the kick; and Morris Dolf was a fraction of an instant slow in sorting out the situation. The Saint's left hand grabbed his automatic around the barrel before the trigger could tighten, twisting it sideways out of line: it exploded once, harmlessly, and then the Saint's right fist slammed squarely on the weasel-faced man's thin nose. Morris Dolf's eyes bleared with agony, and his fingers went limp with the stunning pain. Simon wrenched the gun away and reversed the butt swiftly into his right hand.

The Saint spun round. Hoppy's chunky outline loomed in the doorway, his massive automatic questing for a target, a pleased warrior smile splitting the lower half of his face. But Kaskin was finding solid ground under his feet again, and his right hand was struggling with his hip pocket. The girl's nickel-plated toy was coming back to aim. And behind him, the Saint knew that Morris Dolf was getting out another gun. Simon had only taken back the automatic he had lost a short while earlier. Morris Dolf still had his own gun. The Saint felt goose-pimples rising all over him.

"The lights, Hoppy!" he yelled. "And scram out the front!"

He dived sideways as he spoke; and darkness engulfed the room mercifully as he did it. Cordite barked malignantly out of the blackness, licking hot orange tongues at him from two directions: he heard the hiss and smack of lead, but it did not touch him. And then his dive cannoned him into the man called Verdean.

It was Verdean that he had meant to reach. His instinct had mapped the campaign with a speed and sureness that deliberate logic still had to catch up with. But all the steps were there. The atmosphere of the moment showed no probability of simmering down into that mellow tranquillity in which heart-to-heart talks are exchanged. The Saint very much wanted a heart-to-heart talk with somebody, if only to satisfy a perfectly normal inquisitiveness concerning what all the commotion was about. But since Messrs Dolf and Kaskin had been asking the questions when he arrived, it appeared that Mr Verdean might know more of the answers than they did. Therefore Mr Verdean looked like the prize catch of the evening. Therefore Mr Verdean had to be transported to an atmosphere where heart-to-heart talking might take place. It was as simple as that.

The Saint gripped Verdean by the arm, and said: "Let's go somewhere else, brother. Your friends are getting rough."

Verdean took one step the way the Saint steered him, and then he turned into a convincing impersonation of a hysterical eel. He squirmed against the Saint's grasp with the strength of panic, and his free arm whirled frantically in the air. His knuckles hit the Saint's cheekbone near the eye, sending a shower of sparks across Simon's vision.

Simon might have stopped to reason with him, to persuasively point out the manifest arguments in favour of adjourning to a less hectic neighbourhood; but he had no time. No more shots had been fired, doubtless because it had been borne in upon the ungodly that they stood a two to one chance of doing more damage to each other than to him, but he could hear them blundering in search of him. The Saint raised his gun and brought the barrel down vigorously where he thought Verdean's head ought to be. Mr Verdean's head proved to be in the desired spot; and Simon ducked a shoulder under him and lifted him up as he collapsed.

The actual delay amounted to less than three seconds. The ungodly were still blinded by the dark, but Simon launched himself at the window with the accuracy of a homing pigeon.

He wasted no time fumbling with catches. He hit the centre of it with his shoulder—the shoulder over which Verdean was draped. Verdean, in turn, hit it with his hams; and the fastening was not equal to the combined load. It splintered away with a sharp crack, and the twin casements flew open crashingly. Verdean passed through them into the night, landing in soft earth with a soggy thud; and the Saint went on after him as if he were plunging into a pool. He struck ground with his hands, and rolled over in a fairly graceful somersault as a fourth shot banged out of the room he had just left.

A gorilla paw caught him under the arm and helped him up, and Mr Uniatz's voice croaked anxiously in his ear.

"Ya ain't stopped anyt'ing, boss?"

"No." Simon grinned in the dark. "They aren't that good. Grab hold of this bird and I'll see if the car'll start. They probably left the keys in it."

He had located Mr Verdean lying where he had fallen. Simon raised him by the slack of his coat and slung him into Hoppy's bear-like clutch, and turned back towards the window just as the lights of the living-room went on again behind the disordered curtains.

He crouched in the shadow of a bush with his gun raised, and said in a much more carrying voice: "I bet I can shoot my initials on the face of the first guy who sticks his nose outside."

The lights went out a second time; and there was a considerable silence. The house might have been empty of life. Behind him Simon heard an engine whine into life, drop back to a subdued purr as the starter disconnected. He backed towards the car, his eyes raking the house frontage relentlessly, until he could step on the running-board.

"Okay, Hoppy," he said.

The black sedan slid forward. Another shot whacked out behind as he opened the door and tumbled into the front seat, but it was yards wide of usefulness. The headlights sprang into brilliance as they lurched through an opening ahead and skidded round in the lane beyond. For the first time in several overcrowded minutes, the Saint had leisure to get out his cigarette-case. The flame of his lighter painted jubilantly Mephistophelian highlights on his face.

"Let's pick up our own car," he said. "Then we'll take our prize home and find out what we've won."

He found out sooner than that. He only had to fish out Mr Verdean's wallet to find a half-dozen engraved cards that answered a whole tumult of questions with staggering simplicity. They said:

---

### Mr Robert Verdean

**BRANCH MANAGER**

CITY & CONTINENTAL BANK LTD
STAINES

---

## V

Patricia Holm put two lumps of sugar in her coffee and stirred it. "Well, that's your story," she said coldly. "So I suppose you're sticking to it. But what were you doing there in the first place?"

"I told you," said the Saint. "We were looking for Hogsbotham."

"Why should you be looking for him?"

"Because he annoyed me. You remember. And we had to do something to pass the evening."

"You could have gone to a movie."

"What, and seen a picture about gangsters? You know what a demoralising influence these pictures have. It might have put ideas into my head."

"Of course," she said. "You didn't have any ideas about Hogsbotham."

"Nothing very definite," he admitted. "We might have just wedged his mouth open and poured him full of gin, and then pushed him in the stage door of a leg show, or something like that. Anyway, it didn't come to anything. We got into the wrong house, as you may have gathered. The bloke who told us the way said 'the fourth house', but it was too dark to see houses. I was counting entrances; but I didn't discover until afterwards that Verdean's place has one of those U-shaped drives, with an in and an out gate, so I counted him twice. Hogsbotham's sty must have been the next house on. Verdean's house is called 'The Shutters', but the paint was so bad that I easily took it for 'The Snuggery'. After I'd made the mistake and got in there, I was more or less a pawn on the chessboard of chance. There was obviously something about Verdean that wanted investigating, and the way things panned out it didn't look healthy to investigate him on the spot. So we just had to bring him away with us."

"You didn't have to hit him so hard that he'd get concussion and lose his memory."

Simon rubbed his chin.

"There's certainly something in that, darling. But it was all very difficult. It was too dark for me to see just what I was doing, and I was in rather a rush. However, it does turn out to be a bit of a snag."

He had discovered the calamity the night before, after he had unloaded Verdean at his country house at Weybridge—he had chosen that secluded lair as a destination partly because it was only about five miles from Chertsey, partly because it had more elaborate facilities for concealing captives than his London apartment. The bank manager had taken an alarmingly long time to recover consciousness; and when he eventually came back to life it was only to vomit and moan unintelligibly. In between retchings, his eyes wandered over his surroundings with a vacant stare into which even the use of his own name and the reminders of the plight from which he had been extracted could not bring a single flicker of response. Simon had dosed him with calomel and sedatives and put him to bed, hoping that he would be back to normal in the morning; but he had awakened in very little better condition, clutching his head painfully and mumbling nothing but listless uncomprehending replies to any question he was asked.

He was still in bed, giving no trouble but serving absolutely no useful purpose as a source of information; and the Saint gazed out of the window at the morning sunlight lancing through the birch and pine glade outside, and frowned ruefully over the consummate irony of the impasse.

"I might have known there'd be something like this waiting for me when you phoned me to come down for breakfast," said Patricia stoically. "How soon are you expecting Teal?"

The Saint chuckled.

"He'll probably be sizzling in much sooner than we want him— a tangle like this wouldn't be complete without good old Claud Eustace. But we'll worry about that when it happens. Meanwhile, we've got one consolation. Comrade Verdean seems to be one of those birds who stuff everything in their pockets until the stitches begin to burst. I've been going over his collection of junk again, and it tells quite a story when you put it together."

Half of the breakfast table was taken up with the pot-pourri of relics which he had extracted from various parts of the bank manager's clothing, now sorted out into neat piles. Simon waved a spoon at them.

"Look them over for yourself, Pat. Nearest to you, you've got a couple of interesting souvenirs. Hotel bills. One of 'em is where Mr Robert Verdean stayed in a modest semi-boarding-house at Eastbourne for the first ten days of July. The other one follows straight on for the next five days; only it's from a swank sin-palace at Brighton, and covers the sojourn of a Mr and Mrs Jones who seem to have consumed a large amount of champagne during their stay. If you had a low mind like mine, you might begin to jump to a few conclusions about Comrade Verdean's last vacation."

"I could get ideas."

"Then the feminine handkerchief—a pretty little sentimental souvenir, but rather compromising."

Patricia picked it up and sniffed it.

"Night of Sin," she said with a slight grimace.

"Is that what it's called? I wouldn't know. But I do know that it's the same smell that the blonde floozie brought in with her last night. Her name is Angela Lindsay; and she has quite a reputation in the trade for having made suckers out of a lot of guys who should have been smarter than Comrade Verdean."

She nodded.

"What about the big stack of letters? Are they love-letters?"

"Not exactly. They're bookmaker's accounts. And the little book on top of them isn't a heart-throb diary—it's a betting diary. The name on all of 'em is Joseph Mackintyre. And you'll remember from an old adventure of ours that Comrade Mackintyre has what you might call an elastic conscience about his bookmaking. The story is all there, figured down to pennies. Verdean seems to have started on the sixth of July, and he went off with a bang. By the middle of the month he must have wondered why he ever bothered to work in a bank. I'm not surprised he had champagne every night at Brighton—it was all free. But the luck started to change after that. He had fewer and fewer winners, and he went on plunging more and more heavily. The last entry in the diary, a fortnight ago, left him nearly five thousand pounds in the red. Your first name doesn't have to be Sherlock to put all those notes together and make a tune."

Patricia's sweet face was solemn with thought.

"Those two men," she said. "Dolf and Kaskin. You knew them. What's their racket?"

"Morrie was one of Snake Ganning's spare-time boys once. He's dangerous. Quite a sadist, in his nasty little way. You could hire him for anything up to murder, at a price; but he really enjoys his work. Kaskin has more brains, though. He's more versatile. Confidence work, the old badger game, living off women, protection rackets—he's had a dab at all of them. He's worked around race-tracks quite a bit, too, doping horses and intimidating jockeys and bookmakers and so forth, which makes him an easy link with Mackintyre. His last stretch was for manslaughter. But bank robbery is quite a fancy flight, even for him. He must have been getting ideas."

Patricia's eyes turned slowly towards the morning paper in which the holdup at Staines still had a place in the headlines.

"You mean you think——"

"I think our guardian angel is still trying to take care of us," said the Saint; and all the old impenitent mischief that she knew too well was shimmering at the edges of his smile. "If only we knew a cure for amnesia, I think we could be fifteen thousand pounds richer before bedtime. Add it up for yourself while I take another look at the patient."

He got up from the table and went through to the study which adjoined the dining-room. It was a rather small, comfortably untidy room, and the greater part of its walls were lined with built-in bookshelves. When he went in, one tier of shelving about two feet wide stood open like a door; beyond it, there appeared to be a narrow passage. The passage was actually a tiny cell, artificially lighted and windowless, but perfectly ventilated through a grating that connected with the air-conditioning system which served the rest of the house. The cell was no more than a broad gap between the solid walls of the rooms on either side of it, so ingeniously squeezed into the architecture of the house that it would have taken a clever surveyor many hours of work with a foot-rule to discover its existence. It had very little more than enough room for the cot, in which Verdean lay, and the table and chair at which Hoppy Uniatz was dawdling over his breakfast—if any meal which ended after noon, and was washed down with a bottle of Scotch whisky, could get by with that name.

Simon stood just inside the opening and glanced over the scene.

"Any luck yet?" he asked.

Mr Uniatz shook his head.

"De guy is cuckoo, boss. I even try to give him a drink, an' he don't want it. He t'rows it up like it might be perzon."

He mentioned this with the weighty reluctance of a psychiatrist adducing the ultimate evidence of dementia praecox.

Simon squeezed his way through and slipped a thermometer into the patient's mouth. He held Verdean's wrist with sensitive fingers.

"Don't you want to get up, Mr Verdean?"

The bank manager gazed at him expressionlessly.

"You don't want to be late at the bank, do you?" said the Saint. "You might lose your job."

"What bank?" Verdean asked.

"You know. The one that was robbed."

"I don't know. Where am I?"

"You're safe now. Kaskin is looking for you, but he won't find you."

"Kaskin," Verdean repeated. His face was blank, idiotic. "Is he someone I know?"

"You remember Angela, don't you?" said the Saint. "She wants to see you."

Verdean rolled his head on the pillows.

"I don't know. Who are all these people? I don't want to see anyone. My head's splitting. I want to go to sleep."

His eyes closed under painfully wrinkled brows.

Simon let his wrist fall. He took out the thermometer, read it, and sidled back to the door. Patricia was standing there.

"No change?" she said; and the Saint shrugged.

"His temperature's practically normal, but his pulse is high. God alone knows how long it may take him to get his memory back. He could stay like this for a week; or it might even be years. You never can tell . . . I'm beginning to think I may have been a bit too hasty with my rescuing-hero act. I ought to have let Kaskin and Dolf work him over a bit longer, and heard what he had to tell them before I butted in."

Patricia shook her head.

"You know you couldn't have done that."

"I know." The Saint made a wryly philosophic face. "That's the worst of trying to be a buccaneer with a better nature. But it would have saved the hell of a lot of trouble, just the same. As it is, even if he does recover his memory, we're going to have to do something exciting ourselves to make him open up. Now, if we could only swat him on the head in the opposite direction and knock his memory back again——"

He broke off abruptly, his eyes fixed intently on a corner of the room; but Patricia knew that he was not seeing it. She looked at him with an involuntary tightening in her chest. Her ears had not been quick enough to catch the first swish of tyres on the gravel drive which had cut off what he was saying, but she was able to hear the car outside coming to a stop.

The Saint did not move. He seemed to be waiting, like a watch-dog holding its bark while it tries to identify a stray sound that had pricked its ears. In another moment she knew what he had been waiting for.

The unmistakable limping steps of Orace, Simon Templar's oldest and most devoted retainer, came through the hall from the direction of the kitchen and paused outside the study.

"It's that there detective agyne, sir," he said in a fierce whisper. "I seen 'im fru the winder. Shall I chuck 'im aht?"

"No, let him in," said the Saint quietly. "But give me a couple of seconds first."

He drew Patricia quickly out of the secret cell, and closed the study door. His lips were flirting with the wraith of a Saintly smile, and only Patricia would have seen the steel in his blue eyes.

"What a prophet you are, darling," he said.

He swung the open strip of bookcase back into place. It closed silently, on delicately balanced hinges, filling the aperture in the wall without a visible crack. He moved one of the shelves to lock it. Then he closed a drawer of his desk which had been left open, and there was the faint click of another lock taking hold. Only then did he open the door to the hall—and left it open. And with that, a master lock, electrically operated, took control. Even with the knowledge of the other two operations, nothing short of pickaxes and dynamite could open the secret room when the study door was open; and one of the Saint's best bets was that no one who was searching the house would be likely to make a point of shutting it.

He emerged into the hall just as Chief Inspector Teal's official boots stomped wrathfully over the threshold. The detective saw him as soon as he appeared, and the heightened colour in his chubby face flared up with the perilous surge of his blood-pressure. He took a lurching step forward with one quivering forefinger thrust out ahead of him like a spear.

"You, Saint!" he bellowed. "I want you!"

The Saint smiled at him, carefree and incredibly debonair.

"Why, hullo, Claud, old gumboil," he murmured genially. "You seem to be excited about something. Come in and tell me all about it."

## VI

Simon Templar had never actually been followed into his living-room by an irate mastodon; but if that remarkable experience was ever to befall him in the future, he would have had an excellent standard with which to compare it. The imitation, as rendered by Chief Inspector Claud Eustace Teal, was an impressive performance, but it seemed to leave the Saint singularly unconcerned. He waved towards one armchair and deposited himself in another, reaching for cigarette-box and ashtray.

"Make yourself at home," he invited affably. "Things have been pretty dull lately, as I said last night. What can I do to help you?"

Mr Teal gritted his teeth over a lump of chewing gum with a barbarity which suggested that he found it an inferior substitute for the Saint's jugular vein. Why he should have followed the Saint at all in the first place was a belated question that was doing nothing to improve his temper. He could find no more satisfactory explanation than that the Saint had simply turned and calmly led the way, and he could hardly be expected to go on talking to an empty hall. But in the act of following, he felt that he had already lost a subtle point. It was one of those smoothly infuriating tricks of the Saint to put him at a disadvantage which never failed to lash Mr Teal's unstable temper to the point where he felt as if he were being garrotted with his own collar.

And on this occasion, out of all others, he must control himself. He had no need to get angry. He held all the aces. He had everything that he had prayed for in the long sections of his career that had been consecrated to the heartbreaking task of trying to lay the Saint by the heels. He must not make any mistakes. He must not let himself be baited into any more of those unbelievable indiscretions that had wrecked such opportunities in the past, and that made him sweat all over as soon as he had escaped from the Saint's maddening presence. He told himself so, over and over again, clinging to all the tatters of his self-restraint with the doggedness of a drowning man. He glared at the Saint with an effort of impassivity that made the muscles of his face ache.

"You can help me by taking a trip to the police station with me," he said. "Before you go any further, it's my duty to warn you that you're under arrest. And I've got all the evidence I need to keep you there!"

"Of course you have, Claud," said the Saint soothingly. "Haven't you had it every time you've arrested me? But now that you've got that off your chest, would it be frightfully tactless if I asked you what I'm supposed to have done?"

"Last night," Teal said, grinding his words out under fearful compression, "Mr Robert Verdean, the manager of the City and Continental Bank's branch at Staines, was visited at his home in Chertsey by two men. They tied up his servant in the kitchen, and went on to find him in the living-room. The maid's description of them makes them sound like the two men who held up the same bank that morning. They went into the living-room and turned on the radio."

"How very odd," said the Saint. "I suppose they were trying to console Comrade Verdean for having his bank robbed. But what has that got to do with me? Or do you think I was one of them?"

"Shortly afterwards," Teal went on, ignoring the interruption, "two other men entered the kitchen with handkerchiefs tied over their faces. One of them was about your height and build. The maid heard this one address the other one as 'Hoppy'."

Simon nodded perfunctorily.

"Yes," he said; and then his eyebrows rose. "My God, Claud, that's funny! Of course, you're thinking——"

"That American gangster who follows you around is called Hoppy, isn't he?"

"If you're referring to Mr Uniatz," said the Saint stiffly, "he is sometimes called that. But he hasn't got any copyright in the name."

The detective took a fresh nutcracker purchase of his gum.

"Perhaps he hasn't. But the tall one went into the living-room. The radio was switched off and on and off again, and then it stayed off. So the maid heard quite a bit of the conversation. She heard people talking about the Saint."

"That's one of the penalties of fame," said the Saint sadly. "People are always talking about me, in the weirdest places. It's quite embarrassing sometimes. But do go on telling me about it."

Mr Teal's larynx suffered a spasm which interfered momentarily with his power of speech.

"That's all I have to tell you!" he yelped, when he had partially cleared the obstruction. "I mean that you and that Uniatz creature of yours were the second two men who arrived. After that, according to the maid, there was a lot of shooting, and presently some neighbours arrived and untied her. All the four men who had been there disappeared, and so did Mr Verdean. I want you on suspicion of kidnapping him; and if we don't find him soon there'll probably be a charge of murder as well!"

Simon Templar frowned. His manner was sympathetic rather than disturbed.

"I know how you feel, Claud," he said commiseratingly. "Naturally you want to do something about it; and I know you're quite a miracle worker when you get going. But I wish I could figure out how you're going to tie me up with it, when I wasn't anywhere near the place."

The detective's glare reddened.

"You weren't anywhere near Chertsey, eh? So we've got to break down another of your famous alibis. All right, then. Where were you?"

"I was at home."

"Whose home?"

"My own. This one."

"Yeah? And who else knows about it?"

"Not a lot of people," Simon confessed. "We were being quiet. You know. One of these restful oldfashioned, fireside evenings. If it comes to that, I suppose there isn't an army of witnesses. You can't have a quiet restful evening with an army of witnesses cluttering up the place. It's a contradiction in terms. There was just Pat, and Hoppy, and of course good old Orace——"

"Pat and Hoppy and Orace," jeered the detective. "Just a quiet restful evening. And that's your alibi——"

"I wouldn't say it was entirely my alibi," Simon mentioned diffidently. "After all, there are several other houses in England. And I wouldn't mind betting that in at least half of them, various people were having quiet restful evenings last night. Why don't you go and ask some of them whether they can prove it? Because you know that being a lot less tolerant and forbearing than I am, they'd only tell you to go back to Scotland Yard and sit on a radiator until you'd thawed some of the clotted suet out of your brains. How the hell would you expect anyone to prove he'd spent a quiet evening at home? By bringing in a convocation of bishops for witnesses? In a case like this, it isn't the suspect's job to prove he was home. It's your job to prove he wasn't."

Chief Inspector Teal should have been warned. The ghosts of so many other episodes like this should have risen up to give him caution. But they didn't. Instead, they egged him on. He leaned forward in a glow of vindictive exultation.

"That's just what I'm going to do," he said, and his voice grew rich with the lusciousness of his own triumph. "We aren't always so stupid as you think we are. We found fresh tyre tracks in the drive, and they didn't belong to Verdean's car. We searched every scrap of ground for half a mile to see if we could pick them up again. We found them turning into a field quite close to the end of Greenleaf Road. The car that made 'em was still in the field—it was reported stolen in Windsor early yesterday morning. But there were the tracks of another car in the field, overlapping and underlapping the tracks of the stolen car, so that we know the kidnappers changed to another car for their getaway. I've got casts of those tracks, and I'm going to show that they match the tyres on your car!"

The Saint blinked.

"It would certainly be rather awkward if they did," he said uneasily. "I didn't give anybody permission to borrow my car last night, but of course——"

"But of course somebody might have taken it away and brought it back without your knowing it," Teal said with guttural sarcasm. "Oh, yes." His voice suddenly went into a squeak. "Well, I'm going to be in court and watch the jury laugh themselves sick when you try to tell that story! I'm going to examine your car now, in front of police witnesses, and I'd like them to see your face when I do it!"

It was the detective's turn to march away and leave the Saint to follow. He had a moment of palpitation while he wondered whether the Saint would do it. But as he flung open the front door and crunched into the drive, he heard the Saint's footsteps behind him. The glow of triumph that was in him warmed like a Yule log on a Christmas hearth. The Saint's expression had reverted to blandness quickly enough, but not so quickly that Teal had missed the guilty start which had broken through its smooth surface. He knew, with a blind ecstasy, that at long last the Saint had tripped. . . .

He waved imperiously to the two officers in the prowl car outside, and marched on towards the garage. The Saint's Hirondel stood there in its glory, an engineering symphony in cream and red trimmed with chromium, with the more sedate black Daimler in which Patricia had driven down standing beside it; but Teal had no æsthetic admiration for the sight. He stood by like a pink-faced figure of doom while his assistants reverently unwrapped the moulage impressions; and then, like a master chef taking charge at the vital moment in the preparation of a dish for which his underlings had laid the routine foundations, he took the casts in his own hands and proceeded to compare them with the tyres on the Hirondel.

He went all round the Hirondel twice.

He was breathing a trifle laboriously, and his face was redder than before—probably from stooping—when he turned his attention to the Daimler.

He went all round the Daimler twice, too.

Then he straightened up and came slowly back to the Saint. He came back until his face was only a few inches from the Saint's. His capillaries were congested to the point where his complexion had a dark purple hue. He seemed to be having more trouble with his larynx.

"What have you done to those tyres?" he got out in a hysterical blare.

The Saint's eyebrows drew perplexedly together.

"What have I done to them? I don't get you, Claud. Do you mean to say they don't match?"

"You know damn well they don't match! You knew it all the time." Realisation of the way the Saint had deliberately lured him to greater heights of optimism, only to make his downfall more hideous when it came, brought something like a sob into the detective's gullet. "You've changed the tyres!"

Simon looked aggrieved.

"How could I, Claud? You can see for yourself that these tyres are a long way from being new——"

"What have you done with the tyres you had on the car last night?" Teal almost screamed.

"But these are the only tyres I've had on the car for weeks," Simon protested innocently. "Why do you always suspect me of such horrible deceits? If my tyres don't match the tracks you found in that field, it just looks to me as if you may have made a mistake about my being there."

Chief Inspector Teal did a terrible thing. He raised the casts in his hands and hurled them down on the concrete floor so that they shattered into a thousand fragments. He did not actually dance on them, but he looked as if only an effort of self-control that brought him to the brink of an apoplectic stroke stopped him from doing so.

"What have you done with Verdean?" he yelled.

"I haven't done anything with him. Why should I have? I've never even set eyes on the man."

"I've got a search warrant——"

"Then why don't you search?" demanded the Saint snappily, as though his patience was coming to an end. "You won't believe anything I tell you, anyhow, so why don't you look for yourself? Go ahead and use your warrant. Tear the house apart. I don't mind. I'll be waiting for you in the living-room when you're ready to eat some of your words."

He turned on his heel and strolled back to the house.

He sat down in the living-room, lighted a cigarette, and calmly picked up a magazine. He heard the tramp of Teal and his minions entering the front door, without looking up. For an hour he listened to them moving about in various parts of the house, tapping walls and shifting furniture; but he seemed to have no interest beyond the story he was reading. Even when they invaded the living-room itself, he didn't even glance at them. He went on turning the pages as if they made no more difference to his idleness than a trio of inquisitive puppies.

Teal came to the living-room last. Simon knew from the pregnant stillness that presently supervened that the search had come to a stultifying end, but he continued serenely to finish his page before he looked up.

"Well," he said at length, "have you found him?"

"Where is he?" shouted Teal, with dreadful savagery.

Simon put down the magazine.

"Look here," he said wearily. "I've made a lot of allowances for you, but I give up. What's the use? I tell you I was at home last night, and you can't prove I wasn't; but just because you want me to have been out, I must be faking an alibi. You've got casts of the tyre tracks of a car that was mixed up in some dirty business last night, and they don't match the tracks of either of my cars; but just because you think they ought to match, I must have changed my tyres. I tell you I haven't kidnapped this fellow Verdean, and you can't find him anywhere in my house; but just because you think I ought to have kidnapped him, I must have hidden him somewhere else. Every shred of evidence is against you, and therefore all the evidence must be wrong. You couldn't possibly be wrong yourself, because you're the great Chief Inspector Claud Eustace Teal, who knows everything and always gets his man. All right. Every bit of proof there is shows that I'm innocent, but I must be guilty because your theories would be all wet if I wasn't. So why do we have to waste our time on silly little details like this? Let's just take me down to the police station and lock me up."

"That's just what I'm going to do," Teal raved blindly.

The Saint looked at him for a moment, and stood up.

"Good enough," he said breezily. "I'm ready when you are."

He went to the door and called: "Pat!" She answered him, and came down the stairs. He said: "Darling, Claud Eustace has had an idea. He's going to lug me off and shove me in the cooler on a charge of being above suspicion. It's a new system they've introduced at Scotland Yard, and all the laws are being altered to suit it. So you'd better call one of our lawyers and see if he knows what to do about it. Oh, and you might ring up some of the newspapers while you're on the job—they'll probably want to interview Claud about his brainwave."

"Yes, of course," she said enthusiastically and went towards the telephone in the study.

Something awful, something terrifying, something freezing and paralysing, damp, chilly, appalling, descended over Chief Inspector Teal like a glacial cascade. With the very edge of the precipice crumbling under his toes, his eyes were opened. The delirium of fury that had swept him along so far coagulated sickeningly within him. Cold, pitiless, inescapable facts hammered their bitter way through into the turmoil of his brain. He was too shocked at the moment even to feel the anguish of despair. His mind shuddered under the impact of a new kind of panic. He took a step forward— a step that was, in its own way, the crossing of a harrowing Rubicon.

"Wait a minute," he stammered hoarsely.

## VII

Fifteen minutes later, Simon Templar stood on the front steps and watched the police car crawl out of the drive with its cargo of incarnate woe. He felt Patricia's fingers slide into his hands, and turned to smile at her.

"So far, so good," he said thoughtfully. "But only so far."

"I thought you were joking, at breakfast," she said. "How did he get here so soon?"

He shrugged.

"That wasn't difficult. I suppose he stayed down at Staines last night; and the Chertsey police would have phoned over about the Verdean business first thing this morning, knowing that he was the manager of the bank that had been held up. Claud must have shot off on the scent like a prize greyhound, and I'm afraid I can sympathise with the way he must have felt when he arrived here."

"Well, we're still alive," she said hopefully. "You got rid of him again."

"Only because his nerves are getting a bit shaky from all the times I've slipped through his fingers, and he's so scared of being made a fool of again that he daren't move now without a cast-iron case, and I was able to pick a few awkward holes in this one. But don't begin thinking we've got rid of him for keeps. He's just gone away now to see if he can stop up the holes again and put some more iron in the evidence, and he's sore enough to work overtime at it. He's going to be three times as dangerous from now on. Worse than that, he's not so dumb that he isn't going to put two and two together about all this commotion around Verdean coming right on top of the robbery. You can bet the Crown Jewels to a showgirl's virtue that he's already figured out that Verdean was mixed up in it in some way. While we're stuck with Verdean, and Verdean is stuck with amnesia." The Saint closed the front door with sombre finality. "Which is the hell of a layout from any angle," he said. "Tell Orace to bring me a large mug of beer, darling, because I think I am going to have a headache."

His headache lasted through a lunch which Orace indignantly served even later than he had served breakfast, but it brought forth very little to justify itself. He had gone over the facts at his disposal until he was sick of them, and they fitted together with a complete and sharply-focused deductive picture that Sherlock Holmes himself could not have improved on, without a hiatus or a loose end anywhere—only the picture merely showed a plump rabbit-faced man slinking off with fifteen thousand pounds in a bag, and neglected to show where he went with it. Which was the one detail in which Simon Templar was most urgently interested. He was always on the side of the angels, he told himself, but he had to remember that sanctity had its own overhead to meet.

Verdean showed no improvement in the afternoon. Towards five o'clock the Saint had a flash of inspiration, and put in a long-distance call to a friend in Wolverhampton.

"Dr Turner won't be back till tomorrow morning, and I'm afraid I don't know how to reach him," said the voice at the other end of the wire; and the flash flickered and died out at the sound. "But I can give you Dr Young's number——"

"I am not having a baby," said the Saint coldly, and hung up.

He leaned back in his chair and said, quietly and intensely: "God damn."

"You should complain," said Patricia. "You Mormon."

She had entered the study from the hall, and closed the door again behind her. The Saint looked up from under mildly interrogative brows.

"I knew you adored me," he said, "but you have an original line of endearing epithets. What's the origin of this one?"

"Blonde," she said, "and voluptuous in a careful way. Mushy lips and the-old-baloney eyes. I'll bet she wears black lace undies and cuddles like a kitten. She hasn't brought the baby with her, but she's probably got a picture of it."

The Saint straightened.

"Not Angela?" he ventured breathlessly.

"I'm not so intimate with her," said Patricia primly. "But she gave the name of Miss Lindsay. You ought to recognise your own past when it catches up with you."

Simon stood up slowly. He glanced at the closed section of bookcase, beyond which was the secret room where Hoppy Uniatz was still keeping watch over Mr Verdean and a case of Vat 69; and his eyes were suddenly filled with an unholy peace.

"I do recognise her, darling, now I think about it," he said. "This is the one who had the twins." He gripped her arm, and his smile wavered over her in a flicker of ghostly excitement. "I ought to have known that she'd catch up with me. And I think this is the break I've been waiting for all day. . . ."

He went into the living-room with a new quickness in his step and a new exhilaration sliding along his nerves. Now that this new angle had developed, he was amazed that he had not been expecting it from the beginning. He had considered every other likely eventuality, but not this one; and yet this was the most obvious one of all. Kaskin and Dolf knew who he was, and some of his addresses were to be found in various directories that were at the disposal of anyone who could read: it was not seriously plausible that after the night before they would decide to give up their loot and go away and forget about it, and once they had made up their minds to attempt a comeback it could only have been a matter of time before they looked for him in Weybridge. The only thing he might not have anticipated was that they would send Angela Lindsay in to open the interview. That was a twist which showed a degree of circumspection that made Simon Templar greet her with more than ordinary watchfulness.

"Angela, darling!" he murmured with an air of pleased surprise. "I never thought I should see you in these rural parts. When did you decide to study bird life in the suburbs?"

"It came over me suddenly, last night," she said. "I began to realise that I'd missed something."

His eyes were quizzically sympathetic.

"You shouldn't be too discouraged. I don't think you missed it by more than a couple of inches."

"Perhaps not. But a miss is——"

"I know. As good as in the bush."

"Exactly."

He smiled at her, and offered the cigarette-box. She took one, and he gave her a light. His movements and his tone of voice were almost glisteningly smooth with exaggerated elegance. He was enjoying his act immensely.

"A drink?" he suggested; but she shook her head.

"It mightn't be very good for me, so I won't risk it. Besides, I want to try and make a good impression."

He was studying her more critically than he had been able to the night before, and it seemed to him that Patricia's description of her was a little less than absolutely fair. She had one of those modern streamlined figures that look boyish until they are examined closely, when they prove to have the same fundamental curves that grandma used to have. Her mouth and eyes were effective enough, even if the effect was deplorable from a moral standpoint. And although it was true that even a comparatively unworldly observer would scarcely have hesitated for a moment over placing her in her correct category, it was also very definitely true that if all the other members of that category had looked like her, Mr Ebenezer Hogsbotham would have found himself burning a very solitary candle in a jubilantly naughty world.

The Saint went on looking at her with amiable amusement at the imaginative vistas opened up by that train of thought. He said: "You must have made quite an impression on Comrade Verdean. And you drank champagne with him at Brighton."

She put her cigarette to her lips and drew lightly at it while she gazed at him for a second or two in silence. Her face was perfectly composed, but her eyes were fractionally narrowed.

"I'll give you that one," she said at length. "We've been wondering just how much you really knew. Would you care to tell me the rest, or would that be asking too much?"

"Why, of course," said the Saint obligingly. "If you're interested. It isn't as if I'd be telling you anything you don't know already."

He sat down and stretched out his long legs. He looked at the ceiling. He was bluffing, but he felt sure enough of his ground.

"Kaskin and Dolf picked up Verdean on his holiday at Eastbourne," he said. "Kaskin can make himself easy to like when he wants to—it's his stock in trade. They threw you in for an added attraction. Verdean fell for it all. He was having a swell time with a bunch of good fellows. And you were fairly swooning into his manly arms. It made him feel grand, and a little bit dizzy. He had to live up to it. Kaskin was a sporty gent, and Verdean was ready to show that he was a sporty gent too. They got him to backing horses, and he always backed winners. Money poured into his lap. He felt even grander. It went to his head—where it was meant to go. He left his boarding-house, and pranced off to Brighton with you on a wild and gorgeous jag."

Simon reached for a cigarette.

"Then, the setback," he went on. "You had expensive tastes, and you expected him to go on being a good fellow and a sporty gent. But that looked easy. There was always money in the gee-gees, with Kaskin's expert assistance. So he thought. Only something went haywire. The certainties didn't win. But the next one would always get it back. Verdean began to plunge. He got wilder and wilder as he lost more and more. And he couldn't stop. He was infatuated with you, scared stiff of losing you. He lost more money than he had of his own. He started embezzling a little, maybe. Anyway, he was in the cart. He owed more money than he could hope to pay. Then Kaskin and Dolf started to get tough. They told him how he could pay off his debt, and make a profit as well. There was plenty of money in the bank every week, and it would be very easy to stage a holdup and get away with it if he was cooperating. Kaskin and Dolf would do the job and take all the risk, and all he had to do was to give them the layout and make everything easy for them. He'd never be suspected himself, and he'd get his cut afterwards. But if he didn't string along—well, someone might have to tell the

head office about him. Verdean knew well enough what happens
to bank managers who get into debt, particularly over gambling.
He could either play ball or go down the drain. So he said he'd play
ball. Am I right?"

"So far. But I hope you aren't going to stop before the important
part."

"All right. Verdean thought some more—by himself. He was
sunk, anyhow. He had to rob the bank if he was going to save his
own skin. So why shouldn't he keep all the boodle for himself? . . .
That's just what he decided to do. The branch is a small one, and
nobody would have thought of questioning anything he did. It was
easy for him to pack a load of dough into a small valise and take
it out with him when he went home to lunch—just before the holdup
was timed to take place. Nobody would have thought of asking him
what he had in his bag; and as for the money, well, of course the
holdup men would be blamed for getting away with it. But he didn't
want Judd and Morrie on his tail, so he tipped off the police
anonymously, meaning for them to be caught, and feeling pretty
sure that nobody would believe any accusations they made about
him—or at least not until he had plenty of time to hide it . . . There
were still a few holes in the idea, but he was too desperate to worry
about them. His real tragedy was when Kaskin and Dolf didn't get
caught after all, and came after him to ask questions. And naturally
that's when we all started to get together."

"And then?"

The Saint raised his head and looked at her again.

"Maybe I'm very dense," he said apologetically, "but isn't that
enough?"

"It's almost uncanny. But there's still the most important thing."

"What would that be?"

"Did you find out what happened to the money?'

The Saint was silent for a moment. He elongated his legs still
farther, so that they stretched out over the carpet like a pier; his
recumbent body looked as if it were composing itself for sleep. But
the eyes that he bent on her were bright and amused and very
cheerfully awake.

She said: "What are you grinning about?"

"I'd just been wondering when it was coming, darling," he
murmured. "I know that my dazzling beauty brings admiring sight-
seers from all quarters like moths to a candle, but they usually want
something else as well. And it's been very nice to see you and have

this little chat, but I was always afraid you were hoping to get something out of it. So this is what it is. Morrie and Judd sent you along to get an answer to that question, so they'd know whether it was safe to bump me off or not. If Verdean is still keeping his mouth shut, they can go ahead and fix me a funeral; but if I've found out where it is I may have even moved it somewhere else by now, and it would be awkward to have me buried before I could tell them where I'd moved it to. Is that all that's worrying you?"

"Not altogether," she said, without hesitation. "They didn't have to send me for that. I talked them into letting me come because I told them you'd probably talk to me for longer than you'd talk to them, and anyhow you wouldn't be so likely to punch me on the nose. But I really did it because I wanted to see you myself."

The flicker that passed over Simon's face was almost imperceptible.

"I hope it's been worth it," he said flippantly; but he was watching her with a coolly reserved alertness.

"That's what you've got to tell me," she said. She looked away from him for a moment, stubbed out her cigarette nervously, looked back at him again with difficult frankness. Her hands moved uncertainly. She went on in a rush: "You see I know Judd doesn't mean to give me my share. I could trust you. Whatever happens, they're going to give you trouble. I know you can take care of yourself, but I don't suppose you'd mind having it made easier for you. I could be on your side, without them knowing, and I wouldn't want much."

The Saint blew two smoke-rings with leisured care, placing them side by side like the lenses of a pair of horn-rimmed spectacles. They drifted towards the ceiling, enlarging languidly.

His face was inscrutable, but behind that pleasantly noncommittal mask he was thinking as quickly as he could.

He might have come to any decision. But before he could say anything there was an interruption.

The door was flung open, and Hoppy Uniatz crashed in.

Mr Uniatz's face was not at all inscrutable. It was as elementarily easy to read as an infant's primer. The ecstatic protrusion of his eyes, the lavish enthusiasm of his breathing, the broad beam that divided his physiognomy into two approximately equal halves, and the roseate glow which suffused his homely countenance, were all reminiscent of the symptoms of bliss that must have illuminated the features of Archimedes at the epochal moment of his life. He looked like a man who had just made the inspirational discovery of the century in his bath.

"It woiked, boss," he yawped exultantly, "it woiked! De dough is in Hogsbotham's bedroom!"

## VIII

Simon Templar kept still. It cost him a heroic effort, but he did it. He felt as if he were balanced on top of a thin glass flagpole in the middle of an earthquake, but he managed to keep the surface of his nonchalance intact. He kept Angela Lindsay's hands always within the radius of his field of vision, and said rather faintly: "What woiked?"

Mr Uniatz seemed slightly taken aback.

"Why, de idea you give me dis afternoon, boss," he explained, as though he saw little need for such childish elucidations. "You remember, you are saying why can't we sock dis guy de udder way an' knock his memory back. Well, I am t'inkin' about dat, an' it seems okay to me, an' I ain't got nut'n else to do on account of de door is locked an' I finished all de Scotch; so I haul off an' whop him on de toinip wit' de end of my Betsy. Well, he is out for a long time, an' when he comes round he still don't seem to know what it's all about, but he is talkin' about how dis guy Hogsbotham gives him a key to look after de house when he goes away, so he goes in an' parks de lettuce in Hogsbotham's bedroom. It is a swell idea, boss, an' it woiks," said Mr Uniatz, still marvelling at the genius which had conceived it.

The Saint felt a clutching contraction under his ribs which was not quite like the gastric hollowness of dismay and defensive tension which might reasonably have been there. It was a second or two before he could get a perspective on it; and when he did so, the realisation of what it was made him feel slightly insane.

It was simply a wild desire to collapse into helpless laughter. The whole supernal essence of the situation was so immortally ludicrous that he was temporarily incapable of worrying about the fact that Angela Lindsay was a member of the audience. If she had taken a gun out of her bag and announced that she was going to lock them up while she went back to tell Kaskin and Dolf the glad news, which would have been the most obviously logical thing for her to do, he would probably have been too weak to lift a finger to prevent it.

Perhaps the very fact that she made no move to do so did more

than anything else to restore him to sobriety. The ache in his chest
died away, and his brain forced itself to start work again. He knew
that she had a gun in her bag—he had looked for it and distinguished
the outline of it when he first came into the room to meet her, and
that was why he had never let himself completely lose sight of her
hands. But her hands only moved to take another cigarette. She
smiled at him as if she was sharing the joke, and struck a match.

"Well," he said drily, "it looks like you've got your answer."

"To one question," she said. "You haven't answered the other.
What shall I tell Judd?"

Simon studied her for the space of a couple of pulse-beats. In
that time, he thought with a swiftness and clarity that was almost
clairvoyant. He saw every angle and every prospect and every
possible surprise.

He also saw Patricia standing aghast in the doorway behind the
gorilla shoulders of Mr Uniatz, and grinned impudently at her.

He stood up, and put out his hand to Angela Lindsay.

"Go back and tell Morrie and Judd that we found out where the
dough was last night," he said. "Verdean had buried it in a flower-
bed. A couple of pals of mine dug it out in the small hours of this
morning and took it to London. They're sitting over it with a pair
of machine-guns in my apartment at Cornwall House now, and I
dare anybody to take it away. That ought to hold 'em . . . Then
you shake them off as soon as you can, and meet me at the Stag
and Hounds opposite Weybridge Common in two hours from now.
We'll take you along with us and show you Hogsbotham's night-
shirts!"

She faced him steadily, but with a suppressed eagerness that
played disturbing tricks with her moist lips.

"You mean that? You'll take me in with you?"

"Just as far as you want to be taken in, kid," said the Saint.

He escorted her to the front door. There was no car outside, but
doubtless Messrs Kaskin and Dolf were waiting for her a little way
up the road. He watched her start down the drive, and then he
closed the door and turned back.

"You'd look better without the lipstick," said Patricia judicially.

He thumbed his nose at her and employed his handkerchief.

"Excuse me if I seem slightly scatterbrained," he remarked. "But
all this is rather sudden. Too many things have happened in the
last few minutes. What would you like to do with the change from
fifteen thousand quid? There ought to be a few bob left after I've

paid for my last lot of shirts and bought a new distillery for Hoppy."

"Have you fallen right off the edge," she asked interestedly, "or what is it?"

"At a rough guess, I should say it was probably What." The Saint's happy lunacy was too extravagant to cope with. "But who cares? Why should a little thing like this cause so much commotion? Have you no faith in human nature? The girl's better nature has revived. My pure and holy personality has done its work on her. It never fails. My shining example has made her soul pant for higher things. From now on, she is going to be on the side of the Saints. And she is going to take care of Judd and Morrie. She is going to lead them for us, by the nose, into the soup. Meanwhile, Professor Uniatz has shaken the scientific world to its foundations with his new and startling treatment for cases of concussion. He has whopped Comrade Verdean on the turnip with the end of his Betsy and banged his memory back, and we are going to lay our hands on fifteen thousand smackers before we go to bed tonight. And we are going to find all this boodle in the bedroom of Ebenezer Hogsbotham, of all the superlative places in the world. I ask you, can life hold any more?"

He exploded out of the hall into the study, and went on into the secret room, leaving her staring after him a trifle dazedly.

He was bubbling with blissful idiocy, but his mind was cool. He had already diagnosed the effects of the Uniatz treatment so completely that his visit was really only intended to reassure himself that it had actually worked. He studied Verdean coldbloodedly. The bank manager's eyes were vacant and unrecognising: he rolled his head monotonously from side to side and kept up a delirious mumble from which the main points of the summary that Hoppy Uniatz had made were absurdly easy to pick out. Over and over again he reiterated the story—how Mr Hogsbotham had asked him as a neighbour to keep an eye on the house during some of his absences, how he had been entrusted with a key which he had never remembered to return, and how when he was wondering what to do with the stolen money he had remembered the key and used it to find what should have been an unsuspectable hiding-place for his booty. He went on talking about it. . . .

"He is like dis ever since he wakes up," Hoppy explained, edging proudly in behind him.

The Saint nodded. He did not feel any pity. Robert Verdean was just another man who had strayed unsuccessfully into the paths of common crime; and even though he had been deliberately led astray, the mess that he was in now was directly traceable to nothing but his own weakness and cupidity. In such matters, Simon Templar saved his sympathy for more promising cases.

"Put his clothes back on him," he said. "We'll take him along too. Your operation was miraculous, Hoppy, but the patient is somewhat liable to die; and we don't want to be stuck with his body."

Patricia was sitting on the study desk when he emerged again, and she looked at him with sober consideration.

"I don't want to bore you with the subject," she said, "but are you still sure you haven't gone off your rocker?"

"Perfectly sure," he said. "I was never rocking so smoothly in my life."

"Well, do you happen to remember anyone by the name of Teal?"

He took her arm and chuckled.

"No, I haven't forgotten. But I don't think he'll be ready for this. He may have ideas about keeping an eye on me, but he won't be watching for Verdean. Not here, anyway. Hell, he's just searched the house from top to bottom and convinced himself that we haven't got Verdean here, however much he may be wondering what else we've done with him. And it's getting dark already. By the time we're ready to go, it'll be easy. There may be a patrol car or a motorcycle cop waiting down the road to get on our tail if we go out, but that'll be all. We'll drive around the country a bit first and lose them. And then we will go into this matter of our old-age pensions."

She might have been going to say some more. But she didn't. Her mouth closed again, and a little hopeless grimace that was almost a smile at the same time passed over her lips. Her blue eyes summed up a story that it has already taken all the volumes of the Saint Saga to tell in words. And she kissed him.

"All right, skipper," she said quietly. "I must be as crazy as you are, or I shouldn't be here. We'll do that."

He shook his head, holding her.

"So we shall. But not you."

"But——"

"I'm sorry, darling. I was talking about two other guys. You're going to stay out of it, because we're going to need you on the out- side. Now, in a few minutes I'm going to call Peter, and then I'm going to try and locate Claud Eustace; and if I can get hold of both of them in time the campaign will proceed as follows. . . ."

He told it in quick clean-cut detail, so easily and lucidly that it seemed to be put together with no more effort than it took to understand and remember it. But that was only one of the tricks that sometimes made the Saint's triumphs seem deceptively facile. Behind that apparently random improvisation there was the instant decision and almost supernatural foresightedness of a strategic genius which in another age might have conquered empires as debonairly as in this twentieth century it had conquered its own amazing empire among thieves. And Patricia Holm was a listener to whom very few explanations had to be made more than once.

Hoppy Uniatz was a less gifted audience. The primitive machinery of conditioned reflexes which served him for some of the simpler functions of a brain had never been designed for one-shot lubrication. Simon had to go over the same ground with him at least three times before the scowl of agony smoothed itself out of Mr Uniatz's rough-hewn façade, indicating that the torture of concentration was over and the idea had finally taken root inside his skull, where at least it could be relied upon to remain with the solidity of an amalgam filling in a well-excavated molar.

The evening papers arrived before they left, after the hectic preliminaries of organization were completed, when the Saint was relaxing briefly over a parting glass of sherry, and Mr Uniatz was placidly sluicing his arid tonsils with a fresh bottle of Scotch. Patricia glanced through the *Evening Standard* and giggled.

"Your friend Hogsbotham is still in the news," she said. "He's leading a deputation from the National Society for the Preservation of Public Morals to demonstrate outside the London Casino this evening before the dinner-time show. So it looks as if the coast will be clear for you at Chertsey."

"Probably he heard that Simon was thinking of paying him another call, and hustled himself out of the way like a sensible peace-loving citizen," said Peter Quentin, who had arrived shortly before that. "If I'd known what I was going to be dragged into before I answered the telephone, I'd have gone off and led a demonstration somewhere myself."

The Saint grinned.

"We really must do something about Hogsbotham one of these days," he said.

It was curious that that adventure had begun with Mr Hogsbotham, and had just led back to Mr Hogsbotham; and yet he still did not dream how importantly Mr Hogsbotham was still to be concerned.

## IX

The Hirondel's headlights played briefly over the swinging sign of the Three Horseshoes, in Laleham, and swung off to the left on a road that turned towards the river. In a few seconds they were lighting up the smooth grey water and striking dull reflections from a few cars parked close to the bank; and then they blinked out as Simon pulled the car close to the grass verge and set the handbrake.

"Get him out, darling," he said over his shoulder.

He stepped briskly out from behind the wheel; and Hoppy Uniatz, who had been sitting beside him, slid into his place. The Saint waited a moment to assure himself that Angela Lindsay was having no trouble with the fourth member of the party; and then he leaned over the side and spoke close to Hoppy's ear.

"Well," he said, "do you remember it all?"

"Sure, I remember it," said Mr Uniatz confidently. He paused to refresh himself from the bottle he was still carrying, and replaced the cork with an air of reluctance. "It's in de bag," he said, with the pride of knowing what he was talking about.

"Mind you don't miss the turning, like we did last night. And for God's sake try not to have any kind of noise. You'll have to manage without headlights, too—someone might notice them . . . Once you've got the Beef Trust there, Pat'll take care of keeping them busy. I don't want you to pay any attention to anything except watching for the ungodly and passing the tip to her."

"Okay, boss."

The Saint looked round again. Verdean was out of the car.

"On your way, then."

He stepped back. The gears meshed, and the Hirondel swung round in a tight semicircle and streaked away towards the main road.

Angela Lindsay stared after it, and caught the Saint's sleeve with sudden uncertainty. Her eyes were wide in the gloom.

"What's that for? Where is he going?"

"To look after our alibi," Simon answered truthfully. "Anything may happen here tonight, and you don't know Teal's nasty suspicious mind as well as I do. I'm pretty sure we shook off our shadows in Walton, but there's no need to take any chances."

She was looking about her uneasily.

"But this isn't Chertsey——"

"This is Laleham, on the opposite side of the river. We came this way to make it more confusing, and also because it'll make it a lot harder for our shadows if they're still anywhere behind. Unless my calculations are all wrong, Hogsbotham's sty ought to be right over there." His arm pointed diagonally over the stream. "Let's find out."

His hand took Verdean's arm close up under the shoulder. The girl walked on the bank manager's other side. Verdean was easy to lead. He seemed to have no more will of his own. His head kept rolling idiotically from side to side, and his voice went on unceasingly with an incoherent and practically unintelligible mumbling. His legs tried to fold intermittently at the joints, as if they had turned into putty; but the Saint's powerful grip held him up.

They crossed a short stretch of grass to the water's edge. The Saint also went on talking, loudly and irrelevantly, punctuating himself with squeals of laughter at his own wit. If any of the necking parties in the parked cars had spared them any attention at all, the darkness would have hidden any details, and the sound effects would infallibly have combined to stamp them as nothing but a party of noisy drunks. It must have been successful, for the trip was completed without a hitch. They came down to the river margin in uneventful coordination; and any spectators who may have been there continued to sublimate their biological urges unconcerned.

There was an empty punt moored to the bank at exactly the point where they reached the water. Why it should have been there so fortunately was something that the girl had no time to stop and ask; but the Saint showed no surprise about it. He seemed to have been expecting it. He steered Verdean on board and lowered him on to the cushions, and cast off the mooring chain and settled himself in the stern as she followed.

His paddle dug into the water with long deep strokes, driving the punt out into the dark. The bank which they had just left fell away into blackness behind. For a short while there was nothing near them but the running stream bounded by nebulous masses of deep shadow on either side. Verdean's monotonous muttering went on, but it had become no more obtrusive than the murmur of traffic heard from a closed room in a city building.

She said, after a time: "I wonder why this all seems so different?"

He asked: "Why?"

She was practically invisible from where he sat. Her voice came out of a blurred emptiness.

"I've done all sorts of things before—with Judd," she said. "But doing this with you . . . You make it an adventure. I always wanted it to be an adventure, and yet it never was."

"Adventure is the way you look at it," he said, and did not feel that the reply was trite when he was making it.

For the second time since he had picked her up at the Stag and Hounds he was wondering whether a surprise might still be in store for him that night. All his planning was cut and dried, as far as any of it was under his control; but there could still be surprises. In all his life nothing had ever gone mechanically and unswervingly according to a rigid and inviolable schedule: adventure would soon have become boring if it had. And tonight he had a feeling of fine-drawn aliveness that was the reverse of boredom.

The feeling stayed with him the rest of the way across the water, and through the disembarkation on the other side. It stayed with him on the short walk up Greenleaf Road from the towpath to the gates of Mr Hogsbotham's house. It was keener and more intense as they went up the drive, with Verdean keeping pace in his grasp with docile witlessness. It brought up all the undertones of the night in sharp relief—the stillness everywhere around, the silence of the garden, the whisper of leaves, the sensation of having stepped out of the inhabited world into a shrouded wilderness. Some of that could have been due to the trees that shut them in, isolating them in a tenebrous closeness in which there was no sight or sound of other life, so that even Verdean's own house next door did not intrude on their awareness by so much as a glimmer of light or the silhouette of a roof, and the Saint could not tell whether a light would have been visible in it if there had been a light to see. Some of the feeling was still left unaccounted for even after that. The Saint stood on the porch and wondered if he was misunderstanding his own intuition, while Verdean fumbled with keys at the door, muttering fussily about his stolen fortune. And his mind was still divided when they went into the hall, where a single dim light was burning, and he saw the bank manager stagger drunkenly away and throw himself shakily up the stairs.

He felt the girl's fingers cling to his arm. And in spite of all he knew about her, her physical nearness was something that his senses could not ignore.

"He's going to get it," she breathed.

The Saint nodded. That psychic electricity was still coursing through his nerves, only now he began to find its meaning. From force of habit, his right hand slid under the cuff of his left sleeve and touched the hilt of the razor-edged throwing knife in its sheath strapped to his forearm, the only weapon he had thought it worth while to bring with him, making sure that it would slip easily out if he needed it; but the action was purely automatic. His thoughts were a thousand miles away from such things as his instinct associated with that deadly slender blade. He smiled suddenly.

"We ought to be there to give him a cheer," he said.

He took her up the stairs with him. From the upper landing he saw an open door and a lighted room from which came confused scurrying noises combined with Verdean's imbecile grunting and chattering. Simon went to the door. The room was unquestionably Mr Ebenezer Hogsbotham's bedroom. He would have known it even without being told. Nobody but an Ebenezer Hogsbotham could ever have slept voluntarily in such a dismally austere and mortifying chamber. And he saw Robert Verdean in the centre of the room. The bank manager had lugged a shabby suitcase out of some hiding-place, and he had it open on the bed; he was pawing and crooning crazily over the contents—ruffling the edges of packets of pound notes, crunching the bags of silver. Simon stood for a moment and watched him, and it was like looking at a scene from a play that he had seen before.

Then he stepped quietly in and laid his hand on Verdean's shoulder.

"Shall I help you take care of it?" he said gently.

He had not thought much about how Verdean would be likely to respond to the interruption, but he had certainly not quite expected the response he got.

For the first time since Hoppy had applied his remarkable treatment, the bank manager seemed to become aware of outside personalities in a flash of distorted recognition. He squinted upwards and sidelong at the Saint, and his face twisted.

"I won't give it to you!" he screamed. "I'll kill you first!"

He flung himself at the Saint's throat, his fingers clawing, his eyes red and maniacal.

Simon had very little choice. He felt highly uncertain about the possible results of a third concussion on Verdean's already inflamed cerebral tissue, following so closely upon the two previous whacks which it had suffered in the last twentyfour hours; but on the other hand he felt that in Mr Verdean's present apparent state of mind, to be tied up and gagged and left to struggle impotently while he watched his loot being taken away from him would be hardly less likely to cause a fatal hæmorrhage. He therefore adopted the less troublesome course, and put his trust in any guardian angels that Mr Verdean might have on his overburdened payroll. His fist travelled up about eight explosive inches, and Mr Verdean travelled down. . . .

Simon picked him up and laid him on the bed.

"You know," he remarked regretfully, "if this goes on much longer, there is going to come a time when Comrade Verdean is going to wonder whether fifteen thousand quid is really worth it."

Angela Lindsay did not answer.

He looked at her. She stood close by the bed, gazing without expression at Verdean's unconscious body and the suitcase full of money at his feet. Her face was tired.

Still without saying anything, she went to the window and stood there with her back to him.

She said, after a long silence: "Well, you got what you wanted, as usual."

"I do that sometimes," he said.

"And what happens next?"

"You'll get the share you asked for," he answered carefully. "You can take it now, if you like."

"And that's all."

"Did we agree to anything else?"

She turned round; and he found that he did not want to look at her eyes.

"Are you sure you're never going to need any more help?" she said.

He did not need to hear any more. He had known more than she could have told him, before that. He understood all of the presentiment that had troubled him on the way there. For that moment he was without any common vanity, and very calm.

"I may often need it," he said, and there was nothing but compassion in his voice. "But I must take it where I'm lucky enough to find it . . . I know what you mean. But I never tried to make you fall in love with me. I wouldn't wish that kind of trouble on anyone."

"I knew that," she said, just as quietly. "But I couldn't help wishing it."

She came towards him, and he stood up to meet her. He knew
that she was going to kiss him, and he did not try to stop her.

Her mouth was hot and hungry against his. His own lips could
not be cold. That would have been hypocrisy. Perhaps because his
understanding went so much deeper than the superficial smartness
that any other man might have been feeling at that time, he was
moved in a way that would only have been cheapened if he had
tried to put words to it. He felt her lithe softness pressed against
him, her arms encircling him, her hands moving over him, and did
not try to hold her away.

Presently she drew back from him. Her hands were under his
coat, under his arms, holding him. The expression in her eyes was
curiously hopeless.

"You haven't got any gun," she said.

He smiled faintly. He knew that her hands had been learning that
even while she kissed him; and yet it made no difference.

"I didn't think I should need one," he said.

It seemed as if she wanted to speak, and could not.

"That was your mistake," said the harsh voice of Judd Kaskin.
"Get your hands up."

The Saint turned, without haste. Kaskin stood just inside the door,
with a heavy automatic in his hand. His florid face was savagely
triumphant. Morris Dolf sidled into the room after him.

## X

They were tying the Saint to a massive fake-antique wooden
chair placed close to the bed. His ankles were corded to the legs,
and Kaskin was knotting his wrists behind the back of it. Dolf kept
him covered while it was being done. The gun in his thin hand was
steady and impersonal: his weasel face and bright beady eyes held
a coldblooded sneer which made it plain that he would have welcomed an opportunity to demonstrate that he was not holding his
finger off the trigger because he was afraid of the bang.

But the Saint was not watching him very intently. He was looking
most of the time at Angela Lindsay. To either of the other two men
his face would have seemed utterly impassive, his brow serene and
amazingly unperturbed, the infinitesimal smile that lingered on his
lips only adding to the enigma of his self-control. But that same
inscrutable face talked to the girl as clearly as if it had used spoken
words.

Her eyes stared at him in a blind stunned way that said: "I know. I know. You think I'm a heel. But what could I do? I didn't have long enough to think. . . ."

And his own cool steady eyes, and that faintly lingering smile, all of his face so strangely free from hatred or contempt, answered in the same silent language: "I know, kid. I understand. You couldn't help it. What the hell?"

She looked at him with an incredulity that ached to believe.

Kaskin tightened his last knot and came round from behind the chair.

"Well, smart guy," he said gloatingly. "You weren't so smart, after all."

The Saint had no time to waste. Even with his wrists tied behind him, he could still reach the hilt of his knife with his fingertips. They hadn't thought of searching for a weapon like that, under his sleeve. He eased it out of its sheath until his fingers could close on the handle.

"You certainly did surprise me, Judd," he admitted mildly.

"Thought you were making a big hit with the little lady, didn't you?" Kaskin jeered. "Well, that's what you were meant to think. I never knew a smart guy yet that wasn't a sucker for a jane. We had it all figured out. She tipped us off as soon as she left your house this afternoon. We could have hunted out the dough and got away with it then, but that would have still left you running around. It was worth waiting a bit to get you as well. We knew you'd be here. We just watched the house until you got here, and came in after you. Then we only had to wait until Angela got close enough to you to grab your gun. Directly we heard her say you hadn't got one, we walked in." His arm slid round the girl's waist. "Cute little actress, ain't she, Saint? I'll bet you thought you were in line for a big party."

Simon had his knife in his hand. He had twisted the blade back to saw it across the cords on his wrists, and it was keen enough to lance through them like butter. He could feel them loosening strand by strand, and stopped cutting just before they would have fallen away altogether; but one strong jerk of his arms would have been enough to set him free.

"So what?" he inquired coolly.

"So you get what's coming to you," Kaskin said.

He dug into a bulging coat pocket.

The Saint tensed himself momentarily. Death was still very near.

His hands might be practically free, but his legs were still tied to the chair. And even though he could throw his knife faster than most men could pull a trigger, it could only be thrown once. But he had taken that risk from the beginning, with his eyes open. He could only die once, too; and all his life had been a gamble with death.

He saw Kaskin's hand come out. But it didn't come out with a gun. It came out with something that looked like an ordinary tin can with a length of smooth cord wound round it. Kaskin unwrapped the cord, and laid the can on the edge of the bed, where it was only a few inches both from the Saint's elbow and Verdean's middle. He stretched out the cord, which terminated at one end in a hole in the top of the can, struck a match, and put it to the loose end. The end began to sizzle slowly.

"It's a slow fuse," he explained, with vindictive satisfaction. "It'll take about fifteen minutes to burn. Time enough for us to get a long way off before it goes off, and time enough for you to do plenty of thinking before you go sky-high with Verdean. I'm going to enjoy thinking about you thinking."

Only the Saint's extraordinarily sensitive ears would have caught the tiny mouselike sound that came from somewhere in the depths of the house. And any other ears that had heard it might still have dismissed it as the creak of a dry board.

"The only thing that puzzles me," he said equably, "is what you think you're going to think with."

Kaskin stepped up and hit him unemotionally in the face.

"That's for last night," he said hoarsely, and turned to the others. "Let's get started."

Morris Dolf pocketed his automatic and went out, with a last cold stare over the scene.

Kaskin went to the bed, closed the bulging valise, and picked it up. He put his arm round the girl again and drew her to the door.

"Have a good time," he said.

The Saint looked out on to an empty landing. But what he saw was the last desperate glance that the girl flung at him as Kaskin led her out.

He tensed his arms for an instant, and his wrists separated. The scraps of cord scuffed on the floor behind him. He took a better grip on his knife. But he still made no other movement. He sat where he was, watching the slowly smouldering fuse, waiting and listening for two sounds that all his immobility was tuned for. One of them he knew he would hear, unless some disastrous accident had happened to cheat his calculations; the other he was only hoping for, and yet it was the one that his ears were most wishfully strained to catch.

Then he saw Angela Lindsay's bag lying on a corner of the dresser, and all his doubts were supremely set at rest.

He heard her voice, down on the stairs, only a second after his eyes had told him that he must hear it.

And he heard Kaskin's growling answer.

"Well, hurry up, you fool . . . The car's out in front of the house opposite."

The Saint felt queerly content.

Angela Lindsay stood in the doorway again, looking at him.

She did not speak. She picked up her bag and tucked it under her arm. Then she went quickly over to the bed and took hold of the trailing length of fuse. She wound it round her hand and tore it loose from the bomb, and threw it still smouldering into a far corner.

Then she bent over the Saint and kissed him, very swiftly.

He did not move for a moment. And then, even more swiftly, his free hands came from behind him and caught her wrists.

She tried to snatch herself back in sudden panic, but his grip was too strong. And he smiled at her.

"Don't go for a minute," he said softly.

She stood frozen.

Down on the ground floor, all at once, there were many sounds. The sounds of heavy feet, deep voices that were neither Dolf's nor Kaskin's, quick violent movements . . . Her eyes grew wide, afraid, uncomprehending, questioning. But those were the sounds that he had been sure of hearing. His face was unlined and unstartled. He still smiled. His head moved fractionally in answer to the question she had not found voice to ask.

"Yes," he said evenly. "It is the police. Do you still want to go?"

Her mouth moved.

"You knew they'd be here."

"Of course," he said. "I arranged for it. I wanted them to catch Morrie and Judd with the goods on them. I knew you meant to doublecross me, all the time. So I pulled a double doublecross. That was before you kissed me—so you'd find out where I kept my gun . . . Then I was only hoping you'd make some excuse to come back and do what you just did. You see, everything had to be in your own hands."

Down below, a gun barked. The sound came up the stairs dulled and thickened. Other guns answered it. A man screamed shrilly, and was suddenly silent. The brief fusillade rattled back into throbbing stillness. Gradually the muffled voices droned in again.

The fear and bewilderment died out of the girl's face, and left a shadowy kind of peace.

"It's too late now," she said. "But I'm still glad I did it."

"Like hell it's too late," said the Saint.

He let go of her and put away his knife, and bent to untie his legs. His fingers worked like lightning. He did not need to give any more time to thought. Perhaps in those few seconds after his hands were free and the others had left the room, when he had sat without moving and only listened, wondering whether the girl would come back, his subconscious mind had raced on and worked out what his adaptation would be if she did come back. However it had come to him, the answer was clear in his mind now—as clearly as if he had known that it would be needed when he planned for the other events which had just come to pass.

And the aspect of it that was doing its best to dissolve his seriousness into a spasm of ecstatic daftness was that it would also do something towards taking care of Mr Ebenezer Hogsbotham. He had, he realised, been almost criminally neglectful about Mr Hogsbotham, having used him as an excuse to start the adventure, having just borrowed his house to bring it to a dénouement, and yet having allowed himself to be so led away by the intrusion of mere sordid mercenary objectives that he had had no spare time to devote towards consummating the lofty and purely idealistic mission that had taken him to Chertsey in the first place. Now he could see an atonement for his remissness that would invest the conclusion of that story with a rich completeness which would be something to remember.

"Listen," he said, and the rapture of supreme inspiration was blazing in his eye.

In the hall below, Chief Inspector Claud Eustace Teal straightened up from his businesslike examination of the two still figures sprawled close together on the floor. A knot of uniformed local men, one of whom was twisting a handkerchief round a bleeding wrist, made way for him as he stepped back.

"All right," Teal said grimly. "One of you phone for an ambulance to take them away. Neither of them is going to need a doctor."

He moved to the suitcase which had fallen from Judd Kaskin's hand when three bullets hit him, and opened it. He turned over some of the contents, and closed it again.

A broad-shouldered young officer with a sergeant's stripes on his sleeve shifted up from behind him and said: "Shall I look after it, sir?"

Teal surrendered the bag.

"Put it in the safe at the station for tonight," he said. "I'll get somebody from the bank to check it over in the morning. It looks as if it was all there."

"Yes, sir."

The sergeant stepped back towards the door.

Chief Inspector Teal fumbled in an inner pocket, and drew out a small oblong package. From the package he extracted a thinner oblong of pink paper. From the paper he unwrapped a fresh crisp slice of spearmint. He slid the slice of spearmint into his mouth and champed purposefully on it. His salivary glands reacted exquisitely to succulent stimulus. He began to feel some of the deep spiritual contentment of a cow with a new cud.

Mr Teal, as we know, had had a trying day. But for once he seemed to have earned as satisfactory a reward for his tribulations as any reasonable man had a right to expect. It was true that he had been through one disastrously futile battle with the Saint. But to offset that, he had cleared up the case to which he had been assigned, with the criminals caught redhanded while still in possession of their booty and justifiably shot down after they had tried to shoot their way out, which would eliminate most of the tedious legal rigmaroles which so often formed a wearisome anticlimax to such dramatic victories; and he had recovered the booty itself apparently intact. All in all, he felt that this was one occasion when even his tyrannical superiors at Scotland Yard would be unable to withhold the commendation which was his due. There was something almost like human tolerance in his sleepy eyes as they glanced around and located Hoppy Uniatz leaning against the wall in the background.

"That was quick work," he said, making the advance with some difficulty. "We might have had a lot more trouble if you hadn't been with us."

Mr Uniatz had a jack-knife of fearsome dimensions in one hand. He appeared to be carving some kind of marks on the butt of his gun. He waved the knife without looking up from his work.

"Aw, nuts," he said modestly. "All youse guys need is a little practice."

Mr Teal swallowed.

Patricia Holm squeezed through between two burly constables and smiled at him.

"Well," she said sweetly, "don't you owe us all some thanks? I won't say anything about an apology."

"I suppose I do," Teal said grudgingly. It wasn't easy for him to say it, or even to convince himself that he meant it. The sadly acquired suspiciousness that had become an integral part of his souring nature had driven its roots too deep for him to feel really comfortable in any situation where there was even a hint of the involvement of any member of the Saint's entourage. But for once he was trying nobly to be just. He grumbled half-heartedly: "But you had us in the wrong house, all the same. If Uniatz hadn't happened to notice them coming in here——"

"But he did, didn't he?"

"It was a risk that none of you had any right to take," Teal said starchily. "Why didn't the Saint tell me what he knew this morning?"

"I've told you," she said. "He felt pretty hurt about the way you were trying to pin something on to him. Of course, since he knew he'd never been to Verdean's house, he figured out that the second two men the maid saw were just a couple of other crooks trying to hijack the job. He guessed that Kaskin and Dolf had scared them off and taken Verdean away to go on working him over in their own time——"

That hypersensitive congenital suspicion stabbed Mr Teal again like a needle prodded into a tender boil.

"You never told me he knew their names!" he barked. "How did he know that?"

"Didn't I?" she said ingenuously. "Well, of course he knew. Or at any rate he had a pretty good idea. He'd heard a rumour weeks ago that Kaskin and Dolf were planning a bank holdup with an inside stooge. You know how these rumours get around; only I suppose Scotland Yard doesn't hear them. So naturally he thought of them. He knew their favourite hideouts, so it wasn't hard to find them. And as soon as he knew they'd broken Verdean down, he had me get hold of you while he went on following them. He sent Hoppy to fetch us directly he knew they were coming here. Naturally he thought they'd be going to Verdean's house, but of course Verdean might always have hidden the money somewhere else close by, so that's why I had Hoppy watching outside. Simon just wanted to get even with you by handing you the whole thing on a platter; and you can't really blame him. After all, he was on the side of the law all the time. And it all worked out. Now, why don't you admit that he got the best of you and did you a good turn at the same time?"

Chief Inspector Teal scowled at the toes of his official boots. He had heard it all before, but it was hard for him to believe. And yet it indisputably fitted with the facts as he knew them . . . He hitched his gum stolidly across to the other side of his mouth.

"Well, I'll be glad to thank him," he growled; and then a twinge of surprising alarm came suddenly into his face. "Hey, where is he? If they caught him following them——"

"I was wondering when you'd begin to worry about me," said the Saint's injured voice.

Mr Teal looked up.

Simon Templar was coming down the stairs, lighting a cigarette, mocking and immaculate and quite obviously unharmed.

But it was not the sight of the Saint that petrified Mr Teal into tottering stillness and bulged his china-blue eyes half out of their sockets, exactly as the eyes of all the other men in the hall were also bulged as they looked upwards with him. It was the sight of the girl who was coming down the stairs after the Saint.

It was Angela Lindsay.

The reader has already been made jerry to the fact that the clinging costumes which she ordinarily affected suggested that underneath them she possessed an assortment of curves and contours of exceptionally enticing pulchritude. This suggestion was now elevated to the realms of scientifically observable fact. There was no further doubt about it, for practically all of them were open to inspection. The sheer and diaphanous underwear which was now their only covering, left nothing worth mentioning to the imagination. And she seemed completely unconcerned about the exposure, as if she knew that she had a right to expect a good deal of admiration for what she had to display.

Mr Teal blinked groggily.

"Sorry to be so long," Simon was saying casually, "but our pals left a bomb upstairs, and I thought I'd better put it out of action. They left Verdean lying on top of it. But I'm afraid he didn't really need it. Somebody hit him once too often, and it looks as if he has kind of passed away . . . What's the matter, Claud? You look slightly boiled. The old tum-tum isn't going back on you again, is it?"

The detective found his voice.

"Who is that you've got with you?" he asked in a hushed and quivering voice.

Simon glanced behind him.

"Oh, Miss Lindsay," he said airily. "She was tied up with the bomb, too. You see, it appears that Verdean used to look after this house when the owner was away—it belongs to a guy named Hogsbotham—so he had a key, and when he was looking for a place to cache the boodle, he thought this would be as safe as anywhere. Well, Miss Lindsay was in the bedroom when the boys got here, so they tied her up along with Verdean. I just cut her loose——"

"You found 'er in 'Ogsbotham's bedroom?" repeated one of the local men hoarsely, with his traditional phlegm battered to limpness by the appalling thought.

The Saint raised his eyebrows.

"Why not?" he said innocently. "I should call her an ornament to anyone's bedroom."

"I should say so," flared the girl stridently. "I never had any complaints yet."

The silence was numbing to the ears.

Simon looked over the upturned faces, the open mouths, the protruding eyeballs, and read there everything that he wanted to read. One of the constables finally gave it voice. Gazing upwards with the stalk-eyed stare of a man hypnotised by the sight of a miracle beyond human expectation, he distilled the inarticulate emotions of his comrades into one reverent and pregnant ejaculation.

"Gor-blimy!" he said.

The Saint filled his lungs with a breath of inenarrable peace. Such moments of immortal bliss, so ripe, so full, so perfect, so superb, so flawless and unalloyed and exquisite, were beyond the range of any feeble words. They flooded every corner of the soul and every fibre of the body, so that the heart was filled to overflowing with a nectar of cosmic content. The very tone in which that one word had been spoken was a benediction. It gave indubitable promise that within a few hours the eye-witness evidence of Ebenezer Hogsbotham's depravity would have spread all over Chertsey, within a few hours more it would have reached London, before the next sunset it would have circulated over all England; and all the denials and protestations that Hogsbotham might make would never restore his self-made pedestal again.

## XI

Simon Templar braked the Hirondel to a stop in the pool of blackness under an overhanging tree less than a hundred yards beyond the end of Greenleaf Road. He blinked his lights three times, and lighted a cigarette while he waited. Patricia Holm held his arm tightly. From the back of the car came the gurgling sucking sounds of Hoppy Uniatz renewing his acquaintance with the bottle of Vat 69 which he had been forced by circumstances to neglect for what Mr Uniatz regarded as an indecent length of time.

A shadow loomed out of the darkness beside the road, whistling very softly. The shadow carried a shabby valise in one hand. It climbed into the back seat beside Hoppy.

Simon Templar moved the gear lever, let in the clutch; and the Hirondel rolled decorously and almost noiselessly on its way.

At close quarters, the shadow which had been added to the passenger list could have been observed to be wearing a policeman's uniform with a sergeant's stripes on the sleeve, and a solid black moustache which obscured the shape of its mouth as much as the brim of its police helmet obscured the exact appearance of its eyes. As the car got under way, it was hastily stripping off these deceptive scenic effects and changing into a suit of ordinary clothes piled on the seat.

Simon spoke over his shoulder as the Hirondel gathered speed through the village of Chertsey.

"You really ought to have been a policeman, Peter," he murmured. "You look the part better than anyone I ever saw."

Peter Quentin snorted.

"Why don't you try somebody else in the part?" he inquired acidly. "My nerves won't stand it many more times. I still don't know how I got away with it this time."

The Saint grinned in the dark, his eyes following the road.

"That was just your imagination," he said complacently. "There wasn't really much danger. I knew that Claud wouldn't have been allowed to bring his own team down from Scotland Yard. He was just assigned to take charge of the case. He might have brought an assistant of his own, but he had to use the local cops for the mob work. In the excitement, nobody was going to pay much attention to you. The local men just thought you came down from Scotland Yard with Teal, and Teal just took it for granted that you were one of the local men. It was in the bag—literally and figuratively."

"Of course it was," Peter said sceptically. "And just what do you think is going to happen when Teal discovers that he hasn't got the bag?"

"Why, what on earth could happen?" Simon retorted blandly. "We did our stuff. We produced the criminals, and Hoppy blew them off, and Teal got the boodle. He opened the bag and looked it over right there in the house. And Pat and Hoppy and I were in more or less full view all the time. If he goes and loses it again after we've done all that for him, can he blame us?"

Peter Quentin shrugged himself into a tweed sports jacket, and sighed helplessly. He felt sure that there was a flaw in the Saint's logic somewhere but he knew that it was no use to argue. The Saint's conspiracies always seemed to work out, in defiance of reasonable argument. And this episode had not yet shown any signs of turning into an exception. It would probably work out just like all the rest. And there was unarguably a suitcase containing about fifteen thousand pounds in small change lying on the floor of the car at his feet to lend weight to the probability. The thought made Peter Quentin reach out for Mr Uniatz's bottle with a reckless feeling that he might as well make the best of the crazy life into which his association with the Saint had led him.

Patricia told him what had happened at the house after he faded away unnoticed with the bag.

"And you left her there?" he said, with a trace of wistfulness.

"One of the local cops offered to take her back to town," Simon explained. "I let him do it, because it'll give her a chance to build up the story . . . I don't think we shall hear a lot more about Hogsbotham from now on."

"So while I was sweating blood and risking about five hundred years in penal servitude," Peter said bitterly, "you were having a grand time helping her take her clothes off."

"You have an unusually evil mind," said the Saint, and drove on, one part of his brain working efficiently over the alibi that Peter was still going to need before morning, and all the rest of him singing.

# THE LAST WORD

---

AND SO, MY FRIENDS, *dear bookworms, most noble fellow drinkers, frustrated burglars, affronted policemen, upright citizens with furled umbrellas and secret buccaneering dreams—that seems to be very nearly all for now. It has been nice having you with us, and we hope you will come again, not once, but many times.*

*There is, I think, only one more of those standard questions to forestall. You need not go on writing to ask me whether there are going to be more Saint stories. The standing answer, now and for as long as the pair of us can keep it up, is—*

## WATCH FOR THE SIGN OF THE SAINT

## HE WILL BE BACK